JEWS IN POLAND

A DOCUMENTARY HISTORY
by
Iwo Cyprian Pogonowski

THE RISE OF JEWS AS A NATION FROM *CONGRESSUS JUDAICUS* IN POLAND TO THE *KNESSET* IN ISRAEL

A thousand years in Poland
ended in German mass murders.
The Jews reacted with a dramatic effort and
an extraordinary impetus to establish
the Jewish Nation in Israel.

Hippocrene Books, Inc.
New York

For information, address:
HIPPOCRENE BOOKS, INC.
171 Madison Avenue
New York, NY 10016

Library of Congress Cataloging-in-Publication Data

Pogonowski, Iwo, 1921-
    Jews in Poland : a documentary history : the rise of Jews
as a nation from Congressus Judaicus in Poland to the Knesset
in Israel / by Iwo Cyprian Pogonowski.
        p.   cm.
    Includes bibliographical references and index.
    ISBN 0-7818-0116-8:
    1. Jews--Poland--History--Sources. 2. Poland--Ethnic
relations--Sources. 3. Jews--Poland--History--Maps. 4. Poland-
-Ethnic relations--Maps.   I. Title.
DS135.P6P54 1993
943.8'004924--dc20   92-44706
                                             CIP

Printed in the United States of America.

FOREWORD

More than half a century ago, the writer of these lines attended school in Warsaw with Mr. Pogonowski, the author of this book. The clouds of war were gathering over our heads and there was a premonition of great upheavals. None of us, however, had the slightest suspicion that the Germans, universally regarded as an outstandingly cultured nation, were preparing a massacre of the entire Jewish people. True, Hitler in early 1939 had publicly warned that if the Jews dared to "unleash" another world war, they would be destroyed; but no one took these words seriously. Even today the monstrosity of what the Germans had committed, especially on the territory of Poland, exceeds the capacity of the normal mind to comprehend.

Mr. Pogonowski, who has had his own dreadful experiences with Nazism, has gathered a great deal of material on the history of the Jews in Poland and its tragic finale. Contrary to prevailing opinion, the story of Polish Jewry was not always one of poverty and persecution. For a long time, Jews enjoyed in Poland a safe haven; how else can one explain the extraordinary growth of the Polish Jewish community and its central place in the development of Jewish religious and secular life? The anti-Semitic poison first made itself felt in the nineteenth century, reaching a state of destructive fury in the twentieth. Even though Hitler selected Poland as the principal slaughter house for the "final solution" and too many Poles turned their back on its victims, it must never be mistakenly believed that the Holocaust was perpetrated by Poles. Nor must it be ignored that three million Poles perished at German hands.

The Holocaust is the name given to the sadistic killing of six million individual human beings, a quarter of them children. The materials collected in this volume bring to life some of these tragedies, but also the record of good will and exemplary heroism.

Richard Pipes, Professor of History at Harvard University, former Director of East European and Soviet Affairs in the National Security Council, 1981-1982.

M. E. Andreolli, *Deliberations of H. Ezofowicz with M. Butrymowicz*

CONTENTS

PART I TEXT

PART I APPENDIXES

PART II ILLUSTRATIONS

PART III ATLAS

Wilhelm Leopolski, *A Synagogue in Brody*

8

PART I

CHAPTERS:

I. JEWS IN POLAND SYNOPSIS OF 1000-YEAR HISTORY

II. 1264 STATUTE OF JEWISH LIBERTIES IN POLAND

III. JEWISH AUTONOMY IN POLAND 1264-1795

IV. GERMAN ANNIHILATION OF THE JEWS

GERMAN AND POLISH DOCUMENTS OF SHOAH

Jan Nepomucen Lewicki, *The Last Warsaw Maccabee* (an acquatint)

10

PART I

CHAPTER I

JEWS IN POLAND
SYNOPSIS OF 1000-YEAR HISTORY

During 1000 years in Poland, Jews evolved into a modern nation.
The Jewish nation and the State of Israel would not exist today
without centuries of demographic recovery in Poland.

"... Poland saved Jewry from extinction."
From: "The Burning Bush - Anti-Semitism in World History"
by Barnet Litvinoff, on the late medieval
and early modern times.

The age-old Jewish dilemma:
how to remain Jewish and at the same time
to assimilate to the culture, language,
and politics of a host country.

Until the end of the 18th century,
when the majority of all Jews lived in Poland,
Polish Jews had a very positive view of themselves and
did not see themselves as a marginal minority,
as they did in other countries among
Christians and Muslims.

Henryk Berlewi: Glazier

I. INTRODUCTION

In all of Europe and the Mediterranean basin today, the Jews alone have a national culture with direct and continuous links to antiquity. Their extraordinary history began in the Middle East on the borderlands of Asia and Africa. Expelled from Judaea by the Romans in 117 A.D., the Jewish population gravitated to Europe. There, Jewish culture endured over the centuries, flourishing notably in Arab Spain and later in the Rhineland.

Around the time of the Crusades, from the 11th to the 15th centuries, the Jewish people were repeatedly threatened with extinction. The Polish state proved crucial to their survival. Here, the Jews found refuge; their numbers revived, and their culture blossomed. By the time of the first partition of Poland at the end of the 18th century, over 70 percent of the world's Jewish population lived in the territories annexed from Poland by Russia and Austria, and their numbers continued to expand through the 19th century.

At the end of the 20th century, the Jewish nation no longer has a single center of gravity. The U.S.A. and the State of Israel--two very different countries, each with its own problems--have become determinative in the survival of the Jewish people. The descendants of those who came from Poland's historic lands constitute the most important element of the Jewish population in both America and Israel today.

Judaism, Christianity, and Islam

For two millennia, Jews have lived amongst preponderantly Christian or Muslim populations as a foreign minority in exile. They have considered themselves, and have been so by others, a community with distinct religious beliefs and an enduring link to their distant ancestral land, Zion. The Jewish people believed that divine providence alone would redeem them from exile and make possible their eventual return to Zion. Thus, they developed a wholly quietistic attitude toward the process, regarding with skepticism any human attempt at intervention in the divine plan.

In Christian European states, Judaism was tolerated under conditions of segregation and clearly defined and legitimized discrimination. During the Middle Ages, for example, Jews could not enter into feudal relations and therefore they could not hold land. The social equilibrium which contained the Jews through 18 centuries of exile was based, on the one hand, on the fact that conversion was freely available and encouraged, and on the other hand, that refusal to convert meant social marginalization. Those Jews who chose not to convert reconciled themselves to their inferior status by developing a theology of exile. The Christian community, meanwhile, legitimized its discriminatory practices through a philosophy of religious triumphalism.

In late medieval and early modern times, the Jews were caught between Christian accusations that they had murdered Jesus Christ and Muslim contempt that they had not embraced Islam. Although they were able to survive as Jews, their environment was fundamentally hostile. In such a situation, the age-old mechanism of accommodation and quietism seemed the only solution.

Poland stood for several centuries as a border country between Western and Eastern Christianity. She also shared a long southern frontier with Islam. Thus, the drama of the Jewish Diaspora was epitomized in the history of the territory of the Polish Commonwealth, which comprised the Kingdom of Poland and the Grand Duchy of Lithuania. The demographic fortunes of the Jews provide clear evidence that life was much more tolerable for them in Poland than elsewhere in Europe, despite the turbulent, often tragic, history of the state.

The Demographic Perspective

It has been estimated that as many as eight million Jews lived during the first century of the Christian era (*Encyclopedia Judaica*, vol. 13, pp. 866-903). By A.D. 1000, the world's Jewish population may have dwindled to considerably less than 500,000, or fewer than one for every sixteen living in the first century. The revival of the population to its earlier peak of eight million was achieved by 1880, and occurred almost entirely within the historic lands of Poland.

Between 1340 and 1772, the Jewish population of Poland grew 75-fold, from about 10,000 to over 750,000. During the same period, the Christian population grew only 5-fold. This exceptional increase took place in large part between the 11th and 16th centuries, as a result of a massive movement of Jews from

13

western Europe to greater freedom in Poland. Beginning in the 17th century, a steady trickle of Jews migrated west from the historic Polish lands, prompted by the Cossack uprising led by Khmelnitskyy (Chmelnicki) in 1648. The Ukrainian Cossacks perpetrated the bloodiest massacres of Jews since the Romans. However, the tiny Jewish communities subsequently established in the west were much too small to generate a modern ethnic and political identity comparable to that of their parent community in Poland, which included the largest concentration of Jews in the world at that time.

In the 17th century, the Polish Jewish population began to explode. Widespread teenage marriages resulted in unprecedented birthrates, considerably higher than amongst the rest of the population. Between 1650 and 1770, the number of Jews in Poland increased by over 300 percent to more than 750,000. By 1825, Jews comprised an ethnic and cultural minority of over 1,600,000 in the Polish lands annexed by Russia. The Russian census of 1897 indicated a further 300 percent increase in the Jewish population, to nearly 6 million.

The Jewish population continued to grow throughout the partitions of Poland (1795-1918), even though Jewish communal bodies lost the broad autonomy which they had previously enjoyed. By 1880, about six million Jews lived as an ethnic and cultural minority in the Polish provinces annexed by Russia, known as the Pale of Settlement, while about one million lived in Lesser Poland, renamed Galicia by the Austrians. It should be noted that the Jewish population in the old Polish provinces of Ukraine, Byelorussia, Vholynia, Podolia, and Lithuania grew by some 600 to 700 percent during the 19th century, whereas the Polish population in these areas declined, due to tsarist policies of social engineering and Russification.

Between 1880 and 1940, the world's Jewish population grew dramatically to nearly 17 million, a number of whom migrated further west after 1881, notably the United States. By 1944, the number of Jews had fallen to 11 million as a result of the genocide perpetrated by the Nazi German government. By 1980, the world's Jewry comprised about 13 million people. Demographers, however, forecast a drop to about 12.4 million by the year 2000 (Evyatar Friesel, *Atlas of Modern Jewish History*. Oxford University Press, 1990).

The Polish Context: The Middle Ages and the Early Modern Period

During the Middle Ages, Jews referred to the western Slavic lands as the New Canaan. In time, this biblical name came to denote Poland in Hebrew writings. It reflected certain mystical hopes that Poland would one day become the Holy Land and thus fulfill the Jewish theology of exile.

Poland was the only country to accept a massive influx of Jewish immigrants when they fled from the excesses of the Christian crusades and their aftermath in the 14th and 15th centuries. Thus, the Jews settled in the country just as Poland's distinctive civilization, based on the indigenous democratic process, was coming into being. In the late medieval and early modern period, Poland not only comprised Europe's largest political body of free citizens, but was alone in formulating and upholding the principle of freedom of conscience. This constituted the earliest European experiment with civil and human rights on a large scale. In all of the rest of Europe, less than one-tenth as many people as in Poland enjoyed effective civil rights.

Accordingly, Poland extended unprecedented and long-lasting privileges to more Jews than did any other country during the Diaspora. As early as 1264, the Charter of Jewish Liberties allowed Jews in Poland to set up a system of self-government with exclusive jurisdiction over religious and cultural issues. Unlike in other countries, in Poland Jews were not compelled to live in ghettos or to display the yellow star of David on their clothing. (Jews were compelled by the Germans on December 1, 1939, to wear the Star of David for the duration of World War II. This happened for the first time in the history of Poland.) Moreover, Jews were not subject to discriminatory taxes and could pursue the occupation of their choice. They were granted the right to bear arms, and the laws of the land ensured the freedom and safety of their persons, their property, and their religion. It was an environment uniquely favorable to the flourishing of Jewish heritage and culture.

Professor Wiktor Weintraub of Harvard University has written: "Elsewhere they were molested by city mobs...Poland was attracting

[Jews] from other countries...Life was simply more tolerable for Jews in Poland than elsewhere. In the first place, except for an inconsequential attempt in Lithuania, by the end of the 15th century there were no mass expulsions, nor any massacres. Moreover, the Jews enjoyed a much greater degree of self-government in Poland than in any other country." ("Tolerance and Intolerance in Old Poland," *Canadian Slavic Papers,* vol. 13, spring 1971.)

"As a multi-national and multi-denominational state since the 14th century, Poland did not follow the extreme principle of intolerance according to which the majority imposes its faith upon minority...Poland adhered largely to another trend of the pre-modern state whereby members of minority groups had the right to follow their own religion and customs: autonomy. The Polish state generally gave minorities the right to organize as religious groups and to a certain extent even protected their freedom to exercise their respective religions, even supervising their autonomous organizations." (Bernard D. Weinryb, *The Jews of Poland: A Social and Economic History of the Jewish Community in Poland from 1100 to 1800.* Jewish Publication Society of America, Philadelphia: 1973.)

Toleration lay at the heart of Polish values, and the common European premise that a ruler would impose his own religion on his subjects--*cuius regio, eius religio*--was not accepted. The Polish contribution to the concept of pluralism was first stated in 1415, by Paweł Włodkowicz (Paulus Vladimiri), Poland's ambassador to the Council of Constance. In 1493 it was given further force when Poland became the first state in early modern Europe to be ruled by a bicameral parliamentary government.

Forms of republican government had been introduced by 1454 among the land-owning nobility and gentry who comprised Poland's dominant feudal estate, *szlachta.* This group included over 10 percent of the country's population, and the national parliament which emerged from their deliberations was the most broadly based representative political institution in Europe at the time. Thus, from 1454 on Poland became a Commonwealth of Nobility -- in fact a Commonwealth of Citizen-Soldiers.

Moreover, parliamentary government in Poland was underpinned by the most sophisticated legal system in Europe. Its development had started relatively early. Due process under law, for example, was established in Poland at the beginning of the 15th century, some 250 years earlier than in England. One million landowners, from all ethnic groups, enjoyed active rights of citizenship in Poland -- far more than among the free populations of England, Scandinavia, the Italian city states, or Russian Novgorod.

Polish Jews were given broad cultural and political autonomy on the pattern of the national parliamentary government, as were other minorities, including Armenians and Ukrainian Cossacks. Such ethnic diversity was largely responsible for the great Polish Renaissance, most vibrant during the 15th and 16th centuries. That this was also the "golden age" of Jewish culture in Poland highlights the point ably made by professor Walter Kolarz, that "an intermixture of [ethnic groups], so generally felt as a misfortune, this source of wars, frictions and unrest, has been in reality one of the basic conditions for national development of different peoples, a cause of sustained intellectual fertilization begetting innumerable cultural values. The many-colored map of nationalities has sense when one considers the intellectual benefits derived from the mingling of peoples. It is not the purity of race, nor the national homogeneity in any one territory, which has advanced culture in the European Middle East, but rather the blending of...several peoples. The development of the nations of Central and Eastern Europe attests that in the cosmopolitan character of a state, province, or town lay the best chance for the national advancement of all its inhabitants." (*Myth and Reality in Eastern Europe*, London: Drummond, 1946.)

The peaceful coexistence of diverse ethnic groups in old Poland is well described by Professor Gotthold Rhode of the University of Mainz: "There were few countries in Europe practicing a tolerance in both religious and ethnic-national matters similar to that of the Polish-Lithuanian Union of the 16th and early 17th centuries. No less than six languages (Latin, Polish, German, [Byelo-] Russian, Hebrew, and Armenian) were recognized for use in official documents, and four Christian confessions lived in a perfect coexistence with Judaism and Islam until the Counter-Reformation began its struggle against Protestant and Orthodox denominations." (In David S. Collier and Kurt Glaser, eds., *Berlin and the Future of Eastern Europe*, Chicago: Regency, 1963.)

In 1525, the Catholic King Sigismund of Poland became the first European monarch to accept homage from a Protestant vassal, Albrecht von Hohenzollern. For over a century afterwards, Hohenzollern successors regularly paid homage in Warsaw and Cracow. It is interesting to note that the same Hohenzollerns eventually became emperors of unified Germany (1871-1918).

During the 16th and 17th centuries, "Poland's atmosphere of religious toleration made it an attractive land of settlement for Jews aiming to avoid religiously inspired persecution in Western Europe... In this State Without Stakes Protestant, Catholic, Orthodox, Armenian, Muslim, and Jews managed to practice their respective religions in close proximity without being drawn into holy warfare. This was a remarkable record of ethnic pluralism and religious toleration, considering the seething religious strife in Western Europe and the religious exclusivity and xenophobia of Poland's Russian neighbor.

"Economically, Poland's rich farmlands and forests had given her a lucrative role as the main supplier of food and natural products to Western Europe." (M. J. Rosman, *The Lord's Jews*. Harvard University Press, Cambridge, Mass.: 1990. *State Without Stakes* is a book on Polish religious toleration by J. Tazbir (New York - Warsaw, 1973)

The basic ideals of democracy were also brought to maturity in Poland during the 15th and 16th centuries. These were: a social contract between a government and its citizens; the principles of government by consent, personal and religious freedom, and individual civil rights; the value of self-reliance; and the prevention of authoritarian state power.

The First Polish Republic was formally founded in 1569 with the establishment of the Union of Lublin between Poland and Lithuania. It cemented a process started in 1386, when Lithuania had accepted Western Christianity from Poland. The union of the two nations developed as a single state shaped by Polish culture and the Polish legal system. The principle of the equality of all citizens was articulated by the passage of a law abolishing titles of nobility; the chief executive officer of the new republic was an elected king.

As part of the founding of the First Polish Republic, Muslims and Jews were, for the first time, offered emancipation without having to forswear their own religion. Many Muslim clans, descendants of prisoners of war who had settled in northern Poland, took advantage of this opportunity. The Jewish leadership, however, preferred to maintain its own jurisdiction and cultural distinctiveness within the new republic. The community had developed a vast network of religious, social and political institutions, and Jewish autonomy was subsequently confirmed by the creation of the *Congressus Judaicus* (1592-1764), a Jewish national parliament patterned after that of the larger state. The Congressus Judaicus was unique in the history of Jewish Diaspora.

Besides these political privileges and the safeguards of Polish law, the Jews also enjoyed an economic symbiosis with *szlachta*. Proverbial, every member of *szlachta* had his Jew. In fact, a Jew was required to pay a fee to the Jewish communal government, the *kahal* (elected by each main Jewish community known as *kehilla*), for the exclusive privilege, known as *khazaka*, to do business with a gentile in Poland. Such a Jewish holder of the *khazaka* was known as a *balchazaka*. This arrangement effectively guaranteed that he would not have to submit to competitive bidding against another Jew when negotiating the contract. Thus, *hazaka* constituted a license issued by a *kahal;* it entitled a person to hold the monopoly on some economic enterprise.

The social and economic organization of Jewish life in Poland included a number of institutions such as: the *heter iska* or a legal circumvention of the biblical prohibition of loaning on interest; the elective *kahal*; the licenced rabbinate; occupational societies -- the *hevras*; the letter of credit and travel check, which originated in Poland, was known as the *mamram* (often misspelled as "membron" or "membran").

Those Polish Jews who chose to convert to Christianity between 1588 and 1795 were automatically granted rights as full citizens of the republic, a process known as ennoblement. In the second half of the 18th century, this provision made possible the large-scale conversion of the Jewish Frankist sect. The most massive voluntary conversion of Jews to Christianity during the Diaspora, this was motivated by Frankist hopes that Poland could become their new Holy Land and reflected the political crises and financial insolvency then afflicting the organized Jewish communities.

As many as 50,000 Jews may have obtained full rights as Polish citizens in Lithuania at this time. In addition to some 24,000 Frankists, this figure includes thousands of Jewish women who had married gentiles, and thousands of Jews who worked on manors and on landed estates. Many Frankist families, however, preserved their Jewish heritage for over a century after conversion by marrying only amongst themselves. In Warsaw alone there were 6,000 Frankists.

For 500 years, therefore, from 1264 to the end of the 18th century, Poland afforded the Jews an unparalleled period of protection under the law. Historians have described early modern Poland as "the paradise of the Jews," "heaven for the Jews, paradise for the nobles, hell for the serfs," "the sanctuary of the Jews."

It has rightly been said that "the old Polish State was...the first experiment on a large scale with a federal republic down to the appearance of the United States. In the 16th and 17th centuries this republic was the freest state in Europe, that state in which the greatest degree of constitutional, civic, and intellectual liberty prevailed...Like the United States today, Poland was...heaven for the poor and the oppressed of all neighboring countries--Germans, Jews, Greeks, Magyars, Armenians, Tartars, French, Russians... Finally the oldest republic represented an effort to organize the vast open plain between the Baltic and the Black Seas--a region containing so many weak and underdeveloped areas and a region so much exposed to Germanic ambitions on the one side and the Turko-Tartar onslaughts on the other side--into a compact and powerful realm, which was directed indeed by the strongest and most advanced voice within its borders." (Charles H. Haskins and Robert H. Lord, *Some Problems of the Peace Conference*, Harvard University Press, 1920; as quoted in M.K. Dziewanowski, *Poland in the Twentieth Century*, New York: Columbia University Press, 1977.) This benign picture gradually disintegrated, however, with the decline and fall of Poland at the end of the 18th century.

The Polish Context: The Enlightenment to the Present

The Enlightenment, or the Age of Reason, spanned the 17th and 18th centuries. It was a secular humanist philosophical movement which forcefully questioned traditional religious moral authority. Its exponents attacked social injustice, superstition, and ignorance, arguing that men had the capacity using science and rationalism to better their own world. The Enlightenment generated important advances in such fields as anatomy, astronomy, chemistry, geography, mathematics, and physics. It prompted explorations in education, law, philosophy, and politics. On the other hand, the philosophy of Enlightenment prompted a false sense of security in the conviction that the human mind is perfect and capable of correctly diagnosing and resolving any problem. Its exponents therefore rejected the recognition of human limitations which had underpinned the philosophical and political caution of earlier ages.

The Polish Brethren (Unitarians), an off-shoot of Polish Calvinism, were expelled from their native land in 1658, as conscientious objectors. They settled instead in England and Holland, publishing the monumental *Bibliotheca Fratrum Polonorum* in Amsterdam ten years later. Their rationalist philosophy considerably influenced Enlightenment thinkers such as Baruch Spinosa (1632-1677) and especially John Locke (1632-1704), and they contributed greatly to the development of the modern concept of toleration.

One of the earliest significant attempts to emancipate large numbers of Jews in Europe took place in Poland in 1764, exactly 500 years after the proclamation of the Statute of Jewish Liberties in Kalisz in 1264. It was associated with a fiscal reform occasioned by the collapse of the Jewish banking system in Poland. (The situation reached proportions which resembled the crisis of Savings and Loan institutions in the United States in the 1980s and 1990s.)

The resistance to change by the autonomous Jewish institutions derailed efforts by the Polish government and in the Polish parliament to emancipate the large Jewish population in Poland in 1791. A Jewish general synod, or convention, was organized in 1791 in order to collect funds for a lobbying effort in Warsaw to re-establish *Congressus Judaicus*, which was abolished in 1764 as a part of the emancipation. (It should be noted that this episode long predated the French Revolution, which brought full emancipation of the tiny Jewish community in France.)

The rhetoric of the enlightenment firmly underpinned the revolutions which created the American and French republics at the end of the 18th century and, paradoxically, also fueled the partition of the First Polish Republic at the hands of Russia, Prussia, and Austria in 1772-1795. Whereas the people of America and France won individual liberty and civil rights, the people of Poland faced subjugation to three authoritarian regimes. These rulers pretended to be "enlightened," while in reality they were brutally enforcing the concept of "a well ordered police state." Their purpose was to reshape the society in order to increase the power and wealth of their states. They adapted the concept of "a well ordered police state" from the writings of the exponents of Enlightenment. Their absolutist states were instruments for reshaping and policing society by means of detailed regulations based on "natural law or reason."

Edmund Burke (1729-1797), the progressive British statesman who had ardently supported America's quest for independence, had pronounced Poland's political tradition and its republican constitution of 3 May 1791 "more moderate than the French and more progressive than the English," but many exponents of the Enlightenment, ignorant of Poland's history and values, acted as apologists for the partitions. The skeptic Voltaire, so biting in his criticism of the absolutist monarchs of France, was especially servile to the despotic courts of Prussia and Russia.

Besides providing the motivation and justification for the obliteration of the Polish state, the Enlightenment introduced the hollow notion of emancipation unsupported by pluralism. The fall of the First Polish Republic profoundly altered the situation of Jewish people in the historic Polish lands. The obliteration of the old republic brought replacement of Polish "government-from-below" by foreign "government-from-above" imposed by the three autocratic empires which divided the lands of Poland.

Many of the most significant political and social movements of the 19th and 20th centuries had their roots in the philosophies of the Enlightenment. As Moshe Leshem observed: "The Enlightenment certainly failed the Jews. Consider its legacy. The Enlightenment begat emancipation, emancipation begat anti-Semitism; anti-Semitism begat Zionism, and the Holocaust." (*Balaam's Curse.* New York: Simon and Schuster, 1989.)

Jews in Germanic lands experienced a brief period of toleration in the 19th century. Initially, they were afforded emancipation, or legal equality, by some of the smaller principalities, and after mid-century, by Hapsburg Austria and Hohenzollern Prussia, the two largest German dominated states.

The Kingdom of Prussia, however, bore witness to the fact that German nationalism and militarism was still prevalent. The name "Prussia," which originally denoted a country bordering on Poland and Lithuania, had been adopted by the Hohenzollerns of Berlin in 1701, recalling the bloody 13th-century conquest and genocide of the Balto-Slavic Prussians by the armed monks of Germany, the Teutonic Knights.

The development of such German attitudes reached a critical point in 1859. During that year, Karl Marx (1818-1883) published his critique of political economy, containing the first complete presentation of the materialist interpretation of history; the year 1859 was also noted for the first performance of Richard Wagner's *Tristan und Isolde* (for comments on the influence of Wagner's mythological operas, please, turn to page 255); and Charles Darwin (1809-1882) published *On the Origin of Species by Means of Natural Selection.* Darwin's description of human evolution as a struggle for the survival of the fittest provoked much controversy and was crudely misapplied to contemporary social and political questions. The slow evolutionary process which he had discerned in operation over millions of years was transformed, with the overweening humanist self-confidence characteristic of the Enlightenment, into a rationale for social engineering. "Social Darwinism" presupposed rivalry between ethnic groups and challenged the moral restraints which had traditionally governed social relations. In this way, it fortified the concept of *Lebensraum* (first formulated in 1848) and radicalized German attitudes towards the assimilation of minorities, such as Poles and Jews.

This trend was strengthened in 1871, when more than 350 self-governing states were unified to form a single Germany under Prussia. The event was accompanied by intense nationalism, which lauded "Germanity" as "a touchstone of respectability," and claimed that "the Prussians [were] the best of Germans." Among the lower middle class in particular, anti-Semitism seemed the natural corollary of *voelkisch-racism*, the priority of the German *Volk* (people).

A certain number of assimilated Jews participated in this nationalist fervor, thereby distancing themselves from the Poles who, in general, resisted pressures of Germanization.

Indeed, the 19th century and the legacy of the Enlightenment raised fundamental questions regarding Jewish identity. Individually and collectively, Jews suddenly encountered a host of issues associated with "culture shock." Finding themselves with legal equality, they had to confront the cultural differences between themselves and the non-Jewish majority. "Jewish emancipationist aspirations were understood and evaluated in a special way. The 'falling away' of a caste group from its traditional role evokes anxiety and bewilderment within the larger environment." (Aleksander Hertz, *The Jews in Polish Culture*. Evanston, Illinois: Northwestern University Press, 1988.)

Their situation was accentuated by the fact that Jews were now more visible in European society than ever before. The dramatic growth of Europe's cities during the 19th century reflected a disproportionate influx of Polish Jews, whose cultural traditions had long ensured that they were the most literate sector of the European population. (Jewish literacy in Poland was, however, in Hebrew, rather than in any of the modern European languages.) In the historic lands of Poland, the majority of Jews remained in the provinces annexed by Russia and Austria, but those who migrated to the capitals of Europe contributed in great measure to the arts and sciences of the modern world.

The century between 1815 and 1914 has been called the Jewish Renaissance. Shlomo Avineri, a Jewish scholar, describes it thus: "From any conceivable point of view, the 19th century was the best century Jews had ever experienced, collectively and individually, since the destruction of the Temple. With the French Revolution and Emancipation, Jews were allowed for the first time into European society on an equal footing. For the first time Jews enjoyed equality before the law... schools, universities, and professions were gradually opened to them... Indeed, if one compares the beginning of the 19th century to its end... it becomes dramatically evident that economically, socially, politically, and intellectually, this was the most revolutionary century in history for the Jews... [who] until 1815 hardly... had a major impact on European politics or philosophy, finance or medicine, the arts or the law.

"By 1914... Jewish life [had shifted] from the periphery to the center of European society. Geographically, Jews were now heavily concentrated in the metropolises of Europe. Berlin, Vienna, Budapest, Warsaw--and to a lesser degree London, Paris, Odessa--had a disproportionately high percentage of Jewish inhabitants as did the major urban centers in America. And Jews had achieved prominence far beyond their numbers in the intellectual life of these cities. Jews had achieved important positions in journalism, literature, music, science, engineering, painting, philosophy, and psychology; the world of finance was replete with Jewish magnates, and revolutionary movements abounded with Jewish leaders... Jews might not have been as prominent as some anti-Semites would have liked to believe in the commanding height of society, they were certainly at its center--and very visible." *The Making of Modern Zionism*. New York: Basic Books, 1981.

Yet, the political changes wrought in Europe by the Enlightenment had also transformed the "Jewish Question" into a political problem. Jewish efforts to assimilate to the German nation were eventually rejected by the growing racism of the Germans, despite many interfaith marriages. The resistance of Orthodox Jews was also an important factor. Between 1880 and 1939 the contrast between eastern and western European Jews grew deeper. Individuals might go their own way but within the population as a whole distinct groups began to emerge, defined by their specific religious and linguistic orientations. Those who subscribed to a more strictly religious identity used Hebrew, supplemented by Yiddish, while those who interpreted Judaism in secular terms used Yiddish as their primary language. Jewish secularism found expression in nationalism, socialism, and liberalism.

II. ETHNIC IDENTITY

In considering the phenomenon of the Jewish Diaspora, it is pertinent to ask what motivated so many western European peoples to expel the Jews from their midst on pain of death; and, conversely, why Poland, a Christian state, remained relatively unaffected by such anti-Jewish sentiments?

For five hundred years, Poland provided uniquely favorable conditions for the development of a Jewish ethnic identity by allowing Jews autonomous jurisdiction over political, economic, and cultural affairs within their own communities. The philosophy of freedom which characterized republican Poland, and the pluralistic nature of her parliament, precluded the sweeping draconian decisions imposed upon Jews by absolutist rulers in the rest of Europe. Thus, by 1795 the Jewish community in Poland, with Yiddish as its national language and governed in observance of Talmudic law, was by far the largest and strongest in the world. It included over 70 percent of all Jews. In contrast to the tiny Jewish communities of western Europe, which had to conform to the language and culture of their host nations, the Jews in Poland were able to develop a modern national identity, out of which grew the full-blown Jewish nationalism upon which the State of Israel was founded.

The Development of Jewish Identity in Poland

It is worth noting at the outset that the historic Polish lands comprise a culturally and geographically integral area which should properly be designated east-central Europe. This region, stretching east from Germany to the limits of Western Christianity and bordering on the domains of Russian Christianity (later, communism) has always had its own specific character. Poland provided the main organizational base for its northern reaches, while the south was dominated mainly by Turkish Islam. The establishment of the Soviet bloc in the wake of World War II subjugated this region to communist rule for 50 years.

In American literature, however, Jews from this region are usually misidentified as "east European." This usage probably reflects the derogatory German expression *Ostjuden* applied to Yiddish-speaking Jews living to the east of Germany, who were perceived by the Germans as an economic and cultural threat during the late 19th and early 20th centuries.

Poland, on the other hand, has historically treated Jews with more grace. Its location on the borders of Eastern and Western Christianity taught respect for religious pluralism. Toward the end of the first Christian millennium, Polish princes permitted Jews to settle in their lands because they needed their skills as merchants and craftsmen. Between the 10th and 13th centuries, the everyday language of these Jews was Slavonic, mainly old Polish. In official contexts, however, they used Hebrew to write

the king's name, and the Hebrew script appeared on coins minted by Jews for the Polish monarchy.

Polish Christians were exempted from participating in the Crusades of the 11th to 13th centuries because of their ongoing efforts to convert the pagan Prussians on their borders. Consequently, they did not become involved in the horrific pogroms which resulted when crusading zeal was diverted against local Jewish populations in western and central Europe. In fact, toward the end of this period the Poles themselves were subjected to similar atrocities by the Teutonic Knights, German armed monks.

During the 13th century, therefore, a large number of Yiddish-speaking Jews fled from persecution in the West and settled in Poland. There they were able to use Yiddish freely, and from the 14th century Yiddish became the basic language of all of Poland's Jews, rather than Polish, Ukrainian, Byelorussian, or Lithuanian.

A distinct national language is integral to the cultural independence of a people. The Yiddish language (from *Jud[isch]* + *deutsch*) was derived from the Mittelhochdeutsch of western Germany and was infused with Hebrew -- Aramaic and Slavic elements. As it spread across the vast territories of the Polish state, many local dialects emerged, but it still served as a core of ethnic unity. By the end of the 17th century, Polish Jews wrote Yiddish from right to left in the Hebrew script, from which short vowels are omitted. Over the centuries, the number of Yiddish-speaking Jews in Poland grew dramatically, so that by 1750 they represented 6-10 percent of the country's population, and over 70 percent of the world's Jewry.

Polish Jews were notable for a particularly strong attachment to their people and a confident, positive self-image as Jews. They harbored their cultural integrity in small towns known as *shtetls* (shtey-tels), encountering non-Jews only through trade and extra-marital sex. Moreover, the pluralistic social climate of late medieval and early modern Poland made possible the creation of a parallel school system, based on Talmudic educational traditions. These Talmudic schools were the pride of the Orthodox Jews, who kept them strictly isolated from gentile influences. Bright Jewish children could enter primary schools (*kheders*) at the age of three. The boys would then attend higher schools, (*yeshibots*) from the age of nine.

20

The unique situation of Poland's Jews is all the more striking when compared with that of the small communities in other parts of Europe. In France, for example, Jews did not have an everyday language of their own. Their rabbis knew the scriptures, but most of the congregation could only mouth the Hebrew prayers, unable to understand the words. French Jews aspired to be Frenchmen, just as Dutch Jews hoped to become Dutch. The cultural isolationism of Polish Jews, however, was a deliberate policy, grounded in the lessons of history and the traditional Jewish theology of exile. Jewish culture had to be rebuilt in Poland. The Jewish leadership was conscious of the fact that the integration of Jews into the Italian and Spanish renaissance had ended in catastrophe. Therefore, in Poland the Jews shaped their culture anew, limiting contacts with local Christians despite the important economic role which they themselves played in the community at large. After the partitions, many Polish Jews migrated south to Hungary, Slovakia, and above all to Vienna, where they tried to continue this way of life.

The fall of the Polish state at the end of the 18th century, and the resulting injury to the Polish people, prompted the birth of modern Polish nationalism. Early Polish nationalism, in its turn, became a model for other ethnic groups which had participated in the pluralistic unity of the Polish-Lithuanian Commonwealth (1386-1569) and the First Polish Republic (1569-1795), including Jews, Ukrainians, Byelorussians, Lithuanians, and Latvians.

After the final dismembering of Poland, the Jewish national identity continued to develop in the historic lands of Poland during the 19th and 20th centuries. A great number of Polish Jews were forced to live in the Pale of Settlement established by Russia in the former eastern borderlands of Poland. (The term *Pale* was first used to describe the area of English jurisdiction in Ireland.) Poles and Jews alike were stripped of their freedoms. The Poles struggled to rebuild their state, while the majority of Polish Jews wanted to survive as Jews and therefore sought an accommodation with the three partitioning powers, Austria, Prussia and Russia.

The Enlightenment and its concomitant secularization changed the Jews' perceptions of themselves, as well as how they were perceived by others. They now found themselves in an environment which was gradually pulling them away from their traditional religious background. Gentile society was infused with a new national consciousness which emphasized ethnicity, a common language, and a shared history, either real or imagined. Emancipated Jews who tried to be completely secular and fully assimilated found that non-Jews still perceived them as Jewish, rather than French, German, Russian, or Polish. This was especially true in the historic lands of Poland where they were caught in the cross fire of nationalist struggles between Germans, Russians, Poles, Ukrainians, Byelorussians, Latvians, and Lithuanians.

Like others around them, Jews tried to articulate a national identity by turning back to their historic roots. They looked to Hebrew as a non-religious literary medium -- a language of novels, poems, polemics, and journalism. Indeed, Jews started emigrating to Palestine from the lands of prepartition Poland even before the concept of Zionism was developed by the beginning of the 20th century. After World War I, those Jews living in Poland became the mainstay of the Zionist movement.

Between the two world wars, Jewish culture flourished in Poland, despite competition and at times violent strife between the various ethnic and national groups inhabiting the region. These tense relations were aggravated by the Great Depression, and were radicalized by the threat of National Socialist Germany and by Soviet propaganda and subversion. The extraordinarily vibrant cultural life of the Jews in Poland was terminated by the genocide which the Germans started with the organization of the Warsaw Ghetto in 1940, and pursued in their program of extermination through mass executions which began in the fall of 1941 and a horrific industrial process, 1942-1944.

The population of occupied Poland and the historic eastern borderlands of Poland experienced the harshest regime of any in German occupied Europe. They were unable to prevent the mass murder of more than three million Polish Christians and almost as many Polish Jews.

Descendants of Polish Jews in the United States

In the United States, the most significant phenomenon affecting American Jewry is the process of Americanization, which weakens its traditional Jewish identity. The general abandonment of the Yiddish language and acceptance of English as an everyday language is an important factor in this process. Thus, the preservation of the Jewishness of American Jews is challenged by the pluralism of American society.

In 1980, 5,690,000 people, or 1.8 percent of the population, identified themselves as Jews in the United States. In 1991 the Council of Jewish Federations estimated that 4,300,000 Americans identified themselves as Jews. A below-replacement birthrate and assimilation through intermarriage has resulted in a continuing decline in the Jewish minority in the U.S.A. From 1964 to 1985 the number of interfaith marriages involving Jews increased from 9 to 52 percent, while 75 percent of the children of interfaith marriages were not raised as Jews. In recent years the Jewish community has gained 185,000 while losing 210,000 through conversion according to the 1990 study of the Jewish population by the Council of Jewish Federations.

One approach to this situation is that the Jewish community should welcome anyone who chooses to be identified as a Jew. However, the traditional opinion among Jews is that the survival of the American Jewry depends on the continuity of Jewish thought, values, and institutions. The need of Jewish ideology is stressed as much more important than the prevailing vague pro-Israelism, nostalgia, liberal universalism, and fear of anti-Semitism.

The lack of a strong religious commitment in the Jewish-American community is evidenced by the fact that only 20 percent is seriously religious. In the July 22, 1991, *Newsweek* article "The Intermarrying Kind," Steven Bayme, director of Jewish communal affairs for the American Jewish Committee, is quoted as saying, "We are very good at telling the State Department what to do about Israel, but in the privacy of our homes we can not find words to tell our children why they should be Jewish."

III. JEWISH RELATIONS WITH POLES

Ever since the Nazi German government perpetrated the mass murder of at least two-thirds of the European Jewish population, historians have been trying to assess the tragedy objectively. According to the Zionist interpretation, the genocide of the Jews was the culmination of a long history of western anti-Semitism. Most Jewish historians seem to

agree with this view. Others, especially Germans, prefer to see the Shoah, or Holocaust, as a Nazi aberration. Many historians, including some Germans, identify extreme nationalist arrogance and megalomania as a significant factor in the mentality of the Nazis and the vast majority of German citizens who enthusiastically supported them to the bitter end in 1945.

Relations Between Jews and Poles Prior to the 20th Century

During the first two centuries after the 1264 Charter of Jewish Liberties, the Jewish population of Poland grew. Many Jews leased and managed properties such as the royal mint and salt mines. Others collected customs duties and tolls. In general, Jews were not engaged in agriculture, but a few of them owned villages, manors, fish ponds and mills. In the later Middle Ages, Jews became involved with certain crafts, establishing themselves as, for example, tailors, tanners, and furriers. This brought them into direct competition with Christian burghers and resulted in sporadic anti-Jewish riots in certain cities during the 14th and 15th centuries. Yet, these minor disturbances did not adversely affect the steady Jewish immigration into Poland.

In some instances, competition between Jews and Christian burghers spurred one party to try to exclude the other from a particular town. On the whole, Christians were more successful in obtaining privileges of exclusion against Jews (known as *de non tolerandis Judeis*) than vice versa (*de non tolerandis Christianis*). However, there were many examples of exclusion of Christians (in Kazimierz near Cracow, Poznan, and in many Lithuanian communities, to name a few).

The erosion of the Polish republic began when a deluge of invasions in the 17th century ruined the economy and shifted the political power from the lower and middle gentry to the owners of huge estates. This paralyzed the progress of reforms necessary for updating Poland's constitution of 1505, known as Nihil Novi (nothing new about us without our consent). Instead of further broadening the democratic process, reverse trends were set in motion. The peasants could not pay rents and started paying for land use with very inefficient serf labor. A number of rebellions broke out for diverse reasons, ranging from civil rights of

Ukrainian Cossacks to opposition to needed constitutional reforms.

The expansion of large noble estates in the Ukraine provoked a Cossack uprising in 1648, directed primarily against the local landowners, who by this time had come to accept Polish language and culture and considered themselves fully Polish. The immediate cause of the uprising was the Polish national parliament's failure to pass a bill on the ennoblement of the Ukrainian Cossacks and on mobilization for a crusade against the Crimean Tartars the previous year. The uprising reflected the growing conflict of interest within the Polish electorate. The power struggle between small and medium sized landowners and the landed magnates was won by the latter, to the detriment of the democratic process in Poland.

From the 16th through 18th centuries, Jews lived under the protection of *szlachta*, the noble citizens of Poland. The Jews were perceived as allies of the large landowners and thus also fell victim to the rebellion. Some 20 percent of Poland's Jews, possibly as many as 100,000, were killed.

The city of Lwow was among those beleaguered by the insurgents. Cossack leader Bohdan Khmyelnitskyy (Chmielnicki) demanded that all Jews within the walls be handed over to him before he would lift the siege. But the Poles refused, thereby saving the lives of the Jews. As Henryk Grynberg has pointed out, "in fact, the Polish armies, who were at war with [the Cossacks], were the sole defenders of the Jews." (See Appendix II, p. 147; *Is Polish Anti-Semitism Special? Midstream, Monthly Jewish Review*, August/September 1983)

During the Swedish invasion of Poland (1655-1658), Jews were accused of collaborating with the enemy. Reprisals and anti-Jewish riots occurred in Brzeziny, Gabin, Leczyca, and a few other towns in 1656.

Over the next decades, the urban Jewish population of central Poland increased more rapidly than that of the Christian burghers. Economic rivalries between the two groups became correspondingly more acute.

Through the end of the 17th and the whole of the 18th centuries, the economic situation in Poland grew considerably worse. Declining international trade and the ravages of war led to the pauperization of almost all the urban population, including Jews. Many Jews became peddlers or small traders. Others became traveling craftsmen, such as shoemakers, tailors, carpenters, haberdashers, blacksmiths, and musicians. As such, they were indispensable to the rural economy. The resulting interdependence between Polish villages and Jewish *shtetls* (small towns) was unique in Europe and persisted through the vicissitudes of the following centuries until World War II.

In the wake of the partition of Poland during the 19th century, Jewish relations with Poles in the areas annexed by Russia, Prussia, and Austria were linked to the question of Polish independence. (Some 75 percent of the first Polish Republic was gradually annexed by the Russian Empire. In so doing, it acquired about 80 percent of the Polish Jews and over 50 percent of the ethnic Poles.) The political integration of the annexed lands into the new empires took over a century to complete. This process was primarily directed against the Poles, whereas the Jews were considered a separate ethnic group, of secondary political importance. The Jewish population was allowed to grow, despite Russia's traditional policy of "rendering the Jews harmless."

Those Poles committed to national independence became the most politically persecuted people in the lands of the former multinational Polish Republic. Feudal traditions lived on, however, so that Poles who were recognized as nobility and would accept Russification or Germanization were well treated by the imperial governments. Meanwhile, the large Jewish population of the area suffered various forms of discrimination.

In the Germanic states of the Viennese Hapsburgs and the Hohenzollerns of Berlin, emancipation laws enacted in the 19th century theoretically gave Jews equal rights. In practice, they were never fully accepted as either Germans or Austrians. In the east, the Russians confined the Jews in the Pale of Jewish Settlement, comprising mainly provinces annexed from Poland and small coastal areas won from the Turks on the shores of the Black Sea. The outlook was bleak, especially under the harsh rule of the Russian authorities, who had devised some 600 punitive anti-Jewish laws. In response, modern Jewish nationalism was born in the central, eastern, and southern lands of prepartition Poland; and in its wake came the will to rebuild the State of Israel in Palestine.

The fall of Poland, therefore, led to the separation of the national interests of Poles and

Jews. Their centuries-old relationship marked by symbiosis and interdependence was transformed into one dominated by competition.

While the Poles were rallying their forces in the struggle for the restoration of Poland, over 95 percent of the Jews of Poland's historic lands were primarily concerned to maintain their independent identity as Jews. They did not feel that Polish independence was vital to them. Indeed, the Polish cause was gradually discredited in Jewish eyes, especially after the defeat of national uprisings in 1830 and 1863. The consequences were evident from the 1840s in the eastern regions of the former Polish Republic, where Jews who wished to assimilate with the surrounding gentile population started to adopt the Russian language and culture, rather than the Polish. In Greater Poland, the Berlin government had already begun to exert pressure to induce the Germanization of Polish Jews. The process was facilitated by the fact that Polish Jews spoke Yiddish which, as a Germanic language, gave them an entry into German culture.

The governments of Austria, Germany, and Russia deliberately encouraged and manipulated latent tensions between Poles and Jews in the annexed territories. Although Jews and Poles had lived side-by-side in these areas for nearly one thousand years, they did not have an intimate knowledge of each other's culture, and therefore many of them fell prey to easy generalizations. Any sign of Jewish cooperation with the imperial authorities was seen by Poles as harmful to the central issue of independence and, as such, treacherous. This Polish stereotype of the unpatriotic Jew was intensified by the specter of the Jewish Communist. Jews, for their part, developed stereotypes of Poles. A certain spirit of condescension can be heard in the words of one 18th-century rabbi, who declared, "Were it not that there is some good that [comes from the Poles] they would not have been created at all." By the late 19th century, Jews tended to divide all gentiles into progressive revolutionary philo-Semites and reactionary anti-Semites.

During World War I there were a number of Jews among the volunteers serving in the Polish legions under Józef Piłsudski. At the same time, influential Jewish groups, both of the left and of the right, openly opposed efforts to recreate an independent Poland. The degree of success and visibility which they achieved was in large part due to the fact that they shared with the Berlin government concerns about Russia. The Germans had active economic interests in Russian territory, were engaged in battle against Russian forces, and were desperate to get out of the predicament of a two-front war. They hoped to defeat the Russians, eliminate the eastern front and then be able to win on their western front. The Jews were eager to free themselves of the oppression within the Pale of Settlement under Russia and therefore favored a German victory on the Russian front. Since the Russo-German war theater was located mainly within the Polish ethnic area, these considerations were directly related to Poland's cause.

At the outset of the war, Zionist leaders, seeking to establish a national homeland for the Jews, approached the Berlin government with a proposal for a German protectorate east of Germany and Austria, between the Baltic and the Black seas. Stretching from Riga to Odessa (see map), with its capital in the central Polish town of Lublin, this buffer state was to have a population of some 30 million, including Jews as "the carriers of German culture." In this way, the Jews would have been used to solve the problem of Polish irredentism, which was actively suppressed by Germany and Austria. Yet, although preventing the rebirth of independent Poland was always near the top of the agenda in Berlin and Vienna, the Zionist proposal was plagued with difficulties from the start. Ultimately, the Germanic states had more need of Ukrainian wheat than the political support of Jews on their eastern frontier.

In contrast, the revolutionary socialist sympathies of a number of Jewish intellectuals, natives of the lands of prepartition Poland, aroused active interest in Berlin. On 9 March 1915 one of these radicals presented the German government with a comprehensive and sophisticated strategy to defeat tsarist Russia by means of a socialist revolution supported by Germany (see Appendix I, p. 137; see map, p. 298 and accompanying text, p. 299). Despite the obvious incongruity of an alliance with revolutionary forces of the left, the Berlin government accepted the plan in the hope that it would free German troops from fighting on two fronts. If they could eliminate the eastern front, they could concentrate on achieving victory in France. Then, with France in hand, the "Polish Question" and other European issues could be decided on German terms.

The aim of the socialists who sought German support was revolution, per se. They were motivated by a profound hatred of the tsarist regime, and they believed that their plan would spur capitalism to dig its own grave. They did eventually succeed in using Germany to install the Bolsheviks in power in Russia. Count Brockdorff-Rantzau, a German diplomat in Berlin, admitted on 6 July 1915: "It might be risky to use [revolutionaries], but it would certainly be an admission of our weakness if we refuse their services out of fear of not being able to direct them." (Thirty years later, in 1945, the offer of financial support to Russian revolutionaries proved to be the most fatal miscalculation in German history.)

That such Zionist and socialist proposals had been offered to the German government by prominent Jews gave rise to Polish suspicions that most Jewish politicians supported Poland's enemies and were opposed to the country's independence. The case seemed to be proved by active and vocal radicals like Rosa Luxembourg, a Polish-born Jew who spoke out against the cause of Polish independence. In fact, though, such revolutionaries represented a small fraction of the Jewish population in the provinces annexed from Poland by Russia. The majority of these eastern Jews were Orthodox and conservative.

During World War I, therefore, Poles and Jews did not generally feel that they belonged to one and the same nation. When the Second Polish Republic was established in 1918, Ukrainians and Jews comprised the two largest national minorities within its borders.

The 20th Century Background: The Jews in Russia

As the tsarist empire grew in self-confidence and international stature, a powerful myth was cultivated amongst the ruling elite, that for one thousand years the small Jewish nation was determined to destroy the great Russian nation.

Legend had it that Kiev, the most important city of the eastern Slavs, had been founded by Jewish merchants using Viking Varegian mercenaries in the 9th century. The slave trading activities of Jews in the territory of the Khazars, on the borders of Russia, during the 10th and 11th centuries had also left bad memories.

For centuries, Russian governments had feared that the Jews might succeed in converting Russian Orthodox fundamentalists to their own faith, thereby undermining the state religion. "The latter part of the 15th century...saw the rise of a movement which had serious consequences for the Jews of Russia. Called the "Judaizing heresy" because it resulted in many apostasies from the Christian church, this proselytizing movement added fuel to growing anti-Jewish animosity. Its initiator [was] the learned Jew Zechariah of Kiev, who...converted to Judaism some prominent Russian ecclesiastics. After his departure, missionary activities were carried on by the converts...a number of government officials and high-ranking clergy joined the secret sect, among them the daughter-in-law of the grand duke, and the metropolitan of Moscow... Obviously, the fear of Jewish influence since earliest times, culminating in the Judaizing heresy, lay at the root of the anti-Jewish policies of tsarist Russia... From the 16th century...it became fixed Russian policy not to admit Jews...In 1555 the Polish King Sigismund Augustus demanded Ivan the Terrible...admit Lithuanian Jews for business purposes. The tsar categorically refused...Ivan spoke of Jews as importers of poisonous medicines and as misleaders from the Christian faith...In 1727 a decree was issued that 'all Jews found to be residing in the [eastern] Ukraine and in other Russian towns shall forthwith be expelled beyond the frontier and not permitted under any circumstances to re-enter Russia.' Before leaving the country Jews were to exchange all their gold and silver specie for copper money. In 1742 another edict reaffirmed the decree of banishment and non-admission, an exception being made for those who would embrace the Greek Orthodox faith." (Lois Greenberg, *The Jews in Russia*. New York: Schoken Books, 1976. p. 5-6.)

The persecution of Jews in the Russian Empire intensified dramatically after the assassination of the Tsar on 12 March 1881 by Ignacy Hryniewiecki (1855-1881), a Polish engineering student and a member of Polish and Russian conspiracies. The Russian government was naturally determined to punish the conspirators, some of whom were Jews. However, the main purpose behind stepping up anti-Jewish policies was to use the specter of "Jewish enemies" to divert public attention from the government's own problems. It has also been suggested that some Russian revolutionaries supported anti-Jewish excesses in the hopes of destabilizing the country.

About fifteen years later, an international furor and a terrible wave of domestic anti-Semitism were unleashed by the publication of "The Protocols of the Elders of Zion." This fictitious document, forged by Russian security officers, listed more outrageous "revelations" of Jewish "misdemeanors," and "conspiracies" to rule the world.

As the political climate in Russia deteriorated in the early 1880s, Jews began emigrating to the West. The Russian government maintained its policy of "keeping the Jews harmless" during the 20th century, for both political and religious reasons. This was perpetuated by the Soviet Union, under the guise of anti-Zionism.

The anti-Semitism of Joseph Stalin was about to lead to severe persecution of Jews, had he not died in 1953. It appears that Stalin had become especially suspicious about a suggestion from Golda Meir, then the ambassador of Israel to Moscow. She proposed the creation of a homeland for Soviet Jews in the Crimea. The infamous "doctor's plot" was to open a murderous anti-Jewish campaign in the Soviet Union. Apparently Stalin's death saved Soviet Jews from massive atrocities.

The 20th Century Background: The Jews in Germany, a Racist Death-Trap

Gradually a German racist death-trap for the Jews was formulated in the second half of the 19th century. Earlier, Jews who chose assimilation were able to convert from Judaism to Christianity -- now they could not convert from the newly defined "Jewish race" to the "German race." By setting the parameters of ethnicity in racial terms the Germans made it impossible for a Jew to be accepted as a German.

Anti-Jewish sentiments have had a long history in Germany. The Rhinelanders gave the Ashkenazim the Yiddish language, but most of the states of preunification Germany evicted Jews periodically over the course of one thousand years. During the 19th century, this undercurrent of racism was radicalized among the German population and institutionalized in Berlin, to the detriment of Jews and Poles alike.

When Poland adopted the first modern constitution in Europe, on 3 May 1791, Ewald Friedrich Hertzberg (1725-1795), a minister in the Berlin government, wrote: "The Poles have given the coup de grace to the Prussian monarchy by voting a Constitution better than the English. I think that Poland will regain sooner or later West Prussia [Gdansk Pomerania], and perhaps East Prussia also." (Aleksander Gieysztor, et al., *History of Poland*, Warsaw: PWN--Polish Scientific Publishers, 1979.) The political implications of this observation were compounded by a perceived threat to the racial integrity of the region. The government in Berlin was convinced that "Prussia can be either German or Polish but it cannot be both," and thenceforth it actively pursued policies to fulfill this belief. Hertzberg's prediction came true 150 years later, after the Soviet victory over Germany, when the borders were changed in 1945. Poland had to wait for 50 years longer for independence and a new modern constitution.

In the second half of the 19th century, Bismark revived memories of the German genocide of the Balto-Slavic Prussians in the 13th century. He repeatedly likened the Poles to wolves, which should be "shot to death whenever possible." In 1861 he declared, "Hit the Poles till they despair of their very lives...if we are to survive, our only course is to exterminate them." (Werner Richter, *Bismarck*, New York: Putnam Press, 1964. p.101.) Generally, Bismarck's extremist attitude towards the Poles remains unknown in America. Thus, on March 5, 1990, during progress towards the unification of Germany, a headline of *U.S. News & World Report* stated: "Finishing what Bismarck began." It must have been written without the knowledge of Bismarck's pronouncements such as those quoted above.

Bismarck, the "Iron Chancellor" who unified Germany in 1871, was the first head of government in recent history to proclaim the extermination of another people as one of the desirable objectives of his country. His reasoning was based on the misguided premise that history is a life-and-death struggle culminating in the triumph of the "fittest." Ominously, he himself referred to a "social-Darwinist" idea of the "natural selection." (Adolf Hitler and his wartime government also believed in this life-and-death struggle as they executed genocidal policies similar to those advocated by Bismarck.)

26

At the turn of the 20th century, popular sentiment among the German lower middle class was permeated by *voelkisch-racism.* World War I dealt the country a humiliating defeat, for which many Germans were only too ready to blame the Jews. Their fears were fueled by the Russian anti-Semitism which blossomed as the tsarist regime crumbled; the Bolshevik revolution, too, was allegedly "controlled by the Jews."

In 1933, the *voelkisch-racist* vote (40 percent of the electorate) was decisive in bringing the Nazis to power in Germany. The popular appeal of National Socialism lay in its claims of the superiority of the German "race," and of Germany's "right" to expand into her neighbors' lands. Once again, these beliefs were justified in terms of the racial politics of "Social Darwinism" and were perceived to lay the groundwork for the advancement of culture, the improvement of the legal order, and the general betterment of mankind.

The German preoccupation with racial purity led to the legal prohibition of marriages with Jews in the 1930s and 1940s. Furthermore, during World War II Christian Poles were sentenced to death in German courts for causing "racial injury" to the "German race" by having sexual relations with German women. By that time, the Nazi government had declared that both the "Jewish race" and the "Slavonic race" were "subhuman." In all, the Nazis killed over six million Polish citizens, nearly half of whom were Polish Jews.

Germany never offered any apology for the atrocities which its government committed against the Poles during World War II. Indeed, in 1990 German chancellor Helmut Kohl found it expedient to his domestic political fortunes to demand a Polish apology for alleged mistreatment of Germans during and after the war. Contrast this disingenuous behavior with the magnanimous letter sent by Poland's Catholic bishops to the German episcopate in 1965, in which they said, "We forgive and ask for forgiveness."

The Decline of Polish-Jewish Relations During the 20th Century

Jewish demographic history clearly shows that life was, relatively speaking, much more tolerable for Jews in Poland, despite the turbulent and at times tragic history of the Polish state. Simon Wiesenthal correctly observed: "In the history of Poland, the relations between Poles and Jews never were simple." (Simon Wiesenthal, *Krystyna. A Tragedy of Polish Resistance*, Edition Robert Laffont, Paris 1987.)

During the late 19th century, the governments of both the German states and Russia had played Poles and Jews off against one another. In 1912, political and economic rivalries between Poles and Jews reached boiling points in the regions which Russia had annexed from the Kingdom of Poland. An important factor in the escalation of tensions was the economic boycott of Jews organized by the National Democrats in retaliation for their defeat in an election to the Russian *Duma* (parliament).

The revival of independent Poland in 1918 took place amidst considerable Jewish opposition. The Polish cause had the wholehearted support of the Jews who had assimilated to Polish language and culture, as well as of the local Orthodox Jews. However, the leadership of the international Jewish organizations openly opposed the independence of Poland. The great majority of Jewish activists living in the historic Polish lands believed that they were more likely to find security and stability with the powerful states of Germany and Russia than with a vulnerable free Poland.

Anti-Semitism flared up in Poland over the next twenty years, especially in the 1930s, under the shadow of the Great Depression. Economic hardship prompted numerous riots, the worst of which were in Przytyk, Mińsk, Mazowiecki, and Myślenice (for a detailed discussion of Polish anti-Semitism, see Appendices II and VII, pages: 147 and 157). Paradoxically, the culture of Poland's mainly Yiddish-speaking Jews experienced an unprecedented period of growth and dynamism between the two world wars. This rich cultural life developed despite the competition, at times violent, between the several ethnic and national groups inhabiting Polish territory. The government of Poland used its police force to oppose violence. It also gave Polish citizenship to some 700,000 Jewish refugees from the Soviet Union.

In the national census of 1931, nearly 90 percent of Polish Jews stated that they did not speak Polish at home, thus indicating that they constituted a separate ethnic group. However, professionals of Jewish descent who were assimilated to the Polish culture and language, represented 56 percent of all doctors, 43 percent of teachers, 33 percent of lawyers, and 22 percent of journalists. These figures reflect conditions of access to higher eduction in Poland.

Polish universities were autonomous and were governed by a senate composed of faculty members, but students' education was financed by the state, as was the European tradition. Quotas of all kinds were common in universities throughout Europe; at the medical school of the University of Krakow in the 1930s, for example, 10 percent of the freshman year could comprise women and Jews.

Early in the 1920s, a small but vocal minority of university students began to demand that the Jewish quota be cut back to reflect the proportion of Jews in the population of each region of Poland. Such proposals were considered unconstitutional, however, and the overall participation of Jews in Polish universities continued to exceed their national demographic weight in 1918-1939, despite a noticeably declining trend. Since restrictions applied only to the freshman year, Jewish students who could afford to take their first year of study abroad would enter the university in Prague, Czechoslovakia, for example, and then transfer back into a Polish institution.

In 1926, Jewish members of the Polish *Seym* (house of representatives) were assured that the government of Marshal Piłsudski was absolutely opposed to any student quota system based on nationality or religion. However, these good intentions were severely tested by the anti-Semitic propaganda spawned by the Great Depression. Much was made of the Jews' objection to profaning consecrated corpses in medical school laboratories. A shortage of cadavers, for example, prompted radicals to demand that Jewish students dissect only corpses provided by the Jewish community; an impossible condition, since Orthodox Judaism forbade dissection.

Even though most Polish students opposed anti-Jewish excesses, extremists were able to foment riots from 1931. University lectures were disrupted by shouted demands for segregated classroom seating for Jews. Several dozen Jews were badly beaten. The memory of two victims, in particular, has endured. One was Stanisław Wacławski, a Catholic law student in Wilno, who was killed when a Jewish worker threw a cobblestone at him. The other, Markus Landsberg, a Jewish freshman at Lwów

Polytechnic, died in hospital from injuries incurred in May 1939. In both cases, the faculty senate condemned the violence which caused the loss of young lives.

The transformation of generalized anti-Jewish sentiments into political anti-Semitism was an outgrowth of the rise of nationalism in Europe. However, in Poland it never reached such heights, nor won the support of as large a sector of the population, as in Germany, Austria, Slovakia, Hungary, Romania, Latvia, and Lithuania. Indeed, in light of their country's long tradition of toleration, many Poles felt that the anti-Semitism of their compatriots was a disgrace. Anti-Semitism was widely condemned and ridiculed by Polish authors, such as Prus, Orzeszkowa, Żeromski, Gombrowicz, Miłosz and Roztworowski, to name but a few.

The only political party in Poland which espoused anti-Semitism as part of its program were the National Democrats, who had scant success in national elections. Polish anti-Semitism was not informed by German racism (which was directed equally against Poles), but was born of economic hardship and competition, political manipulation by the partitioning powers, and the conviction that the Polish nation could not integrate millions of Yiddish-speaking Talmudic Jews. Nevertheless, the flood of German propaganda had some influence in Poland, as it did in the rest of Europe. This influence was mitigated by the fact that Polish nationalists saw in Germany the greatest threat to their own survival.

In truth, in 1939 the Poles and the Jews found themselves trapped between two anti-Polish, anti-Jewish totalitarian powers. Germany unquestionably represented a deadly threat to Poles and Jews alike. The Soviet Union, on the other hand, was correctly perceived as much more menacing to the Polish than to the Jewish people. Unfortunately, the trauma of war and occupation bred mutual resentment among its victims. The long night of terror inflicted by the Germans and the Soviets was marked both by heroism and by common human frailty.

Right wing radicals believed that all Jews were Communists or Communist sympathizers. On the verge of war, under threat of German attack, however, extremist groups suspended their anti-Semitic agitations. During the Soviet occupation of eastern Poland, 1939-1941, relations between Poles and Jews again deteriorated, in response to deportations and the very visible support of leftist Jews for the Soviets. Yet, as the war progressed, many Poles who had previously harbored anti-Semitic feelings risked and lost their lives in their efforts to save Jews. Nowhere in Europe did the Germans execute as many gentiles for helping Jews as in Poland.

The organization of an armed resistance movement within Poland served to bring Poles and Jews together. One clandestine agency of the Polish government-in-exile was dedicated to rescuing Jewish victims of German genocidal policies in occupied Poland. It was code-named Żegota. It saved thousands of Jewish lives. Żegota was unique in all of German occupied Europe. More generally, in occupied Poland, extortion and denunciations were punished by summary execution.

Of all of Poland's wartime experiences, Auschwitz has acquired exceptional potency as a symbol. For many Jews, it represents the most important turning point in their history. In the Polish memory, however, it was not a specifically Jewish camp, despite the fact that the majority of its victims were ultimately Jewish.

Auschwitz was opened in 1940, initially as a concentration camp for Polish political prisoners, in accordance with secret provisions in the boundary and friendship treaty signed on 28 September 1939 between Germany and the Soviet Union. By the terms of this treaty, the two powers agreed to cooperate in the extermination of potential Polish opponents to both occupational regimes. The governments of Berlin and Moscow were to take all necessary steps to forestall or contain any Polish campaign directed against territory held by the other. Each promised to crush any sign of agitation within its own occupational zone, and to inform the other of actions employed to this end.

The Soviet Union implemented its side of the agreement by conducting the largest execution of prisoners of war during the entire conflict (1939-1945). Nearly 15,000 Polish officers, 45 percent of the prewar officer corps, were massacred at Katyń, Kharkov, and Kalinin (since renamed Tver) in April/May 1940.

The coverage of the Katyń massacre put out by the German government's news media in 1943 in occupied Poland attempted to break Polish solidarity with the Jewish victims of German genocidal operations. The Germans claimed that the mass murder of Polish officers had been perpetrated by Jewish agents of the NKVD. They stated, moreover, that the head of that organization, Lavrenti Beria, was a Jew because his mother was allegedly Jewish.

For their part, the Germans, at the end of April 1940 came up with Aktion AB, a plan to liquidate "the spiritual and political leaders of the Polish resistance movement," as they defined them. Twenty thousand Poles were immediately arrested and held in concentration camps, to be exterminated gradually. For 21 months, from 14 June 1940, Aushwitz contained only Polish political prisoners.

The Germans decided to locate their prison camp for the Polish elite in Auschwitz because the victims lived nearby, and because the local coal mines could conveniently provide fuel to cremate the bodies. The site lay near Cracow, on Polish territory newly annexed by Germany. By a strange coincidence, this spot had been known in Polish for over 700 years as Oświęcim, meaning "a place to be made holy."

All Poles living in the immediate vicinity of the camp were deported, for reasons of secrecy and security. Some 270,000 Polish prisoners perished in the first camp, Auschwitz I. Jews represented 14 percent of the inmates there. Later, Aushwitz II was added at Birkenau, close by (see map page 338). There, the majority of victims were Jews; some 960,000, as estimated by Israeli and Polish historians.

Between 1939 and 1941 Soviet occupied Poland, more than any country in Europe, witnessed a dramatic collision of the interests and sympathies of the majority of its Jewish population and those of the conquered people among whom they lived. Jewish historians, such as Pawel Korzec and Jean-Charles Szurek have described how young and working class Jews played an important role in the Soviet strategy of oppression, fomenting "class struggle," primarily to the disadvantage of the Poles. However, the Jewish community structure was also destroyed in the process; its leaders, arrested. They were among the nearly two million Polish citizens apprehended by local militia (in which many Jews served) and deported to the Soviet Union.

Of the two million deportees, some 1,200,000 were ethnic Poles, including around 250,000 children under 14 years of age. These represented 25 percent of the Poles under Soviet occupation. About 500,000 of the deportees were sent to Soviet prisons and slave labor camps; few survived.

Under Soviet occupation, therefore, ethnic Poles felt that they were waging war on two fronts, both against Germans and against Soviets. The majority of Polish Jews, on the other hand, refused to identify themselves with the Polish state and regarded the Soviets as a lesser evil than the Germans.

From the summer of 1944, Poland was gradually occupied and subjugated by the Soviets. Polish perceptions of the fate of the Jews during World War II were thenceforth colored by the fact that the new administration and its agencies of repression employed a disproportionately high number of people of non-Polish ethnicity, including a very large number of Jewish Communists. These, however, were only a small and unrepresentative element of the Jewish community as a whole. Not many noticed that, in fact, gentile Poles constituted the majority of the membership both of the Communist party and of the secret police.

In general, Polish Christians fared far worse under the Soviet regime than did Jews, because the Polish-speaking population showed much greater commitment to the defense of Poland and to the opposition to communism than did Yiddish-speaking Jews. Consequently, every Soviet-Polish conflict was reflected by a deterioration in relations between Polish Christians and Jews. Well aware of this trend, the Soviets refined the imperial Russian tradition of "divide and conquer" to exploit differences between the two groups. Immediately after the war, the Soviets used Jews as executioners. Then, with a particularly callous twist, they made them the victims in all their satellite states, especially in the Polish People's Republic.

While Poland was in their hands, the Soviets cleverly played on the revulsion that the German genocide of the Jews had aroused throughout the civilized world. It was convenient for the Communists to make western public opinion believe that Poles were viciously anti-Semitic, and thus deserved to be left to their fate.

Meanwhile, the Soviets were also disseminating propaganda among the Jews. They alleged that, had the Poles lost the war against the Soviets in 1920, the German genocide of the Jews could never have happened because Communist governments would have been firmly in power in Poland and Germany, and Hitler's Nazi party would not have taken hold in Berlin. Some Jews accepted this at face value. The Poles, on the other hand, were proud to have defeated the Soviet and delayed their advance into the center of Europe by a quarter of a century. The Polish victory over the Bolsheviks in 1920 won Poland national independence. It also saved her people, and those of the Baltic states and Romania, from the fate that befell the Ukrainians, many millions of whom died in a terrible famine and in the countless slave labor camps of the Gulag archipelago, as a result of Soviet domination and land collectivization programs in the 1930s.

In 1944, the Soviets encouraged the Polish national uprising against the Nazis in Warsaw. However, once it was underway, the Soviets halted their very successful offensive just short of the Polish capital, thereby interrupting the general rout of the German armed forces (see map) and giving them an opportunity to destroy the Freedom Fighters of the Polish resistance movement within the city. The express purpose of the Soviets was to use the German army to eliminate Polish forces who might resist the Sovietization of Poland after the war. Military historians estimate that the decision to suspend the advance prolonged the war, and the Germans' mass murders of Jews and others, by half a year.

The Soviet takeover of war-torn Poland in 1945 deprived the Poles of a natural period of national mourning for the millions of victims of the conflict, Christian and Jew. Instead, the Poles struggled in vain to resist subjugation to the Soviets. Many Jewish survivors of the Holocaust, most of whom had assimilated into Polish culture, soon fell victim to Soviet policies; anti-Zionism became a cover for anti-Semitism.

After the war, about one-quarter of a million Jews were driven out of Poland under Soviet policies enforced by local Communists, many of them Jewish. There were even reports of "Jewish anti-Semitism" among functionaries of the Communist party, who claimed that they acted "to save their own skins." (See Michael Checinski, *Poland, Communism, Nationalism, Anti-Semitism*, New York: Karz-Cohl Publishing, 1982. p. 72.)

Yet, in truth, between 1945 and 1956 no gentile or Jew in Poland could claim t0 be compelled to participate in the machinery of

Stalinist terror and serve in the political police or the judiciary, any more than former Gestapo officers could legitimately claim that they had no choice but to torture and murder harmless political opponents.

The Soviets deliberately fomented rabid competition between Jew and non-Jew within the Communist party, transforming the organization into a hot-bed of anti-Semitism. Most of the Jews who left Poland after the Soviet takeover were forced out and would have stayed, if they could reestablish their own religious communities.

The legacy of the German genocide and the Soviets' reign of terror was an accumulation of mutual resentments which the surviving Jews and Poles often found very hard to overcome. Poland's intellectual leadership, traditionally pluralistic, has openly and sincerely expressed regret at the loss of the Jews, who had inhabited historic Polish territory for one thousand years. A great deal of Polish literature and many press reports accurately described the fate of Poland's Jews, flouting the official Soviet denial of the unparalleled tragedy which befell the Jewish victims of the German genocide.

The Polish nationals repatriated from Soviet forced labor camps in 1957 included 40,000 Jews. Many of these people spoke Yiddish rather than Polish, and had no attachment to Polish culture. They joined in the exodus of some 50,000 Jews from Poland, 1957-1958.

The Soviet Union did not permit the revival of Jewish culture in postwar Poland, any more than in other countries of the Communist bloc. Instead, the Soviets and their satellite regime evicted a quarter of a million Jews from Poland, many of whom settled in Palestine. The Soviets decided to exploit Jewish efforts to organize a state of Israel. The Soviet aim was to destabilize the Middle East and turn this strategic, oil rich region against the West, and especially against the United States, which was clearly set to become the most powerful guarantor of Israel's survival.

Thus, toward initial efforts to establish the State of Israel, the Soviets offered political support and were the only source of the weapons which brought the Israelis victory in their crucial first struggle against the Arabs. Once Israeli victory was secured, the Soviets proceeded to blackmail both Israel and the Arab states. There is no reason to believe that Soviet support of the Jews was based on new-found altruism, rather, it was motivated by geopolitical considerations.

Accordingly, the Soviets continued to flood Poland with successive waves of anti-Semitic policies, and in 1960 another purge of the local Communist party was initiated. "Jews were being kicked out because they were Jewish, Poles because they were too friendly with the Jews or because they would not vociferate against Jews...preventive action [became] an instrument of widespread terror and blackmail...From 1962 on, the Jewish section of the Ministry of Internal Affairs began preparing for the total elimination of Jews. A card index file of all hidden Jews, which included totally assimilated Poles of Jewish origin, converts and their offspring, mixed marriages, as well as Poles with Jewish relatives or connections was prepared...all senior Jewish officials were placed under police surveillance. [Anti-Polish books such as *Exodus* and *Mila 18* by Leon Uris] published in the West were systematically utilized in anti-Semitic propaganda." (Michael Chęciński, *Poland, Communism, Nationalism, Anti-Semitism.* New York: Karz-Cohl Publishing, 1982.)

Jewish Communists, who had been a major asset during the imposition of the Soviet system in Poland immediately after the war, had come to be considered a handicap to Moscow by 1962. The Soviets found it more convenient to espouse anti-Zionist propaganda and thus expand their influence among the Arabs in the Middle East. The Polish people, however, remained unconvinced. After the Six-Day War in 1967, Poles, including many officers on active duty, openly proclaimed their joy at the ignominious defeat of the Soviet Union's Arab allies. Polish buildings sported such slogans as "Our Polish Jews have thrashed the Russian Arabs."

In the struggle between Gomulka and Moczar for Polish leadership in 1968, anti-Semitism was brought to the fore. Although Gomulka, whose family had Jewish connections, was the victor, he continued to enforce anti-Semitic policies mandated by the Soviet Union. For instance, 30,000 people classified as Jews were evicted from Poland, 1968-1969. Gomulka also used anti-Semitic propaganda to confuse and weaken public support in Poland for Dubcek's reforms in neighboring Czechoslovakia.

31

IV. JEWISH-POLISH DIALOGUE

Jewish-Polish dialogue has proved very difficult in postwar Poland; practically no Jews remained there after 1968. On both sides, perceptions have been clouded by the unthinkable experiences endured under war and occupation, and these selective memories have colored the attitudes of onlookers in the West.

In any society, circumstances such as those created by the Germans in Poland are prone to result in quarrels and abuse among the victims. However, people who find shelter in the homes of others, or who take over whatever is left of the homes and work places of fellow victims, are not motivated by racial hatred, but by normal human impulses and the will to survive. World over, natural and manmade disasters generate examples of such behavior, and in this respect, Poland and her citizens were no exception.

The Seeds of Misunderstanding: Betrayals and Human Loyalty

The traumatic German occupation of Poland gave rise to countless tests of human loyalty. Conscious of a century's worth of ethnic competition between Jews and Poles, Jewish victims of Nazi German terror despaired. Help is not usually forthcoming from one's rivals. Yet, the terrible situation which both groups now faced, while it exposed the inevitable human frailties, also prompted unprecedented acts of physical and moral courage.

Unfortunately, the relatively few Polish and Jewish informers mobilized by the Gestapo were always more efficient than the far greater number of people who risked their lives to save Jewish victims of Nazi German terror. For example, it took considerable time and effort on the part of many people to hide a Jew from the Gestapo for an extended period of time, whereas a single informer could quickly and easily betray a hidden Jew. However, no one in the Polish political establishment collaborated with the German invaders.

The issue of shelter beset Christian and Jewish Poles alike. The involuntary migration of Polish citizens from territories annexed by the Berlin government produced masses of homeless people, who swelled the numbers of those who had lost their homes through the destruction of war. Moreover, there were no Jewish ghettos in prewar Poland. Therefore, in order to isolate the Jews in ghettos, the Germans evicted more than one million Polish Christians and crowded their former homes with Jews.

Poles of Jewish descent who had assimilated into Polish culture, whether or not they had converted to Christianity, constituted a high proportion of the survivors among those classified as Jews by the Germans and destined for extermination in the gas chambers.

Yiddish-speaking, ethnic Talmudic Jews, however, were in the gravest danger in occupied Poland, for they were easily identifiable by the Gestapo. Over 80 percent of the Jewish population did not speak Polish at home, and consequently lived with the fear that their broken Polish would reveal their identity. The Germans forced some of the Jews to travel through the streets of occupied Poland with bandages around their heads, so that they would not display their "Semitic faces."

Contrasting Views of Auschwitz

Jewish people have every right to regard Auschwitz-Birkenau and Treblinka together as the largest and most bitter Jewish cemetery in history. Since the retreating Germans did not have time to destroy the facilities at Auschwitz as they did at their other camps, Auschwitz, rather than Treblinka, came to symbolize the German extermination of six million Jews. Also, more of the Jewish inmates of Auschwitz survived than in any of the other death camps, such as Belzec, Treblinka, Sobibor, or Chelmno (Kulmhof), and thus it has lived on in the collective memory.

The immediate execution of entire Jewish families in Auschwitz II at Birkenau is beyond comparison with the gradual extermination of political prisoners, mostly Poles, in the original camp of Auschwitz I. Nevertheless, the Germans did subject Polish gentiles to horrible deaths, a fact little recognized by Jews who live far from the tragic site. For their part, Poles generally have not been informed of the different fates met by Poles and Jews in the extermination program carried out by the Germans at the Auschwitz complex.

At the time, Poles were aware that, from mid-1941, the German government described Jews and Slavs as subhuman (*Untermensch*), enemy races which were destined to perish in order to bring about the final victory and world domination of the German race. Among the Slavs, Poles were especially hated by the Germans.

Yet, despite their common adversity, Polish gentiles have not, so far, given adequate consideration to the relative suffering of the Jews. In part, this is due to the respective behavior of each group during the war. The Jews did not offer armed resistance to the Germans until they had nothing left to lose. Such was their situation on 19 April 1943 when they started an uprising in the Warsaw Ghetto, and shortly afterwards, in Białystok.

The Poles, on the other hand, fought the Germans throughout World War II. Nine hundred thousand Polish soldiers participated in the fall campaign of 1939. Over 350,000 took part in resistance units; 200,000 Polish units of airmen, sailors, and soldiers fought under allied command on the western and southern fronts of Germany. Some 400,000 Polish soldiers fought alongside the Soviets on the eastern German front. Polish participation in campaigns in France and the Battle of Britain were followed by Narvik, Tobruk, Monte Cassino, and Falaise. Finally, in April 1945 the Poles defeated the main force of the last German offensive (ordered by Hitler in person) to rescue Berlin. Poles served in the only non-Soviet forces to press through to the conquest of the German capital. All these engagements made Poles feel that they had contributed significantly to the defeat of Nazi Germany.

Their unstinting prosecution of the war gave the Polish people a certain feeling of self-righteousness. This was strengthened by the fact that there was no political collaboration with the Germans in Poland, in contrast to France, Norway, and the other occupied countries. Unlike anti-Semitic groups in the rest of occupied Europe, even the Polish right-wing parties were traditionally anti-German and fought vigorously against them. Thus, the fall of Germany did not precipitate a crisis of right-wing ideology in Poland. Those on the right considered themselves impeccably patriotic.

When the outcome of the conferences at Tehran (1943) and Yalta (1945) was made known, the Poles were devastated. They considered themselves twice betrayed. They felt that the western allies had failed them in 1939, by neglecting to act on their declaration of war; and in 1943, by placing Poland in the Soviet sphere of interest. Consequently, they perceived themselves to be among the foremost victims of the war. With six million of her citizens dead, her cities, industry, and agriculture in ruins, not only was Poland now to lose half of her territory, but she was also to be subjugated by a foreign country.

Contrasting Views on Polish Responsibility for the Annihilation of the Jews

Jan Karski, who carried information about the German genocide of the Jews from Poland to the West in 1942, commented on the contrast between the responses of the world leaders whom he met, and those of ordinary people: "Leaders of nations, powerful governments decided about this destruction, or kept indifferent towards it. People, normal people, thousands of people sympathized with the Jews or helped them."

Nothing could be farther from the truth than the central thesis of Claude Lanzmann's film *Shoah*, which claims that the Jews were allowed to meet their end in the gas chambers because the Poles were indifferent to their fate. The horrible fact is that, except for a very few individuals, all Polish Jews were doomed under German occupation, irrespective of Jewish resistance or the assistance of Poles.

Lanzmann claims that the fate of the Jews in occupied Poland would not have been possible in France. It is, however, a well-proven fact that the French offered the Germans indispensable assistance in identifying, arresting, and isolating Jews in prisons and internment camps, and then turning them over to the Gestapo. Vichy, France, helped the Germans much more than did the Poles or most other Europeans, including ostensible allies of the Germans like the Bulgarians, the Romanians, and the Hungarians.

Professor Yisrael Gutman of the Institute of Contemporary Jewry at the Hebrew University and director of the Center of Holocaust Studies at Yad Vashem observed: "For this was, after all, a remarkable Polish phenomenon, this solidarity of the Polish underground...This feeling of identification of Poles from all social spheres and their anti-German solidarity is a previously unheard of historical achievement and one of Europe's greatest under Nazi occupation. I should like to make two things clear here. First, all accusations against the

Poles that they were responsible for what is referred to as the 'Final Solution' are not worth mentioning here. Secondly, there is no validity at all in the contention that Polish anti-Semitism or other Polish attitudes were the reason for siting of the death camps in Poland." (Institute of Polish Studies, *Polin*. vol.2, p.341.)

The Soviets also played a determinative role in the tragic fate of the Jews of Poland. From the signing of the Hitler-Stalin treaty of friendship and cooperation in 1939, which started World War II, the Soviets systematically destroyed the organized religious communities and the culture of the Polish Jews. Rabbis were deported and murdered, together with other prominent Polish citizens whom the Soviets viewed as "class enemies." It was the Soviets' intention to control the Jews and use them whenever possible in anti-Polish programs. In this regard, it is pertinent to quote Simon Wiesenthal on his eightieth birthday: "I know what kind of role Jewish communists played in Poland after the war. And just as I, as a Jew, do not want to shoulder responsibility for the Jewish communists, I cannot blame 36 million Poles for those thousands of [wartime] extortionists (*szmalcownicy*)."

These wartime extortionists were common criminals, such as exist in all human societies. They included both Jews and gentiles. A number of them were sentenced to death by Polish underground courts for betraying Jews and others, and were executed. However, those who volunteered to serve in the Soviet terror apparatus tortured and murdered on behalf of Moscow, in a manner similar to that of the German Gestapo.

The cult of Shoah, however, has assumed a particular significance in the United States of America. In strictly numerical terms, the U.S.A. is the new demographic center of the Jewish world, but it is an increasingly pluralistic society. Thus, as a growing number of young Jews marry outside of the community and fail to pass on their cultural heritage to their children, the commemoration of the enormous Jewish tragedy of World War II serves as a standard around which to rally the Jewish identity.

Contemporary American pluralism offers hope of progress towards equitable assimilation. It corrects the legacy of the Enlightenment, which aroused aspirations for emancipation alongside the fraudulent denationalization of minorities. The impossibility of assimilation without respect for pluralistic values has rendered the 20th century one of the bloodiest in the history of mankind.

Christian-Jewish Dialogue in Poland

Bishop Henryk Muszynski, in charge of the Polish episcopal commission for dialogue with the Jews, attempted to formulate the issues which must be understood in order to prevent another Auschwitz or Shoah. He observed that since Christians and Jews have different customs, opinions, and sensitivities, they need to learn about each other. He felt that the meaning of Auschwitz for Jews can only be grasped by others through an educational process assisted by the Jews themselves. Declaring that Jewish culture constitutes a precious element in Poland's national history, he appealed to Jewish organizations to help preserve the monuments of Jewish culture in that country.

Conversely, he argued that it was also imperative that Jews respect the Christian cross erected to commemorate the spot on which thousands of Poles were executed, just outside the perimeter of the main camp at Auschwitz. The Christian cross was defended in Poland throughout the years of Communist oppression. To Catholic Poles, it symbolizes the redemptive suffering of Jesus.

There is almost no family in Poland which did not lose someone in executions or concentration camps. In fact, millions of Poles were killed simply because they were Poles, and many thousands compounded this "crime" by trying to rescue Jewish neighbors. The wartime suffering of both Jews and Poles was unthinkable, too cruel to comprehend. Thus, fifty years later it still divides Christian and Jew. And the hardships of Soviet occupation have made dialogue even more difficult.

It is hardly possible to discuss the genocide of the Jews as an external matter in Poland. Poles cannot easily grasp the difference between Shoah and Polish martyrdom under German occupation, as can people of other nations, who suffered less. It is indeed tragic that victims of German racism should accuse and defame one another, even if they did not suffer in quite the same way. Jews keep stressing the exceptional nature of Shoah, while Poles remember their martyrs.

34

One outcome of this unhappy quarreling in Poland is the open slander of Polish people in the West. Through pervasive anti-Polish references in films, television programs, novels, and other mass media, the impression has falsely been created that Polish Christians participated in the genocide of Jews during Shoah. It has been proved conclusively that there was no Polish complicity in the German genocide of Jews in occupied Poland. Unfortunately, though, the general public seems rarely to read comprehensive historical accounts and succumbs instead to confusing messages from popularizing sources.

An illustration of an extraordinarily damaging anti-Polish fabrication is William Styron's book *Sophie's Choice*, (Bantam Books New York, 1982 see pp. 289-306), which was printed in 3 million copies, and was also made into a popular movie. Styron erroneously claims that the Poles originated the concept of murdering Jews in gas chambers long before the Nazis came to power in Berlin: "[A fictitious] Zbigniew Biegański, Distinguished Professor of Jurisprudence at the Jagiellonian University of Cracow; Doctor of Law *honoris causa*, Universities of Karlova, Bucharest, Heilderberg and Leipzig... [was a] philosopher whose vision of the "final solution" antedated that of Eichmann and his confederates (even perhaps Adolf Hitler...)." (An exchange of letters between William Styron and Dr. Ralph Slovenko on this subject is included in Appendix VII, p. 160 and 171).

It is in the United States that these poisoned relations are most bitter. Polish and Jewish ethnic groups respond to media messages in different ways. Many Jewish Americans tend to conclude that the Poles share some responsibility for the German genocide of six million Jews. Most of them do not know that more Polish gentiles were killed in occupied Poland than Polish Jews died in the Holocaust. American Poles ask, "How could the Poles save 2,700,000 Jews at a time when they could not save over 3,000,000 of Poland's Christian citizens?"

Obviously, those extortionists and unscrupulous individuals who sought material benefit from the Jewish tragedy must be condemned. However, a double standard is applied to Jews who collaborated with the Germans on the *Judenrate*. These Jewish councils were introduced by the Germans as a form of "self-government," and were then forced to facilitate the destruction of the Jewish people. Jewish extortionists and paid informers of the Gestapo caused endless suffering to fellow Jews under German occupation, but they are rarely mentioned today; whereas their gentile counterparts, the *szmalcowniks*, are cited disproportionately.

American Poles feel slandered and believe that Polish anti-Semitism has deliberately been exaggerated in order to foster general fears of anti-Semitism, and thus prevent the loss of less devoted members from the Jewish community in the United States. Similar situations have developed in western Europe, notably in France.

Anti-Semitism and Anti-Polonism

The history of anti-Semitism in Europe is well-known, and an ample discussion of Polish anti-Semitism can be found in Appendices II to VII, pp. 147 to 178. The persecution of the Poles is much less widely recognized. Viewed over the last three hundred years, anti-Polonism has, in some respects, resembled age-old anti-Semitism.

The Russian government began deporting Poles to Siberian prisons as early as 1770 and later led the effort to defeat the Polish struggle for independence. In 1795 Austria, Prussia, and Russia signed a pact which committed them to erasing the Polish presence from European history. Austria started out as the most severe oppressor of the Poles, while the Berlin government confiscated Polish landholdings and openly attacked Polish culture. During the 19th and 20th centuries, anti-Polonism was pursued with even greater intensity in the official propaganda of the German and Russian states.

The phenomenon of Jewish anti-Polonism also merits consideration. It arose after the partitions of Poland and was strengthened by the mutual resentments of Jewish and Polish victims of German and Soviet terror during and after World War II. Two centuries of competition between Pole and Jew in the historic lands of prepartition Poland have left many bad memories. However, none of the issues raised have concerned the extermination of the Jews in Poland. At their most extreme, radical activists advocated evicting Jews to Palestine and made deals with the Zionists to this end.

Bitter memories of anti-Semitic actions by Poles pale next to the atrocities committed by the Germans against the Jews. Complaints about university quotas, unsuccessful economic boycotts, broken store windows, lost their dramatic impact after the horrors of World War II. Thus, in the West, especially in the United States and France, anti-Polish propaganda has since degenerated into crude, uninformed, accusations of Polish complicity in the genocide of the Jews.

In the 1990s, there are practically no Jews in Poland. However, an anti-Semitic lunatic fringe still exists. It represents a tiny proportion of the Polish electorate and is apparently much smaller, for example, than Jean Marie Le Pen's Front Nacionale in France.

V. CONCLUSION

International political organizations have successfully prevented the disintegration of European Jewry. By the beginning of World War I, massive emigration to America and a much lesser migration to Palestine had cost Poland her position as the demographic center of gravity of the Jews. The German genocide of some six million Jews between 1940 and 1944 constituted the epilogue of the European period in Jewish history.

The End of the European Period in Jewish History

Up until the 18th century, Poland was home to the largest Jewish community in the world. Here, the Jews were able, for the first time, to arrest their thousand-year slide towards extinction and start out on the road to recovery, rebuilding the Jewish ethnic and national identity. These Polish Jews laid the foundations for the modern Jewish world.

Jewish legal and governmental culture, its educational system, philosophical concepts, and religious beliefs evolved in the historic lands of Poland from the 16th through 18th centuries. The region was also the birthplace of many Jewish religious and political movements, including Zionism, socialism, and Orthodoxy. Even under the intense political anti-Semitism of the first half of the 20th century, Jewish culture flourished in Poland as nowhere else.

By 1939, Poland was yet home to the second-largest Jewish community in the world. The Jewish Shoah and the largely forgotten genocide of the Poles, happened side-by-side in Poland, under German occupation. Subsequently, both Jews and Poles became the victims of Soviet terror.

From a historical perspective, it was the pluralism of late medieval and early modern Poland which allowed the Jews to preserve their nationhood. Some Jews were almost willing to accept the homeland of the Poles as their own, a replacement for the Holy Land. To some extent, the partitions of Poland at the end of the 18th century created similar problems for Poles and Jews as they were dispersed throughout the vast multiethnic territories of the former Polish Commonwealth. Living amidst Ukrainians, Byelorussians, Russians, Germans, Lithuanians, and Latvians, neither Poles nor Jews had clearly definable ethnic borders.

The vast majority of Jewish people today have some Polish ancestry. Soviet Jewry originated in the provinces annexed from Poland by Russia, and the world's largest and most vibrant Jewish community, that of the Untied States, is primarily composed of the descendants of Polish Jews. The great Jewish historian Salo Baron has described American Jewry as "a bridge built by Polish Jews" between the old world and the new.

The second most populous center of Judaism is the State of Israel. It too was founded on the ethnic and cultural heritage developed in Poland and in the Polish provinces annexed by Russia and Austria. A continuity of Jewish political culture extends from the *Congressus Judaicus* in early modern Poland to the *Knesset* of the State of Israel.

The State of Israel now faces the challenge of integrating Jews from the areas of Christianity, who created Jewish nationalism in the historic lands of Poland, with the Jews of Islam, who were awakened to a national consciousness by the struggles of the European Jews and the Arabs of Palestine. The current confrontation between European and Afro-Asian Jews in Israel is sometimes interpreted as a clash between Ashkenasim (originally, Yiddish speakers) and Sephardim (originally, Ladino speakers).

European Jews, mainly from the historic lands of Poland, have always constituted the leadership community of the State of Israel. However, the overall number of European, and especially Polish, Jews was so drastically reduced by the genocidal policies of the German Nazis that they now represent a minority of less than one-third of Israel's population. On the other hand, the disintegration of Communist political power in Europe at the end of the 1980s has made possible the large-scale emigration of Jews from the Soviet bloc. As a result, the proportion of Israelis with cultural affinities to the peoples of the Christian world is growing. Optimists hope that Israel will successfully act as a "melting pot" of Jews from the lands of Christianity and of Islam. Pessimists fear that the Jews from the areas of Christianity, who created the State of Israel, will fight to preserve their privileged and dominant status at the expense of the Jews of Islam, thus fomenting domestic strife.

The Scope of This Book

The *Jews in Poland--A Documentary History* attempts to show how the Jews once found sanctuary in Poland, how they lived there with unique autonomy, and how they formed their modern ethnic identity in its historic lands.

Anti-Semitic arguments formulated elsewhere in Europe did resound in Poland over the ages, but they have too often since been quoted out of context and used to confuse the uninformed. In this context, it should be remembered that the system of parliamentary government effective in the old Polish Commonwealth (1386-1569) and the First Polish Republic (1569-1795) was incompatible with the massive persecution of Jews or other minorities. No Polish government was ever elected on the basis of an anti-Semitic political program. In the two-thousand-year history of the Jewish Diaspora, the freedom of the pluralistic society of old Poland provided a uniquely nurturing environment and gave the Jews the only national parliament during the history of Jewish Diaspora, the *Congressus Judaicus*.

The story of Poland as the heartland of the world's Jewry ended in tragedy at the hands of the government in Berlin. And Poland's national tragedy was reflected in the fate of the Jews. Firstly, the partition and destruction of the Polish state brought an end to the unparalleled political freedom of the Jewish population in her territories. The decline of the Polish state exposed latent processes of self-destruction which threaten all elective governments and pluralistic societies. Gravely weakened in this way, Poland could not defend herself against greedy, power hungry neighbors.

The second blow was the unconscionable German genocide of the Jews in the occupied and terrorized Polish lands. One thousand years of Polish Jewish history were abruptly terminated by the German mass murders. Yet the Jewish spirit was not to be stifled. With extraordinary vigor and perseverance, the Jewish nation has been reestablished, in Israel.

Anshel of Cracow, 1534: Frontispiece "Mirkebet ha-Misjnah"
(In Yiddish: concordance and glossary to The Bible.)

38

PART I

CHAPTER II

1264
STATUTE ON
JEWISH LIBERTIES
IN POLAND

Translated from Latin
by
Thomas O. Macadoo
for
Jews in Poland:
A Documentary History

Ever since Alexander the Great permitted Jewish settlements within the Hellenic cities founded by him, the Jews began formulation of the demands for special laws and privileges.

During the next fifteen hundred years they accumulated a great amount of experience in clarifying what laws were convenient and practical for them.

PREFACE

TO THE ENGLISH TRANSLATION FROM THE LATIN

BY PROFESSOR OF CLASSICAL LANGUAGES

DR. THOMAS O. MACADOO

FOR

JEWS IN POLAND: A DOCUMENTARY HISTORY

The Latin text of this statute submitted for translation is a nineteenth-century edition printed in Poznan in 1892 as a part of the German book entitled *Die General-Privilegien der polnischen Judenschaft* by Dr. Philipp Bloch (Enlarged and improved special printing from the Periodical of the Historical Society for the province of Poznan, Bb. VI.)

The Latin text was derived from two previous editions of the statute as found in the archives of Poznan under the year 1539. The section numbers, however, are derived from a third edition not otherwise used, because of its rather arbitrary emendations. The Poznanian archival text appears itself to be derived from the autograph of 1264; that is, of course, except for the introduction of 1539, and the letters of confirmation of 1453 and 1334.

The text itself is obviously corrupt; aside from errors that may have been introduced in the making of one or more copies from the autograph, one feels the presence of a rather bored and sleepy sixteenth-century scribe, who was, moreover, having great difficulty in reading a thirteenth-century, or possibly, a fourteenth-century hand. He seems to have had no difficulty with the fifteenth-century letters.

There are some egregious omissions: introductory dependent clauses that lead to no discoverable independent clause, and the like. In such cases, I have simply given the gist or thrust of the whole context, without attempting to guess exactly what the lost portion may have said. There may well be other omissions here and there that are not so obvious, and for these I take no responsibility.

A second difficulty arises from the fact that the document is legal, and, therefore, repetitive. Where two different words of similar meaning are both employed, it is by no means always clear whether there is a technical difference between the two, or whether we have only the typical lawyer's trick of saying the same thing in as many different ways as possible, so as to cover all bases. For example, the words "pignus" and "vadium" both refer to property (or even an oath) given as security for a debt, or as some other guarantee. I have usually translated either, or both, of these words with the word "security," but in some cases, where it is clear that the personal property was actually held by the creditor during the term of debt, I have used the word "pawn," whether as noun or as verb.

In one or two places, where the Latin verb required an unstated word, I have supplied it (in English) in brackets [ ]; where the Latin did not require such statement, but the English does, I have simply supplied the missing word without the use of brackets. In several places, the Polish equivalent of a Latin word is given, with the word "alias" regularly preceding the Polish word; with equal regularity, I have placed the Polish word within parentheses ( ). In at least one place, however, the Polish word appears immediately following the Latin, without the introductory "alias": "contributiones dany." Here the word "dany" is likely to be a misspelling of the word "dary," meaning gifts or gratuities.

Despite the problems mentioned above, and many others, I can assure the reader that this is an essentially reliable translation, giving at all times the tenor of the statute, if not always its exact details.

The following translator's notes should help in reading of the relevant sections of the statute:

Section 1. note: The first part of this section is horribly corrupt, and shows the kind of omission described in my preface. Apart from that, the words "rodale" and "ferunca" are not to be found in any classical or medieval Latin dictionary. I take "rodale" to be a misspelling of "rotale," a thing equipped with a wheel or other rotary

device, hence, a "scroll," which fits the context perfectly. Etymologically, one would guess "ferunca" to be an iron hook (or a load hook or ring), and this is confirmed by the fact that its Polish equivalent "colche" is also made equivalent of "cathena" (correctly, "catena," a chain). The English word "rote" (a prescribed form or repetition) I have used as a translation of the mysterious word "rotha," presumably a misspelling of "rota," a wheel, although the dictionaries tell us that the English word is not derived from "rota." There is no doubt whatsoever that "rotha" refers to a prescribed form of oath. It appears that a Jew was required to swear, in less important matters, while holding a hook or chain from which, presumably, a scroll of the Ten Commandments was suspended. In more important matters he had to place his hand on the scroll itself. The "Woszny" (Vozhny) was an officer of the court: a justice of the peace, or a bailiff, or a sheriff; the "Scolny" (Szkolony = learned) is the teacher of the synagogue, the rabbi.

Section 32. note: A gross (Latin "grossus") was a gold monetary unit which differed in value in various countries. I do not know how many Polish marks there were in a Polish gross. If, for example, there were 144 marks to the gross, then interest under consideration was limited to an annual rate of approximately 36%. But if there were only 100 marks, the maximum annual rate was about 52%. By the same token, if a gross was worth 1000 marks, the maximum annual interest would have been 5.2%. The phrase "either kind of mark" presumably refers to the coin's composition, whether of gold or of silver. This may imply that there was also such a thing as a silver gross. What is clear from the passage on the interest charges is that they had a definite ceiling, at least in the case of noble debtors; in the light of the remarks about recording of the debt, the securities in this case were parcels of real estate. Even today it is commonplace that statutory limits on debts secured by real estate are lower than those placed on debts secured by chattels. Section 33 also suggests debts secured by real

41

estate.

Section 33 and passim: I have been unable to find the verb "introligari" in any dictionary, classical or medieval. Unfortunately, the relevant volume of the *Thesaurus Linguae Latinae* is (I hope temporarily) missing from our university's library, and I have not been able to consult it. From an etymological viewpoint, the verb's meaning closely parallels the American slang "latch onto;" that is, make one's own. In matters of debt, the formal legal English for this is "foreclose," and I have so translated the word. All the contexts in which this word appears also make it clear that this is what is meant.

Section 41. & 44.: The Latin word "cola" in these passages is certainly a scribal error. I had at first thought to emend to "sola," which would mean "alone," but because I have little expertise in paleography, I consulted Professor R. P. Oliver as to whether the letters "s" and "c" could be confused in medieval manuscripts. He assured me that that would be most unlikely, but suggested that "cola" might easily be confused for "tota," which fits the context perfectly. I have therefore adopted his emendation.

Section 45, note: If any classicist should happen to compare this translation closely with the Latin original, he might well be appalled by the rather cavalier attitude I have taken toward the uses of the moods in hypothetical prepositions, of which there are many throughout. In defense, I would remind him that this is medieval Latin, and provincial medieval Latin at that. There is no very strong reason for assuming that the author observed, or even understood, the classical rules. Another difficulty arises from the fact that the protasis often uses a verb which may be either present perfect indicative subjunctive, indicating (in classical Latin) that the user doubts that the event will happen, or the future perfect indicative, indicating that he strongly expects it to happen. In classical Latin, the verb of the apodosis would ordinarily clarify which is intended. But here the verb of the apodosis is often "debet," which, though indicative, can have a force approximating either the subjunctive or the imperative. In this section, we have a strange construction in which two verbs of the protasis are in different moods, the second being imperfect subjunctive, which should indicate that the user considered the fulfillment impossible; the verbs of the apodosis are also imperfect subjunctive, reinforcing (in classical Latin) the impossibility of the entire hypothesis. Mixed constructions are by no means unheard of in classical Latin, but this one is egregious. "Denegaverit" could be translated "when any...prohibits" (fut. pf. ind.), or "if any... should prohibit" (pf. subj.). But "peturbaret" should require "were disturbing." The apodosis would require "he would be doing this against all our royal statutes, and would be incurring thereby our great indignation." But surely it is less probable that the public official (who alone would have the power of prohibition) would violate the royal decree, than that any ordinary citizen (who could easily foment a disturbance) would. I have, therefore, chosen simply to show the relationship of the proscribed conduct to its result, without any reference to probabilities. And I have done essentially the same thing elsewhere, using what I sensed to be the import of the passage in selecting English phrases, since I can have no confidence that the rules of classical Latin are applicable here.

I must thank my friend and colleague, Dr. J. F. Ferguson, for reading both the Latin and the English texts. He discovered a number of typographical errors and other infelicities that have escaped my notice. It was also he who suggested the desirability of appending the note explaining my treatment of the moods.

A political note: the Latin often makes no distinction between the various parts of eastern Slavic territory, but uses the word "Russia" to refer to all of it. The part that belonged to King Casimir Jagiellon is properly called Ruthenia, and "Russia" is so translated here.

1264 STATUTE ON JEWISH LIBERTIES IN POLAND

THE 1264 ACT OF KALISZ BY DUKE BOLESLAUS THE PIUS

RATIFIED IN 1334 BY KING CASIMIR THE GREAT

RATIFIED IN 1453 BY KING CASIMIR JAGIELLON

RATIFIED IN 1539 BY KING SIGISMUND I THE ELDER

(Text of 1539 Preserved in the Fortress of Poznań)

1539

Constituti personaliter coram judicio domini capitanei seniores judei civitatis Posnaniensis literas sacre regie majestatis serenissimi olim domini domini Kazimiri dei gracia regis Polonie illis et aliis judeis concessas sub sigillo sue sacre regie majestatis in pergameno scriptas exhibuerunt quas propter varios humanos cansus in librum actorum castri Posn. illic referri petiverunt et dominus judex causarum castri Posn. cum dominis judicio presidens prefatorum judeorum petitione audita et exaudita revisis diligenter ipsis literis salvisque per omnia repertis mandavit illas secundum illarum verba in librum presentem referri et inscribi quarum equidem literarum ita verba habent.

Certain duly appointed elder Jews of the state of Posnania displayed in the presence of the court of the lord governor a letter of his sacred royal majesty the most serene lord Casimir, by grace of God late King of Poland, written on parchment under the seal of his sacred royal majesty granted to them and other Jews, which letter for various humane reasons they asked to be entered there in the book of the acts of the town of Poznan; and the lord judge of causes of the town of Poznan, presiding over the court with [other] lords, having heard and reheard the petition of the aforesaid Jews, and having diligently examined the letter itself and found it intact throughout, ordered it to be entered word for word in the present book and to be inscribed therein letter for letter.

1453

In nomine domini amen! Nos Kazimirus dei gracia rex Polonie nec non terrarum Cracovie Sandomirie Siradie Lancicie ac Cujavie, magnus dux Lithvanie Pomoranie Russieque dominus et heres etc. ad perpetuam rei memoriam. Significamus tenore presencium quibus expedit universis presentibus et futuris presencium noticiam habituris, quomodo coram majestate nostra personaliter constituti judei nostri de terris Majoris Polonie videlicet de Posnaniensi Calischiensi Siradiensi Lanciciensi

In the name of the Lord amen! We, Casimir, by the grace of God King of Poland and of the lands of Cracovia, Sandomiria, Siradia, Lancicia, and Cujavia, Grand Duke of Lithuania, Pomorania, and Ruthenia, lord and heir, etc., to the perpetual memory of the matter: We indicate by the content of these presents to all, present and future, whosoever shall have notice of these presents how before our majesty our personally appointed Jews from the lands of Greater Poland, to wit, from the palati-

Brzestensi Wladislaviensi palatinatibus et districtibus ad ipsa spectantibus sua exposicione deduxerunt quod jura, que habuerunt a celebris memorie serenissimo principe domino Kazimiro rege Polonie etc. perdecessore nostro mediato et quibus aliorum regum predecessorum nostrum et nostris temporibus semper et usque in hactenus usi fuerint, tunc quando civitas nostra Posnaniensis voragine ignis nobis presentibus consumpta fuit, ipsis essent eciam per ignem in cinerem redacta, petentes et humiliter nobis supplicantes, quattenus juxta eorundem jurium copiam quam coram nobis exhibuerunt eadem jura innovare ratificare et confirmare dignaremur graciose. Quorum quidem jurium taliter accopiatorum tenor de verbo ad verbum sequitur et est talis.

nates of Posnania, Calischia, Siradia, Lancicia, Brzest, and Wladislavia and the districts pertaining to them demonstrated by their exposition that the rights which they had from the most serene prince of famous memory, lord Casimir King of Poland, etc., our distant predecessor, and which they had enjoyed in the times of other kings our predecessors, and in our times and right up to the present, had also been reduced to ashes at the time when our city of Poznan was consumed by engulfing fire with us present; they asked and humbly supplicated us that we might deign graciously to restore, ratify and confirm the same rights after a copy of the same rights which they displayed before us. Now the content of these rights thus copied follows word for word and is as follows:

1334

In nomine domini amen. Nos Kazimirus dei gracia rex Polonie nec non terrarum Cracovie Siradie Sandomirie Lancicie Cujavie dominus at heres Posnaniensis, volumus devenire ad noticiam universorum tam presencium quam futurorum, quia ad nostre majestatis nostrorumque nobilium terrigenarum presenciam venientes quidam nostri judei de regno nostro mansionem in majori Polonia habentes offerentes privilegium a serenissimo duce Boleslao bone memorie datum qui prius fuit dux et dominus terrarum polonie ipsi judeis ipsorumque jura et statuta in se continens, quandoquidem privilegium cum statutis nostra regalis majestas nostrumque dominorum ac nobilium terrigenarum providencia matura deliberatione ponderantes dicti privilegii seriem de verbo ad verbum legimus in eoque nihil reperientes quod nostre displiceret majestati aut juri modo in aliquo articulo derogare videretur, hoc attendentes dictum privilegium majestatis nostre ac nostrorum dominorum nobiliumque terrigenarum maturo cum consensu jussimus et adhesimus renovare et confirmare acceptum gratum atque firmum statuentes.

In the name of the Lord amen. We Casimir, by the grace of God King of Poland and of the lands of Cracovia, Siradia, Sandomiria, Lancicia, Cujavia, lord and heir of Posnania, wish to bring to the attention of all persons, both present and future, that, coming to the presence of our majesty and of our landed nobles, certain of our Jews from our realm having residence in Greater Poland showed a privilege given to them by the most serene Duke Boleslaus of happy memory, who was earlier the duke and lord of the lands of Poland, and containing in it their laws and statutes; whereas we have considered the privilege and its statutes with the exhaustive deliberation of our royal majesty and with the deliberation and advice of our lords and landed nobles, and have read the aforesaid privilege word for word and have not found in any article anything which should displease our majesty or seem to detract from our right, now therefore with the full agreement of our majesty and of our lords and landed nobles, we order and command the renewal and confirmation of the aforesaid privilege, declaring it acceptable, pleasing, and firm.

44

1. Primo quidem statuimus ut pro pecunia re mobili aut pro qualibet re immobili seu pro causa criminali que tangeret personam aut res judeorum nullus christianus contra judeos pro qualibet re mobili et immobili que tangeret ut prefertur ipsorum judeorum vita vel bona, talis christianus contra prefatos judeos si aliquem inculpaverit pro quacumque re eciam criminali non admittatur ad testimonium nisi cum duobus bonis christianis et eciam cum duobus bonis judeis. Qui omnes supradicti in sua humanitate non essent infames sed cum sint accepti taliter si prefatus christianus convicerit aliquem ex judeis, tunc primo ille judeus puniri debet, pro quo a prefato christiano infammatus seu inculpatus fuerit. Qui duo christiani jurare debent super sacram crucem videlicet sic: ita nos deus adjuvat et sancta crux etc. secundum morem ipsorum christianorum. Judei vero jurabunt super rodale decem preceptorum secundum consuetudinem ipsorum judeorum super summam que se extendetur quinquaginta marcarum fusi argenti puri, et quidquid inferius esset quam se predicta summa fusi argenti quinquaginta marcarum extendere videretur tunc ipsi judei super feruncam alias colcze circa scolam in hostio pendentem debebunt jurare secundum morem ipsorum hoc est tali modo seu rotha: ita nos deus adjuvet qui illuminat et observat et libri Moysi, ita debet fieri juramentum judeorum et aliter non, pro quacunque re sit parva sive magna tenendo se feruncam, et hoc debet mandare ministerialis alias woszni vel scolni cui demandetur.

2. Item si aliquis christianorum judeum impedierit asserens quod sibi pignora sua invadiavit et judeus hoc negaverit, tunc ipse christianus si simplici verbo judei fidem noluerit adhibere judeus jurando sibi christiano debet esse ab eo liber.

3. Ceterum si christianus pignus seu vadium impignoraverit in minori summa pecu-

1. First of all we decree that in any matter of movable or immovable property, or in a criminal case which touches the person or property of Jews, or any movable or immovable property which affects the life or goods of Jews (as previously stated), if any Christian should accuse any of the Jews in any matter whatsoever, even a criminal matter, he shall not be admitted to testimony except with two good Christians and also with two good Jews. None of the above may be of infamous character, but when they have been accepted thus, if the aforesaid Christian shall have convicted one of the Jews, only then must that Jew be punished for the charge brought against him by the aforesaid Christian. The two Christians must swear thus on the Holy Cross, to wit: May God and the Holy Cross so help me, etc., according to the custom of Christians. But the Jews must swear on the "rodale" (scroll) of the Ten Commandments according to the practice of the Jews, over a sum amounting to fifty marks of pure silver ingot, but over a lesser sum the Jews must swear on the "ferunca" or "colcze" hanging in the door of the synagogue, according to their custom. This is the form or rote of the oath: May God who illuminates and observes and the books of Moses help us. Thus must the oath of the Jews be and not otherwise, whether the matter be great or small, while each holds the "ferunca," and the ministerial (Woszny or Scolny) to whom the matter is referred must require this.

2. Furthermore, if any Christian shall sue a Jew, asserting that he has pawned securities with him, and the Jew denies it, then if the Christian refuses to accept the simple word of the Jew, the Jew by taking oath must be free of the Christian.

3. In addition, if a Christian shall have pledged a security for a lesser sum, and

nie et judeus dicens asserit fore majorem summam, extunc judeus prestito sibi juramento secundum morem ipsorum talis christianus sibi judeo solvere debebit et tenebitur principalem summam pecunie pariter cum usura absque omni dilacione dare.

4. Insuper judeus poterit recipere omnia pignora, que ei oblata fuerint quocumque nomine vocitentur, exceptis sangine madefactis seu madidis et sacris vestibus que pro cultu divino sunt dedicate que nullatenus acceptabit, demto quod eadem alicui presbitero ad reservandum daret, quia solus servare non potest.

5. Item si aliquis christianus impediret judeum propter pignus quod judeus habet quod eidem per violenciam furtive sit ablatum, judeus in dando super pignus eo tempore dicet quando mihi tale vadium seu pignus est invadiatum nescivi quod furtive ablatum vel per violenciam raptum fuisset sed credidi fore vadium justum et liberum, judeus jurabit juramento suo, in quantis sit ei hujusmodi pignus invadiatum, et sic judeus expurgacione facta christianus ipse principalem pecuniam, in qua tale vadium sit obligatum et usuram a tempore obligationis excrescentem eidem realiter et cum effectu persolvere debebit.

6. Item quod absit si cansu infortuito incendium ignis evenerit aut furtive res et bona judei unacum aliquibus pignoribus deperderentur, tunc prefatus judeus testimonio aliquorum judeorum sibi vicinorum protestari debet, quod res seu bona unacum pignoribus sibi invadiatis sibi furtive sunt ablata et recepta; et nihilominus christianus volens habere talia pignora invadiata, judeus vero prestito juramento secundum morem ipsorum judeorum erit liber et solutus ab ipso christiano, et si judeus talis jurare non presumpserit, ex tunc ipsi christiano tantum quantum prius super vadium perditum dedit addere tenebitur et erit liber ab ipso christiano.

the Jew shall declare that it was for a greater sum, then when the Jew has taken the appointed oath according to their custom, such a Christian must pay the Jew, and he shall be required to give over the principal sum along with interest, without any delay.

4. Moreover, a Jew shall be able to accept all securities pledged to him, by whatever name they are called, with the exception of articles tainted or wet with blood, and sacred vestments which have been dedicated to divine worship, which he shall under no circumstances accept, unless he give them to a priest for safekeeping, since he alone cannot keep them.

5. Likewise, if any Christian should sue a Jew over a security which the Jew has, saying that it was taken from him by robbery or larceny, the Jew, in handing over the security at that time shall say, "When this security was pawned with me, I did not know that it had been taken by theft or robbery, but I believed that it was a free and proper security." The Jew shall swear by his oath, as to the sum for which the security was pawned, and with the Jew having made expurgation, the Christian shall be obliged to pay over in reality and with effect the principal money for which the security was pawned, and also the interest accruing from the time of the obligation.

6. Likewise, if -- Heaven forbid -- by any chance a fire or theft has occurred, and the property and household goods of a Jew have been destroyed along with some pawned articles, then the aforesaid Jew ought to show by the testimony of several Jewish neighbors that his own property and goods have been stolen along with the articles pledged to him as security; if nonetheless a Christian wishes to have such pledged articles, then the Jew will become free and clear of the Christian by means of the appointed oath in accordance with the custom of the Jews. But if such a Jew does not presume to swear thus, then he shall be required to add only so much as he

46

originally gave for the pledged article, and he will be free of the Christian.

7. Item si judei inter se de facto discordiam contencionis commiserint aut aliquam gwerram vel judeus cum christiano et se mutuo sic contendentes percusserint aut vulneraverint, tunc neque judex civitatis neque consules neque eciam aliquis hominum, tantummodo palatinus ipsorum judeorum aut ille qui loco eius presidet eosdem judicet et illi judicabunt taliter in judicio locando scabellum cum judeis.

7. Likewise if the Jews create dissension among themselves -- or even a riot -- over some act, or if a Jew and a Christian fighting with each other engage in hitting or wounding, then neither the judge of the city, nor the consuls, nor even anybody else, but only the palatine of the Jews or his surrogate shall judge them, and the place of the trial shall be with the Jews.

8. Si vero prefatus judeus sic contendens cum quocumque hominum prefatorum postulaverit repponi talem causam ad nostram majestatem, tunc palatinus vel eciam judex ab eo substitutus quicumque pro tempore fuerit hujusmodi causam ipsius judei ad nos debebit defferre, et eciam quecumque causa verteretur coram palatino inter judeos et palatinum aut substitutum ejus dummodo postulaverint debet differri ad nostre majestatis adventum.

8. But if the aforesaid Jew, contending with any one of the aforesaid people, shall ask that his case be placed before our majesty, then the palatine or his temporary substitute judge must defer the Jew's case to us, and also any case arising before the palatine between Jews and the palatine or his surrogate, provided they request it, must be deferred to the arrival of our majesty.

9. Item nullus palatinus aut capitaneus debent aliquos proventus alias poplathky et contribuciones dany apud judeos, nisi quo eos ipsi judei de sua voluntate donaverit, et hoc ideo quia nos eos reservamus pro nostro thesauro.

9. Nor may any palatine or governor receive any excises (poplathky) or gratuities (dany = dary?) among the Jews, except where the Jews have given them of their own accord; and then only because we reserve such contributions for our own treasury.

10. Et eciam statuimus quod quecumque causa propter discordiam aut contenciones inter judeos oriretur, hoc nullus nisi ipsorum antiquiores judicare debent dempto quod si ipsi veritatem inter eos comperire nequiverint, ex tunc ad dominum palatinum hoc defferre debent.

10. And we also ordain that whatever case arises because of discord or contention among Jews, no one should judge it except their own elders, except when they are unable to ascertain the truth among them; then they must refer it to the lord palatine.

11. Item si aliquis judeorum suis superioribus non esset obediens, ex tunc talis domino palatino luet penam trium marcarum et superioribus suis similiter penam trium marcarum.

11. Likewise, if any of the Jews is not obedient to his own superiors, then he must pay to the lord palatine a penalty of three marks, and to the superiors a similar penalty of three marks.

12. *Insuper si christianus cum judeo contenderit insimul quovismodo et si idem christianus judeum wlneraverit vulnere cruento vel livido aut ipsum in faciem maxillaverit vel ipsius crines de capite erruerit, tunc nos damus ipsi judeo talem nostram jurisdicionem quod prefatus judeus tiliter wlneratus prestito juramento secundum consuetudinem super cathenam alias colcze scole ipsorum judeorum in hostio, tunc talis christianus, si per judeum superjuratus fuerit, debebit et tenebitur dare eidem judeo pro maxilla a quolibet digitto quinque marcas, a vulnere livido decem marcas, a vulnere vero cruento medietatem suorum bonorum tam mobilium quam immobilium predicto judeo, residuam vero medietatem bonorum hujusmodi pro nobis et nostris successoribus et pro palatino hujus districtus reservamus et alias juxta nostram voluntatem prescripta judicabimus, sed pro crinibus extractis de capite judei prefatus christianus sibi solvere tenebitur secundum decretum dominorum in judicio residencium juxta posicionem juris.*

13. *Ceterum quod absit si aliquis christianus aliquem ex judeis occiderit, ex tunc proximior judeus occisi judei si perjuraverit ipsum christianum super rodale decem preceptorum secundum morem judeorum, tunc volumus et statuimus, quod talis christianus sic per judeum superjuratus debet mortifficari morte taxando caput pro capite, et aliter in ea re non sit faciendum.*

14. *Si vero talis christianus qui occiderit judeum aliquomodo evaserit sic quod non possit capi nec haberi in manibus, extunc ipsius christiani bona mobilia et immobilia quecumque habuerit primo medietas dictorum bonorum et hereditatum debet devolvi super propinquiores consaguineos judei interempti, reliqua vero medietas pro camera nostra regia pertinere debet.*

15. *Item si talis profugus judei interempti salwm-conductum habere voluerit, dari sibi non debet nisi cum consensu dicorum*

12. Furthermore, if a Christian gets into an argument with a Jew in any way, and if that Christian wounds the Jew with a bloody or livid wound, or hits him in the face, or rips the hair of his head, then we give to that Jew our jurisdiction that the aforesaid Jew thus wounded take the appointed oath according to custom on the chain (colcze) in the door of the synagogue of the Jews; then the Christian, if he be outsworn by the Jew, must and shall be required to give to that Jew five marks for a blow to the jaw by any finger, ten marks for a livid wound, but for a bloody wound half of all his possessions both movable and immovable to the aforesaid Jew; but we reserve the other half of such possessions for ourselves and our successors, and for the palatine of his district, and we shall otherwise judge the prescribed penalties according to our will; but for hair pulled from the head of the Jew the aforesaid Christian shall be required to absolve himself according to the decree of the lords resident in the court, in respect to the position of the law.

13. Moreover, if -- Heaven forbid -- any Christian kills one of the Jews, then if the Jew next of kin to the slain Jew overswears the Christian on the scroll of the Ten Commandments according to the custom of the Jews, then we will and ordain that such a Christian thus oversworn by the Jew must be punished with the imposition of death, a head for a head, and it is not to be done otherwise in this matter.

14. But if such a Christian who kills a Jew in any way escapes so that it is not possible for him to be taken or held, then of the movable and immovable property of the Christian, whatever he has, the first half of such possessions and inheritances must devolve to the blood kin of the slain Jew, but the rest must be assigned to our royal chamber.

15. Likewise, if such a fugitive of a slain Jew wishes to have a safe-conduct, it must not be given him, except with the consent

consaguineorum ipsius judei interempti.

of the aforesaid kin of the slain Jew.

16. Item volumus et statuimus si aliquis ex judeis intraverit in domum alicujus christiani, nullus hominum christianorum sibi aliquod impedimentum gravamen vel molestiam debet inferre.

16. Likewise, we will and ordain that if any of the Jews enters into the home of any Christian, none of the Christian people must offer him any impediment, physical inconvenience, or annoyance.

17. Item quilibet judeus potest libere et secure ire transire aut equitare sine omni impedimento vel arresto a civitate ab una provincia ad aliam in regno nostro secundum morem secure libertatis sine impedimento et arresto in omnibus civitatibus nostris et ipsorum subditorum vel provinciis, et quilibet judeus in regno nostro potest libere et secure sine omni impedimento secum ducere bona sua et res seu mercancias quascumque que voluerit seu habere poterit ipsasque vendere et alias emere commutare et ad usus beneplacitos convertere ipsius, in locoque civitatis vel oppidi morari stare libere et secure sine omni impedimento et arresto quam, diu sibi opportunum fuerit, in omnibus civitatibus oppidis villis et aliis locis regni nostri, nostra regia quilibet eorum pociatur securitate et salvoconductu, thelonea solita prout alii christiani solverint et non aliter persolvendo.

17. Likewise, any Jew may freely and securely walk or ride without any let or hindrance from city to city and province to province in our realm, in accordance with the law of secure liberty in all our cities or provinces without let or hindrance on the part of their subjects, and any Jew in our realm may freely, securely, and without any let or hindrance take with him his goods, property, or whatsoever merchandise he wishes or is able to have, and to sell such things and buy others, and to alter and convert them to his own satisfactory uses; he may freely and securely delay or stay in a place of the city or town without let or hindrance, for as long as it suits him -- in all the cities, towns, villages, and other places of our realm: by our royal will any of them possesses security and safe-conduct; they shall pay customary tolls just as other [sic!] Christians do, and nothing otherwise.

18. Si vero contingat ipsis judeis secundum consuetudinem ipsorum ducere mortuum judeum vel judeam de una civitate ad aliam civitatem vel provinciam, tunc thelonator loci hujusmodi nulla thelonea a tali mortuo judeo exigere audeat, et si aliquis ex thelonatoribus in contrarium nostrum presencium statutorum et mandatorum theloneum a tali mortuo judeo receperit, ex tunc statuimus et volumus quod talis thelonator judicari debet sicut fur predo et raptor ejusque bona quecumque sint ad nos devolvi debent.

18. But if it becomes necessary for the Jews, in accordance with their custom, to take a dead Jew or Jewess from one city to another city or province, then the toll-collector of such a place must not dare to exact tolls from such a dead Jew, and if any of the toll-collectors, contrary to our present statutes and mandates, should receive a toll from such a dead Jew, then we ordain and will that such a toll-collector be judged as if he were a thief, bandit, and robber, and his goods, whatever they may be, must devolve to us.

19. Item volumus et statuimus quod quilibet judeorum potest libere et secure ad balneum civitatis generale cum christianis

19. Likewise we will and ordain that any of the Jews may freely and securely enter the general bath of a city along with Chri-

49

intrare et nihil superflue solvere debet nisi prout alii incole civitatis.

20. *Eciam ubicumque judei mansionem habuerit in aliqua civitate vel oppido regni nostri, possunt eis mactare pecora et peccudes pro carnibus ad suam utilitatem, et si alique carnes eis secundum morem ad voluntatem et placitum non fuerint, tunc eas vendere possunt quomodo melius poterint vel eis videbitur.*

21 *Item si aliquis ex christianis ipsorum judeorum czimiterium ubi sit sepultura ipsorum lapides violenter ejecerit seu amoverit aut alia loca in dicto ipsorum czmiterio quomodo destruxerit, ille quicumque taliter fecerit res et bona ipsius super cameram nostram regiam devolvi debebunt. Quod volumus fieri et teneri firme secundum jurisdicionem ipsis judeis per nos datum.*

22. *Item si aliquis christianorum temerarie et presumptuose super scolas ipsorum jactaverit, palatino nostro ipsorum tutori talis christianus duo talenta piperis pro tali pena solvere tenebitur et debebit.*

23. *Item si aliquis judeus cittatus fuerit per judicem ipsorum primo et secundo et si non paruerit pro quamcumque cittatus fuerit causa, pro qualibet vice solvere debebit et tenebitur suo judici per unum talentum piperis, si vero cittatus tercio non paruerit, pro quacumque re cittaretur illam eo facto perdet et amittet.*

24. *Item judex ipsorum judeorum non debet aliquam sentenciam promulgare nec profferre aut sentenciare nisi prius habito super hoc speciali ipsorum judeorum consensu.*

stians, and he must not pay anything more than other citizens of the city.

20. Also, wherever the Jews have an inn in any city or town of our realm, they may slaughter sheep and cattle for meats for their own use, and if any meats should be displeasing to them according to their custom and will, then they may sell these in whatever way they are better able or seems good to them.

21. Likewise, in respect to a cemetery of the Jews, where their graves are, if any of the Christians violently throws out or removes the stones, or in any way destroys other places in their aforesaid cemetery, the property and possessions of him who has thus acted must devolve to the royal chamber. We will this to be done and firmly required according to the jurisdiction given by us to the Jews.

22. Likewise, if any of the Christians rashly and presumptuously jeers at their synagogues, such a Christian shall be required to pay and must pay to our palatine their guardian two talents of pepper as punishment.

23. Likewise, if any Jew is summoned by their judge the first and second time, and does not appear in regard to the case for which he is summoned, he must pay and shall be required to pay to his judge for each occasion one talent of pepper, but if, summoned for the third time, he does not appear, he shall by that act forfeit and lose the case for which he was summoned.

24. Likewise, the judge of the Jews shall not promulgate nor propose any sentence, nor shall he impose sentence, unless a special consensus of the Jews is first obtained.

25. Item judex judeorum non debet aliquem judeum judicare in jure suo nisi talis judeus cittatus fuerit cum cittacione per scolni ministerialem, tunc primo judex dictum judeum debet judicare secundum hoc pro quo cittatur.

26. Et si aliquem christianum contigerit vulnera quecumque sint super judeum, tunc debet ea monstrare scolnemu ipsorum judeorum et eciam ministeriali, et ipse judex non debet judicare nec judicium locare in causa tali alibi nisi circa scolam ipsorum judeorum aut eciam ubi dicti judei cum judice ipsorum ex utraque parte consencientes ipsis locum aptum ad hoc elegerint seu deputaverint, et ibidem si adducet christianus duobus judeis et duobus christianis quod sibi idem judeus wlnera dedit et intulit, tunc sibi ea judeus solvere debebit juxta composicionem terrestrem.

27. Ceterum si alicui christiano quodcumque vadium fuerit furtive ablatum et invadiatum inter ipsos judeos, debet interrogare seniorem scole ipsorum et ille senior scole ipsorum sub anathemate ipsorum requiret inter judeos de tali vadio et idem servitor scole debet hoc facere cum scitu senioris judei, et si aliquis ex judeis tale vadium furtive ablatum negaverit ante servitorem scole et judeorum seniorem et postea si arestatum fuerit apud quempiam ex ipsis, talis judeus perdet suas totas pecunias super vadium datas et domino palatino tenetur tres marcas pro pena.

28. Item statuimus et volumus hoc habere quod nullus ex ipsis christianis debet querere aliqua vadia violenter quecumque sint in habitaculis seu in domibus ipsorum judeorum, nisi prius posita una marca auri puri in limitte hostii ipsius judei quam levare debet ipse judeus, tunc primo inquirat de dicto vadio ipse christianus.

25. Likewise, the judge of the Jews shall not judge any Jew in his court, unless the Jew shall have been summoned with a summons from the ministerial "scolny;" then only must he judge the aforesaid Jew in regard to the matter for which he is summoned.

26. And if it should happen to any Christian that he is wounded by a Jew, then he should show the wounds to the "scolny" of the Jews and also to the ministerial, and the judge must not make judgment nor locate the trial anywhere else than at the synagogue of the Jews, or else where the aforesaid Jews, with their judge from each side agreeing, choose and designate an appropriate place, and there if the Christian with two Jews and two Christians shows that that Jew imparted and inflicted wounds upon him, then the Jew must pay him for them according to the system of the region.

27. Furthermore, if any article of value is stolen from a Christian and pawned among the Jews, he should sue the elder of the synagogue, and the elder of the synagogue shall make inquiry under anathema among the Jews concerning such a pawn, and the same servant of the synagogue must do this with the knowledge of the Jewish elder, and if one of the Jews denies before the servant of the synagogue and the elder of the Jews that such a pawn was stolen, and it is later recovered from one of them, that Jew must lose all the money given for the pawn and must pay three marks to the lord palatine as penalty.

28. Likewise we ordain and will this: no Christian must violently seek any pawns whatever in the lodgings or homes of the Jews, unless a mark of pure gold is placed on the threshold of the Jew's door, which the Jew must pick up; only then may the Christian inquire concerning the aforesaid pawn.

29. *Et si aliquis ex christianis non attendens et non curans statuta nostra violenter in dominum judei intraverit, querendo res suas quascumque non ponendo aurum, pretactum talis christianus judicari debet ut predo et raptor.*

29. And if any of the Christians, not observing or heeding our statutes, should violently enter into the home of a Jew seeking whatever property of his own, without depositing the gold, that Christian must be judged as a bandit and robber.

30. *Eciam nullus christianus cittare debet aliquem judeum in judicium spirituale quocumque modo fuerit et pro quacumque re et quacumque cittacione cittatus, nec judeus debet respondere coram judice in judicio spirituali, sed cittetur talis judeus coram ipsius palatinum qui tunc pro tempore fuerit, et ulterius prefatus palatinus cum capitano nostro pro tempore existenti tenebitur deffendere tueri et intercedere ipsum judeum a tali cittacione juris spiritualis.*

30. Also, no Christian may summon any Jew into the ecclesiastical court in any way whatsoever, or for whatever property or summons he be summoned, nor shall the Jew make answer before the judge in the ecclesiastical court, but the Jew shall appear before his palatine appointed for that term, and furthermore the aforesaid palatine, along with our governor for that term, shall be required to defend and protect that Jew, and prohibit his responding to the summons of the ecclesiastical court.

31. *Insuper statuimus quod quilibet judeus qui haberet aliquod vadium quodcumque sit et cujuscumque valoris esset et steterit ultra debitum terminum invadicionis, alias Byssye thaka zasthawa visthala ita quod jam judeus servare nollet quia non staret, prefatus judeus debet tale vadium ostendere et ponere coram ipsorum palatino aut ipsius vicesgerente et postea dictus judeus debet avisare christianum per ministerialem pretacti vadii pro exempcione, et si ipse christianus neglexerit exemere post jam avisacionem ministerialis, ipse judeus potest convertere prefatum vadium ad suos usos beneplacitos ubicumque voluerit, eciam si prefatus judeus pretactum vadium non monstraverit taliter et vendiderit sicut premissum est, tunc tenebitur ipse judeus domino palatino pro pena tres marcas.*

31. Moreover, we ordain that whenever any Jew who has some pawn, whatever it may be, and of whatever value, and it has stood beyond the appointed termination of the pawning (Byssye thaka zasthawa visthala), so that the Jew does not wish to keep it, since the arrangement no longer stands, then the aforesaid Jew must display and deposit the pawn before the palatine or his vicegerent, and afterward the aforesaid Jew must advise the Christian, through the ministerial, of the detention of the affected pawn, and if the Christian neglects to redeem it after notification by the ministerial, the Jew may convert the aforesaid pawn to his own beneficial uses whenever he pleases; and if the aforesaid Jew does not display the affected pawn in this way, and sells it as stated above, then the Jew shall be required to pay to the lord palatine three marks penalty.

32. *Item de speciali consensu majestatis nostre statuimus et volumus habere, quod quilibet judeorum nostrum potest accomodare et inscribere pecunias seu bona sua nobilibus nostris terrigenis cujuscumque status aut condicionis fuerit et illas ipsorum pecunias firmare libris terrestribus*

32. Likewise, by the special intention of our majesty we ordain and will have it that any of our Jews is able to lend and make over moneys or goods to our landed nobles of whatever status or condition, and to record those moneys in the books, both regional, municipal, civil, and praeto-

castrensibus civilibus pretorialibus et scabinorum, et super vadia possunt accomodare suas pecunias cujuscumque valoris fuerint talia, et ipse judeus non plus debebit recipere de usura a talibus vadiis nisi per unum grossum septimanatim a qualibet marca, quam diu talia vadia apud ipsos judeos steterint.

33. Et si contingeret si aliquis ex judeis nostris monuerit aliquem ex suis quibuscumque debitoribus quomodocumque cui ipsi debitores essent obligati sive obligacionibus literarum cum sigillis suis sive inscripcionibus librorum pretactorum, indulsimus etenim ipsis judeis quod possunt accomodare pecunias suas terrigenis super bona oligatoria sigillis ipsorum terrigenarum nostrum ad literas appensis, et ubi prefati debitores ita prout se inscripserunt temerarie non curaverint judeis eciam et pro vadiis sicut sunt obligati plenariam facere solucionem, ex tunc vobis palatinis capitaneis burgrabiis vestrisque vicesgerentibus et quibusvis aliis officialibus pro tempore existentibus precipimus habere volentes, quattenus ipsis nostris judeis finale complementum justicie cum prefatis terrigenis nostris debitoribus eorum ministretis et vestris ministris seu subditis ministrare faciatis ita pro pecunia recepta sicut et pro usura et aliter non facturi, et ad introligacionem bonorum hereditariorum in terris nostris si procederint et ministeriales affectaverint super pignora alias naczansza, nostro regio mandato vos su- pradicti et vestrum quilibet debeatis et tenemini ipsis nostris judeis prebere auxilia et subsidia secundum juris formam eosdem judeos ab omnibus injuriis ipsorum tuentes et deffendentes oesque judeos ad talia bona nostrorum terrigenarum introligantes.

34. Si vero aliqui ex judeis fuerint introligati per vos et subditos vestros in aliqua bona hereditaria nostrum terrigenarum, nos statuimus et decernimus quod in cujus terrigene bona aliqui ex judeis introligarentur talis terrigena noster sibi judeo

rial, and those of the judges, and they are able to lend such moneys for securities of whatever value, and the Jew is not to receive more interest for such debts than either kind of mark weekly per gross, for as long as such debts stand among the Jews.

33. And if it happens that if one of our Jews shall advise one of his debtors of the way in which debtors are obligated to him, whether by obligations of a letter with the debtor's seals or by his signature in books, we grant to our Jews that they are able to lend money to nobles in return for securities obligated by the seal of our nobles appended to a letter, and whenever the aforesaid debtors, having thus bound themselves, boldly do not bother to make full payment for the mortgage as they are obligated to do, then we admonish you palatines, governors, burgraves, your vicegerents, and any other officials appointed for a term -- and we intend to have it this way -- that you administer a full complement of justice to our Jews [in their relations] with our noble debtors, and that you make your ministers or subordinates administer it thus in respect to money received as also for interest, and that they act in no other way, and if they [the Jews] proceed to the foreclosure of hereditary estates in our lands and the ministerials seize them as pledged securities (naczansza), by our royal mandate you who are named above, and any of your people, must and are required to render to our Jews aid and full asistance according to the form of the law, protecting our Jews from all injuries, and defending the same Jews when they foreclose on such properties of our landed nobles.

34. But if any of the Jews shall have foreclosed through you and your subordinates on any hereditary estates of our landed nobles, we ordain and decree that if any of the Jews foreclose on the estate of some noble, then our landed noble must

debet ponere fidejussores bone possessionis, quos eciam ipse judeus acceptaverit, illius distritus in quo bona ipsius sunt sita, quod talis noster judeus eadem bona hereditaria possit pacifice et quiette tenere et possidere absque impedimento cujuslibet hominis tali sub dicione prout eciam bona hereditaria jurisdicionem habebant nihil juris aut dominii ibidem diminuendo.

give to the Jew deeds of good possession, of the district in which his estate is located, and when the Jew has accepted the deeds, that our Jew shall be able to hold and possess the estate peacefully and quietly, without the interference of any person, under the authority [of those who] have jurisdiction in respect to hereditary estates, with no diminution of right or dominion there.

35. Et si contigerit quod aliquis ex nostris terrigenis cujus bona hereditaria aliquis ex judeis tenuerit per introligacionem realiter factam et idem terrigena eadem bona exemere ad decursum annorum secundum consuetudinem terrestrem antiquitatis, nos statuimus quod post decursum trium annorum ipse judeus potest libere vendere prefata bona hereditaria et ad suos proprios usus convertere prout sibi melius et utilius videbitur expedire.

35. And if it happens that any of our landed nobles whose estate one of the Jews holds through foreclosure properly executed..., and the same noble [tries] to redeem the same property at the expiration of [whatever] years [are] in accordance with ancient local custom, we ordain that after the expiration of three years, the Jew is able freely to sell the aforesaid hereditary estate and to convert it to his own personal uses as may seem to him to be more expedient and useful.

36. Et eciam statuimus quod quicumque judeus bona hereditaria per introligacionem tenuerit, ad expedicionem non tenebitur equitare nec aliquid pro expedicione dare, et hoc ideo qui ipsi judei nostri sunt thezauri.

36. And we also ordain that any Jew who holds an hereditary estate through foreclosure shall not be required to ride to a campaign nor to give anything for the campaign, and this because our Jews are treasures.

37. Insuper statuimus quod si aliquis ex nostratibus sit nobilis noster terrigena vel civis qui prefatis judeis aliquam summam pecunie super obligacionem aut librorum inscripcionem sive quovismodo teneretur, et si contigerit ipsum mori et pueri ipsius supervixerint qui nondum annos haberent, ipsi pueri predictos judeos annis puerilibus evadere non debebunt sed debet eisdem judeis subveniri secundum ipsorum obligaciones, et hoc ideo quia ipsi judei debent fieri suis cum pecuniis parati pro necessitatibus nostris sicut subditi nostri.

37. Moreover, we ordain that if one of our countrymen, whether a landed noble or a citizen, is bound to the aforesaid Jews for a sum of money by [a letter of] obligation or the signing of books, and if it happen that he dies and his surviving sons are not yet of legal age, they must not evade the aforesaid Jews by reason of their tender years, but must pay the same Jews according to their obligations, and this because the Jews must be prepared with their funds for our necessities as our subjects.

38. Item si contigerit aliquem ex christia-

38. Likewise, if it happens that any Chris-

54

nis adducere ad quempiam ex judeis infantulum vel juvenem quasi more furti sine ipsorum judeorum scitu, talis christianus quicumque sit non alio modo sit plectendus nisi sicut alius fur.

39. Item statuimus ne decetero aliquis judeus inculpandus ab aliquo christiano pro tali re sic dicente, quod ipsi judei de necessitate uterentur sanguine christianorum annuatim vel sacramentis ecclesie christianorum, ex quo statuta pape Innocencii et constituciones nos edocent quod in talibus rebus non sunt culpabiles quia hoc est contra legem ipsorum, et si ultra aliquis christianus sua temeritate alias vpornossczya aliquem judeum pro talibus rebus inculpaverit alias obvynylby, tunc eis jus tale damus et concedimus, quod talis christianus si voluerit adducere et probare et hanc suam rem finire, tunc debet probare tribus judeis bonis et possesionatis in regno nostro qui in sua humanitate non essent infames et in fide essent immobliles et quattuor christianis qui eciam essent bene possesionati in regno nostro in suaque humanitate non infames et in fide immobiles alias nye porwscheni, et si hujusmodi testimonio christianus probaverit contra judeum, tunc judeus ipse reus erit mortis et ea plectendus, et dum hujusmodi testimonium christianus non adduxerit nec contra judeum probare potuerit, tunc solus morte eadem erit condempnandus qua judeus damnari debuit, et si pro talibus rebus nobiles nostri terrigene vel cives regni nostri ipsis judeis nostris violenciam fecerint jure eos non victo, tunc bona ipsorum pro camera nostra regia devolvi debent et cola pro gracia nostra speciali.

40. Et si quis ex terrigenis regni nostri quempiam judeum cittaverit hoc eciam statuimus, quod prefatus judeus non tenetur coram aliquo judice respondere nisi coram palatino qui pro tempore fuerit et non alibi.

tian should bring to any of the Jews an infant or juvenile as a thief does without the knowledge of the Jews, that Christian must be punished in exactly the same way as any other thief.

39. Likewise we ordain by decree that [if] any Jew is to be prosecuted by any Christian alleging that the Jews of necessity annually use the blood of Christians or the sacraments of the Church of the Christians, concerning which the statutes and constitutions of Pope Innocent teach us that in such matters they are not culpable, since this is against their own law; and if despite this any Christian with temerity (vpornossczya) accuses (obvynylby) any Jew of such things, then we grant and concede to them this right, that if the Christian chooses to adduce and prove and bring to an end this affair of his, then he must prove it with three good propertied Jews in our realm who are not infamous in character and are firm in faith, and with four Christians who also are well propertied in our realm, not infamous in character, but firm in faith (nye porwscheni)[sic]; and if by such testimony the Christian proves [his case] against the Jew, then the Jew shall be deserving of death and must be punished with it; and whenever the Christian does not adduce such testimony, and is not able to prevail against the Jew, then he alone is to be condemned; and if for such matters our landed nobles or the citizens of our realm offer violence to the Jews, when the latter have not been condemned by law, then their property must devolve to our royal chamber, and all of it for our special grace.

40. And if any of the nobles of our realm should summon any Jew, we also ordain this, that the aforesaid Jew shall not be held to answer before any judge except before the palatine for that term, and not elsewhere.

41. *Eciam si contigerit quod aliqui ex christianis nostris vellent exemere vadia ipsorum alicui ex judeis invadiata in ipsorum judeorum die festo sabato aut in aliquo ipsorum festo in quibus ipsi judei non essent ausi tangere pecunias pro vadiis exemendis et pecuniam eandem tollere, et christianus non curans tale festum eorum quodcumque sit, volens rehabere suum vadium temerarie et per violenciam ruptis ipsorum judeorum habitaculis et abstulerint predictum vadium, talis christianus non aliomodo judicari debet nisi ut predo et fur prout jurisdicio exigit super furem et predonem.*

41. And if it should happen that any of our Christians choose to redeem securities pledged to one of the Jews on a Sabbath feast day of the Jews or on any feast of theirs on which feasts the Jews dare not touch the moneys of redemption and pick up the same money, and the Christian, not bothering with such a feast, whatever it may be, and wishing to have his security back, rashly and violently breaks open the lodgings of the Jews and takes away the aforesaid security, the Christian must not be judged otherwise than as a thief and bandit, to the extent that the jurisdiction requires concerning a thief and bandit.

42. *Item possunt accomodare suas pecunias super equos vel alia peccora, sed tantum in die circa evidens testimonium; sed noctis tempore non accomodent.*

42. Likewise they can lend money backed by horses or other farm animals, but only in open daylight; at night they must not lend.

43. *Insuper statuimus et decernimus si aliquis ex judeis fuerit per aliquem ex christianis vel quempiam pro qualibet falsa moneta vel furto vel pro quocumque maleficio parvo vel magno inculpatus fuerit quod tangeret guttura et bona eorum, talis judeus non debet captivari per aliquem dignitarium nostrum in regno nec judicari nisi per palatinum ipsorum judeorum vel ab eo vicesgerente per eundem palatinum debet captivari et super caucionem fidejussoriam dari et pro omnibus articulis, pro quibus inculpatus fuerit, propinquior erit judeus ad expurgandum se de tali infamia assumptis secum aliquibus aliis judeis pro testimonio contra illum qui prefactum judeum inculpavit, et pro omnibus itaque penis que ipsi christiano lueret judeus et palatino solvere debit sicut terrigene secundum consuetudinem terrestrem, quia remansimus dictos judeos nostros circa jura nobilia nostrum terrigenarum.*

43. Moreover we ordain and decree that if any of the Jews shall be accused by one of the Christians, or anybody, for counterfeit money, or theft, or any misdeed great or small which touches upon their throats or possessions, the Jew must not be taken prisoner by any dignitary of our realm nor judged, except by the palatine of the Jews or his vicegerent; he must be taken prisoner by the same palatine and admitted to bail bond, and in respect to all the articles of which he has been accused, the Jew will be closer to clearing himself of the charges if he brings with him several other Jews for testimony against the man who accused the aforesaid Jew; and for all the penalties which the Jew pays the Christian, he must also pay the palatine as if he were a noble according to the regional practice, since we have bound our aforesaid Jews to the noble rights of our landed nobles.

44. *Insuper si contigerit quod aliquis ex judeis clamaret publice super violenciam sibi a quocumque hominum illatam noctis tempore et clamaret super vicinos suos christianos secum in una civitate commo-*

44. Moreover, if it happens that one of the Jews cries out in public about violence committed against him by some man at night, and he cries out to his Christian neighbors abiding with him in one city,

rantes et tales vicini christiani audientes ipsum judeum clamare et a tale violencia deffendere et eum adjuvare nolentes, nos statuimus et decernimus quod omnia bona illorum christianorum vicinorum quecumque sint devolvi super cameram nostram regiam cola vero ipsorum reservantes grecie nostre.

45. Insuper statuimus quod omnes judei morantes in regno nostro possunt libere secure et sine quovis impedimento et arresto omnes mercancias et alias res venales quocumque nomine vocitentur emere comparare et mercari cum eisdem more christianorum in regno nostro existencium, et si aliquis christianorum talia premissa ipsis judeis facere denegaverit aut ipsos in talibus negociis quomodo perturbaret, hoc faceret contra omnia statuta nostra regalia et magnam nostram exinde indignacionem incurreret.

46. Item statuimus quod omnis mercator sive quicumque sit res suas in annali foro sive septimanario foro vendens, sicut christiano sic et judeo vendere debet, quod si aliter fecerit et ipsi judei conquesti fuerint, ex tunc ipsorum bona venalia pro nobis et palatino recipi debent, et ut omnia premissa robur perpetue firmitatis obtineant ad presens privilegium sigillum nostrum est appensum.

and the Christian neighbors hear that Jew cry out and are unwilling to defend him from such violence and to help him, we ordain and decree that all the possessions of those Christian neighbors whatsoever are devolved to our royal chamber, indeed reserving them all to our grace.

45. Moreover, we ordain that all Jews abiding in our realm are able freely, securely, and without let or hindrance to buy all merchandise and other things for sale, by whatever name they may be called, and to trade with them in the manner of the Christians in our realm, and if any of the Christians prohibits the Jews from doing the aforesaid things, or in any way disturbs them in such activities, he does this against all our royal statutes and incurs thereby our great indignation.

46. Likewise we ordain that every merchant or anyone selling in the annual fair or weekly market must sell alike to Christian and Jew, and if he does otherwise and the Jews complain, then all his merchandise must be taken for us and the palatine, and in order that all the foregoing may gain force of perpetual stability, we have appended our seal to the present privilege.

1453

Et nos Kazimirus rex prefatus prefatis juribus judeorum prescriptorum auditis et cum certis regni nostri consiliariis cum debita maturitate revisis ac examinatis ac ponderatis singulis articulis clausulis et condicionibus in eis expressis volentesque ut ipsi judei, quos nobis et regno pro speciali conservamus thesauro, tempore nostri felicis regiminis se agnoscant esse a nobis consolatos pro eisdem judeis in terris Majoris Polonie videlicet in Posnaniensi Calisiensi Siradiensi Lanciciensi Brzestensi Vladislaviensi palatinatibus et omnibus districtibus civitatibus et oppidis ad ipsa spe-

And we, Casimir, the aforesaid king, having heard the aforesaid rights of the described Jews, and with due deliberation having reviewed them with certain counselors of our kingdom, and having examined and pondered the single articles, clauses, and conditions expressed in them, and wishing that the Jews themselves, whom we preserve as a special treasure for ourselves and our kingdom, should acknowledge that in the time of our happy reign they were benefited by us, on behalf of the same Jews in the lands of greater Poland, to wit: in the palatinates of Posna-

ctantibus et in eisdem habitantibus ac degentibus nunc presentibus et aliis undecumque in ipsas Majoris Polonie terras advenientibus hujusmodi jura superius descripta in omnibus eorum punctis condicionibus clausulis et articulis innovamus ratificamus et confirmamus per presentes, decernentes robur habere perpetue firmitatis harum quibus sigillum nostrum presentibus est subappensum testimonio literarum. Actum Cracovie feria secunda ante festum Assumpcionis gloriosissime virginis Marie proxima anno domini millesimo quadrigentesimo quinquagesimo tercio, presentibus ibidem magnificis generosis et strenuis Luca de Gorka Posnaniensi, Stanislao de Ostrorog Calissiensi palatinis, Hyncza de Rogow castellano Siradiensi vicethezaurario, Petro de Sczekocim vicecancellario regni Polonie, Andrea de Thanczin, Joanne Krasska de Lwbnicza pincera Calissiensi et capitaneo Coninensi, et Czrzeslao Woysschik de Woycza supremo cubiculario nostro et aliis pluribus fide dignis circa premissa. Datum per manus magnificorum Joannis de Konieczpolie cancellarii et Petri de Sczekoczini vicecancellarii regni Polonie sincere nobis dilectorum ad relacionem ejusdem magnifici Petri de Sczekocini r. P. vicecancellarii.

nia, Calisia, Siradia, Lancicia, Brzest, Vladislavia, and all districts, cities, and towns pertaining to them, and among the same inhabitants and sojourners now present and others coming from any other place into the lands of Greater Poland, we renew, ratify, and confirm through these presents the rights of this sort hereabove described, in all their points, conditions, clauses, and articles, decreeing that they have the strength of perpetual confirmation of this present letter to which our seal is appended in testimony. Enacted in Cracow on Monday, the day before the Feast of the Assumption of the Most Glorious Virgin Mary, in the year of our Lord one thousand four hundred and fifty-three, there being present there the eminent, distinguished, and able Lucas de Gorka, Palatine of Posnania, Stanislaus de Ostrorog, Palatine of Calissia; Hyncza de Rogow, Castellan of Siradia and Vice-Treasurer, Peter de Sczekocim, Vice-Chancellor of the Kingdom of Poland; Andreas de Thanczin; Joannes Kraska de Lwbnicza, Butler of Calissia and Governor of Coninsia; and Czrzeslaus Woysschik de Woycza, our Supreme Chamberlain; and many others worthy of trust in regard to the foregoing. Given by the hands of the eminent Joannes de Konieczpolia, Chancellor, and Peter de Sczekoczini, Vice-Chancellor of the Kingdom of Poland, who are sincerely esteemed by us, for the archives of the same eminent Peter de Sczekocim, Vice-Chancellor of the Kingdom of Poland.

1539

Sigismundus rex significat.

King Sigismund ratifies.

CHAPTER III

JEWISH AUTONOMY IN POLAND 1264-1795

The Vaad Arba Arazot, or the *Congressus Judaicus*, or *the Jewish Seym* in Poland was a "unique event in the history of Jewish Diaspora."

According to the distinguished historian Heinrich Graetz in his *Geschichte der Juden*, vol. IX, Leipzig, 1866, p.483 and LXXIX

Under the spiritual leadership of the *Vaad Arba Arazot* the spiritual life of Polish Jewry late in the 16th and during the 17th century attained an uncommonly high level. Thanks to the works of Polish rabbis, Jewish ritual and religious laws governing civil and matrimonial life have been accepted by European Jews to the present day. Indeed, without a doubt, the 16th and 17th centuries were the period of spiritual hegemony of Polish Jews in world Jewry.

Isaac Lewin, a noted historian, the representative to the United Nations of the Agudath Israel World Organization, *The Jewish Community in Poland*, Philosophical Library, New York , 1985

The Jewish Seym in Poland, 1581-1764, was a unique Jewish parliament in the history of the Jews between the Sanhedrin of the Biblical times and Knesset of the modern State of Israel.

Modern Jewish legal, governmental, and educational systems, as well as philosophical concepts and religious beliefs, evolved in Poland between the 16th and the 18th centuries.

During the entire history of the Diaspora, the Jewish nation existed only in Poland, where masses of Jews lived and had their own social classes, their own policies and laws, their own parliament and economic system, and their own spiritual and material culture. This is why the Jews once called Poland the New Holy Land.

1. Early Polish Constitutional Development and the General Charter of Jewish Liberties.

The 500 years between 1264 and 1764 was a crucial period not only for Polish Jews, but also for the survival of the entire Jewish people. This period began with the *General Charter of Jewish Liberties*, issued in Kalisz, and ended with the abolition of the autonomous Jewish parliament, when the Jewish banking system failed in Poland. During these 500 years, Jewish life evolved from limited self-government to real autonomy, unique in the long history of the Diaspora.

At the beginning, the Jews governed themselves within the framework of laws laid down by Polish authorities. In the 16th century, they were permitted to proclaim their own laws. At that time, Jews in Poland had the only Jewish parliament that existed between Sanhedrin of antiquity and Knesset of the modern State of Israel. It was known as the Jewish Seym, or the Congressus Judaicus.

The evolution of Jewish self-government paralleled the indigenous Polish development of representative institutions, which included the first bicameral parliament in Europe, formed in 1493. Early modern Polish civilization was unique in Europe. It was shaped by an indigenous democratic process which matured in the 15th century. Unique to Poland, this process yielded good conditions for her Jews, who were persecuted elsewhere in Europe. In fact, for centuries Poland contributed more than any other country to Jewish survival. Modern Jewish legal, governmental, and educational systems, as well as philosophical concepts and religious beliefs, evolved in Poland between the 16th and the 18th centuries.

Jewish historians have viewed the development of the institutions of Polish Jewish autonomy as the most important phenomenon in the history of the Diaspora. For example, in his book *History of the Jews in Russia and Poland from Earliest Times to the Present Day*, S. Dubnow expressed admiration for Polish Jewish autonomy and treated it as a political program at the end of the 19th and the beginning of the 20th century. On the other hand, B. D. Weinryb, in his book *The Jews of Poland: A Social and Economic History of Jewish Community in Poland from 1100 to 1800*, characterized the autonomy of the Polish Jews as an organic tie between Jewry and the Polish state. Thus, in order to understand the autonomous institutions of Polish Jews it is necessary to review the early development of representative forms of government in Poland.

The democracy of the Polish nobility eventually encompassed a population of one million citizens, or about 12 percent of the population of the First Polish Republic, which was formally founded in 1569 in Lublin. Many Polish historians believe that the beginning of the republican form of government in Poland coincided with the Act of Nieszawa of 1454. It confirmed the jurisdiction of unicameral regional legislatures called Seymiki (sey-MEE-kee, pl. of Seymik, SAY-meek). These legislatures acquired the power to approve military mobilization and the right to name four candidates for the local judiciary, out of whom one would be selected by the king, who also functioned as an elective chief executive.

Following the Act of Nieszawa of 1454, open attendance at the legislatures gave way to an orderly national system of representation. Government-from-below was actualized through these regional legislatures, in which ordinary citizens had a dominant voice. This was especially true as the citizen-soldiers (who belonged to the masses of Polish lower and middle nobility) gained power over the landed aristocracy in the 15th and 16th centuries.

In that period regional legislatures, or Seymiks, became platforms for political emancipation and a source of information for the ordinary citizen about the affairs of state. They created the means for mutual consultation through duly elected representatives equipped with a real and clear mandate.

The roots of Polish government-from-below reach back before the empowerment of the Seymiki. Acts limiting the power of the throne are central in this regard. The first such act was issued at Cienia in 1228 by Władysław Laskonogi, or Ladislas III (1161-1231). The Act of Cienia promised to preserve "just and noble laws according to the council of the bishops and barons" in return for succession to the throne in Kraków, then the royal capital of Poland.

In 1264, thirty-six years after the Act of Cienia, the General Charter of Jewish Liberties was issued at Kalish. The text of this act is reprinted in the original Latin in the preceding chapter, accompanied by a recent English translation. Known as the Act, or Statute, of Kalisz by Bolesław Pobożny, or Boleslaus the Pious (1221-1279), it provided the basis for the development of a Jewish sanctuary in Poland. Eventually, it led to the creation of a Yiddish-speaking autonomous Jewish nation which lived by Talmudic law until 1795. Its provisions established Jewish courts and a separate tribunal for matters involving Christians and Jews. Also, the Jews were exempted from slavery and serfdom as well as from any obligation to participate in the defense of Poland or to speak Polish. These provisions created for the Jews in Poland the status of a foreign commercial group, free of any of the national obligations of the exclusively Christian feudal estates of peasants, burghers, and nobles. In Poland, as in the rest of Christian Europe, the feudal estates excluded all non-Christians.

The reign of Casimir the Great, or Kazimierz Wielki (1310-1370), brought codification of the Polish Common Law in 1346-47. The Act of Wiślica applied to Lesser Poland, or Małopolska, and the Act of Piotrków applied to Greater Poland, or Wielkopolska. Casimir the Great ratified the General Charter of Jewish Liberties of 1264, and uniformly extended it throughout Poland, which then had a Jewish population of about 10,000. King Casimir recognized the Jews as a distinct national, religious, linguistic, and cultural group. He established punitive assessments for towns guilty of anti-Jewish activities -- half of the assessed money was used to pay damages to the Jews, and half went to the state treasury. Casimir also banned accusations against Jews for ritual murders of Christians, a superstition brought to Poland by German immigrants.

An important step towards the limitation of the power of the throne in Poland occurred in 1355. The Act of Buda issued that year by Ludwik I, or Louis I (1326-1382), confirmed all previous acts and privileges. Louis I issued the act in order to secure his succession to the Polish throne. He had to overcome the weakness of his succession through a female rather than a male connection to the first Polish dynasty of the Piasts. Thus, Louis I became the first king crowned on the basis of a negotiated royal succession. This procedure was followed until 1572.

The era of negotiated royal succession (1370-1572) overlapped the evolution of constitutional monarchy in Poland (1370-1493). In 1493, Poland became the first constitutional monarchy in Europe. Her newly constituted bicameral national parliament became the supreme political power in the country. In 1505, the first Polish constitution was passed. It represented an important milestone in the history of the European quest for representative government. It is known as the Constitution "Nihil Novi," or "nothing new about us, without us."

The 1374 Act of Koszyce by Louis I bestowed taxing authority on regional legislatures, reduced taxes, promised to nominate local people to territorial offices, and limited military service to national territory. If defensive operations necessitated combat outside of national territory, the act promised special payments for related military service and injuries. It guaranteed the inviolability of the ethnic Polish territory known traditionally as the Corona Regni Poloniae, or the Crown of the Kingdom of Poland. All these guarantees were given by Louis I in return for acceptance of his right of succession to the Polish throne.

The Act of Koszyce strengthened the power of the Seymiki, or regional legislatures. It enfranchised Polish landowners, the very numerous Polish knighthood, and transformed them into a uniquely Polish noble estate of citizen-soldiers. Eventually, about 12 percent of the population of Poland, or over one million persons, belonged to this political nation of citizen-soldiers who gradually evolved the indigenous Polish democratic process. Thus, the Act of Koszyce crystallized the estate system in Poland and reconfirmed the indigenous parliamentary system based on regional legislatures.

2. The Birth of a Unique Polish Civilization Based on an Indigenous Democratic Process

The 1374 Act of Koszyce started Poland on its way to becoming the main scene of development of civil liberties in Europe, especially when England drifted in the direction of absolutism, and the Magna Carta Libertatum of 1215 became ineffectual for several centuries. Cromwell's revolution and the decapitation of King Charles I (in 1649) steered England, recognized as the model of modern democracy, towards a more liberal political system. Meanwhile the Poles progressed in developing a representative form of government.

A unique Polish civilization was born, based on the nascent democracy of citizen-soldiers. This unusually numerous Polish nobility formed the largest political nation of free citizens in Europe for the next four hundred years, during which a unique Jewish self-government and autonomy also evolved in Poland.

With the signing in 1385 of the Union Act of Krewo, the unique Polish civilization started to expand over the huge territory of the Grand Duchy of Lithuania, which included all of Byelorussia, part of Great Russia, and the Ukraine. The Grand Duke Jogaiła (c.1350-1434) committed himself to converting Lithuania to Latin Christianity, uniting with Poland all Lithuanian and Ruthenian lands, and to recovering Polish territories lost to the Germans, in exchange for his marriage to the Polish Queen Jadwiga and his coronation as Catholic King of Poland, Władysław (Ladislas) Jagiełło. In 1386, before the coronation, the future king issued the Act of Kraków, in which he confirmed the 1374 Act of Koszyce.

3. Enactment of Basic Civil Liberties in Poland-Lithuania; Beginning of Polish Political and Cultural Pluralism

In 1387, King Jagiello started spreading Polish civil liberties to the lands of the Grand Duchy of Lithuania by proclaiming the Act of Wilno (Vilnius), in which he bestowed hereditary ownership of land and freedom from taxation by the local princes on the newly converted Lithuanian nobles, the boyars. The borders of Western civilization started to expand to their furthest historic limits in eastern Europe.

In 1388, King Władysław Jagiełło issued the Act of Piotrków, and further limited royal power in Poland by increasing the civil rights of citizen-soldiers and clergy. The next important act by the king emphasized the basic values of political and social pluralism and freedom of conscience. These values were beautifully stated in the Union Act of Horodło in which King Władysław Jagiełło united Poland and Lithuania into a personal union.

The 1413 Union Act of Horodło followed the Polish-Lithuanian victory over the German monastic state of the Teutonic Knights in 1410. It established the office of wojewoda (vo-ye-vo-da) as a provincial governor and initiated a new administrative and defensive organizational model for central and eastern Europe. Polish families extended the use and privileges of their coats-of-arms to Lithuanian and Ruthenian clans. The united Poland and Lithuania became the largest state on the European continent. It was on its way to becoming known not only as the freest country in Europe, but also as the paradise of the Jews, who settled in Poland in large numbers, fleeing persecution.

From the beginning of the crusades in the 11th century, Jewish minorities were persecuted in and evicted from western Europe. The spirit of the crusades was brought to Poland and Lithuania by the German armed monks of the Teutonic Order who committed the genocide of the Balto-Slavic people of Prussia in the 13th century under the pretext of converting them to Christianity, and repeatedly attacked both the Polish and the Lithuanian states. Thus, in 1414-1418 at the Council of Constance Poland condemned the "crusading" practices of the Teutonic Knights, proposed the first seventeen theses of international law based on the principle of freedom of conscience, and stated that license to convert is not a license to kill and expropriate.

The Act of Czerwińsk of 1422, called "Nec Bona Recipiantur," promised not to allow the confiscation of privately held property without a court sentence based on the written law. The court could not include officials of the crown among the judges. In 1423, the Statute of Warka extended the protection of private property to burghers and free peasants -- the hereditary rights of bailiffs were abrogated. Two years later, in 1425, King Władysław Jagiełło proclaimed in the Act of Brześć a fundamental law equivalent to the English Act of Habeas Corpus of 1685, and preceding it by 260 years. "Neminem Captivabimus Nisi Iure Victim," or "no one will be imprisoned without a legal decision by a proper court," became the basic law in Poland for the next 350 years, until the conquest and dismembering of the Polish state in 1795.

Poland was the first country in Europe where due legal process guaranteed the inviolability of the citizen's person and his property. These laws were solemnly reconfirmed in the Act of Kraków of 1433. Subsequent acts reconfirmed these laws throughout the Polish-Lithuanian Commonwealth, and the same laws were spelled out in the Act of Incorporation of Prussia into Poland in 1454. At that time, the Prussian population rebelled against the yoke of the Teutonic Knights and preferred that their lands be a part of Poland.

4. Early Political Programs Advocating Republican Institutions in Poland

In order to understand the environment in which Jewish autonomy evolved in Poland, it is useful to note the early Polish political programs which advocated republican institutions as a form of government. In 1475, the political program of Jan Ostroróg (c.1436-1501), Wojewoda of Poznań, was published under the title "Pro Rei Publicae Ordinatione," or "On Putting the Commonwealth in Order." It advocated the use of the same laws for all inhabitants of Poland without differences for each feudal estate, the codification of Polish laws on the basis of Roman Law, and the use of the Polish language instead of Latin in all court records.

Ostroróg was a Renaissance man. His progressive program included strengthening national defense by including peasants and burghers besides noble citizen-soldiers in the military mobilization. Also, Ostroróg advocated greater control and reduction of the privileges of German immigrant burghers in Polish towns. Under his leadership, in 1488 the first Digest of Polish Law was printed.

Another progressive program of reforms was formulated in the sixteenth century. In 1551, Andrzej Frycz Modrzewski (c.1503-1573) published his socio-political program "De Republica Emendanda," or "On the Improvement of the Republic." Modrzewski advocated legal equality for all and analyzed the conditions of the evolving Polish Nobles' Republic. He was in favor of strengthening the executive powers of the government of the elective king, modernizing the state administration system, using properly trained officials, and observing strict legality in government and courts of law. He also advocated establishing public schools free of religious control. In European literature, Modrzewski is recognized as one of the pioneers of the modern science of government and law. His works were translated into German, French, Spanish, and Russian soon after they first appeared in Latin.

The works of Wawrzyniec Goślicki (1530-1607) constituted another example of early political writings in Poland. He published his program for the Polish republican system in 1568, under the title "De Optimo Senatore," which was translated into English as "The Counselor Exactly Protrayed." Goślicki's program was based on the principle of pluralism and a perfect equilibrium between power and liberty. When his work was published in 1568 in England, it was immediately confiscated, but secretly became popular. One hundred fifty years later, it was analyzed and highly praised by Sir Robert Walpole (1676-1745). Earlier, William Shakespeare (1564-1616) acknowledged the popularity of Goślicki's work when he gave the name "Polonius," or "a Pole," to the chief advisor to Hamlet. However, Shakespeare was parodying the inept use of Goślicki's work by an English dignitary, and therefore Polonius is presented in a rather ironic light.

Dr. Wagner of Indiana University provides a clear characterization of representative government in Poland in his many works. "Beginning in 1573, the newly elected king had to take an oath that he would abide by the laws of the Commonwealth (the so-called Henrician Articles) and that he would respect special conditions, submitted to him by the electors [known as the "pacta conventa"]. A statute of 1609 ("de non preastanda oboedientia") regulated the procedure and the consequences... in case the [elective] king violated his sacred trust. There was no question of a human error, but if the ruler should act with ill will and consciously infringe on the nation's legal order, the Senate should issue a resolution to this effect three times, and the Primate should warn him. If this proved to be ineffective, the Seym could terminate the agreement between the nation and the ruler who did not abide by its terms. This Polish approach preceded by [189] years the 1762 "Contract Social" of Rousseau.

"All the above rights... were fully enjoyed only by the class of gentry (which, however, included as many as twelve percent of the citizens of the Polish-Lithuanian Commonwealth, and about one-third of all ethnic Poles, while, e.g., the upper class in France constituted only one-half of one percent of the whole population)...

"In Poland there were no slaves, but besides the gentry three classes were in existence: the ecclesiastics, the townsmen, and the peasants, some of whom were subject to obligations as serfs. This pattern followed the well-established approach in European nations, but the Polish system had special features. First of all, the gentry class was not closed and many persons born in families of lower classes could ascend to it. (E.g., everyone appointed as professor of the Jagiellonian University was granted nobility.) Many peasants who displayed military prowess in war time merited the same distinction. There were some villages whose inhabitants were all brought into this class. They continued to till their land as they did previously, but they could wear the traditional Polish sword (*karabela*) in their belts at all times; they could elect -- and be elected -- to public office, including the dignity of the king.)...

"The situation of the peasants in Poland was better than in most other countries. In France and Germany, for example, the owners of landed estates had unlimited jurisdiction over them, including the power to punish by death. In Russia their economic oppression was notorious...") (W. J. Wagner, "May 3, 1791, and the Polish Constitutional Tradition." *The Polish Review*, Vol. XXXVI, No. 4, 1991:p.386-387, New York, 1991.

Early political writings by Polish authors and the structure of representative government in Poland, as described by Professor Wagner above, support the thesis of B. D. Weinryb, in his book mentioned previously, that Jewish autonomy in Poland developed on the basis of an organic tie between Polish Jews and the Polish state. The following review of the evolution of this unique Jewish autonomy confirms its close links with Polish parliamentary development.

5. Two Phases of Mass Influx of Ashkenazim Jews to Poland

When Jewish self-government in Poland was first formally defined by the Statute of Kalish of 1264, it affected a relatively small number of Jews who had started coming to the Polish lands by the end of the first millennium of the Christian Era. By the end of the 15th century, the number of Jews in Poland has been estimated at between 10,000 and 30,000, by the mid-16th century about 150,000 to 200,000, and by the end of the 17th century 750,000; by then Polish Jews numbered between one-half and three-quarters of all the Jews on earth. By the end of the 18th century, the Jewish minority in Poland exceeded one million people. At that time, Polish Jews represented up to 80 percent of the world's Jewry.

The massive influx of Jews from the west and south--west to Poland began at the end of the 14th century. This first phase lasted until the end of the 15th century. The new arrivals consisted mainly of Ashkenazim Jews -- very few Sephardic Jews arrived in Poland after 1492; those that did, traveled through Italy and Turkey. The Jewish exodus was a result of a deliberate policy carried out throughout the fragmented German Empire. German towns and monastic orders were persecuting Jews and evicting them from Germany. Some of German monastic orders consisted of armed monks, such as the German brethren known as Teutonic Knights.

The next phase of the influx of Jews into Poland resulted from persecutions in western Europe during the Reformation. Anti-Jewish teachings by Martin Luther sounded similar to Hitler's ravings four hundred years later. By 1570, practically all the Jews were gone from western Europe. They went mainly to Poland.

6. Spiritual Autonomy of Each Ghetto; Institutionalization of Rabbis

The Ashkenazim Jews responded to the persecutions of the 14th century by trying to develop a centralized leadership. The Torah became the only recourse for the Jews. The Chosen People were to study their contract with God more intensely, and the status of scholars gained even more prestige than before. The rabbis became institutionalized. Being a rabbi became the profession of spiritual and practical leaders who naturally could be effective if their leadership was centralized.

By 1500, Jewish urban communities had started to subordinate smaller communities in the vicinity. They all followed the guidance of rabbis who became accepted as authorities on Jewish law, the *Halakhah*. This natural trend towards centralization among the Jews was noticed by princes interested in tax collection within the fragmented Roman Empire of the German nation. Thus, the rabbis were officially appointed by the German princes as leaders of the Jews in order to make the tax collecting system more efficient. As a result, the Ashkenazim Jews fleeing to Poland from persecution in Germany were used to having institutions of territorial leadership and state appointed rabbis. Besides, learned Jews were aware of the old tradition of asking for special laws and privileges for Jewish communities in exile, a tradition which had existed ever since the foundation of Greek cities by Alexander the Great.

The persecution in western Europe destroyed communication among Jewish communities there, and Jews modified the role of Talmud. Scattered Jews needed a simple and universal handbook of Jewish law. Such a Talmud, written for every Jew, was published in 1565 by Joseph Caro, a Sephardic Jew. Its title was *Shulhan Aruch*. Caro's version of the Talmud gave every Jew the chance to be "equal to the sages," and each isolated Jewish community the chance to have spiritual autonomy.

Persecuted Ashkenazim Jews in Germany knew about the 1264 Charter of Jewish Liberties, issued and honored in Poland. With the passage of time, the Ashkenazim learned that Poland was ruled by means of an indigenous democratic process, and that by the end of the 15th century the Polish national parliament had become a supreme power. By its very nature the Polish parliament was tolerant. Harsh persecutions were ordered in western Europe by individual absolute rulers, but such persecutions were never likely to be ordered by a debating and voting body of senators and representatives.

7. Pluralism in Poland

Polish pluralism was based on the multi-ethnic character of the country, and the Jews could consider themselves one of many different ethnic groups. By 1634, as much as 60 percent of Poland's population was not ethnically Polish. Poland was the largest country in Europe. Its territory extended from the Baltic almost to the Black Sea, and from Silesia to about 200 kilometers east of the Dnieper River. At that time, the largest concentration of Jews lived in Poland. Jews in Poland were free men -- never serfs or slaves. They could worship and practice occupations designated to them in privileges. Full civil rights were held by some 12 percent of Poland's population -- the masses of noble citizen-soldiers. The "Jewish paradise" in Poland was in full bloom until the victory of Counter-Reformation, late in the 17th century, and the oligarchic effects of manipulations by the political machines of huge landowners, whose estates were called *latifundia* in the tradition of ancient Rome.

The Polish economy was based on rich farmlands and huge forests. Grain crops and natural products provided the main commodities for export to western Europe. Because of the subordination of most Polish towns to the nobility, Jews in Poland could perform much broader social and economic functions than in western Europe. The noble citizens of Poland successfully prevented an alliance between the throne and royal towns. Such alliances were the backbone of absolute royal power in western Europe. However, in the process of gaining the upper hand, the citizen-soldiers effectively undermined the position of the merchants in the towns chartered by the central government.

Professor Rosman describes well the difference between royal towns and private towns in Poland. "On the other hand, the private towns, owned by noblemen, flourished under their owners' guiding hands. The lords invested in their towns' commercial life and often delegated to their resident merchants the nobility trade privileges to which they themselves were entitled. Hence, even though Polish noblemen generally shunned direct involvement in commerce as a distasteful, ignoble pursuit, the nobility actually determined the contours of Polish commercial life." (M.J. Rosman, *The Lords' Jews*, Harvard University Press, Cambridge, Mass. 1990.)

An important phenomenon was the so-called "secondary serfdom" of peasants, which was legally sanctioned and became particularly oppressive after the shift of European trade from the Baltic to the Atlantic in the 17th century, when the terms of trade for Polish grain fell dismally. Subsidized exports of Russian wheat contributed to the fall of grain prices in western Europe.

As long as the demand for and price of export grain were firm, and the noble citizens grew richer, they did not need to expand the economic strength of the towns. Towns were viewed as a potential source of strength for the executive branch headed in Poland by an elective king who was always suspected of trying to impose absolute rule.

"Secondary serfdom" was also associated with the loss of the power struggle by the small and medium landowners in favor of the land speculators and aristocratic magnates who owned huge landed estates and were gradually acquiring a controlling position in Poland's economy and politics. The citizen-soldiers who owned small and medium estates suffered numerous bankruptcies and were becoming landless while still retaining their full civil rights and privileges. Many of them had to seek employment in the huge estates called *latifundia*. In the period from 1648 to 1763, the political machines of the owners of the *latifundia* enabled them to attain an oligarchic control of the politics of Poland. Their control of the national parliament was based on their grip on the provincial legislatures.

In late medieval and early modern times, during the massive influx of Jews, the intense competition in the Polish towns reached its peak. The Polish economy was dominated by the noble citizens, who were the governing estate in feudal Polish society from the 15th century. During the 17th century, noble citizens were the main driving force in the Polish economy. Most important among them were the successful land speculators and aristocratic noblemen, many of whom acquired estates equal in area to territories of entire states such as Denmark, England, Ireland, the Netherlands, Portugal, Scotland, or Switzerland. These huge estates, or *latifundia*, spread mainly outside of the Polish ethnic area, east of the Bug River, but some spread as far north as the Polish fief of Prussia. Eventually, nearly three-quarters of all Polish Jews were settled east of the Polish ethnic area. The process of building up the latifundia in the mercantilist feudal real estate market in early modern Poland resembled the natural formation of monopolies in economies based on the capitalistic market, unrestrained by the anti-monopoly policies of a central government.

Historians find it difficult to identify the families of the owners of the large estates, because the principle of equality was fundamental in Poland, and the noble citizens did not label the elite among them. Also, one should note that this group was not permanent, as its membership actually changed from generation to generation with economic fortunes, marriage connections, and successful land acquisitions. However, when discussing pluralism, one should note that Poland was unique in the world for having one million people who enjoyed equality of civil rights in the period from the 15th to the end of the 18th centuries. Even a very poor Polish noble, or citizen-soldier, had the potential of attaining economic and political success.

The successful broadening of the indigenous democratic process in Poland was eventually ended by a sharp conflict of interest between the very numerous "middle class" of Polish electorate, which consisted of small and middle size landowners, and those who concentrated huge landed estates in their hands. The turning point came in 1647, when the political machines of the huge landowners defeated in Polish national parliament the drive to extend full civil rights to the Ukrainian Cossacks. From that point on the First Polish Republic began to decline. The aristocratic noblemen remained victorious in maintaining upper hand in the struggle for power and became the primary beneficiaries of the political freedom in feudal Poland.

The most successful period in early modern Polish history and the blossoming of the Polish Renaissance occurred in the 16th century, when the small and middle size landowners controlled the politics of Poland.

8. *Golden Age of Polish Jews 1500-1648*

The Golden Age of Polish Jews lasted from 1500 to 1648. Then the Jews enjoyed very rapid economic development and strong demographic growth. Jewish life in Poland was affected by the founding of the Polish Nobles' Republic in 1569, during the ratification of the Union of Lublin. At that time, a new subdivision was made within the united state of Poland-Lithuania. North-central Poland included Greater Poland, Gdansk Pomerania, Prussia, Lesser Poland and part of Silesia. Eastern Poland included Red Ruthenia, Podolia, Volhynia, the Ukraine, and Inflanty in Latvia. The Lithuanian administration included Lithuania proper and Byelorussia. After the disasters which started in 1648, Jews became economically dependent on the huge landowners. This dependence resulted in political stagnation during which, however, their strong demographic expansion continued.

The Jews settled mainly in the towns of central Poland, in accordance with the privileges granted to them until the middle of the 17th century. However, because of the controlling position held by the Poles in the Polish-Lithuanian state, Jewish opportunities in the Polish ethnic area were limited by the rules of the municipal guarantee system which was controlled by the towns' Christian elite. It regulated prices and limited competition.

European feudal society was based on religion, and municipal citizenship was given only to Christians. Thus, theoretically, European Jews could not engage in crafts, trade, or any other economic activity reserved for Christians. In Poland, unlike elsewhere in Europe, the political and economic domination of towns by noble citizens gave Jews a chance to compete with Christian burghers. However, in 1521 the royal towns organized a common action against the Jews at the parliamentary session in Piotrków. They demanded the legal exclusion of Jews from trade, as had been enacted in western Europe. The action in the national parliament failed, but Christian burghers were more successful in individual localities, where they obtained the privilege "de non tolerandis Judaeis," for the exclusion of Jews.

66

However, in a number of localities in Poland and in Lithuania, Jews were able to obtain the privilege "de non tolerandis Christianis," and were able to exclude the Christians from their neighborhoods.

9. The Alliance of Noble Citizens and Jews.

In the eastern part of the Polish Republic, Jews were accepted as economic, and therefore also political, allies who would complement the activities of the ruling noble estate. The political victory of the noble citizens practically eliminated the towns as an estate by the constitutional acts of 1496, 1507, 1538, and 1565. Jewish economic activity was limited by the act of 1538. It forbade Jews to lease collection of customs, tolls, and other public incomes. Jewish trade in towns and villages was also limited by this law. Despite these laws, the Jews were able to compete with the burghers' system of production and to complement the economic activity of the nobility.

Ethnic Poles represented 40 percent of the country's population. Political and economic conditions in densely populated western and central Poland, which was ethnically Polish, were less favorable to Jewish economic expansion than were the conditions in the eastern borderlands of the Polish state. Thus, traditional Jewish communities, such as those in Cracow and Poznań, gradually stagnated in the 16th century. Meanwhile, the Jews were able to play an important role in the eastern borderlands in the service of the noble citizens who enjoyed a spectacular economic expansion there.

10. Jewish Opportunity in the Eastern Frontier Lands of Western Civilization.

The political and legal situation of the Jews in the eastern borderlands improved after the founding of the Polish Nobles' Republic in 1569. At that time, there were only a few towns in the eastern borderlands, or "Kresy," and they were economically and politically weak. The successful aristocratic magnates, land speculators, and developers became fabulously rich in the borderlands, especially in Red Ruthenia, Ukraine, Podolia, Volhynia, Byelorussia, and Lithuania. These magnates used Jewish middlemen and business experts. Polish Jews had the best opportunity for rapid economic and demographic growth in the lands of Kresy.

Thus, a revitalized Jewish nation emerged primarily in Kresy, the Polish borderlands of western civilization. Polish Jews changed the course of the history of Diaspora for the next four centuries. It was possible to stabilize the favorable conditions in Kresy as long as the Jews could avoid conflict with the noble citizens in the ethnic Polish area in western and central Poland. For this purpose, the Jewish Seym, or the Vaad, passed a law in 1581 prohibiting the Jews from activities which might collide with the interests of the noble citizens in the western and central part of Poland.

In the ethnic Polish area in the mid-16th century, a political movement of noble citizens developed, aimed at enforcing respect for the law. It was called the "Executionist Movement." It pursued and won the 16th century power struggle between the small and middle-size land holders and the elective throne of Poland together with the aristocratic land magnates. The winners became dominant in the parliament, which had supreme power in Poland. This was especially true in the ethnic Polish territory. The social structure was different in the eastern frontier lands, where there was a greater proportion of huge landowners and there were practically no burghers.

In the ethnic Polish territory, a "mixed" form of government was well established. It consisted of the Polish version of "checks and balances," a dynamic equilibrium between the king, whose role gravitated towards that of a chief executive, the lower house of the parliament, which became the supreme political power in Poland, and the senate, dominated by the magnates; a lesser role was also played by the burghers. This system of "checks and balances" worked well in the Polish ethnic area of THE Polish Nobles' Republic -- much better than in Kresy, the frontier lands, where the political influence of huge landowners was very strong, and where this system existed only formally.

The situation of the Jews in the ethnic Polish area was different than in Kresy. In the Polish ethnic area, a pluralistic system was well established. Here the Jews were protected by law, but did not enjoy any social or economic privileges. On the other hand, in the lands of Kresy a unique utilitarian alliance was formed between the huge landowners and the Jewish financial elite. In the eastern frontier lands, the Jews functioned within a system of patronage in which they became the main instrument of colonization and trade. Jewish colonization in the Ukraine was especially intense during the eighty years, from 1569 to 1648.

67

11. Jewish Occupational Structure and Pre-paid Short-Term Leases.

Jewish economic activity evolved steadily in Poland. By the end of the 14th century, the mass exodus of Jews fleeing persecution in Germany increased the size of the Jewish population in Poland greatly and diversified the social and occupational structure of their communities. The main occupations of Polish Jews before the 15th century were usury and local trade, as well as leasing of mints and salt mines. Jewish merchants in Poland borrowed capital from Catholic monasteries and noble landowners, who accumulated money from collection of tolls, customs duties, and market taxes on transported goods, in addition to profits from landed estates.

The nobles were exempted from most customs duties, tolls, and market tax expenses, and therefore could undermine the activities of the merchants. The nobles determined the framework of Polish commercial life, despite the fact that they tried to avoid "ignoble pursuits" such as commerce and trade. The noble owners of the large estates and private towns could delegate to their resident merchants their trade privileges and tax exemptions. In the 16th century, most Jews made their living as craftsmen and traders, while a Jewish business elite prospered in estate administration and in the organization of credit.

In the eastern frontier lands, or Kresy, Jews became middlemen between the nobility (especially the huge landowners) and the peasants. Jews also occupied the position of burghers in private towns in Kresy. Rich Jewish merchants and financiers played a special role in the economic expansion of the frontier lands through a system of short-term prepaid leases. For a pre-set rent, the lessor transferred to the lessee control over property and rights and the income produced by them, to which the lessor was entitled. Whole economic complexes were leased to a general contractor, and their components, such as mills, alcohol distilleries, and inns, were sub-let, usually to the contractor's relatives.

The system of prepaid short-term leases prevailed in Poland. It was called *arenda*. It fueled the expansion of noble estates, and became a major incitement to Ukrainian Cossack uprisings. *Arenda* was a central economic institution of the Jews in Poland. It became a traditional Jewish occupation -- a fact reflected in the language of that time. In 17th and 18th century contracts, the words "arrendator" (in Polish *arendarz* pron.: a-ren-dash) and "Jew" were used interchangeably.

It has been estimated that 15 percent of urban and 80 percent of rural Jewish heads of households were occupied within the arenda system.

In Polish private law, arenda was defined as: "The leasing of immovable property or rights. The subject of the lease might be a whole territory, held either in ownership or in pledge [or] the subject might be a tavern, mill, or the right to collect various payments such as a bridge toll or a payment connected with a jurisdiction." (M. J. Rosman *The Lords' Jews*, Harvard University Press, Cambridge, Mass. 1990.

Arenda-type short-term leases resulted in intensive exploitation of the leased estates, as the lessees tended to overwork the land, peasants, and equipment, without worrying about long-term effects. The peasants experienced additional hardships when Jewish arrendators obtained the right to collect and even impose taxes and fees for church services. The peasants and Cossacks in Kresy bitterly resented having to pay Jews for the use of Eastern Orthodox and Greek-Catholic churches for funerals, baptisms, weddings, and other similar occasions. It was no wonder that in a number of uprisings, especially during the revolution of 1648 led by Bohdan Chmielnicki (Khmelnitski c.1593-1657), the noble citizens and the Jews were murdered together in great numbers.

12. Arenda Leases, Estate structure, Benefits, and Discounts.

Polish landowners used a simplified measure of the profitability of their property: receipts minus expenses were equal to the net income. Cash transactions were watched closely, because there was a shortage of currency in Poland in the 17th and 18th centuries. Thus, lessors wanted to maximize cash income. The income generated annually by arenda leases represented between 20 and 70 percent of the total income of large estates.

The income from *arenda* leases provided the estate owners with needed cash for conspicuous consumption, for covering the legal expenses of the frequent disputes among nobles, and for purchasing new land in order to expand estates. Cash was also necessary for the operating budgets of the manors, which were the basic production elements of Polish agriculture. The manors included the main house, or *dwór* (dvoor), and the working agricultural enterprise called *folwark* (fol-vark). Folwarks were centers of a variety of labor-intensive agricultural and animal husbandry activities, as well as forest industries, mills, liquor production and sale. The peasants' work was supplied through the feudal labor system controlled by the landowner, and to a lesser extent by the village council or *gromada*.

The latifundia of the aristocratic magnates included several contiguous complexes of manors called *dobra*, or *włości* (vwośh-ćhee), and private towns. These complexes were called *klucze* (kloocche).

Landowners viewed the proceeds from *arenda* leases as a means of raising cash to pay bills. *Arenda* rents represented the easiest source of cash, for which the lessors had to contribute a minimum of effort. An arrendator had to set up books and a collection system and to deal with his subarrendators (subcontractors), customers, and taxpayers. Thus, the arrendator simplified the role of the lessors, whether in developing newly acquired property or in producing grain, mining salt, or leasing a tavern (*karczma*) where he marketed liquor produced out of surplus grain. In theory, *arenda* leases reduced risk because the lessee was legally obligated to absorb losses resulting from unforseen events. However, if *arenda* revenues were considerably reduced, the arrendator was usually given a *folga*, or a discount.

Jews also provided banking services to the landowners. The payments for the leases were often made over a period of time. The landowners would issue an equivalent to a modern check, payable to a particular party for a specified amount of money. This check, called *asygnata* (a-sig-na-ta), was cashed by the arrendator so that the landowner did not have to handle the cash himself. This way, no great accumulation of cash at one time was necessary, and safety was combined with convenience.

13. Leases of Monopoly Rights and Estates.

The dislocations after the Cossack uprising of 1648 brought significant changes. The bankruptcies of small and middle-size landowners, discussed before, resulted in an increased demand for land leases by the impoverished noble citizens. In this new situation, the system of leasing was adjusted. The Polish word *dzierżawa* (pron.: dźher-zha-va) described the leases of real estates such as villages, manors, and village and private town complexes called *klucze* (pronounced: kloocche). The term *arenda* was redefined to mean a lease of monopoly rights to a Jewish businessman.

Exposure to the resentment of peasants and Cossacks might have discouraged Jewish arrendators from continuing to lease manors and villages

in the Ukraine. Also, the law of 1633 forbade noble citizens to deal in commerce and sell liquor, although estate leasing was allowed, and it permitted the continuation of a life-style to which the landless nobles were used before they had lost their property. *Dzierżawa*, or a lease of real estate, permitted them to continue in the noble occupation of agriculture.

The system of arenda leases was used much less in the territory of ethnic Poland, known as the *Crown* territory, than in the eastern borderlands, or *Kresy*. As early as the 16th century small holders among the noble citizens, rather than Jews, often leased land in the *Crown* territory.

14. Lease of Monopoly Rights as a Jewish Domain.

A landowner's monopoly rights to produce and sell alcohol gave him a chance to market grain in the form of liquor. This possibility was especially convenient in the regions of Poland far from river transportation. It also permitted the landowners to make money off the local peasants, and made the peasants more dependent on the landowners.

Liquor rights were usually leased for less than three years. These rights could cover a larger territory, or sales in just one *karczma* (tavern) or *szynk* (bar). The bar could be a part of a tavern which also served as a restaurant and general store, where food, fabrics, and consumer goods were sold. A *karczma* could also rent rooms for social occasions such as weddings.

Aristocratic landowners often leased out the right to collect tolls and different kinds of taxes in their domain. All kinds of income producing properties, such as fish ponds, mines, etc. were leased out either separately or in one general lease which then was divided into sub-leases to a number of sub-arrendators. General leases were contracted for one to three years. The rights and obligations under the general lease contract were spelled out in detail. Lucrative leases often generated cut-throat competition.

General leases were contracted by one or a group of wealthy individuals, or by a Jewish communal government, the *kahal*. Dividing the general lease by subleasing gave the Jewish financiers a chance to realize good profit on the capital that had to be invested to obtain the general lease. Subleases provided a means of livelihood (in Hebrew *mihya*) for the poorer members of Jewish community. When conflicts developed between the general arrendator and his sub-arrendator, mediation by a Jewish court could be obtained. However, often the sub-arrendators addressed their petitions to the noble estate owner.

Thus, Jews became the essential element in the organization of the trade of the noble citizens. The Jewish business elite in Poland controlled the eastern section of the trade route from the Black Sea to western Europe. Polish Jews had many international connections with the tiny Jewish business communities which were established in the west by a trickle of Jewish emigrants from Poland in the 16th and 17th centuries.

Jews were acceptable to the noble citizens of Poland as safe middlemen who had no political claims because of the reigning Christian feudal social order, and because of the Jewish self-perception of being outsiders, rooted in their theology of exile. The Jews were more efficient, paid better than others, and therefore they were accepted into this unique alliance with the landowners.

15. The Role of the Jews in River Trade, the Spław (pron.: spwaf).

Polish rivers had always served as transportation arteries. Some of the numerous port towns situated along the major rivers were privately owned in the 16th, 17th, and 18th centuries. Gdańsk was the Polish sea capital on the Baltic, located on the delta of the Vistula River, or "Wisła" (vees-wa), the main river of Poland. Every spring, flotillas of river boats loaded with agricultural, forest, and mineral products traveled to Gdańsk. All their goods were to be sold there and exchanged for imported merchandise, to be carried back. The boat owners were anxious not to return with empty vessels, because this could mean losing money on the whole voyage.

The profitability of these annual voyages depended on the fluctuating crop yields and on the freight fees collected from merchants. River transportation costs represented about 40 percent of the price of grain in Gdańsk. These costs included payments of customs and tolls as well as security arrangements called protekcja (pron.: pro-tek-tsya) against corrupt customs officials and marauders.

By the end of the 17th century, the large landowners achieved a monopoly of the river trade. Only they were able to finance river boat construction and to use their custom and toll privileges effectively, as well as to afford a dependable protekcja.

Spław revenues included freight fees paid by merchants called freighters, in Polish froktarz (pron.: frok-tash). The associated Polish term for freight was frokt. Occasionally, wealthy Jewish merchants rented entire boats. However, usually the freighters rented space left over after the cargo of the boat owners was loaded. The freight tariffs were proportional to the value of the freight.

The general managers of the large estates which owned the river boats coordinated grain deliveries from inland manors and hired a noble citizen to serve as the skipper, in Polish szyper (pron.: shiper), to lead the flotilla. Skippers were in charge of all arrangements for the entire expedition, including preparing the boats, hiring crews, contracting freighters, loading the cargo and necessary supplies for the round trip. The skipper acted as a business agent for the boat owners, and had authority over the crew and the passengers - - freighters (or merchants). He had to sell the owner's merchandise in Gdańsk and to pay all tolls, customs, and bills; he also had to make purchases and re-load for the return trip.

The crew included, beside deck hands, a clerk or pisarz (pron. pee-sash), who kept the books, and a steward, or factor, called szafarz (pron.: sha-fash), who procured and dispensed supplies and acted as a purser. Occasionally, Jews were hired by the skipper to work as a pisarz or a szafarz. The skippers made business trips to sign up freighters, and when faced with competition could offer a discount on the freight rates.

About half of the passenger-freighters would make the round trip to Gdańsk. In the 17th century, Jewish merchants represented about one-third of the freighters; later, in the 18th century, their number increased to over 60 percent. Other freighters (or traveling businessmen) were noblemen, burghers, and peasants. Usually, the cargo of goods owned by the Jewish merchants generated most of the income (about 70 percent) collected from the freighters by the boat owners.

In order to facilitate Jewish participation in the spław voyages, loading and embarkation were not scheduled on the Sabbath or Jewish holidays. When large Jewish participation was expected, the post of clerk was filled by a Jew. Jewish freighters (or traveling businessmen) paid regular fees and were not charged any premiums. The owners of river boats shipped mainly their own agricultural and forest products to Gdańsk. For this reason, they did not depend primarily on Jewish merchants as customers, suppliers, and marketers. On the other hand, Jews dominated small local markets, and found the best business opportunities in the thriving, privately owned towns.

16. Patronage System, Private Towns and Rebirth of Jewish Culture in Shtetls (shtey-tels).

Jewish life in private towns, which were located mostly in Kresy, was shaped by the patronage system, unrestrained by the laws of the royal towns of the ethnic Polish area. In the frontier lands, Jews were able to replace the economically weak Christian burghers and drive many of them into a state of serfdom. When the grain prices began increasing in the west from the 16th century on, the owners of private towns often made their Christian burghers perform agricultural duties. Thus, local Jews would take over municipal occupations under the patronage system.

The *arenda* lease system produced a type of a country Jew who was, at times, the only literate person (generally in Hebrew) in the countryside. Besides him the parish priest and the noble citizen were usually literate in Polish and in Latin. They influenced all aspects of the peasants' life. Country Jews were a part of the patronage system and played an important role in the feudal exploitation of peasants by landowners. Country Jews were conveniently situated to provide landowners with intelligence about the peasants.

The patronage system in the countryside established social and economic structures which produced a special type of Jewish settlement in Poland. It was known as the *shtetl*. For centuries, the shtetls were the mainstay of Jewish culture. These Jewish settlements survived in the historic lands of Poland until World War II and the German genocide of European Jews.

A typical Jewish *shtetl* consisted of a market square surrounded by stores, workshops of different kinds, and small warehouses. Christian inhabitants of the shtetls lived at the outskirts as workers and part-time farmers. It was in the shtetls of early modern Poland that the rebirth of Jewish culture and civilization took place after persecutions and evictions from western Europe.

Thus, Kresy, the eastern frontier lands, became the main theater of Jewish rebirth in Poland. Kresy represented two-thirds of the Polish state's territory. Jewish immigration into Poland in general, and in particular into the lands of Kresy, opened new and greater possibilities of economic advancement for the Jews. It represented a movement of Jewish masses from the rigid and constrained environment of Western Europe into an area of dynamic growth in Poland. By the mid-18th century, when Polish Jews represented some 75 percent of world Jewry, 71 percent of the Jewish minority lived in the frontier lands of Kresy, and only 29 percent in the Crown, or the Polish ethnic area in the western and central part of Poland.

The mass migration of Polish Jews into the frontier lands of Kresy resulted in a Jewish social revolution. It gave the Jews social, economic, political, and cultural emancipation and reshaped Jewish culture by isolating it. Jewish leadership was conscious of the fact that the integration of the Jews into the Italian and Spanish Renaissance had ended in catastrophe. Therefore, once in Poland, the Jews decided to keep to themselves and to isolate their community from the Christian environment.

Polish Jews formed a deliberately isolated culture, despite their important economic role and many business contacts with the Christians in Poland. Jewish culture in Poland influenced all Jews in the Diaspora, including the tiny Jewish communities in western Europe and those living in the area of Islam. Like medieval guilds, Jewish elites maintained close contacts among themselves, while the main body of world's Jewry resided in Poland.

17. Toleration and the Jewish Credit Network.

Western European entrepreneurs and merchants increasingly viewed inconclusive religious wars as bad for business. By the end of the 16th century, the policy of western European governments towards the Jews started to reflect the gradual secularization of politics. The idea of sovereignty was formulated. It led to the acceptance of the principle of toleration, which was for the first time established as a law in the Polish Nobles' Republic in Warsaw on July 7, 1573. However, in western Europe the new toleration was associated with a political order based on the absolute power of the throne.

With the new perception of Jewish usefulness, a trickle of Jews started to immigrate from Poland into Western Europe. They joined, in small but strategically important numbers, the mercantile structures of western Europe at the same time as Jewish masses were colonizing Kresy and building their shtetls in these eastern frontier lands of Poland. Western Europe was in turmoil, and the absolute rulers needed flexible middlemen for the administration of their states. They could use the Jews and the Jewish ability to mediate, based on a long tradition.

Jews were not bound by the economically inefficient ethics of the guilds, and insisted on protection and privileges in return for credit and services rendered. The establishment of tiny new Jewish communities in western Europe was made possible by the number and political organization of the Polish Jews. The elite of Jewish suppliers and financiers served as state functionaries, and at the same time led the European Jewish communities.

The international credit network of Sephardic and Ashkhenazi Jews was formed early in the 17th century. It was able, in a short period of time, to collect large sums of money and deliver them quickly, usually in the form of loans. Until the beginning of the 18th century, the activities of the Jewish credit network were made possible by Polish Jews and their supplies of agricultural products.

The massacres of the 1648 Cossack uprising against Poland did not stop Jewish expansion in Polish eastern frontier lands. The Cossack uprising constituted a turning point in the history of Poland and marked the beginning of the decline of the huge Polish Nobles' Republic. However, when the uprising was over, Jews started coming back to the eastern borderlands from Jewish communities overcrowded by refugees in western and central Poland.

Despite the serious decline in the Polish grain trade and bankruptcies among the small and middle-size landowners, the importance of the Jews in the economy of the thinly populated frontier lands was increasing. This increase was possible because the burghers' estate was very weak in the lands of Kresy and could not compete against Jews protected by large landowners.

18. *Changes in the Legal Status of the Jews.*

Originally, Polish Jews were legally defined as servants of the state treasury, and therefore they were subject to the king. However, Polish government had evolved from a hereditary monarchy (c.840-1370) to transitional stage of constitutional monarchy (1370-1493), then through a period of full constitutional monarchy (1493-1569), leading to the First Polish Republic of the Kingdom of Poland united with the Grand Duchy of Lithuania (1569-1795). The new republic was nominally headed by a king, who in reality was elected to serve as the chief executive of the republic. All these changes had a profound effect on the legal status of Polish Jews.

At first, the life of the Polish Jews was regulated by royal privileges. With time, additional privileges were given to the Jews by the noble citizens of Poland. Jews were also able to negotiate bi-lateral agreements with Polish towns. However, the real status of the world's largest Jewish community depended on the political and economic situation of the Jews within the Polish corporate structure.

Polish Jews lived in their own communities as subjects of the king and governed themselves by their own laws. They were classified as *servi camerae regiae*. Whenever there was a conflict between a Jew and a Christian, it was brought under the jurisdiction of a court of law headed by the provincial governor, or *wojewoda* (vo-ye-vo-da -- in English "voivode").

In western Europe Jews were legally described as *servi camerae*, or servants, rather than slaves of the royal treasury. However, in German states, this description coexisted with the concept of *servitus Judeorum*, or the "slavery of the Jews," advanced by Christian theologians in order to justify the treatment of Jews as the personal property of western European rulers.

According to an early German principle, "the laws should make the Jews the least harmful to the State." In this situation, the Jews were defenseless in western Europe and often given as gifts, or left as pawns to princes, magnates or towns. Influential people who owed money to the Jews could easily cancel their debts.

In Poland, the term *servi camerae* was interpreted in a more humanitarian way than in western Europe. Casimir the Great (1310-1370) ratified the 1264 General Charter of Jewish Liberties for the entire Polish state and referred to the Jews as *utilitates camerae nostrae augere cupientes*, or those who endeavored to multiply the profits of the royal treasury. Thus, rather than treating the Jews as slaves, the Poles preferred to interpret the term *servi camerae* as "the payers of royal tax."

The concept of *servitus Judeorum*, or of the slavery of the Jews, was not used in Poland, where the principle of freedom of conscience was early included among the fundamental values. The principle of toleration was already considered as part of the divine order by Kings Jagiello (c.1350-1434), Casimir Jagiellonian (1427-1492), and Alexander Jagiellonian (1461-1506). It should be remembered that these kings ruled over a realm which was composed of many different ethnic and religious groups.

19. Outlawing of the Holy Inquisition -- Jews as Free People in Poland.

Polish kings protected the Jews, did not evict them, did not cancel debts owed to them, and did not confiscate Jewish property. In late medieval and early modern Poland, Jews were treated better than anywhere else in Europe. The eviction of Jews from Lithuania between 1494 and 1503 as well as the relocation of the Jewish community from Kraków to nearby Kazimerz were minor incidents when compared with the persecution of the Jews in western Europe. In Poland, Jews were given legal protection against false witnesses and never had to take the degrading oath of *more judaico*, which was required of them in Germany.

Polish Jews were free people with status similar to that of the burghers, and personal rights at times almost equal to those of the nobility. In fact, Polish Jews considered themselves as free as the nobles, and at times refused to appear before Polish courts or to pay taxes. Rabbi Luria of Ostroróg wrote that privileges granted to the Jews in Poland made them as free as the Polish nobles. Individual Jews held high posts in the court of Poland.

An act of 1364 by Casimir the Great stated that the fine for wounding a squire was the same as for wounding a Jew, and that the killer of a Jew was subject to the death penalty. This law has been often quoted, for instance in *Polish Legislation Concerning the Jews* by L. Gumplowicz (Kraków 1867). Jews paid the same taxes as the burghers and had the same rights of settlement and trade. They could also carry arms.

In feudal Poland, the estates had legal autonomy and could affect the situation of the Jews. The Catholic Church, which developed an anti-Jewish attitude on religious grounds, could not enforce anti-Jewish policies in Poland as easily as it did in other countries of Europe. The political anti-clericalism of the democracy of the masses of the Polish nobility virtually prevented the excesses of the Holy Inquisition in Poland. In 1552, 1562, and 1565, the Seym, or national parliament, passed laws which banned the Inquisition in the Polish state. These laws were broken in very few cases in Poland, while in the 17th century alone, the Holy Inquisition caused the killing of about one million women accused of witchcraft in western Europe. Jewish losses caused by the Holy Inquisition are estimated at 40,000.

The anti-Jewish resolutions passed by the synods of the Catholic Church in Poland were practically never implemented. Generally, the resolutions of Church synods tried on the one hand to enforce the strict separation of the Christian and Jewish communities, and on the other to make the Jews obey the Church's rules on trade and public behavior. The details of these resolutions are described in the work of L. Gumplowicz mentioned earlier.

20. Decentralization of Government in the Polish Nobles' Republic.

The decentralization of Poland's representative government did not result in a uniform official policy of the noble citizens towards the Jews. In the Polish state, provincial legislatures, or Seymiki, and even the national parliament, or Seym, responded to different political pressures. Laws which regulated the life of the masses of Polish Jews reflected the changing interests of the nobility, the political power of the autonomous Jewish community, and the degree of decentralization of the government of Poland.

Jews were treated as a separate social and economic quasi-estate, or caste. Polish Jews considered themselves exiles and outsiders. As a result, at different periods, in different places, pro-Jewish or anti-Jewish legislation was passed. These enactments were always tempered by the democratic character of Polish parliamentary government. From the second half of the 17th century, Poland suffered from the increasing corruption of her state administration and from the increasingly more effective foreign subversion of her open and decentralized government.

The competition between Polish burghers and Jews led to a political struggle. The burghers repeatedly appealed to the government, led by the king, to issue regulations *de non tolerandis Judaeis*, to exclude Jews from their towns. Occasionally, the burghers also passed anti-Jewish restrictions in their towns. At times, the Christian burghers negotiated with the Jews in order to obtain the support of the Jewish political leadership for self-imposed restrictions on competition for the sake of social peace.

Laws protecting Polish Jews, and their alliance with the powerful noble citizens, equalized their position vis-a-vis the burghers. Sometimes one group and sometimes the other had the upper hand in royal and in private towns. Despite the protection of the Jews by the nobility, they were subjected to sporadic pogroms and accusations of profanation of the host and of ritual murders. Such accusations were prohibited by the Charter of Jewish Liberties of 1264, which was in effect in Poland for five hundred years and generally prevailed. The accusations were relatively rare and insignificant in comparison with similar events in western Europe. The often mentioned 17th century massacres were inflicted equally on Jews and nobles during the Cossack wars against the Polish Nobles' Republic. These mass killings happened during wars against the beleaguered government of Poland. Primarily, they took place outside the Polish ethnic area.

21. Weakening of the Central Government and the Increased Dependence of Jews on Private Towns.

Many factors contributed to the gradual weakening of the authority of the central government in Poland. It had started by the end of the 16th century when the economic position of the noble citizens, who owned small and middle-size estates, started to deteriorate, and that of the huge landowners grew stronger. The shift of commerce from the Baltic to the Atlantic, and the gradual increase of subsidized exports from Russia badly affected the terms of trade and prices for Polish grain in western European markets.

The decentralized structure of Polish government and the increasing difficulty of rebuilding the economy after the destruction of war shaped the strategy of political leadership among the masses of Polish Jews for the two hundred years from the end of the 16th to the end of the 18th centuries. Tiny Jewish communities in western Europe could live under the protection of absolute rulers and their functionaries. The masses of Jews in Poland could not ally themselves with a king who had become the elective chief executive of the Polish Nobles' Republic. For this reason, Polish Jews had to ally themselves with the noble citizens, and especially with the increasingly more powerful huge landowners.

The control of the central government over private towns was progressively weakening. From the beginnings of the private towns in Poland, in the 13th century, they had been under the same public laws as the royal towns. However, from the middle of the 16th century, legal authority over private towns started passing into the hands of their private owners. This change resulted in increasing activity by individual Jewish communities, aimed at obtaining local privileges which would guarantee them protection. This process lasted from 1539 until the destruction of the Polish state at the end of the 18th century.

Jewish privileges were issued by the owners of private towns when these owners obtained the exclusive right to impose duties and taxes. Thus, from 1539, Polish Jews obtained local community privileges, both in private and in royal towns. These Jewish privileges were granted by the squire in private towns and by the king, provincial governor or voivode, or county chief territorial officer, called the *starosta*, in others.

During the intense colonization of the frontier lands, or Kresy, local privileges were used to attract Jewish settlers to the eastern towns. This spreading of local privileges coincided with a period of very rapid demographic growth among Polish Jews. The new use of local privileges as an incentive for the Jews often resulted in the contradiction of privileges enjoyed by the burghers and brought about endless lawsuits, accompanied by intense lobbying.

Private owners tried to organize life in their towns to suit their own interests. However, they were never able to impose a uniform administrative organization. The private owners of towns usually did not interfere with the workings of the organization of Jewish self-government, known as the kahals. Occasionally, the municipal courts would make ineffectual attempts to interfere with the internal structure of the kahals. The kahals had a political advantage over individual municipalities because they were basic units of the unique parliamentary autonomy of the masses of Polish Jews. The Christian burghers who controlled Polish municipalities did not form such a statewide organization, and therefore were politically weaker than the Jews.

22. Maturing of Jewish Autonomy in Poland and the Tollection of Taxes.

Tiny Jewish communities throughout Europe had some degree of state-wide autonomy. However, in Poland, Jews had a unique parliamentary autonomy which included the vast majority of all the Jews in the world. Jewish autonomy in Poland was politically strong and could defend itself against the state government's interference far better than anywhere else in Europe. In fact, Polish Jews were able to negotiate how much they would pay in taxes.

Tax collection was always a difficult problem in Poland, a country which for centuries enjoyed more freedom than any other state in Europe. Attempts were made to have each autonomous group, including the Jews, collect its share of taxes fairly. By 1503, the royal government had already appointed a chief rabbi for Lesser Poland, and another in 1506 for Lithuania, to settle tax disputes among the Jews. The posts of chief tax collector for Lesser Poland, Greater Poland, and Mazovia were established by King Sigismund I in 1512. However, these new chiefs were ineffectual because they did not have jurisdiction over Jewish and other autonomies.

Not long after the 1505 proclamation of the first Polish constitution of "Nihil Novi," or "nothing new about us without us," Jewish autonomy took a giant step forward. The first regional organization was created for Jews. In the four years between 1518 and 1522, King Sigismund I established five autonomous Jewish provinces, or land communities, in Poland. Each acquired the right to elect elders and tax collectors at a convention of representatives of land communities. At the same time, a conciliatory rabbinical court was created in Lublin. It held session during the national trade fairs.

In 1540, the last king of the Jagiellonian dynasty, Sigismundus Augustus (1520-1572), established a permanent arbitrational tribunal in Lublin, which functioned as the highest Jewish court for appeals from the verdicts rendered by land courts and community courts. This jurisdiction of the Jewish appeal court was legalized in Poland by the privileges of 1549 and 1553. In 1551, the king renounced his right to appoint the chief rabbis in central Poland and in Lithuania. In 1553, Sigismund Augustus bestowed the rights of execution and enforcement of the verdicts of the high Jewish courts in Lublin.

There was perennial difficulty over collecting the Jewish head tax, which was passed by the Polish national parliament, the Seym. In 1549, a suggestion was made to assign the responsibility for the collection of Jewish poll-taxes to national Jewish institutions. This solution materialized during the reign of Stephen Bathory (1533-1586), who was the first head of state in Europe to be elected by general election. He was elected in 1575 by the masses of noble citizens to be the head of state as king, and at the same time to act as the chief executive of the First Polish Republic. He was sworn and crowned after signing a detailed social contract to uphold the laws of Poland. It was the first social contract between a head of state and its citizens anywhere in Europe.

23. Jewish National Parliament -- the Jewish Seym and Its Structure.

In 1579, King Stephen Bathory convened the Jewish National Seym, which at first was called the Council of Four Lands and gradually was expanded to include twenty-two lands by the middle of the 18th century. The Jewish Seym was entrusted with assessing the poll tax in Jewish lands within the Polish state. The earliest records of the convening of the Jewish Seym in Lublin are dated 1581. The Jewish Seym, or parliament, then included representatives from Lesser Poland, Greater Poland, Red Ruthenia, and Lithuania.

By 1581, the Seym Walny (val-ny), or Polish national parliament, was at the high point of its development and power. Thus, the first meeting of the Jewish Seym in Poland occurred at an important point in the history of the development of Polish parliamentarianism. The Jewish Seym became the supreme political body of Jewish autonomy in Poland. It represented the vast majority of the entire world's Jewry; it was a unique Jewish institution in the history of the Jewish Diaspora between the Sanhedrin of the biblical times and Knesset of the modern State of Israel.

The structure of the Jewish national parliament in Poland resembled that of the Polish Seym. Poles developed a three-tier structure of representation. There were local circles of the nobles, or koło rycerskie (ko-wo ri-tser-ske), which elected representatives to the regional legislatures, each of which sent two representatives to the national parliament. The same three-tier structure was adopted for the Jewish autonomy. The local Jewish community, the kehilla, had yearly elections for its communal government, the kahal. Representatives from kahals were sent to land assemblies equivalent to Polish regional legislatures. The Jewish national parliament was composed of the representatives of the lands, or regions.

The Jewish parliament met bi-annually, in Lublin in February and in Jarosław in September. It selected one chief lobbyist to represent the entire Jewish population in Poland for negotiations with the Polish government about taxes and other matters, and to lobby for the Jews in the Seym Walny. Thus, the Jews knew well the structure of Polish parliamentary government and were given a chance to duplicate it in their own autonomy in Poland. Despite the Polish influence, the Jewish Seym kept some features of the Sanhedrin, which was established in the third century B.C.

in Judea. Both were composed of a legislative body of 70 delegates. The executive body of the Jewish National Seym in Poland included 21 men -- exactly as many as were in the small Sanhedrin of antiquity in Jerusalem.

24. *The Principle of Unanimity and the Liberum Veto.*

The Jewish parliament accepted the Polish parliamentary principle of unanimity. Poles regarded consent as a basic guarantee of freedom. The deputies defended the will of their electors. They represented tradition and precedent which served as an example or justification, sometimes stronger than law. They strove for full agreement, consensus, and the commitment of all. Thus, a decision by majority vote was considered an expediency, because the efforts to secure a majority were generally viewed as dishonest, as are "pork barrel" politics in America. Poles felt that minority rights had to be respected, and that in general "more numerous" was not necessarily "better." Poles respected consensus reached by "brotherly entreaties." However, on many occasions, a dissenting deputy was "shouted down"; all were not willing to perish because of the obstinacy of one region.

At the regional level, the selection of two deputies to the national parliament, called Seym Walny, required unanimity about the instructions for their action in Warsaw. The national parliament would not accept two deputies from one region who argued and voted against each other. Also, no motions were accepted from deputies who would not present them personally and be present during the resulting debates and voting. Uncontested bills were passed, while questioned motions and proposals were postponed or eventually abandoned. Polish politicians felt that the Seym had a dual responsibility. One was to adopt new laws, and the other, no less important, was to correct any abuses and infringements of the law by the government.

In 1652, 160 years after the Polish national parliament became bicameral, a successful protest against one question by a deputy exercising a "Liberum Veto," or a free veto, led to the break up of the entire session of the Seym. This disastrous legal precedent was created by default. A member of a political machine controlled by the fabulously wealthy governor of Wilno registered a formal veto with the Crown Secretariat and immediately left Warsaw. His sudden departure violated the basic parliamentary rule which required that the deputy had the right to have his motions accepted for consideration only when he was personally present. Absentee motions and votes were not acceptable in the Seym.

The 1652 session of the Seym was presided over by a very unusual speaker named Andrzej Fredro (1620-1679). He was the author of a libertarian "paradoxical philosophy of anarchy." He illegally accepted an absentee protest motion of Liberum Veto which was registered by a departed deputy. The speaker, however, pronounced the Liberum Veto legal and valid. This extremely harmful precedent was followed for one hundred years, despite efforts to eliminate it using established formal and strictly observed parliamentary procedures. Soon, the absolutist regimes of Russia, Prussia, and Austria organized an intense subversive campaign to preserve the Liberum Veto and to cripple the open parliamentary government of Poland.

The Jewish Seym followed the organizational pattern and procedures of the Polish national parliament closely. There was a striking parallelism between Jewish and Polish institutions. The Jewish Seym adopted the Polish type of expense allowances for deputies as well as norms concerning instructions given to the deputies by regional assemblies. The Jews also promptly adopted the Liberum Veto and enforced the practice of unanimity in the Jewish national parliament.

There was one major difference between the Polish Seym Walny and the Jewish Seym. In the Polish Seym, all the deputies from the entire territory of the Polish Nobles' Republic met in Warsaw. In 1620, the Jewish *kahals* of Lithuania seceded from the Jewish parliament in Lublin and organized a separate Seym of their own. This occurred when the central government in Warsaw introduced new legal norms in accordance with the Third Lithuanian Statute, a different fiscal system, and a separate tribunal for Lithuania.

Catherine the Great (1729-1796) of Russia was strongly opposed throughout her reign (1762-1796) to the removal of the Liberum Veto from Poland. Actually, Russian foreign minister Nikita Ivanovich Panin (1718-1783) proposed to help Poles get rid of the Liberum Veto as part of his "Northern Plan" of an alliance that was to include Poland. Catherine declared her solidarity with Frederick the Great of Berlin and rejected Panin's suggestion.

25. Jewish Seym, the Supreme Rabbinic Court and the Kahals.

The parliamentary system of Jewish autonomy in Poland and Lithuania included two institutions: the Seym and the Supreme Rabbinic Tribunal. The delegates to the Jewish Seym were selected by an electoral system which varied throughout the territory of the Polish Nobles' Republic. However, only property owners, or about 1 to 5 percent of the Jewish population could be elected. The electors were enfranchised taxpayers, about 25 percent of Jewish males. The decreasing number of property owners reflected the population explosion of Polish Jews. However, it should be noticed that Jewish electorate in Poland represented the largest percentage of voting people compared with any ethnic group in early modern Europe.

The *kahals* acted as tiny republics and as commercial corporations at the same time. At the basic level of the *kehilla*, or community, the annual elections of the communal government, the *kahal*, were held by the taxpayers, as is shown on the diagram of the autonomous Jewish government in Poland (p. 281). The *Kahal* Communal Government consisted of four *Roshim*, or Elders, five *Tuwim*, or *Meliores*, and fourteen *Kahal* governors. *Kahals* elected nine representatives to the higher Second Electoral College, which in turn elected the Electoral College of five as delegates to the Jewish National Seym.

All Jewish delegates elected at the lower levels carried clearly stated instructions from their constituents to the higher councils. These instructions were patterned after the practice developed in the Polish parliamentary system. They were of four different types:
1. An unlimited power to exercise judgment
2. A specific order to obtain concessions
3. A specific prohibition to agree to new obligations (taxes, etc.)
4. A conditional -- restrictive mandate.

The executives of the Jewish National Seym were: the chairman or president, called *parnas*, the cashier, the writer of records, and the syndic or *shtadlan*, who also acted as a lobbyist at various levels and branches of the central government in Warsaw. An eminent rabbi presided over the Supreme Rabbinic Tribunal, which ceased to be a separate institution when the Jewish National Seym was established.

The Supreme Rabbinic Tribunal was in session during the meetings of the Jewish National Seym. The Jewish Seym referred cases to the Rabbinic Tribunal for interpretation according to Jewish law as written in the Talmud, for censorship of books, etc. The smaller Jewish Seym of Lithuania was initially based on three and later on five communities. It also was composed of two parts: the Seym and the Rabbinic Tribunal.

26. Lobbying and Taxes

Jewish delegates from the entire territory of the Polish state held common conventions of the Polish and the Lithuanian Jewish Seym in Łęczyca, near Lublin. These common conventions dealt with the matter of expenses for lobbying for Jewish interests in the Polish state. Lobbying was used for the prevention as well as the defense in lawsuits stemming from accusations of ritual murder.

The Jewish National Seym and the kahals were very careful to maintain good relations with the political nation of noble citizens of the Polish republic. The alliance of the Jews with the noble citizens of Poland was very important to them. The Jews were also aware of their own importance in the economy of the Polish state, where they represented about 6 to 7 percent of the population. However, with the passage of time, the institutional forms of the alliance of the Jews with the noble citizens of Poland became less important than personal and local relations and connections.

Jewish leadership presented its policies as very favorable to the noble citizens and to the Polish Nobles' Republic. For this reason, the Jewish National Seym and the kahals enforced strict control over their communities throughout Poland. The policies of the Jewish Seym were based on the corporate responsibility of the organized community for the actions of individual Jews.

The Jewish National Seym in Poland had formal fiscal responsibility. An informal responsibility of the Jewish Seym was to defend and protect the interests of the entire Jewish minority in Poland. Jewish syndics, the shtadlans, conducted extensive lobbying throughout the republican institutions of the decentralized governmental system of the Polish state and in the courts of law.

A very important function of the Jewish National Seym was to be the sole leaseholder of the poll-tax collected from Polish Jews. Theoretically, the poll-tax was to be paid by each individual Jew. However, in practice, endless arguments were made that it should be paid only by the head of each family, usually vaguely defined for tax purposes. A law of 1549 stipulated that Jews were to pay only the poll-tax, but special taxes were also paid for various reasons, such as a war-time emergencies, etc.

27. *Negotiated Taxes and the 1569 Offer of Emancipation.*

Large scale negotiations were conducted by the Jewish National Seym with the treasury department about the amount of taxes the Jews would pay. The state treasurer usually felt that the amount of tax actually paid was too low for the number of Jews living in Poland. The co-founder of the Polish Nobles' Republic and the last of the Jagiellonian kings, Sigismund-August, once remarked to the Bishop of Cracow, "Tell me, my Lord Bishop, since you do not believe in sorcery, how is it that only 16,598 Jews pay the poll-tax, whilst two hundred thousand of them apparently live underground."

The taxpayers of the Nobles' Republic paid self-assessed taxes. Masses of noble citizens paid their land-tax, and the burgers paid town taxes in a way similar to how the Jews paid their poll-tax. The treasury officials were never sure whether they were receiving the due amount. Payment of taxes was viewed as a necessary evil in order to maintain the peace and security of the people of the pluralistic Polish state. These taxpayers knew that for centuries Poland had been the freest country on the European continent.

The Seym's 1569 Act of Lublin admitted senators from the Prussian fief of Poland into the Polish National Parliament. At that time, an offer of emancipation was made to Moslem and Jewish minorities without obligation to convert to Christianity. This offer from the Polish National Seym was accepted by the Moslems and rejected by the Jews, who preferred to live within their autonomy governed by Talmudic law. The 16th century brought the final Polonization of the urban population, including the immigrants from Germany. The Jewish population, however, was allowed to continue to speak Yiddish and thus preserve a separate Judeo-Germanic subculture based on its own language and Jewish ethnic and religious traditions.

The arguments about taxes in the Polish republic grew as the government of Poland was increasingly more decentralized and various provinces or voivodships developed various fiscal systems. Since many Jews lived in private towns, and at the same time all Jews were under the jurisdiction of the Jewish National Parliament, jurisdictional and tax-collection problems resulted. The nobles who owned private towns had to negotiate with the Jewish Seym about the taxes of the Jews in their jurisdiction. If the outcome of these negotiations was not satisfactory to them, the noble citizens had to take action in the regional legislature, or in Poland's national parliament, Seym Walny.

Multilateral political deals were concluded between the Jewish Seym and noble owners of private towns. In exchange for a lower tax imposed on local Jews, the town owners would oppose new laws and regulations inconvenient to the Jewish Seym which were under consideration by the regional legislatures or in the national parliament. Individual Jewish business people sought protection from the nobles whom they served in order to avoid paying taxes to the Jewish National Seym. Their argument was that taxes imposed by the Jewish Seym were preventing them from paying rents for mills, inns, etc.

On many occasions, the Jewish Seym had to appeal to the Polish government for help to enforce its tax collecting authority over Jews delinquent in taxes and under the protection of the noble citizens. At times, the Jewish Seym had to appeal to the government of the king to temper irritation against delinquent Jewish tax-payers. The tax collection activities of the Jewish National Seym strengthened the financial situation and orderly administration of the Polish state. However, there was no more unanimity in the Jewish Seym than in Polish republican institutions such as the Seym Walny, regional and provincial Seymiks, or the Nobles Circles in the precincts. All of them experienced at least as much partisanship as can be observed in the Congress of the United States.

28. *Jewish Borrowing from Christians.*

The Jewish Seym was deeply involved in the economic policies of the Polish state. Dynamic economic expansion, especially in the eastern frontier lands of Kresy, necessitated prudent policies. The large expansion of Jewish trade in Poland produced a strong demand for loans. However, borrowing from Christians was risky, especially because if one Jew defaulted on a loan, then the entire Jewish community could be obliged to make the defaulted payment collectively.

In 1607, the Jewish Seym passed a new law regulating credit among the Jews. The new law was well formulated and diminished to some extent Jewish dependence on borrowing money from the gentiles in Poland. In 1673, the Jewish Seym passed a law regulating borrowing by Jews from Christians who wanted to deposit their money in Jewish hands in order to collect interest. This practice was common because Christian real estate owners, monasteries, clergy, and others were forbidden by the Catholic Church to collect interest from other Christians.

The Jewish Seym established a licensing system called *hazaka*, which, among other regulations, also required Jewish borrowers to obtain special permission from their kahal to borrow money from Christians. The Jewish Seym established very severe laws for dealing with bankruptcy. These laws were necessary to stabilize commerce, not only in the Polish state, which occupied the largest territory in Europe, but also in the entire continental east-west trade.

The medieval and early modern Jewish communities, the *kehillas*, acted through their governing elective councils, the *kahals*. They attempted to regulate relations with the surrounding Polish society. This was in accordance with Talmudic law. A *kehilla* was responsible for the behavior of its members and was interested in making sure that individual members would not act against the interest of the Jewish community. Jewish trade secrets were to be kept from Christians. The *kehilla* forbade individual Jews under its jurisdiction to enter into any business arrangements with Polish Christians without the *kahal*'s approval. For this reason, only a Jew licensed by the *kahal* could bid on an arenda lease or try to get a loan from a non-Jew. The *kahal* also issued regulations designed to prevent ostentatious wealth in order to avoid the resentment of the Christians. The kahal forbade individual Jews to turn to non-Jewish courts.

Naturally, the Jewish Seym extended the *hazaka* licencing system to the arenda leasing contracts. The Jewish Seym and the kahals enjoyed the support of the Polish central government which considered them an extension of its administration. Thus, no one could enter into an arenda lease contract without being granted permission from the government of his Jewish community, the kahal. Theoretically, a landowner could not choose his arrendator, and at most could obtain competitive bids only from those who had a licence from the kahal to bid on a contract with him. For issuing a licence, a *kahal* required a licence fee or a commission. Similar payments to the *kahal* were required for renewals of lease contracts.

The control of licencing by the *kahals* was easier when there was no shortage of arenda lease contracts. During times of intense competition for arenda leases, the arrendators could circumvent the *kahal*, and the landowner would grant the lease to the highest bidder. The *kahals* repeatedly issued prohibitions against competitive bidding for arenda contracts. There are records of settlements paid to the kahal by arendators who obtained arenda contracts without license.

Occasionally, very rich aristocratic land magnates granted *arenda* leases on the basis of competitive bidding (*aukcja* pron.: awk-tsya) or favoritism, when their political power grew in Poland in the 17th and 18th centuries. They also preferred to make the leases last one year rather than three years. These conditions prevailed when there were many more potential arrendators than the number of available arenda contracts. In 1637, the Jewish Seym issued a regulation that any 15 householders in a town had the right to sue in a rabbinic court to have the arenda license of the current holder cancelled and competitive bidding opened up for a new arenda license to be issued by the kahal. The market value of lease contracts fluctuated. It was determined by the profitability of leases traded.

When the aristocratic magnates succeeded in building their political machines, they attempted to subordinate and weaken the kahals in their lands. These attempts resulted in a clash of interests between the large landowners and Jewish Seym and the kahals. There are recorded examples of magnate interference in rabbinic courts. A territorial court in the magnate's castle, or *zamek*, could handle some of the cases which belonged to the jurisdiction of rabbinic courts. Therefore, occasionally rabbinic court decisions written in Hebrew can be found inserted in the Polish language files of *zamek* courts. The owners of *latifundia* wanted to maximize the profits from their domain and felt that control of the Jews would be useful to them. They supported the *kahal* when it was convenient for them. When dealing with individual Jews they tried to bypass the *kahal*. There are complaints in the rabbinic literature about the lack of discipline and the selfishness of the Jews who used the *protekcja* of a lord and disobeyed the *kahal*.

An important contribution to national and international trade was the introduction by the Jewish Seym of a law on bills of exchange, called "*mamram*" (often misspelled as "membran" or "membron"). These bills were easily exchangeable and cashed by the bearer in whose name they were issued. "Mamrams" were used to transfer money safely at a time when there was a general lack of money and when travel throughout Europe was hazardous. "Mamrams" became very useful during the mobilization of large loans by the network of international credit organized by Jewish financiers. The "*mamrams*" originated in Poland and were also used as the earliest travel checks.

29. *International Effect of General Elections in Poland.*

The foreign relations of the Polish Nobles' Republic, founded in 1569 in Lublin, became especially complicated in 1573 when the Seym passed the law of general election for the head of state, called "viritim." Masses of the noble citizens of the Polish Nobles' Republic acquired the right to elect the king, who was to serve as the chief executive of the new republic. Exercise of the voting right was not compulsory. Rather than voting by precincts, the voters were to participate in a huge electoral convention in Warsaw. A proposed restrictive law limiting the general elections for the head of state to natives of the Polish Nobles' Republic was tabled and did not pass.

The traditional system of negotiated royal marital alliances and crowning foreign-born rulers was well established in Europe. However, Poland was unique for her republican institutions, decentralized parliamentary government, and general elections for the head of state. The Polish state was a great power and the largest territory in Europe in the 16th and first half of the 17th centuries. Thus, Polish general elections had the potential to suddenly change existing alliances and the European balance of power. No government wanted to be adversely affected by the outcome of Polish elections.

In the capitals of countries adjacent to Poland, lawyers were trained in Polish constitutional law in order to understand how to influence Polish elections and the workings of this republican state, unique in Europe. One of the important avenues of entry into the internal affairs of the Polish state was international commerce and money transfers, dominated by Polish Jews. For this reason, the Jewish National Seym informally could provide important service, or disservice, to the government of the Polish Nobles' Republic in matters related to foreign countries.

The chairman, or *parnas*, of the Jewish National Seym, as well as its syndic, or *shtadlan*, were in regular contact with the central government headed by the elective king. The Jewish syndic dealt most often with the treasurer. In Hebrew sources, the Jewish Council of Warsaw has been called "Vaad Warsza." It was a part of the Jewish National Seym, which had thorough knowledge of the internal politics of Poland. For this reason, foreign powers sometimes tried to enlist Polish Jews for their interference in the internal affairs of the Polish state. Such was the case in 1750, for example, when French and Prussian envoys were attempting to break up the Polish Seym by Liberum Veto. There are not sufficient sources of information to determine whether the Jewish Seym helped them.

30. *Jewish National Parliament in Lublin as the Supreme Power Over All Ashkenazi Jews in Europe.*

In the 17th century, the Polish state was weakened because of the second wave of serfdom and, associated with it, a catastrophic drop in grain crops with a simultaneous growth of the political machines of the huge landowners. As a result of the decline, Poland ceased to have a well planned foreign policy. At that time the Jewish National Seym conducted its own international political and religious activity. In 1956, B. Brilling published in the Jewish Institute, YIVO *Annual* "The Struggle of the Council of Four Lands for the Jewish Right to Worship in Breslau (Wrocław)." He explained that the Jewish National Seym in Poland appealed directly to the Silesian authorities for the right of Jewish merchants from Poland to reside and worship in their own prayer houses in Wroclaw.

The Jewish National Seym, or Congressus Judaicus, in Poland exercised supreme power over all Ashkenazi Jews in Europe. It had the authority to solve their religious and political questions, which were brought to it regularly. Thus, for example, during a controversy in Frankfurt, Germany, in 1615-1678, the Jewish National Seym in Poland established proper procedures for Jewish self-government there, after condemning the local oligarchy.

The decisions of the Jewish National Seym in Poland were considered valid by Ashkenazi Jews throughout Europe. Examples are provided by the anathema of the false Messiah Sabbatai Sevi in 1670, and by support for the community of Polish Jews in Amsterdam in 1660-1673. The Jewish Seym in Poland coordinated annual collections of money for the Jews in the Holy Land and for the ransom of Jewish prisoners. A. Brickner in his *History of Polish Culture* (Warsaw, 1958) stated that the Jewish Seym was accused of illegally transferring Polish laws to Istanbul, Turkey. Jewish Seym appealed successfully to the Vatican when, in the 18th century, the decline of the

Polish state was associated with increasing religious intolerance.

The Jewish National Seym in Poland had jurisdiction over the economic and moral questions of the Ashkenazi Jews. It ruled on the Sabbath work of the peasants in the arenda leaseholds. It published instructions for the proper study of Torah, for the upkeep of the yeshiva (talmudic academies), for admission of Jewish students from all over Europe to schools in Poland, for publishing, and for censoring all Jewish publications.

31. Jews as the Most Influential of All Autonomous Groups in Poland.

The internal affairs of the decentralized Polish state reflected the fact that, for centuries, more people had enjoyed more freedom there than anywhere else in early modern Europe. The Jewish Seym represented the masses of Polish Jews in their relations with other groups. In Poland, the noble citizens were most important. Their number approached one million by the beginning of the 17th century. Nobles were the political nation of free citizens of Poland. As a result of the parliamentary character and decentralization of the Polish state, the Jewish Seym was very influential. It gave the masses of Ashkenazi Jews a feeling of unity similar to the solidarity felt within the political nation of the noble citizens of Poland. This unity contributed to the very positive view Polish Jews held of themselves. The Jewish Seym also organized and performed charity functions for the Ashkenazi Jews.

The real political importance of the Jewish Seym was evident in its influence and initiative in matters important to Jews in the national parliament of Poland, in provincial and regional legislatures, and in the precincts. Thus, the Jewish Seym represented and defended the interests of its constituents by an extensive and well organized system of lobbying, which became an efficient and acceptable institution in the Polish state. Among many autonomous groups in Poland, such as the Ukrainian Cossacks and Armenians, for example, the Jews had the most extensive and influential lobbying organization. This fact reflected the long historic experience of Jewish communities living in foreign lands. Jewish lobbying activities in Poland were informal and not precisely defined by law.

The contemporary Jewish historian Salo Baron has described how efficient the Jewish Seym was in defending its political position and in manipulating social forces in Poland in favor of its constituents. In the case of the killing of a Jew, the Jewish Seym stood on guard to exact legal "vengeance" on the killer. In such murder cases the Jewish Seym often contributed money towards the expenses of Polish state courts in order to speed up the legal proceedings.

The official lobbying activities of the Jewish Seym were performed by the office of shtadlan, or syndic, on all three levels of Jewish autonomy. The governments of Jewish communities, the kahals, performed their lobbying activities at the local level, the lands or regions at the regional legislatures, and the Jewish Seym lobbied through its representative shtadlan at the Polish Seym Walny and at the central government in Warsaw. The shtadlan acted as an advisor, defender and lobbyist. In case of war, when the Jewish Seym could not convene, the shtadlan represented the interests of the Jewish minority in Poland.

32. Lobbying Expenses and Payoffs

The shtadlan, or syndic, was obligated to represent Jewish autonomous institutions as well as individual Jews in lawsuits involving noble citizens, the clergy, burghers, and free peasants. The shtadlan did not participate formally in the republican institutions of Poland. His activity was political and his negotiations with Polish authorities were an accepted part of political life in the First Polish Republic.

The expense of lobbying activities were evident in the budgets of the kahals at the local level. At times some 70 percent of these budgets was assigned to mediation, adjournments, defense in lawsuits, bribes and gifts for dignitaries, etc., and the remaining 30 percent was split evenly between the costs of administration and charities. Despite the fact that the laws of Poland protected Jews from accusations of ritual murder, the courts often had to deal with this problem. T. Czacki wrote in his Discourse on Jews and Karaites, (Kraków, 1860, pp. 45-46) about Jewish economic activity, and concluded that "the money created, prolonged, and warded off persecutions" even though, comparatively speaking, Poland was known for centuries as the paradise of the Jews.

Payoffs and bribes became a form of consulting or permanent protection fees which were paid on a monthly basis as regular salaries of appointed or elected officials. In case of default, such payments would stop. During the lobbying process, bribes were used to obtain specific privileges for a particular kahal or land. The Jewish Seym often cooperated closely with the royal chancellery in the preparation of such privileges.

B. D. Weinryb wrote in *The Jews of Poland* (page 149) that in 1623, for example, the Jewish Seym instructed the *kahals* of Lithuania "to watch that during sessions of the district assemblies held before the National Parliament [or Seym Walny in Warsaw] nothing new which could hurt us should be decided upon." Also, in 1628 a similar instruction issued four weeks before the session of the Seym Walny stated that "the deputies to be elected by the regional legislatures should receive gifts and be asked to be benevolent in the Seym."

33. *Deluge of Invasions in the 17th Century, Oligarchy in Kahals, and Tax Reforms.*

The deluge of invasions, from the 1648 Cossack uprising to the Ottoman Turk occupation of southern Ukraine and Podolia in 1674, resulted in the loss of about one-third of the Christian population of Poland. Massacres by Ukrainian Cossacks brought death to one-fifth of the Polish Jews (about 100,000 people). Recovery was achieved under the leadership of King John III Sobieski, whose victory in 1683 at Vienna ended Turkish expansion into Europe. However, the rape of the Polish election by Peter the Great in 1697, and the illegal placing of a Russian puppet from Saxony on the Polish throne, brought on a crisis of sovereignty. It was the beginning of a century of decline and the open subversion of Poland's parliamentary government and pluralistic way of life by foreign governments.

There are no records of major opposition to the autonomous parliamentary government of the Jewish National Seym until the first half of the 18th century. However, when the decline of Poland was caused by the growing oligarchy of aristocratic magnates, the *kahals* and Jewish lands also became oligarchic -- Jewish self-government started to deteriorate. In parallel with the corruption of Polish republican institutions, Jewish representative government suffered squabbles between the delegates, who experienced difficulty in selecting the parnas, or chairman or president of the Jewish Seym. The sessions of Jewish parliament were broken off by the use of the Liberum Veto. The Jewish Seym was not called to session as scheduled when mounting debts could not be properly accounted for and paid.

Polish political leaders started talking about doing away with lump-sum taxation and increasing Jewish taxes because Jews were alleged to be hiding their real incomes. The declining Polish state was in dire need of a new and well organized fiscal system. The calamities which started in 1648 upset the budgets of the *kahals* with unforeseen expenses for ransoms, protection money, and bribes. Many of these expenses were financed outside of the official budget and kept secret from the Polish treasury -- not even Hebrew records could be kept safely. The deterioration of the Polish state during the first half of the 18th century under the rule of the Saxon puppets of Russia brought a wave of lawsuits against the Jews, including accusations of ritual murder and theft and desecration of the Holy Host (the Eucharist).

The Jewish National Seym had to impose higher taxes, which resulted in opposition by the kahals, already overloaded with their own internal taxes. The *kahals* were suffering from adverse changes in the organization of Jewish credit in Europe in the late 17th century. As a result the *kahals* lost financial control over monies which were invested with them by the noble citizens, Catholic clergy, and monasteries. Christian investors made the *kahals* collectively responsible for the growing Jewish debts.

34. *Derailing of Government-From-Below in Poland and the Hasidic Response.*

Jewish corporate life started to disintegrate. The authority of the *kahals* to issue licenses to borrow money caused general corruption, bribery, kickbacks, and open conflicts. The grievances were increasingly taken to the Christian owners of the private towns and to territorial officers. The Jewish National Parliament threatened "any man of Israel who approaches a landed squire in order to obtain an exemption from taxes" with anathema. Jewish craft guilds demanded the right to share in the decision making (as described by M. Wischnitzer in *A History of Jewish Crafts and Guilds.* New York: 1965). The moral decline of the Jewish National Seym contributed to protest movements initiated by mystics.

The new philosophy of the Enlightenment brought ideas of nation-states, centralization of states, secularization, and radicalization of expansionist policies of states surrounding Poland. All these notions and policies were contrary to the idea of pluralism and autonomy established in Poland among the religious communities, ethnic groups, hereditary castes, and feudal estates. Thus, the breakdown of state institutions and of Jewish autonomy in Poland in the 18th century was to a considerable extent brought about by the ideas and currents of the Enlightenment.

The derailing of Polish government-from-below took a long time. It was the result of the deterioration of grain exports, the reappearance of serfdom, a huge drop in the efficiency of Polish agriculture, the increasing poverty of the masses of the noble citizens, and the political anarchy created by the political machines of aristocratic land magnates, who became huge landowners and cooperated with cynical subversion of Polish parliamentary system and defense establishment by foreign governments. The 18th-century breakdown of Jewish autonomy was caused by the decline of the Polish state and a gradual replacement of the elected *kahal* governments by an oligarchy, which held individual Jews under tight control inside their communities.

The beginnings of the Hassidic movement are described by professor Rosman. "With regard to the rise of Hasidism, the picture of Jewish life on the 18th century magnate *latifundia*... cannot support the idea that Hasidism was a response of downtrodden people seeking a mystical release from desperation of everyday life or disillusioned messianists needing an outlet to diffuse their frustrated beliefs. Hasidism did not begin in the wake of 1648, nor in response to abolition of the Council of Four Lands [Jewish Seym, 1764], nor in the aftermath of Frankism. Hasidism began in 1740s in a town on the Sieniawski-Czartoryski latifundium where Jews were flourishing. Międzybóż, the headquarters of Israel Baal Tov, Hasidism's founder, was not a small secluded village populated by mystics and saintly hermits. It was an important regional center with a Jewish population of over 2000 (large by 18th century standards) where, already in 1730, Jews owned 45 out of 75 stores and 110 out of 124 wooden or stone houses. It was dominated by hard-headed merchants and arrendators." (M.J. Rosman, *The Lords' Jews* p.211, Harvard University Press, Cambridge, Mass., 1990.)

Faced with worsening conditions in the declining Polish state, Jewish masses reacted by seeking refuge in new and uncorrupted social structures provided by the mystical movement of Hasidism. The leadership was provided by *zaddikim*, whose authority grew at the expense of the *kahal* oligarchy. *Zaddikim* provided their followers with spiritual security and freedom from the corruption of the decaying autonomous institutions. Each of the zaddikim started claiming the prerogatives which the Jewish Seym once had.

Hasidic zaddikim organized opposition against the corruption of the oligarchic *kahals*. They collected money from their followers, ransomed imprisoned leaseholders who could not pay their rent, and successfully intervened with the noble owners of the private towns and territorial officers. The Hasidic "reformation" was strong in Podolia and the Ukraine. It did not do as well in the north of Kresy, the eastern Polish frontier lands.

In Wilno (Vilnius), a Jewish conservative "counter-reformation" was successfully organized and stopped the northward advance of the Hasidic reformation, which, however, was equally conservative. Thus, the masses of conservative Jews in the Polish borderlands of the western civilization resisted the Jewish Enlightenment known as *Haskala*. They continued to speak Yiddish and live within the traditions of Jewish orthodoxy. At the same time, the masses of orthodox Jews in the Polish historic lands developed modern Jewish nationalism for several generations, until they fell victim to the German genocide of European Jews.

In 1764, five hundred years after the proclamation of the basic Charter of Jewish Liberties in Poland in 1264, the Polish National Parliament formally dissolved the Jewish National Seym and promised emancipation to the masses of Polish Jews, who by then represented about 75 percent of world Jewry. The dissolution was brought about by the corruption of Jewish leaders, and the insolvency of the *kahal* because of huge debts which caused a crisis within the Jewish autonomy. A new reformist and efficient administration attempted to save the Polish state from catastrophe. In reality, the structures of Jewish autonomy lasted until the conclusion of the partitions and obliteration of the old Polish republic in 1795. Poland was the only major historical state in modern Europe which suffered total destruction. Russia, Prussia, and Austria destabilized the European continent by committing this despicable crime against the Polish state.

35. The Importance of Poland for the Jewish Diaspora. The Fulfillment of the Polish Historic Mission Through Centuries of Pluralism.

Poland was unique in the Christian world in that Polish civilization was pluralistic. It was developed by an indigenous democratic process which for centuries gave more freedom to the people in the Polish state than in any other major country in late medieval and early modern times. Jewish parliamentary autonomy in Poland was unique in the entire history of the Diaspora.

Andrzej Bryk of the University of Kraków wrote on Jewish autonomy in Poland in the *Archivum Iuridicum Cracoviense* (Vol. XXI, 1988) page 68: "The Jewish elites thought highly of life in Poland. They considered the Jewish Seym to be a prestigious institution that enhanced their status. For instance, Ber of Bolechów said in the mid-18th century that the Jewish Seym was 'a small solace and a little honor, too, that Almighty God in his great pity and loving kindness had not deserted us.' Whereas Natan Hanover (?-1683) wrote (in his chronicle) after the [Ukrainian] uprising led by Bohdan Chmielnicki: 'The Pillar of Justice was in the Kingdom of Poland as it was in Jerusalem before destruction of the Temple.. The leaders of the Jewish Seym were like the Sanhedrin... They had the authority to judge all Israel in the Kingdom of Poland... and to punish each man as they saw fit.'" President of Yeshiva Academy in Kraków, Moses Isserles (c.1510-1572), wrote, "It is better to live on dry bread but in peace in Poland [where] the law of the country is to be the law of the Jews." Isserles' commentary and interpretations of the Talmud of Caro were used by all Ashkenazi Jews in Europe.

The obliteration of the original Polish civilization resulted from the initiative of the Brandenburg Hohenzollerns in a political climate radicalized by the ideology of the Enlightenment. The catastrophe touched all ethnic groups in the pluralistic old Polish republic, including Jews. During the entire history of the Diaspora, the Jewish nation existed only in Poland, where masses of Jews lived and had their own social classes, their own policies and laws, their own parliament and economic system, and their own spiritual and material culture. This is why the Jews once called Poland the New Holy Land.

The majority of Jews remained in the Polish frontier lands of the western civilization called, in Polish, Kresy. Jewish culture there was shaped by the indigenous Polish democratic process developed in late medieval and early modern times. Annexation of the lands of Kresy by Russia converted these former provinces of the Polish Nobles' Republic into the so-called Jewish Pale of Settlement -- in the Jewish perception it was a Pale of Confinement, ruled by czarist policy "to keep the Jews harmless," despite all the notions of emancipation propounded by the Enlightenment.

The new problems facing the Jews after the partitions of Poland are described by Professor Pipes of Harvard University. "The experience of the Byelorussian Jews with municipal elections underscored the dilemma which emancipation was in time to bring Jews everywhere. As a pariah nation, confined within their self-governing communities, they had been far less dependent on the fairness of the general administration than they were to become with the attainment of formal equality: in other words, no equality was in many ways preferable to sham equality. The crucial issue was justice. In the *kahal* courts, now abolished, disputes had been settled in accord with Talmudic law. Under the urban reforms, merchants and townsmen came under the jurisdiction of magistrates whose Christian judges knew nothing of Talmudic law and could not even communicate with the Yiddish-speaking litigants. A further complication arose from the fact that Jews could not swear the Christian oath required in city courts". (Richard Pipes, "Catherine II and the Jews," *Soviet Jewish Affairs*, vol. 5, no. 2, 1975, pp. 3-20.)

The loss of the freedom that prevailed in Poland among all segments of the population was felt strongly when people living in the provinces annexed by Russia found themselves in a country in which no civil rights existed. This situation led Polish Jews to think that they were singled out for persecution. Such was not always the case, as the decrees of Empress Catherine clearly indicated.

To quote Richard Pipes again, "The decree of May 7, 1786, constitutes a landmark in the history of modern Jewry. It first formally enunciated the principle that Jews were entitled to all the rights of their estate, and that the discrimination against them on the grounds of religion was illegal. The decree anticipated by more than five years the celebrated declaration of the French National Assembly extending to Jews civil equality. Now, of course, in eighteenth century Russia, when the estate structure was still strictly maintained, equality did not mean the rights of modern "citizenship," for such did not exist. It did mean, however, that Jews had estate equality with Christian merchants and townsmen, which was the only kind of equality then known. Indeed, the decree of May 7 went beyond establishing mere equality with Christians, for it also gave Jews two privileges not accorded to Christians of the *tiers etat*: the right to reside in the countryside and there to deal in spirits. Powers were also vested in the *kahals* (such as the right of self-taxation) which Christian merchants and townsmen could not boast for their communal organizations."

(Richard Pipes, "Catherine II and the Jews," *Soviet Jewish Affairs*, vol. 5, no. 2, 1975, pp. 3-20.)

Unlike Poland, whose freedoms were described in detail earlier in this book, Russia functioned under conditions of military rule and a form of a permanent martial law. Professional army generals served as General-Governors of provinces. The Russian Empire was ruled by a military-police complex which originated during the reign of Ivan the Terrible in the 16th century and was modernized in the passage of time. Thus, in June 1790 Catherine II forbade [Polish-]Byelorussian Jews to import religious books from Poland. General-Governor of Moscow, Prince Alexander Prozorvskii, ordered the handful of Jews living in Moscow to leave (sometimes between February and September 1790). Two years later, the Russian government ordered all foreign Jews to leave Russia. Harsh orders and regulations continued.

In the provinces annexed from Poland, ethnic relations deteriorated. Polish landowners who earlier had protected Jews, assumed the role of Jewish competitors in the conditions created by the Russians. Also, the competition between Polish townspeople and Jews intensified.

During the 19th century, the Russians fossilized the Jewish nation. They locked the Jews in social and cultural forms developed earlier in the freedom of Poland. It was in the Poland of the 16th, 17th, and 18th centuries that Jewish legal and governmental culture, as well as its educational system, philosophical concepts, and religious beliefs evolved.

By 1880, the Jewish population in the Polish historic lands, including the eastern frontier lands of Kresy, reached about 80 percent of the world's Jewry. The culture of the Jewish minority was profoundly influenced by the culture of the Polish republic. This happened despite the absence of integration of the Jewish masses into the gentile society of old Poland -- there, Jews were permitted to follow their own way of life by their own free choice.

The Jews were always welcome to join Polish national life as Poles within the original Polish civilization which was destroyed by the partitions. When Georges Clemenceau reflected on European political history in his book *Grandeur and Misery of Victory* (New York: Harcourt, Brace, and Co., 1930, pp. 193-194) he said: "Let us recall the partitions of Poland, the greatest crime in history, which leaves an everlasting stigma...No outrage had ever less excuse, no violence perpetrated against humanity ever cried louder for a redress that had been indefinitely postponed. The wrong was so great that at no time in the life of Europe, among other acts of violence for which there was no expiation, could it appear less heinous. It has become a byword in history as one of the worst felonies that can be laid to the charge of [European] civilization."

The powerful words of Georges Clemenceau (1841-1929) refresh our memory of the wreckage of the once great and free society of old Poland which blossomed during the splendid Polish Renaissance, followed by the colorful Polish Baroque. This great period of the original Polish civilization also produced the Golden Age of Polish Jews. The Poles lived up to the unique opportunity which presented itself in the geographic center of the European continent, between the declining Mongol and German empires. Polish civilization flourished on the great expanse of central and eastern Europe between the Baltic and the Black seas. There, for centuries, Polish served as the language of elegance and civility; it was used as such in Moscow during the 17th century.

The huge area shaped by Polish civilization extended from the upper Oder River in the west to the upper Dvina and middle Oka rivers, and the area within 100 miles of Moscow, in the east. It extended from the Lithuanian coast on the shores of the Baltic in the north to the shores of the Black Sea and the area between the deltas of the Danube and Dnieper rivers in the south. In Kresy, or the eastern frontier lands of this huge area, the great drama of Polish history took place for six hundred years between 1340 and 1940. The crucial moment came in 1386, when Lithuania, victorious in war against the Mongol invaders, accepted Western Christianity from Poland. This event permitted the rise of east-central Europe under Polish leadership and the creation in the late medieval and early modern period of a unique sanctuary for the Ashkenazi Jews who were severely persecuted in western Europe.

Poland fulfilled her unique historic mission by creating a pluralistic society during the three hundred years from the end of the 14th to the middle of the 17th century. At that time, a vast majority of the world's Jews lived in the Polish Commonwealth.

Basic democratic ideals were crystallized in 15th- and 16th-century Poland as a product of the indigenous Polish democratic process. These ideals were: the social contract between the government and the citizens, the principle of government by consent, personal freedom and civil rights of the individual, freedom of religion, the value of self-reliance, general elections, and prevention of authoritarian power of the state. Thus, Jewish culture in the Polish Commonwealth was shaped by the evolution of the Polish state, in which Jewish autonomy lasted for several hundred years. It encompassed masses of Jews who were ruled by their own national parliament, the Jewish Seym in Poland, a unique Jewish national institution between the Sanhedrin of the Biblical times and the Knesset of the State of Israel.

The Polish democratic form of government, like all open democratic governments, was vulnerable, and its freedom carried the seeds of its own self-destruction such as the expansion of the oligarchy of the aristocratic land magnates and their political machines. This vulnerability was evident in the confrontation of the Polish democratic process with absolute monarchies in the 17th and 18th centuries, in the Polish struggle for independence in the 19th century, and in Poland's confrontation with the totalitarian onslaught of Nazi Germany and Soviet Russia in the 20th century, in which Polish Jews were annihilated in the Holocaust perpetrated by the Germans. In postwar Poland, the Soviets did not permit the revival of Jewish culture.

Poland provided the main organizational basis for the late medieval and early modern history of east-central Europe, a pluralistic unity between the Romano-German and Greco-Slavic absolutist worlds. The Polish indigenous democratic process spread its influence throughout Lithuania, Byelorussia, Ukraine, Latvia (Livonia), Moldavia, and Hungary. Political elites in these countries were composed of very numerous citizen-soldiers who had full civil rights and exercised them through free elections. The political nation of the great multinational Polish Commonwealth was known as *szlachta*. Besides Polish nobles, it encompassed Lithuanian, Byelorussian, Ukrainian, and Moldavian *boyars*, as well as the *ritterschaft* of Livonia (Latvia) and the *komitats* gentry of Hungarian Transylvania when it was in union with Poland. The Cossack *starshyna* of Zaporozhe on the Dnieper enjoyed a similar social position. When the Cossack elite was refused ennoblement and full civil rights by the Seym Walny (Polish National Parliament) in 1647, it elected Bohdan Chmielnicki as its leader (*hetman*). The Cossack rebellion of 1648 ended the great power status of the Polish Nobles' Republic and also put an end to Cossack autonomy.

Poles developed a truly republican legal structure on a grand scale, the only one in Europe between 1454 and 1795. It covered the huge territory between the Baltic and the Black seas. In this period, Poland not only saved Jews from extinction, but also gave them a chance to recover demographically amidst the flowering of Jewish culture in the territory of the multinational Polish state. In Europe, only in Poland were the masses of Jews always free. They were never sold as slaves, nor were they ever made to work as serfs.

In fact, popular foreign opinion about the situation of Polish peasants suggest the atmosphere of relative freedom in Poland during the 18th century. Ever since the tightening of the Russian regime by Peter the Great, large numbers of Russian peasants fled to Poland. This phenomenon continued through the 18th century. A similar situation developed on the Polish-Austrian border. Later, during the preparation of the partitions and destruction of the Polish state, the issue of massive escapes of serfs was used to bring about the coordination of Russian and Austrian plans against Poland. The Polish Constitution of May 3, 1791, clearly stated that Poland would not extradite runaway foreign serfs, and that, in fact, they could remain on Polish territory as free people. Thus, the peasant escapes indicate that relations in Polish villages between nobles, Jews, and peasants in general compared favorably with the conditions then existing in Russia and Austria.

The heritage of the masses of Jews in the world today is based mainly on traditions shaped by centuries of Jewish autonomy in Poland under the leadership of the Jewish Seym -- the Jewish Nation-al Parliament, also known as the Congressus Judaicus, the one and only institution of representative government of masses of Jews in the history of the Diaspora. Thus, out of the long development in old Poland, modern Jewish national identity and nationalism were born in the 19th century to become a powerful force which recreated the State of Israel in the 20th century, despite the German annihilation of six million Jews during World War II.

CHAPTER IV

GERMAN ANNIHILATION OF THE JEWS

A CHRONOLOGY AND ANNOTATIONS
BASIC FACTS AND TYPICAL EVENTS

Based on the files of
Nuremberg Trials of German war crimes,
the Commission Investigating German-Nazi Crimes in Poland,
and the Jewish Historical Institute in Poland which contains
the earliest and most complete archives of
the greatest tragedy in Jewish history

ANORDNUNG
Kennzeichnung der Juden im Distrikt Krakau

[German decree text]

ROZPORZĄDZENIE
Znamionowanie żydów w okręgu Krakowa

[Polish decree text]

Order to wear arm-bands
with the Star of David,
Dec. 1, 1939

L a n d	Zahl
A. Altreich	131.800
Ostmark	43.700
Ostgebiete	420.000
Generalgouvernement	2.284.000
Bialystok	400.000
Protektorat Böhmen und Mähren	74.200
Estland – judenfrei –	
Lettland	3.500
Litauen	34.000
Belgien	43.000
Dänemark	5.600
Frankreich / Besetztes Gebiet	165.000
Unbesetztes Gebiet	700.000
Griechenland	69.600
Niederlande	160.000
Norwegen	1.300
B. Bulgarien	48.000
England	330.000
Finnland	2.300
Irland	4.000
Italien einschl. Sardinien	58.000
Albanien	200
Kroatien	40.000
Portugal	3.000
Rumänien einschl. Bessarabien	342.000
Schweden	8.000
Schweiz	18.000
Serbien	10.000
Slowakei	88.000
Spanien	6.000
Türkei (europ. Teil)	55.500
Ungarn	742.800
UdSSR	5.000.000
Ukraine	2.994.684
Weißrußland ausschl. Bialystok	446.484
Zusammen: über	11.000.000

Berlin-Wannsee plan to exterminate
11,000,000 Jews,
Jan. 20, 1942

REPUBLIC OF POLAND
Ministry of Foreign Affairs
THE MASS EXTERMINATION
of JEWS in
GERMAN OCCUPIED POLAND

NOTE
addressed to the Governments of the
United Nations on December 10th, 1942,
and other documents

*Published on behalf of the Polish
Ministry of Foreign Affairs by*

HUTCHINSON & CO. (Publishers) LTD.
LONDON : NEW YORK : MELBOURNE

Polish Government's appeal to
force stopping of the genocide,
Dec. 10, 1942

Obwieszczenie

Dotyczy: kary śmierci za nieuprawnione opuszczenie żydowskich dzielnic mieszkaniowych.

[Polish proclamation text]

Warszawa, dnia 10 listopada 1941.

(–) Dr FISCHER
Gubernator

Death penalty for Jews leaving the ghetto,
Nov. 10, 1941

BEKANNTMACHUNG

[German text]

1. Książąpolski Kazimierz		6. Zakrzewski Franciszek		
2. Lorkiewicz Jerzy		7. Cabaj Stanisław		
3. Stoń Jan		8. Kondratiuk Bronisław		
4. Stoń Bolesław		9. Zakrzewski Piotr		
5. Zachorczuk Ludwik		10. Włodarczyk Jan		

Der SS- und Polizeiführer

OBWIESZCZENIE.

1. Książąpolski Kazimierz		6. Zakrzewski Franciszek		
2. Lorkiewicz Jerzy		7. Cabaj Stanisław		
3. Stoń Jan		8. Kondratiuk Bronisław		
4. Stoń Bolesław		9. Zakrzewski Piotr		
5. Zachorczuk Ludwik		10. Włodarczyk Jan		

Dowódca SS- i Policji

Death penalty for sheltering Jews,
execution list, March 29, 1942

Death on the sidewalk in the Warsaw Ghetto

Jewish Ghetto Police in Warsaw

Stalin succumbed to the same virus of anti-Semitism as Hitler, substituting the Jewish world-conspiracy of capitalism and Zionism ... for Hitler's Jewish world-conspiracy of Bolshevism...

[Stalin and Hitler regarded their followers as] a resource to be mobilized, not a membership to be represented... [both imposed a] revolution from above.

[Stalin's actions were not merely] an expression of madness [but a deliberate program] with a logic that was consistent both politically and psychologically.

[Genocide of Jews and Gypsies was less rational because German] mass murder became not an instrument but an end in itself.

Alan Bullock *Hitler and Stalin: Parallel lives*
(New York: Knopf, 1992)

The Nazis believed in a life-and-death struggle of the German "master race" against the Jews, Slavs and Bolsheviks. The extermination of Polish, Soviet and other "eastern" Jews was a "practical step" in preparation of the eastern "living space" for colonization by the Germans. Eventually, the sick fantasies of the Nazi government in Berlin led it to its catastrophic mistake -- the invasion of the Soviet Union.

1. 1933-1939
The Prelude to German Mass Murders.

Jan. 30, 1933 Adolf Hitler, the legally appointed Chancellor of Germany, set out to change dramatically the world balance of power in order to achieve the final victory of the German race over all other races. German domination of the world was his ultimate goal. Hitler believed that the "ultimate Jewish goal" was also world domination and therefore he thought of the entire Jewry as Germany's competitor. Almost equally hateful to Hitler were the Slavs. Not only did they inhabit, in Poland and the Soviet Union, most of the areas of the planned German living space (Lebensraum), but the "Jewish-Bolsheviks" were the most important contenders for world supremacy.

The Nazi government in Berlin eventually declared both Jews and Slavs as "subhuman" races which must perish in order to bring about world domination by the German race.

The essence of the policies of the Nazi government at all times was the implementation of the doctrine of Lebensraum, or "German" living space. The aim of the Berlin government was to seize the lands inhabited by others, who were to be enslaved or exterminated and replaced by "racial Germans." These aims were to be realized by a series of wars. Each time Germany was to launch a quick, victorious campaign against a weaker, unprepared, and isolated enemy, whose resources were to help prepare the next war. This sequence was to lead to the conquest of the great agricultural lands of the Slavic two-thirds of Europe, and eventually to Germany's hegemony over the entire world. These lands, located mainly in the Soviet Union and Poland, were to become the German Lebensraum during Hitler's life time. The general Nazi-German plans were fixed, but the actual details and sequence were to be determined as the process of expansion was implemented. Hitler hoped that the German "Aryan" population would double under his rule, thanks to earlier marriages and larger families, while those with hereditary defects were to be sterilized. Eventually, the Berlin government kidnapped some one-half million blond children from occupied Poland to be brought up in Germany as "racial Germans."

The Jewish minority was considered to be the main enemy of internal German racial purity and an important focus for consolidation at home in preparation for expansion abroad. Hitler felt that the wars for German Lebensraum represented an inevitable life-and-death struggle between races for the "survival of the fittest." Hitler was willing to let Germany perish in his attempt to implement the doctrine of Lebensraum rather than to let her turn back and be "disgraced forever."

The doctrine of Lebensraum was first stated in 1848 in an all-German congress at Frankfurt. It is the modern version of the 1000-year-old German "push east to conquer Slavic lands," known as the *Drang nach dem Slavischen Osten*" or simply as the *Drang nach Osten*."

March 20, 1933 Heinrich Himmler obtained authorization from Heinrich Held, Minister-President of Bavaria, who held office for eight years under the Weimar Republic, to organize a model concentration camp in Dachau. Soon Himmler organized sub-camps in Oranienburg, Berlin, Papenburg, Esterwegen, Durrgoy, Kemna near Wuppertal, Sonnenburg, Sachsenburg, and Lichtenburg; in 1934 control of these camps was assigned to the SS-Wirtschaftsvervaltungshauptamt, the Economic and Administrative Headquarters of the SS. Initially, concentration camps were designed to terrorize the small and very weak political opposition to National Socialism which existed in Germany.

In 1933-1939 only 170,000 prisoners were incarcerated in all German concentration camps. Of this total the vast majority were convicted criminals and homosexuals. Thus, the actual number of political prisoners was insignificant. It was so small because of the extraordinary popularity of the Nazi government in Germany. On the other hand, in the same period millions were imprisoned and executed in the Soviet Union in order to keep the Communist party in power. Eventually, the German system of incarceration, slave labor, and extermination encompassed some 9,000 camps which processed 18,000,000 people, of whom 11,000,000 lost their lives. In the camps 8,900,000 people were processed by 1945. At least 7,200,000 or 81 percent died of exhaustion or by summary executions in the German-Nazi death machine.

The Germans organized urban ghettos for people they defined as Jews. Ghettos were a part of the German camp system. 5,100,000 Jews were exterminated by the Germans during World War II as estimated in 1946-1968 by the Main Commission for Investigation of German-Nazi Crimes in Poland and by researchers of the Jewish Historical Institute of Warsaw. By 1990 this estimate was somewhat changed. However, following the early estimates, the victims of the German genocide of the Jews included: 700,000 in Jewish ghettos, about 3,000,000 in extermination camps, and 1,400,000 at the site of arrest. Executions were conducted by firing squads of special forces of the SS, the "Einsatzgruppen der Sicherheitspolizei," German police, the regular German army (the Wehrmacht), and wartime German civilian authorities.

March 1933 "Four Power Pact" of Great Britain, Germany, France, and Italy was proposed by Benito Mussolini. It included provisions which would override the views of Poland and reassure the Berlin government which was convinced that Poland planned to take advantage of its military weakness and launch a preventive war in order to stop German rearmament and secure the Polish western border and Polish rights in Gdańsk-Danzig. Even though it was signed on July 15, 1933, Poland's opposition blocked the implementation of Mussolini's pact.

April 26, 1933 In Berlin, the last dispatch of departing British ambassador Sir Horace Rumbold: "...What Germany needs is an increase in territory in Europe...the new Germany must look for expansion in Russia...To wage war with Russia against the West would be criminal, especially as the aim of the Soviets [according to Hitler] is the triumph of international Judaism."

Jan. 26, 1934 Signing of a Declaration of non-aggression between Germany and Poland for ten years. The pact was advantageous to the Berlin government, because it safeguarded Germany from the danger of Poland launching a preventive war in response to German violations of the Treaty of Versailles. At the time Poland was the only country in Europe willing to enforce militarily the terms of the peace treaty. Poland was assured that Germany would stop her provocations against Polish rights in administration of the harbor of Gdańsk-Danzig and against Poland's western frontier.

This was only a temporary relaxation of German policy with regard to Poland. At the time, it was assumed that the non-aggression pact included secret clauses on Polish-German cooperation against the Soviet Union. Such secret clauses did not exist. When Hermann Goering visited Warsaw and made allusions to a joint attack on the Soviet Union, Marshal Joseph Piłsudski gave a negative answer and in May 1932 concluded an extension of the 1932 non-aggression pact with the USSR for a further ten years and did not oppose Soviet entry into the League of Nations any longer.

June 30, 1934 "The night of long knives" consisted of elimination by Chancellor Hitler of insubordinate individuals in Nazi Sturm-Abteilungen (SA). Hitler's elite body guards, the Sturm-Staffeln (SS) was converted into the most criminal of all organizations of the Nazi government. It was to be used for genocide of enemy races declared "sub-human" by the Berlin government.

June 1934 - Feb. 1938 Heinrich Himmler gradually gained control of the German army and police, both of which continued to be staffed with men appointed by the German Weimar Republic. Both of these branches of the government of Germany were to serve the Nazi regime during German aggression on Poland, and during World War II, which resulted from it. Meanwhile, racist prejudices continued to intensify in Germany. Immediately after the death of Germany's president, Paul von Hindenburg, on Aug. 2, 1934, Hitler combined in his own hands the office of president and chancellor as *Fuhrer und Reichskanzler*.

Anti-Semitism continued to be a powerful vote-catching force in Germany. Amid the growing popularity of the Nazi regime, the tiny opposition to Hitler was terrorized in Germany, and blackmail became the main tool of German diplomacy abroad in order to implement the doctrine of Lebensraum, conquer Europe, and achieve world domination.

Sept. 13, 1934 Poland declared that she would not cooperate with international organizations in matters covered by the treaty on national minorities as long as the said treaty was not binding on the Soviet Union and all other members of the League of Nations. (Poland's main minorities were Ukrainians, Byelorussians, Jews, and Germans.) Poland also opposed the French proposal of an Eastern Pact to guarantee the "status quo" in eastern Europe if the pact was rejected by Germany and exploited by USSR.

End of 1934 German military completed the process of turning the numerous "non-Aryan" officers out of the German army.

Jan. 1935 In Berlin publication of *Das Archiv*, a reference book for "Politics-Economics-Culture" including this statement: "If international finance-Jewry inside and outside Europe should succeed in throwing the nations into another World War, the result will not be the Bolshevisation of the earth and thus the victory of the Jewish race in Europe!"

June 29, 1935 In Berlin Joseph P. Goebbels (1895-1945), German minister for propaganda and national enlightenment, spoke during the celebration of the first "Gau Day" of the Berlin NSDAP. He ridiculed those who spoke of the Jew as a human being.

July 23, 1935 In Baden, Julius Streicher (1885-1946), the Gauleiter of Franconia, stated in a lecture at the Reichsschule Bernau to the Sudeten Germans that "without a solution to the Jewish question there can be no salvation for the German people...it is not sufficient to banish the Jews from Germany, they must be killed the world over in order that mankind will be free of them."

Sept. 13, 1935 In Berlin, Goebbels' speech was reported by *Voelkischer Beobachter*. It was on the ideological war between National Socialism and "Jewish-Bolshevism." It included a warning to the rest of the world -- in particular France and Czechoslovakia, which had concluded pacts with the Soviet Union in May 1935. Goebbels said that there could be no making of pacts "with the Jewish pest without ultimate self-infection...making still worse the fatal disease of this political criminality."

1935 Nuremberg Laws were passed by the German National Assembly (Reichstag) as a basic official document on German citizenship and the defense of German honor and blood. They deprived Jews of German citizenship and made the swastika Germany's official flag and symbol. Marriages and sexual relations with Jews were forbidden -- earlier marriages of Germans with Jews were declared legally null and void (in practice many mixed couples were forced to divorce; a number of women followed their Jewish husbands to "Jewish homes" called *Judenhausen*.) German women younger than 45 years of age were forbidden to work as domestic servants in Jewish homes.

1935 In Berlin Chancellor Adolf Hitler established astrology as an official science of the German state (Reichsfachschaft). In 1939 K.E. Kraft (1900-1944), a Swiss born astrologer, was appointed as the official German government astrologer to work on elaboration of plans for military operations. When Kraft's predictions offended the Nazis, he was arrested, and died in Buchenwald concentration camp. In 1942, after getting unsatisfactory predictions from other astrologers Hitler abolished the official science of astrology and declared it a "useless science." However, the Nazi government used in its propaganda the similarity of name "Hitler" and the word "Hister," which was mentioned in the predictions made by Nostradamus (1503-1566). Nazis claimed that Nostradamus predicted Hitler, when in reality Hister or Ister is the Latin name for the Danube River.

Polish ambassador to Germany, 1934-1939, Józef Lipski (1894-1958), reported that Hitler had spells of hallucinations, both during official receptions and while delivering public speeches. During these spells Hitler's bloodshot eyes would pop out, he would utter irrational words, and make strange gestures.

1936 Sachsenchausen concentration camp was established in Oranienburg near Berlin by the SS-WVHA (Wirtschaftsvervaltungshauptamt), the Main Office of Economy and Administration of the SS. The administrative headquarters in Oranienburg controlled all Nazi-German concentration camps from 1936 to 1945, and established camp districts around the main camps with sub-camps (Nebenlager of Aussenlager) and work detachments (Arbeitskommandos or Aussenkommandos).

Aug. 1936 In Obersalzburg Hitler's memorandum on the Four-Year Plan included clear statements about the coming war between the Soviet Union and Germany as well as the threat posed by world Jewry and its alleged commitment to Bolshevism. Hitler said: "It is Germany's duty to secure her own existence by every means in the face of this catastrophe...a victory of Bolshevism over Germany would...lead to the final destruction, indeed annihilation of the German people..." The Four-Year Plan was accompanied by systematic planning for expropriation and the complete "Aryanisation" of Jewish businesses and property.

End of 1936 Germany was becoming the dominant power on the European continent, while the Soviet Union, despite her huge mechanized armies, was weakened by the Great Purge at the time when the United States was preoccupied with the Great Depression and the New Deal.

National Socialist regime fully consolidated its hold on Germany, initiated rearmament, launched the Four-Year-Plan, remilitarized the Rhineland, created the Berlin-Rome Axis, and formed the Anti-Comintern Pact, which was signed by Germany and Japan on Nov. 25, 1936. Now the German government was determined to implement the expansion of Germany in fulfillment of the Doctrine of Lebensraum by means of war. The process of consolidation of National Socialist Germany was to continue until the end of World War II.

Joint intervention in the Spanish civil war of Italy and Germany was deliberately prolonged by the Berlin government in order to solidify the German-Italian Axis by preventing any deals between Italy and Great Britain and France.

Beginning of 1937 Despite great gaps in the German rearmament program, Germany was considered the most powerful country in Europe. By her head start, she intimidated other European states. At the time when most countries were struggling with the effects of the Great Depression, Germany created full employment and her own version of a welfare state for racial Germans. World mass media was filled with the success story of National Socialist Germany. Adolf Hitler was perceived by many as an incarnation of the German state. Germans saw him as a savior for Germany.

It was becoming obvious that the Versailles treaty potentially strengthened German power in Europe by leaving German industry intact to serve in the thirties as a base for the aggressive growth of German exports and general expansion of Germany's economy, busy with the rearmament program. Germany attracted foreign capital, including investments by American Jews. No one could imagine the catastrophe of war which Germany was about to impose on the world and the unbelievable atrocities soon to be committed by the Germans.

March 21, 1937 Papal condemnation of German racism and of the cult of Hitler, issued by Pope Pius XII, was read during the Masses of the Palm Sunday in Catholic Churches throughout Germany.

May 1937 Cardinal Mundelein lectured several hundred priests of the Chicago archdiocese, deploring the persecution of Catholicism in Germany, and referred to Hitler as the "Austrian wall-paper hanger." Berlin answered with a press campaign, diplomatic protests, and increased animosity towards the Vatican.

June 29, 1937 Hitler disregarded the warning by Canadian Prime Minister MacKenzie King not to underestimate the solidarity and cohesion of the British Commonwealth.

July 17, 1937 Buchenwald concentration camp was established.

July 29, 1937 J.P. Moffat, chief of the European division of the Department of State, recorded in his diary the warning to Great Britain by her dominions that if she wanted to preserve the bonds of the British Empire she should "make friends with (Germany) and if necessary buy her off in Eastern Europe." This warning was immediately reported to Berlin by the defense minister of South Africa, Oswald Pirow, an ardent National Socialist, thereby strengthening the German resolve to make war preparations.

Nov. 5, 1937 Hossbach Memorandum was written on the meeting between Hitler and political and military leaders on readiness for war in 1938 and on the search for the long term objective, the Lebensraum, for which the first moves were to be against Austria and Czechoslovakia. Moves against Poland and Russia were to come later.

Jan. - Feb. 1938 Chancellor Hitler disposed of the crisis in the army resulting from insubordination of Generals Fritsch and Blomberg and took the position of commander-in-chief of German armed forces and minister of war. He nomminated two obedient stooges totally lacking of moral judgment: Wilhelm Keitel as his chief of staff and Walther von Brauchitsch as the commander-in-chief of the German army. These actions crippled the German command and the work of the general staff. They laid the ground for eventual personal domination of German military strategy by Hitler, who was untrained and depended on his intuition.

Since 1936 German agents in France had succeeded in producing highly exaggerated estimates of German strength and brought about the despair of French political and military leaders. Controversies resulted between Polish and French governments because Poland used much lower and more realistic estimates of German strength based on Polish breaking of German code Enigma in 1932-33.

After signing a common defense treaty with them, Poland, on July 25, 1939, gave Great Britain and France each a copy of an electro-mechanical digital computer for deciphering the German code Enigma. It was a key element in the British "Project Ultra." Eventually, it became one of the most important Polish contributions to Allies' victory in World War II.

Jan. 5, 1938 In Berlin, Heinrich Himmler, Reichsfuerer-SS and Chief of the German Police, issued instructions for the expulsion of *Ostjuden*. The term "Ostjuden" meant eastern Jews, who originally inhabited the territories which belonged to Poland before the partitions.

The Ostjude became a cultural symbol in the development of German anti-Semitism. They were disliked by German Gentiles and Jews alike. By 1879 they already were perceived as "a horde of ambitious, pant-selling Jews whose children and grandchildren were the future controllers of Germany's press and stock exchange."

German Jews saw an Ostjude, in his caftan and side-locks, as a "typical east European ghetto Jew: physically filthy, medieval, un-emancipated, alien in appearance, manner, language, culture, and even in their religious extremes such as Hasidism."

Hitler felt that "nine-tenths of the Jews living in Germany had immigrated from the east during the last few decades. Although they arrived with nothing, today they possessed 4.6 times per head as much as their hosts..."

Himmler's instructions for expulsion dealt with the Ostjuden from Russia and with some 50,000 Ostjuden from Poland who had lived abroad for more than five years and were not recognized as Polish citizens any more and therefore were stateless and stranded in Germany.

March 11, 1938 Austria was annexed by Germany amid enthusiastic support of a large number of Austrian National Socialists and their followers. The Nazi government in Berlin proclaimed the *Anschluss*, or formal annexation, of Austria by Germany on March 15, 1938.

180,000 Jews in Vienna, mainly descendants of immigrants from southern Poland, were subjected to persecution. A new and important step in the career of Reinhard Heydrich (1904-1942) was the founding of the Office for Jewish Emigration with Karl Adolf Eichmann as its director.

This agency of the German government extorted all the possessions from about 100,000 Austrian Jews in return for exit visas. Eventually it was responsible for killing some four million people.

Sept. 26, 1938 Hitler stated that the Sudetenland was Germany's last territorial demand in Europe.

Sept. 30, 1938 In Munich, Germany, Great Britain, France, and Italy signed the annexation agreement giving Germany a fifth of Czechoslovakia's land, 800,000 Czechs, over 3,000,000 people of German descent, and most of Czech industry. Hungary annexed Czechoslovak Carpato-Ukraine. Poland occupied the Cieszyn (Tesin) district populated with over 200,000 Poles and including Bogumin (Bohumin). This was the largest railroad yard in Czechoslovakia, located in the strategic Moravian Gate. It was occupied in order to prevent its use during future German aggression against the Polish state. The Czechs took the Bogumin district away from Poland during the Polish-Soviet war of 1920. Poland, in 1938, was in position to take control of Slovakia and prevent its strategic use by the Germans in 1939, but did not do so.

Hitler was deeply disappointed with the Munich agreement because it "cheated him out of war and military victory."

Oct. 23, 1938 Hitler discussed highway and railroad construction across Polish Pomerania from Germany to East Prussia with Fritz Todt.

Oct. 24, 1938 German Foreign Minister von Ribbentrop demanded, in conversation with Polish Ambassador Lipski, that Poland turn over Gdańsk-Danzig to Germany, concede an extra-territorial road and railway across Gdańsk Pomerania, and join the Anti-Comintern Pact.

Poland was to be compensated with special rights in Danzig, a German guarantee of her western border, and an extension of the 1934 non-aggression pact with Germany.

Hitler approved anti-Jewish decrees to be adopted in Danzig in the immediate future despite concern of the administration of the Free City that these might lead to international complications, especially in relations with Poland. Hitler formally reaffirmed the status quo in Gdańsk less than a year earlier.

1938 Mathausen and Flossenburg concentration camps established.

1938-1945 There were, in German concentration camps, on the average, almost 100,000 German speaking internees -- enough to have an internal prison hierarchy made up of residents of Germany. Only a small minority of German internees were classified as political opponents of the Nazi government. The vast majority were criminals. German homosexuals were also incarcerated in concentration camps as "anti-social" elements.

Oct. 29, 1938 German police began driving 20,000 Polish citizens, mainly Jews, at gun point into the no-man's land between Germany and Poland, near the Polish town of Zbąszyń.

Oct. 25, 1938 - Jan. 27, 1939 A German diplomatic offensive against Poland was launched in Berlin in order to convert Poland into a satellite protectorate of Germany by means of:
1. Poland's agreement to the German annexation of the free city of Gdansk-Danzig, in which Germany would promise that it would respect "Polish rights and free access to the Baltic Sea."
2. Poland's acceptance of the German right-of-way for one highway and one railway through Gdańsk Pomerania to East Prussia.
3. Poland's participation with Germany in an anti-Soviet military alliance called the Anti-Comintern Pact, intended to attack the USSR, and create a new Germany, with its border in the Urals. (The German government did not mention in any way the nearly three and a half million Jews who were Polish citizens.) In return for Polish acceptance of German demands, Germany promised to extend the non-aggression pact with Poland for the next 25 years. The Polish government rejected German terms as unacceptable.

Nov. 9-10, 1938 The "Kristallnacht" orgy of destruction -- a massive wave of pogroms in Germany, burning of synagogues, looting of stores, and severe beating and mistreatment of thousands of Jews. It was described as a ritual of public degradation of German Jews. Shortly after the Kristallnacht Hitler told the foreign minister of South Africa, Oswald Pirow, that "one of these days the Jews will disappear from Europe," and that Germany had succeeded in exporting one idea, "not National Socialism -- but anti-Semitism."

Nov. 24, 1938 In Berlin Hitler made a statement on Jewish-Bolshevism: "World Jewry did not want the Jews to disappear from Europe but regarded the Jews in Europe as an outpost for the Bolshevizing of the World. The Jews hated [Hitler] because he had prevented the further Bolshevizing of Europe."

Jan. 21, 1939 Hitler told the Czechoslovak foreign minister, Frantisek Chvalkovski, that "the Jews will be annihilated in our homeland [Germany]. Not for nothing had the Jews made [the communist revolution on] the 9th of November 1918; this day would be avenged."

Jan. 30, 1939 In Berlin, in the Reichstag (German national parliament) Chancellor Hitler stated: "If the international Jewish money power in Europe and beyond again succeeds in enmeshing the peoples in a world war, the result will not be the Bolshevization of the world and a victory for Jewry, but the annihilation of the Jewish race in Europe." (This statement was dated Sept. 1, 1939, in the later editions of Hitler's speeches.)

Feb. 7, 1939 In Berlin, Alfred Rosenberg told foreign diplomats and the foreign press that the immigration restrictions of all countries of the world against German Jewish refugees must be lifted in order to "solve" the German-Jewish question. He also referred to mass migration of "millions of Jews from the whole of central and eastern Europe."

Immigration restrictions against German Jews, especially those imposed by the United States and Great Britain, convinced the German government that there was a very weak support in the world for Jewish victims of German persecution.

March 10, 1939 Stalin's speech to the 18th convention of the Soviet Communist Party was broadcast on Moscow radio. Stalin accused Great Britain and France of trying to foment German and Japanese attacks on the Soviet Union in order to dictate their conditions to the exhausted belligerent. Stalin then suggested a possibility of cooperation between National Socialist Germany and the Soviet Union. This offer came as a complete surprise to Berlin. It provided the Germans with the possibility of buying time by pretending to accept a permanent rapprochement with the Soviets.

Buying time was important for Germany because Poland defended her sovereignty and refused to join Germany against the Soviet Union. By doing so, Poland deprived the Berlin government of the 40 to 50 well trained Polish divisions. Polish forces could have made up the deficiency in German manpower and, together with 100 German divisions, would have been used in a decisive attack on Russia. The Soviet Union was the main target of the planned conquest of Slavic lands in order to create a new Germany "for the next 1000 years." When Poland refused to submit to either the German Nazis or the Soviets, the Berlin government started to gamble with a fake rapprochement with Moscow.

March 15, 1939 Firming up of British resolve not to allow a new Munich -- also a widespread conviction that the Poles definitely would fight for their independence and that Polish leaders would not consider submission to Germany as an acceptable alternative. At the same time the German public was all out to fight Poland but was scared to fight Great Britain and France. It remembered the defeat in the first world war. However, the extraordinary support of the German people for Hitler was growing. They placed him in position to make key decisions alone and they were ready to carry out those decisions without any reservations.

March 28, 1939 Poland's foreign minister, Józef Beck (1894-1944), stated in Warsaw that any change in the status of the free city of Gdańsk-Danzig would be an aggression against Poland. Commander-in-Chief of the Polish Army, Marshal Edward Śmigły-Rydz (1886-1941), ordered mobilization in Poland.

March 31, 1939 British Prime Minister Neville Chamberlain (1869-1940) stated in Parliament in London, after consultation with French Prime Minister Edouard Daladier (1884-1970), that Great Britain and France would fight on the side of Poland if the Polish government could be driven to use its armed forces to defend its independence or its vital interests.

April 6, 1939 Common defense treaty was signed in London by Great Britain, France, and Poland.

April 11, 1939 In Berlin Chancellor Hitler signed the White Plan *Fall Weiss* ordering preparations for a German attack on Poland on Sept. 1, 1939.

April 28, 1939 Germany declared its non-aggression pact with Poland null and void, after assurances of the Soviet ambassador in Berlin on April 17, 1939, that "there is no reason why the relations between Soviet Union and Germany could not keep on improving very much."

May 5, 1939 Poland rejected the German demand for a right-of-way through Polish Pomerania to East Prussia and the annexation of the free city of Gdańsk-Danzig, as a prelude to conversion of Poland into a German protectorate, and subordination of the Polish armed forces to Germany within an anti-Soviet military pact. Poland's foreign minister, Józef Beck, stated that "the Poles will not accept peace at any price." Beck hoped that the German government would realize that an attack on Poland would lead to World War II, and eventual German defeat.

Marshal Śmigły-Rydz felt that a Soviet attack on Poland was a strong possibility if a war was started by Germany. Polish mobilization eventually included 1,500,000 men of which 1,200,000 reached their units, and 900,000 eventually took part in the defensive battle of Poland in Sept.-Oct. 1939. The combat units of the Polish army included about 25,000 Jews. Each year only 40 percent of available men were drafted and the quota was filled primarily with ethnic Poles. This policy aimed at economizing on the costs of feeding the soldiers in order to spend more on modernization of equipment, such as conversion of cavalry into armored brigades. Jews represented about 5 percent of all officers and much less among the ranks, because of relatively poor condition of their health as well as language and cultural differences. Language difficulties of the potential Jewish recruits stemmed from the fact that most spoke Yiddish as their first language and very few spoke Polish at home.

Aug. 14, 1939 The USSR demanded a permission for the Red Army to enter Poland and Romania. Poland rejected the Soviet demand. Such a permission would lead to partition of Poland by Germany and the USSR as there was no guarantee that the Red Army would fight against German aggression on the side of the Poles.

Aug. 17, 1939 German Admiral Canaris formed the K-force, recruited from people classified as "racial Germans" living in Poland, to attempt to secure industrial installations and bridges before Polish soldiers could execute their orders to blow them up.

Aug. 20, 1939 Public announcement of agreement by Germany and Soviet Union to sign a long-term trade treaty.

Aug. 22, 1939 Public announcement of next-day arrival in Moscow of German foreign minister to sign a nonaggression pact with Soviet Union. The pact was to encourage a German attack on Poland and therefore it did not include the clause used in all previous nonaggression pacts signed by Soviet Union, which stated that the treaty would be invalid if either party attacked a third power.

The Soviets were soon to participate in the (fourth) partition of Poland and hoped for a long war of attrition on Germany's western front, as Great Britain and France would declare war on Germany in fulfillment of their common-defense treaty with Poland. The Soviet Union would stay out of the conflict while capitalist nations of Europe would fight among themselves.

The pact with Germany was strengthening the Soviet position in negotiations for conclusion of the armistice with Japan and for ending the military confrontation, which Japan started in 1938. The Soviets were anxious to deflect Japanese expansionism from themselves towards the colonial empires of Great Britain and France as well as against the United States. The Japanese, who signed, with the Germans, the Anti-Cominform Pact in Nov. 1936, now felt betrayed by Germany. Thus, Stalin felt that Berlin was willing to pay a good price for Soviet cooperation without which Germans this time might not go to war at all.

The Soviets were anxious to get Germany entangled into a war of attrition as soon as possible. Moscow was aware that the Germans were discouraged by simultaneous difficulties with the Japanese because of the conflicting German ties to both China and Japan. Stalin's disastrous miscalculation became apparent with the collapse of France in 1940, which freed the Germans to implement the doctrine of Lebensraum and attack the Soviet Union under particularly dangerous conditions.

Aug. 22, 1939 In a secret speech Hitler referred to the imminent conquest and colonization of Poland and ordered his military commanders to use the utmost ferocity against both Polish armed forces and Polish civilians. Hitler's orders issued at this crucial moment a in world history had nothing whatever to do with the extermination of the Jews.

Aug. 23, 1939 Signing of German-Soviet Non-agression Pact for the purpose of implementation of the planned conquest and colonization of Poland.

Aug. 25, 1939 In response to the German-Soviet pact of Aug. 23, the government of Great Britain clarified and confirmed its commitment to the treaty of common defense with Poland and the inviolability of Polish borders.

Aug. 31, 1939 In Gleiwitz (Gliwice), Operation Himmler by General SS Reinhard Heydrich (1904-1942). The body of a prisoner from a concentration camp, dressed in a Polish army uniform, was delivered as "canned goods" to a local radio station seized by the Gestapo. A short message in Polish was broadcast as "proof" of "Polish aggression." The Polish uniform for Operation Himmler was requested by Admiral Canaris on Aug. 10, 1939, from the German High Command.

Operation Himmler was a classical example of German tactics during the implementation of their doctrine of Lebensraum. German strategists believed that the assassination of Archduke Francis F. Habsburg in Sarajevo had led to World War I too late. Generally, they felt that an earlier start would have improved German chances. Hitler expressed this view in *Mein Kampf* and in a speech on June 26, 1944. For this reason Germany would first decide when to attack and then be in control of incidents that would provide a pretext for military action at a convenient time. Thus, the Sudeten German thugs were organized earlier into a Free Corps and assigned fixed quotas of border provocations. Now, finally, Hitler was getting his war.

2. Fall 1939 - Winter 1941
High Tide of German Conquests in Europe.
German aggression resulted in a complete destruction of the power basis for the control of the globe by Europeans which Germany began with the First World War.

In reality from 1941 Germany was short of 1,000,000 men per year for the rest of the war. A severe problem for German armaments was inadequate transportation. Germany had too few personnel carriers, so that her infantry could not keep up with tanks. Also, most German transport had to be based on horses, which perished in World War II in greater numbers than ever before in history.

Manpower shortage resulted in massive use of slave labor imported to Germany from occupied lands, especially from Poland and the USSR. These people were permanently prohibited from cultural Germanization and were destined for slave labor and eventual extermination.

Hitler was supported by the Germans as a man of destiny and an incarnation of Germany. He himself believed in this preposterous notion and repeatedly stated that he preferred to go to war in 1939 when he was fifty, rather than later, when he was less vigorous, at fifty-five or sixty. Warnings about the risks of a world war by several leaders of the German military-industrial complex served to reinforce Hitler's belief in his role as the only leader in German history who, thanks to almost total public support, could lead Germany to start a global war for Lebensraum and world supremacy by the German race. Germany was about to bring a tragic end to the European phase of Jewish history, when the vast majority of all Jews lived in Europe.

The Jewish population of 8,700,000 was trapped under the control of the Berlin government. At least 60 percent (or about 5,100,000) were exterminated by the Germans during World War II. The second world war was not fought to save the Jews.

"World Jewry," that supposedly powerful international force considered to be the most dangerous enemy by Nazi Germany, stood nakedly exposed in its true defenselessness. Meanwhile a general retreat from the perception of the Jews as a nation occurred in the West. This happened despite the fact that the Jewish people were persecuted as Jews and not as Poles or other nationalities.

Sept. 1, 1939 World War II started with the German attack on Poland. Mass killings of over six million Polish citizens -- almost half of them Jews -- began. During the first years of war the rate of German murder of Poles was much higher than that of the Jews.

Sept. 5, 1939 The German army (the Wehrmacht) conducted mass murders of 20,000 Poles in Bydgoszcz in Gdańsk Pomerania, where by 1945 over 50,000 Polish Catholics had been killed. In western Polish provinces the Germans started executing Poles immediately, using lists prepared well in advance of their attack on Poland.

With the events in Bydgoszcz the Germans initiated a new and total type of modern warfare. It took the form of a wholesale slaughter of the Polish civilian population, and especially the cultural elite, long before German genocide of European Jews began on a massive scale.

Sept. 7, 1939 In Limanowa, near Kraków, nine Jews were executed by the Germans together with a Catholic mailman, Jan Semik, who tried to stop their execution.

Sept. 1939 False dating of the gassing of about 70,000 mentally handicapped Germans in the name of "social hygiene." German propaganda pretended that it began while the first battles of World War II were raging in Poland. In fact the gassing occurred in October 1939. German political decisions and military operations were out of step with the production of weapons. The leadership of the German military-industrial complex estimated that the German arsenal would only have been ready for a quick and decisive victory in a world war if the conflict had started in 1944 or 1945.

Polish resistance derailed the Nazi agenda and Poland's army destroyed about one-third of the attacking German tanks and one-fourth of the Luftwaffe.

Sept. 15, 1939 An armistice was signed between the Soviet Union and Japan. It was followed the next day by the Soviet government's order to the Red Army to attack Poland.

Sept. 17, 1939 The Soviet Union invaded Poland using "hyena" tactics, stabbing the Polish army in the back. At the same time the tempo of the German offensive markedly slowed down.

The Germans were running out of ammunition, their cracked units were decimated and exhausted, while they lost about one-third of all tanks used in the invasion of Poland. The Poles still had some 26 full strength divisions and were locked in twentyfive major battles,

which were not going well for the Germans. Had the Red Army not invaded Poland at that time, the Polish-German war could have dragged on for several more weeks, as the Polish defense lines became shorter and the German striking capability was weakening.

The fall 1939 campaign of the fourth partition of Poland and with it the outbreak of the Second World War was made possible by the Ribbentrop-Molotov pacts of Aug. 23 and Sept. 28, 1939. These pacts included secret protocols on the partition of Poland, joint action against Polish resistance and extermination of the Polish leadership community. Eventually, the Soviets captured nearly three hundred thousand Polish soldiers.

A very visible part of the Jewish and Byelorussian population in eastern Poland received the Soviets with triumphal arches, flowers, and symbolic gifts of bread and salt, trying to ally themselves with the invaders. Before long, many were collaborating in NKVD arrests, deportations, and the killings of Polish officials, political and cultural leaders, business people, and their families. A Jewish lawyer from Lvov observed: "When there was a political meeting, parade, or any other happy occasion the visual impression was always the same... the Jews [were most visible]."

Anti-Semitism grew enormously under Soviet occupation. Poles heard derisive slogans: "You wanted Poland without Jews. Now you have Jews without Poland." A paradoxical situation developed. Jews started feeling themselves the first class citizens, while the Soviets in a short time abolished all Jewish communal institutions and destroyed the rich cultural heritage of the Jews in eastern Poland. Jewish religious schools were closed, teaching of the Hebrew language was forbidden, Zionist movement and youth organizations were declared illegal, Jewish political parties were liquidated, and members of the traditional Jewish leadership community were arrested.

The Soviets deprived the Jews of eastern Poland of their ethnic and cultural identity while they made the Jewish people feel more equal than others in their access to government jobs, universities, professions, etc. However, anyone, whether Jew or Christian, who lived comfortably before the war, was automatically considered by the Soviets to be an enemy of the Soviet Union.

Before long, many Jewish refugees from central and western Poland decided to go back home, now under the German occupation. Thousands lined up in front of the German-Soviet Population Exchange commissions. A German officer told the waiting crowd: "Jews! where are you going? Don't you see that we are going to kill you?" Few paid attention. When German commissions arrived in Lvov, Vlodimir and Brest, crowds of Jewish refugees asked for permission to return home under German occupation. Thousands of them shouted "Long live Hitler."

In reality very few Jews were permitted to go west. Instead their registration lists were used by the NKVD to deport them east.

The Soviets immediately enforced a two-fold policy, which consisted of systematic extermination of class enemies accompanied by a massive recruitment of collaborators. Social outcasts and criminals, even convicted murderers, were organized into a new police force on the theory that convicts from Polish prisons were more trustworthy to the Soviets than people who had no criminal record.

Sovietization of occupied Poland was the main aim of the Soviets and according to it they conducted their extermination and exploitation programs. Soviet use of universal socialist slogans helped them to penetrate society much more effectively than could the primitive ethnocentric German propaganda. For this reason, from the beginning it was much harder to organize an effective resistance movement against the Soviets than against the German occupation.

The Soviets were by far more systematic and thorough than the Germans in collecting detailed information on each individual in the newly occupied territory. The Soviets wanted to evaluate everyone's potential to be a loyal and obedient Soviet citizen.

An immediate equalization of the value of Soviet rubles with Polish currency resulted in the wholesale robbery of goods in the hands of Polish citizens and institutions. Hospitals, electric power plants, power lines, apartments, private homes and businesses were stripped and their contents shipped to the Soviet Union by trucks and by railroad. Poland, with her relatively low standard of living, in comparison with western Europe, appeared to the newly arriving Soviet people, to be an extraordinary land of plenty.

Sept. 21, 1939 Reinhard Heydrich, the head of German National Security Office (which united the German state and party police) officially stated the policy of the German government towards the Jews in occupied Poland long before the military campaign was over. He ordered commanders of operational groups of German security police (*Sicherheitpolizei*) to distinguish between "the final solution of the Jewish problem (which required longer time) and a number of necessary stages (which must be conducted during short periods of time) leading to the final solution... The planned operations were to be kept secret."

Heydrich gave orders to concentrate the Jews and isolate them from the Poles in newly created ghettos, each administered by a Jewish council called *Judenrat*. Each local Jewish council was to be "fully responsible... for precise and timely execution of all orders [given by the German authorities]" and for all matters related to the very existence of the population in their communities. Jews were to wear bands displaying the Star of David. Jews 14 to 60 years old were to be used as a slave labor force. The Jewish militia was to enforce German policies towards the Jews in each ghetto.

In order to facilitate the creation of ghettos and confuse the Jews, Heydrich formulated a vicious ruse. He started a campaign to establish the notion that Jews must seek German protection against persecution by the Polish population. Jewish councils of the major ghettos were to prepare detailed reports showing the need for German protection for Jewish lives and properties. These reports were presented in March 1940 to the German occupational authorities in Cracow. Meanwhile German agents-provocateur were to stage anti-Semitic incidents, such as rock throwing by racial Germans residing in Poland.

The reports prepared by the Jewish councils were actually used to help formulate German programs for confiscation of the property of the Jews in occupied Poland. They also provided the Germans with a record of wealthy Jews.

Jewish ghetto police were to arrest non-Jews who made purchases in stores exclusively designated for the Jews. Arrested Polish gentiles were to be turned over to the Germans for execution. (A number of such executions actually took place.) This procedure was designed to ruin relations between Jews and gentiles in occupied Poland.

General Reinhard Heydrich was allegedly of Jewish blood and therefore could be blackmailed by other leaders of the German-Nazi government. Both Hitler and Himmler knew this.

Hitler was very sensitive to matters of Jewish ancestry because his own father, born out of wedlock, under the name of Alois Schicklgruber, allegedly had an Jewish father.

Eventually, as expected and intended by Hitler and Himmler, Heydrich conducted the program of annihilation of the Jews with a vengeance, when he was made to assume the guilt for German genocide of the Jews and in turn made the Jews their own executioners in ghettos and death camps.

Heydrich's, and possibly Hitler's, hatred for their own Jewish blood was a product of the racist German society in which they grew up. To deal with the Jewish problem and eventually plan and enforce the "Final Solution," Heydrich selected others, whom he believed to have this "pathological Jewish self-hate," such as Globocnik, Eichmann, Knochen, Dannecker, etc.

Sept. 28, 1939 Conclusion of the Boundary and Friendship Treaty between governments of Germany and the Soviet Union included an agreement on a common program to exterminate Poland's intellectual elite and leadership community.

The treaty contained secret provisions for a coordinated program for the mutual extermination of potential Polish opponents of both regimes. Germany and the Soviet Union were to take all necessary measures to contain and prevent any hostile action directed against the territory of the other partner. They committed themselves to crush any agitation within their part of occupied Poland and inform each other of means employed to achieve this goal.

A joint Soviet-German victory parade took place in Brześć (Brest) on the Bug. Beginning of close cooperation of German Gestapo with the Soviet NKVD. Zakopane and Cracow were selected and used until June 1941 as meeting places to coordinate German and Soviet extermination programs directed against Poles.

Terror campaigns and mass murders of the Polish population by the Germans were to continue until 1945, and by the Soviets and their henchmen until 1956.

Oct. 3, 1939 In Berlin German government appealed for peace to the Great Britain and France. The appeal was rejected on October 5.

Oct. 3, 1939 In Moscow, in fulfillment of the secret provision of the German-Soviet Boundary and Friendship Treaty, the head of NKVD,

Lavrenti Beria, started to prepare the largest execution of prisoners of war during the Second World War. For this purpose Beria ordered the selection of officers from the quarter of a million Polish prisoners of war in Soviet hands. He issued order no. 4441/b on handling of Polish prisoners of war:

"Until special orders are issued the camp in Kozielsk is to contain prisoners of war who were born in the area of German occupation of Poland.

"The camp in Starobielsk is to contain Polish army generals, officers, high ranking administrative officers, both military and state. The camp in Ostashkov is to contain officers of Polish intelligence, counter-intelligence, prison administration and police officers...

"The commandants of all NKVD prisoner-of-war camps are to check thoroughly the identity of each individual prisoner. The selection process is to be completed by Oct. 8, 1939..."

Each of the thousands of selected Polish officers was presented with a self-incriminating questionnaire which was to document that the Poles were enemies of the Soviet state. Each man was individually interrogated by NKVD officers and each individual dossier was to be presented to the highest NKVD (Troyka) court appointed and instructed by the Politburo to issue death sentences. 21,857 Polish officers held in Soviet prisons were then sentenced to death in absentia, without any attorneys present during the NKVD court proceedings. The paragraph 58 of the penal code of the Soviet Socialist Federated Russian Republic, which dealt with the enemies of the Soviet state, was used as the "legal basis" for the largest execution of prisoners-of-war during World War II, which the NKVD committed on the Polish officers. In accordance with the German-Soviet Boundary Treaty of Sept. 28, 1939, Soviet authorities informed the German government about the execution of their Polish enemies.

Oct. 1939 The first ghetto was established in occupied Poland at Piotrków. All Jewish men between 14 and 60 years of age were compelled to register for work. By the end of 1939 there were 85 Jewish labor camps in German-occupied Poland.

Oct. 30, 1939 The SS-Reichsfuhrer Heinrich Himmler ordered deportation of hundreds of thousands of Poles and Jews from Polish provinces newly annexed by Germany in 1939, into the "General Gouvernement" formed in central Poland, which then had a population of 11,800,000, including 1,500,000 Jews. The only Jewish people not expelled from the annexed Polish provinces were the Jews of Łódź -- a city renamed "Litzmannstadt" by the Germans. The deportations were conducted with utmost severity during four winter months 1939/40 by railroad, in unheated cattle cars. Many people died of exposure and hunger during these deportations which were directed mainly to central Polish regions of Lublin, Kielce, and Kraków.

Oct. 31, 1939, Public proclamation of the death penalty for insubordination to German rule. Countless executions of Poles by German firing squads took place throughout occupied Poland.

Oct. 31, 1939 In Moscow, Vyacheslav M. Molotov (Skryabin, 1890-1982), Commissar of Foreign Affairs, admitted openly in his speech to the Supreme Soviet that the military defeat of Poland was brought about by the attacks of German and Soviet armies.

Nov. 1939 In Lublin, Odilo Globocnik was nominated head of the local SS and police with orders to prepare a "reserve" for expelled Jews.

Nov. 22, 1939 Germans executed 53 Jews who lived at 9 Nalewki Street in Warsaw and made a public announcement of the execution in Warsaw and in Kraków, in order to terrorize the Jews into subordination to German orders. However, the Jewish population interpreted the restriction of their movements by the Germans as part of a slave labor control program and not as a prelude to mass murders.

Dec. 7, 1939 The beginning of mass executions of Poles from Warsaw in the Kampinos Forest, near Palmiry. The fact that at the beginning of World War II Germans executed very large numbers of Polish Catholics and did not conduct mass executions of the Jewish population misled the Jews into believing that they were not threatened with genocide.

German propaganda was very successful in spreading the false notion that Poland and the Poles caused Jewish suffering. The early conviction of the Jews that they were relatively safe was based on the fact that Germans and Soviets concluded an anti-Polish alliance for the purpose of the destruction of the Polish state

and extermination of the Polish population. When the Germans and the Soviets were executing this plan, primarily the Poles, and not the Jews, were the victims of their genocide.

In the eastern part of occupied Poland thousands of Jews were employed by the Soviets in their massive program of incarceration, deportation, and execution of Polish citizens. Among the deportees 52 percent were Poles, 30 percent were Jews and 18 percent were Ukrainians and Byelorussians.

Dec. 19, 1939 In Cracow, German Governor Hans Frank wrote in his diary: "Jews represent for us extraordinarily malignant gluttons" who will be "extirpated."

Jan. 1940 Germans began to set up forced labor camps for Jews, where their sadistic practices caused many deaths. However, the Jewish population did not expect extermination as a whole since the Germans concentrated on executing members of the Polish elite.

Jan. 14, 1940 in Warsaw the first execution of a Catholic Pole, Maria Brodacka, for sheltering a Jew. In her apartment the Germans found the broken shackles of Andrzej Kott, a prison escapee who was classified as a Jew. Kott's resistance activities provided the Germans with the pretext to kill about 100 Jewish intellectuals taken as hostages.

In the next 105 cases, when the Germans established that help was given to individual Jews by Polish Catholics, 333 Poles were executed. A typical ratio was established: for hiding one Jew, three Poles were murdered by the Germans. Thus, it was determined that during the early war years, in 90 localities in central Poland, 1,335 Poles were executed for giving shelter to the Jews.

Jan. 25, 1940 SS-Reichsfuhrer Heinrich Himmler selected Auschwitz, in southwestern Poland (newly annexed by Germany), as the site for a new concentration camp for Poles. During World War II, German concentration camps became sites for mass extermination of prisoners, either gradually by hard work on a starvation diet, or immediately by execution by gassing or shooting.

Auschwitz originally was designed for the extermination of Poles and other Slavs at a rate of 5,000,000 per year. It was a major railroad junction centrally located in German-controlled

Europe. It also was in proximity to major coal fields. Coal was a convenient fuel for the cremation of large number of bodies.

Feb. 1940 Litzmannstadt Ghetto was established in Łódź, the second largest Jewish community in Poland. By the end of April 1940, 165,000 Jews were sealed there, crowded in only four sq. km.

Feb. 10, 1940 Deportation from the annexed Polish provinces to the Soviet Union of 220,000 former Polish officials and their families, to be followed on April 13, 1940, by deportation of 325,000 relatives of previously deported men, to be followed in June 1940, by deportation of 300,000 and then in June-July by deportation of 240,000 war refugees from western Poland.

Soviet deportation, internment, and resettlement programs during the Second World War involved an estimated two million Polish citizens. Among 1,140,000 civilian deportees taken from areas annexed by the Soviets, there were: 703,000 Poles, 217,000 Ukrainians, 83,-000 Jews, 56,000 Byelorussians, 35,000 Polesians, and 20,000 Russians and Lithuanians; of the 336,000 Polish citizens, refugees from German occupied central and western Poland, 198,-000 were classified by the Soviets as Jews and the remaining 138,000 as Poles.

Soviet authorities also deported about 210,000 Polish citizens in 1940-1941 after declaring them citizens of the USSR and drafting them into the Red Army. 250,000 Polish citizens were arrested individually in 1939-1941 and deported to prisons and labor camps in the Soviet Union, which then contained a total of 440,000 Polish citizens. About 240,000 deportees were children below fourteen years of age.

The Soviets acknowledged taking 181,000 Polish prisoners of war in 1939 and in 1940 deporting an additional 12,000 Polish prisoners of war who had been interned since 1939 in Lithuania -- these figures are considered too low and the actual number of Polish prisoners of war deported to the USSR is estimated to be close to 300,000. Additional tens of thousands of Poles were arrested and deported to the Soviet Union in 1944. In 1945, 9877 Polish coal miners were deported from Silesia to USSR.

Of the earlier deportations the number of Jews was estimated at up to 30 percent. Some of the deported Jews considered themselves to be of Polish nationality and some of Jewish --

all Jews were registered by the Soviets as being of Jewish nationality.

It is estimated that by October 1, 1942, about 900,000 of the deportees, including 50,-000 children, were dead. Over 2,500 books, publications, and articles were printed in Poland and abroad after the war on the subject of deportations of Polish citizens to the Soviet Union during 1939-1945.

Feb. 12, 1940 Himmler planned to resettle 30,000 racial Germans from the Lublin province in Germany in order to make room for Jews and 30,000 German Gypsies. Trains with frozen corpses of Jewish children infected with typhus arrived at villages in the Lublinland.

Feb. 12, 1940 headquarters of the NKVD started to prepare the liquidation of three prisoner of war camps in Kozielsk, Ostashkov, and Starobielsk following Stalin's decision to comply with the joint German-Soviet program of Sept. 28, 1939, to liquidate the Polish resistance, intellectual elite, and leadership community. The liquidation of Polish officers was the largest execution of POWs during World War II.

March 5, 1940 In Moscow Stalin and all members of the Central Committee of the Communist Party of the USSR signed an order to execute 21,857 Poles listed by Beria. Top NKVD officers were nominated to the Troyka court.

By June 6, 1940, the execution of 21,857 Polish officers (mostly reservists and college graduates) was reported by the NKVD as completed. The victims, were captured by the Soviets in the fall of 1939, together with about three hundred thousand Polish soldiers (including some 50,000 men captured later in Lithuania).

The Soviet report for the first quarter of 1940 by Major P. Soprunienko, the chief of NKVD administration of POW camps, listed imprisoned officers of Polish armed forces: one admiral, 12 generals, 82 colonels, 200 lieutenant colonels, 555 majors, 1507 captains, 13 navy captains, 2 commodores, 3 lieutenant commodores, 6049 lieutenants, second lieutenants, and ensigns. (Intelligence, police, and administrative officers were not included.)

Some 4421 officers from the camp in Kozielsk were murdered. They were buried in Katyń forest on the upper Dnieper River between March 1 and May 3, 1940, under the supervision of the regional command of NKVD in

Mińsk, Byelorussia. The 190th infantry regiment provided security for the execution at Katyń (near the NKVD rest home). About 200 of the victims buried in Katyń graves were Jews, including the chief rabbi of the Polish army, Major Baruch Steinberg (1897-1940). Other rabbis, together with many Catholic priests and a few Lutheran pastors were among the chaplains of the Polish armed forces executed.

Katyń became a symbol of the execution of the 21,857 captive Poles (including about 700 Jews) when at the end of February 1943 the 537th German Signal Regiment reported finding mass graves of Polish officers.

The evidence, in the form of diaries and Red Cross and other forensic medicine reports, indicates that the victims were transported and executed at Katyń in the following manner:

1. Polish officers and prisoners of war were searched and then driven in vans from the camp at Kozielsk to a railroad station. All of a sudden they realized that their new guards were grim and very brutal men.
2. The prisoners were loaded into a special prison train. Each prison car, called *Stolypinka* (after tsarist minister of interior and head of government Piotr A. Stolypin), was divided into compartments for six to eight people. These compartments were crowded with up to sixteen Polish officers.
3. The prisoners spent one or two nights in the prison train.
4. Hungry and dehydrated, the prisoners arrived at the Gniezdovo railroad station.
5. The prisoners were gradually transferred to a small bus with its windows painted over. During the transfer the Gniezdovo station was encircled by a large number of NKVD soldiers.
6. In groups of thirty, Polish officers were made to file through the rear door of the bus, passing between NKVD soldiers standing with bayonets on the ready.
7. Each man was pressed into a small and very tight cubicle. (There were 15 cubicles on each side of a central corridor of the bus. It was returning to the train at half hour intervals.)
8. Hunched in a cramped position and suffering physical discomfort, the victims, in batches of thirty, were driven to the grave site at Katyń.
9. Upon arrival, one at a time, the victims were taken out of the cubicles. One NKVD man opened the cubicle door so that the door would divide him from the prisoner. The prisoner was directed towards the rear door of the bus.

10. At the door two NKVD men grabbed each prisoner by his arms. They quickly determined whether to tie his hands and put a choke knot on his neck or whether just to control him with the grip of their own hands while leading him directly to the nearby grave. Polish officers who were still strong enough to struggle were attacked by additional NKVD men. A number suffered crushed skulls, some had their overcoats tied around their heads, some were gagged by stuffing sawdust into their mouths. A number had their elbows tied tightly together behind their backs. Many were stabbed with four-cornered Soviet bayonets. All rope used by the NKVD at Katyń was manufactured in the Soviet Union and pre-cut to the same length. It was secured with metal clasps while the victim was held down. Some of the victims were searched and robbed.
11. At the grave site each victim was held by two NKVD men for execution by shooting from the back at the base of his skull to produce minimum bleeding. The exit holes of most of the bullets were in the forehead of the victims. A vast majority of NKVD executioners were armed with German "Walther" 7.65 millimeter pistols and used German ammunition manufactured by Geco. A small number of 6.35 millimeter shells, made by the same German manufacturer, were also found at Katyń.
12. Some of the victims were stacked in layers inside a large L shaped grave. Others were thrown in a disorderly fashion into a ditch.
13. Bodies of the victims were covered with dirt. Pine trees were planted on the mass graves.

Polish officers imprisoned in the camps of Starobielsk and Ostashkov were executed inside special NKVD buildings, within special enclosures equipped with floor gutters for draining the blood. Polish prisoners wore their uniforms during the execution. The usual NKVD procedure was to execute naked prisoners after prison clothing was taken away from them. Generally, the victims were shackled for the execution and positioned over the blood gutter. They were then shot in the back of the head.

The mass murder of the 3820 Polish officers held in Starobielsk was conducted under the supervision of the regional command of NKVD in Kharkov, Ukraine. The 68th Ukrainian infantry regiment provided security for the execution of Polish prisoners of war there. Officers from the camp of Starobielsk were murdered in Kharkov prison and buried near the village of

Piatikhatki. Multiple wounds were inflicted at the grave side. Many skulls were penetrated by several bullets. Some had bullet wounds in the legs and in the other parts of the body as a result of a last minute struggle. The graves at Piatikhatki appear to have been dug and later covered by hands.

Today, the mass graves of Polish officers imprisoned in Starobielsk are within the 6th quadrant of parks and woods encircling the city of Kharkov, some 8 kilometers from the center.

The Ostashkov camp was actually located on the nearby lake island of Stolbnyj. The mass murder of 6311 Polish officers held there was conducted in Kalinin in the NKVD building (which now houses a medical academy). The 129th infantry regiment based in Vyelke Luki provided security for the execution in Kalinin under the regional command of the NKVD in Smoleńsk. The bodies of Polish officers were transported to Myednoye near the railroad station of Bologoye (near Kalinin, now Tver, 90 miles north of Moscow, on the Moscow-Leningrad highway). The NKVD built its resort in Myednoye and placed the watchman's house and a latrine at the grave site. The rest of the grave site was covered with pine growth.

Deputy Minister of the Interior and a member of the Central Committee of the Communist party of USSR, Vsevolod Nikolayevich Merkulov was in charge of the entire operation of murdering Polish officers described above. He also signed the death sentence for each of the 21,857 selected Polish prisoners. Other Troyka Court members were the Head of the First Special Section of the NKVD, Bashtakov and another top echelon NKVD-man, Kabulov.

On April 13, 1990 the president of the USSR, Mikhail Gorbachev, officially admitted Soviet guilt in the mass murder of the 21,857 captured Poles. The actual order signed by Stalin and other members of the Central Committee was made public by the Russian President, Boris Yeltsin, in October 1992.

April 1940 Closing by the Germans of the Jewish ghetto in Łódź (renamed "Litzmannstadt" and located on land recently annexed by Germany). The ghetto was surrounded with barbed wire and watched by German guards, spaced 50 to 100 yards apart. Any person attempting to cross the fence was shot without warning. It was almost impossible to smuggle supplies into the Łódź Ghetto. Of the 48,102 rooms assigned to 160,000 Jews, only 382 had indoor plumbing. 90 percent of Jewish inmates, including children over ten years of age, were employed in workshops as virtually free labor. Many inmates were very well trained and experienced craftsmen and technicians. The Łódź Ghetto had a large number of professional, business, and cultural leaders from Poland, Germany, Austria, and Czechoslovakia. The Jewish Council in Łódź was dominated by a former Zionist politician, Mordechaj Chaim Rumkowski (1877-1944).

From 1940 to 1944 starvation and disease caused the deaths of 43,411 people in the Łódź Ghetto. By mid-01944 there were 68,000 Jews there. In 1941-1942 alone 70,000 Jews, classified by Rumkowski as not fit for work, were sent from Łódź to gas chambers, mainly to the death camp in Kulmhof on the Ner.

April 21, 1940 In London, Reginald Leeper, Asst. Under-Secretary at the Foreign Office, received with skepticism an account by two Jewish refugees of conditions in German-occupied Poland. He commented: "As a general rule Jews are inclined to magnify their persecutions. I remember the exaggerated stories of Jewish pogroms in Poland after the last war which, when fully examined, were found to have little substance."

April 27, 1940 In London, Sir John Shuckburgh, Deputy Under-Secretary at the Colonial Office wrote of Jews: "I am convinced that in their hearts they hate us and have always hated us; they hate all Gentiles..."

April 29, 1940 An ex-convict, SS-Sturmbannfuhrer Rudolf Hoess arrived in Auschwitz to serve as the camp commandant and to prepare to take part in the "extraordinary pacification program" ordered by Heinrich Himmler in fulfillment of the secret provisions of the Boundary and Friendship Treaty between Germany and the Soviet Union. Immediately 20,000 Poles were sent to other German concentration camps already in operation.

Auschwitz was located near Cracow and it offered the most practical way to carry out the destruction of the Polish elite, close to where they lived, but on the territory recently annexed by Germany. In order to isolate the future inmates and keep the extermination process secret, the Germans deported east all the Poles who inhabited the vicinity of the future camp.

May 1940 Beginning of the "Aktion AB" (*Auserordentliche Befriedungsaktion*), the "extraordinary pacification program," ordered by Himmler. It was a grand design to exterminate Polish intelligentsia, "the spiritual and political leaders of the Polish resistance movement" within German occupied Poland. This program, which involved an immediate arrest of 20,000 Polish profesionals, was coordinated with similar operations within the Polish territory occupied by the Soviets. Both of these programs were conducted in fulfillment of the secret clauses of the Boundary and Friendship Treaty between Germany and the Soviet Union. The immediate purpose was to contain and prevent the emergence of any hostile campaign directed against the territory of the other side. Both parties were determined to crush any signs of agitation within their own territories. They would inform each other of means employed to achieve this aim.

German and Soviet representatives regularly exchanged progress reports on their joint program of extermination of the Polish leadership community. Their meetings took place in Cracow and Zakopane.

June 14, 1940 Arrival at Auschwitz of the first 728 Polish (Christian) prisoners - the official beginning of the extermination program in the camp. For the next 21 months Auschwitz was to be inhabited almost exclusively by Poles.

June 21, 1940 At Compiegne surrender of France to Germany after an unexpectedly short campaign, which started with the German attack on France proper on June 5, 1940. Thus, the French military resistance did not last as long as the battle of Poland in the fall of 1939.

The German breakthrough to Dunkirk was executed by 500 tanks alone, without infantry, artillery, and supplies of fuel and food, on the insistence of Hitler against the advice of German High Command. German generals were aware that the French had more munerous and better tanks than the Germans and that Hitler's plan involved a very risky massive and rapid transit of armored vehicles through the mountainous terrain of southern Belgium. The attacking Germans were to depend on captured local French fuel and food, which the French could have destroyed rather than surrendering to the invaders. Since his gamble worked, Hitler gained credit in Germany as a "military genius" and started his personal domination of

German military strategy, despite the fact that he was a complete dilettante in the military art.

July 6, 1940 The first Polish prisoner escaped from Auschwitz.

July 10 - 12, 1940 In Warsaw, the Gestapo arrested and deported the Board of Directors of the Polish Bar Association -- a total of eighty Polish Catholic lawyers -- to Auschwitz for refusing to disbar Jewish lawyers. Practically all of them perished.

July 1940 The German government in Berlin devised a plan to deport Jews from Europe to Madagascar and collect ransom for them.

Sept. 6-9, 1940 Emanuel Ringelblum noted in his chronicle "improved spirits" among Warsaw Jews, as rumors spread of possible payment of ransom money by the Western allies to free Jews.

Sept. 7, 1940 Himmler stated in Metz that "we must attract all the Nordic blood of the world to us and deprive our adversaries of it." He was finally aware of the shortage of German manpower to establish the "1000 year Germany."

Sept. 21, 1940 The second transport arrived at Auschwitz from Warsaw, including the Polish officer, Witold Pilecki, who volunteered to have himself arrested by the Gestapo under the name of Tomasz Serafiński and became prisoner number 4859. He organized several clandestine battalions among the inmates of Auschwitz, as instructed by his superiors, in order to take over the camp during the requested allied bombings, or drops of weapons or parachutists. Meanwhile the military organization of prisoners was to disseminate news from outside and supply camp news to the Polish resistance, and organize additional food, clothing, and medical supplies for the inmates.

Oct. 1940 In Lańcut, Germans executed a Catholic, Aniela Kozioł, along with the Jewish Wolkenfeld family whom she was sheltering in her home.

Oct. 12, 1940 The Germans decided to quarantine Jews as "immune carriers of germs and epidemics." Warsaw was divided into German, Polish, and Jewish sections. Resettlement of

138,000 Jews and 113,000 Poles occurred within a week. The death penalty was enacted for possession of weapons or any action suspected of being inimical to the German forces or individual soldiers.

Nov. 15, 1940 In Warsaw the Germans began the construction of a wall encircling Europe's largest ghetto, where some 400,000 Jews were sealed.

Nov. 19, 1940 An entry of a typical event in the ghetto chronicle of E. Ringelblum stated: "A Christian who threw a sack of bread over the [ghetto] wall was killed."

Jan. 1941 In occupied and unincorporated central Poland, the General Gouvernement absorbed 1,200,000 Poles and 300,000 Jews expelled from Polish provinces newly annexed by Germany. In their place 497,000 racial Germans arrived from Soviet controlled eastern Poland, the Baltic states, Bukovina, and Yugoslavia. By then 99,500 racial Germans remained to be absorbed into the economy and 22,000 were still in resettlement camps. Thus, in 1939 the Berlin government initiated the German refugee problem.

Jan. 9, 1941 In Warsaw an information bulletin was issued by Polish Armed Resistance (*Związek Walki Zbrojnej*). It stated that "Jewish labor camps, in fact, do not differ from Auschwitz [which then contained exclusively Polish gentiles]. People completely unprepared to work outdoors in winter cold, wearing inadequate clothing and starved, are driven from cold farm shacks (where they are kept overnight) to work on German fortifications. The treatment [of the Jewish slave laborers] is sadistic and their mortality is very high."

March 1, 1941 Heinrich Himmler inspected Auschwitz for the first time.

April 18, 1941 In London, J. S. Bennet, Middle East expert in British Colonial Office commented: "The Jews have done nothing but add to our difficulties by propaganda and deeds since the war began..." Bennet was irritated with "the persistence, ubiquity, and selfishness of Jewish complaints, demands, and pleas."

April 21, 1941 In the Łódź Ghetto, a Jewish policeman named Ginsberg was killed by German guards for intervening on behalf of another Jew.

May 10, 1941 Rudolf Hess (1894-1988), Hitler's deputy and head of Nazi party arrived in Scotland for the purpose of negotiating an armistice with Great Britain. Hess had a vain hope that he would not be imprisoned, but be allowed to return with a British agreement which would facilitate the planned German attack on the USSR. Albrecht Haushofer, a great supporter of German expansionism and a man accused of "non-Aryan" ancestry, was the architect of Hess's flight.

May 23, 1941 Polish Armed Resistance reported that 500,000 Jews were crowded into the Warsaw Ghetto: 600 people per acre. Hunger, and unspeakably poor hygienic and sanitary conditions resulted in the spreading of tuberculosis and other contagious diseases. "Isolated ghetto is restricted to internal trade which consist of people's private property, clothing, and household goods are sold at low prices for extremely expensive food... There is no heating fuel in the ghetto... The health and sanitary conditions are beyond description -- there is a monstrous hunger and poverty... Overcrowded streets are full of aimless, pale, and starving people... People die in the streets... Orphanage is being overcrowded with daily arrivals of newborn babies... Germans plunder of once affluent Jews continues... and treat Jews in an exceptionally brutal manner... also daily, Germans savagely amuse themselves in a beastly war torturing Jews."

German plans for the starvation of ghetto inmates was sabotaged by illegal deliveries of about 250 tons of flour daily. Józef Dąbrowski and others were shot by the Germans for such deliveries. By then the daily food ration in Warsaw was 184 calories for a Jew, 669 for a Pole, and 2,613 for a German. 80 percent of the food consumed in the ghetto was smuggled in by Poles.

Despite these facts, German propaganda, stating that the Poles rather than the Germans were the principal enemies of the Jews, was still effective in the ghetto. Neither the extensive smuggling of food into the ghetto by the Poles nor the illegal Polish trade with the ghetto convinced the Jews that Germans, not Poles, were their deadly enemies.

The Polish trade with the Jewish ghetto consisted of illegally supplying raw materials on a huge scale and carrying out large quantities of finished products. The supply of raw materials into the ghetto was forty times greater than that officially permitted by the Germans, according to the records of the Jewish Council of the Warsaw Ghetto.

June 6, 1941 The first transport of Czechs signaling the beginning of transports of prisoners of at least 30 nationalities to Auschwitz, including: Americans, Austrians, Belgians, British, Bulgars, Croats, Czechs, Dutch, French, Germans, Greeks, Hungarians, Italians, Latvians, Lithuanians, Norwegians, Poles, Rumanians, Russians, Serbs, Slovaks, Slovenians, Swiss, Turks, Ukrainians, Gypsies, and Jews from all over Europe and Palestine; also one man each from China, Egypt, and Persia.

June 22, 1941 German attack on the Soviet Union -- execution of the "Barbarossa Plan" (of Dec. 18, 1940). Nazi Germany finally felt free to execute policies which her leadership had desired for a long time. The chief point of German focus now was the destruction of the USSR as the "Jewish-Bolshevik" state in order to prevent "Bolshevization of the earth" and "the victory of the Jewish race."

Nazi Germans were finally able to realize their long held hope to win a major battle in the life and death struggle of the fittest race and to exterminate European Jews starting with the hated and feared Ostjuden of the Soviet Union.

Special German SS-Einsatzgruppen were ordered to execute entire families of Communists and Jews by firing squads. Between June and December 1941 almost 500,000 Jews were killed in this way. Eventually, about 1,400,000 Jews were killed at the place of their arrest by the Einsatzgruppen, SS, police, Wehrmacht, and German civil authorities. Secret German formulation of the "Final Solution of the Jewish Question," or *Endloesung der Judenfrage*, was in the beginning stage.

Extermination was begun of three and one-half million Soviet prisoners-of-war taken by the Germans. About 250,000 Polish Jews survived until the end of the war in the USSR.

June 29, 1941 In Zborów, near Tarnopol, in southeastern Poland, the "Viking" division of Scandinavian SS executed 600 Jews accused of collaboration with the Soviets "as a reprisal for Soviet cruelties," as well as for the mass execution of prisoners held in jails by the NKVD.

July 1941 A resistance radio message from occupied Poland to the Polish Government-in-Exile in London said: "Jews despite all [are] optimistic." (The "Final Solution" as yet was not even imaginable in occupied Poland.) Almost daily radio reports by Polish resistance were sent to the Polish Government-in-Exile throughout the war. Polish Jews, refugees in Great Britain, Switzerland, and Sweden, regularly heard these radio reports.

July 1941 Polish prisoner Father Maximilian Maria Kolbe (1894-1941) offered his own life for another prisoner. Father Kolbe was arrested by the Gestapo for hiding and caring for up to 2000 Jews in his Franciscan monastery in Niepokalanów. Kolbe died in the "bunker" on August 14, 1941, and was canonized as a saint by the Catholic Church on Oct. 10, 1982. A total of 2512 Polish Catholic priests were killed by the Germans during World War II. Catholic orders of nuns in Warsaw, Niepokalanów, Szymanów, Otwock, Płudy, Laski, Turkowice, and other convents saved at least 5000 Jewish children.

July 1941 - June 1942 In Poland, German personnel murdered approximately 600,000 Jews according to Ringelblum Archives (Ring I, position 144). In 1941 Polish Jews did not believe that the German government intended to commit genocide on all Jews under its occupation. German propaganda stressed that work for the needs of the Wehrmacht provided safety for the Jewish workers in the ghettos in the form of a German pass (*Ausweis*).

An exceptional German, sensitive to the Jewish tragedy, noticed that the Jews in the ghetto were making too much out of these passes. He said: "*Du dummer Kerl, das ist alles quatsch! Der bester Ausweis ist und bleibt der Keller Ausweis.*" (You fool, all this is nonsense! The best pass is and always will be the cellar pass.) He meant that hiding in bunkers and shelters offered the only hope of survival for the Jews under German occupation.

A number of German businessmen, such as Bernard Hallmann, organized their own workshops by robbing Jewish factories of their equipment and employing the former owners in the production of furniture and other items at starvation wages.

July 14, 1941 The *Gazeta Żydowska* (Jewish Gazette nr. 58), published in Cracow (7/14/-1940 -- 7/28/1942) as an official newspaper of anti-Polish German propaganda for the Jews, reported on very popular theater performances in the ghetto by Jewish actors such as Stefania Grodzieńska and Jerzy Jurandot -- later, both of them were rescued by the Poles. Synagogues, theatres, and elementary schools were temporarily permitted to reopen in the ghettos.

July 31, 1941 Heydrich received authorization from Goering to extend the "Final Solution to the Jewish problem" to all of German controlled Europe. In order to obtain coordinated cooperation from all German government agencies, Heydrich started to prepare an intra-ministerial conference to convene at the Interpol office at Wannsee, in Berlin. At the same time, Himmler made his first visit to Russia. In Minsk he witnessed a mass execution of Jews and Communists for the first time. He nearly fainted, shouted hysterically and was deeply shocked. Himmler ordered the German police to design a more efficient method of killing. This incident resulted in the use of gassing vans which were the forerunners of the standard German extermination system of 1942-1944. Eventually, gassing killed a vast majority of Jewish victims of the German genocide of Jewish people.

Aug.-Sept. 1941 The gradual formulation of the policy for the extermination of all Jews under German occupation was reflected in the orders issued by Himmler and Heydrich. The Commandant of Auschwitz, Rudolf Hoess, was called to Berlin and ordered to make preparations for mass extermination of the Jews. The Berlin government used competitive bidding by German industry to design and equip an industrial process for human extermination.

Sept. 1941 German gas Zyklon-B was first tested in Auschwitz (in a provisional building) on 250 Polish political prisoners, sick with tuberculosis, and 600 Soviet prisoners of war. The design of an industrial extermination system began. It was based on blue hydrogen-cyanide crystals which were more reliable than carbon monoxide from old diesel engines. At first Germans used carbon monoxide in their gassing-vans which caused a painful and slow death for the victims.

Sept.-Oct. 1941 12,000 Soviet prisoners of war arrived in Auschwitz.

Oct. 7, 1941 Berlin authorities approved the building of a sub-camp for 200,000 prisoners at Birkenau, two miles from Auschwitz.

Oct. 1941 German experts on euthanasia chose extermination sites at Bełżec and Chełmno (Kulmhof) on the Ner in the part of Poland recently annexed by Germany.

3. Oct. 1941 - March 1943
Recession in the German Military Situation
Germany bogged down the Russian front, she lost the advantage of her head start and allowed her adversaries to put into production their greater economic resources and make far more numerous and more modern weapons.

The German war gamble was failing as Germany was losing the arms race -- formation and beginning of the "Final Solution to the Jewish Problem" as an industrial genocidal process.

The recession started on the Moscow front with a foolish entanglement in the north. Germany was losing the chance to maximize efforts to capture the huge oil fields in the south, which were urgently needed in view of the German fuel shortage and at the same time were the only source of petroleum of the Red Army.

The German troops were also poorly equipped for the winter cold. As late as October 1941, Field Marshal Wilhelm Keitel (1882-1946) refused to admit that there would be any winter fighting in Russia. In addition, the Germans badly underestimated the strength of the Siberian divisions. When the situation worsened, Chancellor Hitler forbade his generals to withdraw and shorten the front, as they wanted to do.

From now on German military strategy was guided by Hitler's intuition. Gone was the German systematic approach and careful planning of operations. Paradoxically these features, for which the Germans were so famous, now characterized the Soviet conduct of war. Stalin's General Staff employed two thousand officers who were working in three eight-hour shifts around the clock and attended to smallest details of Soviet military operations. Stalin never initiated any strategic moves himself. He always had several alternatives prepared for him. Stalin's military initiatives were limited to choosing what seemed to him to be the best alternative. Marshal G. K. Zhukov wrote later that with time Stalin's choice of the best military alternative became quite frequent. Thus, after their initial successes, the Germans lost every major battle fought on the eastern front.

The critical activity of German military intelligence was failing badly on the eastern front. The Germans were never able to foresee any of the major Soviet offensive operations. They paid for this deficiency very dearly, not withstanding the boastful reports by the chief of their eastern front intelligence, Reinhardt Gehlen, who in fact depended too heavily on monitoring Soviet radio communications. The Soviets, aware of this monitoring, fed the Germans false information which they substantiated by placing dummy tanks, cannons, and other equipment to be "verified" by Luftwaffe reconnaissance sorties.

Also, it should be noted that the German wartime government was so obsessed with its own ravings about Jewish domination of the world that even at this stage of the war it believed that the Jews, rather than Stalin, were in control of the Soviet Union.

A fearful notion started to spread in Berlin that the "1000 year Reich" and the war-time German government were doomed. The country's leaders were slowly coming to the conclusion that the extermination of the Jews was the only part of the "New Europe" of the German super-race which could be achieved, even if they did not win the war.

The leadership of the German nation needed to reassure itself of its own power, and to act out the depraved pseudo-scientific fantasies which had circulated for a century in opposition to Jewish emancipation in Germany and Austria.

When in the 19th century, Germans, under the influence of the Darwinian theory of evolution, falsely defined Jews as a separate race, the Jewish situation in Germany and in the rest of Europe changed dramatically. In the past the Jews were perceived as the people of the Old Testament from which came both Christianity and Islam. Within their "religious identity" the Jews could continue to be Jewish or they could choose to convert to any other religion.

The new "racial identity" given to the Jews in 19th century Germany, put them on a dead end street. By the new definition there could be no conversion from the "Jewish race" to any other race.

By the end of 1941 the Berlin government saw a brief window of opportunity to win a major battle in the imaginary life and death struggle between the German and Jewish "races" for the survival of the fittest, and thereby to exterminate one-third of all the members of the entire "Jewish race."

"The Final Solution to the Jewish Problem" was formulated by the Berlin government during the military recession, and it was during this period that most of the mass murders of the Jews were committed by German personnel.

Oct. 8, 1941 Secret mass killing began in the first extermination camp in Chelmno (Kulmhof), where eventually 360,000 Jews were gassed, and only three were known to survive.

Oct. 16, 1941 Hans Frank, Governor of the General Gouvernement, announced to his staff that "a great Jewish migration will begin... rid yourself of all feelings of pity."

Nov. 1941 A small slave labor camp opened at Treblinka for Poles and Jews employed in building an extermination camp.

Nov. 1, 1941 In Słuck, a report was issued on the massacre of Jews, mostly craftsmen, by a German police battalion. The report by the head of German civil administration, Wilhelm Kube (1887-1943), to the Berlin government stated that many wounded were buried alive and some of them later crawled out of their graves.

Nov. 10, 1941 Warsaw German Commandant Fischer issued a decree which made the act of providing "Aryan" identification cards to Jews punishable by death. At least eleven Polish municipal employees in the Department of Registration were murdered by the Gestapo for giving false papers to thousands of Jews during the war. Also, the Head of the Municipal Employment Office, Kazimierz Wendt, was arrested and executed by the Germans for providing Jews with the uniforms and fake identity cards of streetcar workers.

Late Fall, 1941 A cottage was converted into the first gas chamber in Section B III of Birkenau-Auschwitz. Hitler's government still considered massive emigration and expulsion of Jews as a solution to the "Jewish problem." In

November 1941 all Jewish emigration from German controlled Europe was prohibited.

Dec. 6, 1941 In the Warsaw Ghetto legal deliveries of food represented a monthly value of 1,800,000 zlotys, and the illegal, 70 to 80 million zlotys. Among the Jews in the ghetto there were 10,000 rich "capitalists," 250,000 working people, and 150,000 who lived on the meager social assistance, according to records of the Jewish Council. 96,000 Jews had died since November 1939 in Warsaw. The "capitalists" with their families represented some 30,000 people. A few were wealthy pre-war business people -- most of them were the newly rich and wartime collaborators who did not show any solidarity with the suffering masses of ghetto Jews.

Dec. 21, 1941 In Wilno, Mania Liffe Ainsztein saw Germans killing a Jewish woman and a Soviet prisoner of war who had received a piece of bread from her. (Just one instance...)

1942-1944 In Warsaw, Dr. Tadeusz Charemza, with a group of Polish doctors, performed plastic surgery on Jewish patients to remove scars of circumcision in order to prevent their identification as Jews during inspection by the Gestapo.

In occupied Poland an increasingly large number of suspected people were picked off the streets and inspected for circumcision in the hallways of nearby apartment houses and other buildings. Jews were the only people circumcised in northern Europe. Performing such plastic surgery, Polish doctors risked their lives.

1942-1944 In Stockholm, "The Specter of a Separate Peace in the East: Russo-German Peace Feelers." (H.W. Koch, Journal of Contemporary History, Vol. X no. 3., July 1975.) Germany was trying to split the Allies. Soviets were blackmailing the West for concessions. Polish position in the western alliance became increasingly more difficult because not much attention was paid to reports of German atrocities on Jewish and Polish population in occupied Poland.

Jan. 10, 1942 In Kraków, the German governor, Dr. Hans Frank, informed his cabinet that the "Final Solution is to be extended to 3,000,000 Jews in Poland." German doctors from the euthanasia organization were sent to assist Gen. Odilo Globocnik in Lublin.

Jan. 19, 1942 Polish-Jewish Senator Czerniaków, the head of Jewish Council of the Warsaw Ghetto, reported that 443 men and 213 teenagers were arrested by the Germans for participating in the massive smuggling of food from the Polish side. A huge Polish-Jewish organization smuggled food and raw materials into the ghetto and smuggled out finished products in exchange. Bribes associated with the operation were making the local German government officials rich. Czerniaków stated that without it "very few Jews would have survived the first year of confinement inside the ghetto walls." The Polish Christian population did not object to the "illegal" shipments of food to the ghetto, despite the scarcity of food in Warsaw on the "Aryan" side.

Jan. 20, 1942 The Wannsee Conference in Berlin finalized the plans for implementation of the "Final Solution of the Jewish Question." The Berlin government announced new invitations for bids from German industry for equipment for an industrial process of extermination for eleven million European Jews. Occupied Europe was to be searched from west to east during the practical realization of the "final solution." Terrorized Jewish personnel were to be used in the extermination process, with the nominal involvement of Germans. No Jewish "germ cell" was to be allowed to survive. Procedural guidelines were specified:

1. Jews to be made to believe that they are going to some unidentified labor camp in the occupied east.
2. Extermination camp sites to be near centers of Jewish population.
3. Camp sites to be isolated from local population for maximum secrecy.
4. Sites to be close to railways.
5. New arrivals to be made to believe that they are in a transit or a labor camp.
6. Gas chambers to be disguised as shower rooms.
7. Victims to be rushed through the extermination process.
8. Victims to be disoriented.
9. Resistance by the victims to be prevented.
10. Men to be separated from women and children.
11. Potentially "useful" victims to be separated from the weak and "useless."

110

12. Victims to be stripped of their clothing and belongings.

13. Victims' hair to be shaved and collected.

14. No reprieve to be granted to anyone who arrived in the death transport, even if the person could prove to be a Christian or an "Aryan."

15. Process of extermination to proceed with maximum possible speed, involving the smallest possible number of German personnel.

(In Treblinka the process took less than two hours from opening the train doors to pushing the victims into the gas chamber.)

The minutes of the Wannsee conference included a statement by Secretary of State, Dr. Buhler, "German authorities in occupied Poland volunteered to start the 'final solution' there because of short transport distances which would require a minimum of [German] personnel and... a priority should be given to liquidation of all Jews in the Polish territory... because the vast majority of Jewish population there is unfit for work."

Feb. 1942 The Berlin government decided to abolish collective responsibility for escapes from concentration camps, in order to reduce the growing threat of prison revolt in Auschwitz and other camps. The German government was preparing for massive extermination of the ghetto Jews and wanted to prevent revolts by camp inmates.

Feb. 16, 1942 In Terezin (Teresienstadt), in northwestern Czechoslovakia, the camp started receiving Jews from Germany, Austria, Holland, and Denmark. The 140,000 Jewish inmates at Terezin included 74,000 Czech Jews. 33,419 Jews died in Terezin and 17,000 survived. Eventually, transports totaling 86,954 Jews were sent to Auschwitz and other death-camps for extermination.

The victims included several hundred Jews from Denmark, who were betrayed by pro-Nazi Danes. While Denmark was under the mildest regime of German occupation, the Danes had their share of blackmailers and collaborators. However, of a total of some 7,800 Danish Jews, including 1,300 half-Jews, some 90 percent were smuggled across the narrows to Sweden in Oct. 1943 and saved.

In Mala Pevnost, two kilometers south of Teresienstadt, starting in 1940 to May 1945, about 35,000 Czech political prisoners were held. About 25,000 of them were murdered or wasted there during the war.

Feb. 21, 1942 In Lwów, two Catholic priests were shot to death by the Germans for trying to give shelter in their monastery to two Jewish families.

Feb. 25, 1942 The sinking of the Panamanian flag ship *Struma* with 768 Jewish refugees from Romania took place in the Black Sea, ten kilometers from the Turkish coast, near Istanbul. The tragedy happened after the British government refused to permit the *Struma* to sail to Palestine. The *Struma* was towed from Istanbul by the Turks towards the Black Sea with a disabled engine and was cast adrift during the disaster.

David Stoliar, the solitary survivor, reported that the *Struma* was sunk by a torpedo which may have been fired in error by a Soviet vessel. A British naval intelligence report of Feb. 27, 1942, stated that the *Struma* was torpedoed.

Feb. 27, 1942 Einsatzgruppen reported on killing of Jews in the Baltic states. In Estonia all Jews were murdered. In Latvia only 7 percent and in Lithuania only 12 percent of the Jews survived. In nearby Byelorussia 75 percent of the Jews were still surviving -- many hid in forests after escaping from ghettos designated for them by the Germans.

March 1942 Opening of the camp in Bełżec at which 600,000 Jews were gassed. Only two were known to survive. Bełżec marked the beginning of a massive German program of extermination of Jews held in German-built ghettos. All ghettos were liquidated in 1942-1943, with the exception of the Łódź Ghetto, which lasted through 1944.

March 26, 1942 999 women from Rawensbruck concentration camp, north of Berlin, arrived in Auschwitz - the number of women there eventually reached 20,000.

March 26, 1942 Another 999 Jewish women arrived in Auschwitz with the first *Transport-Juden* directly from Slovakia.

April, 1942 In Mlawa, Gestapo conducted a public execution of 50 Jews. A Polish bystander shouted: "They are spilling innocent blood." He was murdered along with Jewish victims.

April 1942 The camp at Sobibór opened. Eventually 250,000 Jews were gassed there, only sixty-four were known to survive.

April 27, 1942 In Berlin, RSHA (*Reichssicherheithauptamt*, or Head Office of State Security) a German plan was formed for annihilation of the Slavic nations of eastern and central Europe, starting with the Poles. The execution of the plan was based primarily on the system of extermination camps, which continued to be expanded. The code name of the German genocidal program was "Generalplan Ost" (general plan east). By 1945 the design of the gas chambers was expanded by German civil service officials to exterminate over 100,000 people daily. By then the stocks of the poison gas, Zyklon-B, were large enough to kill some 15 million people, although less than two million Jews were left in German occupied Europe.

May 1, 1942 In Warsaw, arrival of German film propaganda specialists to record scenes in the ghetto including the workings of the Jewish Council, the use of the public bath by three Orthodox Jews with side-curls and 20 prominent Jewish women, and a demonstration of circumcision.

May 3, 1942 In Biłgoraj, near Lublin, Jewish Council members Hillel Janower, Szymon Bin, Shmuel Leib, and Ephraim Waksschul were murdered by the Germans for refusing to compile a list of Jews for transport to the death camp in Bełżec.

May 5, 1942 In Dąbrowa Górnicza, near Katowice, the Chairman of the Jewish Council, Adolf Weinberg, refused to compile a list of Jews for "resettlement." He was sent to the gas chamber with his entire family.

May, 1942 In Tarnów, near Chełm, German military police executed 15 Polish farmers together with 25 Jews whom they sheltered, and their homes and farm buildings were burned to the ground.

May 8, 1942 In Sobujew, the Germans executed Jan Machulski for harboring a group of Jews who managed to escape from Machulski's farm.

May 12, 1942 In Auschwitz, the first transport of 1,500 Jews arrived from Sosnowiec. It was sent directly from the railway ramp to the gas chamber. Eventually about 960,000 Jews were gassed there. In addition 404,000 men and women were registered in Auschwitz -- 75,000 Polish Catholics, 25,000 Gypsies, and 15,000 Soviet prisoners of war also died there; several thousand Jews survived as slave laborers.

May 17-18, 1942 In the Warsaw Ghetto, nighttime street Gestapo executed, without trial, 52 Jewish members of the Anti-Fascist Bloc who had been betrayed by informers and the Jewish police. During May, German courts sentenced 187 Jews to death for resistance activities.

Gestapo acted on the basis of name lists prepared by the Jewish police and other collaborators, most prominent among whom was Abraham Gancwajch. He apparently was recruited by the Gestapo before the war started and spied for the Germans on Soviet subversive activities in Białystok, Wilno, and Lwów at that time.

Gancwajch was a very intelligent man who spoke Yiddish, German, Hebrew, and Polish fluently and taught Hebrew and published Zionist articles in newspapers before the war. He organized a spy agency at 13 Leszno Street in the Warsaw Ghetto, under the name of the Office for Combatting Usury and Bribery. He claimed to be dedicated to the welfare of the Jews on the basis of his good relations with the Germans. Gancwajch was a gifted demagogue and provocateur who specialized in breaking down the morale of the Jews by explaining that the German-Nazi victory was "inevitable" and therefore any resistance was useless.

Gancwajch became very wealthy by collecting protection money from some 100 large apartment buildings along Leszno Street. Daily, he sold 30 German passes from the ghetto to the "Aryan" side at exorbitant prices. He also sold "safe" appointments to the ambulance service, for which people were willing to pay fortunes. He promised to convert the Warsaw Ghetto into a German army workshop, free from hunger, beatings and arrests. Gancwajch and his associates Moryc Kon and Zelig Heller were able, as Gestapo agents, to earn huge sums of money for smuggling Jews from Lodz and Białystok to the Warsaw Ghetto, releasing people from jail, returning confiscated property, etc. A change in the Gestapo personnel in June 1942 ended the career of Gancwajch in the Warsaw Ghetto, and all the members of his band were executed.

May 20, 1942 In Czarny Dunajec, Karol Chraca, a Catholic, was murdered by the Germans together with Jews Józef Lehrer and his daughter for providing them with food. The three were buried in a common grave in the Jewish cemetery.

May 22, 1942 In Ozorków, near Łódź, a Jewish teacher, Mania Rzepkowicz, joined a transport of some 300 Jewish children sent to the death camp in Chelmno rather than serve as secretary of the Jewish Council.

May, 26, 1942 In Kronosz, near Chełm, the Gestapo, with help of regular German army units killed 15 Poles in reprisal for sheltering Jews and Soviet prisoners. Twenty-six groups of homes and farm buildings were burned to the ground.

May 26, 1942 In Widły, near Chełm, German army units and SS murdered the game warden, Pawel Wawer, and eleven farmers for "aiding Jews and guerrillas."

May 28, 1942 In the Warsaw Ghetto, Gypsies were forced to join the Jews, contributing to further overcrowding, hunger, and disease.

May 29, 1942 At Moldau Bridge, near Prague, two members of Czechoslovak forces, Jan Kubis and Józef Gabcik, parachuted from a British plane and mortally wounded Reinhard Heydrich. In reprisal the Germans under Col. Max Rastock executed 199 men and sent 195 women to the Ravensbruck concentration camp. Also between June 10 and 12 three trains with more than 3,000 Czech Jews from the Teresienstadt Ghetto were sent to the gas chambers under code name Einsatz Reinhard.

Heydrich died on June 10. His disgraced doctor, Karl Gebhardt, assigned to Ravensbruck, murdered many hundreds of women there, experimenting with the use of sulphanilamide. In further reprisal, executions were conducted in Prague and its vicinity. 1,331 people were killed there, including 201 women.

May 29, 1942 In Berlin, Joseph Goebbels (1897-1945), German minister for propaganda and national enlightenment, ordered the arrest of 500 Berlin Jews as hostages against "Jewish plots." The Gestapo reported to the Berlin Finance President that, in reprisal for the attack on Heydrich, 152 Jews were killed in prison in a "special action," and that their property was forfeited to the German state.

Goebbels was the first to suggest extermination by working people to death while in "protective custody."

The noticeable overlapping of the fields of competence of such men as Himmler, Goering, and Goebbels weakened the command in Berlin and contributed to eventual German defeat.

June - Nov. 1942 Himmler's statistics showed that 136,700 new prisoners were registered in concentration camps and in this period of six months 70,610 had died, 9,267 were executed, 28,846 had been sent to gas chambers, and 4,711 had been released. This represented a monthly rate of wastage of 19,000 prisoners ostensibly "suitable for work." Himmler ordered a reduction in the death rate and eventually families of prisoners were allowed and encouraged to send in food packages to supplement the diet in concentration camps. In Auschwitz-Monowitz, the I.G. Farben plant added a midday bowl of soup, but in Essen, Krupp continued to exploit Jewish women from Hungary under murderous conditions.

June 7, 1942 In Wlodawa, near Lublin, a young Jew tried to impersonate the local rabbi in order to save him from arrest. Germans realized the deception and killed both the rabbi and his impersonator.

June 10, 1942 A mass escape was attempted at men's penal company at Auschwitz.

June 17, 1942 In Warsaw, Emanuel Ringelblum noted in his diary that it was completely incomprehensible why Jews from villages "were evacuated under a guard of Jewish policemen. Not one of them escaped, although all of them knew where and towards what they were going... One [German] gendarme is sufficient to slaughter a whole town." Ringelblum was amazed by the ease with which small units of German soldiers were able to subjugate and put to death very large numbers of Jews.

Polish responses to what they perceived as the passivity of the Jews during the war were negative. Thus, Jews were perceived as cowards, unsuitable for armed resistance to the Germans, which the Poles considered honorable and vitally necessary. The Poles believed that many more Jews could have survived, had they resisted. Unfortunately, these notions freed some people from any moral obligation towards the Jewish victims of the Germans and allowed some witnesses of the horrible genocide of the Jews to preserve a clear conscience.

In retrospect, an officer of the Polish Home Army, Władysław Siła-Nowicki wrote, "passive behavior -- seeking security by staying with the group and by accepting German orders -- was the first and principal obstacle to the possibility of extending help to the Jews."

June 22, 1942 In London, appeal to Prime Minister Winston Churchill was made by Wladyslaw Sikorski, the Prime Minister of Poland and Commander-in-Chief of Polish Armed Forces. He was pressing the British for retributive bombing of Germany in retaliation for German savagery towards the Jews in occupied Poland. General Sikorski also demanded the confiscation of German property and drastic measures against German citizens in allied countries. The British government rejected Sikorski's idea of announcing reprisal air raids in retaliation for German atrocities against Poles and Jews.

June 23, 1942 German doctors arrived in Lublin to assist Gen. Odilo Globocnik. They were the second group sent from the "euthanasia staff" in Berlin to help in the extermination program in "Jewish Lublin State."

June 26, 1942 The first BBC broadcast about the fate of Polish Jewry. Jews of Warsaw reacted with joy that finally their horrible situation was recognized by the British.

June 30, 1942 The second temporary gas chamber was put in operation in Section B III, in Birkenau-Auschwitz.

July 1, 1942 In Białobrzegi, near Opoczno, German military police executed a Pole, Maxymilian Gruszczyński, for letting Jews bake bread in his home.

July 11, 1942 The first Jewish transport was sent to Auschwitz by the RSHA, the Head Office of State Security (*Reichssicherheitshauptamt*).

July 15, 1942 In Molczadź, near Słonim, the chairman of the Jewish Council, Ehrlich, and a Council member, Leib Gilerowicz were beaten and killed by the Germans when they protested against the German "resettlement" scheme as a cover-up for the gassing of Jews.

July 17-18, 1942 The second inspection visit to Auschwitz was made by Himmler.

July 19, 1942 The first rumors about the Wannsee decision to exterminate all Jews reached Warsaw. Senator Czerniaków, the head of the Jewish Council, made the rounds to reassure the panic-stricken Jews. Czerniaków wrote: "I did what I could. I am also trying to lift the spirits of the delegations which come to see me."

July 20, 1942 In Warsaw, Polish Socialists Tadeusz Koral and Ferdynand Grzesik were arrested by the Germans for teaching tactics of diversion and sabotage in the ghetto; Koral was murdered and Grzesik sent to a concentration camp by the Gestapo.

July 21, 1942 In Warsaw, the Germans murdered Dr. Franciszek Raszeja, an outstanding scientist and professor of medicine at the University of Poznan, together with his assistant, Dr. Kazimierz Polak, and his nurse while they were administering to a Jewish patient, Mr. Abe Gutmajer, a prominent antique art dealer in Warsaw. Mr. Gutmajer was murdered with all members of his family. The tragic death of Dr. Raszeja, who gave his life to treat Mr. Gutmajer, symbolized the moral attitude of Polish intelligentsia and was consistent with Polish national values.

July 23, 1942 Mass murders began in Treblinka II, the most efficient of German extermination camps, where up to 15,000 people could be gassed daily. The total number of victims is estimated between 750,000 and 870,000; about forty are known to have survived. A German staff of some 24 people was operating the extermination camp with the assistance of some 120 Lithuanian, Latvian and Ukrainian guards. The actual extermination process was executed by terrorized Jewish inmates. The procedure in Treblinka II generally followed the guidelines established in Wannsee Conference on Jan. 20, 1942. It consisted of:
1. Clothing and belongings were to be taken up for disinfection.
2. Valuables were to be deposited for a receipt.

3. Victims were to be shaved and their hair collected.

4. Victims were to enter gas chambers disguised as "showers."

5. Carbon monoxide was to be pumped through "shower" pipes for 30 minutes using gas from dismounted diesel engines taken from tanks and lorries.

6. Dead Jewish victims were to be separated out, their bodies to be removed from gas chambers with meat hooks.

7. The "dentists" were to extract gold and platinum teeth from the bodies using pliers.

8. Jewish prisoners were to carry the bodies of victims to the ditches for a preliminary burial.

9. Excrement and blood were to be cleaned off the gas chambers by Jewish inmates and the "shower rooms" were to be made ready for the next batch of victims.

July 23, 1942 The leader of the Jewish Council of Warsaw committed suicide. He was the senator, Adam Czerniaków, who initially disregarded warnings from the Polish Underground. At first he issued orders to Jewish police to make a list of 6,000 Jews daily to be "resettled" in the east until the ghetto was empty. However, when Germans raised their daily quota to 8,000 he realized that these people were to be gassed. Czerniaków wrote in his diary: "It is 3:00 P.M. So far 4,000 people are ready for transport. By 4:00 P.M. according to German orders the next 4,000 are to be ready." Then he broke down and wrote to his wife and to the other members of the Jewish Council of Warsaw: "I could not kill my people with my own hands," and he took his own life. (Senator Czerniaków served in the Polish Senate in 1931-1935 and belonged to BBWR political group of senators.)

July 23 - Sept. 30, 1942 The Warsaw Ghetto lost at least 275,000 people. 265,000 were deported to Treblinka and other death camps, 5422 people were killed being loaded on the death trains and the rest were murdered by the Germans in the streets of the ghetto.

July 25, 1942 Jewish police delivered 7,000 victims for transport to Treblinka and from then on delivered them at a minimum daily rate of 10,000. The average Jewish policeman in the Warsaw Ghetto sent two thousand Jews to their death, in order to save his own life. Jewish police became notorious for their corruption and demoralization. They were hated in the ghetto as the symbol of German authority and terror. On the other hand, the Polish "navy blue" police, which was recruited from pre-war Polish police and certified racial Germans (former Polish citizens), did not take part in sending Jews from the Warsaw Ghetto to extermination camps.

July 26, 1942 Radio broadcasts by the underground Directorate of Civil Defense in Warsaw provided up-to-date information, including reports by the chiefs of the Jewish sections in the Office of the Delegate of the Polish Government-in-Exile and of the High Command of the Home Army with up-to-date information: "The Germans commenced the liquidation of the Warsaw Ghetto. Wall posters ordered the deportation of 6,000 persons, each allowed 15 kilograms of personal effects, plus valuables. Departures to date included two trainloads, obviously scheduled for execution. There was despair and suicide. Polish police were removed, to be replaced by Lithuanians, Latvians, and Ukrainians. Summary shooting in homes and streets are common. [The broadcast repeated that] Dr. Raszeja, professor at the Poznań University, was killed during consultation with a Jewish patient."

July 29 - Aug. 4, 1942 In the Warsaw Ghetto, daily proclamations were made to the starving Jews by the commander (Jozef Szerynski) of the Jewish police, who stated that "people who would come to the loading ramp at the Umschlagplatz of their own free will would receive six pounds of bread and two pounds of jam." Dr. E. Ringelblum was scandalized by this cynical luring of hungry Jews to the death trains. He stated that "Jewish police were known for their terrible corruption, but they have reached the apogee of depravity at the time of the deportations."

Aug. 4, 1942 In Holland, Anne Frank (1929-1944) was arrested, after being betrayed to the Gestapo by a Dutchman. She died in the Bergen-Belsen concentration camp in Germany. Her diary survived her and became famous world-wide. She perished together with most of the Jews from Holland. The percentage of Jews saved in the Netherlands was the same as that saved in Poland. The Dutch had many blackmailers and collaborators. Thousands of Dutchmen volunteered to serve in the Dutch SS and fought alongside the Germans. A far greater number of Jews survived in Poland and lived to tell about the horrors of German occupation and extermination of the Jewish people.

Aug. 1942 In Warsaw, an appeal was made in the underground press by Zofia Kossak-Szczucka, a writer and an activist in Catholic charities, for organized help for the Jews in form of shelter, money, false papers, etc. to be organized by a new Council for Aid to Jews, a unique organization in occupied Europe. The appeal called the destruction of Jews then in progress "the most terrible crime history has ever witnessed," and declared that anyone remaining silent was an accomplice because "he who does not condemn, condones." The appeal also stated that the Poles were morally obligated to give help to the Jews and oppose German atrocities even if some of them perceived the Jews as political, economic, and ideological enemies of Poland.

Aug. 1942 In Adamów, near Łuków, a resistance unit attacked a German military transport of Jews sent to Treblinka. Two hundred Jews were freed by this partisan unit, led by Serafin Aleksiejew.

Aug. 5, 1942 Children from Jewish orphanages in Warsaw were transported to Treblinka. Dr. Janusz Korczak (Henryk Goldszmit, 1878-1942) in his Polish major's uniform, and Dr. Stefania Wilczyńska voluntarily accompanied them, instead of accepting help to escape to safety outside the ghetto. They carried small orphans in their arms and led the others, to save them the horrors of being beaten and shoved into the death train by force. Dr. Korczak was a prominent educator and writer. He was one of the first to formulate the human and civil rights of children.

Aug. 17, 1942 Jewish resistance posters accused the entire Jewish police of the Warsaw Ghetto, including all officers and functionaries, of eager cooperation with the German program of mass-extermination of Jews.

Aug. 21, 1942, Jewish Police Chief, Józef Szeryński was wounded in his apartment at 10 Nowolipki Street by Israel Kanał, a member of the "Akiba," Jewish nationalist-conservative group.

Aug. 28, 1942 The reorganization of the Treblinka extermination camp began. Jewish prisoners in work crews at the unloading ramp, gas chambers, preliminary burials, and crematories were executed in order to preserve secrecy. A new system of burning bodies day and night inside large ditches was begun.

Aug. 28, 1942 In the Warsaw Ghetto a meeting with Dawid Nowodworski, who escaped from Treblinka, brought information that in the last few weeks at least 300,000 Jews from Warsaw, Radom, Siedlce, and other towns were exterminated. They had not been resettled or relocated to a labor camp as the Germans had announced.

Sept. 4, 1942 The extermination process in Treblinka was restarted after interruption for reorganization on Aug. 28 1942.

Sept. 4, 1942 In Łachwa, near Pińsk, Yisrael Dubski, a member of the Jewish Council, refused to compile a list of Jews for transport to gas chambers, and was murdered by the Germans.

Sept. 12, 1942 The end of deportation for Warsaw Ghetto of 310,000 Jewish men, women, and children to death camps. Officially, some 35,000 Jews remained working in German shops -- another 35,000 hid inside the ghetto and between 10 and 20 thousand Jews crossed to the "Aryan" side to hide there.

Sept. 17, 1942 The underground Directorate of Civil Resistance in occupied Poland proclaimed: "The tragic fate of the Polish people is compounded by the monstrous, planned slaughter of the Jews that has been carried on (by the Germans) in our country for nearly a year. These mass murders are without precedent in the history of the world, and all the cruelties known to man pale beside them. Infants, children, young people, men, women, whether of Catholic or of the Hebrew faith, are being mercilessly murdered, poisoned by gas, buried alive, thrown out of windows onto the pavements below -- for no other reason but that they are (classified as) Jewish... More than a million victims have already been slaughtered... Unable to counteract these crimes, the Directorate of Civil Defense protested in the name of the entire Polish nation against the atrocities perpetrated on the Jews..."

116

Sept. 21, 1942 In Warsaw, on the Jewish Day of Atonement, Jewish policemen and their families were deported to Treblinka in the final stage of the *Selektion*, or German selection, of victims. The ghetto police was reduced to 380 men. Germans transported 235,741 people to the gas chambers. Some 10,000 Jews were killed during the violent assembling and loading, 12,000 were sent to other labor camps and 8,000 escaped to the Polish "Aryan" side.

Sept. 21, 1942 In Stalowa Wola Death Camp (Vernichtungslager) under the local Gestapo, on the Yom Kippur day, Rabbi Frenkel of Wieliczka was murdered by the camp commander named Swamberger because another prisoner reported that the rabbi was praying instead of working on this important Jewish holy day.

Sept. 25, 1942 In Kałuszyn, near Warsaw, the chairman of the Jewish Council, Abraham Gamz, refused to make a list of Jews for deportation and was murdered by the Germans.

Sept. 1942 In Włodzimierz, a member of the Jewish Council, Jakub Kogen, took his life together with those of his wife and 13-year-old son in protest against the German demand that he must prepare a shipment of 7,000 Jews for one of the death camps.

Oct. 5, 1942 A revolt broke out in the women's penal company in Auschwitz.

Oct. 6, 1942 In Bidaczów Nowy, near Biłgoraj, Germans murdered 22 Polish farmers for sheltering Jews. Their homes and farm buildings were burned to the ground.

Oct. 1942 In Treblinka, new gas chambers were built for the simultaneous gassing of 3,800 people. By Nov. 1942 a total of 750,600 verified (actual total was estimated at 870,000) victims were gassed. About 24 German SS-men and 125 guards (Ukrainian, Latvian, and Lithuanian) operated the Treblinka camp, which depended on huge German occupational forces for security against outside interference by the Polish underground.

Oct. 14, 1942 In Piotrków Trybunalski, near Łódź, Yehuda Russak, a Jewish baker, was murdered by the Germans because he refused to part with his paralyzed wife.

Oct. 21, 1942 In Kobryń, near Brześć, two Polish farming families were massacred by the Germans for "maintaining contacts with Jewish guerrillas."

Oct. 25, 1942 In Poręba, Germans executed Zofia Wójcik with her two children, aged two and three, along with a Jewish man she was harboring.

Oct. 30, 1942 An Auschwitz sub-camp at Monowitz (Monowice) was established in the area of the Buna-Werke as a concentration camp fully owned by the IG-Farbenindustrie of Germany. Prisoners were exploited with the lowest possible expenditure on food and shelter.

In German industry, the labor of inmates was treated as a consumable raw material; human life was treated as a mineral systematically extracted; used up and exhausted inmates were shipped to gas chambers and cremated.

Nov. 8, 1942 In Oborki, near Łuck, Gestapo and the German military police massacred over 70 people from 22 Polish families named Trusiewicz and Domalewski for feeding and giving shelter to Jews.

Nov. 14, 1942 In Kraków, a decree was issued by Wilhelm Kreuger, German Secretary of State for Security, ordering establishment of "remnant ghettos" inside the largest ghettos throughout occupied Poland to be completed by Nov. 30, 1942. The purpose was to concentrate the surviving Jews for execution and to liquidate empty ghettos in order to conceal the evidence of German crimes committed there.

Nov. 1942 In Łomża, near Białystok, a member of the Jewish Council, Dr. Joseph Hepner, took his life "rather than cooperate with the Nazis in the extermination of Jews."

Nov. 1942 The Polish emissary from Warsaw, Jan Karski, arrived in London. He brought extensive documentation of the horrors of German occupation of Poland and a message from Jewish leaders Leon Feiner and Adolf Berman, addressed to American Rabbis Stephen Wise and Nahum Goldmann, as well as to Ignacy Schwartzbart, a Zionist, and Szmul Zygielbojm, a Bundist, both members of the Polish National Council in London:

"We want you to tell the Polish government, the Allied governments, and the Allied leaders that we are helpless against the German criminals. We cannot defend ourselves, and no one in Poland can possibly defend us. The Polish underground authorities can save some of us, but they cannot save the masses. The Germans do not try to enslave us the way they do other peoples. We are being systematically murdered... All Jews in Poland will perish. It is possible that some few will be saved. But three millions of Polish Jews are doomed to extinction.

"There is no power in Poland able to forestall this fact; neither the Polish nor the Jewish underground can do it. You have to place the responsibility squarely on the shoulders of the Allies. No leader of the United Nations should ever be able to say that he did not know that we were being murdered in Poland and that only outside assistance could help us."

This message was delivered to the Polish Government-in-Exile and to the following dignitaries in London: Anthony Eden, Foreign Secretary; Arthur Greenwood, leader of the Labor Party; Lord Selbourne; Lord Cranborne; Hugh Dalton, the Chairman of the Board of Trade; Ellen Wilkinson, member of the House of Commons; Sir Owen O'Malley, British Ambassador to the Polish Government-in-Exile; Anthony Drexel Biddle, American Ambassador to the Polish Government-in-Exile and Richard Law, Foreign Affairs Under-Secretary as well as representatives of the United Nations War Crimes Commission including its Chairman.

The Polish diplomat Jan Karski, eye witness to the German extermination of the Jews in the death camps and ghettos, accomplished his mission and passed on to Allied leaders the desperate message about the fate of Jews in occupied Poland. However, until the end of 1942 many British and American officials refused to believe most of the reports of German atrocities against the Jews. They excused themselves by mentioning the atrocity propaganda of the first world war and the exaggerated accounts of pogroms in Poland in the period 1918-1921. In reality the western officials knew the facts but simply did not want to act on behalf of Jewish victims. Typical were the conversations between Jan Karski and prominent literary men, whom he tried to mobilize to use their great talent and describe the plight of European Jewry in order to appeal to the conscience of the world. Typically, the English author Goeffrey Wells and Hungarian-Jewish author Arthur Koestler did not respond to Karski's pleading.

Dec. 1, 1942 In Studziniec, near Rzeszów, German military police executed 16 people: 5 Jews and 11 Poles whom they betrayed, after receiving help and supplies from them.

Dec. 1, 1942 In Przewrota, Germans executed five members of the Zeller family together with six Polish Catholic farmers who sheltered them.

Dec. 1942 In Białka, near Biała Podlaska, Germans executed one hundred Polish hostages for aiding Jewish guerrillas and hiding Jews.

Dec. 2, 1942 In the Warsaw Ghetto the Jewish National Committee founded the Jewish Fighting Organization for protection of the Jewish people of Warsaw against the Germans and their collaborators in the ghetto.

Dec. 4, 1942 In Przeworsk, 6 Catholics were executed by the Germans as a reprisal for the aid given to Jews by Polish Christian townspeople.

Dec. 4, 1942 The headquarters of the Council of Assistance for the Jews, code name *Żegota*, was established in Warsaw with the approval of the Polish Government-in-Exile. Pre-war political leaders were in charge of the operation, which was unique in occupied Europe. Julian Grobelny was the chairman, Leon Feiner, vice-chairman, and Adolf Berman, secretary. The Council had branches in Kraków, Lwów, Zamość, Lublin, Radom, Kielce, and Piotrków. It expanded and improved the existing forms of assistance to Jews who lived in hiding outside of ghettos.

Zegota provided over 100,000 Jews with living quarters, "Aryan" documents, food, medical care, and financial help. It also established communication between family members living in different localities. In the small area of Nowy Sącz alone, 210 Polish Catholics were executed by the Germans for their participation in Żegota. For example, 18-year-old Stefan Kiełbasa was executed in Nowy Sącz for providing a Jewish friend with false "Aryan" papers. Żegota also donated 500,000 zloties for the purpose of acquiring weapons for Jewish resistance fighters.

Dec. 5, 1942 In Rzeszów the arrival at the "remnant ghetto" and the Jewish Slave Labor Camp (*Judisches Zwangsarbeitslager*) of 600 Jews from the liquidated ghetto of Krosno was reported. The Jewish Slave Labor Camp was organized as a concentration camp for working prisoners only. It was under control of the central German authorities in Kraków.

The "remnant ghetto," or the "scrap ghetto" (*szmelc-getto*), was administrated by the Jewish Council (*Judenrat*) under strict supervision of the local Gestapo. Many families had members in both ghettos. The scrap ghetto suffered terribly from hunger and diseases. An epidemic of typhoid fever developed there. It was concealed from the Germans by a local Polish doctor in order to prevent the gassing of the entire scrap ghetto. In two months the typhoid epidemic died out.

Dec.6, 1942 In Ciepielów Stary, near Kielce, a motorized detachment of the SS, under Officer Berner, burned alive 21 Poles of the Kosior, Kowalski, and Obuchiewicz families for harboring Jews. A neighbor, Mrs. Stanisława Lewandowska, hid and kept little Dawid Semkowicz, who survived and after the war moved to Haifa, Israel.

Dec. 6, 1942 In Kłamocha Forest, near Kielce, Polish partisans battled German forces surrounding a hideout of Jews from Radom, Ostrow, and Starachowice. Twenty Poles were killed; two captured Jews died without betraying names of Polish game wardens who had helped them.

Dec. 10, 1942 An urgent appeal to the Allies was made by the Polish Government-in-Exile, addressed primarily to the governments of the United States and Great Britain, to stop the German genocidal operation by bombing the access railways, gas chambers, and crematoria, among other measures of retaliation and punishment against Germany. The Poles cited the complete record of German crimes as reported on radio by Stefan Korboński (1901-1989), the Head of the Directorate of Civil Resistance in Warsaw, and by numerous emissaries from Poland. At the same time Polish reports were confirmed independently by the intelligence work of Allen Dulles in Geneva, Switzerland, where German industrialists were reporting and cooperating with the U.S. Office of Strategic Studies (now Central Intelligence Agency) in

order to ensure their personal security in the face of the dwindling prospect of German victory in World War II.

Dec. 17, 1942 In London, Edward Raczyński, the Director of the Foreign Office of the Polish Government-in-exile, made an urgent appeal to the conscience of the world, in English, on British radio. He described the gigantic proportions of the German crimes committed on Polish Jews. He ended with words: "How small-minded is the powerful German nation and how infinite is its disgrace!"

Dec. 17, 1942 Twelve Allied governments issued a joint statement, announcing that persons responsible for the extermination of the Jews would be punished. However, Allied air planes did not scatter any leaflets protesting genocide of the Jews during the bombing of German cities. Polish requests for bombing of access railroads leading to the extermination camps, as well as gas chambers and crematoria, were ignored. Many British and American officials persisted in their criticism of reports of Jewish mass murders as exaggerations similar to the accounts of pogroms in Poland immediately after the First World War.

Dec. 19, 1942 Execution in Warsaw by the Gestapo of Rev. Father Marian Malicki, betrayed by a Jew for providing him with baptismal certificates and "Aryan" I.D. cards for a number of Jews. Malicki's brother, a municipal employee, and his wife were tortured and with broken limbs were loaded on death trains to be gassed in Treblinka. This information was given by Maria Reibenbach and her sister, two Jews who survived, thanks to the false documents supplied to them by the Malickis.

Dec. 28, 1942 The German physician, Professor Carl Clauberg, started an extensive program of pseudo-medical experiments on thousands of prisoners in Auschwitz and the other camps. Many of these experiments were ordered by the German pharmaceutical industry. Prisoners were infected with typhoid fever, malaria, tuberculosis, etc. Experimental bone and muscle transplants were performed and extensive frost bites were inflicted on the prisoners.

1942 In Warsaw, two members of the Polish Underground Scouting Organization, "Szare

Szeregi," were arrested by the Gestapo for bringing aid and weapons to the Jews in the Ghetto. Zdzisław Grecki was publicly executed while his friend was tortured in the Pawiak prison and then executed.

Jan. 1943 A series of meetings started between the officers of the Polish Home Army and representatives of the Jewish Fighting Organization. Planning began for joint action on both sides of ghetto walls at the outbreak of the Jewish uprising in Warsaw. Poles were to dynamite the ghetto walls to open the way for the retreat of Jewish fighters, who knew that the uprising would inevitably end in disaster. The Home Army supplied the Jewish Fighting Organization with: 1 light machine gun, 2 submachine guns, 50 handguns (all with magazines and ammunition), 10 rifles, 600 hand grenades with detonators, 30 kilograms of plastic explosives, 120 kilograms of regular explosives, 400 detonators for bombs and grenades, 30 kilograms of potassium to make the incendiary "Molotov cocktails," and also large quantities of saltpeter for the manufacture of gun powder.

The Jewish Fighting Organization was supplied by the Home Army with instructions on how to manufacture bombs, hand grenades, and incendiary bottles; how to build strongholds, and where to get the building supplies.

The Home Army's supplies to the Jewish Fighting Organization represented a considerable portion of its own stocks within the city of Warsaw. Thus, for example, the entire stock of weapons which Polish resistance held in the suburb of Wola was transferred by the Polish Home Army to the Jewish Fighting Organization in the ghetto. However, the primary goal of the Home Army was to build a secret armed force able to rise against Germany when the Reich was on the verge of defeat. The Home Army shared scarce weapons only with groups which manifested their overt resistance to the Germans. The totality of German domination of occupied Poland was the key factor that doomed the Polish Jews and millions of other victims.

Jan. 2, 1943 In London, the British Foreign Office and Air Ministry rejected renewed demands by the Polish Government for reprisal bombing of German cities in retaliation for German mass murders of Jews and Poles in occupied Poland. Earlier, Polish Prime Minister General Władysław Sikorski actually secured Winston Churchill's agreement to bomb the access railroads, gas chambers, and crematoria at Auschwitz. Churchill's clear instruction to bomb Auschwitz was endlessly delayed by the British Foreign Office and Air Ministry.

Jan. 14, 1943 Himmler paid a surprise visit to Warsaw to find out why the ghetto had not been evacuated. Himmler had apparently tried to do too much. He ran the Waffen SS, the entire German police, and all the anti-partisan actions in occupied countries. All along he tried to set a good example to the German nation which was enthusiastically supporting the war effort.

Jan. 15, 1943 In Aleksandrówka, near Biała Podlaska, Germans executed four Catholic Poles for aiding Jews.

Jan. 15, 1943 In Pilica-Zamek, German policemen executed Maria Rogozińska with her one-year-old son, for harboring Jews; a local Polish policeman was executed with her because he did not report the presence of Jews in the village.

Jan. 18, 1943 In the Warsaw Ghetto, the first clash between Germans and the Jewish resistance force took place. Jews marked for transport to Treblinka fired on their guards and succeeded in escaping. Armed resistance was encountered by the Germans.

Jan. 29, 1943 A radio message from the underground Directorate of Civil Resistance said: "In recent days, Jews in the Warsaw Ghetto defended themselves, arms in hand, and killed a few Germans. The Jewish National Committee requested that this information be passed on to the Histadrut in Palestine."

Jan. 29, 1943 In Wierzbica, near Miechów, a Jew named Naftul betrayed the hide-outs of a number of Jews, including his own in-laws, the Wandelmans. They and six members of another Jewish family were executed. Naftul also precipitated execution by the Germans of several Catholic farming families: four Książeks, seven Kucharskis, and three Nowaks.

Feb. 24, 1943 In Paulinów, near Sokołów Podlaski, German SS executed 14 Poles who gave aid to a German agent provocateur disguised as a Jew.

Feb. - July, 1943 Four hundred and forty-six Poles were executed by the Germans in the village of Aleksandrów near Lublin in reprisal for sheltering Jews, guerrillas, and Soviet prisoners of war.

4. March 1943 - Nov. 1944
Critical Decline of German Military Situation
The completion of the last stages of the "Final Solution to the Jewish Problem" came after German disaster at Stalingrad.

Despite limited counter-offensives the Germans were rapidly losing ground in the east. In the west, they lost France in this period. German fury concentrated on Jews within the reach of the Berlin government. Germans were venting on the Jewish population frustration caused by the impending total defeat of Germany in the world war and the bankruptcy of the struggle for the Lebensraum, the "1000 year Reich," and the domination of the world by the German race.

At the end of November 1944, Himmler issued the final orders to destroy the industrial installations of huge gas chambers and crematoria in the death camps in order to remove the evidence of German war crimes of genocide.

March 1943 The deportation of all the Jews of Berlin to death camps in the east was completed.

March 5 - July 8, 1943 Julius Gebler, the head of the Gestapo in Dębica, near Rzeszów, personally led raids on farms in the vicinity to trap Catholic families sheltering Jews. Gabler conducted the executions of 70 Poles and had their homes and farm buildings burned.

March 16 - 31, 1943 In Zarzętka, near Węgrow, sixteen Catholic farmers were tortured and murdered by the Gestapo during investigation of aid given to Jewish escapees from Treblinka.

March 18, 1943 A proclamation was issued by the underground Directorate of Civil Defense in Warsaw:

"The Polish people, themselves the victims of a horrible reign of [German] terror, are witnessing with horror and compassion the slaughter of the remnants of the Jewish population in Poland. Their protest against this crime has reached the ears of the free world. Their assistance to Jews escaping from ghettos or extermination camps prompted the German occupiers to publish a decree, threatening with death all Poles who render help to Jews... Some individuals from the criminal world [are] blackmailing the Poles who shelter Jews, and the Jews themselves. The Directorate of Civil Defense warns that every instance of such blackmail will be recorded and prosecuted with all the severity of the law -- immediately, whenever possible, but in any event in the near future."

March 18, 1943 A radio message from the underground Directorate of Civil Defense in Warsaw stated: "Jews remaining in Radomsk, Ujazd, Sobolew, Radzymin, and Szczerzec near Lwów have been liquidated."

March 22, 1943 In Rzeszow, in connection with the bribery of a German official named Brehmer, 27 Jews were murdered. They included: Mr. Pinek Goldberg, the owner of the largest printing shop in Rzeszow, Dr. Szmelkes, Dr. Stierer, a lawyer, Srul Turne, and other professional people.

March 22-23, 1943 Auschwitz-Birkenau: the construction of large scale gas chambers and crematoria was completed.

March 23, 1943 A radio message reached London from the underground Directorate of Civil Defense in Warsaw: "Tests on the sterilization of women are being conducted in Auschwitz. New crematoria have a capacity of 3,000 persons per day."

March 25, 1943 In Sterdyń, near Sokolów, German SS executed 47 Polish farmers and deported 140 to concentration camps for the "crime" of *Judenherbergerung*, or harboring of Jews.

March 30, 1943 A radio message from the underground Directorate of Civil Defense in Warsaw said:
"On March 13, 14, and 15 truck convoys loaded with Jews left the Kraków Ghetto en route to Auschwitz. About 1,000 people were killed in the ghetto. Jews from Łódź are being taken to Ozorków and exterminated there."

April 9, 1943 The Gestapo arrested Jerzy Vogel (a Polish citizen who had a German name) for smuggling about three hundred Jews out of the Warsaw Ghetto, hiding a Jewish girl,

Dorota Gelbert, with his family, and refusing to sign the Volksliste as a "racial German" -- he and most of his family perished in concentration camps.

April 13, 1943 German government radio announced finding the Katyń graves of Polish officers. Germans claimed that the Soviet Union, allied to the United States and Great Britain, murdered nearly half of all the officers of Poland's armed forces. Even though the Soviets murdered Polish officers while allied and cooperating with Germany in 1940, now the Germans tried to use this Soviet crime to split the allies. German propaganda also used the Katyń murders to deflect the world's attention from the mass murders in the Warsaw Ghetto.

April 14 to Aug. 4, 1943 In occupied Poland, German press and radio gave most of its attention to the Katyń massacre. German propaganda claimed that the mass murders of Polish officers were committed by Jewish agents of the NKVD. The Germans claimed that Soviet Marshal Lavrenti P. Beria, who was in charge of the NKVD, was Jewish because allegedly he had a Jewish mother.

April 19, 1943 In Berlin, the office of Foreign Minister Joachim Ribbentrop sent coded telegrams to German embassies in Switzerland and Hungary to recruit, from thousands of Poles in those countries, at least four anti-Semitic and anti-Soviet emigre Poles who would be willing to visit Katyń and make pronouncements convenient to German propaganda. German efforts in this matter failed.

April 19, 1943 An uprising began in the Warsaw Ghetto as Germans started the final liquidation of the Jewish population there (approx. 70,000 people). Polish and Jewish flags were raised by the (approx. 600) Jewish fighters. Germans used tanks and armored cars and began killing the 35,000 people in the ghetto. Within the ghetto, 7,000 Jews were killed during the uprising -- 6,000 were burned alive in the buildings. All buildings in the ghetto were destroyed. Germans used a total of about 2,000 men in combat, including Alsatian SS, who were French citizens. Casualties were suffered by both sides - Jewish fighters, and Polish resistance soldiers; German SS-men, military police, and Wehrmacht as well as Lithuanian guards. The ghetto walls were broken in several places and hundreds of Jews were able to cross to the "Aryan" side. The struggle lasted until May 8. After May 10 sporadic fighting went on in the ruins.

Marian Fuks analyzed Polish help to Jewish fighters in the Warsaw Ghetto in the bulletin of the Jewish Historical Institute in Poland (July-December 1989); he stated on p.44:

"It is an absolutely certain fact that without help and even the active participation of the Polish resistance movement it would have not been possible at all to bring about the uprising in the Warsaw Ghetto."

April 20, 1943 In Warsaw, Michal Klepfisz stepped in front of a German machine gun to save other Jews. He was decorated with the cross of *Virtuti Militari* by the Commander-in-Chief of the Polish Armed Forces, Gen. Władysław Sikorski (1881-1943), a fact immediately broadcast by radio from London to lift the spirits of Jewish fighters in the ghetto.

April 20, 1943 - May 16, 1943 In Warsaw, in the ghetto, the Germans destroyed 631 underground bunkers in which groups of Jews were hiding. In addition hundreds of secret shelters were destroyed in the demolished buildings. The increasing threat of execution and the need to hide had led the Jews to build shelters and bunkers. A diary stated: "During the night one could hear throughout the ghetto the rasp of saws, knocks of hammers, and blows of pick axes. Jews were digging for themselves another ghetto below the surface of the ground."

A poet of the ghetto, Władysław Szengel, wrote: "The cave age is returning. People are going back to live underground." Many shelters were overcrowded as another diary described: "200 unwashed persons, stuffy, hot, stench. Two cases of open tuberculosis, one case of measles. I could not find any spot for myself and my baby, there was no room to put the child even on the floor."

April 22, 1943 German commander Gen. J. Stroop in Warsaw ordered the execution of 35 Poles who fought in the ghetto in the Jewish uprising. Stroop described many of them as communists who belonged to the Soviet sponsored, and numerically small People's Guard. Before execution some of them shouted, "Long Live Poland!" and "Long Live Moscow!". However, Soviet help to the Jews was conspicuously absent despite the fact that there was an obvious Communist presence in the ghetto.

April 25, 1943 In Warsaw, additional executions were ordered by the German commander Gen. Jurgen Stroop. 17 Catholic Poles who fought in the ghetto in the Jewish uprising were condemned to death.

April 26, 1943 The Soviet Union broke diplomatic relations with Polish Government-in-Exile under the pretext that the Poles refused to accept Soviet (false) claims that the Germans murdered Polish officers at Katyń. The Soviets cynically claimed that in this matter the Poles collaborated with the Germans and thus betrayed the anti-German alliance. Moscow complained that the Poles did not address pertinent questions about the Katyń murders directly to the Soviet government and therefore insulted it. Thus, the Soviets not only committed the mass murder of 15,000 Polish officers, but also used the murder itself as a political weapon to gradually deprive Poland of independence.

Immediately, they succeeded in weakening Polish position with the western allies despite the fact that allied governments in London and Washington were aware that the Soviets, and not the Germans, had committed the Katyń massacre and other mass murders on Polish citizens in Soviet held territory in 1939-1941. At this stage of the war London and Washington were willing to betray Poland rather than to antagonize the Soviets. Moscow wanted to have diplomatic relations with a new government of Poland which would be fully controlled by the Soviets.

In 1952 a Special Committee of the U.S. Congress unanimously concluded that the security police of the Soviet Union were responsible for the Katyń massacre. It recommended that its investigations of the Katyń crime, depositions, evidence and findings "should be presented to the General Assembly of the United Nations, with the end in view of seeking action before the International World Court of Justice against the Soviet Union for a crime of violation of the law recognized by all civilized nations." (82nd Congress, Congressional Record 8864, 1952)

April 27, 1943 In Warsaw, eighteen men from the Security Corps of the Polish Home Army cooperating with the Jewish Military Organization entered the ghetto area through a tunnel on Muranowska Street, carrying arms, hand grenades and ammunition, under the command of Major Henryk Iwański and Wladyslaw Zarski (Zajdler). All were wounded or killed in action. Iwański's brother, Wacław, and son, Roman (16), were killed together with Wincenty Jędrychowski (30), and "Czapa" Pilichowski (35) as soldiers of the Polish Home Army. When they had used up all their ammunition the survivors retreated through storm sewers, taking with them 34 wounded Jewish fighters, including Ber Mark, the author of the *Uprising in the Warsaw Ghetto* (Schocken Books).

May, 1943 In Warsaw, 15 men of the Security Corps of the Polish Home Army under Major Henryk Iwański, brought food, drugs, and munitions from the "Aryan" side to the ghetto. They rescued wounded Jewish fighters on their way back. The older son of Major Iwański, Zbigniew (18), lost his life together with Stanisław Gładkowski and Jan Cieplikowski.

May, 1943 In Brody, near Tarnopol, German military police surrounded a house where two Jewish guerrillas had found shelter. Polish inhabitants were shot after they refused to show where the two Jews were hiding. Both Jews committed suicide.

May 6, 1943 The underground newspaper *Rzeczpospolita* printed an official statement by the Delegate of the Polish Government-in-Exile, which denounced German crimes in the Warsaw Ghetto and paid homage to the Jewish fighters. It voiced Polish solidarity, and called on all Poles to help Jews who had escaped from the ghetto.

May 8, 1943 Massada-like suicides of Jews and one Polish girl took place at the Jewish headquarters of Mordechai Anielewicz (1920-1943) at 18 Mila Street in Warsaw, only moments before an underground passage was found nearby and provided escape for a number of Jewish fighters. Of the four deputy commanders of the Jewish uprising in the Warsaw Ghetto, two survived: Marek Edelman (a cardiologist and Solidarity activist in Poland) and Icchok Cukierman (now residing in Israel). The last message from the Jewish Fighting Organization in Warsaw, addressed to Jewish leaders in New York, pleaded:

"Brothers! Speak up! The surviving Jews in Poland live convinced that in the most horrible moments of our history you did not help us. Speak up! This is our last appeal."

May 8, 1943 In Brody, a German infantry battalion surrounded and massacred a Polish resistance group assembled to free Jews (including the poet Shudryk) from the Lwów Ghetto.

May 8, 1943 A radio message from the Directorate of Civil Defense in Warsaw said: "Germans are finishing off the ghetto. Two hundred apartment houses were burned down. The members of the Jewish Council, held since April 19 as hostages, were shot. They were: the chairman, Lichtenbaum, the deputy chairman, Gustaw Wielikowski, Alfred Sztocman, and Stanisław Szereszewski. Their bodies were thrown into a pile of garbage."

May 12, 1943 A Soviet Air Force attack on Warsaw ended up killing more Poles and Jews than Germans. No Soviet help was given to the fighting ghetto despite the fact that Warsaw was clearly within range of Soviet aircraft, while Moscow government had detailed current information on the situation of the Jews in occupied Poland.

May 13, 1943 Szmul Zygielbojm (1895-1943), a member of the Polish National Council, committed suicide in London to protest the indifference of the Allies and neutral countries to the German genocide of the Jews and in particular to the suffering of the Warsaw Ghetto. Zygielbojm, as a member of the Polish National Council in exile, had been in charge of informing western allies about the horrible fate of Jews under German-Nazi rule since 1941. He arrived from occupied Poland in London as one of the leaders of Jewish socialist labor union movement called "Bund." His office gathered radio reports, documents brought by couriers, and all information related to the tragedy of European Jews for the purpose of broadcasting them to the world.

The British coroner who investigated Zygielbojm's suicide described it as "the death of a Polish gentleman." Although Zygielbojm's death was widely reported in the British and American press, the motive behind it received little notice.

May 15, 1943 Polish resistance radio SWIT (which was located in England and worked in close cooperation with the Home Army in Poland) reported:

"The horrible massacre of the remnants of the Warsaw Ghetto has been going on for three weeks now. Led by the Jewish Fighting Organization, armed Jews defended themselves heroically. The Germans used artillery and armored cars. Over 300 Germans were killed by the Jewish fighters; some 1,000 Germans have been wounded. Tens of thousands of Jews have been deported, murdered, or burned alive by the Germans.

The underground *Economic Bulletin* reported that 100,000 dwellings, 2,000 industrial locations, 3,000 commercial establishments and several factories have been burned or blown up in the Warsaw Ghetto. This was greater destruction than that caused by the Germans in the battle of Warsaw in September 1939.

May 16, 1943 SS General Juergen Stroop reported that "the Warsaw Ghetto is no more." He later stated that 56,065 Jews were apprehended. Of these, 7,000 were immediately executed and the rest were sent to the death camps; an additional 5565 people were killed during the fighting, and Germans destroyed 631 bunkers in the ghetto.

May 29, 1943 In Warsaw, the Gestapo executed a "blue" police lieutenant, Riszard Stolkiewicz, who, together with Capt. Tadeusz Żmudziński, served in the underground Polish Home Army, and provided Jews with "Aryan" I.D. cards and gave shelter to Jewish refugees from the ghetto.

June 3, 1943 In Warsaw, radio messages were repeated throughout the day with instructions from the Polish underground Directorate of Civil Defense on helping Jews hiding throughout occupied Poland.

June 8, 1943 In Zwieczyce, near Rzeszów, 19 Polish farmers were executed by the German Gestapo and Ukrainian SS Galizien for aiding Jews and Communists.

June 10, 1943 In Hucisko, near Głogow Małopolski, 21 Poles were massacred for sheltering Jews. Seventeen farm houses, homes of the executed Poles, were burned together with a large number of farm buildings.

June 10, 1943 A radio message was heard in London from the underground Directorate of Civil Defense in Warsaw:

"In Auschwitz, Block X is scheduled to become an experimental station of the Central Institute of Hygiene in Berlin for castration, sterilization, and artificial insemination. At present, 200 Jewish men and 25 Jewish women are there."

June 17, 1943 A radio dispatch to the Polish Government-in-Exile in London from the Chief of the Directorate of Civil Defense of the Polish underground in Warsaw said:

"Public opinion here demands that the attention of the Anglo-Saxons turn to Poland, and it calls for retaliation against the [German] Reich, in line with the demands, reiterated over the past year, listing the crimes for which the bombardment of Germany should be conducted... I beg and urge you that declarations be made simultaneously with bombing raids over the Reich that these are in retaliation for the latest German bestialities."

Spring 1943 The completion of the hunt for the remaining Jews in Poland, known as the operation "Reinhard," was reported by the SS. In effect, no more Jews were left in German hands to be gassed by the administration of the General Gouvernment in occupied Poland.

Himmler ordered exhuming and burning over 700,000 bodies temporarily buried in Treblinka and Sobibor, including 135,000 from Yugoslavia, Greece, and France. French police arrested 70,000 Jews and sent them from Paris to German death camps.

French help was indispensable to the Germans in identifying, locating, and isolating Jews in internment camps and then delivering them to the Gestapo entirely on their own initiative. Vichy France offered more help to the Germans in the destruction of European Jewry than any other western European country and most eastern European countries which were actually allied with Germany, such as Romania and Hungary.

June 28, 1943 The director of the SS-Central Building Office in Auschwitz reported to the Wirtschaftsverwaltungshauptamt (WVHA), or the Chief Economic and Administrative Offices of the German Government in Berlin, that the four big, new gas chambers and crematoria numbers II, III, IV, and V were exterminating and cremating 4756 people daily.

June 28, 1943 A radio message from the underground Directorate of Civil Defense in Warsaw stated: "In Lwów there are still about 4,000 Jews gathered in the labor camp at Janowskie. During the roll call each morning, two rabbis are forced to fox-trot before the assembled inmates, to the tune of a Jewish band."

Volumes could be written on the macabre and sadistic use of music by the Germans in ghettos, prisons, and concentration camps.

Music in these places of confinement has been the tool of a refined and vicious German sadism. It was used to inflict moral and physical tortures.

June 28, 1943 In the village of Ciesie, near Mińsk Mazowiecki, a raid by Gestapo, SS, and German military police searched for Jewish escapees from a death train to Treblinka.

Twenty-one Poles and three Jews were burned alive as the village was set on fire. Several Polish families were executed, one Jew escaped.

June 29, 1943 Resistance radio SWIT reported: "All inhabitants of the ghetto, in Stanisławów, Łuków, Węgrów, and Żółkiew have been murdered. In Warsaw some 2,000 Jews are breathing their last in cellars and ruins. There is still some fighting during the night. At Sobibór, German bands are playing music at the station to greet Jews arriving from abroad."

June 31, 1943 In Bobowiska, near Puławy, Germans executed Kazimierz Hołaj (35), Michał Podolski (32), Feliks Pecuła (45), and Stanisław Pecuła (30), for hiding Jews.

July 4, 1943 Near Gibraltar, General Władysław Sikorski, Prime Minister of Poland and Commander-in-Chief of Polish Armed Forces, died in a sabotaged British airplane.

At that time the notorious Kim Philby served as the British security chief in Gibraltar. He was a Soviet spy, who later died in Moscow and was given a Soviet state funeral with full honors. He was one of the few foreigners who achieved a rank of a general in the NKVD - KGB. Philby was in position to sabotage Sikorski's plane, possibly using an NKVD team, which traveled with ambassador E.M. Maisky.

Ever since the breaking of diplomatic relations with Poland the Soviets had wanted to liquidate the legal Polish government headed by Sikorski. German radio called General Sikorski "the last victim of the crime of Katyń."

Among others, British Secretary of State for Foreign Affairs R.A. Eden exerted heavy pressure on General Sikorski, shortly before his death, to accept the false Soviet version of the Katyń crime "for the sake of unity of the anti-German alliance." Sikorski resisted British and American pressure to falsify the truth. Thus, Poland lost an able leader of international stature and a great spokesman for all Polish citizens living through the horrors of German occupation. More than any other head of government, Sikorski repeatedly appealed to the conscience of the world on behalf of the Jews suffering in occupied Poland the unbelievable atrocities of the German "Final Solution."

July 4, 1943 In Bór Kunowski, near Starachowice, Germans murdered 43 Poles for helping Jews hidden in a nearby forest, who had escaped from the ghetto and formed a guerrilla unit. Twenty-three Poles were burned alive, and twenty were killed with pistols.

July 5, 1943 In Szarwark, near Kraków, Gestapo aided by the "navy blue" police murdered the Mendala family of five for having prepared 300 hard boiled eggs for Jews (hiding in a nearby forest), and Władysław Starzec for sheltering a Jew (who managed to escape from the Germans). Both Polish farms were burned to the ground and never rebuilt. Thousands of such Polish tragedies were never recorded in the Yad Vashem memorial of the Holocaust in Israel.

July 12 - Aug. 17, 1943 In Michniów, near Kielce, the German reprisal surpassed the famous massacres in Lidice, in Czechoslovakia and in Oradour-sur-Glane, in France. Two hundred and fifty families of Polish farmers were exterminated and their farms burned, for helping Jewish guerrillas. Only three Poles survived.

July 16, 1943 In Wilno (Vilnius), Ichok Wittenberg was delivered by the Jewish ghetto police to the Gestapo. He took his life by swallowing poison rather than risk betraying his co-conspirators under torture.

July 20, 1943 In Mińsk, 70 Jews working for the German civil administration were executed by the German police.

July 25, 1943 In Berlin, Admiral Canaris warned Colonel Ame of the Italian Intelligence that Himmler planned to kidnap the Pope in order to stop the Catholic Church's sheltering of the Jews. However, Himmler was not fully aware of the fact that as many as 700,000 Jews were helped by the Catholic Church.

Aug. 1943 Jan Karski, a Polish diplomat and an eye witness to German extermination of the Jews in the death camps and ghetto, arrived in Washington. Karski reported to President Roosevelt on the horrible situation in occupied Poland and the German genocide of the Jews. Karski presented the true dimensions of the mass murders committed under the full authority of the German government. President Franklin D. Roosevelt kept asking specific questions about the extermination of Jews in occupied Poland long past the time allotted for Karski's audience.

On behalf of the Polish Government-in-Exile and with the help of the Polish diplomatic service, Karski organized a campaign of speeches and conferences advocating immediate measures, especially the bombing of the access railways, gas chambers, and crematoria. These measures could still have saved millions of Jewish and other victims. Karski's efforts were directed at American dignitaries including the Under-Secretary of State, Adolf Berle, Attorney General Biddle, Supreme Court Justice Felix Frankfurter and Catholic Archbishops Mooney and Strich.

Karski spoke to many Jewish-American community leaders and rabbis, such as Stephen Wise, Nahum Goldmann and others requesting in vain their political support for the Allied bombings needed to disable the huge extermination plant in the death camps.

Aug. 16 - 20, 1943 An uprising in the Bialystok Ghetto was led by Daniel Moszkowicz and B. Tanenbaum, who was killed Aug. 20. It was precipitated by German moves to liquidate the Bialystok Ghetto. Some Jews were able to escape and join guerrilla forces.

Aug. 31, 1943 A radio message from the underground Directorate of Civil Defense in Warsaw said:

126

"Liquidation of Jews in Będzin started at the beginning of this month. About 7,000 were taken to Auschwitz. The young are liquidated first. As of July 1 of this year, the total number of Jews in Poland -- including those who were in camps, in ghettos, and in hiding -- is 250 to 300 thousand. Of these, 15,000 are in Warsaw; 80,000 in Łódź; 30,000 in Będzin; 12,000 in Wilno; 20,000 in Białystok; 8,000 in Kraków; 4,000 in Lublin; 5,000 in Lwów."

Aug. 1943 In Polish provinces newly annexed by Germany, 566,000 Germans were resettled in accordance with the German "blood and soil" theories; they were removed from areas east of the borders of Germany, such as the Baltic states, Romania, and Hungary. They were to be placed in properties confiscated from Poles and Jews. 25 percent of them were still in the resettlement camps. Thus, the growing problem of displaced people classified as "racial Germans" from eastern and southern Europe was caused initially by German racist programs of the wartime government in Berlin. It was to continue for the next fifty years.

Sept. 22, 1943 In Dobrucowa, SS guards from the camp at Szebnie murdered about 700 Jews, mostly old people, women, and children. Bodies of the victims were burned. The victims included the wife of a lawyer from Rzeszów, Mrs. Schildkrant, and her daughter.

Sept. 23, 1943 A radio message from the underground Directorate of Civil Defense in Warsaw said:
"The Będzin Ghetto has been liquidated. The Germans murdered 30,000 people."

Oct. 1943 In Warsaw, Gestapo arrested the rector (president) of the Catholic Seminary, Rev. Monsignor Roman Archutowski. The Gestapo sent him to the Majdanek concentration camp where he died after being tortured for helping hundreds of Jews.

Oct. 15, 1943 In Tyczyn, German Gestapo agents executed five Polish farmers "for helping and hiding Jews."

Nov. 3, 1943 In Warsaw, Aleksander Weiss was arrested and tortured to death by the Gestapo. He was the manager of a Polish underground printing office which provided thousands of Jews with "Aryan" I.D. cards.

Nov. 3, 1943 In Szebnie, upon arrival the SS-Obersturmfuhrer, Wilhelm Hasse, together with Ukrainian police, conducted the liquidation of a Jewish camp. 2800 Jews were loaded completely unclothed for transport to Auschwitz. They were deprived of their clothing in order to prevent escapes. After arrival, a few persons considered fit for hard physical work were selected, the others were gassed.

Nov. 5, 1943 In Szebnie, 500 Jewish prisoners were executed by the SS guards.

Nov. 11, 1943 SS-Obersturmbannfuhrer Arthur Liebehenschel replaced Rudolf Hoess as commandant of Auschwitz.

Nov. 11, 1943 In Kraków, a member of the "navy blue" Polish police, who was a soldier of the Polish Home Army, was executed for providing Jews with "Aryan" papers.

Nov. 18, 1943 In Białystok, German authorities exterminated 22 Poles affiliated with the Home Army for providing Jews with "Aryan" identity cards.

Nov. 19, 1943 A radio message to London from the underground Directorate of Civil Defense in Warsaw said:
"Slaughter of Jews in Trawniki goes on. Massacres also in Poniatowa and Lwów."

Nov. 20, 1943 In Lwów, Professor of the University of Lwów, Chairman of the Department of Polish Literature, Kazimierz Kołbuszewski died after being sent to Majdanek, where he was tortured for harboring one of his Jewish students.

Nov. 28 - Dec. 1, 1943 Poland was betrayed in Teheran by Churchill and Roosevelt, who recognized the Stalin-Hitler line of partition of the Polish state drawn along the Bug River in September of 1939, as the Soviet postwar border. They also agreed to make postwar Poland part of the Soviet zone of influence and thereby deprive their ally of national independence.
(In order to cover up the recognition of the Stalin-Hitler, or Ribbentrop-Molotov, line they called it the "Curzon Line" as of 1920. This line was proposed by the Allies' ambassadors on July 10, 1920, and then it was falsified on

July 11, 1920 in Lloyd George's office before its delivery to Moscow.)

The rape of Poland had to be enforced by the use of Stalin's terror apparatus. Poland was to become the most important Soviet conquest in World War II. Practically the entire area, where German genocide of one-third of world's Jewry was taking place, was to become separated from the West. The Soviets would not permit the revival of the traditional Talmudic culture of Yiddish-speaking Jews after the Germans were gone from war-torn Poland.

1943 In Stryj, Gestapo executed a local schoolteacher and his wife by public hanging for harboring a Jewish family.

Jan. 6, 1944 In Kraków, Germans executed Helena Jabłkowska and Janina Kowalik for assisting scores of Jews and sheltering several Jewish families, including a prominent Jewish family, the Bardachs.

Jan. 20, 1944 The prisoner count then in Auschwitz included 18,418 in the main camp, 8649 Poles, 3830 Jews, 2989 Soviets, 742 Germans, 155 French, 66 Serbs, and other nationalities. Polish Catholics were always the most numerous of the inmates of Auschwitz; German prisoners were brought there to serve as an internal prison hierarchy, which distributed (and stole) prison food and terrorized the other inmates. The total number of victims murdered in Auschwitz included approximately 960,000 Jews, 275,000 Polish Catholics, 25,000 Gypsies, and 15,000 Soviet prisoners of war (according to the estimates accepted in 1990 by Raul Hillberg and other researchers).

Jan. 29, 1944 In Kraków, the head of the SS and military police condemned 73 Poles to death for helping Jews. The names of the executed people were listed on an official German poster displayed in Krakow.

Feb. 1944 In Sasów, Germans burned alive or shot the entire population of the village of several hundred Polish Catholics for bringing aid to about 100 Jews hiding in the local forest.

Feb. 1, 1944 In Warsaw, SS and Police General Frantz Kutschera (1904-1944) was killed in reprisal for conducting mass executions in the streets of Warsaw. The sentence of the Polish resistance court was carried out by the soldiers of the Polish Home Army under Bronisław Pietraszewicz (1922-1944).

Feb. 2, 1944 In Warsaw eighty Poles were executed in the street by the German military police. They included the editor of *Gazeta Rolnicza*, Mikołaj Łażecki, and others arrested for giving shelter to Jews who escaped from the ghetto.

Feb. 5, 1944 In Szerzyny, near Jasło, the Polish family of Józef Augustyniak was executed by German military police together with two Jewish families related to Eliasz and Hersz Heskel, and found on their farm. Neighboring farmers, Franciszek Figura and Jędryś as well as Bronisław Mitoraj were sent to Auschwitz for sheltering Jews, never to return. Mitoraj was betrayed by a Jew who was taken into his home.

Feb. 25, 1944 In Rzeszów, Michał Stasiuk was executed by the Gestapo for sheltering 15 Jews, most of whom were killed with him.

March 7, 1944 In Warsaw, a Catholic midwife was executed in the ruins of the ghetto when she went to a hide-out at Grojecka Street to deliver a Jewish baby.

March 7, 1944 In Warsaw, 34 Jews who were hiding under the floor of a greenhouse at 84 Grójecka Street were executed, together with 6 Poles who built the shelter and supplied it with food.

April 19, 1944 In Brzozow, near Krosno, a German court of three judges, Dr. Aldenhoff, Dr. Naumann, and Dr. Stumpel, presided over by Judge Pooth, with court reporter Hagelstein, sentenced to death an American Seventh Day Adventist, Jakub Gargasz (62), and his Polish wife, Zofia (44), for harboring Mrs. Katz, a Jew.

May 3, 1944 In Rzeszow, a "blue" policeman named Jarocki caught and killed Szymek Unger, a Jew. Later, Jarocki was sentenced to death by a clandestine resistance court and executed near Łańcut by a patrol of the Polish Home Army.

May 16, 1944 The first transport of Hungarian Jews arrived in Auschwitz. They were marched straight to the gas chambers, the first of the

400,000 Hungarian Jews who were murdered there.

May 18, 1944 The Polish 2nd Corps entered Monte Cassino opening the road to Rome after a long and bloody up-hill battle with German paratroopers and panzer grenadiers. Near the monastery of Monte Cassino there is a Polish military cemetery for the 924 men killed there in action plus some veterans of the battle who were buried there later. Among the many Christian crosses, there is a group of graves marked with the Star of David for Polish Jews buried during services conducted by rabbis, chaplains of the 2nd Polish Corps.

May 19, 1944 In Istanbul, Germans offered to the Allies the lives of 700,000 Hungarian Jews against payment of 10,000 lorries, 2,000,000 bars of soap, 800 tons of coffee, 200 tons of cocoa, and 800 tons of tea. The Germans offered a guarantee that the lorries would be used "on the eastern front only." Meanwhile Jews already deported to Germany from Hungary were to be kept alive for fourteen days, pending the transaction (which never materialized).

The Germans sent Joel Brand of the Hungarian Zionist Relief and Rescue Committee with their exchange offer. He was accompanied by a Gestapo agent, a converted Jew, Bandi Grosz, alias Andre Gyorgy, entrusted to arrange a meeting on neutral ground between senior SS and Allied officers in order to discuss terms for a separate peace.

The British government concluded that the German exchange offer was a cover for a separate peace intrigue designed to embroil Britain with the USSR -- a scheme to split the western allies from Russia. The *Manchester Guardian* called it "the depth of satanic wickedness and perverted ingenuity of the Germans." (July 20, 1944). During the war the Soviet and German governments conducted negotiations in Stockholm, Sweden, in 1942-1944. The Germans wanted to produce disunity between Allies and the USSR while the Soviets wanted to blackmail their Western partners with the "specter of a separate peace in the East" and the possible conversion of the weakening German state into a satellite of the Soviet Union.

June 14, 1944, in Budapest, Germans offered to exchange 30,000 Jews for twenty million Swiss francs. The Bergen-Belsen concentration camp was to serve as an "exchange camp." The exchange did not take place.

June 20, 1944 A radio message to London from the underground Directorate of Civil Defense in Warsaw stated:

"Since May 15, mass murders have been carried out in Auschwitz. Jews are taken first, then the Soviet prisoners of war, and the so-called sick. Mass transports of Hungarian Jews arrive. Thirteen trains per day, 40-50 cars each. Victims convinced [that] they will be exchanged for [German] POW's or resettled in the east. Corpses are burned in crematoria and out in the open. Over 100,000 people [from Hungary] have been gassed to date."

July 19, 1944 A radio message to London from the underground Directorate of Civil Defense in Warsaw said:

"Murder of Jews in Auschwitz is conducted under the code name Operation Hoess -- read: Hess."

July 24, 1944 In Lublin Polish prisoners resisted evacuation, captured the SS guards and turned them over, together with an intact gas chamber and crematorium, to the Red Army. Himmler ordered the evacuation of major camps, as well as hundreds Jewish labor camps in central Poland and in Latvia, in a westward direction.

July 29, 1944, SS-Hauptsturmfuhrer Richard Baer was put in charge of the whole extermination complex at Auschwitz.

Aug. 1 - Oct. 2, 1944 The Warsaw Uprising against the Germans at first was encouraged by the Soviets. However, later they watched from across the Vistula River as German forces slaughtered nearly a quarter of a million people and destroyed over 70 percent of the Polish capital. There are indications that the uprising in Warsaw altered Soviet strategic objectives.

Originally the Soviet intent was to fully exploit the breakdown of German defenses by Marshal Rokossowski's surprise offensive on the first Byelorussian Front, starting in the north at Bobruisk and Vitebsk on July 4, 1944, capturing Minsk, and reaching the outskirts of Warsaw and the Vistula River in August 1944. A critical fuel shortage immobilized German tanks and converted them into "sitting ducks" while the Soviets had ample fuel supplies and enjoyed decisive superiority on the battlefield. The Germans lost to Rokossowski's forces some 600000 men killed, wounded and taken prisoner, 900 tanks, and thousands of motor vehicles. By then the Germans and their allies had about 2 million men in less than 200 divisions, decimated and poorly equipped. The Soviets were pushing them with an army of 5 million men in more than 300 divisions, with about 31,000 field guns, 5,200 tanks, and 6,000 aircraft.

On Aug. 1, 1944, a political decision was made in Moscow to stop the Soviet advance across Vistula River and wait until the Germans destroyed in Warsaw the forces of Polish Home Army dedicated to the independence of Poland. The decision to stop the front idled the elite troops of Marshall Rokossowski. These forces were shifted to the Romanian front for an advance into Hungary and Bulgaria -- both located south of the Carpathian Mountains and therefore strategically much less important regions than the area of Poznan on the Warthe River which was on the road to the German capital of Berlin. The Soviets were giving up the opportunity to capture Berlin in the autumn of 1944, in order to convert Poland into their satellite state.

Of the 50000 Poles who took part in the uprising, only 10 percent had guns. Against them the Germans assembled about 55000 soldiers of the Wehrmacht and SS, equipped with tanks, artillery, mortars, rockets, and dive bombers -- all these forces were made available to the Germans by the sudden halt of the Soviet offensive. The few survivors of the Jewish ghetto uprising joined Poles in the struggle against the regular German army, which suffered about 26000 dead and wounded. About 17000 Poles, soldiers of the Polish Home Army, were killed in combat and 25000 wounded. As a reprisal for the uprising, Germans destroyed buildings in Warsaw after the battle was over, and conducted a massive expulsion of the population of the capital in which the remaining Jews suffered along with the Poles. German expulsions in occupied Poland during 1939-1944 included over two and half million Polish citizens, including Jews.

After the collapse of the uprising, some of the Jews who earlier fought in the ghetto uprising, and later fought in the Warsaw uprising of 1944, remained in the Polish resistance. Among them were Icchak Cukierman ("Antek"), Cywia Lubetkin ("Celina"), Tuwie Borzykowski ("Tadek"), Marek Edelman ("Marek"), Salo Fiszgrund ("Julek"), and others. A number of them hid in the ruins of the Warsaw Ghetto in underground bunkers, which the Germans did not manage to destroy. For example, Dawid Fogelman and three other Jews survived until the liberation of Warsaw in the bunker at 5 Szczęśliwa Street.

German forces, which destroyed Warsaw and caused death of about a quarter of a million people in the Polish capital during the uprising, included ex-convicts, known for hideous bestialities. These professional criminals were led by Maj. General Oskar Dirlewanger (1895-?), who was decorated with the German Cross of Gold.

Aug. 2, 1944 In Auschwitz, 2897 prisoners from the "Gypsy Family Camp at Birkenau" were executed.The total population of German concentration camps was recorded at 524,286 and an additional 1,100,000 were expected soon by the government in Berlin.

Aug. 3, 1944 In Poznań (Posen), Himmler fearfully addressed the Gauleiters:

"A half-million [detainees] of the most embittered political and criminal enemies of the Reich...would be poured out over Germany."

Perceived by the Berlin government as a danger to the German public, the inmates of concentration camps were murdered en masse during the evacuations and death marches at the end of the war.

Aug. 21, 1944 In Switzerland, the arrival of the first of 2700 Jews in exchange for payment of 20 million Swiss francs by the Jewish International Charity to the German government took place. The last shipment of 1100 Jews arrived on Feb. 6, 1945 and was noted by the Swiss Press. The German government reacted by ordering "that no concentration-camp inmate should fall into Allied hands alive."

Aug. 22, 1944 The current prisoner count in the Auschwitz complex, including Birkenau and the nearest sub-camps, exceeded 130,000, which were guarded by 2250 SS and Wehrmacht soldiers.

Sept. 1, 1944 In London, A.R. Dew, head of the Southern Department of the British Foreign Office commented:

"In my opinion a disproportionate amount of time of this office is wasted in dealing with these wailing Jews." (Dew was answering the submissions made by the Board of Deputies of British Jews urging help for Jews in Hungary and Rumania.)

Sept. 1944 In Berlin, Heinrich Himmler was nominated Commander-in-Chief of the Replacement Army of "Germanic SS." It was recruited from outside Germany since the best sources of German manpower had been drained on the eastern front.

Sept. 13, 1944 The American Air Force bombed the Auschwitz-Monowitz Buna-Werke concentration camp owned by I.G. Farbenindustrie, Auschwitz division.

Sept, 1944 In Warsaw, Germans murdered eight Catholic nuns for harboring Jews in their shelter.

October 1944 Eleven transports from Theresienstadt in Bohemia were brought to Auschwitz -- over 18000 people were gassed.

Nov. 7, 1944 Prisoners of the Sonderkommando revolted at crematoria II and IV at Auschwitz-Birkenau.

Nov. 29, 1944 Himmler ordered the destruction of the industrial installations of huge gas chambers and crematoria in German extermination camps in order to prevent them falling into the hands of the Allies as evidence of German crimes of genocide.

5. Dec. 1944 - May 1945
The last frantic struggles of the disintegrating German state. Dismantling of death camps in the east and deadly evacuation marches. German army's losses in 1944 were immense, and represented more than one hundred divisions.

The December 16 counter-offensive on the German western front in the Ardennes failed miserably. The Americans, British, Poles, and French forced their way forwards over the Rhine River. The Soviet and Polish armies burst across the Vistula River and then cleared Pomerania and Silesia to reach the Oder-Neisse river line, which was to become the border between Poland and Germany after the war.

By mid-March, the German government of Adolf Hitler had been directing operations from a bomb-proof bunker deep under the chancellery in Berlin, while the Allied forces progressed far into Germany.

After the April 16 attack across the Oder River by the Russians and Poles, Hitler composed his political testament. He repudiated the German people as unworthy of him and he denounced the members of the German government as traitors. He believed that the Jewish conspiracy had brought him down.

Hitler took his own life on April 30, 1945, when the news came that the powerful German army group "Mitte," ordered by him to rescue Berlin had been defeated by the 2nd Polish army near Bautzen (*Budziszyn*) on April 21-27. It was the bloodiest battle fought by Poles in World War II. 26,000 German elite soldiers of the Berlin rescue force were killed there and 314 of their best tanks and 135 self-propelled guns were lost. 27,000 Germans were taken prisoner, most of them wounded in combat.

The Germans were under the command of one of their ablest officers, Field Marshal Ferdinand Schoerner, and the Poles, mostly former soldiers of the Home Army, were led by General Karol "Walter" Swierczewski, who had commanded the International Brigade in Spain and was one of the heroes of Hemingway's *For Whom the Bell Tolls*.

In the final assault on Berlin, units of the Polish 1st Army took part and were the first to take the Brandenburg Gate (erected in 1791 during the partitions of Poland which were initiated by the Berlin government). The Poles were also the first to capture (on May 8, 1945) the Siegessaule, or the Victory Column (erected in 1873 to commemorate the defeat of France and the unification of Germany in 1871 as well as the establishment of the short-lived German Empire, which was very oppressive to the Poles. It ended forty-seven years later, in 1918). Polish 1st Army units were the only non-Soviet forces in the Berlin operation.

The history of the combat of the elite Hermann Goering Panzer Division with the Poles is almost symbolic of the war. In Sept. 1939 it defeated the 10th Brigade of Polish motorized cavalry under General Stanislaw Maczek. In Aug. 1944 the 10th Brigade of Polish motorized cavalry, reorganized as the 1st Polish Armored Division and still under General Maczek, decimated the Hermann Goering Panzer Division in the battle of Falaise, Normandy. Finally, in April 1945 the Polish 2nd Army destroyed the Hermann Goering Division together with the Grossdeutschland Corps and other German elite troops in the battle of Bautzen. Hitler personally ordered the Berlin rescue operation. The Polish victory at Bautzen ended the desperate German attempt to rescue Berlin from encirclement.

600,000 Polish soldiers were in combat on the fronts of collapsing Germany; 200,000 of them on the western and southern fronts and 400,000 on the eastern front. There were more Polish Jews on the western and southern fronts than on the eastern front. Many Jews joined the 1942 evacuation of Polish ex-prisoners from the Soviet Union to Iran. A large number of them, including Menachem Begin, remained in Palestine and joined the fight for independence of Israel. During the Second World War 6,028,000 citizens of Poland were killed (out of population of about 36,000,000). Jews represented about one-half of the victims (out of a community of three and half million people).

Meanwhile the last act of the tragedy of the prisoners of German concentration camps was unfolding amid evacuations, disease, starvation and executions. The war, which had cost some fifty million lives, was coming to a close. As stated before, the war started with the German-Soviet pact in 1939; it led to mass murders committed by both totalitarian states. German genocide of the Jews annihilated one-third of world's Jewry. Jews were murdered by the Germans just because they were Jewish. The genocide gave the German Nazis an illusion of an unlimited power midst vanishing prospects of German victory.

Jan. 19, 1945 Germans finally left the Łódź Ghetto in which 887 people were still alive. Ten mass graves were prepared for their execution near the wall of a Jewish cemetery. German executioners were not able to murder the last victims because they had to retreat with the routed German army. The liquidation of the Łódź Ghetto started in June 1944 and transports of inmates were sent to the gas chambers in Auschwitz. Before departure, the victims received German assurances that all of them would be assigned to agricultural labor in work camps.

Jan. 27, 1945 The Soviet Red Army's patrols reached Auschwitz and found the remaining prisoners who had not been included in the massive evacuation of prisoners to the concentration camps which were still operating in Germany. All German archives of Auschwitz were taken to Soviet Union. A Soviet estimate of about four million victims of Auschwitz-Birkenau was later revised.

Dr. Franciszek Piper of the Polish Museum of Auschwitz estimated that in 1940-1945 the Germans brought to Auschwitz at least 1,300,-000 people, including 1,100,000 Jews, about 150,000 Poles, 23,000 Gypsies, 15,000 Soviet prisoners of war, and 25,000 people of other nationalities. Of these at least 1,100,000 were exterminated, including 960,000 Jews, 75,000 Poles, 21,000 Gypsies, and 15,000 Soviet prisoners of war. These minimum figures were based on German transport lists, lists of numbered prisoners, and on statistics kept in Jewish ghettos. Dr. Piper estimated that the total victims of Auschwitz-Birkenau did not exceed 1,500,000 people.

Feb. 4 to Feb. 11, 1945 In Yalta, F.D. Roosevelt, W. Churchill, and J.V. Stalin agreed on the terms of unconditional surrender by Germany, the Soviet Union's entry into the war against Japan, and the structure of the United Nations. The Teheran agreement to make Poland a part of the Soviet zone of influence was reconfirmed, as well as the line of the 1939 partition of Poland between Germany and the Soviet Union, along the Bug River, as the postwar Polish-Soviet border. The United States and Great Britain agreed to withdraw their recognition from the legitimate Polish Government-in-Exile in London and to accept a new, Soviet controlled government of Poland. Poland's territorial losses in the east were to be compensated by acquisition of smaller territories held by Germany in 1939. These were, centuries earlier, a part of the original Polish ethnic lands during the rule of the first Polish dynasty, the Piasts.

President Roosevelt felt uneasy about his treatment of Poland. He was a part of the Western cover-up (in 1943-1945) of the 1940 Soviet massacre of 21,857 captured Poles. Especially embarrassing was the matter of the mass graves in Katyń Forest. He also was annoyed with the repeated demands of the Polish wartime government to put pressure on Germany to stop the murders of millions of Jews and Poles in occupied Poland. Churchill described in his *Triumph and Tragedy* how President Roosevelt was anxious to end the discussion about Poland with Stalin and made the incredible statement: "Poland has been the source of trouble for over five hundred years."

(President F.D. Roosevelt died two months later on Apr. 12, 1945, and the Yalta agreements, which never were ratified by the United States Congress, nevertheless became the corner-stone of the postwar Soviet empire.)

The Second World War was entered in 1939 by Great Britain and France in defense of the freedom of Poland. The war was ending in 1945 with the betrayal and surrender of Poland to Soviet control by Great Britain and the United States of America.

April 10, 1945 Carpet bombing by the American Air Force destroyed the sub-camp of Sachsenhausen concentration camp at Klinkerwerk (it was one of several bombings killing thousands of inmates at the end of the war). The Klinkerwerk plant owned by Deutsche Erd und Steinwerke (DEST), was the largest brickwork formed by Himmler in 1938-1939.

April 20 - May 2, 1945 The death march of Brandenburg took place. No one marked with Jewish Stars of David was observed among the 33,500 prisoners evacuated in front of advancing Soviet and Polish armies. Approximately 6,000 prisoners were executed during the march and 18,000 reached American positions near Schwerin, East Germany. Similar evacuation marches and transports engulfed hundreds of thousands of camp inmates. Many died from hunger and cold, or were shot by the guards. Barges loaded with prisoners from concentration camps were sunk by the Germans in the North Sea and in the Baltic.

In 1945 German concentration camps were guarded by about 45,000 SSmen and 10,000 soldiers of the Wehrmacht. The process of extermination of prisoners was conducted in close cooperation with German industrial organizations. These firms developed various time and motion studies as well as calorie intake studies for the purpose of achieving the most efficient exploitation of the prisoners. The most prominent among them were IG-Farbenindustrie, Siemens, Roechling, Flick, Krupp, Mannesman, Hoesch, Hawiel, AEG, and "H. Goering."

6. May 2, 1945 -- The aftermath of German mass murders and the unconditional surrender of Germany. Trials of German war criminals. Soviet anti-Jewish policies.

The entire area of German genocide of the Jews in occupied Poland fell under Soviet control. In subsequent years the Soviet government created conditions which did not allow the revival of Jewish culture and Yiddish language in Poland and other areas under its control.

The Soviets ruled by provocation in postwar Poland and other satellite states. They staffed their newly organized terror apparatus in Poland with a large and disproportionate number of Jews. They used the Jews as very visible executioners and then turned them into victims in the following purges.

Soviet policies forced a quarter of a million Jews out of Poland during the first years after the war. As the Soviets expected, many of these people went to Palestine. The Soviets helped initial efforts to establish the State of Israel. The first and crucial struggle against the Arabs was won by Israelis using Soviet Bloc weapons. Soviets were exploiting the rebuilding of the Jewish state in order to destabilize the Arab world and turn it against the West, and especially the United States, which was rapidly becoming the main force guaranteeing the survival of Israel. The Soviet aim was always to destabilize the oil-rich area of the Middle East, which has been critically important for the free world.

Polish-Jewish relations reached a new low when the Soviets first used many Jews as executioners and then purged them. The forcing of masses of Polish Jews out of Poland by the Soviets further aggravated Polish-Jewish relations. Both of these policies helped the Soviets to present to the world all those who resisted postwar Sovietization as anti-Semites. Naturally, the accusation of anti-Semitism in the wake of the Nazi murders of Jews was a potent propaganda weapon against the victims of Soviet oppression in Poland.

Aug. 1945 Representatives of the United States, Great Britain, France, and the Soviet Union agreed in London to set up the International Military Tribunal in Nuremberg to try German war criminals, and thereby further developed international law for the preservation of peace and civilization.

Sept. 20, 1945 - Oct. 1, 1946 Trials were held in Nuremberg by the International Military Tribunal. 22 officials of the German wartime government were treated as war criminals. 19 defendants were convicted, 9 were sentenced to death, 8 were hanged on Oct. 16, 1946, the day after Hermann Goering (1893-1946) committed suicide in prison. Soviet representatives falsely accused the German wartime government of the massacre at Katyń of 11,000 (sic) Polish officers.

American and British judges decided that Germans were not guilty of the Katyń murders and decided to drop this matter without reviewing available evidence, which clearly indicated that Soviet security forces were responsible. Allied trials of German war criminals continued in countries occupied during the war and in the four zones of occupation of Germany, until the incorporation of the West and East German states in 1949. Very few war criminals were tried in the two newly created German states after 1949.

July 4, 1946 42 Jews were killed and 80 injured at 7 Planty Street, Kielce, Poland. The pogrom was apparently staged by Soviet NKVD officer Mihail A. Dyomin (or, Demin) who ordered security officers to disarm the victimized Jews, shoot them, and throw them out of windows. In the meantime Soviet agent provocateurs assembled a mob using the "ritual murder" of a young Christian boy and other accusations. Later, while acknowledging that organized provocation caused the killings, the local court was not permitted to reveal who was responsible.

The ghastly pogrom of Kielce was used by the Soviets to pressure Jews out of Poland. It also diverted the attention of foreign correspondents from the Soviet falsification of a crucial election in Poland. It also served to divert the attention of the world press from the massive use of Soviet terror in postwar Poland.

The trauma of Poland during the Soviet takeover in 1945-47 was well described by the American ambassador in Warsaw, Arthur Bliss-Lane in his book *I Saw Poland Betrayed* (New York: 1948, p.19). He reported that the 4th of July, 1946 pogrom was staged in Kielce in order to overshadow the Soviet election tampering and to discredit Polish opposition to the Soviet takeover "especially among the Jewish circles in the United States."

Soviet postwar policy to force hundreds of thousands of Jews out of Poland and direct as many of them as possible to Palestine was served well by the killings of Jews in Kielce and in other locations.

The Soviet government decided not to allow the revival of Jewish culture in Poland. The Soviet policy was to exploit the desire of Polish Jews to reestablish a country of their own after the horrors of the German genocide of European Jewry in occupied Poland. As mentioned before, immediately after the war, the Soviets forced out of Poland over a quarter of a million Polish Jews, many of whom went to Palestine. During the first postwar years Soviet terror and the resulting turmoil caused the killing of some 300,000 people including about 1,500 Jews. It is impossible to determine how many Jews were killed in 1945-1947 by common criminals and how many were victims of pogroms staged or provoked by Soviet agents provocateurs.

June 16, 1948 In Kraków, the District Court sentenced to death Kurt Schupke. He was the former commandant of the Rzeszów Ghetto and of the Płaszów concentration camp. Schupke personally conducted executions by shooting Jews in the back of their heads. He was executed on Nov. 27, 1948. Schupke was one of the very few German mass murderers who were punished.

Dec. 5, 1948 A United Nations Convention on prevention and punishing of crimes of genocide was established.

May 1960 Adolf Eichmann (1906-1962), lieutenant colonel in German secret police, was seized in Argentina by Israeli agents and taken to Israel for trial on charges of directing the deportation of Jews from Germany and occupied countries to extermination camps; Eichmann was sentenced to death in Dec. 1961 and hanged in 1962.

Nov. 27, 1968 A United Nations Convention declared that war crimes and crimes against humanity, such as genocide, are not subject to legal limitation with the passage of time. The United Nations recognized that the German genocide of the Jews was committed under the full authority of the German government and in the name of German people. Direct responsibility was held by the German war criminals, the ruling German National Socialist Labor party, the Gestapo terror apparatus, and German police composed of the Security Service (Sicherheitsdienst, or SD), SS (Schutzstaffeln), SA (Sturmabteilungen), etc. The German army, or the Wehrmacht, also bears grave responsibility for the wartime mass killings.

7. Notes on the German "Final Solution to the Jewish Problem"

The destruction of the Jewish race was not the main purpose of the political program and conquests of Nazi Germans; it was only one of the ultimate consequences of German racism expressed in the ideology of pan-Germanism.

The enormity of the crime committed against the Jews under the full authority of the German government and in the name of German people is impossible to grasp without reviewing the crucial events which led to the formulation and execution of the program of the "Final Solution" for the genocide of European Jews.

Once the Berlin government decided on the "Final Solution," Jews were murdered by the Germans in occupied Poland because the vast majority of them lived there. Mainly Jews and Gypsies were brought from other countries of Europe to be destroyed in German death camps built on Polish soil. Jews represented almost half of all citizens of Poland killed in World War II. The fact and scale of German genocide of the Jews remains incomprehensible.

Michael T. Kaufman observed in his book *Mad Dreams, Saving Graces* (New York: Random House, 1989, page 180) that "Jews lived in Poland for a longer time and in greater numbers than anywhere else in their long history. Less than a century ago, 75 percent of all the European, or Ashkenazi, Jews in the world lived in the then trisected historical Polish commonwealth. On the eve of the Second World War, 10 percent of Poland's population was Jewish, a level that until the establishment of Israel was unmatched in any other country. All the Jewish religious, national, and cultural movements -- Hasidism, Zionism, Bundism, Hebraism, -- and the rise of Yiddish literature originated or grew largely in Poland, often in an awkward symbiosis with Poles. Only in Poland were there Jewish masses belonging to all levels of society, poor and rich, pious and secular, rural and urban, illiterate and highly educated."

"No one asked the Poles how one should treat the Jews," observed Professor Yisrael Gutman, Max and Rita Haber Professor at the Institute of Contemporary Jewry and at the Hebrew University and Director of the Center of Holocaust Studies at Yad Vashem. He stated in *Polin - A Journal of Polish-Jewish Studies,* (vol. 2, 1987, page 431) speaking about the German genocide of the Jews: "This feeling of identification of Poles from all social spheres and their anti-German solidarity is a previously unheard of historical achievement and one of Europe's greatest under Nazi occupation. I should like to make two things clear here. First, all accusations against the Poles that they were responsible for what is referred to as the 'Final Solution' are not even worth mentioning. Secondly, there is no validity at all in the contention that Polish anti-Semitism or other Polish attitudes were the reason for the siting of the death camps in Poland."

Fritz Stern wrote in his *Dreams and Delusions - The Drama of German History* (A.A. Knopf, New York: 1987, p.13) that historians have recently suggested that the decision of the German wartime government "systematically to exterminate the Jews was made in the wake of the battle of Moscow [in 1941], in apprehension of the ultimate defeat." The German aberration resulted because of a "dream of the past that never was and future that never would be."

By January 20, 1942, Nazi Germany had already declared war against the United States and was on the road to defeat. The Nazi government concluded that the Jewish population under German occupation had lost its value as a useful hostage to keep America out of the war and to collect ransom money for the release of the Jews.

As stated earlier the direct responsibility for the Nazi crimes of genocide is that of the German war criminals and the German National-Socialist party. The power of the wartime German government was primarily based on control of the police and armed forces, whose staff were mainly appointed during the Weimar Republic, long before the Nazi party legally assumed power in Germany. The National Socialist government was very popular in Germany up to the bitter end, which many Germans liked to dignify by calling it the *Goetterdaemmerung* or the "Twilight of the Gods" (after Wagnerian operas).

Gerald Reitlinger expressed his conviction that the vast majority of the German people were racist and did not object to the crimes of their wartime government, when he summarized the critical years of German history in the title : *The SS: Alibi of a Nation, 1922-1945.* In fact not only the SS, but the entire Nazi party in Germany has been an alibi of the German nation -- a nation which was largely permeated with racism and ideas which embraced the megalomaniac ideology of pan-Germanism.

Throughout the 19th century, after the partitions and obliteration of Poland had been initiated by the Germans, and after the murders of the French Revolution, Europe started on a reckless path of social engineering. It was a legacy of the Enlightenment, which spread the notion that the human mind is perfect, that man can diagnose any problem correctly and then cure it. The nation states born out of the Enlightenment practiced the fraudulent denationalization of ethnic minorities. They rejected pluralism. Germans added racist notions of the "survival of the fittest" to their old tradition of the "push to the east to conquer the Slavonic lands."

The Enlightenment gave the Jews emancipation without pluralism. The resulting counter-emancipation brought the political anti-Semitism, which led the Germans to the genocide of one-third of all Jews and two-thirds of European Jewry. Thus, out of the ideas of the Enlightenment came the practices of German and Soviet totalitarian states of the 20th century.

As early as 1856, German Chancellor Otto Bismarck (1815-1898), Berlin's ambassador to the all-German Parliament in Frankfurt, wrote that the Polish minority must be exterminated. Such ideas were a prelude to the genocides and mass murders of the 20th century -- the century in which more people were killed than ever before in the entire history of mankind.

In the aftermath of the horrors and trauma of German occupation and genocidal policies, the reconciliation of Jewish and Polish victims has made little progress. Unfortunately many statements in the western mass-media have had the effect of shifting the responsibility for the Jewish catastrophe from the Germans to Poles in public opinion.

Marian Fuks wrote in the bulletin of the Jewish Historical Institute in Poland (Jan.-March 1989, page 49): "Often in conferences dedicated to the Holocaust and the uprising of the Warsaw Ghetto -- one hears voices intending to minimize Polish help for dying and fighting Jews. These views are not just. One should remember that Poland was the only country in Europe, where any help, even the least important, even alms given to a Jew constituted a threat of a summary execution. At the same time saving and hiding Jews was more difficult in Poland than in any other country in Europe, because in a large part the Jewish population markedly differed from the 'Aryans' surrounding it. However, without demonizing the shabby and abominable activity of the criminals (known as the *szmalcowniks*), thousands of Poles risked their own lives, and often the lives of their families to give shelter, as well as individual and collective help to Jews. If this problem is analyzed in the context of the dreadful indifference of the West, in particular of England and America to what was happening in occupied Poland, or the complete lack of energetic, even impetuous action by the powerful American-Jewish lobby -- the effort of the Poles deserves so much more respect and gratitude."

Polish historians generally express the opinion that Poles should have done much more for the Jews during the war. Considering the magnitude of German crimes against the Jews no one has done enough to oppose them except the people who were murdered by the Germans for helping innocent Jewish victims. However, the Poles should not be singled out because people in occupied Europe, in countries much less terrorized than Poland was, helped the Jewish victims even less than did the Poles. No other country suffered as much as Poland and the fact is that the Germans were murdering the Polish leadership community on the theory that any intelligent Pole might be a potential threat to the "new German order."

136

PART I

APPENDIX I

BASIC PLAN FOR BERLIN'S STRATEGY

FOR ELIMINATION OF THE EASTERN FRONT

BY CRUCIAL GERMAN SUPPORT

OF REVOLUTION IN RUSSIA

The architect of Berlin's eastern policy, Dr. Helphand, obtained virtually unlimited German money to convert a clique of conspirators into Russian revolutionary power.

Memorandum by Dr. Helphand

Note: The memorandum is undated.
It was registered in
the *Journal of the German Foreign Ministry* on March 9, 1917.

A 86₂₉ in WK ₁₁c   9th March 1915
secr, volume ₅

A 86_{29} *in WK* $_{11c}$
secr, volume $_{5}$

Preparations for a Political Mass Strike in Russia

Preparations are to be made for a political mass strike in Russia, to take place in spring, under the slogan "Freedom and Peace." The center of the movement will be Petrograd, and within Petrograd, the Obnuhov, Putilov, and Baltic works. The strike is to halt railway communications between Petrograd and Warsaw and Moscow and Warsaw, and to immobilize the Southwestern Railway. The railway strike will be principally conducted to affect the large centers with considerable labor forces, the railway workshops, etc. In order to widen the scope of the strike, as many railway bridges as possible will be blown up, as during the strike movement of 1904 and 1905.

Conference of Russian Socialist Leaders

The task can only be fulfilled under the leadership of the Russian Social Democrats. The radical wing of this party has already gone into action, but it is essential that they be joined by the moderate minority group. So far it has been mainly the radicals who have prevented unification. However, two weeks ago their leader, Lenin, himself threw open the question of unification with the minority. It should be possible to achieve unity on a compromise policy, based on the necessity of exploiting the weakening of the administrative apparatus inside the country brought about by the war, and thus to initiate positive action. It should be understood that the moderate group has always been more strongly influenced by the German Social Democrats, and amongst them the personal authority of some of the German and Austrian Social Democratic leaders could still achieve a great deal. After careful preliminary probing, it is essential that a congress of Russian Social Democratic leaders be arranged in Switzerland or in some other neutral country. The following should take part in such a congress: (1) the Social Democratic majority party; (2) the minority party; (3) the Jewish League (the Bund); (4) the Ukrainian organization, Spilka; (5) the Polish Social Democratic party; (6) the Social Democratic Party of Poland [*sic*]; (7) the Lithuanian Social Democratic party; (8) the Finnish Social Democrats. The congress can only take place if unanimous decisions on starting immediate action against Tsarism can be assured beforehand.

The congress might have to be preceded by a discussion between the Russian Social Democratic majority and minority parties. Possible additions to the list of participants in the congress might be: (9) the Armenian party Dashnackzutiun; (10) Hindshak.

Apart from its enormous significance in terms of organization, the congress would also, by its decisions, have a tremendous effect on public opinion in France and England.

The Russian Social Revolutionaries

Separate negotiations must be held with the Russian Social Revolutionary party. Its members are more inclined to nationalism, and its influence on the workers is minimal. In Petrograd it only has a few followers in the Baltic works. For the purposes of a mass strike, it can safely be ignored. On the other hand, the peasants are its sphere, and, with them, it wields considerable influence through the medium of the primary school teachers.

Local Movements

At the same time as these preparations to create a basis for the organization of a mass strike, agitation must also be begun immediately. Through Bulgaria and Rumania communications can be established with Odessa, Nikolaiev, Sevastopol, Rostov (on the Don), Batum, and Baku. During the revolution, the Russian workers in these areas made local and occupational demands which were first granted, but later repudiated, and they have not abandoned these demands. Only two years ago there was a strike of sailors and dock workers which brought these old wishes into the limelight once again. Agitation should be based on these points, and then also take a political direction. While a general strike could probably not be achieved in the Black Sea basin, it might be possible, in view of the current unemployment there, to arrange local strikes in Nikolaiev, in Rostov, and among certain trades in Odessa. Such strikes would take on symptomatic significance by disturbing the peace which descended on internal strife within the Tsarist Empire at the beginning of the war.

For this agitation to be carried out, the Russian seamen's organization, which, in recent years, had its base first on Constantinople and then in Alexandria, must be re-established, and it would now have to have its center in Constanta or Galati. The fact that the towns on the Black Sea will be severely disturbed by the war at sea will make them especially amenable to political agitation. A special effort must be made to ensure that, as in 1905, the revolutionary organizations, supported by the workers, gain control of the city administration, so that they can alleviate the misery of the poorer classes, who are suffering terribly from the war. This, too, would serve the purpose of giving a new impulse to the general revolutionary movement. Should a rising occur in Odessa, it could be supported by the Turkish navy.

The prospects of a mutiny in the Black Sea fleet cannot be assessed until closer contact has been established with Sevastopol.

In Baku and the region of the oil-fields a strike could be organized relatively easily. Moreover, it is important that a considerable proportion of the workers there are Tartars, that is, Moslems. If a strike occurs, attempts will be made to set fire to the naphtha wells and the oil depots, as in 1905. There would also be a possibility of organizing strikes in the mining district on the Donets, and conditions in the Urals, where the Socialist majority party has a strong following, are particularly favorable. Political strikes could easily be organized among the miners there, if a little money were available, for the population is extremely poor.

Siberia

Special attention should be devoted to Siberia. In Europe, it is only known as the land of exile, but throughout the great tracts of Siberia, along the railways and the rivers, lives a strong peasant class, proud and independent, which would be happiest completely undisturbed by the central government.

In the towns there are lively business circles and a layer of intellectuals, consisting of political exiles and others influenced by them. The Siberian constituencies send Socialist deputies to the Duma. During the revolutionary movement of 1905, the entire administration lay in the hands of the revolutionary committee. The administrative apparatus is extremely weak, and, now that it is felt that there is no danger threatening from Japan, the military organization has been reduced to a minimum. These conditions make it possible to set up several centers of activity in Siberia. At the same time, preparations should be made to allow the political exiles to escape to European Russia, which would be a purely financial problem. In this way, several thousand of the best agitators, who have important connections and enjoy unlimited authority, could be directed to the centers of agitation mentioned above and to Petrograd. This measure could, of course, only be carried through by the Socialist organizations themselves, as only they have sufficient knowledge of the usefulness of individual personalities.

The more determinedly the Socialist organizations take their stand and the more their activities are co-ordinated, the more all these undertakings will develop and interlock. On the other hand, the undertakings themselves--and they should be taken in hand immediately for this reason, if for no other--will act as a spur to the nuclei of the Socialist parties and will encourage them to achieve unity.

Press Campaign

At the same time, the general trend of the undertakings must be emphasized inside the Russian Socialist parties by discussion in the press, in pamphlets, etc. Pamphlets in Russian can be published in Switzerland. A Russian newspaper, *Golos*, which is edited by several leaders of the Socialist minority party, is published in Paris, and, in spite of the exceptional circumstances in which it appears, it has maintained a completely objective attitude to the war. This paper will not be able to avoid taking part in a discussion of party tactics. The Swiss and Italian Socialist newspapers can also be called on to publish these comments, as can the Danish, the Dutch, the Swedish, and the American Socialist press. Internationally reputed German Socialist leaders could easily take part in this discussion.

A press campaign would have a considerable effect on the attitude of the neutral states, especially on Italy, and this effect would be transmitted to Socialist circles in France and England.

Even an objective portrayal of the course of the war, which could only be given in England and France under the aegis of the Socialists, and even then only with great difficulty, would be of great value.

The Socialist press in Bulgaria and Rumania could easily be influenced to wage a lively struggle against Tsarism.

Since the center for revolutionary agitation in Southern Russia will be Rumania, the attitude of the Rumanian daily press is important for this reason alone, and it is, of course, even more important in determining Rumania's own attitude to the war. The large Rumanian newspapers are all in the service of the Russians, and their financial obligations are supposed to be such as would be difficult to overcome. However, it would not be very difficult to organize a group of reputable journalists to publish a large, independent daily newspaper with an explicit policy of closer contact with Germany. As the Rumanian press is tuned to a Russian victory, it has lost a great deal of prestige as a result of the course of the war so far, whereas this new paper would win itself a public through its objective news reports. The development of events would concentrate public opinion on it more and more, and would even force the other newspapers to change their attitude.

Agitation in North America

The United States demand special attention. The enormous number of Jews and Slavs there represent a very receptive element for anti-Tsarist agitation, and both the Russian Social Democrats and the Jewish League have important contacts there. A few agitators must be sent out to make a tour of these areas. Besides making a personal appearance, they would stimulate the existing forces on the spot into energetic action, strengthen the organizations, reinforce the many Russian and Jewish press undertakings, and thus bring about the development of systematic activity.

In view of the many contacts with Russia which the millions of Russian *emigres*, most of whom have only recently left their own country, must have, this could well be of great importance. Moreover, a movement among the Russian *emigres* in America could not fail to have an effect on public opinion there. Agitators from among these circles could also be sent to Russia. In the present war, in which the future of the German nation is at stake, the German element, too, should become more active. A strong anti-Tsarist movement among the Russians and the Russian Jews in America would favor action by the Germans. A few German and Austrian Social Democratic speakers should be sent over.

The Growth of the Revolutionary Movement

Agitation in the neutral states will have powerful repercussions on agitation in Russia, and vice versa. Further developments depend, to a large extent, on the course of the war. The jubilant mood which reigned in Russia in the first few days has already sobered considerably. Tsarism needs quick victories, while it is, in fact, suffering bloody reverses. Even if the Russian army merely remains pinned to its present positions throughout the winter, there will be grave dissatisfaction throughout the country. This mass mood will be exploited, deepened, extended, and spread in all directions by the apparatus for agitation sketched above. Strikes here and there, the risings produced by distress and the increase in political agitation will all embarrass the Tsarist government. If it takes reprisals, this will result in growing bitterness: if it shows indulgence, this will be interpreted as a sign of weakness and fan the flames of the revolutionary movement even more. Ample experience of this was gained in 1904 and 1905. If, on the other hand, the Russian army suffers a severe reverse, then the movement opposing the government may quickly assume undreamed-of proportions. In any case, it can be assumed that a political mass strike will take place in the spring, if all available forces are mobilized according to the plan sketched above. If the mass strike grows to any considerable extent, the Tsarist regime will be forced to concentrate the military forces at its disposal inside Russia principally on Petrograd and Moscow. In addition, the government will need troops to protect railway communication. During the strike of December 1905, two regiments were needed merely to protect the line between Petrograd and Moscow. Only by these means was it possible to counter the repeated attempts made by the strikers to blow up the railway bridges near Tver and in other places, and to throw the guards regiments, who alone were able to suppress the rising, into Moscow. Although the main preoccupation is to be the imminent railway strike in the West, efforts will also be made to start other railway strikes wherever possible. Even if this does not succeed everywhere, the Tsarist government will have to employ large military forces for the protection of bridges, stations, etc., and, at the same time, the administrative apparatus will be thrown into confusion and will begin to disintegrate.

The Peasant Movement and the Ukraine

As in 1905, the peasant movements may be an important accompanying phenomenon alongside the events outlined above. The conditions in which the peasants in Russia are living have not improved since then; on the contrary, they have deteriorated. In the eyes of the Russian peasants, the whole problem is one of land. The peasants will therefore bring manorial land under the plough again, and thus threaten the landowners.

The fundamental basis of the Russian peasant problem is, of course, the question of land ownership, but the solution of this question is also closely linked with the formation of co-operatives and of organizations granting credit at low interest, with school education, and with the taxation system and the administration of the state in general. In the Ukraine, all these factors combine to produce a demand for autonomy. As long as Tsarism maintains its domination, which, in the Ukraine, follows a policy of giving the land to the Muscovite aristocracy and protecting the great Muscovite landowners against the Ukrainian peasants with all available means, the peasants have no alternative but to rebel as soon as they realize that the power of the government is weakening or that the regime is in difficulties. One of the first tasks facing a Ukrainian government will be to establish law and order in place of the conditions of anarchy which resulted from the Muscovite regime, and, supported by the confidence of the Ukrainian people, it will easily achieve this end. The formation of an independent Ukraine will be seen both as a liberation from the Tsarist regime and as a salvation from the chaos of peasant unrest.

If there is peasant unrest in Central Russia--and the peasants of Greater Russia will certainly not remain quiet if the Ukrainian peasants rise close by them--then the Social Revolutionary party will also have to abandon its policy of inactivity. Through the medium of the primary school teachers this party has considerable influence among the peasants of Greater Russia, and it is authoritative among the Trudovniki, the Peasants' Peoples' Party in the Duma. The attitude of the Russian Social Democrats to peasant unrest would emerge at once if the peasants decided to oppose Tsarism.

The Movement in Finland

Within this general movement, important activities could be undertaken in Finland. The Finnish parties are in an awkward position, for there are considerable Russian military forces in the country. On the other hand, the Finns do not simply want to be annexed by Sweden. But the Swedes do not want to annex Finland: they simply want to turn it into a buffer state, i.e. an independent state. The Swedish party is a small minority in Finland. Therefore attempts must be made, above all, to achieve an agreement between the Swedish government and the more powerful Finnish parties, amongst which the Social Democratic party is the most important. This could probably be achieved by the Swedes guaranteeing the Finns the widest possible measure of autonomy and leaving it to them to decide to which group of states they wish to attach themselves. Once such an agreement is reached, preparations for a general rising in Finland can be made quietly and systematically. The Finnish Social Democrats have excellent organizations, similar to those of the German Social Democrats, at their disposal. The obstinate defense of its rights against Tsarist despotism has trained the whole Finnish people in discretion and silent co-operation, in which the difference of language also helps a great deal. All the preparations are to be made secretly until some considerable wave of strikes breaks out in Russia. This would be the moment for a general rising in Finland. Because of Finland's large area, the Tsarist government would be faced with the choice of breaking down the military forces at their disposal into small, independent units which could attack the various storm centers, or concentrating their forces on the most important administrative and strategic points, thus abandoning the country to the rebels. The former were the tactics used by the Tsarists to defeat the revolutionary movement of 1905. Numerous expeditionary forces were formed, both large and small, and their commanders were given complete military and civil powers. The plan was worked out in Petrograd by a special commission, on which sat members both of the General Staff and of the highest administrative bodies. The revolutionaries' executive was well informed about the work of this commission, but was not able to frustrate its plan. Nevertheless, it took the Tsarist government the whole strength of its army and a period of two years to quash the rising. If the Tsarist government were now to adopt the same course in Finland, the Swedish army would have to intervene to protect Finnish independence, for, while this course is probably the best way to quash a rising, it makes the army absolutely defenseless against the intervention of hostile forces. The Tsarist government will therefore probably decide for the second course and withdraw the army to the administrative centers, i.e. to the coast and the railway just behind. They may even destroy the railway links with Sweden. In practice, the Russians will then only dominate the coast of the Gulf of Bothnia. Masters of their own house, the rebels will then form a National Guard, as in 1904 and 1905, take defensive measures, and make other provisions to permit the Swedish troops entry, which may have been complicated by the destruction of the railways. Naturally, a great deal depends on the development of events in Petrograd.

The Finns could be of great service, even before the general rising. They could provide information about the numbers, the disposition and the movements of Russian troops in Finland, and about the movements of the Russian navy. They could set up a signal service for directing the activities of aircraft. (The Finnish custom of painting country houses, and especially their roofs, red would be useful in this. An unpainted section on a red roof would act as a land-mark.) They could also set up wireless telegraphy stations and make provisions for blowing up bridges and buildings. Above all, they could permit the Russian revolutionaries to communicate with Petrograd. Since the country is very large, is immediately adjacent to the Petrograd region, and has regular, hourly traffic to Petrograd, they could set up an information and transport service, in spite of the military occupation. Stores of arms could be built up, and arms, explosives, etc., smuggled across to Petrograd.

The Caucasus

At the time of the revolution, the Tsarist government for a long time practically ignored the Caucasus. As the Caucasus was not threatened from outside, they began by allowing anything that might happen there to happen. This state of affairs was allowed to reach the point where the government tolerated governors who were in open contact with the revolutionary committee to head the administration. They were certain that, once they had re-established their domination in Russia proper, they would be able to subdue the Caucasus once again, and in this they have been proved perfectly right. This time, however, because of the Russo-Turkish war, the situation is quite different. There is a possibility of the secession of the Caucasus, and the significance of a rising to the rear of the fighting armies needs no further explanation. However, in contrast to Finland, where a well-organized, general rising is possible, the movement in the Caucasus will always suffer from national divisions and party struggles. In the years of the revolution, it was the Georgians who emerged as the most forceful of the Caucasians.

At that time, with the support of the small holders' masses, they gained complete control of the government of Kutai, setting up their own administration, law-courts, &c. However, it was not the separatists but the Social Democrats who headed this movement. Some of the Armenians fought in the ranks of the Social Democrats, while the rest grouped themselves around the Armenian nationalist parties, which had long ago abandoned their separatist tendencies. However, it must be realized that, after the disappointments of the revolution and in face of the war, the separatist tendencies have naturally gained in popularity.

The Tartar workers took part in the strikes. In general, the Tartar masses played a reactionary role; they allowed themselves to be incited against the Armenians by agents of the Petrograd government, and this resulted in bloody encounters between the two national elements. However, since the call for a holy war, the Tsarist government will no longer be able to rely openly on the support of the Moslem population. They will nevertheless secretly foster religious hatred, and will encourage the Armenians' fear of just this holy war. It is therefore essential that first of all everything possible be done on the Turkish side to make it clear to the Caucasian Moslems that it is in fact the achievement of the aims of their holy war which demands their close co-operation with their Christian neighbors in the struggle against Tsarism. An agreement must be made at once between the Young Turks and the Armenian parties in Turkey, which are identical with those in Russia. The details of this project, which will involve a variety of difficulties in its realization, do not fall within the scope of this memorandum. However, attention must be drawn to the fact that a determined attitude on the part of the Russian Social Democrats would have enormous effects on the activities of the Armenians and Georgians in the Caucasus. The Social Democrats could perhaps take control of the whole movement, and they would therefore certainly encourage the national parties to join in the struggle by their attitude. This is another reason why the conference of Russian Socialist party leaders suggested above is an urgent necessity.

A holy war, which has the power to produce large movements in Persia, Egypt, North Africa, etc., will hardly have much effect in Russia. The Tartars on the Volga and the Koma will certainly make no move, for they are a peaceful and completely subjugated people, who would face the opposition of the overwhelming numerical superiority of the Russian population. The situation in the Caucasus is slightly different, but one must realize that the Tartars there were pacified long ago. The memory of the heroic struggle for independence fought in the past has faded, and the Moslem population is not yet sufficiently civilized to begin a modern revolutionary movement. The old conflict between the Caucasian mountain tribes and the Russians was simply a fight against any kind of centralized state. Since then, the tribal organization has completely disintegrated. The tribal chiefs have become landowners; the contact between them and the masses is now only slight, and the people have lost their sense of independence. Because the Moslems feel economically and culturally inferior to the Christian population, they look to the government, as the most powerful among powerful forces, for support. They would certainly prefer a Moslem government, but such a government would first of all have to prove itself strong enough to defeat the Tsarist government. The Turkish army will be favorably received, but it will have to conquer the might of the Russians with the strength of its own arms. This does not, of course, entirely exclude the possibility of the formation of isolated rebel bands, especially on the Persian border. There is no prospect of a large-scale partisan war being waged by the Moslem population in the Caucasus. However, a rising of the Kuban cossacks is not beyond the realms of possibility, and Ukrainian propaganda could be useful in preparing such a rising.

The Culmination of the Movement

The growth of the revolutionary movement within the Tsarist Empire will, among other things, produce a state of general unrest. In addition to the effects of the general course of the war, special measures could be adopted to aggravate this unrest. For obvious reasons, the Black Sea basin and the Caucasian basin are the most favorable districts. Particular attention should be devoted to Nikolaiev, as the shipyards there are working at great pressure for the launching of two large warships. Efforts are to be made to start a strike among the workers there. This strike need not necessarily be political in character; it could just as well be based on the workers' economic demands.

It can be accepted as a fact that the Tsarist government needs quick victories to maintain itself. If it lasts until the spring, even the present situation, in which the Russian army is being systematically harried without achieving any progress, can only result in a revolution. However, the difficulties facing the movement must not be overlooked.

First and foremost, there is mobilization, which has stripped the country of its most active younger elements; and then there is also the growth of national feeling which has resulted from the war. However, in face of the failure of the war, this very feeling is bound to turn into bitterness and be directed against Tsarism. It must be realized that, unlike the Ukrainian or the Finnish Social Democrats, the Russian Social Democratic party will never adopt a position hostile to the Russian Empire. Even at the time of the revolution, this party included over a million workers within its organizations, and, since then, its following among the masses has increased to such an extent that the government has twice been forced to alter the electoral law, for fear of allowing the Duma to be flooded with Social Democratic deputies. Such a party must surely represent the interests and the moods of the masses, who did not want the war, and are now merely taking part in it. The Social Democrats are in determined opposition to the unlimited external extension of power which is the aim of Tsarist diplomacy. They see this as a severe obstacle to the internal development of the nations forming the Empire--including the Russian nation. They consider the Tsarist government responsible for this war, and will therefore hold it responsible for the futility and the failure of the war. They will demand the fall of the government and a quick conclusion of peace.

If the revolutionary movement achieves any considerable scale, and even if the Tsarist government is still in power in Petrograd, a provisional government can be set up to raise the question of an armistice and a peace treaty and to open diplomatic negotiations.

If the Tsarists should actually be forced to make an armistice before this occurs, then the better the revolutionary movement is prepared, the more violently it will break out then. Even if the Tsarist government succeeds in retaining power for the duration of the war, it will never be able to maintain itself after a peace dictated from abroad.

Thus the armies of the Central Powers and the revolutionary movement will shatter the colossal political centralization which is the embodiment of the Tsarist Empire and which will be a danger to world peace for as long as it is allowed to survive, and will conquer the stronghold of political reaction in Europe.

Siberia

Note: The rest of the memorandum forms a separate unit. It was written on a different typewriter; it contains Helphand's afterthoughts.

Particular attention should also be devoted to Siberia because the enormous deliveries of artillery and other arms from the United States to Russia will probably pass through Siberia. The Siberian project must therefore be treated separately from the rest. A few energetic and sufficiently equipped agents should be sent to Siberia on special missions to blow up the railway bridges. They would find a sufficient number of assistants among the exiles. Explosives would have to be provided from the mines in the Urals, but small quantities could probably be smuggled over from Finland. Technical instructions would have to be worked out here.

Press Campaign

The predictions made about Rumania and Bulgaria have been proved correct by the course of developments since the completion of this memorandum. The Bulgarian press is now completely pro-German, and there is a noticeable swing in the attitude of the Rumanian press. The provisions which we have made will soon show even better results. It is now of particular importance to begin work on [word missing].

1. Financial support for the majority group of the Russian Social Democrats, which is fighting the Tsarist government with all the means at its disposal. Its leaders are in Switzerland.
2. The setting up of direct communications with the revolutionary organizations in Odessa and Nikolaiev, via Bucharest and Jassy.
3. The creation of contacts with the Russian seamen's organization. Some contact has already been made through a gentleman in Sofia, and further contacts are possible via Amsterdam.
4. Support for the activities of the Jewish Socialist organization, "The League" (Bund, not Zionists).
5. Finding authoritative Russian Social Democratic and Social Revolutionary personalities in Switzerland, Italy, Copenhagen, and Stockholm and furthering the efforts of such of them as are determined on immediate and vigorous action against Tsarism.
6. Support for those Russian revolutionary writers who will continue to take part in the struggle against Czarism, even while the war is still on.
7. Connections with the Finnish Social Democrats.
8. The organization of congresses of Russian revolutionaries.
9. Influencing public opinion in the neutral states, especially the opinions of the Socialist press and the Socialist organizations, favorably towards the struggle against Tsarism and towards connections with the Central Powers. This has already been done successfully in Bulgaria and Rumania, but efforts to do so in Holland, Denmark, Sweden, Norway, Switzerland, and Italy must be continued.
10. The equipment of an expedition to Siberia, with the specific mission of blowing up the most important railway bridges and preventing the transport of arms from America to Russia. The expedition should also be provided with sufficient financial means to make it possible for a number of deported political prisoners to escape into the interior.

II. Technical preparations for a rising in Russia:

(a) Provision of accurate maps of the Russian railways, showing the most important bridges which must be destroyed if traffic is to be crippled, and also showing the main administrative buildings, depots, and workshops to which most attention should be devoted.
(b) Exact figures for the amount of explosives required to achieve the aim in every case. Here, consideration must be given to the shortage of materials and to the difficult circumstances in which the tasks will be carried out.
(c) Clear and simple instructions for the handling of explosives in blowing up bridges, blowing up large buildings, etc.
(d) Simple formulas for the preparation of explosives.
(e) Preparation of a plan for resistance to armed forces by the rebel population in Petrograd, including special consideration of the workers' quarters, the defence of houses and streets, the construction of barricades, and defence against cavalry and infiltrating infantry.

The Jewish Socialist "League" (the Bund) in Russia is a revolutionary organization, supported by the workers, which gave considerable service even in 1904. It has nothing to do with the Zionists, from whom, by contrast, nothing can be expected:

      1. Because their party structure is extremely loose.
      2. Because a strong Russian patriotic trend has made itself felt in their ranks since the beginning of the war.
      3. Because, after the Balkan War, the nucleus of their leadership actively sought to win the favor of English and Russian diplomatic circles--though this did not stop them from lobbying the German Imperial government as well.
      4. Because they are incapable of any political action.

Dr. Alexander Helphand
Born: August 27, 1867 -- died of heart attack: December 12, 1924

Born: Israel Elephand, in Berezino, 90 miles east of Vilno, in Minsk province, where Jews (mostly literate) accounted for about half of population.

First language: Yiddish, -- learned to read, write, and count in Yiddish written in Hebrew characters -- as a child spoke very little Russian or Polish. He lived in a self-contained Jewish community. (Trade and sex outside marriage were the only links with the gentiles.)

About 1870 was moved to Odessa, learned Russian, and discarded rigid ritual. Developed revolutionary faith -- influenced by the 1872 Russian translation of Marx' *Das Kapital*. Admired the Ukrainian "Haydamak" uprising of 1768-1772, despite its anti-Jewish pogroms.

1886 first travel outside Russia at nineteen (to resolve political doubts).

1888-1891 studied: History and Political Economy at the University of Basle. Major subject: Contemporary Economic and Political Problems of Capitalism and Socialism.
Doctor of Philosophy degree: July 8, 1891 (accepted Marx' revolutionary doctrine).

At 23 considered Germany as the key to western Europe, did not want to go back to Russia. Poverty stricken, started using pen-name "Parvus," or "barefoot" in the Bavarian dialect.

In 1893 deported from Berlin -- "Looking for a (cheap) fatherland." In 1894 in Leipzig working for "Volkszeitung." In 1896 in Dresden editor of the "Arbeiterzeitung."

In 1900 wrote "Proletariat to use social revolution to destroy capitalism." - "Revolution as the main aim." "Only power mattered -- everything was permissible." 1903, tutored Leon Trotsky -- advocated "mass strike." In 1906, as "Karl Wawerk" travelled in Russia. -- sentenced to three years in Siberia by an administrative decision, without trial -- escaped.

Nov. 1906 returned to Germany, received mail as "Peter Klein." Wrote on unity of world market and need for free trade as good for revolution. Had an affair with Rosa Luxemburg.

Nov. 1910 arrived to Turkey becoming an arms merchant, trader, and political consultant.

June 28, 1914 on news of killings in Sarayevo preached that "German victory is best for the Turks." Propagandist of German victory. Author of a plan for subversion of Russia March 9, 1915. Leading advisor of the Berlin government -- obtained withdrawal of deportation order of 1893 and received permit to travel freely. Obtained unlimited German money to convert a clique of conspirators into Russian revolutionary power. Supported an independent Ukraine - very strongly opposed independence of Poland. Became Prussian citizen in 1916 as a "bearer of German civilization." Died: in 1924 as the richest man in Berlin.

PART I

APPENDIX II

Is Polish Anti-Semitism Special ?

Henryk Grynberg

Henryk Grynberg is a poet, novelist and essayist who left Poland in 1967 because of the anti-Semitic campaign following the Six-Day War and now lives in the United States. This article, reprinted in excerpts here, was published in the **Midstream, Monthly Jewish Review**, August/September 1983.

The common phrase "traditional Polish anti-Semitism" is a platitude with very little historical justification. Anti-Semitism came to Poland as part of Western culture and civilization. The word "pogrom" is Russian and the phenomenon is Western European, originated by the crusaders who massacred Jewish communities while marching to free the Holy Land from the "infidels". The blood libel, first used against the Jews in 12th-century England, triggered the "pogrom" of York. It was also a Western idea to accuse the Jews of "desecrating the Host," or poisoning Christian wells. When a Polish prince (Bolesław Pobożny) issued a charter for the protection of Jews on his territory (1265), he did so primarily to protect them from attacks by their Christian neighbors of German origin or descent who were also settling on Polish lands bringing with them their religious intolerance and -- as Abba Eban writes in *My People* -- "their custom of political oppression."

Nothing anti-Semitic was ever invented in Poland - almost everything came from a centuries-old Western European tradition. There was very little new even in the Nazi Nuremberg Laws. Jewish book-burning was pioneered in France by Louis IX (in 1242); he was considered a "moral authority" among contemporary European rulers and a "patron of scholarship," and eventually became a saint. Another tradition which has reached our times is burning Jews alive: all the Jews of Jerusalem were burned alive in the main synagogue after the city was finally "liberated" by the Crusaders in 1099. Pope Innocent III introduced, in 1215, still another anti-Jewish tradition which reappeared in the 20th century: laws forcing the Jews to wear special badges in public, and forbidding Jews to live in the same house as Christians or to hold offices giving them control over a Christian. These medieval inventions were revived in the Age of Enlightenment by Pius VI, who issued his own "Edict Against the Jews," which provided for yellow badges, the censorship of Jewish books, a ban on Jewish shops outside the ghetto, and even introduced a ban on tombstones in Jewish cemeteries -- the latter is practiced in some countries even today with the same purpose: to erase the memory of any Jewish presence.

Europeans had a habit of making pogroms also during their "progressive" or patriotic uprisings. This was the case during the Munzer peasant battles in Germany, Chmielnicki's revolt in the Ukraine, and the White and Red Guard campaign during the Russian Civil War, not to mention the acts committed by the Ukrainian peasant army lead by Makhno. True, some pogroms were committed by the Polish troops of Stefan Czarnecki during his uprising against the Swedes (mid-17th century), but in all the pogroms through Polish history up to World War II, fewer Jews were killed than in one such slaughter in Prague -- then considered an important center of Western culture -- in 1389, when 4,000 Jews were put to death by a fanatical mob. The Chmielnicki pogroms are often misunderstood by those with no knowledge of Eastern European history: it is true they happened on "Polish territories" (the entire Ukraine was a part of the Polish empire in those days), but the pogroms took place in the Ukraine and were perpetrated not by Poles but exclusively by Cossacks and Ukrainian peasants (people often mistakenly assume that Chmielnicki was a Pole because of the Polish sound of his name). In fact, the Polish armies, who were at war with them, were the sole defenders of the Jews, for the Jews and Polish nobility were allies against a rebellion which viewed them both as enemy.

Jews were commonly invited by Western European rulers to develop trade and business, and then, after native Christians had learned and mastered those trades themselves, a vocal majority would cry: "Jews have taken over our trades and business!" That example was merely followed by Poland, where such cries could be heard until World War II.

During the Dreyfus affair, it was France who set the example for anti-Semitic behavior typical of a modern European society. Crowds beat up Jews in the streets of Paris, plundered Jewish stores, shouted "Death to the Jews!", wrote petitions demanding the expulsion of all Jews from France; the nationalist press urged that all Jews be fired from their jobs. Herzl as an eyewitness stressed in his diary that all this was happening in "republican, modern, civilized France, one hundred years after the Declaration of the Rights of Man." If similar moods and slogans were to be observed in Poland in 1936-39 and 1968-70, it should be pointed out that they were not manifestations of any "traditional Polish anti-Semitism," but rather a letter-perfect copy of the French tradition, with the exception of the irrational element: in Poland, "treason" was assumed a priori -- without any pretexts of mock-trials.

When speaking of Paris -- the capital of European culture for at least two centuries -- one should remember also that in that famous city, on July 16-17, 1942, the French police handed over 13,000 Jews to the Germans. Jews were taken out of hiding places, not just rounded up in a ghetto. I doubt if there were 13,000 cases of Jews being handed over to the Germans throughout the German occupation in Poland. Many thousand more were seized in unoccupied France (under the Vichy regime) in August 1942. Michael R. Marrus and Robert O. Paxton, in their book *Vichy France and the Jews*, stressed the fact that the Vichy legislation of October, 1940 "Status des Juifs" went beyond the German regulations of that time. The authors also point out that when the Italians (then German allies) occupied part of southern France, they felt they had to protect the Jews there from the Vichyists. And yet it is not the French but Poles who are singled out as "collaborators" in the Nazi extermination of Jews.

The anti-Semite needs anti-Semitism in order to project his own vices onto somebody else; to be able to blame someone else for his own failures (a device needed by individuals as well as by governments and whole political, social, and philosophical systems); to work off his frustrations (as husband and wife use each other); anti-Semitism is at times as necessary as a dog is for an Englishman or a German (who feels he has to be someone's master). Deprived of any other virtues or merits, an anti-Semite sees his not-being-Jewish as a decided virtue and therefore he denies any positive qualities in Jews, refuses to grant any praise or recognition to Jews, and sees their success as a result of some deceit or swindle -- not a fruit of talent, genius, or courage. Thus an anti-Semite cannot tolerate the emancipation of Jews and equality with Jews, or the existence of an independent Jewish state with equal rights and in free competition with other nations. "Not being a Jew provides them consolation for not being a state councillor," said Ludwig Borne about the German anti-Semites of the early 19th century. The fact that Jews are the chosen people for such a psychological device is no more than the product of certain historical and religious circumstances.

Anti-Semitism is an anomaly of the human mind, and its most characteristic symptom is the confusion of cause and effect. Russian anti-Semites still justify their hatred for the Jews by accusing them of being enemies of Old Russia who worked for the downfall of the Tsarist regime. They do not take into account the "Pale of Settlement" and 600 other anti-Jewish laws of that regime, the Okhrana's (tsarist police) anti-Semitic campaigns at the turn of the century, and the Bailis blood-libel trial as manifestations of Tsarist Russia's hatred for the Jews and perhaps an explanation for a reciprocation of feelings....

....Poland's World War II record is better than that of many of the other occupied countries. Just as the term "traditional Polish anti-Semitism" is historically a great exaggeration, the accusation that Polish society collaborated with the Nazis in the extermination of Jews is equally unjust. In fact most other occupied nations collaborated to a greater degree. There is absolutely no basis to the theory that Poland was chosen for the Holocaust because of "Polish anti-Semitism." It was chosen because it contained the largest concentration of Jews in Europe and because the territory itself was convenniently isolated by the war situation. In both absolute and relative numbers, more Jews were murdered by Austrians (the Nazi core in charge of the death camps and concentration camps), Rumanians (the Bucharest pogrom of 1941 and the extermination of Jews in Bessarabia and Odessa), Ukrainians, Lithuanians, and Latvians (police detachments engaged in the liquidation of Warsaw, Białystok, and Vilna Ghettos), Croats (particularly on Serbian territory), and Bulgarians (also on occupied Yugoslav lands). Very few historians seem to recall the fact that 100,000 Slovakian Jews were deported to the Majdanek death and concentration camp (it had a double function) by an action requested and even petitioned (in writing, to Berlin) by the autonomous Slovakian authorities, who finally, after getting Berlin's permission, executed the deportation with their own police.

Polish anti-Semitism, which never displayed such a murderous component as in the above examples, was never any nastier than French, Russian, Hungarian, or Argentinean anti-Semitism. To stigmatize the Poles in this case is very much like the irrational stigmatizing of Jews by anti-Semites. Accusations against the Poles resulted partly from the fact that Poland became the site of the largest extermination of Jews. That fact causes one to remember all the cases of blackmail and betrayal which took place there, although they were less numerous than in other countries, not only in relation to the number of Jews, but often in absolute numbers (as in the case of Paris and Vichy). Poland got a bad name once again in the late sixties when anti-Semitism, as in the 1930s, became a card in a political gamble. In both cases anti-Semitism was bid for: the competition for power demanded more anti-Semitism and the government gave in to that pressure in order not to leave such an effective and popular weapon in the hands of its rivals. In both cases, the blows fell on the Jews. The anti-Semitic campaign of the 1960s seemed even more morbid since there were very few Jews left in Poland, and more shameless, coming, as it did, after the Holocaust and at the site of the Holocaust. Yes, the anti-Semitic campaigns of the 1930s and 1960s were the most compromising episodes in the history of Polish-Jewish relations, but not so behavior of the Poles during the Holocaust (Poles outnumber other nationalities among the Righteous Gentiles at Yad Vashem) and those episodes still do not make Poland traditionally more anti-Semitic than most other nations.

This is especially obvious now, when the "Jewish question" comes up with increasing frequency and under code names. Until recently, it used to be an "internal affair" (as *Gazeta Polska* stressed in 1939), but in today's more confused world the Judeo-centric obsession and anti-Semitic pathology have assumed an international dimension, appearing under the euphemism of the "Middle East problem," then with increasing frequency as the "Palestinian question," and may soon become an "Israeli question," with the clear implication that something has to be done about Israel, whose existence is, symptomatically, a hindrance to so many states and nations. This disease is the more ominous in that it is now spreading throughout the post-Holocaust world, which knows its potential for cruelty and ruthlessness, while the "bothersome" Jewish state is a creation of a refuge for those who miraculously escaped from the international murderers. Pathology like this on an international scale is very dangerous especially in a world prone to inflection and mental plague because of extreme centralization and the technology of communication and information -- the latter always accompanied by misinformation.

Neither the past nor the present of such a world justifies stigmatizing the Poles.

Midstream, Monthly Jewish Review
February 1983
Henryk Grynberg replies his critics:

Bernard Goldstein doesn't seem to understand my article. I presented any anti-Semitism as an aberration and never asked for excuses. I pointed out that Polish anti-Semitism was a late immitation of both Western and Russian anti-Semitism and much less murderous in its nature than either. There is plenty of historic evidence that Polish anti-Semitism was never more nasty or more "sickening" than in most other countries. The misunderstanding stems from the fact that Poland was for centuries the country of the biggest Jewish settlement, so most of our memories of anti-Semitism is always uncivilized, as was that in pre-war Poland, but a statement that "the Poles achieved the runner-up position to the Nazis" reveals ignorance as well as a kind of "anti-Semitism" in reverse. Unfortunately, some Polish Jews borrowed something from anti-Semitic Poles, and one can find some similarity in their mentality and attitude.

No anti-Semite, Polish or otherwise, should look for his defense in my writing. My point is that anti-Semitism is much more universal; a distortion of this reality, while it hurts the Poles, can only help all the other anti-Semites and not the Jews. What happened to the Germans, by the way? They are hardly ever mentioned. The Poles, as in Goldstein's opinion are the "runner-up" only to the "Nazis," as if Nazis were some sort of nationality. Another explanation can be that only some Germans and some Austrians were Nazis, while the runner-up was all "the Poles" -- this is classic anti--Semitism in reverse.

Anti-Semites are wrong: Jews are not worse that anybody else. But they may not be better either.

The much more objective and balanced argumentation of Abraham Melezin includes some obvious mistakes. Perhaps Poles "retained every anti-Semitic stratagem longer than any other Western Europeans. Even their Roman Catholicism has a clearly Eastern character, with its cult of the God's Mother and of her Byzantine image in Częstochowa. And didn't other Eastern European nations -- Russians, Ukrainians, Latvians, Lithuanians, Slovaks, Hungarians, Rumanians, Croats -- retain all those anti-Semitic "stratagems" as well? The anti-Semitism which we don't know always seems much more benign. Melezin points out the Polish folkloristic expressions, but what about Latin America? All those characterizations of Jews found in Poland by Professor Łukaszewicz are synthesized by the Latin Americans in two words "vena Judia," "the Jewish vein."

The frequency of the ritual murder trials in 18th century Poland can also be easily explained by the fact that the Jewish population was much larger in Poland than in any other country of that period. But the modern pogroms, which started in the 1880s, were much more frequent and much more murderous on territories inhabited by Russians and Ukrainians than by Poles. It is true that up to World War II the Polish clergy was traditionally very hostile to Jews, but no more than the Spanish and German clergy of the past centuries and Russian, Ukrainian or Rumanian clergy in modern times. The truth is that Polish peasants were much less anti-Semitic than the peasants of almost any other Eastern European country and Polish nobility or gentry were hardly anti-Semitic at all.

Again, my point is that augmentation of Polish anti-Semitism serves as a cover-up for all the remaining anti-Semitism in the world. Why blame the Polish Catholic Congress of 1883 if anti-Semitic resolutions are being passed on a regular basis by the United Nations in our own day?

I wonder where Melezin found the information that in 1349, "during the Black Death epidemic in Poland, 10,000 Jews were exterminated -- almost the entire Jewish community." The fact is that the epidemic never reached Poland, and it was the period of Kazimierz the Great, a famous protector of Jews, whom he brought to his kingdom in large numbers. Why does Melezin see "medieval Judophobic tradition... in an unbroken historical continuity" only in Poland and not in Germany, Russia, all over Eastern Europe, or in Latin America? The Jew was a "scab" also in the opinion of so many more Russians, and the cry "Beat the Jews to save Russia!" was certainly not a cry of the "Polish masses." Melezin's idea that "centuries-old (anti-Semitic) perceptions have grown into the Polish soul" is very reminiscent of Dmowski's statements about the "Jewish soul" and everything with which it allegedly "has become imbued in the course of immutable generations" as a clear borrowing in both -- terminology and prejudice. Obviously, Poland was chosen as a cemetery for European Jewry because of logistic considerations. It was easier to transport 400,000 Hungarian Jews to Poland than 3,000,000 Polish Jews to Hungary. Otherwise, at least a dozen other countries could successfully have competed for that role. Germany itself could be a perfect spot for extermination not only of the Jews but of almost anybody else.

Claire Huchet-Bishop's defense of France is quite insufficient. The latest pogroms were not in 1378 but in 1942, when the French police dragged thousands of Jews out of their hidings in Paris and in the Vichy zone and smaller pogroms were still taking place in Paris and in the provinces with the help of bombs, machine guns, and hand grenades (pogroms were always committed by small groups of individuals). Neither Huchet-Bishop nor I can quote the number of Jews saved by friendly French people, but 40,000 Frenchmen were on the payroll of the Gestapo. What I am trying to explain is that the French are neither worse nor better than the Poles. Dryfus was a captain and not a "high-ranking officer." The high-ranking officers were his Gentile accusers and the real traitors. His rehabilitation came very late and not by any popular demand but due to the intransigence of very few intellectuals. Not only in France, but also in some places in Poland, people wouldn't mention their role in rescuing Jews because they were afraid to be branded friends of the Jews. In some places such people were simply ostracized.

PART I

APPENDIX III

POLISH-JEWISH APPEAL FOR RECONCILIATION ON THE FORTIETH ANNIVERSARY OF THE UPRISING IN THE WARSAW GHETTO

Forty years ago, two flags were hoisted side by side on the roof of a building inside the embattled Warsaw ghetto. One was white and blue, and the other was white and red.

The Jewish fighters had only hours left to live when they sent this message to the Polish people:

"We send you our fraternal greetings from amidst the flames and blood of the murdered Warsaw ghetto... The struggle raging here is for your freedom and ours. For the human, social and national honor and dignity of us all...long live the brotherhood and the blood of fighting Poland..."

This was a farewell that struck a tragic yet beautiful final note after nearly a thousand years in which Jews and Poles had lived together on Polish soil.

Forty years after the uprising in the Warsaw ghetto, the culminating point of the greatest tragedy in mankind's history, we, the undersigned, feel it is our moral duty to keep that message from the twentieth-century Masada from being forgotten.

During World War II, three of us were emissaries between the Polish Underground Army fighting in Poland and the Polish government in exile in London.

Across frontiers and battlefronts, we carried eye-witness accounts and documentary evidence of the mass extermination of the Jews, together with desperate appeals from the dying--appeals meant to rouse and awaken the conscience of an indifferent world.

The other three of us are active in Jewish affairs in the West. Each has a record of many years of struggle behind him. Each has a keen sense of fidelity to the heritage of Polish Jewry.

Before the war, the Jewish community in Poland numbered three million people. Today only a few thousand remain. The Jewish quarters and the walls the Nazis put up around them have since been leveled by a common enemy.

And yet, another kind of wall is being erected today to separate the Poles and Jews. On both sides of this wall, mutual resentment and a sense of injustice are spawning enmity and hatred.

Hatred is a boomerang which returns to everyone and spares no one, be he the stronger or the weaker party. The harvest of the hatred that was sown in the soul of Germany was Hitlerism. The human tyranny of the Soviet Union also is the offspring of hatred.

Poles and Jews both have been the victims of hatred. Hatred and deep resentment can spring up when an entire nation or community is burdened with the collective responsibility for the crimes and sins of an individual or a minority -- when blame is laid indiscriminately on all the people of the same nationality, religion or race.

Vengeful hatred is blind to all that is good, beautiful and noble in another people or nation. It sees only what is wicked and criminal.

The Jews remember Polish anti-Semitism, which made itself felt to a substantial degree only at the turn of the present century. They also should remember that this anti-Semitism was deplored by broad sectors of Poland's liberal and democratic intelligentsia, by the Polish labor movement and by the outstanding figures of Polish culture.

Among the strongest supporters of the Jews were such great Polish writers as Adam Mickiewicz, Józef Ignacy Krasicki, Bolesław Prus, Eliza Orzeszkowa, Maria Konopnicka and Andrzej Strug.

There were few cases of outright cruelty and physical violence to Jews in the independent Republic of Poland. But Polish anti-Semites should remember that even a Jew brought up as a Pole, and steeped in its cultural tradition, never felt he was a full-fledged citizen.

He was keenly aware of the school-bench ghetto at the universities. He was treated with scorn and mistrust. He was subjected to boycott and discrimination for which there was no justification in Polish law.

The familiar epithet "Judeo-Communism" cast every Jew in the role of a potential enemy of the Polish state and as a foreign agent. But Jews played a significant part in the Kościuszko insurrection of 1794 and in the uprisings of 1831 and 1863. Jewish volunteers fought in the Polish legions and other military units during World War I -- in the struggle for an independent Poland.

It was the British historian Norman Davies, a great friend of the Poles, who recently reminded the world of the Jews who volunteered to fight the Bolsheviks in the Polish-Russian War of 1920-21. These Jews were thrown out of the army and interned in camps.

It is also important to remember a famous paragraph in the Petersburg manifesto of March 27,1917. In it, the Council of Workers' and Soldiers' Delegates demanded that Poland be granted "the right to total independence." This paragraph was drawn up not by the Russians but by Polish Jew, Henryk Ehrlich, leader of BUND, the Jewish Socialist Party.

Communist propagandists make much of that paragraph, but they do not mention that Ehrlich was its author--or that he was executed on Stalin's orders during World War II.

The Jews, in turn, blame the entire Polish nation for the acts of the *szmalcowniks* -- criminal elements that turned Jews over to Nazi murderers in all the occupied countries.

Resentment has made Jews forget that the majority of Jews who survived the Holocaust outside the extermination camps owe their survival to the heroism of Poles. These Polish people risked their lives and the lives of their families in the rescue efforts. And at least 621 Poles, according to a list that is no doubt incomplete, were executed for hiding Jews.

Jews should remember as well that Poles outnumber all other nationalities on the honor rolls of Yad Vashem in Israel. And that a number of Polish Underground Army soldiers were killed and wounded trying to bring aid to the Jews fighting in the Warsaw ghetto.

Resentment makes many of today's Jewish writers overlook or undervalue the work of the Council for Aid to Jews -- created by the high command of the Polish Underground Army. They forget or undervalue the efforts of Polish authorities in occupied Poland -- and in exile in London. These Poles did everything in their power to bring the Western governments' and the world's attention to the dying Jews' desperate call for help.

Poles consider themselves deeply wronged when they are held responsible for that mass murder of which they too were victims.

Jews feel equally hurt when they are blamed for the crimes committed by the Polish Communist Security Police during the Stalinist era, when several high positions in the terror machine and in the party were held by Jews. They remind the anti-Semites that Poles of Jewish origin have been in the forefront of the freedom movement in Poland since 1956, braving threats of reprisal with courage and self-sacrifice.

The time has come to lay aside the ghost of mutual antagonism. It is harmful to Poles and Jews alike. It is particularly painful to Jews who are Polish patriots but also must remain faithful to their Jewish heritage and religion.

Mutual recrimination serves no useful purpose. Men of good will -- Poles and Jews alike -- are trying to create a real dialogue and mutual understanding. Let us use this dialogue to find what unites Poles and Jews.

There is unity in a shared determination that there should never again be an attempt at the total physical annihilation of any nation. Unfortunately, the Poles and the Jews still live with that threat hanging over them.

Poland's geographical position makes it particularly vulnerable to the current Soviet menace. And Israel is surrounded by a sea of hostile Arab countries looking for the chance to destroy a young state miraculously reborn after two thousand years.

No one more than the Poles -- eyewitnesses to the Holocaust and themselves victims of Nazi terror throughout World War II -- understands the sense of jeopardy of the Jewish survivors who have gone back to their Promised Land.

A substantial number of Israeli citizens come from Poland. A newspaper for them is published in Polish. *Kultura*, the Polish monthly published in France, and other Polish publications are widely read in Israel. Polish musical and theatrical performances in Israel are welcomed by the older generation of Jews; they are nostalgic for the land of their youth -- that "little town of Belz" immortalized in Jewish song.

Any gesture or sign of solidarity from Poles at home or abroad, demonstrating their interest in the fate of the State of Israel, would do more to eliminate Polish-Jewish friction than volumes of apologetic, self-justifying prose.

Poles and Jews are fellows in misfortune in the Soviet Union, where they are the two most persecuted minorities -- both of them victims of cruel discrimination and injustice.

Jews living outside Israel have considerable influence in the Western world. They are struggling to obtain for Soviet Jewry the right to emigrate from the Soviet Union. If they were to broaden their effort and seek the same right for Poles and other nationalities and religions wishing to return to their homelands, the effort surely would be welcomed by Poles everywhere.

In advancing these first thoughts concerning the rapprochement of Jews and Poles, we are fully cognizant of the risk of attack by extremists on both sides.

But we will not be turned aside from our undertaking. We are determined to serve the idea of the brotherhood of mankind regardless of origin, nationality, religion, color or race.

We are acting in obedience to the Ten Commandments, the fountainhead of both our religions and the foundation on which the supreme values of our civilization rest. We are convinced that this is the best way we can serve the cause of Poles and Jews.

Signed:

Michael BORWICZ
Jan KARSKI
Joseph LICHTEN
Jerzy LERSKI
Simon WIESENTAL
Jan NOWAK

September 1, 1983

PART I

APPENDIX IV

POLISH BISHOPS' PASTORAL LETTER

ON ANTI-SEMITISM

This is a press release of the bishops' pastoral letter on the occasion of the 25th anniversary of the announcement of the conciliar declaration Nostra Aetate from the Embassy of the Republic of Poland, dated January 1991.

Today we address ourselves to the extremely important issue of our attitude towards the Jewish nation and the Mosaic faith with which we Christians are linked with unique and unparalleled ties. We are doing this in connection with the 25th anniversary of the announcement of the conciliar declaration Nostra Aetate in which the Church more precisely determined its relation towards non-Christian religions, including the Jewish one, it was stated in a pastoral letter read out at all churches and chapels during holy masses on 20 January 1991.

The conciliar declaration points, first of all, to the multitude and diversification of ties between the Church and the Mosaic faith and the Jewish nation. With no other religion has the Church developed such a close relationship, and with no other nation is it linked with such close ties.

With the Jewish nation we Poles are linked with special ties as early as the first centuries of our history. Poland has become another homeland for many Jews. The majority of Jews living all over the world at present originate from the territories of the former and present Republic of Poland. Unfortunately, it is exactly this land that became the grave of several million Jews in our century, not by our will and not by our hand.

This is what not long ago, on 26 September, 1990, the Holy Father said about our common history: "There is one more nation, one more special people: the people of patriarchs, Moses and the prophets, the legacy of the faith of Abraham. These people lived with us for generations, shoulder to shoulder, on the same land which somehow became the new land for its Diaspora.

Horrible death was inflicted on millions of sons and daughters of this nation. First they were branded with a special stigma. Then they were pushed to ghettoes in separated districts. Next they were transported to gas chambers and killed, only because they were children of this nation.

[German] Murderers did this on our soil, perhaps in order to defile it. But earth cannot be defiled by the blood of innocent victims. Earth becomes a holy relic due to such deaths." (Address to Poles at a Wednesday audience on 26 September 1990.)

Many Poles saved Jewish lives during the last war. Hundreds, if not thousands paid with their own lives and the lives of their families

153

for that assistance. A long chain of hearts of people of goodwill and of helping hands stood behind each of the saved Jews. A significant evidence of the assistance for Jews during the cruel years of Nazi occupation is given by the numerous trees devoted to Poles in the Yad Vashem National Memorial site in Jerusalem and the honorable title of the righteous among the nations of the world granted to many Poles.

Despite such a large number of examples of heroic assistance on the part of Christian Poles, there were also people who remained indifferent to that inconceivable tragedy. We particularly suffer because of those Catholics who were in any way instrumental in causing the death of Jews. They will forever remain a pang of conscience for us, also in the social dimension.

If there was only one Christian who could have helped a Jew in danger but he did not give him a helping hand or had a share in his death, we must ask our Jewish sisters and brothers for forgiveness.

We are aware that many of our compatriots still nurse in their memory the harm and injustice inflicted by the post-war Communist rule, in which people of Jewish origin participated as well. But we must admit that the source of inspiration for their actions hardly lay in their Jewish origin, or religion, or the Communist ideology from which Jews suffered much injustice too.

We also express our sincere regret at all cases of anti-Semitism that have taken place on the Polish soil. We are doing this deeply convinced that all signs of anti-Semitism are contrary to the spirit of the Gospel and, as John Paul II has recently underlined: "will remain totally contrary to the Christian vision of human dignity." (John Paul II on the 50th anniversary of the outbreak of World War II in September, 1989.)

While expressing our regret at all injustice and harm inflicted on Jews, we must mention that we feel it unjust and deeply unfair that many use the notion of the so-called Polish anti-Semitism in general, or that sometimes concen-

tration camps are attributed to Poles in Poland occupied by Germans instead to their actual [German] originators.

Speaking about the unprecedented extermination of Jews, one must not forget, or pass it in silence, that also Poles as a nation became one of the first victims of the same criminal, racist ideology of [German] Nazism.

The same soil that has been a common motherland of Poles and Jews for centuries, the blood shed together, the sea of atrocious pain, the harm suffered by both nations should unite rather then divide them. In particular the sites of torture and, in many cases, common graves call for this unity.

We, Christians and Jews, are united by the belief in one God, the Creator and the Lord of the whole universe, who created man in his own image. We are united by the ethical principles included in the Decalog which may be reduced to the Commandment of the Love of God and Fellow Man.

We are united by our veneration for the Old Testament as the Holy Scripture and common traditions of prayer.

And we are united by the hope for the final coming of the Kingdom of God. We wait together for the Messiah, the Saviour, although we believe that he is Jesus Christ of Nazareth and await not the first but his last coming in might and glory, and not in the poverty of the Bethlehem stable.

The crucial way to overcome the still existing difficulties is to assume the attitude of dialogue which will lead to the elimination of distrust, prejudice, and the stereotypes, which will allow us to get to know and understand each other better, based on the respect for our separate religious traditions, which will open up the road to cooperation in many fields.

It is important too that we learn to experience and evaluate the religious beliefs of Jews and Christians in the way Jews and Christians themselves experience them today.

PART I

APPENDIX V

President Lech Wałęsa's Speech
to the Israeli Parliament
May 20, 1991

During his visit to Israel in May 1991, President of Poland Lech Wałęsa delivered the following speech to the Israeli Parliament. Admitting "there were some malefactors among us," he asked for mutual forgiveness. He met with another cool reception.

I wish to express my great satisfaction at our meeting here today. It has a singular meaning just as the relationship uniting Poles and Jews is singular. History has interwoven the fates of both nations.

Jews came to Poland from all parts of Europe and found a climate of tolerance and hospitality. They felt and found conditions in which they could develop their great culture. Outstanding Jewish intellectuals and religious leaders were able to act and work. Poland was a common home for Poles and Jews. There was a time when more than half of all Jews in the world lived in Poland.

Before World War II the diaspora in Poland was second in size in the world. This war brought to the Jewish people the greatest tragedy in their history. Hitler devised a diabolical plan of total extermination for them. The invader established ghettos and death camps in Auschwitz, Treblinka and Sobibor.

We too, the Poles, were victims of Nazism. Although we tried to help, it was not easy for us -- because the same fate awaited us. And yet, there were many "Righteous" Poles and they have their trees planted in the Avenue of the Righteous.

In the Talmud we read: "Whosoever saves the life of one human being, saves the whole world -- and who takes one life kills the whole world." There were among us some malefactors. I am a Christian and I cannot measure by human reckoning the wrongs of both nations, but here in Israel, the land of your birth and rebirth, I ask your forgiveness.

The Warsaw Ghetto Uprising preceded by almost a year the Warsaw Uprising by people who understood that sometimes you have to die so that a nation does not live on its knees. The cooperation of the Home Army and the Jewish Combat Units were a tradition to which we often refer. From you, our older brothers, with whom we were not always successful in arranging our lives, we can learn much about national solidarity, the building of a nation and the spiritual strength of the nation.

Polish-Jewish relations were at their worst when foreign powers were ruling the country. The principle of "Divide and Conquer" was also the modus operandi of the communists. Both our nations, deprived of their freedom, looked at each other and saw themselves in a distorted mirror. How alike we are in our mix of good and bad characteristics. In giving into foreign influences and in our aspirations for freedom. We are alike in our quarrelsomeness and solidarity, in our generosity and our petty envy. How much aggression our similarities arouse in each other.

Today, as Poland returns to the family of free nations, let us be open with each other. As the representative of a nation that has regained its freedom and is trying to regain its independence -- in the name of Polish honor I ask you for fairness in remembering our mutual past. Today we are building a free, democratic Poland, we are building a nation which is a home for all citizens, irrespective of their religion or origin.

A free and independent Poland refers to the best Polish traditions. We do not limit ourselves to words. I intend to form a State Council for Polish-Jewish matters. It will signal everything which may hinder our cooperation. We are forming far-reaching education programs. Polish youngsters will be able to study the common history of both our nations. After 20 years we have reestablished our diplomatic relations. We are expanding our contacts. Young Poles and Jews should visit each other and cultural, educational and economic ties should be broadened.

I am impressed by the achievements of the Israelis. In 40 years you have established a strong, democratic nation in spite of great difficulties and impending dangers.

At the present time we are experiencing historic changes. We are returning to tried and true values of democracy, personal freedoms, free market economy, and the free enterprise.

Poland's foreign affairs reflect an important transformation in the political system which favors the respect for human and international rights. Our faith in you was underscored during the war in the Persian Gulf, when despite falling rockets and dangers your people respected the coalition and helped it win the war. We support the search for a permanent solution for peace in the Near East. We feel it is possible if it will guarantee the safety of all the nations in the region. I wish you peace and success in building your nation.

Dear ladies and gentlemen -- I know what this land means to you. Here your great prophets lived. This is where God entered into a covenant with his chosen people. Here is where the ten commandments appeared. The Great Diaspora began when Jerusalem was destroyed by the Romans. Your people have survived and have returned to the land of their fathers. This is an accomplishment of world shaking proportions.

I hope that our meeting today will serve to erase all former prejudices and that it would become an impetus for cooperation between Poland and Israel. And that it would be conducive to the rebirth of brotherly association between Poles and Jews in Poland, in Israel and in the whole world.

PART I

APPENDIX VI

The Poles Innocent of the Genocide of the Jews,

Polish American Congress Protests

An Open Slander and the Genocide Libel--

The Problem of "Reverse Anti-Semitism"

Facing distorted interpretation of President Wałęsa's speech [of May 20, 1991) at the Israeli Knesset (parliament), by the American and international media, the Polish American Congress issued the following protest:

The Polish-American Community once again was shocked by the insensitivity of the American mass media towards the genocide of over 3 million Polish Catholics by the German Nazis. After years of referring to the German concentration camps as "Polish death camps," after years of blaming the victims for the crimes of their oppressors, the American media continue to falsify the history, and to twist the facts in a truly Orwellian fashion. It is particularly sad that the latest instance of the anti-Polish bias took place with regard to the courageous step of Poland's President, Lech Wałęsa, whom the World still owes an unpaid dept for freeing it from the communist nightmare.

In May 20, 1991, President Wałęsa delivered a speech to the Israeli Knesset, in which, as a true Christian, he asked all Jews for forgiveness for any wrongs any of them might have suffered at the hands of any Poles. "Forgive us, as we forgive those who trespass against us,"-- taught us Christ. Nevertheless, one can hardly ask to be forgiven sins one has never committed. Nowhere in his speech did President Wałęsa acknowledge, as he could not have, Polish responsibility for the Jewish Holocaust which was prepared and called out by the Germans [under the

full authority of the German government and in the name of the German people].

In general, the American media completely ignored this clear sign of good faith on the part of the Polish leadership. Instead, by quoting President Wałęsa's words out of context, and by coupling them with provocative remarks of Prime Minister Shamir, they created a grave misconception among the American public of Polish apology for the Jewish Holocaust. The full and complete text of President Wałęsa's speech to the Knesset is too plain to be misunderstood. A sizable amount of bad faith and anti-Polish bias is required in order to read an acknowledgment of Polish responsibility for the Jewish Holocaust into it.

The past experience of the Polish American Congress indicates that the American media will remain immune to the protests on this subject, and will continue to blame the victims of German Nazism for the tragedy of other victims of the same German Nazism. If suffering and deaths of millions of Polish Catholics, old and young, men, women and children, who were gassed, starved, hanged, burned and shot, in the concentration camps, in the Polish streets and in the Polish villages, who were killed simply for being Polish or for attempting to help the Jews; if the deaths and suffering of those millions of human beings cannot soften the anti-Polish prejudice in the American media, probably nothing will. But in the end, the history can only be falsified, it cannot be rewritten.

PART I

APPENDIX VII
On Polish-Jewish Relations
Commentary By Professor Ralph Slovenko

Quoted and excerpted from: The Journal of
Psychiatry & Law/Winter 1987 (C) 1988 by Federal Legal Publications, Inc.

*"The paths of the two saddest nations
on this earth have parted forever."*
     --Rafael Scharf

*"Life can only be understood backwards,
but it must be lived forwards."*
     -Kierkegaard

[The Rector (President) of the University of Cracow, Professor Dr. Józef A. Gierowski, headed a 4-week session on Polish-Jewish relations in Cracow in 1987.]
... an indication of willingness on the part of Poland to discuss its Jewish past, frankly and fully... Approximately 25 delegates from Australia, England, Israel, and the United States were there; I participated.[1][2]

Poles and Jews lived through their history in Poland as though in separate worlds. Few peoples in history have lived so closely together yet so far apart.[3]

Professor Andrzej Brożek of Jagiellonian University in his book "Poles in America" writes not a word about Jews from Poland who emigrated to the United States. In an epilogue in the English edition, he mentions the critics who noted this and he replies, Jews constitute an entirely different topic.[4]

Poles in America are known as Polish-Americans and Jews are known as American Jews, sometimes as Jewish-Americans. Immigrants in the United States, at least until the third generation, are generally known as hyphenated Americans.[5] On the other hand, a Pole in Germany would be known either as a Pole or as a German; one could not say "Polish-German," whatever the assimilation. In the concentration camps, Jews from Germany (who were highly assimilated) argued with the guards, "We're not Jews, we're Germans." And they said, "We want to fight for the Fatherland."[6]

In Poland, on the other hand, there was little question: Jews were Jews. With some exception, Jews neither considered themselves nor were they regarded by others as Polish or Polish Jews. As is well known, Jews in Poland were allowed to have their own laws and institutions. They were a nation unto themselves and they maintained their nationhood in Poland. From the time of their arrival and through the centuries, they sought to protect their way of life. They were not merely a separate religion but a tightly-knit community, leading life largely separate from Poles. They had their own customs, culture, dress, schools, courts, community government, and language (in the 1930 census almost 80 percent declared Yiddish as their mother tongue). Menachem Begin's father refused to learn Polish. In a word, the vast majority of Jews were unintegrated socially and culturally in the fabric of the larger society. They shared little or no national sentiment or common allegiance with the Poles. They and the Poles were almost strangers. They avoided association with the vast majority of the population, the Polish peasantry, not wanting to live like, or with, them.

The phenomenon is surely not unique. Birds of a feather flock together. That people group with those similar to themselves is one of the most well-established replicable findings in the psychology and biology of human behavior. People of whatever race or religion have always tried to insulate and remove themselves from what is perceived as different behavior, whatever its origins.[7]

Professor Andrzej Kapiszewski of Jagiellonian University said at the conference, "Jews fostered their own nationalism without concern for Poland." "Jews did as much harm to Poles as Poles did to Jews." This observation aroused the ire of the Jewish participants. Professor Kapiszewski retracted. He conceded that he had overstated the case. "How can one compare the injuries?" asked one Jew. Professor Kapiszewski's book on Polish-Jewish relations is about to be published in the United States.

... the Jews, they did not consider Poland as their country--it was their land, but not their state. Poles to this day say, "Our country was destroyed, but the Jews separated themselves." The vast majority of Jews, they note, never displayed any Polonist passion,- not for the language of Poland, its culture, its history, or its politics. As recent as the 1930s only about 10 percent of the Jewish population was assimilated.[8][9]

Paul Johnson in his recent book, "A History of the Jews," says the Versailles treaty was an important element in the greatest of all Jewish tragedies, for it was a covenant without a sword. It introduced years of growing instability, dominated by the hatreds its own provisions had engendered. In this atmosphere of discontent and uncertainty, the position of the Jews, far from improving, grew more insecure. And now there was an additional cause of hostility--the Jewish identification with Bolshevism.[10]

The publicity about anti-Semitism in Poland gave rise to a negative attitude about Poland in the Western world. According to Polish historians, the Western press often overstated the extent and number of pogroms in Poland. For this adverse publicity, the Pole blamed the Jew. Jews in the West, it is also alleged, because of anti-Semitism in Poland, lobbied against providing credits to Poland, and it hurt the country.[11] A leading Polish-American paper wrote that the Jews were the greatest enemy [of the good name] of Poland.[12] Fights broke out in the United States between Poles and Jews. "Jews are our enemy," said the Poles. "Poles are a despicable race," said the Jews. Jews in the West urged that Poland be denied a seat in the League of Nations.[13]

The image of Poland in the United States in the aftermath of World War I was that it was on the verge of destroying Jewry.[14] ... anti-Semitism grew in Poland.[15] In 1936, Cardinal Augustus Hlond, Primate of Poland, wrote a pastoral letter in which he declared: "The Jewish problem is there and will be there as long as Jews remain Jews....It is a fact that Jews are in opposition to the Catholic Church, that they are freethinkers, the vanguard of godlessness, bolshevism, and subversion. It is a fact that they exert a pernicious influence on public morality and that their publishing houses are spreading pornography. It is true that Jews are swindlers, usurers, and that they are engaged in fostering immoral earnings. It is true that the effect of the Jewish youth upon the Catholic is--in the religious and ethical sense--negative." "But," he urged, "we must not be unjust. This does not apply to all Jews. There are very many Jews who are believers, honest, righteous, merciful, doing good works. The family life of many Jews is healthy and edifying. And there are among Jews people morally quite outstanding, noble and honorable people."[16][17]

In the context of the Church and its history at that time, the position of the Primate could be described as moderate.[18]...Cardinal Hlond advocated the economic boycott of Jewish businesses.[19]

On the other side, Zionists were interested in having Jews settle in Palestine. They too were interested in building a nation. They played up news about anti-Semitism.[20]...Jews cannot feel secure living in Poland, they said.[21] The love of the land of Israel has been central to Jewish thinking for millennia, but the Zionist movement was a consequence of the anti-Semitism.[22][23]

...In the course of its history Poland has taken a large number of different forms--almost every century has seen its territory modified and the political lines that bounded it changed.[24]... The titles of historian Norman Davies' books about Poland capture the plight of the country: "Heart of Europe" and "God's Playground."[25] "Poland is the Jesus Christ of nations," wrote Juliusz Slowacki, the great Romantic poet. Polish messianism showed no hesitation in identifying the country as "the Christ of Nations."[26]

Out of their history, the Poles have distilled a fervent, romantic nationalism.[27]...[28] University students in Poland regard Marshal Pilsudski as a sort of cult figure.[29] In 1980, during the time of Solidarnosc, there appeared another stirring nationalistic song, "Zeby Polska byla Polska" (Let Poland Be Poland), written by Jan Pietrzak.[30] On July 12 and 13, 1987, the main item on nightly television newscasts was the 577th anniversary of the victory of the Polish army over the Teutonic Knights.[31]

...The Jewish community did not support Polish nationalism. They sought a homeland in Palestine or autonomy in those areas of Eastern Europe where they were heavily concentrated. And a substantial number of Jews were revolutionary. As a handicapped people, they wanted a change. Marian Adler, an elderly Jew living in Poland, recalls: "Communism was a beautiful, noble idea." In 1931, Poland's Communist Party had only 10,000 members, but three-quarters of them were Jews. This was a small percentage of the Jewish population (the 1931 census listed 3.1 million Jews in Poland, or ten percent of the population), but they constituted a large percentage of the membership of the Communist Party. The proportionally large presence of Jews in the pre-war Communist Party of Poland served to confirm the slogans about the *Zydokomuna* (the Jew-Communist).

The history of Jews in the diaspora needs no retelling, but their life in Poland was of a different order than elsewhere in the diaspora. Jews came to Poland in large numbers, and lived there for centuries, because in Poland they found a haven. Jews first began coming to Poland over a thousand years ago, with the great influx beginning in the 14th century, when the many-sided pressures on the part of the Christian European states caused a migration to the east. By the year 1500, Poland was regarded as the safest country in Europe for Jews, and for centuries, Poland was known as the "country of heretics." "The kingdom of justice was the kingdom of Poland." Poland was the leader among the countries of the continent in the protection of liberty. In the 16th century it was a country without censorship, where anything and everything was published. The Statute of Kalisz (1264) was the first general law to give protection to Jews in Europe, guaranteeing them full religious liberty, freedom of trade and protection against offenders of their rights. For centuries, Jews in Poland found unparalleled protection.[32]

Out of a desire to have the Jews build up Poland's economy, and as a genuine friend of the Jews, King Casimir III in the 14th century granted Jews special privileges. Casimir is known as "Casimir the Great" but the feudalists lambasted and nicknamed him "king of the serfs and Jews." He was animated by a determination to transform Poland into a great Western power (and as the story goes, he had a Jewish girlfriend, Esther). He exempted the Jews from any dominion by church or guilds. As "king's servants" (servi camerae), Jews were placed under the special protection of the crown. Holding this honorary title, they were under the direct jurisdiction of the king and were exempt from any other jurisdiction and most taxation or custom duties...The kings and nobles valued their skills as merchants and artisans.

Poland soon had the largest population of Jews in the world. Not since the dispersion of the Jews from the Holy Land in 70 A.D. had there been such an ingathering of world Jewry. By 1800 three-quarters of all Jews lived in Poland. In 1939, the Jewish population in Poland numbered 3.5 million. More than 30 percent of the population of Warsaw (some half a million people) was Jewish, and the proportion was similar in other Polish cities. Kazimierz, a quarter of Krakow, was a thriving center of Eastern European Jewry. Unlike Warsaw, where the Germans razed the entire city, the war left Krakow relatively unscathed, so the old Jewish Quarter remains. In rebuilt Warsaw, one of the main streets is still called "Jerusalem" (Aleje Jerozolimskie).

The Jews lived in Poland for centuries in relative peace and stability. In cases of attacks on Jews, the king held the city authorities responsible and demanded that the transgressors be caught.[33] Jews, disinherited and persecuted elsewhere, thus found rather

secure asylum in Poland and long possessed an autonomy that was close to sovereignty, with its own parliament, legal system, religious and civil administration. Poland was the center of Jewish religious and cultural life in the world. It was the home of the most powerful currents of Jewish religion, Hassidism. It was the home of Jewish giants of literature and philosophy. It was where the Yiddish language was formed.[34] At the turn of the 20th century, Jews, 10 percent of the population, constituted 30 percent of university students, 49 percent of all lawyers and 46 percent of doctors, and made up 59 percent of Poland's population engaged in commerce and 21 percent in industry. At Wilno (Vilnius) [the "Jerusalem of the North"] a flourishing center of Judaic studies existed until World War II. Lublin was known as the "Jewish Oxford." In 1937 the Jewish community in Poland published some 250 periodicals and over 700 books.

In the 1930s, when economic depression swept the world, there was a marked rise of anti-Semitism, which manifested itself in efforts to enforce segregation at universities, economic boycotts to reduce Jewish preponderance in commerce, violence, and destruction of property. In that period Polish Prime Minister Slawoj-Skladkowski stated in public, referring to Jews: "Economic boycott, yes; but physical harm, no." On the walls of buildings one could read such slogans as "Shame and hideousness for buying at Jews' shops."[35] Slogans echoed in the streets--"Long live free Poland without Jews," "We want a Warsaw without Jews." Propaganda from Hitler's Germany further incited Polish anti-Semites. Signs reading "Jews to Palestine" or "Jews to Madagascar" appeared.

The climate of anti-Semitism grew...Though without formal regulations, the medical and polytechnic schools of fully autonomous universities restricted enrollment by Jews to eight or nine percent of the student body, and they had in their auditoriums separate benches for Jews.[36] Among the student extremists there were those who made it a practice to beat Jewish students and other Jews in the streets (and also Poles who were political opponents). During the period 1937-1938 some universities had to suspend classes because of the violence against the Jews. [In December 1937, 53 professors of the universities of Warsaw, Wilno, and Poznan signed a declaration "In defense of the Polish culture" in which they condemned all forms of discrimination against Jewish students.] Between 1925 and 1939 the proportion of Jewish students at Polish universities dropped from 21.5 to 8.2 percent.[37]

When war broke out in 1939, Poles faced two enemies at once, Germany and the Soviet Union, but that is not the way Jews saw it. Large numbers of Jews welcomed the Soviet invasion, imprinting in Polish memory the image of Jewish crowds greeting the invading Red Army as their liberators. By 1939, the alienation of the Jewish community had reached its zenith...even quite assimilated Jews welcomed the Soviet invader.[38] Shunned and persecuted...the Jews reacted as a wounded people might be expected to react. In any case, it only deepened the hostility of the Poles, confirming their suspicions about the loyalty of Jews to the Polish state.[39]

And as it turned out, with German occupation, Poland became a graveyard for Polish Jews, and European Jews. It became the land of the Holocaust, the land marked with the stigma of [German] crime. As Malgorzata Niezabitowska, a young Pole, put it: "Though that crime was planned and carried out by the Germans, its shadow fell upon Poland and the people who were its witnesses, and, what is worse, who did not always sympathize."[40] In the last days of the Polish state, in 1939, Polish anti-Semitism flared up in the prisoner-of-war camps...[41] The rightist militia group, *Narodowe Sily Zbrojne* (National Armed Forces), refused to admit Jews into its ranks; survivors of the ruins of the Warsaw Ghetto were afraid to seek their assistance or protection lest they be killed by them.[42] In other German-occupied countries the resistance, as a rule, was anti-antiSemitic...

Yet, of all the countries in the world, it was Poland that first and until the latter part of the 19th century represented, as the Jews themselves defined it, a paradise for the Jews (Paradisus Judeorum).[43] Poland did not follow the Catholic Church's declaration, *"Extra ecclesiam nulla salus"* (outside the church no salvation).[44] At the Council of Constance (1414-18), one of the great diplomatic conferences of the middle ages, Poland's representative, Paulus

158

Vladimiri, rector of the University of Krakow, submitted to the Council his memorial, "*De potestatae papae et imperatoris respectu infidelium*," in which he formulated his, and his country's, thesis that Christianity should not be forced upon infidels, and that all forcible conversion was immoral. In contrast to other countries in Europe, where religious differences led to bloody civil wars, religious tolerance reigned in Poland. An apt phrase for Poland in the 16th century was, "a country without stakes."[45]

Jews in Poland occupied a place between the nobility and the peasants. That changed in the middle of the 19th century but it was impressed in the mind of the peasantry. The Jews collected taxes for the nobility and managed their estates. They represented the nobility who were often in France or other places. They were known as *pachciarz*, or "commercial agent."[46] The Jew, on behalf of the noblemen, controlled the life of the village. The peasants lost legal protection in 1518, when the king ceased to consider their complaints against the nobles. The peasants now remained virtually at the mercy of the nobles, who decided on the levies to be imposed upon them in the form of services and the use of monopolies and held jurisdiction over them. The nobles, with Jews as their agents, often misused their privileges to exploit the peasants subject to their whims.[47] Poland in the 16th and 17th centuries has often been described as "heaven for the Jews, paradise for the nobles, hell for the serfs."[48] The result was inevitable: strong resentment.[49]

The partition of [Poland] at the end of the 18th century was a disaster for the Jews. In 1569, to recall, the personal Polish-Lithuanian union (based on marriage) was changed into a real union, forming one state called the Commonwealth of Two Nations (*Rzeczpospolita Obojga Narodów*). The problem of royal power was solved in such a way that each monarch was chosen by the entire gentry [which included about one million people].[50]

As the power of the kings decreased, the Jews became more vulnerable to political and physical attack by their adversaries. Jewish corporate life disintegrated with that of the disintegration of the Polish-Lithuanian commonwealth. Zionism likely would not have had appeal if it had continued.

Most Poles viewed the Jews as a strange people, a foreign body thrust into the midst of Polish society. For the most part, as we have noted, Jews in Poland were different from the rest of the population in their dress, language and speech mannerisms, their gestures, and facial expressions. They wore beards and long earlocks, yarmulkes on their heads, and black caftans.[51] They worshipped differently. They circumcised their male offspring. They did not for the most part engage in menial labor.[52]...[53]

Historically, what was unique in Poland of all European countries was that it was the only one in which Jews were allowed to participate in a wide range of trades, crafts and skills. They were the indispensable craftsmen of the rural economy in the villages and small towns, and they were the shopkeepers. A typical expression attributed to Jews, told among Poles, was: "The Jews own the buildings, the Poles have the streets."[54] However, in truth, what was most in common was that both Poles and Jews, in the vast majority, were poor.[55]

Differences can create tensions, we know, even within a group. The acculturated German Jew, we may recall, looked with contempt on the Jews who lived to the east of Germany--the "Ostjuden." The "snobbish" German Jew regarded the Polish Jew as "barbarous," "vulgar", an "aversion to civilization."[56] Indeed, in the United States the tensions between Jew and Gentile often pale in comparison to that between orthodox and reform Jews, and in Israel, were it not for the Arab threat, civil war would likely erupt between the religious and secular Jew.[57]

The church, often a magnificent structure, contrasted sharply with the poverty of the peasants' houses. The priest, the trusted adviser, was obeyed more readily than any secular power.[58]...[59]

The situation of Jews in 20th century Poland was in some respects similar to that in the Ukraine, but it would be an overstatement to say that the situations were identical. There were no "pogroms" (Russian word) in Poland, except for sporadic instances. In the Ukraine, my family would run for cover on Christian holidays, especially at Easter. Jewish boys, my father included (though he had a Ukrainian name), were forced to lower their pants to show their circumcised body part. The Christian Church everywhere fomented anti-Jewish prejudice. Prayers were said at Mass for the conversion of the perfidious Jew. Jews were thought of as Christ killers and as users of Christian blood for baking their matzos. Rabbi Marc Tanenbaum of the American Jewish Committee relates that near his family's home in a tiny Jewish village in the Ukraine was a Russian Orthodox church where on Good Friday the priest, celebrating the liturgy commemorating the death and resurrection of Jesus, would be emotionally carried away by the imagery of "the Jews killing Christ," and through his sermon would convert the congregation into an angry mob that descended on their home.[60]

The question has been put in various ways: Did the crucifixion set the stage for the Holocaust? Was the Holocaust the natural outcome of the centuries-old condemnation of the Jews as the Christ-killer?[61] Is the Christian symbol of the crucified Christ an incitement to violence (comparable to the now much-discussed violence in the media)? Did it contribute to the extermination, the *shoah*, suffered by the Jews?...[62]

Was the doctrine, "You can't be a Jew" (convert or die), the predecessor for, "You can't be" (genocide)? Professor Raoul Hilberg, author of a 4-volume work on the extermination of the Jews, says "yes."[63]...[64]

Indeed, in the eyes of many Jews (as well as others), the Holocaust was the consummation of centuries of Christian hate and contempt; this was the punishment for the alleged crime of deicide, the final result of the Gospel's "His blood be upon us and upon our children."[65] Rabbi Mordecai Waxman, honorary president of the Synagogue Council of America, said to Pope John Paul II on his visit to the United States that the Holocaust was "the culmination of centuries of anti-Semitism in European culture for which Christian teachings bear a heavy responsibility."[66]

In an interview in a recent issue of *Tikkun*, a Jewish quarterly, Nobel Prize-winning poet Czeslaw Milosz argues "no." He says: "I basically don't agree with the argument with Lanzmann in Shoah or Professor Raoul Hilberg that the Holocaust is nothing else but intensification of anti-Semitism which existed in Christianity for centuries. I do not believe it at all, because it was not a gradual increase. The Holocaust was a qualitative jump which was created by a pagan movement of Nazis. Nazism was not Christian at all."[67]

Milosz contends, as others, that socio-economic rather than religious considerations underlie 20th century anti-Semitism. According to Erich Goldhagen, a Jewish-American historian, anti-Semitism in the 20th century in Poland was of an "objective" or "realistic" variety: it represented mainly a manifestation of hostility "born of a genuine conflict of interests between the Jews and their host people."[68] But "subjective," or "unrealistic," ideological anti-Semitism was not lacking either.[69]...[70]

Detroit psychiatrist Emanuel Tanay responded to Milosz in an (unpublished) open letter. Dr. Tanay, born in 1928 in Poland, survived the war on false papers, partly in a monastery (where a priest sought to convert him). He is one of the two survivors depicted in the Oscar-nominated documentary, "Courage to Care," which deals with rescue efforts by Christians in Europe.[71]

In the Kielce pogrom, [a monstrous provocation apparently engineered and supervised by the Soviet government in order to trigger an immediate and massive exodus of Jews from Poland to Palestine, to create a dramatic diversion to draw attention from the falsification of the crucial Polish national referendum of June 30, 1946, and to compromise the Polish people with mob violence in which police and military took part] in 1946, some 42 Jewish survivors were killed and others injured by local Poles.[72] Every few years, even after the war, anti-Semitic demonstrations occurred throughout the country.[73] To be sure, lawless behavior occurs everywhere, but what was again frightening was that the [communist] authorities closed their eyes to it, if not actually encouraging it. As a result of re-immigration from the USSR, there were 240,000 Jews in 1946 in Poland. After the Kielce pogrom, 100,000 Jews emigrated. The successive emigrations of 1956 and 1968 left Poland with only a tiny Jewish population. In his response to Milosz, Dr. Tanay wrote:[74]

Your explanation of the "legitimate resentment" which Poles have toward Jews is a thinly disguised accusation that Jews were hated because they were traitors... you...claim that "there was the fact the young generation of Jews was very sympathetic towards the Soviet Union, and of course greeted the Red Army to the eastern

159

part of Poland very favorably, immediately after the Stalin-Hitler pact."...

Did the Poles collaborate with the Nazis in the destruction of Jewry? One hears the expression, "Polish concentration camp."[75] William Styron's "Sophie's Choice" depicts [an imaginary] Polish professor as the one who sets out the plan for extermination of the Jews.[76] In actual fact, however, no Poles made any such plan...- The Nazis called in Latvians and Lithuanians to help in roundups of Jews, and Ukrainians to serve as guards at the camps. Nechama Tec, a survivor in Nazi-occupied Poland, writes:[77]

There is no evidence...that any Polish leaders collaborated with the Nazis, either in the rounding up of Jews or in any other way. There was not, for example, on the political level, a Polish Quisling. Similarly, I know of no Polish concentration camp guard...- Struggling themselves to survive, they neither aided the Germans nor hindered them... Well aware of the Polish anti-Semitism, the Germans invested much time and effort in keeping it alive.

Professor Yisrael Gutman, head of the Institute of Contemporary Jewry at Hebrew University in Jerusalem and vice-president of the Institute of Polish-Jewish studies at Oxford, has this to say:[78]

I am against the attempt to blame Polish people in total as anti-Semitic or anti-Jewish, and also I do not accept the assumption that the Nazis established the killing camps in Poland because of the consent and the collaboration of the Poles. Moreover, I admired many Poles who despite the pressure and danger around, delivered help to the Jews and rescued many Jewish lives. On the other hand, the recognition and admission of the truth should not bring into oblivion the other side of the coin. The fact is that the majority of Poles during this tragic period were indifferent with regard to the Jewish fate. The Polish underground, generally speaking, did not include Jews and for a long time did not help the Jews (until the end of the year 1942).

By the end of the war, of the six million Polish citizens who died, one-fifth of its total population, approximately three million were Jews, while the other three million were mostly ethnic Poles. In the notorious Auschwitz concentration camp, thousands of Poles died before the first transport with Jews reached its gates.[79] Unlike Jews and Gypsies who mostly died in gas chambers, most Poles perished as a result of mass or individual executions, malnutrition or overwork. However...many Poles died in the extermination camps too.[80]

To wipe out Polish culture, the Nazis rounded up Polish professors and other intellectuals, putting them in concentration camps or killing them by firing squads. Under orders from Hitler, Himmler directed his SS and police forces to liquidate the elite of Poland. The SS lost little time. In November 1939, they arrested almost 200 professors and fellows of Jagiellonian University and sent them to the Sachsenhausen concentration camp, where many of them died. And as the church was the bulwark of Polish nationalism, many clergymen and nuns were sent to the camps. Poland during the war lost almost half of its educated people--45 percent of its physicians and dentists, 57 percent of its attorneys, 15 percent of its teachers, 40 percent of its professors, 30 percent of its technicians, 18 percent of its clergy, and the majority of its journalists.

Nazi Germany launched a concerted attack on Polish culture and history. There was to be no schooling of Poles beyond the fourth grade. History books were confiscated, and teachers were prohibited to teach any history. Monuments, memorials, and inscriptions of Polish heroes were removed. Poland's cities were de-Polonized: their names were changed--Gdynia became Gotenhafen, Lodz was renamed Litzmannstadt, Rzeszow was now Reichshof--along with street names.

Poles under Hitler were to be "a reservation, a vast Polish labor camp. Poles will never be raised to a higher level." The Germans used every means of violence and physical extermination in order to transform Poland into a colony. "From now on," said Dr. Hans Frank, the head of German-occupied Poland, "the political role of the Polish nation is ended. It is our aim that the very concept *Polak* be erased for centuries to come. Neither the Republic nor any other form of Polish state will ever be reborn. Poland will be treated as a colony and Poles will become slaves in the German empire.[81] In 1944, Frank reflected that when the war was over and Polish labor was not required, the remnants of the Polish people had a grim future.[82] Over 1.6 million Poles were deported to the Reich as factory and agricultural laborers--they had to wear a violet letter "P" on their clothing to distinguish them from the German population, who were admonished not to have any social relations with them.[83]

The Nazis, said Jan Karski (Kozielewski), the Polish emissary who gave a forceful interview in "Shoah," were able to make of the Jewish question "something akin to a narrow bridge upon which the Germans and a large portion of Polish society are finding agreement." This was before the period of systematic killings of the Jews by the Nazis. What the "large portion of Polish society" agreed to, in Karski's observation, was not murder but the isolation of the Jewish people as well as the economic squeeze to which they felt they were subjected.[84]

At the conference at Jagiellonian University, Professor Norman Davies, the author of the widely acclaimed books on Poland, was asked: Did the Poles collaborate in the Holocaust? "Nonsense," he replied...one and all were delighted by his appearance.

Davies, professor of history at the University of London, came to Poland by chance some 20 years ago, he married a Pole, he lived and studied in Poland, and he became a renowned Polish historian. He spent the last year teaching at Stanford where he would be considered for an endowed chair in East European history. Students there found his lectures immensely interesting. He was, however, denied the position. As widely reported in the U.S. media, he contends he was denied the position because Jewish faculty members considered his work "insensitive" toward Jews and "unacceptably defensive" of Polish gentiles in World War II.[85]

In "God's Playground," Davies wrote that while Jews in Poland experienced considerable discrimination before the war, other ethnic groups and social classes also suffered from the effects of discrimination and that conditions facing Jews at that time were "nothing exceptional." And during the first two years of the war, Davies maintains, the Poles suffered more than the Jews.

...Davies maintains that some Jewish scholars and writers "have spread the view that the Poles actually rejoiced at the fate of the Jews or at best were indifferent 'bystanders' to the Holocaust." Disputing this view, Davies asserts that the Nazi occupation force terrorized all Poles, and adds, "To ask why the Poles did little to help the Jews is rather like asking why the Jews did nothing to assist the Poles."[86] And he writes, "Polish hostility toward the Jews is complemented by Jewish hostility toward the Poles."[87]...[88]

Davies filed a lawsuit seeking damages from Stanford and some staff members for what he called fraud, misrepresentation, breach of contract, discrimination and defamation. The lawsuit accused the defendants of making slanderous statements by alleging that his scholarship was defective. Davies contended that the vote against him, 12-to-11, was based not on bona fide academic criteria.[89] To add fuel to the fire, Davies engaged as his lawyer former (seven-term) U.S. Congressman Paul N. McCloskey Jr., a Stanford alumnus who had at one time clashed with pro-Israeli activists on.[90] Davies' defenders at Stanford say: "If Davies does not qualify for the chair, who does?"[91]

Why is it necessary to ask which people suffered more? Why the statistical competition on who lost more people? Is it relevant to the question whether Poles did all that they could to help the Jews? Few questions have generated such conflicting passions.[92] Some facts though are undeniable: For aiding a Jew in any way, a Pole and his entire family--three generations (his parents and children)--faced death. That was not the case in other occupied countries. In Holland, the family who hid Anne Frank remained alive.[93] The Jews did not jump Germans armed with machine guns; could the Poles? Davies puts it this way: If the Poles had it within their power to save the three million Polish Jews killed by the Nazis, and failed to do so because of anti-Semitism, why did they not save the three million murdered non-Jewish Poles, to whom that prejudice would not apply?[94] In the eyes of many, passivity can be justified in a situation in which every action is heroic. Can ordinary people be blamed for not behaving as heroes?[95]

The Nazis gave rewards to anyone reporting the concealment of a Jew. To assist a Jew required not merely an individual act but a network of support. To provide food, clothing and shelter to a people who looked and spoke differently was no simple task. Jews in Denmark looked, acted and spoke like Danes but the vast majority of Jews in Poland were readily distinguishable from Poles--Jews and Poles lived in separated and different worlds and their diverse experiences made for easy identification.[96] As Nechama Tec observes in her book about Christians who sheltered Jews, "obstacles and barriers to Jewish rescue were the most formidable in Poland."[97] At the Yad Vashem Memorial in Jerusalem, honoring those who helped, the "Righteous among Nations," the number of Polish names exceeds all others but the Dutch.[98] As of December 1986, of the 5,800 people honored, 2,072 are of Polish descent.[99] The surprise is not how few Poles helped Jews, but given the anti-Semitism and the threat of death, that any did at all.[100] Those guilty of passivity are in the West.[101] Some 150,000 Jews survived in Poland because Poles provided hiding places, food, clothing and false documents. Other Poles blackmailed Jews or turned them in for rewards, but there were also Jewish blackmailers, some of them, even quite famous by name, who were neither better nor worse than the Polish ones, and also Jewish policemen in the Ghetto whose duty was to deliver a specified number of Jewish victims to "be sent" to extermination. In psychiatric terms, the process is called identification with the aggressor.[102]

The fact is, though, that Jews did find protectors, despite the fact that their appearance made them hard to conceal and the additional circumstance that assistance to them in any form was punishable with death, and while...the so-called *szmalcownicy*, hunted down Jewish fugitives from the ghettos and blackmailed and denounced Poles who protected them. (The term *szmalcownik* is literally a greased palm, a word of unequivocal shame in Polish, reserved exclusively to designate a blackmailer of Jews during World War II.) As Professor Wenceslas Wagner of the University of Detroit Law School puts it, "The *general* reaction of the Poles to the German persecution of Jews was sympathy and willingness to help, even on the part of those who were not considered as friends of the Jews."[103] Thousands of Poles risked their lives to save Poles, and lived in fear of betrayal by fellow Poles. The Poles were unique among countries under occupation in forming an underground organization specifically designed to aid Jews, the Council for Aid to Jews, or *Zegota*, which had its headquarters in Warsaw, and which sought to provide fugitives with food, shelter, medical assistance, and forged documents. A recent estimate puts the number of Poles, either as members of such organizations or as private citizens, who aided Jews at the risk of their own lives at [at least] one million.[104] [A fraction of aided Jews survived the war.]

There was a saying in France, "Better the Germans than the Reds or Jews." In contrast with France (or some of the other occupied countries), cooperation with the Nazis and denunciations were a rarity in Poland.[105] And those who would denounce a Jew one day would just as well do the same with a Polish patriot some other day. Denunciation of Jews was punishable by death by the Polish Home Army, and the sentences were published in its official secret paper *Biuletyn Informacyjny*.[106]

The Poles were...the first to inform the Western allies of the Nazi program of exterminating the Jews and to ask for action to stop it. At the end of 1942, Karski, then a young member of the Polish underground who had observed conditions in the Warsaw ghetto and even managed to penetrate the Belzec death camp, made his way to England and the United States and reported to government officials (including President Roosevelt); he spoke to Justice Frankfurter; he made over 200 public addresses; his mission had no lasting effect. The Polish government in exile suggested that German cities be bombed mercilessly and that leaflets be dropped telling the German people that this was in retaliation for what they were doing to the Jews, but the proposal fell on deaf ears. The Allies did not want to fight a "Jewish war."[107],[108]

Karski contacted Walter Lippmann, then the foremost and most influential journalist in the United States, as well as other journalists. Lippmann was a Jew, the son of rich clothing manufacturers from Germany, and an ultra-assimilationist. He ignored the plight of European Jewry. He considered anti-Semitism a punishment that Jews invited, by making themselves "conspicuous." He called one Hitler speech "statesmanlike," the "authentic voice of a genuinely civilized people." He not once wrote about the death camps.[109] His failure to speak out--unlike that of people in the occupied countries--may not be excused as calling for heroic action. His life would not have been put in peril.[110]

Lippmann was not a socialist, but in the United States many Jews in the early part of the century embraced socialism, of the utopian variety or whatever, and until the late 1930s, quite a number looked upon Hitler as a socialist who, in order to carry out his program, had to remove Jews from positions of influence. As a boy growing up in New Orleans, I heard that explanation time beyond count.

Lanzmann's film "Shoah" accuses the Poles, themselves locked in a deadly struggle for survival, not only of refusing to provide any effective assistance to the Jews but of actual complicity in their extermination by the Germans...Czeslaw Milosz said, "In his treatment of the Polish peasants, Lanzmann was more a Parisian intellectual than a Jew, and exhibits the scorn shown for specimens by an anthropologist. But, I disagree precisely in one aspect...he draws a line of continuity between Christianity and Shoah."[111] ...Every bit of evidence indicates that the Nazis were mindful of the cost and the military need of transport, and that meant that the camps were to be established in the area of the greatest concentration of victims...[112] Others complain about the way the interviews were excerpted. Karski, who has received the award, "Righteous among Nations," has praised the film[113] but has said:[114]

"...The time devoted to my account and the construction of *Shoah* forced Lanzmann to omit the section of the interview which I felt was the most important part of my Jewish mission at the end of 1942. As a courier of the Polish Underground State, who had personally witnessed beginnings of the final solution, I was sent to alarm the Western world to the fate of the European Jews under the Nazi occupation. The suffering of the Jews was described by others in the movie for more than seven hours. Many did it better than I. For me, the central point of my interview was that having made my way to the West, I described the tragedy and demands of the Jews to four members of the British War Cabinet including Eden; President Roosevelt and three key members of the American government; the Apostolic Delegate in Washington; Jewish leaders in the United States; distinguished writers and political commentators such as Walter Lippmann and George Sokolsky. None of these matters could be discussed by anyone else. After all, this would have demonstrated how the allied governments, which alone were capable of providing assistance to the Jews, left the Jews to their own fate."

"Including this material in the movie, as well as general information about those who attempted to help the Jews, would have presented the Holocaust in a historically more accurate perspective. The leaders of nations, powerful governments either decided about the extermination or took part in the extermination or acted indifferently toward the extermination. People, ordinary people, millions of people sympathized with the Jews or provided assistance."

In the final analysis, the film is an anti-Polish film, a vendetta against the Poles. "There is no business like Shoah business," say Poles.[115] A headline in the Paris daily *Liberation* read, "Poland on Trial." In his press statements, Lanzmann stated that it was his intention to set out this thesis. In an interview in *L'Express*, Lanzmann states that his film puts the blame on the Poles.[116] At Oxford, at a meeting organized by the new Institute for Polish-Jewish Studies, he was asked about his criteria of selection. He replied, "The film is made around my own obsessions, it wouldn't have been possible otherwise..."

Lanzmann, in newspaper interviews and in the Oxford discussion, waxed and waned. "The film, you are aware, is an act of accusation against Poland?" he was asked by *L'Express*. "Yes," he replied... But in the Oxford discussion he said, "It's not an accusation...against the Poles, because I don't think they could do much."...[117] Subsequently, Lanzmann... declared categorically, "There could not have been extermination camps in France."[118]

Another widely seen film, "The Struggle for Poland," brought a protest from Professor Yisrael Gutman. In a letter to a Polish weekly published in England he wrote:[119]

During a short trip to London I had the occasion to see one of the television series, "The Struggle for Poland," which dealt with Polish-Jewish relations entitled "The Different World." This fragment was rich in documentary material. The scenes and the way they were presented, using this material, showed a distant and complicated reality--they made an impression on both the audience familiar with this reality through their own experience, as in my case, and on the audience for the first time encountering this reality.

...As a result, the facts as presented are not the real historical facts. I myself, having a part in the film, know that from my 30-minute interview, only a few sentences were chosen which in no way presented my point of view. Of the facts presented in the film, I must say, however, that there was only one factual error (one of the witnesses stated that Einsatz Gruppen was also Polish--but that was not the case).

I am very annoyed about the way the various interviews were put together in order to accentuate some events. There are many scenes which present the Polish people in a very negative light and too little about the Polish people providing help and assistance to the Jewish people. ...I cannot agree with the suggestion that Polish society took part in the Holocaust...

Karski has suggested that the movie "Shoah" by its self-limitation has created a need for a next movie which will present the second reality of the Holocaust--not in order to contradict that which "Shoah" shows but to complement it.[120]

At the end of the second week at the Jagiellonian conference a Felician nun from Baltimore broke her silence and took the floor: "I have been listening quietly for two weeks and now I must speak. All I have been hearing is Polish anti-Semitism and Polish responsibility for the Holocaust. I have not heard one word, not a single word, about the Germans."

Is it because Poles have been cowed by a blanket of implied guilt and official silence into avoiding the subject? Germany has officially acknowledged guilt and has made reparations. Poles say, to put it briefly, "Why should we acknowledge guilt? What are we guilty of? Poland for centuries was a haven for Jews. Poland was the first to stand up to German terrorism."[121]

The concept of culpability may signify one thing to the ethicist and another to a jurist, but in this case, most would agree: the identity of the party who actually plans and carries out an execution is the primary culprit. It is a "quantum jump," most would say, from evidence of anti-Semitism to the charge of approving or participating in mass murder. It is a fact of human behavior, illogical as it may be, that people who tolerate one sort of crime when done by others will not do it themselves, and expulsion (or forced emigration) is not in the same category as extermination, and should not be assumed to influence each other.[122] In the law of torts, courts have distinguished between the active "cause" of a harm and the existing "conditions" upon which that cause operated. If the defendant has created only a passive, static condition which made the harm possible, the defendant is said not to be liable.[123]

Oft-forgotten is the fact that it was Germany, not Poland, that carried out the destruction of European Jewry. When I would make a trip to Poland, my Jewish friends in the United States would say, "Why do you go to that anti-Semitic country? That is the land of the Holocaust." Little or nothing would be said when I would go to Germany, Austria or the Ukraine, though anti-Semitism in ...Poland pales in comparison to that in those places... Under German occupation, the French denounced the Jews and delivered them to the Germans.[124] In comparison to the talk about Polish anti-Semitism, no one talks about French anti-Semitism, yesterday's or today's, or about German, Austrian, Ukrainian, Lithuanian or Latvian anti-Semitism. Anti-Semitism is deeply imbedded in the minds of the people throughout a large part of Eastern or Western Europe. Of yesterday's Poland, one must go by the historical record; of today's, I have my experiences.[125] Though I am a Jew, I have a Ukrainian name and I believe that it has made me privy to attitudes, when at times I would raise the discussion about Jewry, that I would not otherwise have heard.[126]

Spending six summers in Poland, I have developed a feeling of empathy for the Polish people. As my parents were immigrants from a Slavic country (the Ukraine), I must say that I feel quite at home in Poland. The Ostjuden, as I sense it, have more in common with the Poles than with Israelis or American Jews.[127] Studies show that husband and wife after years of living together begin to look and act alike. So too is it with peoples who are exposed to each other. Jews and Poles in Poland, though they lived as though in separate worlds, interpenetrated. They are similar in many ways. Both people are family-oriented, both are religious, both are nationalistic, both are individualistic, both value education as the key to the future, and both focus on food.[128]...both believe chicken soup is the remedy for any ailment.[129]

Collectively, the Jews through the ages have been blamed for the crucifixion of Christ and they have suffered for it.[130] Likewise, Poland as a nation or Poles collectively are called anti-Semitic. On the other hand, on the occasion when Germany is blamed for the

extermination of Jews, the guilt is limited to "Nazi Germany." A study carried out in a New York high school found that students do not link "Nazis" to Germans--the "Nazis" are people from outer space. And when one travels in Germany, one never meets a Nazi or anyone acquainted with a Nazi. Elie Wiesel, the well-known survivor of the camps, rejects the notion of collective responsibility and favors the use of the adjective "Nazi" so as to limit the responsibility. Others would agree, but there is no counterpart, in time or place, in speaking about Poles. The entire nation is blamed. We hear, "Polish anti-Semitism" or "the Poles beat the Jews." Collective guilt is forbidden in the Bible: Abraham begged God to spare Sodom if there were 50 just men, or 10.

In the post-World War II period, Poles...felt that they were under the reign of the Jews. In the early 1960s Jews numbered less than 100,000 but a disproportionate number of them held high positions, including posts in the security apparatus. Following the war when the future of Poland was at stake, Stalin put Jews in positions of power, knowing that he could rely on them in installing a Communist system. They became actively engaged in the consolidation of Soviet power. In some instances, they even helped hunt down Polish officers and members of the deposed Polish administration. In the eyes of many Poles, the Jews were quislings.[131]

In 1945, at Potsdam, the country was physically moved westward, and the population as well, but politically it was forced into the Eastern orbit and saddled with a Communist-dominated government that had little to do with the wishes or sentiments of the great majority of the Polish people.[132] One might say that the Jews in power were not Jews, as they were not seeking to further Judaism, but rather they were Communists. They renounced Judaism. The Poles, nonetheless, saw them as Jews.[133]

In times of stress, people give up their critical faculties, and they develop tunnel vision. In a little book called *The Ordeal of Change*," Eric Hoffer wrote: "It has been often said that power corrupts. But it is perhaps equally important to realize that weakness too corrupts. Power corrupts the few, while weakness corrupts the many. Hatred, malice, rudeness, intolerance, and suspicion are the fruits of weakness."[134]...

In any sense, could the Poles' actions against the Jews be called self-defense? The "objective" versus "subjective" analysis in discussing anti-Semitism has a variation in assessing the legitimacy of a claim of self-defense in tort or criminal law...[135]

For most Poles, for a mixture of religious, economic and political reasons, it would have been difficult not to have internalized an anti-Semitic ideology. For "anti-Semitism," the word might be "Judeophobia," fear; fear of a people who live among them, growing in number, wealth, importance and influence.

The Soviet takeover of Eastern Europe after World War II brought large numbers of Jews to high official positions in many countries, and Poland was no exception. The Red Army entering Poland had a large contingent of Polish Jews. Many of the Jews in the Polish Communist Party escaped to the USSR and after 1944 they returned to hold high offices in the Polish government, Party, and army during that crucial period.[136]

Few peoples in the world are less suited to communism than the Poles; and their long distrust of the Russians reinforces their nationalism. In 1947, Stalin said that taking communism to Poland was like saddling a cow.[137] By that, Stalin meant that it would be pointless, and probably cause a lot of trouble; so Stalin recommended capitalism for the Poles--privately, at least.[138]...

Zygmunt Warszawer, a surviving Jew in Poland, recalls: "After World War II so many Jews signed up for the police and for the secret police. I would shout at them: Why are you doing this? What do you need it for? You want to beat people up and shoot people? So go to Israel. You want to be a colonel or something in the government? Do it in your own country with your own people, but not here. There's a handful of us left and still you're pushing."[139]

The father of one of my closest friends, Ernest Lederman, was among the Jews holding a position of power... Ernest's father and others were jailed on trumped-up grounds. The virulent anti-Semitic campaign of March 1968 caused a mass emigration, including the Lederman family. They say in Poland that the Jews gave Poland communism and then escaped to Israel themselves. Of the less than 30,000 Jews in Poland in 1968, only about 5,000 now remain (mostly old, lonely, ill people).[140]...[141]

Nikita Khrushchev repeatedly admonished Wladyslaw Gomulka, who headed Poland from 1956 to 1970, saying that there were too many Jews in the Polish Communist Party.[142] The split between Gomulka and his Jewish colleagues came with the outbreak of the six-day Arab-Israeli war of June 1967. A week after the break in diplomatic relations the party launched the intense domestic anti-Zionist campaign. In a speech of June 19, Gomulka issued a solemn warning to those who "applauded the Israeli aggression" and stressed that Poland would not tolerate a fifth column in its midst. In the purge of the Communist party in 1968 led by General Moczar, some 9,000 people lost their jobs over accusations of Jewish origin. In his reminiscences, Gomulka admitted that the anti-Zionist campaign was unleashed on the insistence of Moscow.[143]

The film produced in 1975 by Andrzej Wajda, "Land of Promise" (based on the 1898 novel by the Noble laureate Wladyslaw Reymont), was shown at the Jagiellonian conference. Wajda is Poland's foremost director. The film depicted the conflicts in capitalist Lodz at the end of the 19th century shown through the careers of three friends--a German, a Pole, and a Jew--who give up their youthful ideals and act according to ruthless rules of the business world in order to achieve great fortune. The Jews in the film are shown without any saving grace--they are greedy, ugly, uncouth. The Poles at the conference claimed that the picture was not anti-Semitic but rather that it also showed the corruption of Germans and Poles under capitalism, but the Jewish participants were unsatisfied.[144]...[145]

Malgorzata Niezabitowska, ...along with her husband, Tomasz Tomaszewski, a photographer, produced a magnificent book, *Remnants/The Last Jews of Poland*." [146]...[147]

Generally speaking, however, young people in Poland know little or nothing about the history of Jews or of their life in Poland.[148] Schoolbooks may have only a passage or two. The concentration camps that are now museums are described as places where peoples of all nationalities perished.[149]...[150]

At the Jagiellonian conference Professor Andrzej Bryk, a leading Polish historian, said: "There's an enormous amount of ignorance in Poland about Jewry. The young generation must come to terms with their history. The Catholic Church has yet to come to terms with its anti-Semitic past. There are no services, no flowers, no plaques in memory of the Jews."[151] "The paths of 'two of the saddest nations on this earth' have parted forever," writes Rafael F. Scharf, a graduate of Jagellonian University. "I wonder how far the Poles are aware of the fact that with the Jews an authentic part of their Poland was obliterated. The question begs to be asked: will that Poland one day be better, and richer spiritually and materially, without the Jews?"[152]

In April 1987 Jaruzelski signed a cultural treaty with Soviet leader Mikhail Gorbachev calling for a "public examination of the blank spots in our history," a statement interpreted by Polish historians to include the Katyn massacres,[153] the Hitler-Stalin pact, the deportation of Poles after World War II, and the error of Polish Stalinism, all taboo subjects since the 1950s. Jewry was not mentioned.

The Jewish card was played again by the authorities in the early 1980s, claiming that Solidarnosc was manipulated by the Jews. This time, the card did not work...[154]... (The contemporary heroes for the Polish people are Pope John Paul II, Lech Walesa, and President Reagan. The Poles are strongly pro-America as any visitor quickly learns. They celebrated when Soviet leader Brezhnev died.)

Polish nationalism is synonymous with Catholicism. The Catholicism has been so bred into successive generations that it is almost as much a culture as a faith. Through a thousand years of invasion, oppression and dismemberment, it was the church that had kept alive Polish culture, language, intellectual life and sense of nationhood. *Polak, to Katolik*, they still say: To be Polish is to be Catholic. When Karol Wojtyla of Krakow, was elected pope, the Polish people were seized by immense and irresistible emotion. A Polish pope! Polish-Americans have the bumper sticker, "Happiness is a Polish Pope." In public opinion polls conducted by the University of Warsaw over the past few years, about 95 percent of Poles singled out John Paul II (the name taken by Karol Wojtyla) as the public figure they trusted most. The pope "represents for us

that part of Poland which is beyond all manipulation by the great powers," says Krzysztof Sliwinski, a Catholic journalist in Poland. "He is independent, free Poland. He represents the freedom, which is in the dreams of everybody. The pope doesn't take orders from anyone."[155]...

In actuality, at least in today's world, Polish-Americans are more anti-Semitic than are the Poles in Poland. Jews and Poles both left Poland looking for paradise in the United States. To a greater extent, Jews found it. The Poles were among the most disadvantaged of American immigrants... Recent Polish immigrants wonder why, with Poles constituting one of America's larger ethnic groups, there are no Polish institutions, like the Jewish institutions, to offer assistance in obtaining employment or housing...

For the many insulting Polish jokes that abound, Poles in America in large measure blame Jewish comedians.[156]...[157]

In the interwar period the Zionist press in the United States was particularly anti-Polish. It was aimed at getting support for going to Palestine. And in the Polish press, one may find anti-Semitic editorials and letters-to-the-editor. Even today, the letters-to-the-editor, in particular, in both the Polish and Jewish papers in the United States reveal the hard feelings between the two groups.[158]

As a rule, Jews from Poland (and their offspring) do not participate in Polish-American organizations or activities (a notable exception is the cooperation at the Polish Institute in New York). Generally speaking, American Jews are staunchly anti-Polish and frequently publish books, articles and films that are highly negative about Poland. They speak about the "traditional" Polish anti-Semitism, forgetting centuries-long cooperation, about the "Polish" concentration camps (where Poles were exterminated by the Germans along with the Jews), etcetera. Poles blame these distortions, frequently taken as true by the general public, on the Jews, who are reputed to have better access to the mass media than the Poles.

Some Jewish leaders and writers (like Leon Uris) have refused to speak to Poles and examine documents offered for their examination, while continuing anti-Polish propaganda. ...Jews ...do not acknowledge that the Poles also suffered and were persecuted by the Germans.[159] In the U.S. Holocaust Council, a number of Jews opposed or tried to minimize all references to the German mistreatment of the Poles.[160] Recently, in some states (Calif., N.J., N.Y.), Jewish teachers strongly insisted on the elimination from high school manuals of all mention about Polish losses during the war. The other day at a social gathering a Pole mentioned that he had been an inmate in a concentration camp, whereupon a Jewish lady accused him of lying because "the camps were established only for Jews."...[161]...

Poles and Jews, while they have lived separately, share a common heritage. They both view the world as one of terrible trouble, of being persecuted, of being surrounded by enemies. To keep body and soul together, they focused on themselves. Anything that is perceived as negative--any tap from behind--is immediately responded to as an attack. "A Jew's joy," says a proverb, "is not without fright"--and the same may be said of the Pole.[162]...

The Jews wail at a wall in Jerusalem.[163]...[164]

Poles and Jews are wounded people, sensitive people, so one must be careful what is said. Say the same thing about a Russian and he would laugh. For good reason, Poles and Jews do not feel secure with their place in the world. In a report on Poland, Lawrence Weschler, a young Jewish writer, had this to say, and with it I will close:[165]

...I have come to a deeper appreciation of the tragic nature of the historical inter-penetration of these two peoples in this hopeless land where ironies fold in and in and in on themselves. For, apart from anything else, Polish history and Jewish history seem to illuminate each other. If Poland, as Słowacki claimed, is the Jesus Christ of nations, then we are speaking of Jesus the Jew, the martyr to the Roman occupation of Palestine. The situation of the Poles during much of the last two centuries--a people, a language, a religion, a literature, a culture, all without a state--is uncannily congruent with the simultaneous situation of the Jews. Much has been written of the messianic longing with which Polish Jewish Chassidism was rife during the early nineteenth century--but Polish Catholic romanticism during that period likewise conceived of a national messianic mission. It is one of the cruellest ironies of history that these two stateless, visionary people came to share the same meagre plot of land at the same moment.

163

NOTES

This paper was the basis of a presentation at the annual meeting
of the American Association for Social Psychiatry
on September 4, 1987, in New Orleans.

1.   July 10 - August 7, 1987. In another conference, one on Jewish life in medieval and Renaissance Poland, held in 1986 also at Jagiellonian University, Anthony Polonsky, a historian at Oxford, said he was gratified that such a gathering in Poland, unthinkable in the past, was taking place. Quoted in M.T. Kaufman, "Jews Return to Examine Poland's Past," New York Times, Sept. 30, 1986, p. 6.

More and more young people in Poland, who do not know Jews, who know next to nothing about their past in Poland, are having their consciousness raised by accusations coming from distant places. A. Zamoyski, "What has gone, what is left," Spectator, Feb. 6, 1988, p. 27. Not long ago a passionate controversy over whether Poles bear any special responsibility for the deaths of millions of Jews in World War II appeared in Tygodnik Powszechny, Poland's most influential Roman Catholic newspaper. M.T. Kaufman, "Debate Over the Holocaust Stirs Poles," New York Times, March 8, 1987, p. 3.

In recent years a number of books have been published in Poland on the history of the Jews in Poland, their traditions and culture, their language, and their cuisine. One of these books opens with these words: "This is an exceptional and unusual book we are presenting our readers. This is a book about a world which is no more. Though there are among us people who remember this world, it belongs to the past which was destroyed by the Second World War." M. Fuks, Z. Hoffman, M. Horn & J. Tomaszewski, Polish Jewry/History and Culture (Warsaw: Interpress, 1982), p. 7. See also A. Bieberstein, Zaglada Zydow w Krakowie (Krakow: Wydawnictwo Literackie, 1985).

An Institute for Polish-Jewish studies at Oxford, and its U.S. wing the American Foundation for Polish-Jewish Studies in Boston, Chicago, New York and Miami, emerged out of an International Conference on Polish-Jewish Studies held at Oxford in September 1984. The Institute publishes an international year book under the title POLIN: A Journal of Polish-Jewish Studies (London: Blackwell)—Polin is the Jewish name for Poland (derived from the Hebrew poh lin) ("there shalt thou dwell"). It also publishes books on the history and culture of Polish Jews.   It provides scholars with facilities enabling them to come to Oxford to study Polish-Jewish topics, and provides grants to students and scholars from Jagiellonian University to study in Israel and vice-versa (in association with the Hebrew University of Jerusalem).

2.   ...M. Visser, *Much Depends on Dinner/The Extraordinary History and Mythology, Allure and Obsessions, Perils and Taboos, of an Ordinary Meal* (New York: Grove Press, 1987).

3.   Jew and Arab in Israel is another example of peoples living closely together yet far apart. D. Grossman, The Yellow Wind (New York: Farrar, Straus & Giroux, 1988; tr. by H. Watzman); D.K. Shipler, Arab and Jew/Wounded Spirits in a Promised Land (New York: Penguin, 1987); D. Pipes, "Two Bus Lines to Bethlehem," National Interest, Winter 1986/7, p. 95; L. Rotenberk, "A 'nightmare' splits Israeli Arabs, Jews," Chicago Sun-Times, March 4, 1988, p. 3.

4.   A. Brozek, The Polish Americans, 1854-1939 (Warsaw: Interpress, 1985). Nearly all Jews from Poland are not part of "Polonia," the name given to Poles living outside Poland. Books about Polish-Americans written in the U.S. are, like Professor Brozek's book, about Poland's Catholic emigrants and their descendants. See, e.g., J.J. Bukowczyk, And My Children Did Not Know Me/a History of the Polish-Americans (Bloomington: Indiana University Press, 1987).

5.   In general, people in the U.S. have no difficulty in saying, "I am an American," without any other qualification. Theodore Roosevelt in 1915 said, "There is no room in this country for hyphenated Americanism....The one absolutely certain way of bringing this nation to ruin, of preventing all possibility of its continuing to be a nation at all, would be to permit it to become a tangle of squabbling nationalities." Speech on October 12, 1915 before the Knights of Columbus in New York.

6.   Reported by Stanley Krajewski (communication of Sept. 24, 1987 to Ralph Slovenko). Krajewski is now editor of the Polish Daily News in Detroit. He was inmate no. 495, from October 1942 to January 1945, at the camp for internees at Tittmoning and Laufen in upper Bavaria, where he heard these arguments.
To the Nazis, "Jewish blood" was a contamination, a virus to be exterminated; so no distinction was made between types of Jews, orthodox or reform, or between a half-Jew or full Jew.

7.   Many say that living separate and apart is not conducive to the development of good relations, but rather creates antagonisms and resentment. K. Lukomski, "Polish-Jewish Relations: In Search of a Meaningful Perspective," Zgoda (official publication of the Polish National Alliance of North America), Jan. 15, 1988, p. 1... "Glasnost and Perestroika: Prof. Gitelman's Analyses," Detroit Jewish News, Feb. 19, 1988, p. 40. Poland's population today is one of the most homogeneous yet conflicts surely abound, but that's another story...
In the history of man, conflicts often stop being about its root causes and become just about hatred. The conflict becomes no longer one for resolution but a way of life--or, more appropriately, a way of death.

8.   The minority of Jews who were assimilated considered themselves as Polish Jews or simply Poles and were taken as such by others. Examples include Jewish generals just before World War II like General Mond (his son, Jerzy Mond, professor of sociology is now Secretary General of the Polish Museum in Paris); Jerzy Langrod, professor of law at Jagiellonian University; Dr. Joseph Lichten, the representative of B'nai B'rith and at the same time a Polish patriot; and Jewish members of the Polish pre-war government like Floyar Rajchman.
The physician, educator and author Janusz Korczak, born Henryk Goldszmidt, was a founder and administrator of two Warsaw orphanages, one housing Jewish children and the other Catholic. When the Nazis invaded Poland in 1939, Korczak, then 61, served in the army--for the fourth time in his life. He perished in Treblinka. He is honored by monuments in Warsaw and Jerusalem. The Committee on Polish and Jewish Relations in Detroit describes him in their literature as "a heroic Pole who assisted Jewish children."
The family of Dr. Nahum Sokolow, Zionist leader, passionately loved Poland. His grandson, Jerzyk (George), when a child paraded in a Polish uniform; Jerzyk later was killed by a German shot as he was standing at BBC in London broadcasting the war news. Dr. Sokolow's son (Jerzyk's father) was also a passionate Polish patriot, and his daughter constantly yearned for her native land, despite her ardent Zionism. Today, while not common, one may meet Jews who, with tears in their eyes, will tell of their longing for their birthland.
The great pianist Arthur Rubenstein was deeply Polonized while at the same time a Jew. At the founding of the United Nations in San Francisco, he played the Polish national anthem--Poland was not represented at the conference because of the conflict between the Polish government in exile and the government installed in Warsaw. Rubenstein's wife was a Pole.
An anecdote of the interwar period tells about the great Jewish philanthropist Baron de Hirsch visiting Leo Poznanski in Lodz, the leading textile industrialist in Poland, who was highly assimilated. The Baron asked Poznanski, "How many employees do you have?" Poznanski answered, "2750." "How many of them are Jewish?" asked the Baron. Poznanski replied, "Four." Embarrassed by having to

give such an answer, he added, "But I have built for the Jews one of the finest hospitals in Eastern Europe." The Baron replied, "It seems to me it would have been better if you gave jobs to the Jews and a hospital to the Poles."

9.   C.S. Heller, On the Edge of Destruction (New York: Columbia University Press, 1977), p. 57.

10.   P. Johnson, A History of the Jews (New York: Harper & Row, 1987), p. 447.

11.   Reported by Professor Andrzej Kapiszewski at Jagiellonian conference. Growing up in Poland in the interwar years, Professor Wenceslas J. Wagner of the University of Detroit School of Law recalls the news in Poland that Jewish financial leaders like Baron Rothschild ruled the West and they were sympathetic to the Jewish movement; and that the Bolshevik revolution was led by Jews in Russia and supported by banks in the West run by Jews. It was said that Polish endeavors to fight Soviet Russia were hindered by failure to get loans. Communication of Professor Wenceslas Wagner to Ralph Slovenko (Oct. 5, 1987). For the record, however, it must be noted that in the 1920s the U.S. Government did not make loans or give credits to foreign countries. The Export-Import Bank dates from 1933. Banks in the U.S. were Judenrein and would hardly have refrained from lending to a good credit risk just because Jews were opposed to it. Neal Pease writes: "The Poles hurt their own cause by slipshod conduct of their first financial transactions in the United States. The 6 percent loan of 1920 had ended in a fiasco of litigation and ill-will, and its failure cast a pall over Polish credit in America." N. Pease, Poland, the United States, and the Stabilization of Europe, 1919-1933 (New York: Oxford University Press, 1986), p. 14.

12.   Reported by Professor Kapiszewski at Jagiellonian conference.

13.   Reported by Professor Kapiszewski at Jagiellonian conference. On the interwar years in Poland, see N. Pease, Poland, The United States, and the Stabilization of Europe, 1919-1933 (New York: Oxford University Press, 1986); P.S. Wandycz, The United States and Poland (Cambridge: Harvard University Press, 1980).

14.   A.H. Sakier (now age 94) recalls that on May 2, 1920, as a member of an American group in Warsaw, they patrolled the Jewish Quarter of the city in (imitation) U.S. Army uniforms because May 3 was a special Polish holiday... Communication from A.H. Sakier to Ralph Slovenko (March 12, 1988).

15.   Reported by Professor Kapiszewski at Jagiellonian conference. There was a period in the early 1920s when there was a sudden surge of emigration of Jews from Poland to Palestine--and the worst anti-Semitic paper of Poland, Dwa Grosze, came out with a headline, "We are losing some of our best Poles!" Jews were bemused by it. Communication from A.H. Sakier (age 94) to Ralph Slovenko (Feb. 2, 1988).

16.   Pastoral letter of February 29, 1936, "O Katolickie zasady moralne," published in Listy Pasterskie, Poznan, 1936. I am grateful to Professor Kapiszewski for providing me with a copy of the letter.

17.   Comment by Professor Kapiszewski at Jagiellonian conference. Professor Kapiszewski claims that only the first part of the letter, describing the Jew in a negative way, was published in the United States.

18.   A. Smolar, "Jews as a Polish Problem," Daedalus, Spring 1987, p. 31. Following a conversation with Cardinal Hlond, Professor O. Forst de Battzglia of Vienna wrote in 1937: "In treating the most thorny problem of Polish life, Mgr. Hlond has unloosed against himself the hardly conceivable rage of the extreme anti-Semites and the impertinence of a few more arrogant members of Jewry." He describes the influence of Cardinal Hlond: "The Cardinal Primate of Poland, August Hlond, is one among three men who stand at the head of their country's affairs. With the President, Mościcki, and the Marshal, Smigły-Rydz, he embodies the supreme authority, and his is the greatest moral influence of the three. Like them, he is an abiding and stable element in the State of Poland, whilst heads of governments come and go according to the necessities of the hour." O.F. de Battzglia, "The Primate of Poland/A Conversation," The Tablet, Jan. 9, 1937,   p. 48.

19.   M. Chęciński, Poland (New York: Karz-Cohl, 1982), p. 22.

20.   Historian Norman Davies writes, "(Poland) is remembered as a land inhabited by anti-Semites and infested by everday pogroms-- and as nothing else.
   The myth was a necessary instrument in the hands of the Zionist movement for persuading the Jewish masses to leave Poland for Palestine. By the same token, the extreme Polish nationalists, while castigating the Zionists, have shared their outlook, for they too were working for a separation of the two peoples." N. Davies, "The Survivor's Voice," New York Review of Books Nov. 20, 1986, p. 21.

21.   Isaac Bashevis Singer recalls in a memoir: "The Warsaw communists, Jews nearly all, heaped brimstone and fire upon all the parties and insisted that only in Soviet Russia did true social justice prevail. The Zionists argued that there was no longer any hope for Jews in the lands of the Diaspora. Only in Palestine would the Jew be able to live freely and develop." I.B. Singer, Love and Exile (New York: Doubleday, 1984), p. 48. In 1937 A.H. Sakier decided to take over the management of the somnolent American Federation of Polish Jews, and the first thing he did was to begin a campaign to help Jews to leave Poland for Palestine. He and the president of the organization were invited to come to a small private meeting of assimilated German Jewish leaders and the head of the (Socialist) Jewish Labor Committee, and were angrily told that "if you do not at once stop propaganda of this kind, you will find it impossible to find a job with any reputable Jewish organization." The real tragedy, Sakier recounts, is that as soon as the Mandate for Palestine was issued, the Jews did not rush to take advantage of it. He says, "How different things might have been! We had men on the ground; all that was needed was money, which there was plenty of. Marshal Józef Piłsudski promised military help without limit in free rolling-stock and transport, weapons, etc. He was a friend. For a half century, I have been tormented by nightmares. Why did I give up so easily?" Communication from A.H. Sakier (now age 94, living in New York) to Ralph Slovenko (Feb. 13, 1988).

22.   L.S. Dawidowicz, "The Curious Case of Marek Edelman," Commentary, March 1987, p. 66.

23.   P. Friedman, "The Lublin Reservation and the Madagascar Policy," 8 YIVO Annual of Social Science 151 (1958).

24.   J. Tagliabue, "Once Prussian Baroque, Now Polish," New York Times, Sept. 12, 1987, p. 4.

25.   The full titles are Heart of Europe: A Short History of Poland (New York: Oxford University Press, 1986); God's Playground: A History of Poland (New York: Columbia University Press, 1982), 2 vols.

26.   The seminal text on Polish Romantic ideology is to be found in Adam Mickiewicz's Ksiegi narodu i pielgrzymstwa polskiego (Books of the Polish Nation and Pilgrimage, 1832). Here, in biblical cadences can be found that strong Romantic metaphor, "Poland, the Christ of Nations."...

27.   The Polish writer Witold Gombrowicz in the 1930s wrote about the "Polish complex." He derided his country's infantile yearning for romantic and heroic father figures and for moralistic works of art that teach patriotic lessons.

28.   George Orwell in his famous "Notes on Nationalism" writes that characteristic for the nationalism of the victim is a reluctance to acknowledge in just measure the sufferings of other peoples, and an inability to admit that the victim can also victimize.

29.   In 1920, Soviet Russia appeared to have been weakened by civil war... Josef Pilsudski (criticized by some Polish political parties) intended to reestablish the "Polish Commonwealth" as it existed before the partitions. Poland's push into the Ukraine met with initial success, but a Red Army counteroffensive halted the advance and drove the Polish forces in full retreat. The Polish Army rallied at Warsaw and regained the offensive, ...but for the Poles, at this critical time in Poland's revival as a sovereign nation, Pilsudski emerged as a man of Polish destiny, the man who forced the Bolsheviks back. This action turned out to be "the only time from Poland's re-birth at the end of World War I that the Poles were able to determine their own fate," writes Norman Davies in White Eagle, Red Star: Polish Soviet War 1919-1920 (London: Orbis, 1985).

30.   For over 30 years Jan Pietrzak has been a satirist in Poland, delighting his countrymen, and on tours in the United States, he also draws large crowds, of Polish-Americans. M.A. Uhlig, "Barbs of Polish Satirist Bring Cheers on U.S. Tour," New York Times, April 4, 1988, p. 19.

31.   K. McKinsey, "Poles Obsessed with Historical Anniversaries," Detroit Free Press, Aug. 27, 1987, p. 10.

32.   I. Halevi, A History of the Jews (London: Zed Books, 1987).
On various aspects of Polish legal systems, see W.J. Wagner et al., Polish Law Throughout the Ages: One Thousand Years of Legal Thought in Poland (Stanford: Hoover Institution Press, 1970).

33.   The incidents of attacks on Jews are set out in B.D. Weinryb, The Jews of Poland/Social and Economic History of the Jewish Community in Poland from 1100 to 1800 (Philadelphia: Jewish Publication Society of America, 1972), p. 46.

34.   Jews in old Poland used two languages. Hebrew was the language which prevailed in the liturgy, schools and religious and philosophical writings. The colloquial language, at least from the beginning of the 15th century, became Yiddish which, though derived from German vocabulary and syntax, differed from German dialects. In later periods the vocabulary acquired a strong Slavonic element.

35.   For photos illustrating the impact of the economic boycott, see R. Vishniac, A Vanished World (New York: Farrar, Straus & Giroux, 1986). At p. 21: Because of the boycott of Jewish merchants, the shopkeeper could not pay his rent, and so the [usually Jewish] landlord locked him out (Lodz, 1938). At p. 23: Peddling bagels on a street that is off-limits to Jews (Warsaw, 1937). At p. 26: A shopkeeper, forced out of business by the boycott, passing by his old store. The new, non-Jewish merchant is having it renovated (Lodz, 1937). At p. 50: The boycott changed peddlers into beggars (Warsaw, 1937). At p. 74: Another shopkeeper locked out of his store because of the boycott (Makachevo, 1938).

36.   Dr. A.L. Halpern of United Hospital in Port Chester, N.Y., says: "It always pains me when I think about the cruel treatment suffered by Jewish medical students at the hands of the learned professors and administrators of the medical schools in Poland. Jewish-American physicians from Poland have often told me about the humiliation and degradation they experienced in the Polish higher halls of learning. We are not talking here about ignorant and superstitious peasants, but about the cream of Poland's non-Jewish intellectuals." Communication from Dr. A.L. Halpern to Ralph Slovenko (Oct. 5, 1987). Dr. Halpern was born in Poland and came to the U.S. as an infant.

37.   J. Lestchinsky, Crisis, Catastrophe and Survival: A Jewish Balance Sheet, 1914-1948 (New York: Institute of Jewish Affairs of the World Jewish Congress, 1948), p. 33; N. Tec, When Light Pierced the Darkness (New York: Oxford, 1986), p. 17. In the documentary, "Image Before My Eyes," produced by Susan Lazarus and the Yivo Institute for Jewish Research, a Jew recalls that a non-Jewish worker would have been deferential upon meeting him, "but if he found out I was Jew in the next three minutes, he might spit on me."
Henry Galler, who now lives in New Orleans, provided me with a remembrance of his life in Poland. When the Germans took Oleszyce in southern Poland, his hometown, they badly beat him. Then the Russians arrived, arrested him, and sent him to Siberia. When they began recruiting for the Polish army, he volunteered and was released to return to Poland to fight the Nazis. He served as an officer (as a non-Jew). His entire family--parents, grandparents, and six brothers and sisters--were killed at the Belzec extermination camp. Recalling his life in Poland, he says (communication of September 22, 1987 to Ralph Slovenko):
We grew up in an atmosphere of anti-Semitism. We felt it in the schools and on the streets of our city. In the school we were singled out by being segregated in separate seats, and not being able to participate in school plays or any other school activities. Many high schools and universities had a quota system, and accepted very few Jewish students.
In the streets we walked mostly in groups to avoid physical attacks by Polish boys, who called us names and told us to go to Palestine. "Żydy do Palestyny." The worst time was around Easter and Christmas holidays. After listening to the sermon in church about the killing of Christ, some of the young people were aroused with hatred, that they could beat up any Jew-Christ killer. At that time most of us tried to stay inside to avoid beatings. We had no protection.
According to our observation and experience, the Polish anti-Semitism was rooted in the religion. The religious teaching and the sermons in church were anti-Jewish. The blood libels that Christian blood was used at Passover for matzo was taught in the church.
Mr. Galler is now a tailor in New Orleans; his wife, also a survivor, teaches Hebrew at Touro Synagogue. Their eldest daughter, Janina, is a child psychiatrist who recently received the American Psychiatric Association's Ittleson award for research; another daughter, Linda, is a tax lawyer on Wall Street; a third daughter, Marilyn, runs Pappagallo in Dallas. A story of the family is reported in M. Fuller, "They Came in search of liberty," New Orleans Times-Picayune, June 29, 1986, p. F-3.

38.   Some Jews even welcomed the German invader. On September 1, 1939, the first day of the German invasion of Poland, Chaim A. Kaplan wrote in his Warsaw Diary (New York: Collier Books, rev. ed. 1973; tr. and edited by A.I. Katsh): "We are witnessing the dawn of a new era in the history of the world. This war will indeed bring destruction upon human civilization. But this is a civilization which merits annihilation and destruction. Now the Poles themselves will receive our revenge through the hands of our cruel enemy."

39.   A. Smolnar, "Jews as a Polish Problem," Daedalus, Spring 1987, p. 31.

40.   M. Niezabitowska & T. Tomaszewski, Remnants/The Last Jews of Poland (New York: Friendly Press, 1986), p. 10. The writer Kazimierz Wyka said, "The Germans have committed a crime murdering the Jews. It is on their conscience—but for us it is a sheer benefit, and in the future we shall reap more benefits, with a clear conscience, without blood on our hands." K. Wyka, Życie na niby (Warsaw: Książka i Wiedza, 1959), p. 199.

41.   E. Ringelblum, <u>Polish-Jewish Relations During the Second World War</u> (New York: Fertig, 1976), p. xxxvii.

42.   The "National Armed Forces" was never incorporated into the Home Army. In the Home Army there were some Jews, among them the officer Dr. Borwicz, who is now teaching sociology in Paris. Marek Edelman was saved by the Home Army, but his recent accounts are contradictory. H. Krall, <u>Shielding the Flame: An Intimate Conversation with Dr. Marek Edelman, the Last Surviving Leader of the Warsaw Ghetto Uprising</u> (New York: Henry Holt, 1986, tr. by J. Stasinska & L. Weschler); reviewed in N. Davies, "The Survivor's Voice," <u>N.Y. Review of Books</u>, Nov. 20, 1986, p. 21.

43.   Wiktor Weintraub, a Harvard scholar, writes: "...while elsewhere [Jews] were molested by city mobs and students...Poland was attracting [Jews] from other countries, and during the sixteenth century and the first half of the following century their numbers grew rapidly -- from about fifty thousand around 1500 to half a million a century and a half later. Life was simply more tolerable for Jews in Poland than elsewhere. In the first place, except for an inconsequential attempt in Lithuania, by the end of the fifteenth century there were no mass expulsions, nor any massacres. Moreover, the Jews enjoyed a much greater degree of self-government in Poland than in any other country." W. Weintraub, "Tolerance and Intolerance in Old Poland," <u>Canadian Slavic Papers</u>, Spring 1971, p. 13.
    Sholem Asch in <u>Kiddush hai Shem</u> wrote (quoted in <u>Polin/A Journal of Polish-Jewish Studies</u>, 1986, vol. 1, p. xi):
    "God took a piece of Eretz Yisroel, which he had hidden away in the heavens at the time when the Temple was destroyed, and sent it down upon the earth and said, "Be My resting place for My children in their exile." That is why it is called Poland (Polin), from the Hebrew <u>poh lin</u>, which means: "Here shalt thou lodge" in the exile. That is why Satan has no power over us here, and the Torah is spread broadcast over the whole country. There are synagogues and schools and Yeshivahs, God be thanked.
    "'And what will happen in the great future when the Messiah will come? What are we going to do with the synagogues and the settlements which we shall have built up in Poland?' asked Mendel...
    "'How can you ask? In the great future, when the Messiah will come, God will certainly transport Poland with all its settlements, synagogues and Yeshivahs to Eretz Yisroel. How else could it be?'"

44.   Christianity claims to be the right religion for everyone. T.S. Szasz, "Justifying Coercion Through Theology and Therapy," in J.K. Zeig (ed.), <u>The Evolution of Psychotherapy</u> (New York: Brunner/Mazel, 1987), p. 413.

45.   In his history on the Jews of Poland, Bernard D. Weinryb writes: "The religious freedom of non-Catholics in Poland, as in many other Catholic states before the French revolution, was limited.   As a multinational and multidenominational state since the fourteenth century, Poland did not follow the extreme principle of intolerance according to which the majority imposes its faith upon the minority (<u>Cuius regio eius religio</u>; He whose state it is, his is the religion). Poland adhered largely to another trend of the pre-modern state whereby members of minority groups had the right to follow their own religion and customs: autonomy. The Polish state generally gave minorities the right to organize as religious groups and to a certain extent even protected their freedom to exercise their respective religions, even supervising their autonomous organizations." B.D. Weinryb, <u>The Jews of Poland: A Social and Economic History of the Jewish Community in Poland from 1100 to 1800</u> (Philadelphia: Jewish Publication Society of America, 1973), p. 134.

46.   The translation "commercial agent" is loose. The Jew on a <u>majatek</u> (estate) was called <u>pachciarz</u>, which is literally defined as "tenant." His function was to buy and sell for the <u>pan dziedzic</u> (squire). Therefore, the non-literal translation "commercial agent" conveys the sense of his role.

47.   B.D. Weinryb, <u>The Jews of Poland/A Social and Economic History of the Jewish Community in Poland from 1100 to 1800</u> (Philadelphia: Jewish Publication Society of America, 1972), p. 9. In the first quarter of the 16th century, wrote in 1521 Justus Ludwik Decius, the chronicler of Sigismund the Old, "Jews are gaining in importance; there is hardly any toll or tax for which they would not be responsible or at least to which they would not aspire. Christians are generally subordinate to the Jews. Among the rich and noble families of the Commonwealth you will not find one who would not favor the Jews on their estates and give them power over Christians." M. Fuks et al., <u>Polish Jewry/History and Culture</u> (Warsaw: Interpress, 1982), p. 13.

48.   C. Abramsky, M. Jachimczyk & A. Polonsky (eds.), <u>The Jews in Poland</u> (Oxford: Blackwell, 1986), p. 3.

49.   Weinryb writes: "Living in the villages as innkeepers and as managers of the lords' estates and collectors of revenues, the Jews came into close contact with the most numerous and most exploited sector of the Polish population -- the peasants. The Jew became the middleman between the lord and the peasant, partly as a handmaid of the former, partly fulfilling some functions for the latter (selling to him and buying from him). In time the Jews became entrenched in the villages (mostly in the southeastern parts) and to some extent became identified by the peasant with the exploiter -- the landlord -- while at the same time culturally they were growing somewhat nearer to the peasants. Both these developments were bound to have repercussions in subsequent centuries." B.D. Weinryb, <u>The Jews of Poland/A Social and Economic History of the Jewish Community in Poland from 1100 to 1800</u> (Philadelphia: Jewish Publication Society of America, 1972), p. 10.

50.   Writing shortly after the end of World War I, Charles H. Haskins and Robert H. Lord of Harvard University characterized the historic importance of the Polish-Lithuanian commonwealth as a structure of peculiar civic nature: "The old Polish State was...the first experiment on a large scale with a federal republic down to the appearance of the United States. In the sixteenth and seventeenth centuries this republic was the freest state in Europe, that state in which the greatest degree of constitutional, civic, and intellectual liberty prevailed.....Like the United States today, Poland was at that time the melting pot of Europe, the haven for the poor and the oppressed of all the neighboring countries--Germans, Jews, Greeks, Magyars, Armenians, Tartars, Russians... Finally the oldest republic represented an effort to organize the vast open plain between the Baltic and the Black Seas--a region containing so many weak and underdeveloped areas and a region so much exposed to Germanic ambitions on the one side and the Turco-Tartar onslaughts on the other side--into a compact and powerful realm, which was directed indeed by the strongest and most advanced voice within its borders...but which in its better period allowed a genuine equality to the other voices and extensive self-government of some of them." C.H. Haskins & R.H. Ford, <u>Some Problems of the Peace Conference</u> (Cambridge: Harvard University Press, 1920), p. 160.

51.   Later, when a number of Jews tried to become assimilated into Polish society, some Poles resented that too. Jews were thus faced with a dilemma: if they kept to their traditional language and culture, they were disliked and mocked for being different; when they tried to behave like Poles, they were laughed at, and rejected. H. Orenstein <u>I Shall Live</u> (New York: Beaufort Books, 1987), p. 5. Jews in Germany, as we have noted, were highly assimilated but that did not help them. In Poland, as it turned out, the Poles opined that they were controlled by the Jews, and in Germany the Hitlerite message was that German culture was dominated by the Jews...

52.   Aaron David Gordon, born in 1856 to Orthodox parents in Russia, believed that through physical labor in Palestine both he and the Jewish people would be recreated...
    A new Jew, in tune with nature, would be born, as a long-exiled people rebuilt a land and was rebuilt by it. In pre-World War I Palestine Gordon became a spiritual hero for the "Young Workers Labor Zionist" party. The words "Man and Nature" were engraved on his tombstone. R. Siegel & C. Rheins (eds.), The Jewish Almanac (New York: Bantam, 1980), p. 170. William Simon of Israel wrote recently: "A.D. Gordon wrote of the redemptive powers of physical labour for restoring the Jewish people. Possibly the most disastrous development since the 1967 war has been the fact that we allowed this country to become hostage to a non-Jewish and hostile labour force." Ltr., "Jewish Labour," Jerusalem Post, March 19, 1988, p. 23.

53.   M. Brzezina, Polszczyzna Zydow (Warsaw: Panstwowe Wydawnictwo Naukowe, 1986), p. 84, quoting from S. Skorupki, Slownika frazeologicznego jezyka polskiego (Warsaw, 1967-1968). In Poland, a Jew was a "zhid"--a hateful word in any Slavic language. In Russia, the word "yevrei" was used in speaking decently of a Jew, and "zhid" when the intention was pejorative, insulting - in Poland it was in reverse.

54.   "Nasze kamienice, wasze ulice," literally, "our buildings, your streets."...

55.   The people in the Austrian and Prussian parts of Poland were better educated than in the part under Russia, where Tsarist anti-semitism was added to the stew. A British colonel, John Seymour Mellon, who was sent out to advise the Poles as to how they should establish a police force, wrote from Warsaw in 1919: "...It is all rot to say there are pogroms in Poland....It is all Jewish propaganda, in my opinion they are very dangerous people in these days and are at the bottom of all Bolshevism in Russia...a dishonest, unpatriotic crew" (a line that must reflect what Mellor heard from his friends). N. Stone, "An Englishman in Old Poland," Spectator, July 11, 1987, p. 14.

56.   One does not hear it said, "He (she) is too (or very) Spanish" or "too French" but one hears, "He's too Jewish." R. Patai, The Jewish Mind (New York: Scribner's Sons, 77), p. 468. See also J.M. Cuddihy, The Ordeal of Civility (New York: Delta, 1974).

57.   T.L. Friedman, "Rage in Jerusalem on Sabbath Films," New York Times, Aug. 25, 1987, p. 1; "Police and Religious Clash Again in Jerusalem," New York Times, Aug. 30, 1987, p.8.

58.   R. Patai, supra at p. 186.

59.   M. Myant, Poland: A Crisis for Socialism (London: Lawrence & Wishart, 1982), p. 9.

60.   M. Tanenbaum, "A revolution in mutual esteem," Newsweek, Sept. 21, 1987, p. 9. Nikita Khrushchev remembers too, as he should. S. Talbott (ed.), Khrushchev Remembers (Boston: Little, Brown, 1970), p. 284. It is estimated that in the years 1917-1921, the years of revolution, more than 2,000 pogroms took place in the Ukraine. In 1919, more than 30,000 Jews were slain instantly. Together with those who died from wounds, contagious and other illnesses, the number of Jewish dead probably reached 150,000, or some ten percent of the Jewish population. These estimates are cited in Z. Gitelman, Jewish Nationality and Soviet Politics (Princeton, N.J.: Princeton University Press, 1972), p. 162; and in his recent book A Century of Ambivalence (New York: Schocken, 1988), reviewed in R. Sokolov, "Jews in Russia," Wall Street Journal, March 1, 1988, p. 28; and in S.W. Baron, The Russian Jew Under Tsars and Soviets (New York: Macmillan, 1964). In the years following World War I, Jews all too often found themselves either caught between competing nationalisms or branded as agents of the revolution. R. Sanders, Shores of Refuge/A Hundred Years of Jewish Emigration (New York: Henry Holt, 1988), reviewed in J. Gross, "Books of the Times," New York Times, Feb. 23, 1988, p. 21.

61.   In 1965, after centuries of enmity and periods of persecution, the Vatican said, in carefully chosen words, that Jews as a group were not to be blamed for the death of Jesus.

62.   French historian Jules Isaac, by the title of his book "The Teaching of Contempt," epitomized its central thesis: the dissemination of the Church's doctrine of the contemptible character of Jews and the Jewish mentality prepared the ground for the defamation and ultimate proscription of Jews in modern times. J. Isaac, L'Enseignement du mepris (Paris: Fasquelle, 1962); English version, The Teaching of Contempt/Christian Roots of Anti-Semitism (New York: Holt, Rinehart & Winston, 1964). The difference between ancient anti-Semitism and its Christian version has been much discussed in the literature. See, e.g., E.H. Flannery, The Anguish of the Jews (New York: Macmillan, 1965). The most powerful argument that has been adduced, by Christian apologists, to acquit Christianity of the charge of having fostered anti-Semitism is the fact that anti-Jewish sentiments and even atrocities existed in Hellenistic Alexandria, as well as in the Roman world long before Christianity. If animosity against Jews in antiquity was basically the same as in Christian and modern times, then anti-Semitism could not be attributed to a factor that emerged only later. Discussed in J. Katz, From Prejudice to Destruction/Anti-Semitism, 1700-1933 (Cambridge: Harvard University Press, 1980).
    Though the roots of anti-Semitism pre-date Christianity, it might be argued that the early Christians utilized the prevalent anti-Semitism to attract pagans and this may account for the unfortunate portrayal of the Jew in the gospels and much of early Christian thought. As we point out, some attribute the "radicalization" of anti-Semitism in the form of the Holocaust to Christianity; others attribute it to the very opposite--i.e., the unmoorings of Nazism from Christianity which had tolerated continued Jewish existence for the purposes of a witness on the "final day of judgment" and in fulfillment of the curse of the "Wandering Jew." Hannah Arendt attributes the Holocaust to the fall of the centralized nation state and the rise of totalitarianism. The Jews, who had played a vital role in the development of the centralized nation state, were left unprotected when this crumbled.

63.   R. Hilberg, The Destruction of the European Jews (New York: Holmes and Meier, rev. ed. 1985; originally published 1961).

64.   Query: Did Christianity in fact say to the Jews "You may not live amongst us as Jews"? Professor Israel Shahak of Jerusalem writes: "....although Christian churches insisted on serious limitation of the rights of Jews, on their humiliation and degradation, Jews were allowed to live as Jews in Christian countries with a rather full protection of their own religion and their right as Jews not to be Christians, more than any other non-Christian or heretical group. In the Middle Ages and long afterward, the sole non-Christian group in most Christian countries was Jewish. Pagans, witches, heretics (and other groups as well) were exterminated or persecuted with much greater ferocity than the Jews." I. Shahak, "The Life of Death': An Exchange," New York Review of Books,, Jan. 29, 1987, p. 45.

65.   At an open day for Christians, the first, held recently by the Auckland (New Zealand) Jewish community at the Beth-Israel Synagogue, Rev. Selwyn Dawson commented, "Christians and Jews have been separated from each other by misunderstandings over the centuries. The Jewish community has been blamed by the Christians for crucifying Christ--and some aspects of the Holocaust and the anti-Semitism movement can be traced to this Christian misconception. Hitler was only able to do what he did because there had been long years of misunderstandings." L. Clifton, "Synagogue to Hold More Get-togethers," New Zealand Herald, Dec. 14, 1987, p. 17.

66.   J. Berger, "Pope Defends Vatican's Response to Holocaust in Talks with Jews," New York Times, Sept. 12, 1987, p. 1.

67.   "Poland and the Jews: An Interview with Czeslaw Milosz," 2 Tikkun 36 (May/June 1987). Arthur Brumberg responds to Milosz in "Poland and the Jews," 2 Tikkun 15 (July/August 1987).

68.   E. Goldhagen, "Pragmatism, Function and Belief in Nazi Anti- Semitism," Midstream, Dec. 1972, p. 52.

69.   M.K. Dziewanowski, Poland in the Twentieth Century (New York: Columbia University Press, 1977), p. 88. Witold Olszewski in a Polish daily wrote: "Anti-Semitism can be everything: breathing the air around the camps of death, living in the post-Jewish houses, the number of the camps of death in the occupied Poland, the number of Jews saved, the counting of Jews living among us, the lack of love to the country of Israel, and even--the prayer for the Jews murdered. Because there are people who think that Oswiecim (Auschwitz) should be the only place on the earth, from which should never rise the prayer, because 'God was silent' when millions of the sons of the Chosen Nation perished there. Is it not the obsession, when the specific anti-Semitism is ascribed even to God?" W. Olszewski, "The Wicked Beginning," Slowo Powszechne ("The Universal Word"), May 12, 1986. In his study of Jewish life in Poland, Weinryb writes: "True, one can find in Poland through the centuries counless anti-Jewish trends and a great deal of opposition to the Jew. The Catholic was opposed to the Jew from a religious point of view. The city burgher and the artisan sought to exclude the Jew. But part of this and similar opposition to Jews could hardly be classified as blanket anti-Semitism. The concept anti-Semitism signifies a value judgment. We define and condemn anti-Semitism on moral grounds. But the opposition of the burgher or the artisans' guild member to the foreigner and the Jew in earlier ages was for the most part no more immoral, according to the opinion of those times, than is present-day opposition by union members to the employment of nonorganized labor. It became immoral (or anti-Semitic) when illegal means--extreme violence, staging blood libels, or expulsion--were employed to achieve the economic goals." B.D. Weinryb, The Jews of Poland/A Social and Economic History of the Jewish Community in Poland from 1100 to 1800 (Philadelphia: Jewish Publication Society of America, 1972), p. 134. I once asked Dr. I.S. Kulcsar, the psychiatrist who examined Adolph Eichmann awaiting trial in Israel, for his definition of "anti-Semitism." With wry humor, he replied, "Disliking Jews more than is necessary."
    For a discussion of Jewish anti-Semitism, see P. Roth, "A Talk with Aharon Appelfeld," New York Times Book Review, Feb. 28, 1988, p. 1.

70.   F. Schauer, "Thinking About Causation," Law Quadrangle Notes (University of Michigan), Winter 1987, vol. 31, no. 2, p. 24.

71.   The documentary, "Courage to Care," was produced by Sister Carol Ritter of Mercy College, Detroit. It highlights personal interviews with those who survived and those who protected and sheltered Jews during the Holocaust.

72.   On the eve of World War II about 25,000 Jews lived in Kielce. Of this number only some 250 survived the Holocaust and returned to the town, and these came mostly from the Soviet Union. In 1946 they represented not more than one-half of one percent of the total population of about 50,000. Some 200 of them occupied a block of apartments in a building on Planty Street which also housed all the Jewish social and religious institutions. In December 1945, during the Jewish Chanuka feast, a grenade was thrown into the building. The explosion caused no major damage, but it aroused anxiety among the Jews. To forestall other outbursts, the Jewish Committee asked the bishop of Kielce, Czeslaw Kaczmarek, to use his influence and appeal to the population to leave the remnants of the Jewish community in peace. They asked him to issue an appropriate pastoral letter. The bishop refused. The bishop's reply can be summed up as follows: Jews are good physicians and good lawyers, and they have a strong tradition as merchants and craftsmen. Poland needs people with such skills. But when they meddle in politics and interfere in Polish public affairs, they offend Poles' national feelings. It is therefore hardly surprising that the Polish population reacts violently--as it did in Kielce. M. Checinski, Poland (New York: Karz-Cohl, 1982), p. 21.
    Likewise, the primate of Poland, Cardinal August Hlond, refused a request by the Jewish community that he issue a pastoral letter officially condemning anti-Semitism. Even after the Kielce pogrom when the Communist authorities challenged the Church for its failure to suppress anti-Semitism and the U.S. ambassador urged the primate to make a statement to the press, the cardinal censured the pogrom as a "painful" event caused by political rather than racial animosity and blamed "Jews in the government for creating animosities" leading to such events. The Church took this attitude not only because of its traditional religious anti-Semitism, but mainly because it regarded anti-Semitism as a powerful weapon against Communist rule and enforced Sovietization. S. Segal, The New Poland and the Jews (New York: L. Furman, 1948), p. 80.
    In July 1946 the pogrom at Kielce occurred killing 42 Jews and wounding 70 to 80 others. The circumstances surrounding it remain shrouded in mystery. The (Soviet controlled) Polish government claimed that it was organized by the anti-Communist underground linked with the Polish emigres in the West and in collusion with the opposition Polish Peasants' Party. The pretext apparently was an accusation that Jews abducted a Polish youth (presumably for the purpose of carrying out a ritual murder) M. Checinski, Poland (New York: Karz-Cohl, 1982), p. 22. [Checinski identifies NKVD agent, Mikhail A. Dyomin, p. 24-26, who allegedly supervised the staging of the 4th of July pogrom to draw attention from Soviet falsification of a crucial election in Poland (June 30, 1946), to discredit Polish opposition to the Soviet takeover, to trigger an immediate exodus of Jews from Poland to Palestine, and to exploit the Jewish effort to establish the state of Israel. The Soviets gained an important propaganda asset against the Polish people by compromising them with criminal mob violence in which Soviet controlled Polish police and military took part. One could easily imagine a terrible loss of life in Brooklin, New York, for example, if during the recent riots the police would have joined the rioters in attacking the Hassidic Jews, one of whom accidentally killed a black child. Excerpts from Checiński's chapter 2 "The Kielce Pogrom," pages 21-32 follow:]
    [At 10 a.m. militiamen appeared on the scene and entered the building with some onlookers to assist in the search. No children were found. The building stood on the bank of a river and therefore had no cellar at all. Nevertheless, the crowd began harassing the Jews and smashing windows. Jewish ex-servicemen fired warning shots in the air to prevent the crowd from storming the building. At about 10:30 a.m. Berel Frydman, a tinsmith, was thrown out of the building by the militiamen and killed: his death was the first. At 11 a.m. two army officers appeared accompanied by several soldiers from the local military garrison, and they were let into the building. Once inside they disarmed the Jewish defenders. One of the officers then shot Dr. Kahane dead, the chairman of the Kielce Jewish Committee, while the soldiers began throwing the Jews out the windows and doors into the hands of the mob, which murdered them on the spot. Soldiers and militiamen joined the lynchers and even fired at the windows....
    The circumstances surrounding the pogrom and its aftermath remain to this day shrouded in mystery. Many aspects of the riots have been consistently concealed or distorted by the authorities and later by official Polish historiography. Of the 100 people arrested for participating in the pogrom, 12 were openly tried, 9 of whom were sentenced to death. In his final plea the prosecutor admitted that "this was an organized provocation. An investigation is under way against the perpetrators of the provocation: its findings cannot yet be revealed, but they, too, will be made public before long...." (Życie Warszawy, 11 July 1946.) This promise has never been kept. The semiofficial progovernment paper Rzeczpospolita wrote that it was not sufficient merely to arrest a few murderers: the whole matter should be cleared up, and all who permitted the pogrom to take place should be found. (Rzeczpospolita, 10 July 1946.) These, too, have remained idle words.
    From ...interviews with people who were employees of the Kielce District Public Security Office at the time, it turns out that the kidnapping case was the subject of intensive investigation and was indeed followed closely by a group of Soviet advisers. According to Mrs. Eta Lewkowicz-Ajzenman, then chief of the Secretariat of the District Public Security Office in Kielce, the day after the pogrom the

investigation officers established that the boy had been abducted by two men to the vicinity of Końskie , where they instructed him to accuse the Jews of having kidnapped him. Here follows ...the ...interview:

Q. Why any attempt made to establish who the organizer of the pogrom was?

E.L-A. Answer Yes, but it was unsuccessful.

Q. Was any attempt made at the trial to establish who had abducted the boy and where he had been taken?

E.L-A. Answer: This matter did not come up at all.... When the trial was over I wondered why it had not been established who the kidnapper had been and why it had all been limited to the prosecution of the murderers alone. The child's mother was not even called to give evidence, though she had been interrogated several times by the security organs, as had the boy. The mother and little Henryk were, incidentally, questioned by a Soviet advisor as well, in my presence.

Q. What was the advisor's name?

E.L-A. Answer: Dyomin... I no longer recall his function or military rank, but he was an intelligent man, with a good command of French and German and fairly fluent Polish. He was blond, tall, with a touch of "Western" refinement about him-a gentleman....

As it turns out, Dyomin was assigned to Kielce, an unlikely place for a highly-educated Soviet intelligence officer, a few months before the pogrom, and he left two weeks after the pogrom. As a rule, Soviet intelligence officers were sent abroad if delicate political provocations were needed. Further, it should be noted that the KGB did not usually shift its officers around and rather insisted on their specialization. Any officer sent to Poland might be assumed to be an expert on Polish, or at least East European affairs.

While agreeing that Dyomin was probably an intelligence, and not a counterintelligence, officer, Mrs. Lewkowicz-Ajzenman added: "When years later I found myself in Israel, a newspaper referred to a Mikhail Dyomin, the secretary of the commercial attache at the Soviet embassy in Tel-Aviv. This aroused my curiosity, and I decided to go and have a look at him ...it was undoubtedly the same Dyomin. Interesting, isn't it?...

Dyomin's later assignment to Israel would suggest that he was a specialist in Jewish affairs. Whether he was an expert on Jewish matters as early as 1945-46, when employed in Kielce, no one can know. That Dyomin was used for very important tasks is borne out by the evidence of an American historian of the KGB who lists Mikhail Aleksandrovich Dyomin (also transliterated Demin) as an officer of Soviet military intelligence (GRU) in Israel in 1964-67, and West Germany since 1969. (John Barron, KGB: The Secret Work of Soviet Secret Agents, New York, p. 385.)

....the investigation of Colonel Adam Kornecki, former chief of the District Security Office in Kielce. He was reassigned to this city on the day after the pogrom by the minister of public security as part of a commission to investigate the activities of its local network of agents both before and after the riots...

Q. Then the Kielce pogrom was organized by NSZ (National Armed Forces)?

Col. A.K. Answer: Not at all. In my opinion, both the Soviet advisors and the Ministry of Public Security tried to implicate the (right-wing) underground... Only one answer could suit the government: that it was the underground which had organized the pogrom. ...being informed by Błaszczyk of NSZ's plans to have him abduct his own son to discredit the Jews, the authorities (supervised by Soviet advisors) then went about planning the pogrom to discredit the NSZ.... The instigation of the pogrom and the trial itself all seem to have been stage managed. Here is an eyewitness account by one of the victims, Mr. Israel Terkieltaub:

Soon [after the pogrom started] three army lieutenants arrived [at the Jewish Committee's building]. At that moment I was in the room of Dr. Kahane, the chairman of the congregation. When the officers entered the room, Dr. Kahane had the receiver in his hand and was trying to get in touch with the city, but by then the telephone was out of order. The officers said they had come to take away the arms, which some of the Jews had permission to carry. One of them came to Dr. Kahane and told him to keep calm because everything would soon be over ...and then he crept up on him from behind and shot him at close range through the head. This could have been around 11 a.m.

The next thing I remember I was lying naked among the corpses....I was saved from being buried alive by Dr. Bałanowski, who had noticed that I was moving my arm. I was taken, seriously wounded, to a hospital in Łódź, where I was laid up for two months. In the hospital I was interrogated by a man from the Security Office. I testified among other things that Dr. Kahane had been shot before my eyes by a lieutenant of the Polish army. The interrogator was to return three days later to repeat questioning, but he never showed up again. I was never summoned to the prosecutor's office or to the court to give evidence on the murder of Dr. Kahane or to identify his murderer.

When I recovered I was summoned to the Jewish Committee, where I was questioned about the pogrom in Kielce by a representative of some party authority, a Jew. He put down what I said but did not ask me to sign my statement.

....The rest of Mrs. Lewkowicz-Ajzenman's account:

During the funeral of the pogrom victims I stood close to the grave. Next to me stood a major, a captain, and two lieutenants, one of them of rather small build who was with the local Informacja (military counterintelligence), a Pole. Opposite me at the grave-side stood Dębski, a Jew who had been in the building during the pogrom... Dębski came to me and said: "Edzia, the small lieutenant who was standing next to you, he is the one who disarmed us." ...chief of the Soviet military advisers to the Kielce Informacja, was present throughout. He also represented the Soviet military at the funeral of the victims.

At the public trial the question of an army officer who disarmed the Jews and killed the leader of the Jewish community was never mentioned. His name was probably Krawczyk, and he was listed by Mr. Mikołajczyk as among the officers suspected of complicity in the massacres. (S.Mikołajczyk, The Pattern of Soviet Domination, London, 1948, p. 188.).... The evidence pointing to the involvement of Soviet and Polish security officers, while inconclusive, is consistent with their well-known global aims and tactics ... The mass emigration of Jews from Poland played into the hands of the Soviet Union by... taxing British rule in Palestine.... Certainly the Polish press was virtually unanimous in its condemnation of the hideous crime committed in Kielce and in its demands for a full investigation and punishment not only of the perpetrators but also of the instigators.]

Polish officials explained that the anti-Jewish currents in postwar Poland represented an expression of hostility toward the Polish [communist] and Soviet regimes. Foreign minister Rzymowski said that the outbreaks were "aimed primarily against the present regime in Poland and only in the second place against the Jews." Since most Poles regarded the regime as an alien-imposed system, the obvious prominence of Jews within the government, along with those who returned to Poland from the Soviet Union after the war, created an extremely tense situation. The American charge d'affaires in Warsaw, Gerald Keith, described it this way: "It is a paradox that after a period of six years when Jews were more mercilessly killed off than any other race, this country finds itself under a very marked Jewish governing and industrial influence." And he added, "I consider it difficult to estimate what proportion of the resentment towards the government may be attributed to the part played by the Jews in the government and government-controlled industry, but it is surely of considerable consequence." Quoted in R.C. Lukas, Bitter Legacy/Polish-American Relations in the Wake of World War II (Lexington: University Press of Kentucky, 1982), p. 57. An American Jewish journalist visiting the scene of the tragedy at Kielce conveyed his view that the attack had been directed against Jews "as an easier way of showing displeasure against the government than to attack the government directly." Quoted in R.C. Lukas, op. cit. supra at p. 58. Still others say the pogrom was designed to intimidate the Jews from reclaiming their property. Far from welcoming back the Jewish survivors, the Poles refused to restore Jewish property to their owners. The situation was the same in the Ukraine and other parts of East Europe. The Nazis had turned over homes confiscated from the Jews to the local population and when survivors returned after the war, the occupants (given the critical housing shortage) were not at all pleased to see them.

73.   Professor Richard C. Lukas claims that "the scope and effect of the attacks were exaggerated in the western press" and that most were "the work of criminal elements associated with the nationalistic right wing of the Polish underground."   R.C. Lukas, Bitter Legacy/Polish-American Relations in the Wake of World War II (Lexington: University Press of Kentucky, 1982), p. 57.

74.   E. Tanay, "An Open Letter to Professor Czeslaw Milosz," July 15, 1987, submitted to Tikkun.

75.   Ltrs., Detroit Free Press, June 9, 1987, p. 10.

76.   New York: Bantam, 1980. In response to my query about depicting a Polish professor as setting out the plan for the extermination of Jews, William Styron replied: "There are great numbers of episodes, incidents and characters in Sophie's Choice which are, to use your phrase, 'contrary to fact.' That is because the book is a novel, not a work of historiography, and a novelist is free to invent situations which are imaginary, so long as he does not violate the general historical record and the spirit of the historical moment. That there was no actual professor like the one I wrote about is true. It is also true that at that place and at that time there could have existed a professor like him, and therefore I was in my novelist's rights to create such a man." Communication from William Styron to Ralph Slovenko (Aug. 25, 1987). There's a saying: Be reasonable--unless you're a writer.
[Contrary to his statement quoted above William Styron violated "the general historical record..."   The actual quotations from "Sophie's Choice" illustrate his historically false statements: "...[the imaginary] Profesor Zbigniew Biegański, Distinguished Professor of Jurisprudece at the Jagiellonian University of Cracov; Doctor of Law honoris causa, Universities of Karlova, Bucharest, Heilderberg and Leipzig... philosopher whose vision of the "final solution" antedated that of Eichmann and his confederates (even perhaps of Adolf Hitler, the dreamer and conceiver of it all), and who had a message tangibly in his possession... he was an aspiring Jew-killer... Murder Jews... he began methodically to philosophize about the necessity of eliminating Jews from all walks of life..."]

77.   N. Tec, When Light Pierced the Darkness/Christian Rescue of Jews in Nazi-Occupied Poland (New York: Oxford, 1986), p. 40.

78.   Communication from Yisrael Gutman to Ralph Slovenko (Nov. 3, 1987).

79.   Remarks by Professor Wenceslas Wagner as chairman of a panel discussion on Jews and Poles as co-victims of the Holocaust, at Wayne State University, March 16, 1986. Auschwitz (in Polish, Oswiecim) was set up as a concentration camp in 1940. From June 1940 to June 1941 the camp was used only for Poles; then, also for others, particularly Soviet POWs (to March 1942); then, it became an extermination camp for Jews. The mass extermination camp, Auschwitz II Birkenau, was constructed in 1942, where Jews and Gypsies were murdered. Treblinka, northeast of Warsaw, constructed in 1942, was a mass extermination camp for Jews, and in the neighborhood was a penal labor camp through which about 10,000 prisoners passed, mainly Poles, of whom about 7,000 perished. Belzec (district Lublin) functioned as a forced labor camp for Jews from June to December 1940, and in 1942 an extermination camp was set up, with gas chambers and crematorium, which functioned until early 1943. A likely estimate of those murdered in this camp is 600,000 Jews and 2,000 Poles. Sobibor (district Lublin), a mass extermination camp for Jews, existed from March 1942 to October 1943. Chelmno on the Ner (northwest of Lodz), the first mass extermination camp for Jews on Polish territory to be equipped with gas chambers and a crematorium, operated from December 1941 to April 1943 and was set working again for some months early in 1944. About 360,000 Jews, mainly from the western territories of Poland that had been annexed to the Reich, as well as some thousands of Gypsies were murdered in this camp. Majdanek, a concentration camp and mass extermination camp in a suburb of Lublin, was set up in the autumn of 1941, first as a camp for Soviet prisoners-of-war and afterwards as a concentration camp. About 300,000 registered prisoners passed through this camp, mainly Jews and Poles, of whom 160,000 perished. From May 1942, the camp also became an extermination camp for Jews; about 200,000 Jews who were not registered at all were murdered there.
Total Polish losses--Jews and non-Jews--are generally estimated by Polish research workers at 6,028,000... As regards the non-Jewish Poles, the Nazi terror was directed particularly against the intelligentsia. One of the first terror operations against the Poles was the so-called Aktion A-B--Ausserordentliche Befriedungsaktion--in which the Germans murdered about 3,500 representatives of the Polish intelligentsia. In all, in the years of German occupation in Poland 28.5 percent of the professors, lecturers and teachers in institutions of higher learning were murdered, as well as 27.2 percent of the Catholic clergy. E. Ringelblum, Polish-Jewish Relations During the Second World War (New York: Fertig, 1976), pp. 4-6. The suffering of the Poles under the Nazi occupation is described in R.C. Lukas, The Forgotten Holocaust: The Poles under German Occupation, 1939-1944 (Lexington: University Press of Kentucky, 1986). A history of concentration camps located in Poland and of Polish losses during World War II is presented in F.J. Proch, Poland's Way of the Cross: 1939-1945 (New York: Polish Association of Former Political Prisoners of Nazi and Soviet Concentration Camps, 1987).
A modern-day commandment, however, is: "Thou shalt have no other holocaust before the Holocaust of the Jews of Europe." A. Ophir, "On Sanctifying the Holocaust: An Anti-Theological Treatise," 2 Tikkun 61 (1987). Jewish historians, educators and politicians tell and retell the difference between the destruction of the Jews of Europe and all other mass murders. As Elie Wiesel says, "There were victims who were not Jews but all Jews were victims."   And as Rabbi Marvin Hier, dean of the Simon Wiesenthal Center, a Holocaust research and educational institution in Los Angeles, says, "The Jewish tragedy during the Holocaust was unique." A.L. Goldman, "Jewish Groups Continue Plans to Push Protest," New York Times, Sept. 2, 1987, p. 9.
What, however, was the total extermination of the Tasmanians in the second quarter of the 19th century carried out by the British settlers, the nearly complete extermination of the Armenians in a great area of the Ottoman Empire in 1915-1917, the wholesale murder of Gypsies in World War II, or the later genocide in Cambodia? Many Poles say that Jews get more attention about their suffering because Jews write books and control the media. To be sure, Jews have for centuries referred to themselves as a nation of the book (Am Ha-Sefer), not only because they possessed the Torah, a book which they believed to contain the principles and commandments of their religion coming from God, but also because they could read and write...
Detroit psychiatrist Victor Bloom has this to say: "It is certainly true that Jews were a minority of those who were killed, so why do we think of the Holocaust as six million Jews rather than 30 million Slavs? It is because of such questions that Jews are accused of "controlling the media." The fact is that the Slavs do not think of the Holocaust as 30 million Slavs deliberately and routinely exterminated because Slavs as such never faced an actual, workable plan of genocide. The Slavs consisted of Russians, Poles, Czechs, Bulgars, Croats and others who were not united as Slavs or singled out as Slavs. These people were mostly Gentiles with a long history of anti-Semitism who eagerly helped the Nazis in this most monstrous endeavor to rid the world of Jews once and for all."
Dr. Bloom continues: "The Jews have a stake in the concept, "Remember, lest we forget." That is why the Holocaust has become synonymous with a plan to destroy Jews. Jews have been victims of anti-Semitism throughout recorded history... If the Slavs want the world to remember that 30 million Slavs were killed in World War II, why don't they bring it up as intensely and repeatedly as the Jews?..." V. Bloom (ltr.), Detroit Free Press, April 9, 1983, p. 8.

The uniqueness of the extermination of European Jewry called for a special term, "Holocaust"; it would not be sufficient to say "mass murder." In English, the word "holocaust" (from the Greek holokaustos, "burnt whole") first appeared in the language around 1250, in a biblical song telling the story of Abraham's willingness to sacrifice his son, Isaac, as a burnt offering to God. In its application to the Nazi era, the capitalized word was used first in the title of a 1965 book of memoirs about the Warsaw ghetto by Alexander Donat, "The Holocaust Kingdom." To note the uniqueness of Jewish suffering, Weisel brought the term Holocaust out of scholarly usage into common parlance in a book review in the New York Times some 30 years ago. As Ophir puts it, it has given rise to another modern-day commandment: "Thou shalt not take the name 'Holocaust' in vain"—it shall not be used for other calamities and atrocities. A. Ophir, op. cit. supra. To universalize the Holocaust is to assuage guilt, says Rabbi Charles H. Rosenzweig, founder and executive vice-president of the Holocaust Memorial Center in suburban Detroit. He writes, "Attempts to trivialize, rationalize and universalize the Holocaust cannot erase the fact that the Holocaust represents Christianity's epochal sin against the Jewish people." C.H. Rosenzweig (ltr.), "Historic opportunity," Detroit Free Press, Sept. 18, 1987, p. 10.

Lanzmann used "shoah," a Hebrew word, as the name for the tragedy befallen the Jews.

80. The first killing by poison gas at Auschwitz involved 300 Poles and 700 Soviet prisoners of war. M. Gilbert, Auschwitz and the Allies (New York: Holt, Reinhart & Winston, 1981), p. 16; R.C. Lukas, The Forgotten Holocaust/The Poles Under German Occupation 1939-1944

(Lexington: University Press of Kentucky, 1986), p. 38. On February 17, 1941, five Franciscan monks were arrested in Niepokalanow, near Warsaw. Three of these men later died in concentration camps, including Father Maximilian Kolbe, who offered his life for another man. Kolbe died from an injection of phenol on August 14, 1941. Kolbe was recently canonized a saint of the Roman Catholic Church. R.C. Lukas, op. cit. supra at p. 228.

81. Quoted in M.K. Dziewanowski, Poland in the Twentieth Century (New York: Columbia University Press, 1977), p. 114. For a comprehensive study of the subject, see C. Madajczyk, Polityka Trzeciej Rzeszy w okupowanej Polsce (Warsaw: Panstwowe wydanictwo naukowe, 1970), 2 vols.

82. Central Commission for Investigation of German Crimes in Poland, German Crimes in Poland (New York: Fertig, 1982), 2 vols. Actually, all Slav peoples east of Germany were intended by the Nazis for an ultimate fate not very much better than the fate assigned by them to the Jews, while the fate of the French and others in Western Europe was to be much less bad, because of a measure of respect and snobbery that the Nazis, including especially Hitler, had towards them. I. Shahak, "'The Life of Death': An Exchange," New York Review of Books, Jan. 29, 1987, p. 45. On January 20, 1942, 14 representatives of the Nazi party, the Gestapo and the government convened in a house in a Berlin suburb--Wannsee--under the direction of Reinhard Heydrich, head of the security police and Hitler's heir apparent. The topic was "the final solution of the Jewish problem," the plan to exterminate the 11 million Jews the Germans expected to eventually be under their control. And according to the records of the meeting: "With the Germanization of Poland, the majority of Poles will disappear with the Jews."...

83. R.C. Lukas, The Forgotten Holocaust/The Poles Under German Occupation 1939-1944 (Lexington: University Press of Kentucky, 1986), p. 33.

84. J.T. Gross, "Polish-Jewish Relations During the War: an Interpretation (lecture at Oxford University on November 30, 1985), published in Dissent, Winter 1987, p. 73.

85. R. Lindsey, "Scholar Says His Views on Jews Cost Him a Post at Stanford," New York Times, March 13, 1987; J. Wiener, "The Case of Norman Davies/When Historians Judge Their Own," The Nation, Nov. 21, 1987, p. 584.

86. N. Davies, Heart of Europe (New York: Oxford University Press, 1984), p. 72.

87. Ibid.

88. Dawidowicz says Davies' chapter on Polish Jews in "God's Playground" is "replete with errors, misconceptions, misrepresentations, and prejudices." L.S. Dawidowicz, "The Curious Case of Marek Edelman," Commentary, March 1987, p. 66. Dawidowicz is the author of, among other books, The War Against the Jews 1933-1945. For other criticism, see M. Leski, "Glossa do 'Żydów Polskich' Normana Daviesa" (Gloss on Norman Davies's "Polish Jews"), Arka (Krakow, 1985), no. 10. Abraham Brumberg has an exchange with Norman Davies in The New York Review of Books, April 9, 1987, p 41. Jon Wiener, professor of history at the University of California, Irvine, writes, "(Davies) distorts evidence to fit his conclusions, he ignores evidence that disproves his arguments, and his thesis that Poles were as helpless as Jews under the Nazi occupation is simply untenable." J. Wiener, "The Case of Norman Davies/When Historians Judge Their Own," The Nation, Nov. 21, 1987, p. 584 at 588. Norman Davies replies: "Wiener belongs to the relatively small school of historians who believe in judging their colleagues' work on the basis of one sentence. At Stanford, the decisive majority is at least thought to make its judgment on the basis of a whole chapter....I do not believe that Wiener has ever read (my) book, or, if he did try to read it, that he is capable of understanding it." Ltr., "Davies on Davies," The Nation, March 5, 1988, p. 290.

89. Professor James J. Sheehan, chairman of the history department at Stanford, declines to comment: "I have been instructed by the University lawyers not to comment about the Davies' case while litigation is in progress." Communication to Ralph Slovenko (Aug. 27, 1987).

90. J. Mathews, "Politics in Academia Questioned at Stanford," Washington Post, May 25, 1986, p. A-4; Reuters North European Service, "British Scholar Files Multimillion-Dollar Job Loss Suit," May 10, 1986; P. N. McCloskey (ltr.), "Unsuited," The Nation, March 5, 1988, p. 320. A ruling favorable to the University's demurrer and motion to strike, going to the substantial bulk of the complaint, was rendered on March 2, 1988. Superior Court, County of Santa Clara, Case No. P48041.

91. Professor Davies' books have been widely praised in the United States and abroad, especially among Poles. He is often called the leading historian on Poland in the West. My colleague, Frank Corliss, chairman of the Slavic Department at Wayne State University, calls Davies "the most prominent historian in the West on Poland" (communication to Ralph Slovenko, Sept. 10, 1987)... L.S. Dawidowicz, "The Curious Case of Marek Edelman," Commentary, March 1987, p. 66. Davies' books, I can attest, are acclaimed by historians and sociologists in Poland.

Zygmunt Nagorski, the Polish-born director of the Center for International Leadership, calls Davies' "Heart of Europe" a "masterpiece" with "sweep, a rare analytical depth and a courageous display of the author's personal convictions." Z. Nagorski, New York Times Book Review, Dec. 23, 1984, sec. 7, p 5. Professor Leszek Kołakowski, professor at the University of Chicago and senior research fellow of All Souls College, Oxford, says of Davies' two-volume "God's Playground" that it "is beyond doubt not only the best book on Poland in the English language; it is the book on Poland." Professor Wallace J. Kosinski, history professor at John Carroll University, says, "[If those who condemn Poles on the subject of anti-Semitism] are sincerely interested in gaining a more accurate version than they now entertain of how Jews fared in Poland over long centuries....they might begin with a magisterial history of the people they so evidently dislike. I suggest a new work by a highly respected and disinterested British historian, Norman Davies's God's Playground." W.J. Kosinski (ltr.), "Two professors rebut views on Poland and Jewry," Plain Dealer (Cleveland), Jan. 11, 1983, p. 8.

92. Professor Piotr S. Wandycz of Yale University asks: "How many people who proffer advice (now) would have been willing to risk their own life and that of their family by harboring a Jew under Nazi occupation?" Ltr., "Historic Responsibility," The Nation, March 5, 1988, p. 319. Did not Bulgaria and Denmark save its Jews? On the other hand, crowds of Poles and Lithuanians watching the roundup of Jews in Vilna (the "Jerusalem of Lithuania") shouted taunts and insults at the Jews. In the first few days of the German occupation, Lithuanian groups murdered some 8,000 Jews. Y. Arad, Ghetto in Flames (Jerusalem: Yad Vashem, 1980)...

93. When the Franks were arrested, Miep Gies, who hid the Franks, went to the Gestapo, talked to officials and offered them a bribe. That kind of effrontery would not have been tolerated in Poland. The collaborator, the man or woman who betrayed Anne and her family, still isn't known. M. Gies, The Story of the Woman Who Helped to Hide the Frank Family (New York: Simon & Schuster, 1987).

94. Question posed by C. Chotkowski (ltr.), "Poles' Own Plight," New York Times, June 6, 1987, p. 14. One answer is: 27 million (90 percent) of Poles were saved; only about 150,000 (5 percent) of Jews.

95. Nietzsche's conception of the uber-mensch, however, is that man must transcend himself, that ordinariness is not acceptable...
Slawomir Mrozek has written, "After all, what the Germans did to the Jews was a matter between Germans and Jews. No concern of ours, no need to stick your head out. A very, very unpleasant business, perhaps even more than unpleasant, perhaps even horrible, but not ours." S. Mrozek, "Nos," Kultura, 1984, no. 7, p. 8...

96. For the majority of Jews, as we have noted, Polish was not the mother tongue, and they did not speak good Polish. Some hardly spoke it at all, and particularly the 600,000 Jews from Soviet Russia who were admitted to Poland and given Polish citizenship upon an express order of Marshal Pilsudski when he assumed power in 1926. This made it very difficult to harbor the Jews. In most cases, they were distinguishable as non-Poles. This was facilitated by the Germans in Poland (the Volksdeutsche) who were more than a million, spoke excellent Polish and knew everything that was going on in the Polish community. In case of doubt, the Germans would check if the suspect was circumcised (in Europe, Aryans are not circumcised). Further difficulties in harboring the Jews consisted in the fact that lodging was very scarce (1939 bombings, influx of refugees from the eastern provinces occupied by the Soviets), and lack of food (strictly rationed). Besides, the Germans requisitioned all better houses and apartments.

97. Nechama Tec tells the story of Jewish survivors and their rescuers in Nazi-occupied Poland in her book, When Light Pierced the Darkness/Christian Rescue of Jews in Nazi-Occupied Poland (New York: Oxford University Press, 1986). Tec herself lived through the war in Poland. Her family was assisted by a number of people, including the German manager of a factory the family had owned before the war. They paid some of their helpers, not ransom money but [cost refunds and] agreed-upon fees for services; others helped them without being paid. Since Tec had what was called a "good appearance" (she didn't look Jewish), she could move around and even work, passing as non-Jewish. Tec's memoir, "Dry Tears" (New York: Oxford University Press, 1984), describes her experiences.

98. ... Jewish population in Holland was 140,000; in Poland, 3,500,000.

99. Tec points out that Poles who lost their lives because they were protecting Jews died together with their charges, as a rule, and Yad Vashem distinctions are not offered to them. How many such Poles were there? The efforts of Tec to count some of those who died while saving Jews and who were identified by name have resulted in numbers ranging from 343 to 668. Recalling that at times the Germans would surround and burn entire villages accused of harboring Jews, annihilating every inhabitant, neither the names nor the numbers of the resulting fatalities can ever be known. N. Tec., op. cit. supra at p. 84 (her book is dedicated "to the rescuers, with gratitude and admiration").
A documentary work, published by Ministerstwo Sprawiedliwosci, Glowna Komisja Badania Zbrodni Hitlerowskich w Polsce, entitled Zbrodnie na Polakach Dokonane Przez Hitlerowcow za Pomoc Udzielana Zydom, documents the deaths of approximately 1,000 Poles who died helping Jews. The compilers of the book indicate that this is not intended to be a definitive figure. Waclaw Zajaczkowski in Martyrs of Charity (Washington, D.C.: St. Maximilian Kolbe Foundation, 1987) gives [as examples] accounts of hundreds of instances in which Poles were murdered because they had befriended Jews.
Professor Richard C. Lukas in The Forgotten Holocaust/The Poles Under German Occupation 1939-1944 (Lexington: University Press of Kentucky, 1986), at p. 150, cites estimates of the number of Poles who perished for aiding Jews ranging from a few thousand to 50,000. Professor Lukas says that based on his own research recently (that is, since the publication of The Forgotten Holocaust), he thinks the number of Poles who died helping Jews went well beyond a few thousand, but he is not prepared yet to offer a figure. Communication from Professor Lukas to Ralph Slovenko (Sept. 18, 1987).
Yisrael Gutman, a survivor, acknowledges that some Poles helped Jews... The vast majority of Poles, he feels, "adhered to the view that the Jews were an alien body and that their fate neither concerned the Poles nor obliged special action on the part of Poland's underground or clandestine armed forces." Y. Gutman, The Jews of Warsaw 1939-1943: Ghetto, Underground, Revolt (Bloomington: Indiana University Press, 1982), p. 252.

100. Walter Laqueur writes: "That there has been a great deal of anti-semitism in modern Polish history is not a matter of dispute, but it is also true that help was extended to the Jews after 1939 precisely by some who had been their bitterest enemies before. Those who represented Poland after 1940 were by and large people who had been in opposition in the 1930s to the rabidly anti-semitic Government and they tried to eliminate the forces who had caused Poland's ruin. All this is not to say that the Government-in-exile and its representatives at home were liberal internationalists who saw their first duty in helping the persecuted Jews. If the Poles showed less sympathy and solidarity with Jews than many Danes and Dutch, they behaved far more humanely than Romanians or Ukrainians, than Lithuanians and Latvians. A comparison with France would be by no means unfavorable for Poland. In view of the Polish pre-war attitudes towards Jews, it is not surprising that there was so little help, but that there was so much." W. Laqueur, The Terrible Secret (Boston: Little, Brown, 1981), pp. 106-107.
See also B. Shatyn, A Private War: Surviving on False Papers, 1941-1945 (Detroit: Wayne State University Press, 1985; foreword by Norman Davies); The Extermination of 500,000 Jews in the Warsaw Ghetto (New York: American Council of Warsaw Jews and American Friends of Polish Jews, 1944); J. Lichten, "Kronika Zbrodni Podstępnej i Oszukańczej," Dziennik Związkowy (Chicago), Dec. 24, 1984; J. Lichten, "'Kalendarz żydowski' i refleksje na zblizony temat," Dziennik Polski/Dodatek Tygodniowy, April 18-19, 1986, p. 6; J. Łobodowski, "Żydzi w okupowanej Francji," Tydzień Polski (London), Dec. 5, 1987, p. 16.

101.   See D.S. Wyman, <u>The Abandonment of the Jews</u> (New York: Pantheon, 1984). On the public response of American Jews to the Holocaust during the years 1938-1944, see H. Lookstein, <u>Were We Our Brothers' Keepers?</u> (New York: Random House, 1985).

102.   In the process of identification with the aggressor, passivity is transformed into activity. A. Freud, <u>The Ego and the Mechanisms of Defense</u> (New York: International Universities Press, l966), p. 134.

103.   Communication from Professor Wenceslas Wagner to Ralph Slovenko (Feb. 6, 1988). Professor Wagner lived in Warsaw until the uprising of 1944.

104.   G.A. Craig, "'Schreibt un Farschreibt!'" <u>New York Review of Books</u>, April 10, 1986, p. 7 at 10. Emmanuel Ringelblum estimated that in Warsaw alone 40,000 to 60,000 Poles were involved in hiding Jews, E. Ringelblum, <u>Notes from the Warsaw Ghetto: The Journal of Emmanuel Ringelblum</u> (New York: McGraw-Hill, 1958, ed. and trans. J. Sloan). Tadeusz Bednarczyk in <u>Obowiazek Silniejszy od Smierci</u> (Duty Stronger Than Death) (Warsaw: Grunwald, 1986), describes the assistance Poles provided Jews in Warsaw during the years 1939-1944. Piotr S. Wandycz writes in <u>The United States and Poland</u> (Cambridge: Harvard University Press, 1980), at p. 242:
    ... It is necessary to reiterate that Poland was the only occupied country where aiding or sheltering a Jew was punishable by death, and where German terror was about the worst in Europe. If one can speak of indifference of the Polish masses to the fate of the separated and isolated Jewish community, it must be seen in the context of the ongoing struggle for survival. Sublime courage or villany are always the attributes of a minority. Blackmailers and informers who denounced the Jews were threatened with severe penalties by the Polish underground. While anti-Semitism persisted and was fed by stories of pro-Soviet Jewish behavior in eastern Poland, some of the formerly notorious anti-Semites helped Jews, and not only individuals but numerous churches and convents provided them with places of refuge.

105.   W. Laqueur, <u>The Terrible Secret</u> (Boston: Little, Brown, 1981), pp. 106-107.

106.   One of the Home Army judges who sentenced such a person to death for denouncing a Jew (and the sentence was carried out) lives now in Washington, D.C.: Dr. Andrew Pomian. The executed person was a Pole of German extraction.

107.   When the United States entered World War II, there was confusion among many Americans about their role in it... N. Sayre, <u>Running Time: Films of the Cold War</u> (New York: Dial Press, 1980), p. 6.

108.   Quoted in G.A. Craig, <u>op. cit. supra</u> at p.10. Walter Laqueur writes: "The Polish case is very briefly that they did what they could, usually at great risk and in difficult conditions. If the news about the mass murders was not believed abroad this was not the fault of the Poles. It was, at least in part, the fault of the Polish Jews who, in the beginning, refused to believe it; it was also the responsibility of the Jewish leaders abroad who were initially quite skeptical." W. Laqueur, <u>The Terrible Secret</u> (Boston: Little, Brown, 1981), p. 106. A private commission of prominent American Jews, set up in 1981 to examine the behavior of Jewish organizations in the United States at the time of the Nazi campaign to annihilate European Jews, split up 15 months later in anger and dissension. B. Weinraub, "Panel on U.S. Jews and Holocaust Is Dissolved," <u>New York Times</u>, Jan. 4, 1983, p. l. Western countries were closed to immigration. Canada, a huge land then thought of as underpopulated, admitted only a trickle of the millions of Jews who hoped to flee Europe. Irving Abella and Harold Troper, <u>None Is Too Many</u> (New York: Random House, l983). For a criticism of U.S. efforts to rescue Jews, see D.S. Wyman, <u>The Abandonment of the Jews</u> (New York: Pantheon, 1984).

109.   P. Johnson, <u>A History of the Jews</u> (New York: Harper & Row, 1987); R. Steel, <u>Walter Lippmann and The American Century</u> (Boston: Little, Brown, 1980).

110.   The Front for the Rebirth of Poland (<u>Front Odrodzenia Polski</u>) issued a protest against the crimes occurring in the Warsaw ghetto. It stated:
    "...the world looks upon this murder, more horrible than anything that history has ever seen, and stays silent. The slaughter of millions of defenseless people is being carried out amid general sinister silence. Silent are the executioners; they do not boast about their deed. England and America are not saying anything. Silent is the ever-influential international Jewry, which was previously oversensitive of wrongdoing to their own. Silent are Poles. Polish political friends of Jews limit themselves to newspaper notes; Polish opponents of Jews show lack of interest in the problem, which is foreign to them. The perishing Jews are surrounded by Pilates who deny all guilt.
    "This silence can no longer be tolerated. Whatever the reason for it, it is vile. In the face of murder it is wrong to remain passive. Whoever is silent witnessing murder becomes a partner to the murder. Whoever does not condemn, consents.
    "Therefore we--Catholics, Poles--raise our voices. Our feeling toward the Jews has not changed. We continue to deem them political, economic, and ideological enemies of Poland. Moreover, we realize that they hate us more than they hate the Germans, and that they make us responsible for their misfortune. Why, and on what basis, remains a mystery of the Jewish soul. Nevertheless, this is a decided fact. Awareness of this fact, however, does not release us from the duty of damnation of murder.
    "We do not want to be Pilates. We have no means actively to counteract the German murders; we cannot help, nor can we rescue anybody. But we protest from the bottom of our hearts filled with pity, indignation, and horror. This protest is demanded of us by God, who does not allow us to kill. It is demanded by our Christian conscience. Every being calling itself human has the right to love his fellow man. The blood of the defenseless victims is calling for revenge. Who does not support the protest with us, is not a Catholic.
    "We protest also as Poles. We do not believe that Poland could benefit from the horrible Nazi deeds. Just the opposite; we detect hostility toward us, caused by the silence of world Jewry and by the German propaganda, already in process to shift from themselves the blame for the slaughter of Jews to Lithuanians and--Poles.
    "The forced participation of the Polish nation in the bloody spectacle taking place on Polish soil may breed indifference, sadism, and, above all, belief that murder is not punishable.
    "Whoever does not understand this, and whoever dares to connect the future of the proud, free Poland, with the vile enjoyment of your fellow man's calamity--is, therefore, not a Catholic and not a Pole."
    The protest appears in full in N. Tec, <u>When Light Pierced the Darkness/Christian Rescue of Jews in Nazi-Occupied Poland</u> (New York: Oxford University Press, 1986), pp. ll0-112.

111.   "Poland and the Jews: An Interview with Czeslaw Milosz," 2 <u>Tikkun</u> 36 at 40 (l987).

112.   Documentary film, "The Wannsee Conference," based on records of meeting held on January 20, 1942 at a house in the quiet Berlin suburb of Wannsee. Fourteen key representatives of the SS, the Nazi Party and the government bureaucracy attended the meeting at the invitation of Reinhard Heydrich, head of the Security Police and Secret Service. The meeting lasted 85 minutes. There was only one item on the agenda: the Final Solution. The word "murder" was not once used.   Milton Dank writes: "The Nazi goal was clear, and they never wavered from it despite the vicissitudes of war. They were determined to eliminate the Jews from Europe--by emigration if possible, by extermination if necessary--but in dealing with the Jews of Western Europe they knew that they were being watched by the

rest of the world and therefore could not apply the murderous tactics which had been so successful in Poland and the other eastern territories of the Reich." M. Dank, The French Against the French (Philadelphia: Lippincott, 1974), at p. 225.

113.   "Lanzmann made a great film..." An interview with Jan Karski, "The Mission That Failed," Dissent, Summer 1987, p. 326 at 334. See also "Refleksje na Marginesie Filmu 'Shoah'", Relax/Ilustrowany Magazyn Polski, June 20, 1987, p. 6. Of publications that quote Karski as critical of the film, he says they take his comments out of context... Communication from Jan Karski to Ralph Slovenko (Sept. 15, 1987).

114.   "Polish Americans Reflect on Shoah" (Chicago: Polish American Congress, 1986), p. 4.

115.   W. Zajaczkowski, Martyrs of Charity (Washington, D.C.: St. Maximilian Kolbe Foundation, 1987), p. 22.

116.   Interview published in May 1985.

117.   T.G. Ash, "The Life of Death," New York Review of Books, Dec. 19, 1985, p. 26.

118.   Quoted in T.G. Ash, "The Life of Death," New York Review of Books, Dec. 19, 1985, p. 26. A survivor, Professor Israel Shahak of Jerusalem, calls Lanzmann "a prisoner of his own prejudices." He writes: "Lanzmann simply heard what he wanted to hear, that Poles are such and such and that Jews are chosen people whose behavior should not be investigated. He did not want to hear the real truth, that both of them, and of course all other peoples too, are human beings who behave more or less in the same way in similar circumstances." I. Shahak, "'The Life of Death': An Exchange," New York Review of Books, Jan. 29, 1987, p. 45. In actual fact, the Polish record of aid to Jews was better than many Eastern Europeans—Romanians, Ukrainians, Lithuanians, Latvians—and, as Jewish historian Walter Laqueur has stated, "a comparison with France would be by no means unfavorable to Poland." W. Laqueur, The Terrible Secret/Suppression of the Truth about Hitler's Final Solution (Boston: Little, Brown, 1980), p. 106.

119.   Y. Gutman (ltr.), "Unikac bezpodstawnych ocen," Tydzien Polski, Aug. 8, 1987, p. 13. But Gutman observes in his book, The Jews of Warsaw, op. cit. supra, and in a recent communication to the author, as quoted, relatively few Poles were rescuers.

120.   Reported in "Polish Americans Reflect on Shoah" (Chicago: Polish American Congress, 1986), p. 7. Dr. Karski is now Professor of Government at Georgetown University in Washington D.C. He is most recently the author of The Great Powers and Poland 1919-1945/From Versailles to Yalta (New York: University Press of America, 1985). Dr. Karski married a Jewess.

121.   J. Szapiro, "Warsaw Defiant," New York Times, April 29, 1939, p. 1; "Roosevelt Silent on Hitler," New York Times, Feb. 21, 1938, p. 1. See M.T. Kaufman, "Debate Over the Holocaust Stirs Poles/A Confession of Shame Has Provoked Outrage," New York Times, March 8, 1987, p. 3; K. Kawon, "Odczyt Jana Karskiego," Dziennik Polski, Dec. 11-12, 1987, p. 2; K. Lukomski, "W poszukiwaniu prawdy beznamietnej i obiektytwnej," Dziennik Polski (Polish Daily News, Detroit), Jan. 15-16, 1988, p. 5. Norman Davies writes, "'After all, it's the Germans who were responsible' (quoting a young Pole). To hear how some people speak, one might overlook the fact that both Poles and Jews were common victims of the Nazis." N. Davies, "The Survivor's Voice," New York Review of Books, Nov. 20, 1986, p. 21.
    "Money cannot restore a life or rewrite the past, but reparations can begin to heal certain wounds." Editorial, New York Times, April 3, 1988, p. E-16. To that end in 1951, Chancellor Adenauer of the Federal Republic of Germany acknowledged the "immeasurable suffering" inflicted on Jews by Germany and proposed joint talks with Israel "to bring about a solution of the material indemnity problem, thus easing the way to the spiritual settlement of infinited suffering." (Menachem Begin, the opposition leader in Israel at the time, was totally opposed: "Whoever heard of the son of the murdered going to the murderer to ask for compensation?") Austria has offered modest pensions to some individuals who had suffered during Nazi rule, but it has rejected large-scale reparations on the ground that they were "Hitler's first victim," coerced into union with the Nazi Reich. Editorial, New York Times, April 3, 1988, p. E-16.

122.   I. Shahak, "'The Life of Death': An Exchange," New York Review of Books, Jan. 29, 1987, p. 45. As the activity of one is made possible or influenced by the inactivity of another, many would say: both are culpable. W. Safire, "Silence is Guilt," New York Times, April 24, 1978, p. 23. The Vatican, better informed than anyone else by its priests and its faithful throughout Central and Eastern Europe, knew beyond a shadow of doubt in the summer, even in the spring, of 1942 of the gas chambers. W. Laqueur, The Terrible Secret/The Suppression of the Truth About Hitler's Final Solution (Boston: Little, Brown, 1981). There was, however, no papal encyclical that might have created a crisis of conscience among the Catholics in the German nation and the German army. Pius XII maintained diplomatic silence while the furnaces worked full blast. He blessed the German weaponry and German soldiers wore the insignia on their belt, "Gott mit uns" (God is with us). Rabbi Charles H. Rosenzveig, a survivor, says: "Germany's objective, to murder the entire Jewish people, was partially made possible through the indifference and silence of the many, and the voluntary collaboration of a significant number of Christians in Europe." C.H. Rosenzveig (ltr.), "Learning the Lessons of the Holocaust," Detroit News, Sept. 22, 1987, p. 8. Rabbi Rosenzveig is founder ...of the Holocaust Memorial Center in suburban Detroit.

123.   Gilman v. Central Vermont Ry. Co., 93 Vt. 340, 107 A. 122 (1919); W.P. Keeton (ed.), Prosser and Keeton on the Law of Torts (St. Paul: West, 5th ed. 1984), p. 277.

124.   On the fate of the Jews in France, see M. Dank, The French Against the French (Philadelphia: Lippincott, 1974), chap. 12, pp. 224-244.

125.   "A new wind is blowing," says Mordechai Palzur, who arrived in Warsaw at the end of 1986 to head the Israel Interest Section in Poland. Much of its force, he says, is directed by the Pope, who has urged his followers to look on Jews as their older spiritual brothers. A native Pole, who was in Siberia during the Stalinist era, he is happily surprised by the gracious reception he has received in Poland. He is often invited to lecture or to participate in symposia. G.F. Cashman, "Ambassador to the Past," Jerusalem Post, Jan. 16, 1988, p. 13. A lengthy interview with Palzur on the history of Jews in Poland appears in W. Piasecki, "Myslac o Przyszlosci," Przeglad Tygodniowy, 1987, no. 31 (279).

126.   Of anti-Semitism in Austria, Mervyn S. Feinstein of England, a Jewish student who has spent six months living in Vienna, writes: "The Jews of Austria are constantly being blamed by people of other religions for crimes such as muggings, burglaries and shoplifting. The Jewish family I stayed with received regular intimidation in retaliation for crimes supposedly committed by Jews. I also witnessed several incidents where orthodox Jews were attacked by gangs of youths. The authorities in Vienna take absolutely no notice of this anti-semitic behavior, which leads me to believe that they are glad to see our persecution." M.F. Feinstein (ltr.), "Austria," Economist, July 11, 1987, p. 6. "Ours is an old, Christian anti-Semitism, as old as the empire," says Ruth Beckermann, a young Austrian film maker and writer who actively opposed Kurt Waldheim's election. "In Austria, even the Jews are anti-Semitic." Quoted in J. Miller, "Erasing the

Past/Europe's Amnesia About the Holocaust," <u>New York Times Magazine</u>, Nov. 16, 1986, p. 30 at 34. See also W. Stricker (ltr.), "Austria Welcomed Hitler, and Its Anti-Semitism Lingers," <u>New York Times</u>, March 30, 1985, p. 14.

Of anti-Semitism in Hungary, Erwin Fuchs of Seattle writes: "It is nothing short of amazing that during all these years when people talk about the Holocaust in Europe....I never hear about Hungary, which was for generations the most rabidly anti-semitic country... I think that as a Jew of Hungarian origin I'm well qualified to say this. My great-grandfather from my mother's side was murdered during a pogrom... E. Fuchs (ltr.), "Holocaust," <u>Tikkun</u>, Sept./Oct. 1987, p. 2.

127.   Dr. Marek Edelman, a cardiologist and Solidarity activist in Lodz, and the last surviving leader of the 1944 Warsaw   ghetto uprising, puts it thus: "Jewry was the basin between the Vistula and the Dnieper. What existed in America, in France, in England didn't create Jewish culture. What is a people anyway? A people is a group of individuals who create a common culture, a sense of progress. It's not necessary or sufficient for a people to have a common ideology or religion. There are millions of Moslems in the world, but they're not all of the same culture. Those 5 million Jews from Odessa to Warsaw had a single culture, even the same economic conditions. And that no longer exists." He continues: "The state of Israel has a totally different culture. Even if it survives, after a certain amount of time it will become culturally Arabic. And there's no way around that. You see, it's not a Jewish state but a mosaic state. Jews were brought to Israel from Ethiopia, Egypt, China. Apart from sharing the faith of Moses they have nothing at all in common with each other. And so if they do hold out, a new people, a new culture will eventually arise that won't have anything to do with Europe, with Chagall, with the Jewry that used to exist here." Interview with Dr. Marek Edelman, "Poland's 'Jewish Problem,'" <u>Harper's</u>, August 1987, p. 21.

In one story, Shlomo goes back home to Poland to visit his mother after living in the United States for two years. "Shlomo, why aren't you wearing a beard?" his mother asks. "Mother, there's no time to grow a beard in America." "Shlomo, do you keep kosher?" "Mother, there's no time in America." "Shlomo, do you work on Shabbos?" "Mother, you have to work on Shabbos in America." The mother then pauses, "Tell me, Shlomo, are you still circumcised?"

128.   Paul Johnson says he undertook the writing of his book, "A History of the Jews," when he became aware of the magnitude of the debt Christianity owes to Judaism. Quoted in A. Goldman, "They Gave Birth to His Faith," <u>New York Times Book Review</u>, April 19, 1987, p. 11. Pope John Paul II on his visit in the U.S. emphasized the common heritage of Jew and Christian. "The Papal Visit," <u>New York Times,</u> Sept. 12, 1987, p. 8.

129.   H. Golden, <u>Ess, Ess, Mein Kindt</u> (Eat, Eat, My Child) (New York: Putnam, 1967);   C.E. Silberman, <u>A Certain People/American Jews and Their Lives Today</u> (New York: Simon & Schuster, 1985), p. 74. Jews in Poland loved herring and onions. Eating so much onion, Jews were called "onions." Dr. Emanuel Tanay reports that in Nazi-occupied Poland he would say that he hated onions--to show that he was not Jewish (communication to Ralph Slovenko, Sept. 23, 1987). Today, a favorite food of Poles is herring or tomatoes covered with onions. E. Wirkowski, <u>Cooking the Jewish Way</u> (Warsaw: Interpress, 1983). Dr. de Pomian Pozerski, the most famous French expert on gastronomy of Polish descent (his father fled Poland after the collapse of an uprising against the Russians) wrote a well-known book about Jewish cuisine ("La Cuisine Juive"); he died in the 1960s.

130.   The concept of collective responsibility is linked to the idea of national character. The term "character" is often used to describe those traits that are characteristic of a particular individual. One might say, "You could expect that of him." In collective usage, that is said of the group of which that person is a member. Jews are blamed collectively for just about anything. More often than not, when a Jew causes someone harm, the aggrieved party is heard to say, "Those damn Jews!" Call it collective guilt, or collective prejudice.

The festival of Purim, based on the biblical Book of Esther, celebrates the victory of Jews at a time when there seemed to be no hope... Purim has been a form of celebrating a political victory against anti-Semitism.

131.   A. Smolar, "Jews as a Polish Problem," <u>Daedalus</u>, Spring 1987, p. 31. Czeslaw Milosz asserts that Jewish Communists after the war "occupied all the top positions in Poland and also in the very cruel security police." C. Milosz, "Anti-Semitism in Poland," <u>Problems of Communism,</u> 1957, no. 3, p. 35. See M. Checinski, <u>Poland: Communism, Nationalism, Anti-Semitism</u> (New York: Karz-Cohn, 1982).

132.   T. Toranska, <u>Them: Stalin's Polish Puppets</u> (New York: Harper & Row, 1987).

133.   When Russian Communism emerged after World War I, many Jews saw in its egalitarian philosophy a chance of finally escaping discrimination, if not persecution. Then, when these hopes proved spurious, many of them defected again from "the God that failed." Many more left the party again after the so-called Doctors' Plot was announced in 1953 in Moscow--"murderers in white aprons," most of them Jewish, were accused of attempting to poison the highest Soviet party and army leaders. Many of the German and Austrian exiles who fled to the Soviet Union were banished or exterminated, or returned to the Nazis during the Stalin-Hitler Pact. Equally harsh treatment was given to the many valiant Communist Jews who had fought on the side of the Republic during the Spanish Civil War. Be that as it may, the reasons for Poland's falling under the Russian orbit are more related to inter-Allied agreements at Yalta than to any internalia.

134.   E. Hoffer, <u>The Ordeal of Change</u> (New York: Harper & Row, 1963).

135.   K. Johnson, "2 Years Later, Goetz Case Remains Legal Puzzle," <u>New York Times</u>, March 23, 1987, p. 11.

136.   Czeslaw Milosz has written: "When Sikorski's Polish Army was being formed in the Soviet Union during the war, the Jews who tried to join it encountered two obstacles: exclusion by anti-Semitic Polish officers and the refusal of the Soviet authorities to permit Poles from the 'incorporated' Polish eastern territories, now Soviet 'citizens,' to join a Polish army. The same authorities, however, did not create difficulties when another Polish army, a Communist one, was formed. The Jews joined it en masse because it was an opportunity to get out of a country in which they no longer wished to live. In the army they passed through a period of indoctrination that qualified them as members of the <u>apparatus</u>. The first <u>cadres</u> of the Polish Comunist Party in 1945, it must be remembered, were composed of men in uniform, a very large proportion of them intellectuals of Jewish descent. The Russians regarded them as more reliable instruments of Soviet desires in the belief that they would be less inclined to Polish patriotism because of the discrimination to which the Polish rightists had subjected them before the war....While the hatred of the masses was directed against the whole privileged group, that is, all of the top party officials, through a reversion to primitive mentality it was only such 'outsiders' as the political directors of the Security Police, Colonel Rozanski, who were held responsible for the general poverty and terror. In other words, the hostility of the masses focused on people who were somehow distinguished by their Jewish descent, although they were no more zealous in enforcing the orders of Moscow that thousands of higher officials of non-Jewish descent." C. Milosz, "Anti-Semitism in Poland," <u>Problems in Communism</u>, 1957, vol. 3, p. 35.

R.V. Burks, an American historian, points out the significant role that the Jews played generally in Communist-oriented East Europe: "Just below the summit of power, the party Jews tended to concentrate in certain ministries and functions. They congregated in the foreign ministry and the ministry of foreign trade, because they were almost the only ones whom the party could trust who had the requisite knowledge of foreign languages and high finance. They also flooded into the central committee and the security police, perhaps because they felt safer near the centers of decision-making. In Bucharest, Budapest, and Warsaw virtually every important police official was Jewish....Often these police officials were survivors of Nazi extermination camps, and they did not let mercy or other humanitarian considerations stand in their way when it came to dealing with the class enemy. Indeed, many Jews were publicly associated with the extremist policy followed by the Satellite regimes...." R.V. Burks, The Dynamics of Communism in Eastern Europe (Princeton: Princeton University Press, 1961), p. 166.

137. Quoted in F. Kempe, "The Black Veil of Poland's Long History," Wall Street Journal, Dec. 17, 1981, p. 29.

138. A 1948 book on Poland quotes Stalin as saying, "Communism does not fit the Poles—Poland's future economy should be based on private enterprise." S. Mikolajczyk, The Rape of Poland: The Pattern of Soviet Aggression (New York: Whittlesey, 1948), p. 100.

139. Quoted in M. Niezabitowska & T. Tomaszewski, Remnants/The Last Jews of Poland (New York: Friendly Press, 1986), p. 125.

140. The American Jewish Yearbook reports 25,000 Jews living in Poland in 1967, 21,000 at the end of 1968, 15,000 at the end of 1969, and 5,000 in 1987. American Jewish Yearbook (Philadelphia: Jewish Publication Society of America, annual publication). See also J. Banas, The Scapegoats/The Exodus of the Remnants of Polish Jewry (New York: Holmes & Meier, 1979). The Polish government spokesman, Jerzy Urban, though himself Jewish, has described the Catholic weekly Tygodnik Powszechny (Everybody's Weekly) as "idolatrously philosemitic." ... J. De Lacy, "Someone from Cracow," Atlantic, Nov. 1986, p. 95.

141. A. Bromberg, "Poland and the Jews," 2 Tikkun 15 (July/August 1987). Spurious? In the 1930s, Isaac Bashevis Singer recalls, the Warsaw communists were nearly all Jews. I.B. Singer, Love and Exile (New York: Doubleday, 1984), p. 48. The point to be made is that, while all (or a disportionately large number of) communists were Jews, not all Jews were communists. Natan (formerly Anatoly) Sharansky, the well-known dissident in the Soviet Union, now living in Israel, says about Jews and revolution: "Perhaps because they have always been considered outsiders, or because their own cultural heritage served as a powerful counterinfluence, the Jews never quite accepted enforced conformity and the obliteration of individualism... Jews have never been considered loyal Soviet citizens." N. Sharansky, "As I See Gorbachev," Commentary, March 1988, p. 29 at 31.

142. Radio Free Europe Situation Reports (June 22, 1967). For testimony of the Soviet pressure on the Polish party concerning its Jewish membership, see G. Mond, "A Conversation in Warsaw," Problems of Communism (May-June 1964).

143. Nowiny-Kurier, May 18, 1973. Recently two Polish professors read a strongly worded condemnation of Poland's anti-Semitic purges of 1967-68 at a Jerusalem conference on Polish Jewry. They announced that Gen. Jaruzelski, the country's leader, had authorized them to publicize the statement, but three weeks later the government spokesman in Warsaw categorically denied that the general had sent any message to Jerusalem. "A tale of two statements," U.S. News & World Report, March 14, 1988, p. 12.

144. The film had its first commercial run in New York in 1988, at which time film critic of the New York Times wrote: "Too many secondary characters are stereotypes of Jews, especially a repulsive, piggish woman with whom (a Polish nobleman of diminished fortunes) has an affair, and her merciless, vengeful husband. There is so little historical perspective on these characters that Mr. Wajda's own judgment seems to have failed him." C. James, "Film: 'Land of Promise,' 1975 Work by Wajda," New York Times, Feb. 5, 1988, p.18.

145. Reported in T.G. Ash, "The Life of Death," New York Review of Books, Dec. 19, 1985, p. 26. An anecdote told in Poland goes like this: A Jew says to a Pole: "I'm leaving for Israel." "Why?" asks the Pole. "Don't you have friends here, and roots here?" The Jew says, "I hear they are going to kill Jews and pipe-smokers." The Pole... "Why the pipe-smokers?" "You see," says the Jew, "you didn't ask about the Jews."

146. M. Niezabitowska & T. Tomaszewski, Remnants/The Last Jews of Poland (New York: Friendly Press, 1986). Their book is devoted to the Polish Jews: "To those we came to know during the five years of our work, to those who became our friends, and also to those whom we never managed to meet--in the hope that nevertheless and despite everything they are not the last." The book is reviewed in A. Brumberg, "A Last Stand in Poland," New York Times Book Review, Oct. 19, 1986, p. 11.

147. M. Miro, "Remnants: The Last Jews of Poland," Detroit Free Press, March 21, 1987, p. 1-D.

148. Poles immigrating now to the United States are, in general, surprised to hear so much discussion about Jewry and they are surprised to learn that many of their favorite authors were Jews--J. Tuwin, A. Slonimski, B. Lesmian, M. Jastrun, J. Brzechwa, B. Schulz, J. Korczak, B. Jasienski, S.J. Lec, A. Rudnicki.

149. Rev. Witold Kiedrowski, a priest from the Chelmo diocese in Poland and now residing in France, writes: Poland has recognized the site of the Auschwitz camp as a monument commemorating the crimes against humanity and the sacrifice made by the people massacred by Nazi barbarity. Consequently, commemorative plaques honoring all nationalities massacred there have been placed there. They are identical, no matter what the actual number of victims of a given nationality. It is a monument to man's martyrdom, irrespective of his nationality, convictions or religion. The strange persistence of the Jews demanding to make Auschwitz exclusively a monument to their martyrology may evoke a painful impression that for them other peoples are not important. That only the Jews and Jewish victims have a right to be honored. In a painful way this attitude reminds of the theory which held that only a German could be a superman ...When sensitiveness, even the most justified, is becoming hypersensitivity it may lead us astray.
The Jewish argument that, proportionally speaking, their people suffered the most in Auschwitz, or rather Birkenau, and this gives them a right to "own" Auschwitz is inadmissible. If Auschwitz or Birkenau were to go to the nationality which suffered the most there, then they should be granted to the Gypsies who lost 600,000 people in Auschwitz, that is, proportionally many more than any other nationality.
Auschwitz is a monument to the martyrdom of man and a protest against barbarity, no matter what the nationality of its victims.
W. Kiedrowski, "The World Needs a Monument of the Living Prayer," in A. Kaplinski (ed.), Christian Life in Poland (Warsaw: Christian Social Thought Centre, 1986), p. 50. Rev. Kiedrowski was an inmate of the concentration camps in Majdanek, Auschwitz and Buchenwald. Nobel Laureate Czeslaw Milosz is anxious "when the meaning of the word Holocaust undergoes gradual modifications, so that the word begins to belong to the history of the Jews exclusively, as if among the victims there were not also millions of Poles, Russians, Ukrainians, and prisoners of other nationalities." Quoted in R.C. Lucas, The Forgotten Holocaust/The Poles Under German Occupation 1939-1944 (Lexington: University Press of Kentucky, 1986), p. ix. See also G.A. Craig, "'Schreibt un Farschreibt!'" New York Review of Books, April 10, 1986, p. 7. Poles (and others) say, "It is a curious elitism of the Jews to claim that they and only they suffered." Elie Wiesel's reply is oft-quoted: "Not all victims were Jews, but all Jews were victims."

150. Communications in Poland by university students to author.

151.   Actually there is a monument in Warsaw honoring those who perished during the Ghetto uprising.

152.   R.F. Scharf, "In Anger and In Sorrow," 1 Polin/A Journal of Polish-Jewish Studies 270 (1986).

153.   Several thousand Polish officers were killed in three places that have come to be known collectively as Katyn--a village in western Russia. According to official Polish and Soviet state versions, the massacre took place in 1941 as Hitler's armies headed toward Moscow, and the victims were martyrs to Nazism. But most Poles know better: the massacres took place in 1940, when Soviet forces occupied eastern Poland in the aftermath of the Hitler-Stalin non-aggression pact. There is no official memorial to Katyn, but every year at the Powazki cemetery in Warsaw there is a spontaneous laying of wreaths and flowers.

154.   Among the publications of Moscow's Novosti Press Agency Publishing House is "Zionism: Instrument of Imperialist Reaction" (1970). It states: "We are legitimately incensed at the fuss raised by the Pied Pipers of international Zionism to get Soviet Jews to move to Israel" (p. 18). "The atrocities they are committing on Arab land are no different from what the Nazis did" (p. 52). "The Soviet people demand that the Israeli invaders stop military provocations and get out of the Arab lands they have occupied" (p. 57). "Let the Israeli aggressors and their imperialist patrons know that they shall not escape the judgment of the people." (p. 62).

155.   Reported in K. McKinsey, "To Poles, the pope is one of their own," Detroit Free Press, Sept. 8, 1987, p. 1; K. McKinsey & B. Stanton, "The Charisma of John Paul II," Detroit Free Press, Sept. 9, l987, p. B-1.

156.   J.J. Bukowczyk. And My Children Did Not Know Me/A History of the Polish-Americans (Indiana University Press, 1987), p. 111.

157.   Marian Szczepanski, a Polish American, says he "will not rest until such jokes are no longer told." A. Cohen, "Polish fighter now fights Polish jokes," Detroit News, Nov. 4, 1982, p. B-3. See also M. Wowk, "'Polish' math quiz angers Sterling Heights parent," Detroit News, March 5, 1988, p. B-6. Tom Shovan in a New York-based weekly, The Pulse of Radio, described polka as the "same song over and over again with slightly different words," and said the ability to tell the difference beween polkas was akin to "dogs sniffing other dogs' urine on fire hydrants and trees." The article was reprinted in The Polska, a musical supplement to the Polish American Journal. He received from the Polish community in Detroit about 700 letters by way of protest, but instead of demands for apologies, they wrote anti-Semitic insults. "I'm not even Jewish," Shovan said. L. Jones, "Polka lovers are hopping mad over critic's remarks," Detroit News, March 10, 1988, p. 1.

158.   By way of illustration, see W. Zajaczkowski, "Martyrs of Charity," New Horizon/Polish American Review, Aug. 1987, p. 8. At a recent large gathering of Polish-Americans at a ball sponsored by Radio Poland of Detroit (Feb. 13, 1988), the popular Polish actor Jan Tadeusz Stanislawski told an anecdote involving the would-be assassin of Pope John Paul II. According to the story, he was not told to shoot the Pole in Rome but the Pole in Jerusalem, Menachim Begin. The humor escaped me but the audience roared.

159.   "(The Slavs) participated in starting the fire, fanning the flames, and pouring gasoline on the raging inferno that was the Holocaust. If 30 million Slavs were killed in World War II, who can be blamed (but themselves)?" V. Bloom (ltr.), Detroit Free Press, April 9, 1983, p. 8.

160.   Communication from Professor Wenceslas Wagner to Ralph Slovenko (Feb. 6, 1988); confirmed by council member Raoul Hilberg (communication of March 14, 1988).

161.   K. Lukomski, "Polish-Jewish Relations: In Search of a Meaningful Perspective," Zgoda (Official Publication of the Polish National Alliance of North America), Jan. 15, l988, p. l. See also Z. Zaniewicki, "Antysemityzm?--a Moze Polonofobia," Dziennik Zwiazkowy (Chicago), Oct. 2, 1985, p. 4; N. Gross, "Przywileje Zydow Polskich," Dziennik Zwiazkowy, Jan. 29, l986, p. 4.

162.   On the role of the territorial imperative in human power struggles, see R. Ardrey, The Territorial Imperative (New York: Dell, 1966). Dr. Gerald J. Sarwer-Foner's work on human territoriality points out its importance to instinct theory, its place in human power struggles and its representation in the visualization and treatment of the phobic disorders. G.J. Sarwer-Foner, "On Social Paranoia--The Psychotic Fear of the Stranger and He Who is Alien," 4 Psychiatr. J. Univ. Ottawa 21 (1979); "On Human Territoriality: A Contribution to Instinct Theory," 17 Can. Psychiatr. Assoc. J. 169 (Supp. II, 1972).

163.   Universities in the U.S. with large Jewish enrollment are known (by Jewish students) as the "Oy Vey League" [from AJ-VAJ used in the shtetles in Poland]. S. Ludmer-Gliebe, "Not So Funny," Detroit Jewish News, March 4, 1988, p. 73. Of the Jew as eternal victim, Rabbi Pinchas H. Peli of Ben-Gurion University of the Negev writes: "[O]ne element must be firmly reiterated: that the very fact of the existence of Israel makes it possible and obligatory for the new Jew who rose from the ashes of Auschwitz and Treblinka to declare to himself and the world that he is no longer ready to be the eternal victim, whether of satanically-contrived gas chambers or colorfully keffiyeh-wrapped teenagers." P.H. Peli, "A time to speak out," Jerusalem Post, March 19, 1988, p. 22.

164.   Quoted in F. Lewis, "Bad News Gives a Better Chance," New York Times, March 13, 1988, p. 27.

165.   L. Weschler, "A Reporter in Poland/And There Was Light," New Yorker, Nov. 9, 1981, p. 59 at 114; reprinted in L. Weschler, The Passion of Poland, From Solidarity Through the State of War (New York: Pantheon, 1984).
[In the summer of 1941 Abraham Stern, the leader of Irgun Zwei Leumi, to which belonged Yitzhak Shamir, sent a message to Beirut to contact the German Nazis and offer them the following proposal: "The establishment of the historical Jewish state, on a nationalist and totalitarian basis, tied by treaty to the German Reich, in accordance with the preservation and strengthening of future German power position in the Near East." In the fall of 1941 Stern was determined to renew his connections with the Nazis and made a second attempt to contact them in December 1941. It was shortly before Stern was murdered by the British in Tel Aviv in February 1942. His, second attempt to make contact with the German Nazis failed. Yitzhak Shamir was then a member of the command of Stern's group and chose as his assistant Ghiladi. Later Shamir decided that Ghiladi had to be killed. Avishai Margalit, "His Violent Career" The New York Review of Books, May 14, 1992, p. 21. On the political career of Yitzhak Shamir (Yezernitzky).]
[The Jews in Poland were not forced to convert to Christianity. Those who did maintained a positive attitude towards their Jewish heritage and towards Jewish people. Reasons for conversion were: 1. a true conviction, 2. an advancement, social and material, 3. personal difficulties, 4. an obligation for help, upbringing etc. Most Jewish converts intermarried with Christians and some, eventually, joined the ranks of Polish intelligentsia. Jakub Goldberg "Jewish Converts in the Old Poland" Jahrbucher fur Geschichte Osteuropas 30 (1982), p: 45-99. Mateusz Mieses Patriotic Polish Families, Once of Jewish Blood, WEMA, Warsaw 1991. On the Jewish descent of the mother of Adam Mickiewicz and his connections with the Jewish world: Jadwiga Maurer Of A Foreign Mother ("Z Matki Obcej...") Polska Fundacja Kulturalna, London 1990. The Encyclopedia Judaica lists Adam Mickiewicz as a Jew (because of Jewish mother).

LIST OF RECOMMENDED READINGS:

which together with standard atlases and encyclopedias were used in writing of
Jews in Poland: A Documentary History

BOOKS:

Abramsky, Chimen at al. ed., *The Jews in Poland*. New York: Basil Blackwell Inc. 1986

Bałaban, Majer, *Dzieje Żydów*. Kraków: Ireon Frommer, 1912

Baron, S.W., *The Russian Jew Under Tsars and Soviets*. New York: Macmillan, 1964

Ben-Sasson, H. H. et al., *A History of the Jewish People*. Cambridge, Mass.: Harvard University Press, 1976

Bieberstein, A., *Zagłda Żydów w Krakowie. Kraków: Wydawnictwo Literackie, 1985*

Brikner, A., *History of Polish Culture*. Warsaw: 1958

Brożek, A., *The Polish Americans, 1854-1939*. Warsaw: Interpress, 1985

Bukowczyk, J.J., *And My Children Did Not Know Me / A History of the Polish-Americans*. Bloomington: Indiana University Press, 1987

Chęciński, Michael., *Poland: Communism, Nationalism, Anti-Semitism*. New York: Karz-Cohl Publishing, 1982

Cohn, Norman, *Warrant for Genocide*. Chico, California: Scholar Press, 1981

Comay, Joan, *The Diaspora Story*. N. Y.: Random House, 1980

Cuddihy, J.M., *The Ordeal of Civility*. New York: Delta, 1974

Curry, Jane Leftwich, *The Black Book of Polish Censorship*. New York: Random House, 1984

Czapliński Władysław, ed., *The Polish Parliament at the Summit of Its Development: 16th - 17th Centuries*. Wrocław, Warsaw, Cracow, Łódź: Ossolineum, 1985

Davies, Norman, *God's Playground: A History of Poland*. New York: Columbia University Press, 1982

Davies, Norman, *Heart of Europe: A Short History of Poland*. Oxford: Clarendon Press, 1984.

Davies, Norman, *White Eagle, Red Star: The Polish-Soviet War, 1919-1920*. London: McDonald & Co. Ltd. 1972

de Lange, Nicholas, *Atlas of the Jewish World*. Facts on File Publications, New York, 1984

Dodd, Martha, *Through Embassy Eyes*. New York: Harcourt, Brace and Co. 1939

Dziewanowski, M. K., *Poland in the Twentieth Century*. New York: Colombia University Press, 1977

Dziewanowski, M.K., *War at Any Price, World War II In Europe, 1939-1945*. Second edition. Englewood Cliffs, New Jersey: Prentice Hall, 1991, 1987

Feuer, Lewis S., *The Scientific Intellectual - The Psychological & Sociological Origins of Modern Science*. New York: Basic Books, 1963

Fishman, Samuel, *The Polish Ranaissance in Its European Context*. Bloomington, Indiana: Polish Institute of Arts and Sciences of America and Indiana University Press, 1988

Fuks, Marian and others, *Polish Jewry: History and Culture*. Warsaw: Interpress Publishers,1982

Gieysztor, Aleksander; Kieniewicz, Stefan; Roztworowski, Emanuel; Tazbir, Janusz; Wereszycki, Henryk, *History of Poland*. Warsaw: PWN – Polish Scientific Publishers, 1979

Gitelman, Z., *Jewish Nationality and Soviet Politics*. Princeton, N.J.: Princeton University Press, 1972

Goldberg, Jacob, *Jewish Privileges in the Polish Commonwealth*. Jerusalem: The Israel Academy of Sciences and Humanities, 1985

Gross, Jan T., *Revolution from Abroad: The Soviet Conquest of Poland's Western Ukraine and Western Byelorussia*. Princeton, N.J.: Princeton University Press, 1988

Gross, Jan T. and Grudzińska-Gross, Irena, *Poland and Russia*, (Polska a Rosja 1939-1942.). London: An-eks, 1983

A Guide: *Scenes of Fighting and Martyrdom, War Years in Poland 1939-1945*. Warsaw: Council for the Preservation of Monuments to Resistance and Martyrdom, 1968

Gutman, Y., *The Jews of Warsaw 1939-1943: Ghetto, Underground, Revolt*. Bloomington: Indiana University Press, 1982

Halevi, I., *A History of the Jews*. London: Zed Books, 1987

Haskins, C.H. & Lord, R.H., *Some Problems of the Peace Conference*. Cambridge: Harvard University Press, 1920

Heller, C.S., *On the Edge of Destruction*. New York: Columbia University Press, 1977

Hertz, Aleksander, *The Jews in Polish Culture*. Evanston, IL 60201, North Western University Press, 1988.

Hilberg, R., *The Destruction of the European Jews*. New York: Holmes and Meier, 1985

Iranek-Osmecki, Kazimierz, *He Who Saves One Life*. New York: Crown Publishers, Inc. 1971

Jędruch, Jacek, *Constitutions, Elections, and Legislatures of Poland, 1493-1977: A Guide to Their History*. Washington, D.C.: University Press of America, Inc., 1982

Jędrzejewicz, Wacław, *Piłsudski: A Life for Poland*. New York: Hippocrene Books, Inc. 1982

Johnson, P., *A History of the Jews*. New York: Harper & Row, 1987

Karski, Jan, *The Great Powers & Poland: 1919-1945, From Versailles to Yalta*. Lanham, MD.: University Press of America, TM Inc., 1985

Krall, H., *Shielding the Flame: An Intimate Conversation with Dr. Marek Edelman, the Last Surviving Leader of the Warsaw Ghetto Uprising.* New York: Henry Holt, 1986

Kaplan, Chaim A., *Warsaw Diary.* New York: Collier Books, 1973

Katz, J., *From Prejudice to Destruction / Anti-Semitism, 1700-1933.* Cambridge: Hravard Univesity Press, 1980

Kielar, Wiesław, *Anus Mundi: 1500 Days in Auschwitz/Birkenau.* New York: New York Times Book Co., 1980

Kieniewicz, Stefan, et al., *History of Poland.* Warsaw: P.W.N., 1979

Klier, John Doyle, *Russia Gathers Her Jews.* Dekalb Illinois: Northern University Press, 1986

Korboński, Stefan, *The Polish Underground State: A Guide to the Underground 1939-1945.* New York: Hippocrene Books, Inc., 1978, 1981

Korboński, Stefan, *Jews and Poles in World War II.* New York. Hippocrene Books. 1989

Lerski, George J. and Lerski Halina, eds., *Jewish-Polish Coexistence, 1772-1939: A Topical Bibliography.* Westport, Ct.: Greenwood Press, 1986

Leshem, Moshe, *Balaam's Curse.* New York: Simon and Schuster, 1989

Laqueur, W., *The Terrible Secret / The Suppression of the Truth About Hitler's Final Solution.* Boston: Little, Brown, 1981

Lestchinsky, J., *Crisis, Catastrophe, and Survival: A Jewish Balance Sheet, 1914-1948.* New York: Institute of Jewish Affairs of the World Jewish Congress, 1948

Levine, Isaac, Don, *Eyewitness to History.* New York: Hawthorn Books, Inc., 1973

Lewin, Abraham, *A Diary of the Warsaw Ghetto.* New York: Basil Blackwell Inc. 1988

Lewin, Isaac, *The Jewish Community in Poland.* New York: Philosophical Library, 1985

Lewis, Bernard, *Semites and Anti-Semites.* New York: W.W. Norton and Co, 1986

Litvinoff, Barbet, *The Burning Bush: Anti-Semitism and World History.* London: Collins, 1988

Lukas, R.C., *Bitter Legacy / Polish-American Relations in the Wake of World War II.* Lexington: Univeristy Press of Kentucky, 1992

Lukas, Richard C., *Forgotten Holocaust: The Poles Under German Occupation, 1939-1944.* Lexington, Ky.: The University Press of Kentucky, 1986

Miłosz, Czesław, *History of Polish Literature.* London: Macmillan Co., 1969

Moczarski, Kazimierz, *Conversations With an Executioner: An Incredible 255-day Long Interview With the Man Who Destroyed the Warsaw Ghetto.* Englewood Cliffs, N.J.: Prentice-Hall, Inc., 1981

Mosley, Leonard, *On Borrowed Time - How World War II Began.* New York: Random House, 1969

Myant, M., Poland: *A Crisis for Socialism.* London: Lawrence & Wishart, 1982

Niezabitowska, Malgorzata, *Remnants: The Last Jews in Poland.* New York: Friendly Press, 1986

Nova, Fritz, *Alfred Rosenberg - Nazi Theorist of the Holocaust.* New York: Hippocrene Books Inc. 1986

Oliner, Samuel P. and Pearl M., *The Altruistic Personality: Rescuers of Jews in Nazi Europe.* New York: Free Press, 1988

Oliver, Revilo P., *Conspiracy or Degeneracy?* New York: Power Products, Publishers, 1967

Olszer, Krystyna M. ed., *For Your Freedom and Ours.* New York: Frederic Ungar Publishing Co. 1981

Patai, R., *The Jewish Mind,* New York: Scribner's Sons. 1977

Pease, N., *Poland, the United States, and the Stabilization of Europe, 1919-1933,* New York: Oxford University Press. 1986

Piłsudski Institute. *Niepodległość.* Volume XXI. N. York: 1988

Pipes, Richard, *The Russian Revolution.* New York: Alfred A. Knopf: 1990

Pipes, Richard, *Russia Observed. Catherine II and the Jews.* San Francisco: 1975

Pogonowski, Iwo Cyprian, *Poland: A Historical Atlas.* New York: Hippocrene Books Inc., 1987

Proch, F.J., *Poland's Way of the Cross: 1939-1945.* New York: Polish Association of Former Political Prisoners of Nazi and Soviet Concentration Camps, 1987

Reinhold, Meyer, *Diaspora: The Jews among the Greeks and Romans.* Sarasota: Samuel Stevens and Co. 1983

Reitlinger, Gerald *The SS - Alibi of a Nation 1922-1945.* Englewood Cliffs, New Jersey, Prentice-Hall, Inc. 1981 (1956)

Ringelblum, E., *Notes from the Warsaw Ghetto: The Journal of Emmanuel Ringelblum.* New York: McGraw-Hill, 1958

Ringelblum, E., *Polish-Jewish Relations During the Second World War.* New York: Fertig, 1976

Rosman, M. J., *The Lords' Jews: Magnate-Jewish Relations in the Polish-Lithuanian Commonwealth during the Eighteenth Century.* Cambridge, Mass., Harvard University Press, 1990

Sanders, R., *Shores of Refuge / A Hundred Years of Jewish Emigration.* New York: Henry Holt, 1988

Shatyn, B., *A Private War: Surviving on False Papers, 1941-1945.* Detroit: Wyane State University Press, 1985

Shipler, D.K., *Arab and Jew / Wounded Spirits in a Promised Land.* New York: Penguin, 1987

Singer, I.B., *Love and Exile.* New York: Doubleday, 1984

Stankiewicz, W. J., ed., *The Tradition of Polish Ideals.* London: Orbis Books, Ltd., 1981

Stern, Fritz, *Dreams and Delusions - The Drama of German History.* New York, Alfred A. Knopf. 1987

Steven, Stewart, *The Poles*. New York: Macmillan Publishing Co., Inc. 1982

Steven, Stewart, *The Spy-Mastres of Israel*. New York: Macmillan Publishing Co. Inc., 1980
Sukhanov (Himmer), Nikolai Nikolayevich, *The Russian Revolution 1917*. Princeton, New Jersey, Princeton University Press, 1955

Szasz, T.S., "Justifying Coercion Through Theology and Therapy," in J.K. Zeig, *The Evolution of Psychotherapy*. New York: Brunner/Mazel, 1987

Tazbir, Janusz, *A State without Stakes - Polish Religious Toleration in the Sixteenth and Seventeenth Centuries*. Warsaw: P.I.W. 1973

Tcherikover, Victor, *Hellenistic Civilization and the Jews*. New York: Atheneum, 1975

Tec, Nechama, *In Lion's Den. The Life of Oskar Rufeisen*. New York: Oxford University Press. 1990

Tec, Nechama, *When Light Pierced the Darkness: Righteous Christians and the Polish Jews*. New York: Oxford University Press, 1986

Vinecour, Earl, *Polish Jews: The Final Chapter*. New York: McGraw-Hill Book Company

Wagner, W.J. et al., *Polish Law Throughout the Ages: One Thousand Years of Legal Tought in Poland*. Stanford: Hoover Institution Press, 1970

Wandycz, P.S., *The United States and Poland*. Cambridge: Harvard University Press, 1980

Wasserstein, Bernard, *Britain and the Jews of Europe 1939-1045*. Institute of Jewish Affairs, London, Oxford University Press, Oxford, New York, 1988

Watt, Richard M., *Bitter Glory: Poland and Its Fate*. New York: Simon and Schuster, 1979

Wechsler, Lawrence, *Solidarity: Poland in the Season of Its Passion*. New York: Simon and Schuster, 1982

Weinberg, Gerhard L., *The Foriegn Policy of Hitler's Germany - Starting World War II, 1937-1939*. Chicago and London: The University of Chicago Press, 1980

Wienryb, B.D., *The Jews of Poland / Social and Economic History of the Jewish Community in Poland from 1100 to 1800*. Philadelphia: Jewish Publication Society of America, 1972

Willenberg, Samuel, *Surviving Treblinka*. New York: Basil Blackwell Inc. 1989

Wirth, Andrzej, *The Stroop Report: The Jewish Quarter of Warsaw Is No More*. New York: Pantheon Books, 1979

Wyka, K., *Życie na niby*. Warsaw: Książka i Wiedza, 1959

Wyman, D.S., *The Abandonment of the Jews*. New York: Pantheon, 1984

Zajączkowski, Wacław *Martyrs of Charity*. Washington, D.C. St. Maximillian Kolbe Foundation, Vol. 1: 1987 and Vol. 1989

Zawodny, J.K., *Death in the Forest - The Story of the Katyń Forest Massacre*, Hippocrene Books, 1988

Zeman, Z.A.B., *Germany and the Revolution in Russia 1915-1918*. London, Oxford University Press, 1958

Zeman, Z.A.B. and Scharlau, W.B., *The Merchant of Revolution - The Life of Alexander Israel Helphand (Pravus)*. London, Oxford University Press, 1965

JOURNALS:

Canadian Psychiatr. Assoc. Journal (Supp. II, 1972), "On Human Territoriality: A Contribution to Instinct Theory," by G.J. Sarwer-Foner

Canadian Slavic Papers, Spring 1971, "Tolerance and Intolerance in Old Poland" by W. Weintraub

Commentary March 1987, "The Curious Case of Marek Edelman" by L.S. Dawidowicz

Daedalus, Spring 1987, "Jews as a Polish Problem" by A. Smolnar

Institute for Polish-Jewish Studies, Oxford, "Polin: A Journal of Polish-Jewish Studies Vol. I, 1986, Vol. II, 1987, Vol. III, 1988, Vol. IV, 1989, and Vol. V, 1990. New York: Basil Blackwell Inc.

Institute for Polish-Jewish Studies, Oxford. "Polin: A Journal of Polish-Jewish Studies Vol. II, 1987. New York: Basil Blackwell Inc., "Dmowski, Paderewski, and American Jews" by George J. Lerski

Journal of Contemporary History, vol. X, no July, 3, 1975, H. W. Koch, "The Spectre of a Separate Peace in the East: Russo-German 'Peace Feelers,' 1942-44.

Midstream, A Monthly Jewish Review, New York: Hertzl Press, August-September, 1983 and February, 1984, "Is Polish Anti-Semitism Special?" by Henryk Grynberg

Midstream, A Monthly Jewish Review, New York: Hertzl Press, April and May, 1988 and January 1991, "Collective Guilt of the Poles -- An Appeal from a Frustrated Philosemite" by George Lerski

New York Review of Books, Dec. 19, 1985, "The Life of Death" by T. G. Ash

New York Review of Books, New York, Nov. 20, 1986, "The Survivor's Voice" by N. Davies

Polish Institute of Arts and Sciences of America. New York: A Quarterly: "The Polish Review." Special Issue: Polish-Jewish Cultural Relations. Vol. XXXII, No. 4, 1987 New York: A Quarterly: "The Polish Review." Vol. XXXVI, No. 4, 1991, New York, "May 3, 1791, and the Polish Constitutional Tradition" by W.J. Wagner

Psychiatry Journal University of Ottawa (1979) "On Social Paranoia -- The Psychotic Fear of the Stranger and He Who is Alien," by G.J. Sarwer-Foner

"Soviet Jewish Affairs," Vol. 5, No.2, 1975. The Institute of Jewish Affairs, Ltd., "Catherine II and the Jews: The Origins of the Pale of Settlement." by Richard Pipes

Tikkun 36 (May/June 1987), "Poland and the Jews: An Interview with Czesław Miłosz"

YIVO Annual of Social Science, 151 (1958), "The Lublin Reservation and the Madagascar Policy" by P. Friedman

a oseph iłsudski

Artur Szyk, *The Statute of Kalisz, Engravings Dedicated to Józef Piłsudski*

PART II

ILLUSTRATIONS

JEWS IN POLISH PAINTINGS

AND

JEWISH PRESS IN POLAND

SAMPLES OF TITLES AND HEADLINES

Marcin Bielski (1495 -1575), *History of the Entire World*, Patriarch Abraham, engraving

184

Arthur Szyk, *The Statute of Kalisz*, Jewish minters striking the first Polish coins, in the tenth and eleventh centuries, engraving

Artur Szyk, *The Statue of Kalisz*, Bolesław Pobożny Signs the Statute of Kalisz, 1264 , engraving

Artur Szyk, *The Statute of Kalisz,* English version, engraving

187

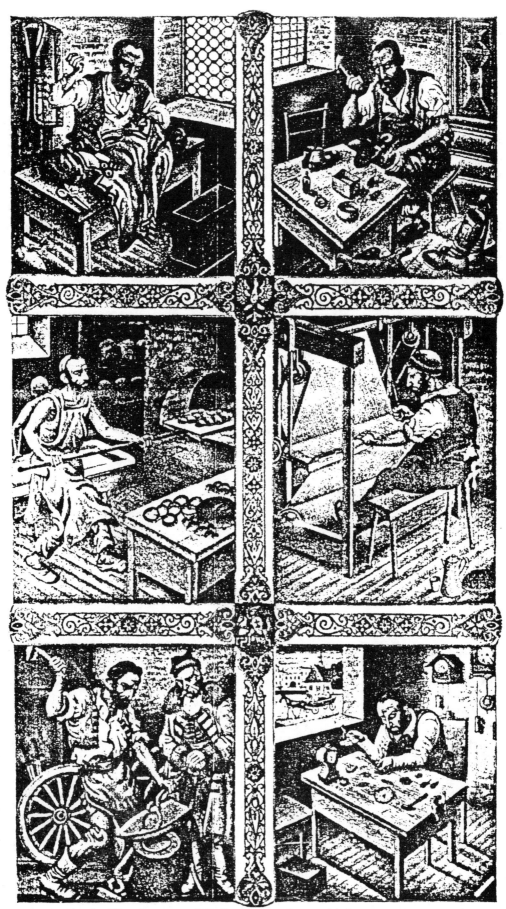

Artur Szyk, The Statute of Kalisz, Jews in crafts in Poland, engraving

Artur Szyk, *The Statute of Kalisz*, Jews merchants in Gdańsk, engraving

Artur Szyk, (1894-1951) *The Statute of Kalisz Illuminated*, engraving

Artur Szyk, *The Statute of Kalisz*, Jews at the Court of Casimir the Great, engraving

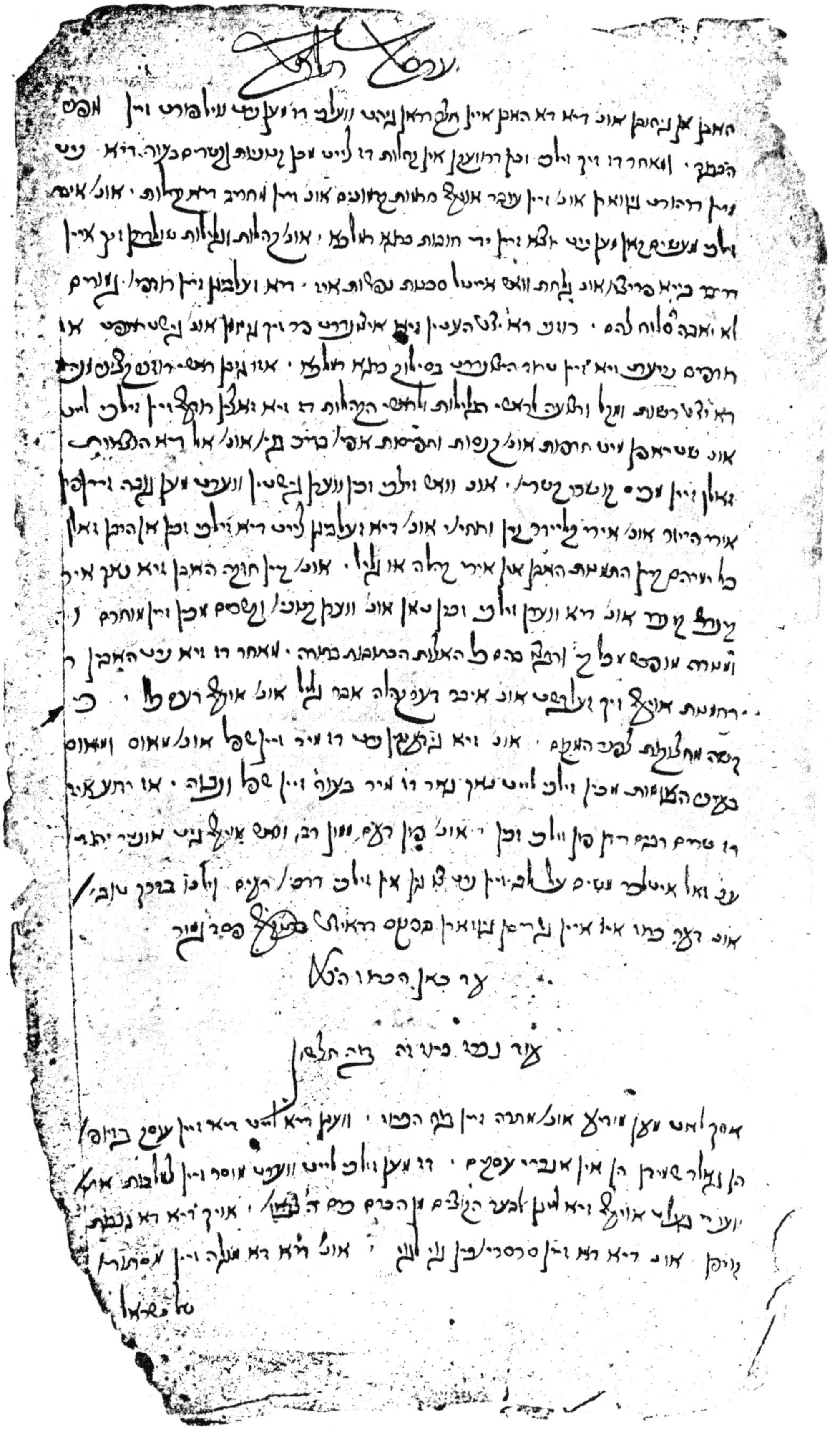

האבן אן נעמן אונ דיא דא האבן אין חלק ראן נעבט וועלב רי ועלכטי שילורט וין אפש
הבתך · ואחרי דו זיך ולב וכך רמושען אין נעלות דו ליט צ'ך נעטוף ושרם בעוה.דיא עש
זיך רהורש שואת אונ זיך עבר אונך מהות קדונעם אונ זיך אחרב רוא קלות · אונ אים
ואוב עשישפ אן ען עט אלא זיך יר חומת כתא ואלא · אונ קרלות ונקרות סלבן וך אין
חזב ביא פריבא אונ נלחת וואס ארוו סכמת נפ'וא'אונ · ריא ועלבן נ'ך חומ'/ נ'ורים
לא יאהב פלות לדם · רנ'ט רא'נלהעזין נ'א אילוורב בר'וך ענוך אונ נפ'שחבש או
חודם ועעט וא'זיך שחר סאענ'ורב בי'ון מ'א חולא · אוו'נעו ואש'רוב'ן ג'בן ועב
רא'וא'ר'רשות ועף ואלעב'ארא'- תל'לות ואהב'ה'רלות דו ויא ואלכ'ן ראק'איי'ן וילוב לש
אונ ט'ראא'ך ליט חסהות אונ נפשות · וחפ'סת אפ'/'ברב בך'/אונ'/ או'ראא הל'אות'נ
נאן זין דב'- ע'וטבך פ'שר'- אוו ווא'וילב וכך'ועבך'ב'שוין'וועבי'עך נעבב'וי'ק'פך
אור היוד אונ איר עלירו'נך וחת'יל'אונ'ריא ועל'בן'ליט ריא'ז'ילב'וכך'אך'א'הך'ואך
בל ייחרפ'רך הא'אות האבן אך איר אלה או נל'יל · אונ'ן'ך חפ'ך האבן ראא ויא טאן איך
ענ'ב'ק'עב'אונ ריא ונעך ו'ילב'וכך'אך'אוב'ונעך ק'ב'ב'וטב'/ נ'שסם'אבך'זן'צוחרפ'וי
ואוחת עוכש'א'ב'ך'ורפא בר'ם'בל האלת הבחמות במ'ה · לאחר'רו'ויא'עב'האבן'/'ק
רחמות אוק'וין'ועל'בפ'אוו'איבב'רעע'על'ה'אבר'נ'ל'ל'אונ'אוק'עש'ל' כ
נשא אחל'ול'ת'לפ'ב'העם · אונ'ויא'נ'ק'שן'ט'ר'דו'איר'ו'ך'א'ל'אוב'/'אאוס'ואוס
בעט'הצ'וות'אבך'ו'לב'ל'יט'שאך'נ'יר'דו'איר'בע'וה'וין'א'ל'ונע'ה · או'יחע'א'ו
דו'שרח'ונ'פ'רק'ק'ין'וי'לב'וכך'-'אוב'/'פ'ך'רק'מ'וין'רב'וסש'ע'ע'ל'בע'ט'אונ'ב'י'חד
עב'ואל'אולבר'עע'ם'על'ה'וין'ע'ב'ב'ל'אך'א'ך'וילב'רחס'/'חנ'יש · ואלא'ן'בדק'ע'לב'/
אונ'רף'כ'מו'א'ל'א'ין'ע'ר'ן'שואך'בס'טפ'ה'ולא · מ'שט'י'פ'ב'ד'/ע'ר

עד'ט'ן'הכח'ד'הבא

עד'נכד'ב'ד'ה'בת'חל'ב'ל

א'ך'לאש'ען'וד'א'צ'ורא'אוב'/'אתדה'ו'ך'ב'ה'הבד · ו'ע'ך'ר'א'ל'בט'ד'א'ו'ך'ע'ם'ב'ו'י'ם'/
ה'ן'נ'ל'ורר'ה'ך'ה'ן'אין'א'ב'ב'י'ע'פ'ך · דו'וע'ך'ו'לב'ליט'וועב'/'ע'וסר'וין'ל'ו'ב'ת'אנ'א
ועע'ר'בע'ל'אורא'וי'א'לן'ובע'ה'ל'ב'בם'ו'ה'בר'ם'מ'ס'ד'ב'צ'ל'/ · א'ך'ך'ר'א'ר'א'נ'ט'נ
ניק'ן'אונ'רא'רא'וך'ן'ק'ש'ל'בן'ע'ל'ע'ל'ן · אונ'ר'א'רא'על'ה'וין'ע'ש'ת'ל
ט'ל'ב'אאו'ל

Menora at the Central Synagogue at the Jewish Cemetery in Lublin, engraving

Gniezno Cathedral Ornamental Door Element - *The Slave Trade*

Tadeusz Popiel, *The Feast of the Torah*

Von den Jü-
den vnd jren
Lügen.

D. M. Luth.

Gedruckt zu Wittemberg/
Durch Hans Lufft.

M. D. XLIII.

Martin Luther (1483-1546), Father of the Reformation in Germany.
On Jews and Their Lies
Title page of the most virulent of Luther's anti-Jewish pamphlets, Wittenburg 1543

Luther publicized his arguments by pamphlets and translated both New and Old testament into German. A protest of six principalities and 14 towns in 1529 on behalf of Luther originated the term "Protestantism." Luther advocated burning of synagogues, destroying Jewish houses, confiscating of Jewish prayerbooks and Talmud as well as all cash, silver and gold owned by Jews. Rabbis were to be prohibited to teach, Jews to travel and to lend money. For centuries no one in Polish literature has ever written in such an inflammatory way against Jews.

195

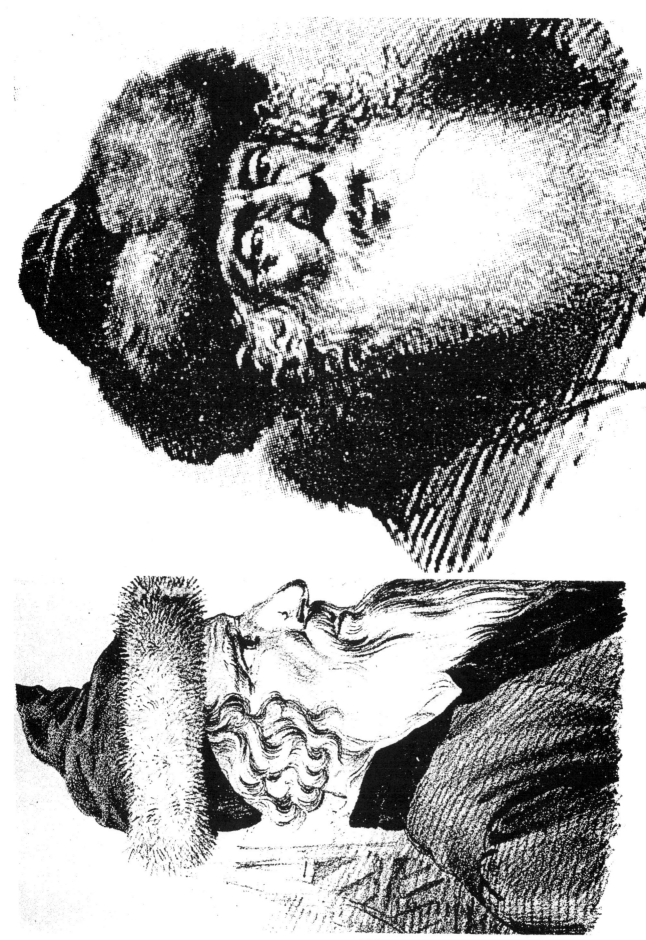

Jan Feliks Piwarski, *Head of a Jew*, a lithograph

Kysztalewicz, *Lithuanian Jew*, a lithograph

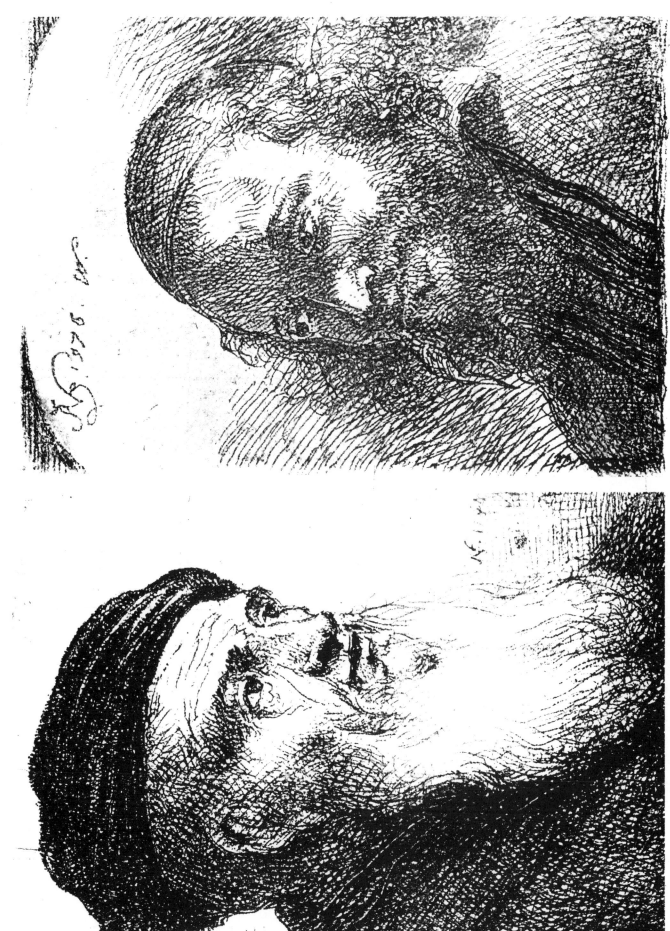

Jean Pierre Norblin, *Head of an Older Jew, an* etching

Jean Pierre Norblin, *Smiling Jew, a* 1776 etching

Jan Matejko: "Arrival of Jews to Poland" (oil painting)

Zygmunt Vogel, *The Synagogue in Łańcut*, an ink drawing

Photograph: *Shtetl in Szydłów*

200

Photograph: Kazimierz Dolny, Fajersztajn's Granary

201

Wojciech Grabowski, *Jewish Wedding*, 1878

Photograph: Kraków, *Jewish Town of Kazimierz*

203

Aleksander Gierymski, *Jews Praying*

204

Władysław Skoczylas, Shtetl Market, Kazimierz Dolny

Shtetl or miasteczko (myas-tech-ko) Staszów

The Yiddish word *shtetl* was popularized in the Polish language by Isaac Bashevis Singer when his novels and short stories were translated into Polish in 1960s. Until then the Polish population was unfamiliar with it despite centuries of presence of Jewish masses in Poland, for whom it was a common word. The word *shtetl* was not used in the pre-war homes of assimilated Jewish intelligentsia who, besides Polish, used proper German, rather than Yiddish. This fact exemplifies the profound cultural gap which existed for centuries between the Jewish masses and the rest of the population of Poland. The word *shtetl* (usually pronounced shtey-tel) is a diminutive of the word *shtot* or "town." Poles usually called it "a small Jewish town" or *miasteczko żydowskie* (myas-tech-ko zhi-dos-ke). The *shtetl* was a unique Jewish phenomenon formed in Poland long before the partitions (1772-1795). German genocide of the Jews in 1940-1944 brought a tragic end to the small Jewish towns in Poland. Now *shtetls* live only in the literature and in anthropological writings. Once they were the places where the Scriptures were studied, provincial backwaters with muddy often unpaved streets. In them Catholic monasteries and churches were surrounded by Jewish dwellings because the vast majority of *shtetl* population was Jewish. The *shtetl* was a typical element of the Polish landscape, especially in central Poland and in the eastern borderlands known as "Kresy." Stetls played a fundamental role in recognizing, understanding, and experiencing Jewish identity. Its patriarchal elders were embodying Jewish values and were dedicated to the traditional Jewish religion. The heritage of *shtetls* gave roots to the majority of contemporary Jews. The destruction of the *shtetls* became a symbol of the disappearance of the Jewish patriarchal world in Poland. The inter-war *shtetl* was invaded by waves of Polonization and secularization -- a place of dispute between traditional faith, Zionism, and socialism intermingled with words of longing for Jerusalem.

Aleksander Gierymski, *Loading River Sand, an oil painting*

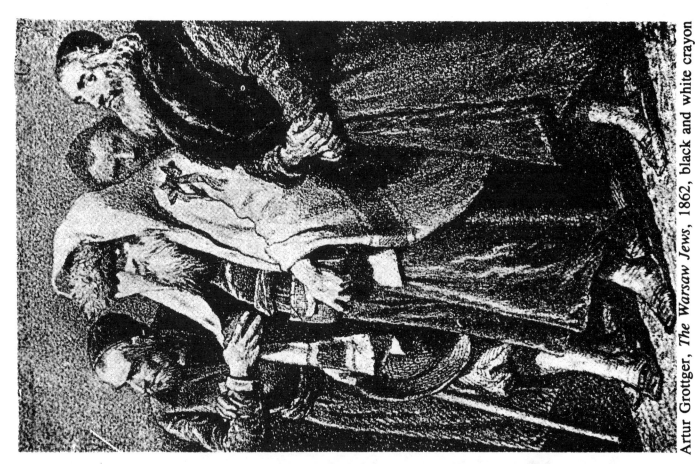

Artur Grottger, *The Warsaw Jews*, 1862, black and white crayon

Jacek Malczewski, *The Sage*, charcoal and white chalk on cardboard

Wincenty Smorakowski, *Jewish Wedding*, a detail

209

Old Szapsa with Matches, a zincograph

Return from Auction, a zincograph

Money Lenders, a zincograph
Jan Feliks Piwarski

The Pawnbroker from Jelen, a zincograph

210

Elwiro Andreoli, *Jankiel's Patriotic Concert, 1812*

Władysław Podkowinski, *Street in Siennica Shtetl*, an oil painting

212

Tadeusz Rybkowski, *The Jewish School*

Old Synagogue of Kazimierz, Kraków, Photograph

Kajetan Wincenty Kielisiński, *Synagogue in Przeworsk*, 1838

Anonymous, *Inaguration of the New Synagogue in Warsaw*, 1878

Artur Szyk, *Jew Michał Landy Holding The Cross*, Warsaw, Apr. 12, 1861
(taken from a fallen friend, shortly before Landy's own death)

Friedreich Nietzsche
(1844-1900)
Philosopher, poet, and
classical scholar

Nietzsche formulated a revolutionary theory about nature and civilization in which he contrasted two basic human tendencies: a desire for order and clarity, on one hand, and a drive toward a wild, irrational disorder, on the other. He criticized all religion and proclaimed that "God is dead." He tried to re-evaluate all values in light of the "will to power" to control one's own passions the way it is done by ascetics and artists. Such men Nietzsche called *overman* or *superman* as contrasted with *undermen* or *subhumans*. He said "men are not equal." In 1870 Nietzsche became the close friend of Richard Wagner. However, soon he disapproved of Wagner's mythological operas as disorienting Germans and leading to German national megalomania. Their friendship ended in hostility.

Nietzsche resented misuse of his terminology, radical ideas, and criticism of religion. Will Durant summarized Nietzsche's reaction:

"Protestantism and beer have dulled German wit; add, now, Wagnerian opera. As a result, 'the present-day Prussian is one of the most dangerous enemies of culture.' 'The presence of a German retards my digestion.' 'If, as Gibbon says, nothing but time -- though a long time -- is required for a world to perish; so nothing but time -- though still more time -- is required for a false idea to be destroyed in Germany.' When Germany defeated Napoleon it was as disastrous to culture as when Luther defeated the Church; thenceforward Germany put away her Goetes, her Schopenhauers and her Beethovens, and began to worship 'patriots;' '*Deutschland uber Alles* [Germany above all others] -- I fear that was the end of German philosophy.' 'We require an intergrowth of the German and Slav races; and we require, too, the cleverest financiers, the Jews, that we may become the masters of the world."

Nietzsche thought himself a Pole when he wrote:

"People will say, some day, that Heine [a Jew] and I [a Pole] were the greatest artists, by far, that ever wrote in German, and that we left the best any mere German could do an incalculable distance behind us." (Will Durant. *The Story of Philosophy*. New York 1926.) Heinrich Heine (1797-1856), lyric poet and literary critic, converted to Christianity in 1825. His books were burned on orders of the Nazi-German government in the 1930s.

Nietzsche, made solitary by illness, thought himself at war against the sluggishness and mediocrity of men. "Sensing that his time was running out, he no longer was content in being the witness. Nietzsche craved and claimed real influence -- to wield an ultimate veto, one held by the philosopher over his age.... In *Ecce Homo* (1888) he wrote: 'Even by virtue of my descent I am granted an eye beyond all merely local, merely national conditioned perspectives; it is not difficult for me to be a *good European*. On the other hand, I am perhaps more German than present day Germans, mere citizens of the German Reich could be -- I, the last *antipolitical* German. And yet my ancestors were Polish noblemen: I have many racial instincts from that source -- who knows? In the end perhaps even the *liberum veto*'.... He sought to exercise a veto as if in the Polish Diet by declaring: 'I disapprove.' He pronounced 'war to the Death against the House of [German Emperors] the Hohenzollern.' He issued epistles for the Polish nation to rise, a war council against the Reich, and execution of anti-Semites." (Peter Borgmann: *Nietzsche -- The Last Antipolitical German*. Indiana University Press, 1987.)

Nietzsche has unjustly suffered notoriety as a racist, anti-Semite, and forerunner of German Nazism and the Holocaust. German racists edited his writings and misinterpreted his ideas. German Nazis perverted them to commit some of the worst crimes in human history.

Ch. Burstin, *Theological Dispute*, (oil painting)

Mojżesz Rynecki, *Chess players*, a water color

Aleksander Lesser, *Burial of Five Demonstrators*, Warsaw, 1861, an oil painting

Piotr Michałowski, *Jews*, an oil painting

Bruno Schultz, *Self Portrait*, (pencil, 1919)   220

Bruno Schultz, *Visiting Sick Friend*, self portrait, 1926, a pencil drawing

Bruno Schultz, *Two Girls*, a pencil drawing

XIĘGA
BAŁWOCHWALCZA
GRAFIKI ORYGINALNE
BRUNONA SCHULZA

TREŚĆ:

Bruno Schultz: title page of *The Book on Idolatry*, and self portrait

Bruno Schultz: *Self Portrait*

Janusz Krajewski: "An Unexpected Guest" (oil painting)

Leopold Horowicz: *Portrait of Loepold Kronenberg*, (oil painting)

Romàn Kramsztyk, *Man Wearing Glasses*, an oil painting

Jacek Malczewski, Portrait of Dr. Józef Tislowitz, *Return from Siberia*, (oil painting)　224

Samuel Hirszenberg (1864-1908), portrait of *Dr. Anszel Siódmak*, an oil painting

Aleksander Kotsis (1885-1960), portrait of
Rabbi Józef Habner, (oil painting)

Ignacy Pinkas, *Tadeusz Epstein,*
President of Cracow Chamber of Commerce, (oil
painting)

Władysław Aer, *Miss S.,* a detail

Maurycy Gottlieb (1856-1879), *Young Jewess*

225

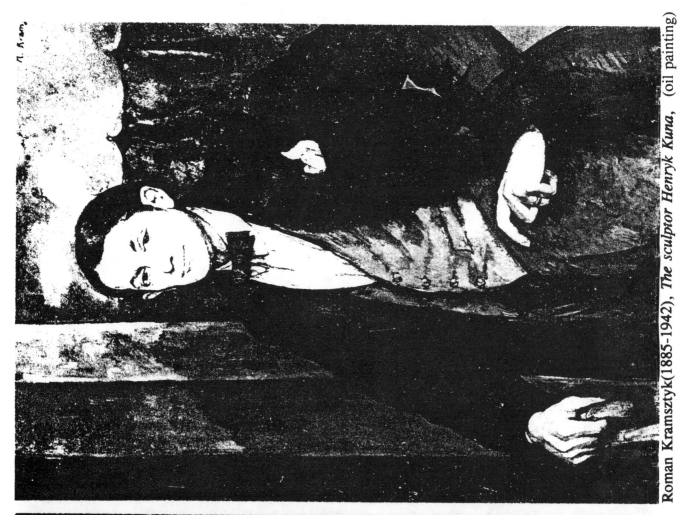

Roman Kramsztyk(1885-1942), *The sculptor Henryk Kuna*, (oil painting)

Janusz P. Janowski, portrait of *Józef Lewartowski*, (1895-1942), (oil)

Maria Blomberg (1883-1956), portrati of *Stanislaw Stern*,

oil on plywood

Józef Mehoffer(1864-1946), *Mrs. Zofia Minder*,

an oil painting

227

Edward Kokoszko (1900-1962), portrait of *Mrs. Krammer*, an oil painting

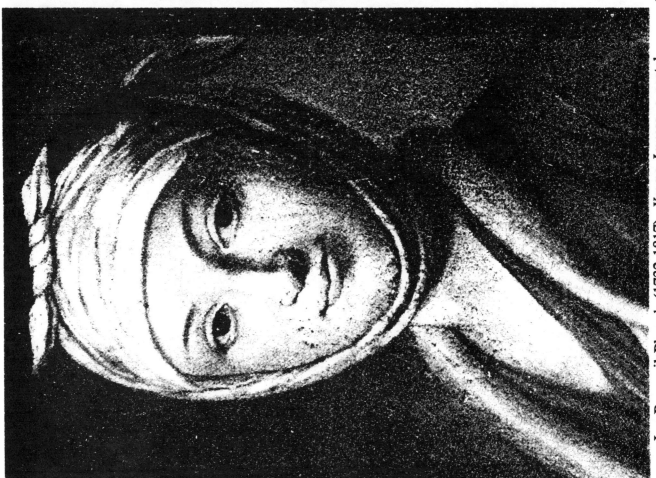

Jan Bogumił Plersch (1732-1817), *Young Jewess*, a pastel

228

Stanisław Ignacy Witkiewicz (Witkacy 1885-1939),
The poet Julian Tuwim, a pastel

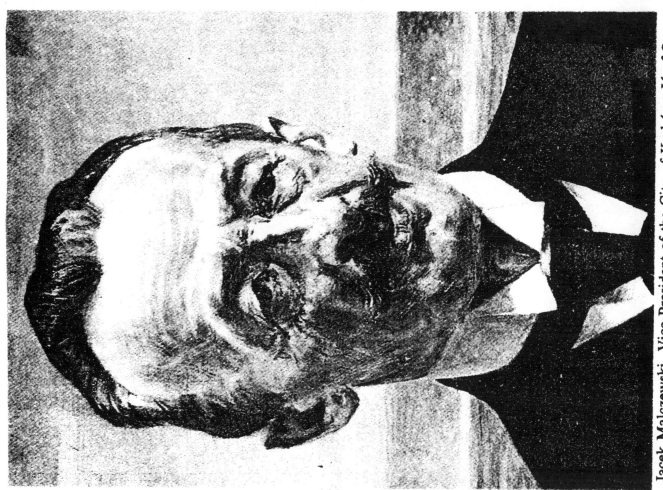

Jacek Malczewski, Vice-President of the City of Kraków, *Józef Sary*
(1850-1929)

Jakub Wienles (1870-1938), *On the Shores of Vistula*, a water color

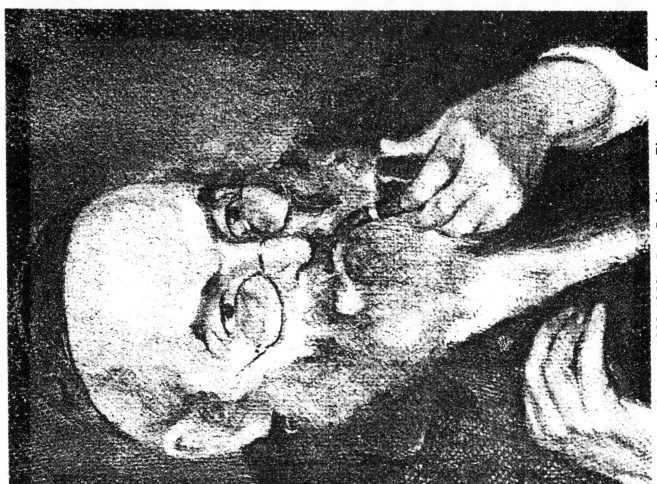

Leon Lewkowicz (1888-1950), *Jew Smoking a Pipe*, an oil painting

Józef Pankiewicz, *Jewish Porter with a Basket*

Stanisław Lentz: "Warsaw Newspaper-boy" (oil painting)

Józef Charyton (1910-1975),

Beating a Ghetto Escapee Before Execution,

Wysokie Litewskie, 1942

Józef Charyton, *Picture Taking*

(A common sight during WWII)

Artur Szyk, *German-Nazi Leadership Shown as a Human Garbage"*
title page *Ink and Blood* (sangwina)

Szmul Zygielbojm (1895-1943), member of Polish National Council in London, leader of the Bund. He committed suicide to protest the indifference of the Allies

Roman Kramsztyk, *A Jewish Family in the Ghetto*, 1942

235

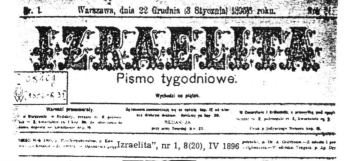

nr 20, 15 XI 1861

„Głos Żydowski", nr 1, 20 II 1917

„Izraelita", nr 1, 8(20), IV 1896

nr 102, 29 IV 1913

Tygodnik „Teater-Welt", nr 1-2, 8 X 1908

Ch. Z. Słonimski   N. Sokołów

„Unzer Leben", nr 255, 2 XI 1909

Dziennik „Der Weg", nr 37, 25 II 1908

Bundu „Lebens-Fragen", nr 47(95), 23 XI 1917

DI FRAJE JUGENT · פרײז 60 גראשן · דריטער יארגאנג נומער 4 ו

פרײַנע יוגנט

אילוסטרירטער חודש-ארגאן פאר דער פראלעטארישער יוגנט

W-wo, Kwiecien Maj 1926 · P. K. O. 9938 געלט-אדרעס: · 1926 וואַרשע, אַפּריל מאַי
Warszawa, Skrzynka-poczt. 561 · ביוראדרעס:

דער נומער האלט

20 זײַטן

אינהאלט:

„Di Fraje Jugent", 1926, nr 4-5

Der BLOFER · פרײז 25 גראשען · 4 · Nr. 38

בלאפער

וואכענבלאט פאר וויץ, הומאר אוז סאטירע

Warszawa, 13-go września · 1929

אלץ הײם א קריזיס!...

„Der Blofer", nr 38, 13 IX 1929.

אילוסטרירטע וואך

Warszawa, 20 Lutego 1924 · צווייטער יארגאנג נומער 8 (10)

„Ilustrirte Woch", nr 8(10), 28 II 1924. Sikorski

שיקארסקי ווידער בײַ דער מאכט

אזוי פיל אוית אין פאסאזשן

„Der Blofer"

Blagier

פרײז 60 גר. אוסלאנד: 20 סענטים · 40 זײַטן

№ 39-40 · 21 październ. 1938 · 21 אקטאבער 1938

ליטעראריטע בלעטער

אילוסטרירטע וואכנשריפט פאר ליטעראטור טעאטער און קונסט

„Literarisze Bleter", nr 39-40, 21 X 1938. Nr 750

238

"Hajnt", nr 277A, 5 XII 1929.

"Welt Szpigiel", nr 9, 28 II 1928

"Wochenszrift far Literatur, Kunst un Kultur" nr 86, 2 IX 1932.

"Unzer Ekspres", nr 49A, 26 II 1932

Naje Fołks-Cajtung", 132, 11 V 1935.

Dziennik "Frajnd", nr 53A, 26 VI 1934. Skonfiskowany

Dziennik "Naje Fołks-Cajtung", nr 173, 8 VI 1937. Skonfiskowany

m.in. Beck i amb. Kennard

"Der Moment", nr 191A, 5 IX 1939.

"Handels-Welt", nr 3, 16 II 1938.

Warszawer Radio", nr 94A, 12 VIII 1939.

"Hajntige Najes", nr 192, 20 VIII 1939.

PART III

ATLAS

JEWS IN POLAND

MAPS AND ANNOTATIONS

POLAND IN JEWISH HISTORY
A PERSPECTIVE

EARLY SETTLEMENT IN POLAND
966 -- 1264
THE CRUCIAL 500 YEARS
1264 -- 1795
UNFER FOREIGN RULE
ECONOMIC AND POLITICAL COMPETITION
1795 -- 1918
THE LAST BLOSSOMING
OF JEWISH CULTURE IN POLAND
1918 -- 1939
SHOAH -- THE GERMAN GENOCIDE
OF THE JEWS
1940 -- 1944
BRIHA
THE ESCAPE FROM EUROPE
1945 --

241

E. Grozdowski, *The Synagogue on Tłomackie Street in Warsaw*, wood engraving

A. Regulski, *The Synagogue in Włocławek*, wood engraving

242

POLAND IN

JEWISH HISTORY

A PERSPECTIVE

THE LEGAL STATUTES

OF JEWS IN

THE DIASPORA

THE UNIQUENESS OF POLAND'S

STATUTE OF JEWISH LIBERTIES

IT LASTED 500 YEARS

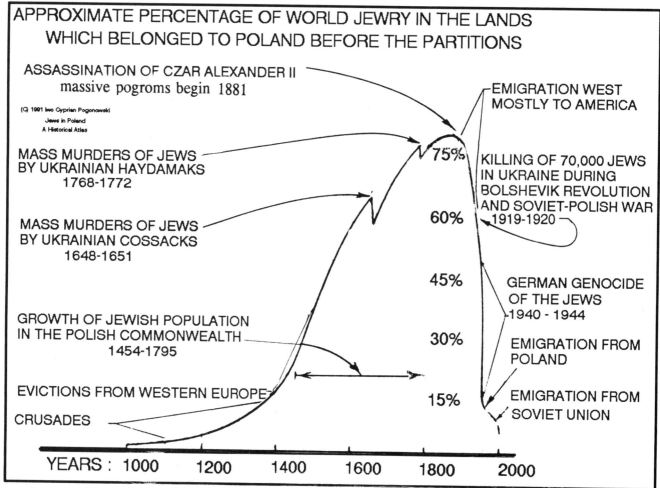

APPROXIMATE PERCENTAGE OF WORLD JEWRY IN THE LANDS WHICH BELONGED TO POLAND BEFORE THE PARTITIONS

ASSASSINATION OF CZAR ALEXANDER II
massive pogroms begin 1881

(C) 1991 Iwo Cyprian Pogonowski
Jews in Poland
A Historical Atlas

MASS MURDERS OF JEWS BY UKRAINIAN HAYDAMAKS 1768-1772

MASS MURDERS OF JEWS BY UKRAINIAN COSSACKS 1648-1651

GROWTH OF JEWISH POPULATION IN THE POLISH COMMONWEALTH 1454-1795

EVICTIONS FROM WESTERN EUROPE

CRUSADES

EMIGRATION WEST MOSTLY TO AMERICA

75%

KILLING OF 70,000 JEWS IN UKRAINE DURING BOLSHEVIK REVOLUTION AND SOVIET-POLISH WAR 1919-1920

60%

45%

GERMAN GENOCIDE OF THE JEWS 1940 - 1944

30%

EMIGRATION FROM POLAND

15%

EMIGRATION FROM SOVIET UNION

YEARS : 1000   1200   1400   1600   1800   2000

At best, the number of Jews in the world can only be estimated to show the broad outlines. The earliest estimates were very approximate. The fact that many European countries used a head tax to collect money from the Jews often resulted in low estimates by Jewish communities of the total number of their members. Thus, for example, in Poland, in the 1550's only about seven percent of the Jews paid the poll-tax.

The graph showing an approximate percentage of world Jewry in the lands which belonged to the Polish state before the partitions (1772-1795) includes the entire second millennium of the Christian Era. The graph includes the European period of Jewish history, when a vast majority of world Jewry lived in Europe.

The difficulties in estimatind the number of Jews in the past may be illustrated by the reports of Jewish losses during Cossack uprisings against Poland in 1648-51. Polish estimates are at about 120,000, while an Israeli textbook by H.H. Ben-Sasson, gives the total number of Jews shortly before 1648 in the Polish Ukraine as "51,325 residents, according to an official count."

Jews of the territory of pre-partitioned Poland evolved into a modern nation in the 19th and 20th centuries. They could do this because of the continuity of their settlement there, their numbers, a relatively complete social structure, and the unique parliamentary autonomy given to them earlier by the Republic of Polish Nobles.

Once the Polish State was partitioned and obliterated four distinct areas were created out of its territory. They were: the truncated Kingdom of Poland under the Czar, the Pale of Settlement (or confinement) in the other Polish provinces annexed by Russia, the Lesser Poland called "Galicia" by the Austrians, and the Greater Poland, Pomerania, and East Prussia annexed by the Berlin government. The conditions of Jewish communities in each of these areas were different. However, the estimates of the percentage of world Jewry living in these four areas by 1880 vary between 75% and 90%. The Ben-Sasson "History of the Jewish People," (mentioned above) gave the following numbers of Jews for 1880: Russia (four million), Austria-Hungary (one and a half million), Germany (550,000), the Ottoman Empire (300,000), and the United States of America (250,000).

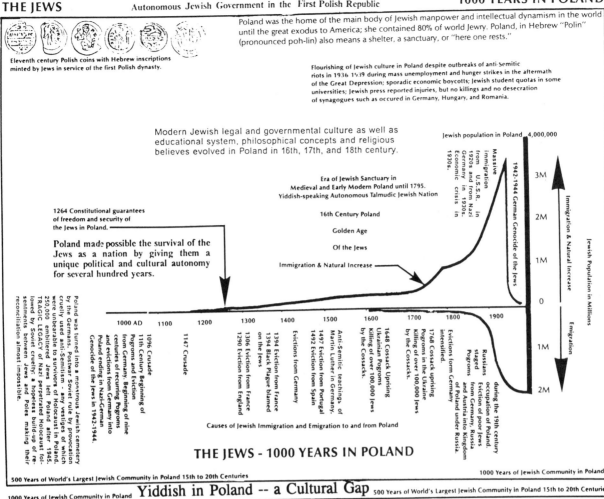

Eleventh century Polish coins with Hebrew inscriptions minted by Jews in service of the first Polish dynasty.

Poland was the home of the main body of Jewish manpower and intellectual dynamism in the world until the great exodus to America; she contained 80% of world Jewry. Poland, in Hebrew "Polin" (pronounced poh-lin) also means a shelter, a sanctuary, or "here one rests."

Flourishing of Jewish culture in Poland despite outbreaks of anti-Semitic riots in 1936–1939 during mass unemployment and hunger strikes in the aftermath of the Great Depression; sporadic economic boycotts; Jewish student quotas in some universities; Jewish press reported injuries, but no killings and no desecration of synagogues such as occured in Germany, Hungary, and Romania.

Modern Jewish legal and governmental culture as well as educational system, philosophical concepts and religious believes evolved in Poland in 16th, 17th, and 18th century.

Jewish population in Poland 4,000,000

Massive immigration from U.S.S.R. in 1920s and from Nazi Germany in 1930s. Economic crisis in 1930s.

1942–1944 German Genocide of the Jews

Era of Jewish Sanctuary in Medieval and Early Modern Poland until 1795. Yiddish-speaking Autonomous Talmudic Jewish Nation

16th Century Poland

Golden Age

Of the Jews

1264 Constitutional guarantees of freedom and security of the Jews in Poland.

Poland made possible the survival of the Jews as a nation by giving them a unique political and cultural autonomy for several hundred years.

Immigration & Natural Increase

Immigration & Natural Increase

Emigration

Jewish Population in Millions

3M / 2M / 1M / 0 / 1M / 2M

1000 AD 1100 1200 1300 1400 1500 1600 1700 1800 1900

Poland was turned into a monstrous Jewish cemetery by the Germans. Postwar Soviet rule by provocation cruelly used anti-Semitism - any vestiges of which were unbearable to survivors of Holocaust in Poland. 250,000 embittered Jews left Poland after 1945. TRAGIC LEGACY of Nazi perpetrated Holocaust followed by Soviet cruelty a hopeless build-up of resentments between Jews and Poles making their reconciliation almost impossible.

1096 Crusade 11th Century Beginning of Pogroms and Eviction from Germany. Beginning of nine centuries of recurring Pogroms and evictions from Germany into Poland ending in Nazi-German Genocide of the Jews in 1942-1944.

1147 Crusade

1306 Eviction from France 1290 Eviction from England

1394 Eviction from France 1394 Black Plague blamed on the Jews

Evictions from Germany

1497 Eviction from Portugal 1492 Eviction from Spain

Anti-Semitic teachings of Martin Luther in Germany.

1648 Cossack Uprising Ukrainian Pogroms Killing of over 100,000 Jews by the Cossacks.

1768 Cossack uprising Pogroms in the Ukraine Killing of over 100,000 Jews by the Cossacks.

Evictions from Germany intensified.

during the 19th century occupation of Poland. Eviction of poor Jews from Germany, Russia and Austria into Kingdom of Poland under Russia.

Russians staged Pogroms

Causes of Jewish Immigration and Emigration to and from Poland

THE JEWS - 1000 YEARS IN POLAND

500 Years of World's Largest Jewish Community in Poland 15th to 20th Centuries

1000 Years of Jewish Community in Poland

1000 Years of Jewish Community in Poland   ## Yiddish in Poland -- a Cultural Gap   500 Years of World's Largest Jewish Community in Poland 15th to 20th Centuries

Yiddish, a Judeo-German language, was the basic language spoken by the Jews in Poland until 1944. In national census of 1931 nearly ninety percent of the Jew reported that they did not speak Polish at home. Educated Jews were fluent in Polish and German but in general did not cultivate Yiddish language.

When the martyrdom of Polish Jews began under German occupation all of the Jews were condemned to death just because they were Jewish. Poland was the only country in Europe where the Germans established a death penalty for helping the Jews. Under this law entire Polish Christian families were executed for helping the Jews.

The hunt for the Jews organized by the Nazis was facilitated by hair and clothing styles of the Jews, lack of knowledge of unaccented Polish, and the fact that the Jews were the only people circumcised in Northern Europe.

Yiddish language came to Poland thousand years ago when it started forming as a high German dialect in the Rhine Basin. Large Jewish immigration in 14th century established Yiddish throughout Jewish communities in Poland. By the end of the 15th century an autonomous Talmudic school system was permitted in Poland. During the following 400 years Jews were educated (many of them since the age of three) in Talmudic schools. This resulted in a complete cultural isolation. Polish offers of emancipation with the right to continue in Jewish faith were rejected by Jewish leadership in 1569 and in 1764. In the Second Polish Republic (1918-1939) there was equality of all and there were 14% of Jews in the Polish parliament out of 9% of Jewish minority. Educated Jews constituted an important part of the leadership community of Polish culture

The medieval western anti-Semitism eventually culminated in the Nazi death camps. In comparison with the rest of Europe of the last 1000 years Poland has by far the best record of toleration towards the Jews as evidenced by mass migration of the Jews to Poland - even including in this perspective the most regrettable events of the thirties. Germany is responsible for the breakdowns in morality within Polish and Jewish community under wartime Nazi terror. The Soviets produced such breakdowns in 1939-1941 and from 1944 on. It should be noticed that the well educated people in Poland behaved unusually well under Nazi and Communist terror. Before the years 1936-9 anti-Semitism in Poland had characteristics of a "normal" ethnic antagonism between people of different language and culture. For the last 1000 years Christianity's preoccupation with the Jews took by far less drastic forms in Poland than it did in the other countries of Europe. Thus, for centuries some 80% of the world's Jews lived in Poland.

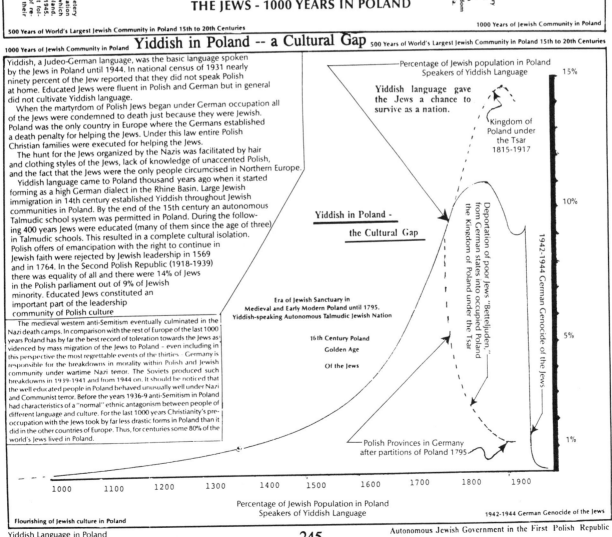

Percentage of Jewish population in Poland Speakers of Yiddish Language

15% / 10% / 5% / 1%

Yiddish language gave the Jews a chance to survive as a nation.

Kingdom of Poland under the Tsar 1815-1917

Yiddish in Poland - the Cultural Gap

Deportation of poor Jews "Betteljuden," from German states into occupied Poland the Kingdom of Poland under the Tsar

1942-1944 German Genocide of the Jews

Era of Jewish Sanctuary in Medieval and Early Modern Poland until 1795. Yiddish-speaking Autonomous Talmudic Jewish Nation

16th Century Poland

Golden Age

Of the Jews

Polish Provinces in Germany after partitions of Poland 1795

1000 1100 1200 1300 1400 1500 1600 1700 1800 1900

Percentage of Jewish Population in Poland Speakers of Yiddish Language

Flourishing of Jewish culture in Poland

1942-1944 German Genocide of the Jews

APPROXIMATE DEMOGRAPHIC GROWTH OF JEWS IN POLAND

THE CRITICAL YEARS OF WORLD JEWRY

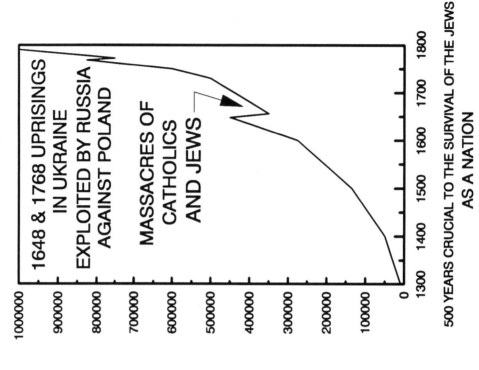

JEWISH MINORITY IN POLAND

1648 & 1768 UPRISINGS IN UKRAINE EXPLOITED BY RUSSIA AGAINST POLAND

MASSACRES OF CATHOLICS AND JEWS

500 YEARS CRUCIAL TO THE SURVIVAL OF THE JEWS AS A NATION

APPROXIMATE DEMOGRAPHY OF THE JEWS

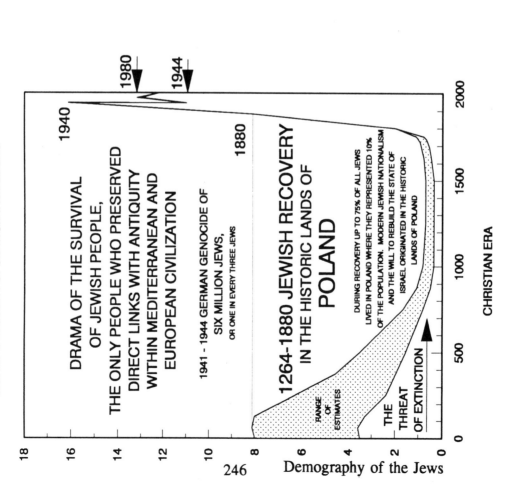

WORLD'S JEWISH POPULATION IN MILLIONS

1940

1980

1944

DRAMA OF THE SURVIVAL OF JEWISH PEOPLE, THE ONLY PEOPLE WHO PRESERVED DIRECT LINKS WITH ANTIQUITY WITHIN MEDITERRANEAN AND EUROPEAN CIVILIZATION

1941 - 1944 GERMAN GENOCIDE OF SIX MILLION JEWS, OR ONE IN EVERY THREE JEWS

1880

1264-1880 JEWISH RECOVERY IN THE HISTORIC LANDS OF POLAND

DURING RECOVERY UP TO 75% OF ALL JEWS LIVED IN POLAND WHERE THEY REPRESENTED 10% OF THE POPULATION. MODERN JEWISH NATIONALISM AND THE WILL TO REBUILD THE STATE OF ISRAEL ORIGINATED IN THE HISTORIC LANDS OF POLAND

RANGE OF ESTIMATES

THE THREAT OF EXTINCTION

CHRISTIAN ERA

246   Demography of the Jews

Demographic growth of Jews in Poland has been the most important element in the survival of Jewish people. During the period of Christian triumphalism in late medieval and early modern times, Jews lived as a minority in exile. Although Jews were a marginal and persecuted community in western Europe, Poland accepted and encouraged Jewish immigration. In Poland, Jewish life shifted from the periphery of western European society to a well-established position in which Jews prospered and grew in numbers. At the same time, Jews were eliminated in the rest of Europe. Thus, conceivably, Poland saved Jews from extinction.

During the era when individual and group identity was perceived in religious terms, the Jewish distinctiveness was seen by Jews and gentiles alike in a strictly religious context. At that time Poland, one of the great powers of Europe and the country with the largest territory, had been the most tolerant state on the European continent. Jews in Poland lived through a social revolution. They achieved social, economic, political, and cultural emancipation at a time when elsewhere they had to limit themselves to the traditional mechanism of Jewish accommodation and quietism.

Jewish culture was reshaped in Poland. Jewish leadership was conscious of the fact that the integration of Jews into the Italian and Spanish Renaissance had ended in catastrophe. Therefore, once in Poland, the Jews decided to keep to themselves and to isolate their community from the Christian environment. Thus, Polish Jews formed a deliberately isolated culture despite their important economic role and business contacts with the Christians in Poland.

During the turbulent history of the Polish state, both Poles and Jews lived through good and bad times. These experiences were reflected in the relations between Poles and Jews. During the golden age of Poland in the 15th, 16th and the first half of 17th centuries the Jewish community flourished. For centuries, the most important center of Jewish life was in Poland. During the Crusades Jewish immigrants came to Poland from Rhineland and Bohemia. The Black Death caused their expulsion from France. They were expelled from Spain and Portugal in 1492. Eventually, three-quarters of world Jewry lived in Poland. In the relative freedom of Poland, Jews produced a great flowering of intellectual and religious creativity as well as material prosperity.

Enlightenment and secularization changed European society. Jews appeared to be the great beneficiaries of the Enlightenment, Emancipation, and the Industrial Revolution. However, the problems of Jewish identity had not been solved by emancipation and liberalism. In fact, they were exacerbated during the 18th century decline of Poland and during her partitions in the 19th century. In this period the great Polish Jewish movements of Hasidism, socialism and Zionism arose in the historic lands of Poland.

Before World War II Jews were an economically and culturally powerful force in Poland. They had been a large part of the middle class. A third of Poland's lawyers and half of her doctors were Jewish. Jews had a strong representation in Poland's Parliament. Jewish culture flourished in Poland more than anywhere else. Anti-Semitic violence was opposed by the government. It was largely the work of small radical groups during and after the Great Depression. Poland had no anti-Jewish laws, except some restriction on kosher slaughtering.

The assimilation and integration of Jews into the German society during the second half of the 19th and the beginning of 20th centuries had ended in disaster. German aggression and World War II resulted in the greatest catastrophe of Poland's history. It brought even greater tragedy for Polish Jews. Their community of over three million was wiped out by German genocide while a numerically greater number of Polish Christians was killed. The losses of all Polish citizens approached 20 percent while the losses of Polish Jews approached 90 percent. Unfortunately the suffering inflicted by the Germans, and to considerable extent by the Soviets, resulted in mutual resentments. Many Jews talked about "Polish anti-Semitism without Jews" and about Poland, the "most anti-Semitic country in which anti-Semitism is transmitted together with mother's milk." Poles answered with pride in their historic tolerance and hospitality.

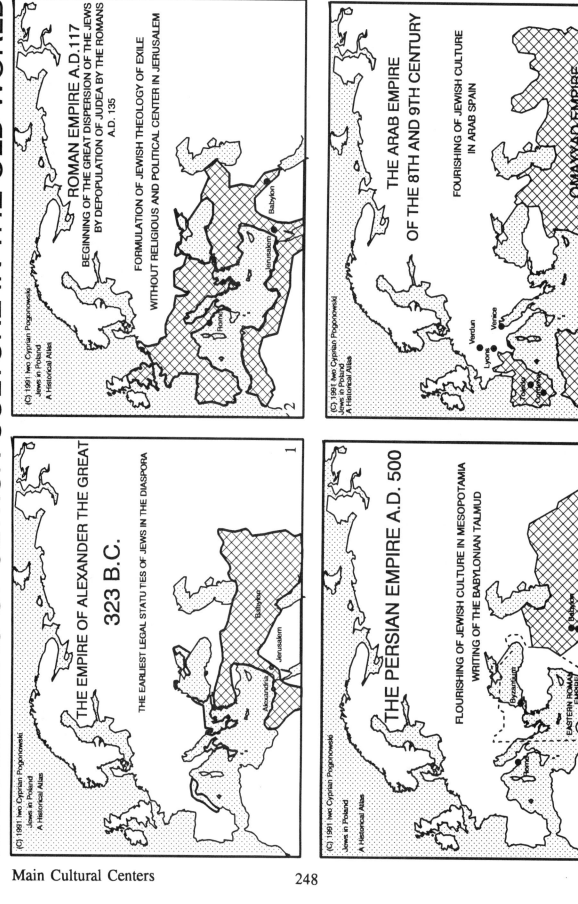

1. THE EMPIRE OF ALEXANDER THE GREAT
323 B.C.

THE EARLIEST LEGAL STATUTES OF JEWS IN THE DIASPORA

(C) 1991 Iwo Cyprian Pogonowski
Jews in Poland
A Historical Atlas

Babylon
Jerusalem
Alexandria

2. ROMAN EMPIRE A.D. 117

BEGINNING OF THE GREAT DISPERSION OF THE JEWS
BY DEPOPULATION OF JUDEA BY THE ROMANS
A.D. 135

FORMULATION OF JEWISH THEOLOGY OF EXILE
WITHOUT RELIGIOUS AND POLITICAL CENTER IN JERUSALEM

(C) 1991 Iwo Cyprian Pogonowski
Jews in Poland
A Historical Atlas

Rome
Jerusalem
Babylon

3. THE PERSIAN EMPIRE A.D. 500

FLOURISHING OF JEWISH CULTURE IN MESOPOTAMIA
WRITING OF THE BABYLONIAN TALMUD

(C) 1991 Iwo Cyprian Pogonowski
Jews in Poland
A Historical Atlas

Rome
Byzantium
EASTERN ROMAN EMPIRE
Jerusalem
Babylon

4. THE ARAB EMPIRE
OF THE 8TH AND 9TH CENTURY

FOURISHING OF JEWISH CULTURE
IN ARAB SPAIN

(C) 1991 Iwo Cyprian Pogonowski
Jews in Poland
A Historical Atlas

OMAYYAD EMPIRE

Verdun
Lyons
Venice
Toledo
Cordova

Main Cultural Centers

248

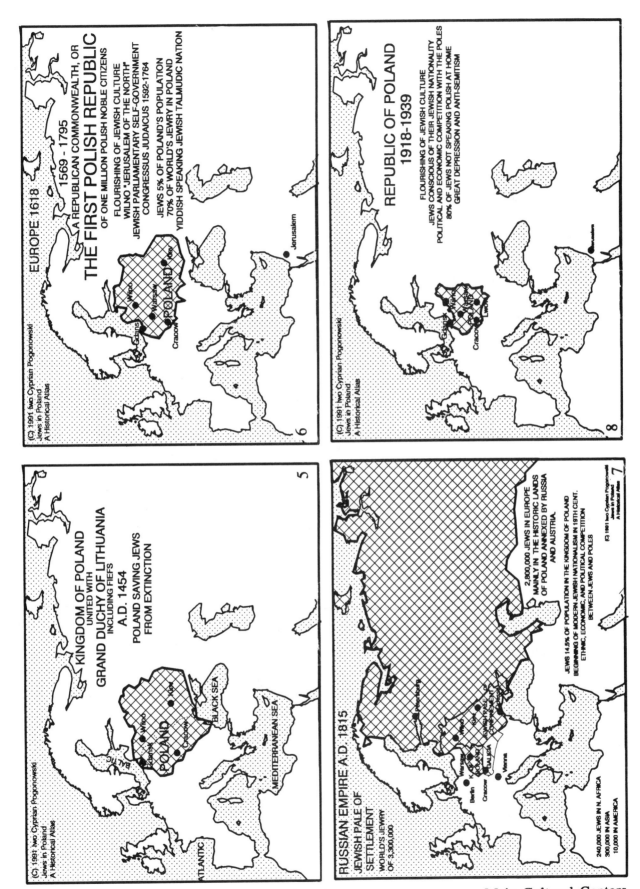

EUROPE 1618

1569 - 1795

THE FIRST POLISH REPUBLIC

A REPUBLICAN COMMONWEALTH, OR
OF ONE MILLION POLISH NOBLE CITIZENS

FLOURISHING OF JEWISH CULTURE
WILNO "JERUSALEM OF THE NORTH"
JEWISH PARLIAMENTARY SELF-GOVERNMENT
CONGRESSUS JUDAICUS 1592-1764

JEWS 5% OF POLAND'S POPULATION
70% OF WORLD'S JEWRY IN POLAND
YIDDISH SPEAKING JEWISH TALMUDIC NATION

(C) 1991 Iwo Cyprian Pogonowski
Jews in Poland
A Historical Atlas

Jerusalem

Wilno
POLAND
Warsaw
Kiev
Gdansk
Cracow

6

REPUBLIC OF POLAND
1918-1939

FLOURISHING OF JEWISH CULTURE
JEWS CONSCIOUS OF THEIR JEWISH NATIONALITY
POLITICAL AND ECONOMIC COMPETITION WITH THE POLES
80% OF JEWS NOT SPEAKING POLISH AT HOME
GREAT DEPRESSION AND ANTI-SEMITISM

(C) 1991 Iwo Cyprian Pogonowski
Jews in Poland
A Historical Atlas

Gdansk
Vilna
POLAND
Cracow
Lwow

8

KINGDOM OF POLAND
UNITED WITH
GRAND DUCHY OF LITHUANIA
INCLUDING FIEFS
A.D. 1454
POLAND SAVING JEWS
FROM EXTINCTION

(C) 1991 Iwo Cyprian Pogonowski
Jews in Poland
A Historical Atlas

BALTIC
Gdansk
Wilno
POLAND
Kiev
Cracow
BLACK SEA
MEDITERRANEAN SEA
ATLANTIC

5

RUSSIAN EMPIRE A.D. 1815
JEWISH PALE OF
SETTLEMENT

WORLD'S JEWRY
OF 3,300,000

2,800,000 JEWS IN EUROPE
MAINLY IN THE HISTORIC LANDS
OF POLAND ANNEXED BY RUSSIA
AND AUSTRIA.

JEWS 14.5% OF POPULATION IN THE KINGDOM OF POLAND
BEGINNING OF MODERN JEWISH NATIONALISM IN 19TH CENT.
ETHNIC, ECONOMIC, AND POLITICAL COMPETITION
BETWEEN JEWS AND POLES

240,000 JEWS IN N. AFRICA
300,000 IN ASIA
10,000 IN AMERICA

(C) 1991 Iwo Cyprian Pogonowski
Jews in Poland
A Historical Atlas

Petersburg
Wilno
JEWISH PALE OF
Berlin
POLAND
Warsaw
GALICIA
SETTLEMENT
Cracow
Vienna

7

249   Main Cultural Centers

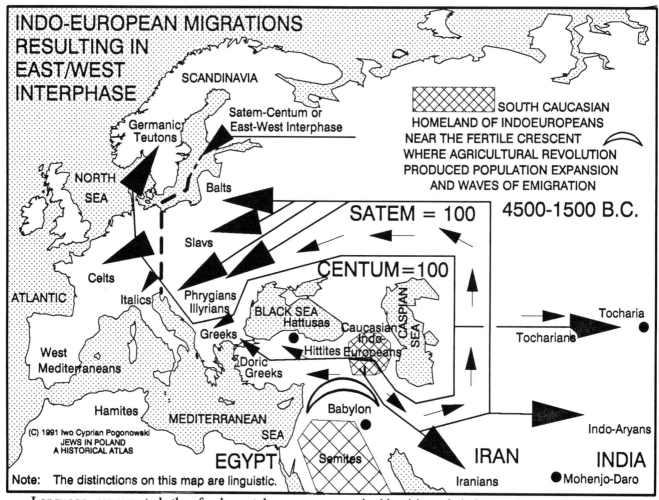

INDO-EUROPEAN MIGRATIONS RESULTING IN EAST/WEST INTERPHASE

SOUTH CAUCASIAN HOMELAND OF INDOEUROPEANS NEAR THE FERTILE CRESCENT WHERE AGRICULTURAL REVOLUTION PRODUCED POPULATION EXPANSION AND WAVES OF EMIGRATION

4500-1500 B.C.

SATEM = 100

CENTUM = 100

SCANDINAVIA

Germanic Teutons

Satem-Centum or East-West Interphase

NORTH SEA

Balts

Slavs

Celts

ATLANTIC

Italics

Phrygians Illyrians

BLACK SEA

Hattusas

Caucasian Indo-Europeans

Hittites Europeans

CASPIAN SEA

Tocharia

Tocharians

Greeks

West Mediterraneans

Doric Greeks

Hamites

Babylon

Indo-Aryans

MEDITERRANEAN SEA

(C) 1991 Iwo Cyprian Pogonowski
JEWS IN POLAND
A HISTORICAL ATLAS

EGYPT

Semites

IRAN

Iranians

INDIA

Mohenjo-Daro

Note: The distinctions on this map are linguistic.

Language represented the fundamental pre-requisite for development of human intelligence and therefore of humanity itself. The evolution which led to modern human speech took some 30,000 years.

An important turning point occurred when in 8500 B.C. glaciers were receding and agriculture was beginning in the fertile crescent which included the Biblical Garden of Eden and was populated by Semitic and other people of the remote antiquity. Eventually the progress of agriculture brought population expansion and emigration.

About 4500 B.C. Caucasians speaking the early Indo-European language started moving out of their homeland which apparently was located in the southern Caucasus north of the fertile crescent. The oldest inscriptions about them were dated in the end of the third millennium B.C. and were written in Akkadian, a Semitic language. Thus, migrations and cultural diffusion took the speakers of the early Indo-European language away from the proximity of Semites in Mesopotamia, where they adopted many Semitic words.

Each language, starting with the remote antiquity, evolved its own perception of the world, its own logic, and its own way of communication. Languages helped to shape the special and very diverse eth-nic identities of their speakers. Thus, the farther apart their ancient roots were the stranger different people appeared to each other.

The most tragic recent example in European history has been the German formation of a racist society, which during the 19th and 20th centuries rejected assimilation of immigrant Polish Jews, killed one third of all Jews during World War II and eliminated the Yiddish language in Europe. Poland, which saved Jews from extinction in the late medieval and early modern period, could not save the Jewish Nation from the German onslaught in the middle of the 20th century.

Earlier in the vicinity of Poland the Germans obliterated other languages. During the 10th to 13th centuries Germans destroyed a number of western Slavic languages in the large area centered on the Elbe River where until present time Slavic geographic names predominate. In the 13th century during the German aggression on the southern and eastern Baltic Sea the Germans committed the genocide of the Balto-Slavic Prussians and caused the extinction of the Prussian language (a close relative of the Lithuanian). However, German genocides reached unprecedented scale in the 20th century when during the Second World War they killed 20 percent of the population of Poland.

250

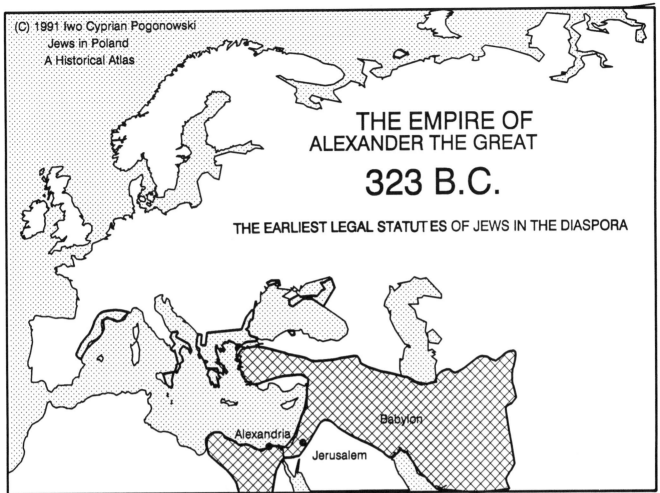

THE EMPIRE OF ALEXANDER THE GREAT

323 B.C.

THE EARLIEST LEGAL STATUTES OF JEWS IN THE DIASPORA

Alexandria

Jerusalem

Babylon

Beginning of a new epoch was the founding of Alexandria and thirty other cities in which Jewish communities were gradually settled and organized.

Jewish communities had begun formulating their social and legal relations with the gentiles in the Greek cities of antiquity. It was a new development in their long struggle for survival as Jews in diaspora. Eventually, after sixteen hundred years of experience in negotiating for a special legal status the Jews found a success in 1264 in Kalisz, Poland. The Polish Statute of Jewish Liberties was unique because it was in force for 500 years. It was basic to the extraordinary survival of Jews, who were permitted to establish an autonomous Jewish nation in modern times (1550-1795) under the protection of the government of Poland.

The historians of the empire of Alexander the Great also recorded that Jewish separateness and the alien character of the Jews brought about the beginnings of anti-Semitism in Greek cities. Jewish belief in one God, circumcision, the Sabbath and religious festivals based on the Mosaic Law were often resented by the ancient Greeks.

Greek cities and immigrant Jewish communities in them were becoming political institutions based on mutually exclusive religious traditions.

The empire of Alexander the Great brought the beginning of penetration of the Orient by Greek culture and the beginning of the Orient's influence on the Greeks. This historic process continued between Alexander's death and the Roman conquest.

During the Hellenic period Greek cities had to depend on the favor of the kings. There was competition between Greek cities and Jewish communities. Often the Greeks had difficulty in defending their autonomy while the Jews, under the protection of the monarch, could enjoy considerable internal autonomy equal even to that of the Greeks. The Jews demanded of the Greek city the recognition of Jewish privileges such as exemption from military service and from its associated taxes as well as permission to collect money and to send it to the temple in Jerusalem. The Jews insisted that they should not be forced to desecrate the Sabbath or to pay for Greek schools, organization of athletic events and the building of the Greek temples. For these reasons the Greeks did not consider the Jews to be good citizens.

Outside Judea, Jewish communities had already begun to form before the Christian era, in the 7th and 6th century B.C.

251

THE START OF THE GREAT DISPERSION

ROMAN RULE OF THE EASTERN MEDITERRANEAN LASTED 667 YEARS

(C) 1991 Iwo Cyprian Pogonowski
Jews in Poland
A Historical Atlas

THE GREAT DISPERSION OF THE JEWS STARTED IN A.D. 135 WHEN THE ROMANS BROKE THE POWER OF THE CELTS AND OPENED THE GERMANIC FLOOD OUT OF SCANDINAVIA AND TOWARDS THE NORTHERN ROMAN FRONTIERS. GERMANIC SLAVES WERE SOLD TO THE ROMANS BY JEWISH SLAVE TRADERS.

JEWISH POPULATION OF THE EMPIRE WAS ESTIMATED FOR A.D. 65 AT UP TO 8,000,000.

THE TEMPLE BUILT BY KING HEROD WAS DESTROYED IN A.D.70 BY ROMAN EMPEROR TRAJAN WHO DEPORTED MANY JEWS. EMPEROR HADRIAN DEFEATED BAR KOCHBA REVOLT IN A.D. 135. SOME 500,000 JEWS WERE KILLED AND JUDEA DEPOPULATED BY MASS DEPORTATIONS TO ROME, GALLIA, PANNONIA, HISPANIA, AND OTHER PARTS OF THE ROMAN EMPIRE. THUS BEGUN THE GREAT DISPERSION OF THE JEWS. BY A.D. 300 JEWISH POPULATION DECLINED BY 1/2 TO 2/3 & TO ABOUT 3,000,000 OR LESS; ABOUT 1,000,000 LIVED WEST OF MACEDONIA.

THE TEMPLE OF JERUSALEM FIRST BUILT BY KING SOLOMON IN ABOUT 1000 B.C. IN 586 B.C. THE BABYLONIANS DESTROYED IT IN 19 B.C. KING HEROD STARTED BUILDING A MAGNIFICENT TEMPLE IN JERUSALEM. IN 64 B.C. THE DECORATIONS WERE FINISHED IN A.D. 70 THE ROMANS AGAIN DESTROYED THE TEMPLE OF JERUSALEM, LEAVING ONLY A SMALL SECTION OF THE WALL WHICH IS KNOWN AS THE WEST WALL

BY 1988: IN THE 20 YEARS SINCE JERUSALEM BECAME THE CAPITAL OF THE STATE OF ISRAEL NO RECONSTRUCTION OF THE TEMPLE OF JERUSALEM HAS BEEN ATTEMPTED.

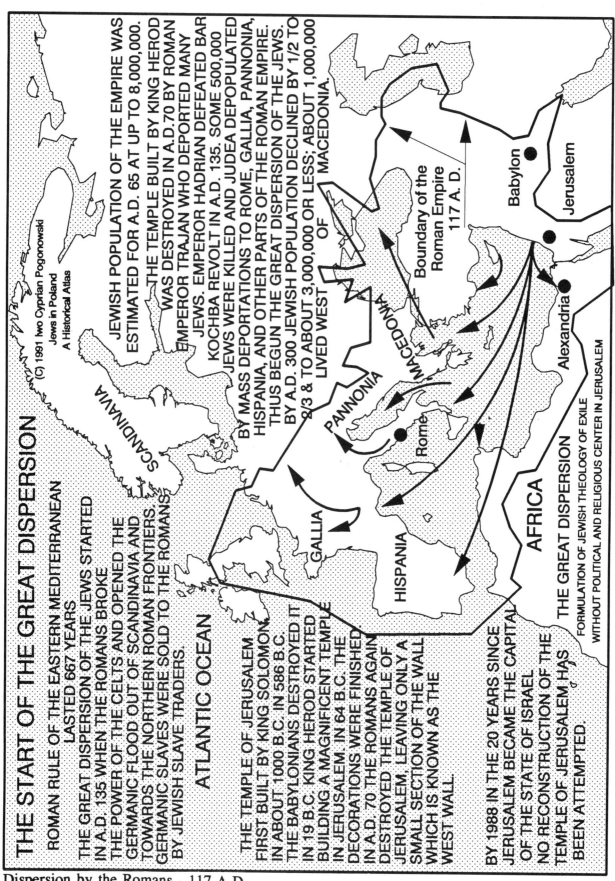

ATLANTIC OCEAN

SCANDINAVIA

GALLIA

PANNONIA

MACEDONIA

Boundary of the Roman Empire 117 A.D.

Babylon

Jerusalem

Rome

HISPANIA

Alexandria

AFRICA

THE GREAT DISPERSION

FORMULATION OF JEWISH THEOLOGY OF EXILE WITHOUT POLITICAL AND RELIGIOUS CENTER IN JERUSALEM

Dispersion by the Romans - 117 A.D.

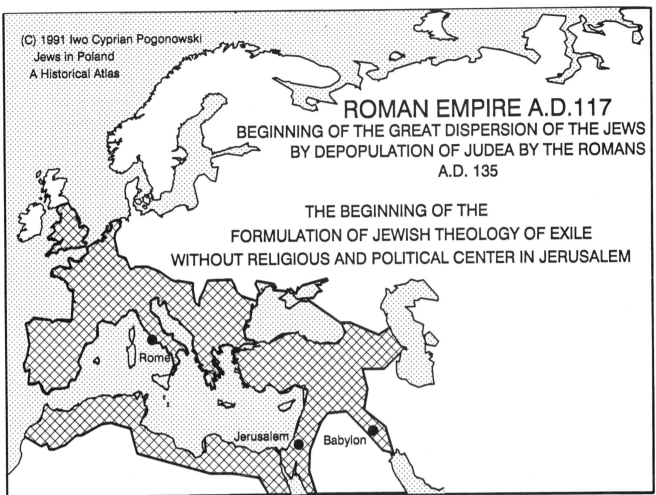

ROMAN EMPIRE A.D.117
BEGINNING OF THE GREAT DISPERSION OF THE JEWS BY DEPOPULATION OF JUDEA BY THE ROMANS A.D. 135

THE BEGINNING OF THE FORMULATION OF JEWISH THEOLOGY OF EXILE WITHOUT RELIGIOUS AND POLITICAL CENTER IN JERUSALEM

Rome

Jerusalem   Babylon

Roman rule of eastern Mediterranean lasted 667 years. The Romans destroyed the 2nd Jewish Temple in Jerusalem in A.D. 70, six years after its construction. Only a small section of the wall was left. It is known as the "Wailing Wall." Israelis call it the "Western Wall."

In **A.D. 65** the Jewish population of the Roman Empire was estimated at up to 8,000,000. (Scholars differ in their estimates: Baron - eight million of whom three million in Palestine and five million in the Diaspora; Beloch - six million of whom two million in Palestine and four in the rest of the Roman Empire; Juster - seven million of whom five million in Palestine and two million in the Diaspora; Harnack - over four millions of whom 700,000 in Palestine and the rest in the Diaspora.) It is estimated that during the fight for independence from Rome about 1,500,000 Jews were killed by **A.D. 70**.

In **A.D. 117**, during the Roman war with Persia, the Jews took advantage of the movement when almost all Roman forces went to the front in Mesopotamia. A Jewish uprising engulfed southern Mediterranean from the Atlantic to Mesopotamia. Killings of many Greco-Romans were reported: 240,000 on Cyprus, 220,000 at Cyrene, etc. Persian victories and the Jewish struggle for independence were important factors in bringing an end to the territorial growth and the beginning of the decline of the Roman Empire.

In **A.D. 135** the Romans defeated the Bar Kochba uprising, killed 500,000 Jews and deported all Jews from Judea. Thus started the great dispersion of the Jews and with it began the **Jewish theology of exile,** which was formulated in the absence of the temple and of a political and religious center in Jerusalem.

By **A.D. 300** Jewish population declined by 50 to 70 percent. It was estimated at less than 3,000,000 of which about 1,000,000 lived in Europe, west of Macedonia. It was estimated that by **A.D. 1000** the total number of Jews in the world was below 500,000 and falling. Jews were the only people in Europe with direct links to antiquity. It appeared that they were headed for extinction like all other peoples of antiquity. However, an extraordinary Jewish demographic recovery occurred in Poland between 1264 and 1795, when the Polish Jewish population multiplied itself over one hundred fold. By 1880 Jewish population had again reached eight million, of whom over 80 percent lived in the territory which belonged to Poland before the partitions.

253

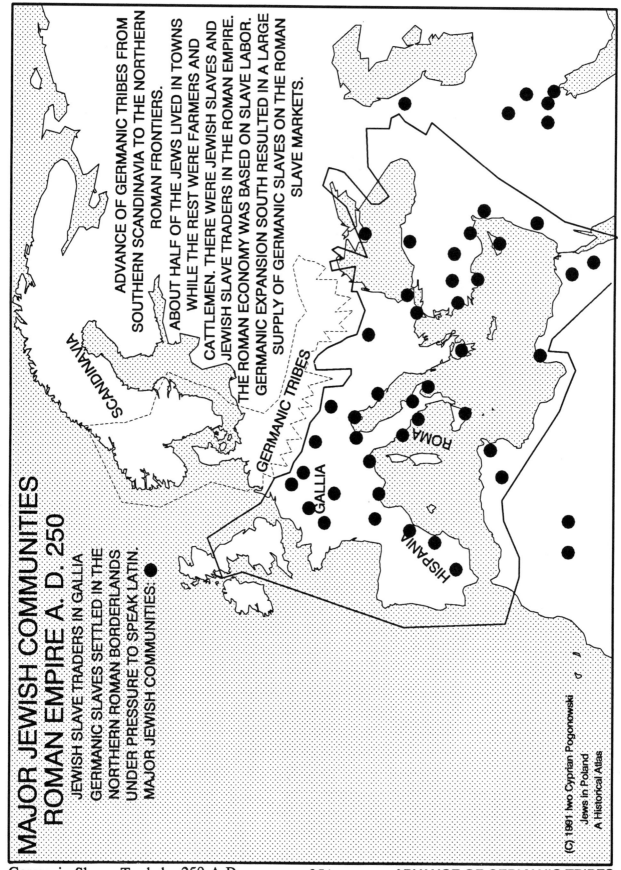

MAJOR JEWISH COMMUNITIES ROMAN EMPIRE A. D. 250

JEWISH SLAVE TRADERS IN GALLIA

GERMANIC SLAVES SETTLED IN THE NORTHERN ROMAN BORDERLANDS UNDER PRESSURE TO SPEAK LATIN.

MAJOR JEWISH COMMUNITIES: ●

ADVANCE OF GERMANIC TRIBES FROM SOUTHERN SCANDINAVIA TO THE NORTHERN ROMAN FRONTIERS.

ABOUT HALF OF THE JEWS LIVED IN TOWNS WHILE THE REST WERE FARMERS AND CATTLEMEN. THERE WERE JEWISH SLAVES AND JEWISH SLAVE TRADERS IN THE ROMAN EMPIRE. THE ROMAN ECONOMY WAS BASED ON SLAVE LABOR. GERMANIC EXPANSION SOUTH RESULTED IN A LARGE SUPPLY OF GERMANIC SLAVES ON THE ROMAN SLAVE MARKETS.

SCANDINAVIA

GERMANIC TRIBES

GALLIA

ROMA

HISPANIA

Artur Szyk, *Ink and Blood*, Plate IV,
THE NIEBELUNGEN marching into the night of the witches —
the Walpurgis Night

Jewish settlements in Gallia and on the Rhine were established after mass deportations of Jews from Judea when the Romans retaliated for the Jewish Bar-Kochba uprising of 117 A.D.

The pressure of Scandinavian Tribes on the northern Roman frontiers brought many Germanic slaves to Roman slave markets. Jewish slave-traders supplied these slaves primarily to Gallia, where they supplemented the native population reduced by Roman legions.

Most of the Germanic slaves in Gallia came from Franconian and Burgundian tribes. Romans gave them the name "Germans," and forced them to speak Latin, which they mispronounced and eventually helped to produce the French language.

Germanic tribes advancing along northern Roman borders brought with them Scandinavian myths to central and southern Europe. These myths reflected the gloom of Scandinavian cold winters. Cold was the main evil of the north while the warmth of the sun has personified the good. The evil cold was believed to have eventually an upper hand over the good sun. Thus, in the Germanic languages the moon of cold nights had a masculine gender while the caressing warm sun had feminine gender. In Latin it was the reverse and in agreement with the Mediterranean tradition. The sun was masculine because at times it produced excessive heat, while the moon was associated with pleasantly cool nights and therefore was given the feminine gender.

The Slavs originated south of the Baltic Sea and gave masculine gender to the moon. However, the Slavic sun had a neuter gender.

The ancient Scandinavian myths became fashionable among Germans during the 19th and 20th centuries. This popularity was strengthened with the monumental and overpowering mythological operas of Richard Wagner. These operas cultivated an overbearing German national identity, which eventually progressed to megalomania.

Naturally, Wagner's operas were loved by the Nazis. Hitler praised them highly and claimed personally to have a gift of an extraordinary "musicality," which was supposed to let him read the inner feelings of the German people. Hitler was perceived by his country men and perceived himself as a personification of Germany.

German fascination with Scandinavian myth and Wagner's music was known in Poland. Polish-Jewish artist Artur Szyk embodied this German craze in the above engraving showing the mythical Siegfried, with Hitler's face, leading the army of legendary dwarfs, the Niebelungen, from the region of foggy mist, into the night of the witches — the Walpurgis night (the eve of the first of May).

Germans were full of mythical notions. Thus, before they started the Second World War by an attack on Poland the Germans built as a precaution a defense line along their western frontier. They called it the "Siegfried Line."

255

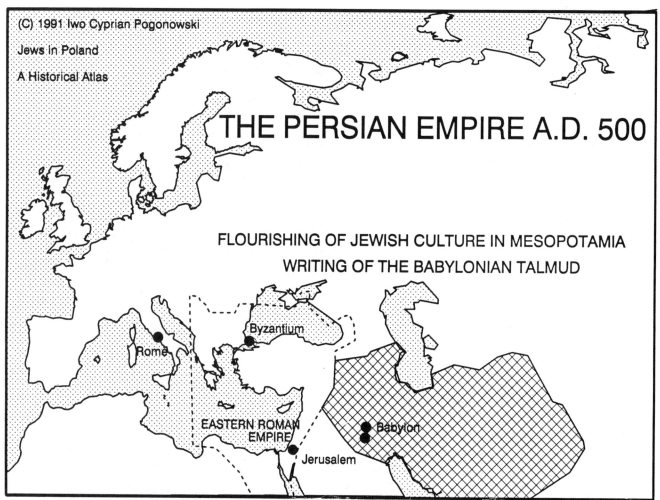

THE PERSIAN EMPIRE A.D. 500

FLOURISHING OF JEWISH CULTURE IN MESOPOTAMIA
WRITING OF THE BABYLONIAN TALMUD

Rome

Byzantium

EASTERN ROMAN EMPIRE

Jerusalem

Babylon

After the establishment of Christianity as the state religion of the Roman Empire in A. D. 380, the situation of the Jews seriously deteriorated. Of all the communities of the diaspora of the 5th century, Jewish culture in Mesopotamia was the most prominent. By A.D. 500 the Babylonian Talmud was written determining the character of Judaism as a national religion. It became a code of religious and civil law observed by the vast majority of Jewish communities in Europe, Africa, and Asia.

Two versions of the Talmud, including Gemara and Mishnah, were prepared. The Palestinian Talmud was written in Jerusalem. It contained 39 treatises. The other version was written in Mesopotamia. It is known as the Babylonian Talmud. It is four times longer than the Palestinian Talmud. The Babylonian Talmud included 63 treatises.

The Babylonian Talmud was written in a mixture of Hebrew and Aramaic languages. It interpreted the first five books of the Old Testament and replaced the earlier Palestinian Mishnah of A.D. 200, which was edited by Rabbi Jehuda Hanasi and interpreted in Gemara by scholars in Palestine and Mesopotamia. Gemara included Halacha, or legal and ritual rules, as well as Agada, or early Jewish history

presented in a literary form. The Palestinian Talmud was completed by A.D. 300.

The Babylonian Talmud emphasized that Jews were a chosen people and therefore superior to others. It helped to create Jewish charisma and served as the basic text of Judaism. It was the basic law of the autonomous Yiddish speaking Talmudic Jewish Nation in Poland (1264-1795) where 80 percent of the world's Jewry lived as 6 percent of the population of the Polish state. Jews in Poland had their own parliament called *Congressus Judaicus*, or Jewish Seym (1581-1764). It was a unique Jewish parliament in the history of the Jewish Diaspora between Sanhedrin of the biblical times and Knesset of the modern State of Israel. Laws passed by the Congressus Judaicus in Poland conformed with the Babylonian Talmud.

The Babylonian Talmud was the basis for the ethical and cultural development of the masses of Orthodox Jews in central and eastern Europe until German genocide of the Jews in World War II. It has formed the mentality and specific way of thinking of Orthodox Jews. It inspired the development of modern Jewish nationalism. The Babylonian Talmud gave to Judaism the character of an exclusive national religion of the Jews in Europe, Asia, and Africa.

256

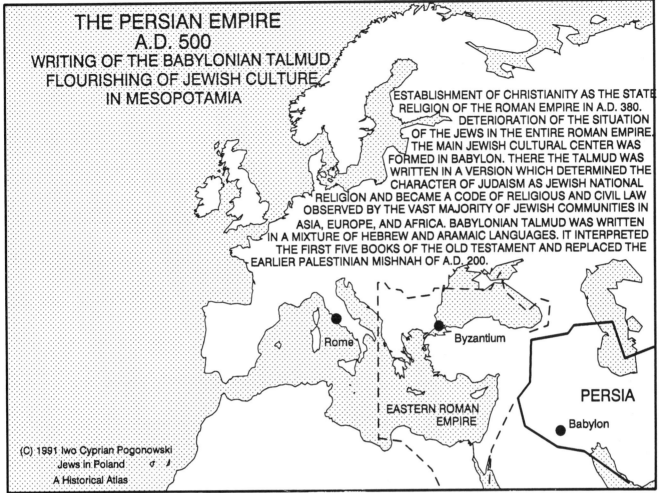

THE PERSIAN EMPIRE
A.D. 500
WRITING OF THE BABYLONIAN TALMUD
FLOURISHING OF JEWISH CULTURE
IN MESOPOTAMIA

ESTABLISHMENT OF CHRISTIANITY AS THE STATE RELIGION OF THE ROMAN EMPIRE IN A.D. 380. DETERIORATION OF THE SITUATION OF THE JEWS IN THE ENTIRE ROMAN EMPIRE. THE MAIN JEWISH CULTURAL CENTER WAS FORMED IN BABYLON. THERE THE TALMUD WAS WRITTEN IN A VERSION WHICH DETERMINED THE CHARACTER OF JUDAISM AS JEWISH NATIONAL RELIGION AND BECAME A CODE OF RELIGIOUS AND CIVIL LAW OBSERVED BY THE VAST MAJORITY OF JEWISH COMMUNITIES IN ASIA, EUROPE, AND AFRICA. BABYLONIAN TALMUD WAS WRITTEN IN A MIXTURE OF HEBREW AND ARAMAIC LANGUAGES. IT INTERPRETED THE FIRST FIVE BOOKS OF THE OLD TESTAMENT AND REPLACED THE EARLIER PALESTINIAN MISHNAH OF A.D. 200.

Rome

Byzantium

EASTERN ROMAN EMPIRE

PERSIA

Babylon

(C) 1991 Iwo Cyprian Pogonowski
Jews in Poland
A Historical Atlas

After completion of the Babylonian Talmud in Mesopotamia the next most important cultural center of Jewish Diaspora was established within the Arab Empire, in Arab Spain, the most civilized country in Europe in the 8th, 9th, and 10th centuries. Arab Spain was the scene of flourishing Jewish culture between the 8th and 15th centuries. Jewish quarters in Spanish towns were known as *Juderias*. The majority of Spanish Jews worked in agriculture. There was a thriving community of Jewish merchants in Arab Spain.

The situation of Jews within the Arab Empire was normalized in A.D. 637 by the decree of Omar I. Jews in Islam were recognized as "tolerated infidels." Most medieval Jews resided in Spain. Jewish medieval merchants were known as "Radanites." They included western European Jews from France and Germany, as well as those from Arab Spain.

The term "Radanites" was derived from the name of the Arab-Christian border along the river Rhone (in Latin *Rodanus*) because of an intense slave trade which was conducted across it. The slaves were castrated in Verdun, Venice, and Lyon and sold by Jewish Radanite slave-traders to the Arabs of Spain. This Jewish slave trade also included girls and small boys who were properly indoctrinated in order to be used later by Arab rulers as body guards, slave soldiers, and bureaucrats.

An alternate origin of the name "Radanite" was a Persian word for those who "knew the way." This explanation was related to the leading role of Jewish merchants in trade after the fall of the Roman Empire. From the 7th century to mid-10th century Radanites controlled the trade which encompassed Europe, North Africa, and southern Asia including China. It was a period when Hebrew was the only language of world trade.

Radanites in the service of the Arabs made advances in geography. The first detailed written description of Poland as a powerful "Kingdom of the North" was provided in 966 by a Radanite trader and geographer from Arab Spain, Ibrahim ibn-Yaqub. Radanites called the Slavic lands the "New Canaan" (from "ebed Kna'an," the Canaanite slave, the non-Jew) because from there originated slaves captured by the Germanic tribes and later sold to Jewish slave traders. At about the same time the Latin term *servus*, or slave, was substituted by the term *sclavus*, which was derived from the ethnic name of the Slavs as was Slovinian, Slovak, etc. The term *sclavus* gave origin to the word *slave* in western Europe.

257

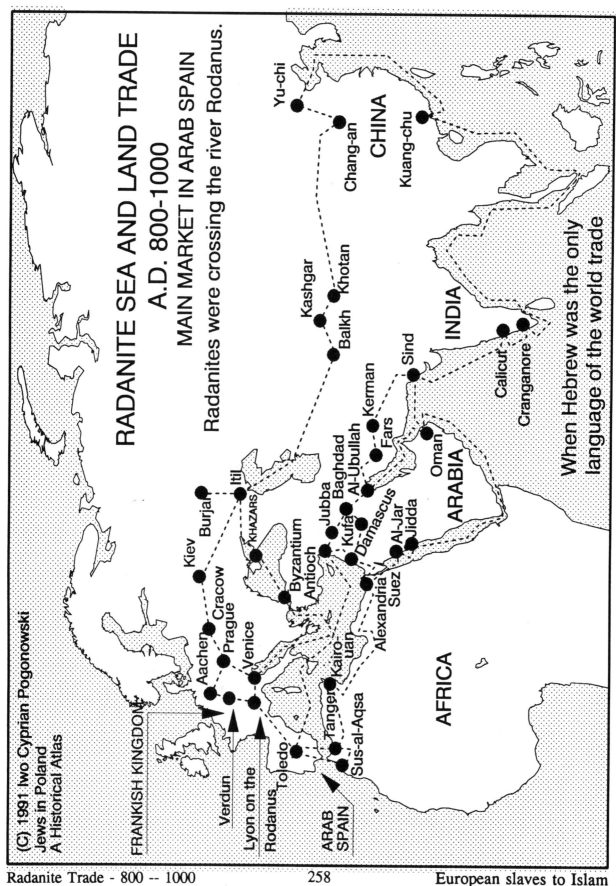

RADANITE SEA AND LAND TRADE
A.D. 800-1000

MAIN MARKET IN ARAB SPAIN

Radanites were crossing the river Rodanus.

When Hebrew was the only language of the world trade

CHINA

Yu-chi
Chang-an
Kuang-chu

Kashgar
Khotan
Balkh

INDIA

Sind

Calicut
Cranganore

Kerman
Fars

Oman

ARABIA

Baghdad
Al-Ubullah
Jubba
Kufa
Damascus
Al-Jar
Jidda

Antioch
Byzantium
Suez
Alexandria

AFRICA

Itil
Burjan
KHAZARS

Kiev
Cracow
Prague
Aachen
Venice

Kairouan
Tanger
Sus-al-Aqsa
Toledo

FRANKISH KINGDOM

Verdun
Lyon on the Rodanus

ARAB SPAIN

(C) 1991 Iwo Cyprian Pogonowski
Jews in Poland
A Historical Atlas

Radanite Trade - 800 -- 1000

European slaves to Islam

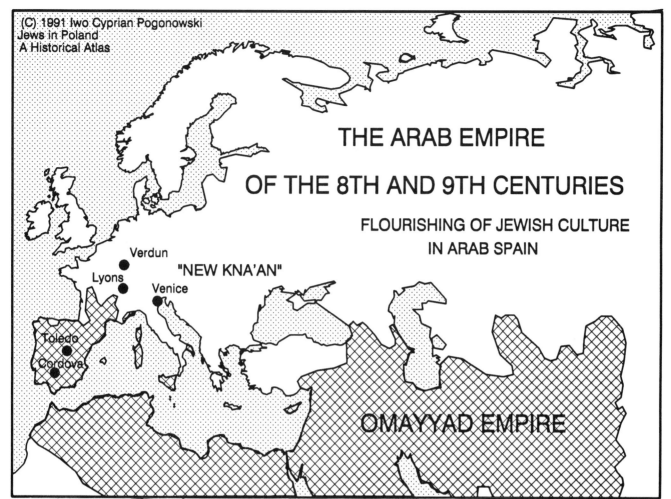

THE ARAB EMPIRE

OF THE 8TH AND 9TH CENTURIES

FLOURISHING OF JEWISH CULTURE
IN ARAB SPAIN

Verdun

"NEW KNA'AN"

Lyons

Venice

Toledo

Cordova

OMAYYAD EMPIRE

Jewish Radanite slave traders were named after the River Rodanus (Rhone) on the border between Christian and Muslim territory. By an alternative explanation the name "Radanite" originates from the Persian phrase meaning "knowing the way." Best known Radanite traders were Jews from Arab Spain. Besides trading, many Jews were in Spanish agriculture. Radanite traders left a number of geographic descriptions of lands through which they traveled.

Ibrahim Ben Ya'qub, a Jew from the Spanish town of Tortosa, traveled by sea to Friaul near Venice, crossed the eastern Alps, and stayed in Prague for a longer time before visiting Cracow, Poland, in A.D. 966. He spoke Arabic, Hebrew, Italian, French, Greek, and understood Slavic.

In the middle of the 10th century Italians gained control of the Mediterranean Sea and its trading ports. They forced their Radanite competitors to use land routes. Radanite traders were arriving in Prague from Venice. The Venetian word for a Jew was adopted, with minor phonetic changes, first into Czech and then into the Polish language.

Arab Spain was the main market for slaves (eunuchs, girls, and young boys). Some slaves were sold as far away as China, which also bought furs, beaver skins, silk, and weapons. Exports from China to Europe included cinnamon, spices, musk, and camphor. The capital of Khazaria, Itil, was an important Jewish trading center. Jewish merchants played an important role in international trade after the fall of the Roman Empire. For two centuries they made Hebrew the only language of world commerce. Slavery, which was the foundation of the Roman economy, was important in the Arab Empire in which the Jews became the main merchants, trading with the infidels and bringing European slaves to Islam.

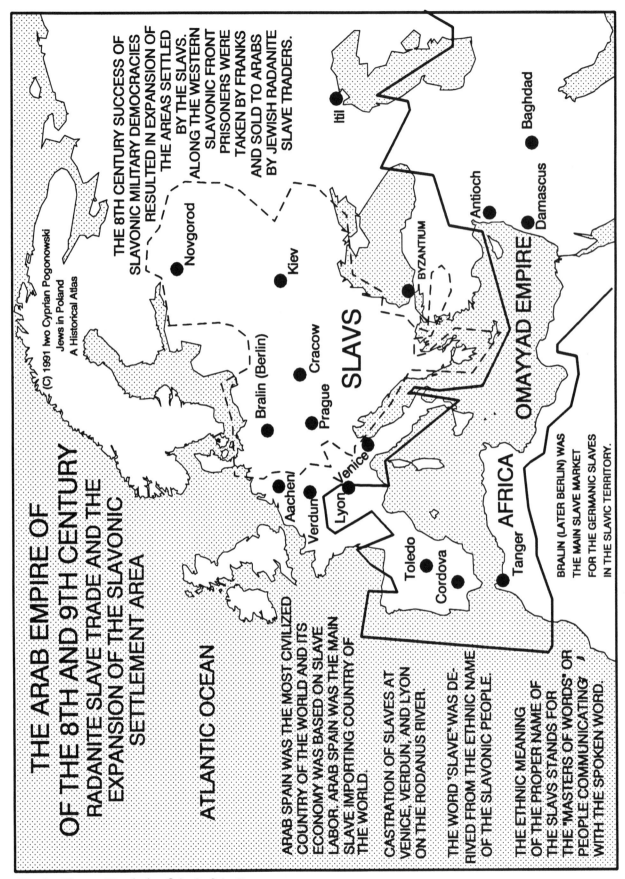

THE ARAB EMPIRE OF OF THE 8TH AND 9TH CENTURY

RADANITE SLAVE TRADE AND THE EXPANSION OF THE SLAVONIC SETTLEMENT AREA

THE 8TH CENTURY SUCCESS OF SLAVONIC MILITARY DEMOCRACIES RESULTED IN EXPANSION OF THE AREAS SETTLED BY THE SLAVS. ALONG THE WESTERN SLAVONIC FRONT PRISONERS WERE TAKEN BY FRANKS AND SOLD TO ARABS BY JEWISH RADANITE SLAVE TRADERS.

(C) 1991 Iwo Cypian Pogonowski
Jews in Poland
A Historical Atlas

ATLANTIC OCEAN

Novgorod

Kiev

Bralin (Berlin)

Cracow

Prague

SLAVS

BYZANTIUM

Venice

Lyon

Aachen

Verdun

Itil

Baghdad

Antioch

Damascus

OMAYYAD EMPIRE

AFRICA

Toledo

Cordova

Tanger

BRALIN (LATER BERLIN) WAS THE MAIN SLAVE MARKET FOR THE GERMANIC SLAVES IN THE SLAVIC TERRITORY.

ARAB SPAIN WAS THE MOST CIVILIZED COUNTRY OF THE WORLD AND ITS ECONOMY WAS BASED ON SLAVE LABOR. ARAB SPAIN WAS THE MAIN SLAVE IMPORTING COUNTRY OF THE WORLD.

CASTRATION OF SLAVES AT VENICE, VERDUN, AND LYON ON THE RODANUS RIVER.

THE WORD "SLAVE" WAS DE-RIVED FROM THE ETHNIC NAME OF THE SLAVONIC PEOPLE.

THE ETHNIC MEANING OF THE PROPER NAME OF THE SLAVS STANDS FOR THE "MASTERS OF WORDS" OR PEOPLE COMMUNICATING J WITH THE SPOKEN WORD.

Slavic Slaves Traded - 8th & 9th Cent.   260

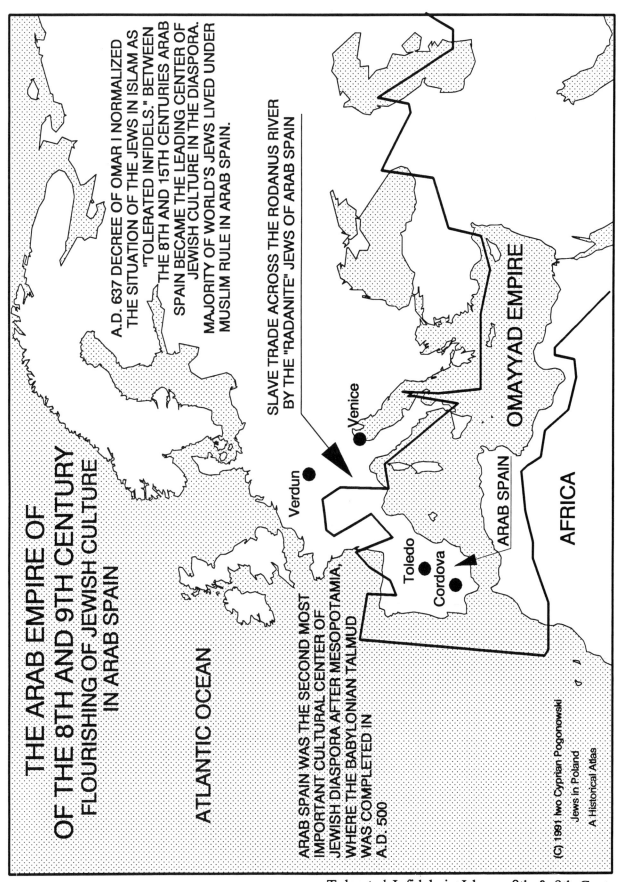

THE ARAB EMPIRE OF
OF THE 8TH AND 9TH CENTURY
FLOURISHING OF JEWISH CULTURE
IN ARAB SPAIN

A.D. 637 DECREE OF OMAR I NORMALIZED THE SITUATION OF THE JEWS IN ISLAM AS "TOLERATED INFIDELS." BETWEEN THE 8TH AND 15TH CENTURIES ARAB SPAIN BECAME THE LEADING CENTER OF JEWISH CULTURE IN THE DIASPORA. MAJORITY OF WORLD'S JEWS LIVED UNDER MUSLIM RULE IN ARAB SPAIN.

SLAVE TRADE ACROSS THE RODANUS RIVER BY THE "RADANITE" JEWS OF ARAB SPAIN

ATLANTIC OCEAN

Venice

Verdun

OMAYYAD EMPIRE

ARAB SPAIN

Toledo

Cordova

AFRICA

ARAB SPAIN WAS THE SECOND MOST IMPORTANT CULTURAL CENTER OF JEWISH DIASPORA AFTER MESOPOTAMIA, WHERE THE BABYLONIAN TALMUD WAS COMPLETED IN A.D. 500

(C) 1991 Iwo Cyprian Pogonowski
Jews in Poland
A Historical Atlas

Jean Pierre Norblin, *Jewish Children*, 1818

EARLY SETTLEMENTS

IN POLAND

966-1264

The oldest Jewish community in Poland existed in Przemysl. It was apparently composed of Jews from Khazar kingdom which was conquered in A.D. 965 by the Kievian Rus. The Turkmen Khazar state was located between the Black and Caspian Seas. The first Jewish colonies in southern Poland were apparently organized to exchange forest products, horses, hides, furs, swords, and slaves of both sexes from the west for luxury goods from the east. The Jews generally used Arab money mostly from Spain and their main operation was in the Czech capital of Prague where Boleslaus the Great ruled in 1003-1004, when Bohemia was a part of his empire. Jewish community in Cracow was first mentioned in 1028 together with Przemysl spelled "Primis." 11th century Jews in Poland spoke Polish rather than Yiddish. Polish word for a Jew is "zyd" (zhid); it is believed to be an adaptation of the Venecian word "giudeo." Venice was then the principal slave market developed on the Adriatic coast.

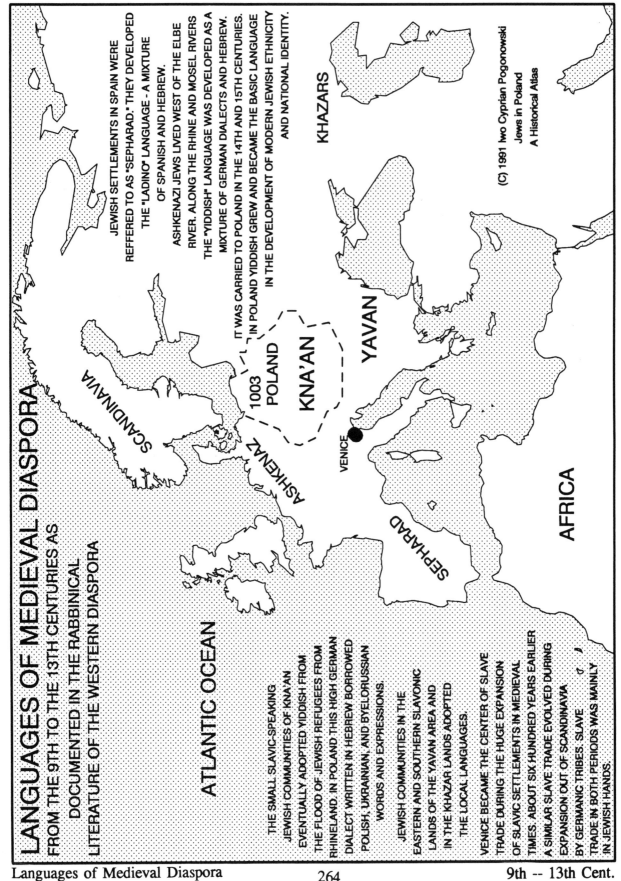

LANGUAGES OF MEDIEVAL DIASPORA

FROM THE 9TH TO THE 13TH CENTURIES AS
DOCUMENTED IN THE RABBINICAL
LITERATURE OF THE WESTERN DIASPORA

JEWISH SETTLEMENTS IN SPAIN WERE
REFFERED TO AS "SEPHARAD." THEY DEVELOPED
THE "LADINO" LANGUAGE - A MIXTURE
OF SPANISH AND HEBREW.

ASHKENAZI JEWS LIVED WEST OF THE ELBE
RIVER, ALONG THE RHINE AND MOSEL RIVERS
THE "YIDDISH" LANGUAGE WAS DEVELOPED AS A
MIXTURE OF GERMAN DIALECTS AND HEBREW.
IT WAS CARRIED TO POLAND IN THE 14TH AND 15TH CENTURIES.
IN POLAND YIDDISH GREW AND BECAME THE BASIC LANGUAGE
IN THE DEVELOPMENT OF MODERN JEWISH ETHNICITY
AND NATIONAL IDENTITY.

KHAZARS

YAVAN

1003 POLAND

KNA'AN

VENICE

SCANDINAVIA

ASHKENAZ

AFRICA

SEPHARAD

ATLANTIC OCEAN

(C) 1991 Iwo Cyprian Pogonowski
Jews in Poland
A Historical Atlas

THE SMALL SLAVIC-SPEAKING
JEWISH COMMUNITIES OF KNA'AN
EVENTUALLY ADOPTED YIDDISH FROM
THE FLOOD OF JEWISH REFUGEES FROM
RHINELAND. IN POLAND THIS HIGH GERMAN
DIALECT WRITTEN IN HEBREW, BORROWED
POLISH, UKRAINIAN, AND BYELORUSSIAN
WORDS AND EXPRESSIONS.

JEWISH COMMUNITIES IN THE
EASTERN AND SOUTHERN SLAVONIC
LANDS OF THE YAVAN AREA AND
IN THE KHAZAR LANDS ADOPTED
THE LOCAL LANGUAGES.

VENICE BECAME THE CENTER OF SLAVE
TRADE DURING THE HUGE EXPANSION
OF SLAVIC SETTLEMENTS IN MEDIEVAL
TIMES. ABOUT SIX HUNDRED YEARS EARLIER
A SIMILAR SLAVE TRADE EVOLVED DURING
EXPANSION OUT OF SCANDINAVIA
BY GERMANIC TRIBES. SLAVE
TRADE IN BOTH PERIODS WAS MAINLY
IN JEWISH HANDS.

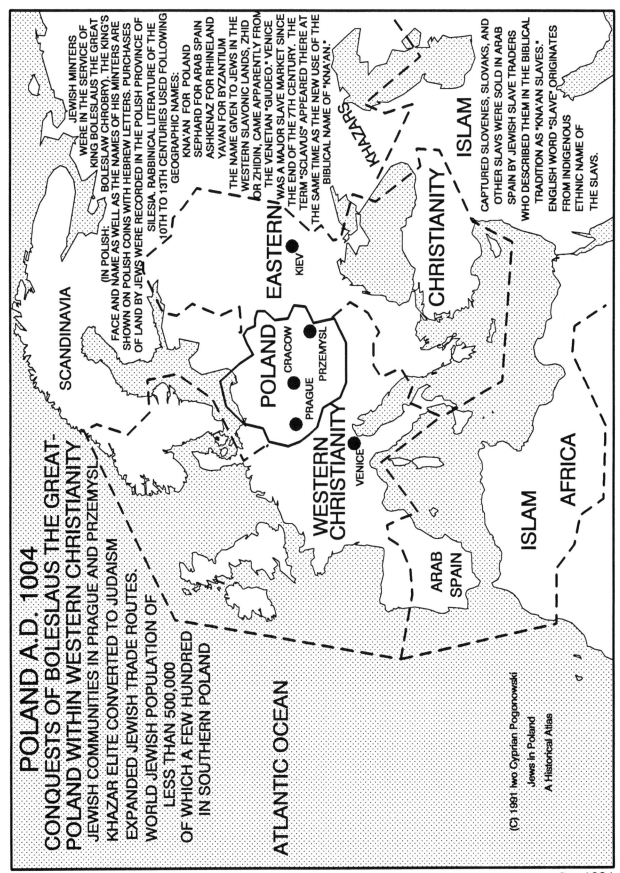

POLAND A.D. 1004

CONQUESTS OF BOLESLAUS THE GREAT-
POLAND WITHIN WESTERN CHRISTIANITY

JEWISH COMMUNITIES IN PRAGUE AND PRZEMYSL.
KHAZAR ELITE CONVERTED TO JUDAISM
EXPANDED JEWISH TRADE ROUTES
WORLD JEWISH POPULATION OF
LESS THAN 500,000
OF WHICH A FEW HUNDRED
IN SOUTHERN POLAND

ATLANTIC OCEAN

(C) 1991 Iwo Cyprian Pogonowski
Jews in Poland
A Historical Atlas

SCANDINAVIA

JEWISH MINTERS
WERE IN THE SERVICE OF
KING BOLESLAUS THE GREAT
(BOLESLAW CHROBRY). THE KING'S
JEWISH MINTERS ARE
SHOWN ON POLISH COINS WITH HEBREW LETTERS. PURCHASES
OF LAND BY JEWS WERE RECORDED IN THE POLISH PROVINCE OF
SILESIA. RABBINICAL LITERATURE OF THE
10TH TO 13TH CENTURIES USED FOLLOWING
GEOGRAPHIC NAMES:
KNA'AN FOR POLAND
SEPHARD FOR ARAB SPAIN
ASHKENAZ FOR RHINELAND
YAVAN FOR BYZANTIUM
THE NAME GIVEN TO JEWS IN THE
WESTERN SLAVONIC LANDS, ZHID
OR ZHIDIN, CAME APPARENTLY FROM
THE VENETIAN "GIUDEO." VENICE
WAS A MAJOR SLAVE MARKET SINCE
THE END OF THE 7TH CENTURY. THE
TERM "SCLAVUS" APPEARED THERE AT
THE SAME TIME AS THE NEW USE OF THE
BIBLICAL NAME OF "KNA'AN."

(IN POLISH:
FACE AND NAME AS WELL AS THE NAMES OF HIS MINTERS ARE

EASTERN

KIEV

POLAND

CRACOW
PRZEMYSL
PRAGUE

VENICE

WESTERN
CHRISTIANITY

ARAB
SPAIN

KHAZARS

CHRISTIANITY

ISLAM

CAPTURED SLOVENES, SLOVAKS, AND
OTHER SLAVS WERE SOLD IN ARAB
SPAIN BY JEWISH SLAVE TRADERS
WHO DESCRIBED THEM IN THE BIBLICAL
TRADITION AS "KNA'AN SLAVES."
ENGLISH WORD "SLAVE" ORIGINATES
FROM INDIGENOUS
ETHNIC NAME OF
THE SLAVS.

ISLAM

AFRICA

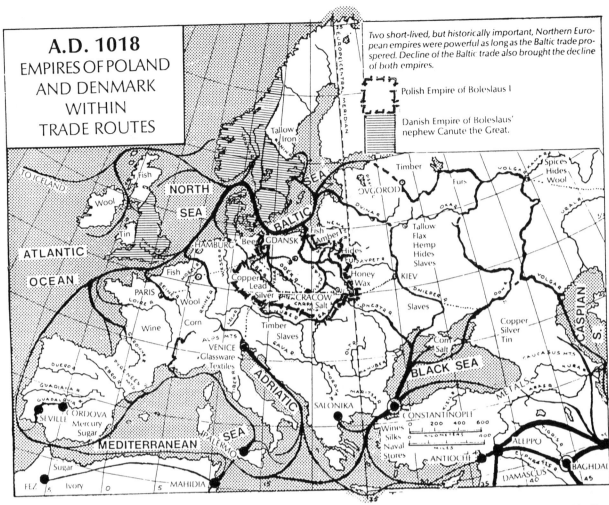

Two short-lived, but historically important, Northern European empires were powerful as long as the Baltic trade prospered. Decline of the Baltic trade also brought the decline of both empires.

Polish Empire of Boleslaus I

Danish Empire of Boleslaus' nephew Canute the Great.

King of Poland Boleslaus I the Great (992-1025), as he was called in the 1116 chronicle of Gallus Anonimus, clearly formulated Polish rejection of the Germans' claim of superiority. He defeated Henry II, the last Saxon Holy Roman Emperor (1002-1024), during the protracted wars of German aggression against Poland (1003-1018). In the treaty of 1018 Boleslaus the Great won from Henry II the German confirmation of Polish fiefs of Lusatia and Milzi and Polish border on the River Saale, southwest of Berlin. The Lusatian Sorbs called Boleslaus the Great "Chrobry" (Khrobry) meaning "great or mighty." This Sorbish nickname became generally accepted in Polish history books.

Jews in service of Boleslaus the Great minted his coins and inscribed on them the name of the Polish sovereign with Hebrew letters. Besides such highly valued craftsmen there were active in Poland Jewish slave-traders. Ever since the time when the economy of Rome was based on slavery the slave trade has continued. In the 11th century the main slave market was in Arab Spain, then the most civilized country in Europe. The Catholic Church fought against slavery and this fight is documented in treatise "Infelix Aurum" by the first patron saint of Poland, and since A.D. 997 the first bishop of Gdansk, Adalbert or Wojciech (voy-chekh). In the struggle

against the slave trade the family of St. Abalbert lost the Czech throne in Prague to their opponents supported by Jewish slave traders. One of 18 sculptures on the 1170 bronze door (please see p.194) made for the cathedral of Gniezno depicted the scene of redeeming manacled Christian slaves by a Polish bishop from Jewish merchants in the presence of the son of King Boleslaus the Great, the second formally crowned King of Poland, Mieszko II (990-1034).

The oldest Jewish community in Poland existed in Przemysl. It was apparently composed of Jews from Khazar kingdom which was conquered in A.D. 965 by the Kievian Rus. The Turkmen Khazar state was located between the Black and Caspian Seas. The first Jewish colonies in southern Poland were apparently organized to exchange forest products, horses, hides, furs, swords, and slaves of both sexes from the west for luxury goods from the east. The Jews generally used Arab money mostly from Spain and their main operation was in the Czech capital of Prague where Boleslaus the Great ruled in 1003-1004, when Bohemia was a part of his empire. The Jewish community in Cracow was first mentioned in 1028 together with Przemysl spelled "Primis." 11th century Jews in Poland spoke Polish rather than Yiddish.

266

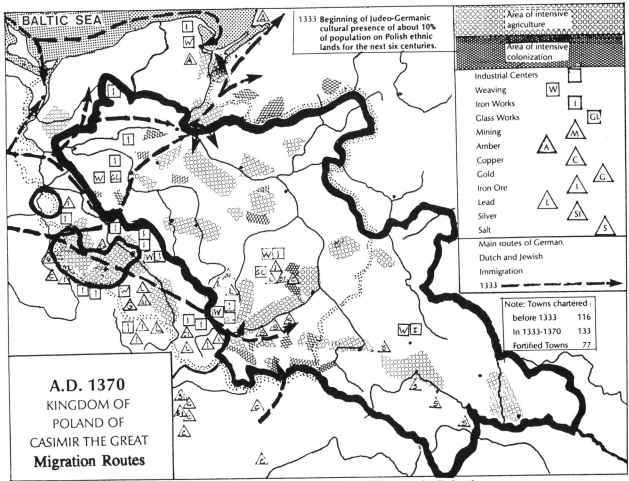

1333 Beginning of Judeo-Germanic cultural presence of about 10% of population on Polish ethnic lands for the next six centuries.

BALTIC SEA

Area of intensive agriculture

Area of intensive colonization

Industrial Centers — W

Weaving — W

Iron Works — I

Glass Works — GL

Mining — M

Amber — A

Copper — C

Gold — G

Iron Ore — I

Lead — L

Silver — SI

Salt — S

Main routes of German, Dutch and Jewish Immigration

1333 ▪ ▪ ▪ ▪ ▶

Note: Towns chartered :
before 1333   116
In 1333-1370   133
Fortified Towns   77

A.D. 1370
KINGDOM OF
POLAND OF
CASIMIR THE GREAT
Migration Routes

The reign of the King Casimir the Great (1333-1370) of the first Polish dynasty (c.840-1370) concluded the period of the development of the Polish State as a hereditary monarchy. Jewish immigration to Poland started as a tiny trickle in the tenth century. Jews were viewed as a "treasure of the throne" - people who were experienced in commerce, minting of money, and money lending procedures developed within the Mediterranean civilization.

Reconstruction from the devastation by the Mongol invasion of 1241 led to encouragement of the further immigration of town people. Jews were coming to Poland together with Germans, Dutchmen, and others. Thus, the move to the east was a part of the larger migration movement of western colonists. This gradual movement and the favorable climate within the Polish State permitted eventual creation in Poland of the most important Jewish settlement in the world.

The positive view of the Jews in Poland was strengthened by the political and national security problems caused by the immigrant Christian German burghers who acquired economic and political power and looked for support to the neighboring German states. German uprisings in Polish towns, such as the one led by mayor Albert in Kraków in 1312, convinced Polish rulers that the economic and political strength of the German burghers should be limited and that the Jews could help in this matter.

Jews immigrating to Poland were steadily increasing in numbers and so did their occupational variation. By the time of Casimir the Great there were about 10,000 Jews in Poland.

Jewish immigrants were proving themselves by displaying their usefulness to the emerging political power of citizen-soldiers who eventually by 1454 became the ruling agricultural elite (ten percent of the population). Kingdom of Poland united with the Grand Duchy of Lithuania in 1386, saved the Jews from extinction by providing the Jewish people with a sanctuary and an opportunity to recover from centuries of numerical decline. Poland gave to the Jews new economic, social and spiritual opportunities, as well as problems within new types of settlements and new circumstances vastly different from those which they experienced in western Europe.

In the 15th century Jews began to turn to additional and new sources of livelihood as they experienced an increasing instability of money-lending especially within German areas. Jewish middlemen were able to serve the people who grew crops and raised livestock by handling their produce and taking it for profitable sale in the urban markets. Thus, Jews became active in the trade of crops as well as in peddling in the towns and villages. Jewish women participated in village trade. Many Jews made their living from handicrafts. Jews were becoming inn-keepers and engaged in trade on the side. Jews in Poland were increasingly engaged in commerce and handicrafts. These activities produced new economic and social development of Jews in Poland as well as an increase of tension between them and German immigrants and other burghers in Polish towns.

267

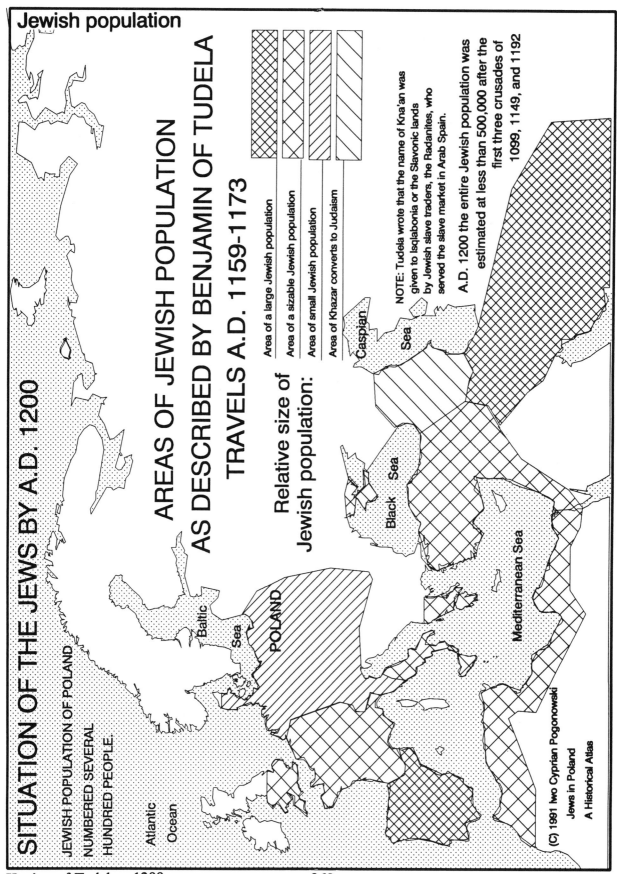

Jewish population

SITUATION OF THE JEWS BY A.D. 1200

JEWISH POPULATION OF POLAND NUMBERED SEVERAL HUNDRED PEOPLE.

Atlantic Ocean

Baltic Sea

POLAND

AREAS OF JEWISH POPULATION AS DESCRIBED BY BENJAMIN OF TUDELA TRAVELS A.D. 1159-1173

Relative size of Jewish population:

Area of a large Jewish population

Area of a sizable Jewish population

Area of small Jewish population

Area of Khazar converts to Judaism

Caspian Sea

Black Sea

Mediterranean Sea

NOTE: Tudela wrote that the name of Kna'an was given to Isqlabonia or the Slavonic lands by Jewish slave traders, the Radanites, who served the slave market in Arab Spain.

A.D. 1200 the entire Jewish population was estimated at less than 500,000 after the first three crusades of 1099, 1149, and 1192

THE CRUCIAL

500 YEARS

1264 -- 1795

Polish-Jewish Relations

" The history of Jews in the diaspora needs no retelling, but their life in Poland was of a different order than elsewhere in the diaspora. Jews came to Poland in large numbers, and lived there for centuries, because in Poland they found a haven. Jews first began coming to Poland over a thousand years ago, with the great influx beginning in the 14th century, when the many-sided pressures on the part of the Christian European states caused a migration to the east. By the year 1500, Poland was regarded as the safest country in Europe for Jews, and for centuries, Poland was known as the "country of heretics." "The kingdom of justice was the kingdom of Poland." Poland was the leader among the countries of the continent in the protection of liberty. In the 16th century it was a country without censorship, where anything and everything was published. The Statute of Kalisz (1264) was the first general law to give protection to Jews in Europe, guaranteeing them full religious liberty, freedom of trade and protection against offenders of their rights. For centuries, Jews in Poland found unparalleled protection.

Out of a desire to have the Jews build up Poland's economy, and as a genuine friend of the Jews, King Casimir III in the 14th century granted Jews special privileges. Casimir is known as "Casimir the Great" but the feudalists lambasted and nicknamed him "king of the serfs and Jews." He was animated by a determination to transform Poland into a great Western power."

Dr. R. Slovenko

269

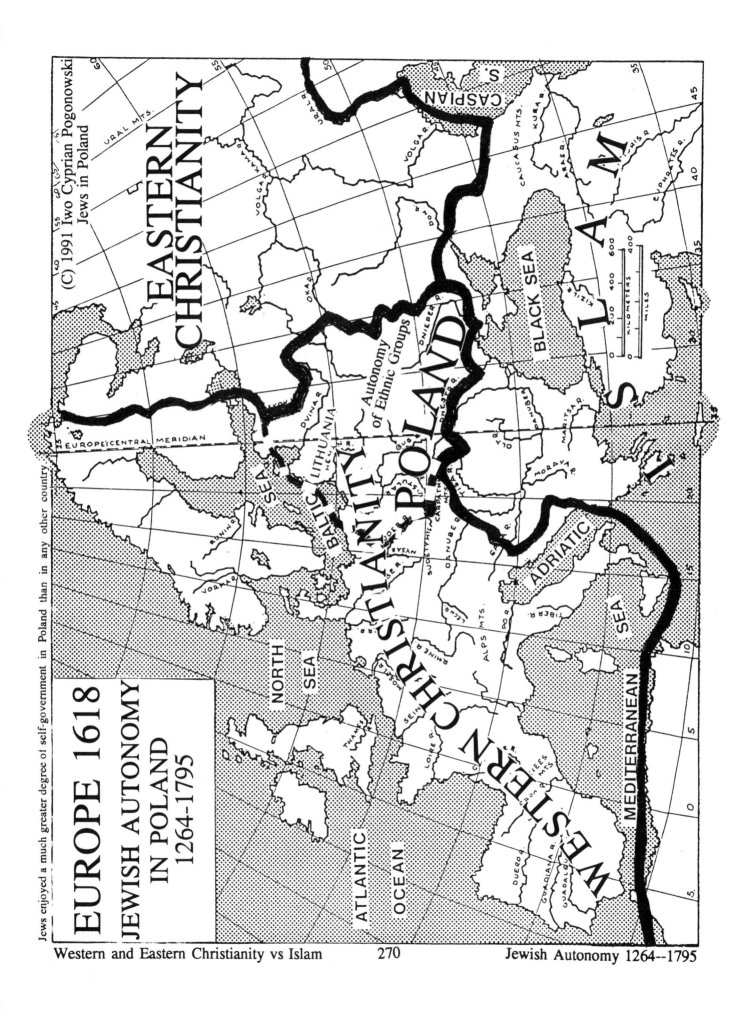

Jews enjoyed a much greater degree of self-government in Poland than in any other country.

EUROPE 1618

JEWISH AUTONOMY IN POLAND 1264-1795

(C) 1991 Iwo Cyprian Pogonowski
Jews in Poland

EASTERN CHRISTIANITY

WESTERN CHRISTIANITY

POLAND

Autonomy of Ethnic Groups

I S L A M

EUROPE CENTRAL MERIDIAN

BALTIC SEA

LITHUANIA

NORTH SEA

ATLANTIC OCEAN

BLACK SEA

ADRIATIC SEA

MEDITERRANEAN SEA

CASPIAN S.

URAL MTS.

VOLGA R.

CAUCASUS MTS.

KURA R.

ARAS R.

TIGRIS R.

EUPHRATES R.

KAMA R.

OKA R.

DON R.

DNIEPER R.

DNIESTER R.

DANUBE R.

MARITSA R.

MORAVA R.

ALPS MTS.

CARPATH. MTS.

DVINA R.

NEMEN R.

VISTULA R.

BUG R.

OLT R.

RHINE R.

TIBER R.

PO R.

DUERO R.

GUADIANA R.

GUADALQUIVIR R.

LOIRE R.

THAMES R.

SEINE R.

MOSELLE R.

SUDETEN MTS.

PYRENEES MTS.

ODER R.

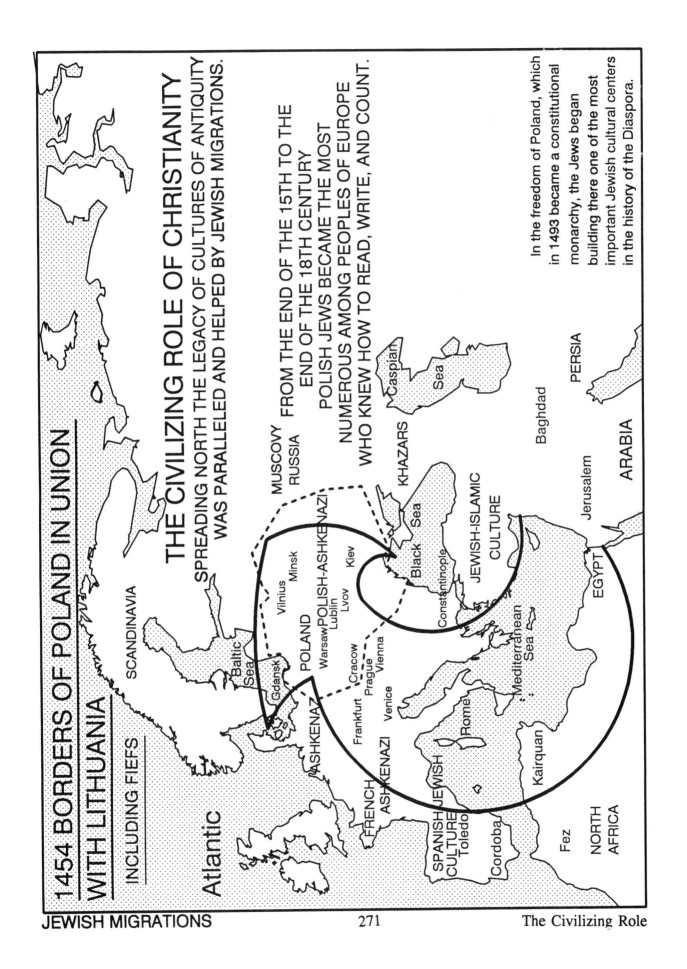

1454 BORDERS OF POLAND IN UNION WITH LITHUANIA

INCLUDING FIEFS

THE CIVILIZING ROLE OF CHRISTIANITY

SPREADING NORTH THE LEGACY OF CULTURES OF ANTIQUITY WAS PARALLELED AND HELPED BY JEWISH MIGRATIONS.

FROM THE END OF THE 15TH TO THE END OF THE 18TH CENTURY POLISH JEWS BECAME THE MOST NUMEROUS AMONG PEOPLES OF EUROPE WHO KNEW HOW TO READ, WRITE, AND COUNT.

In the freedom of Poland, which in 1493 became a constitutional monarchy, the Jews began building there one of the most important Jewish cultural centers in the history of the Diaspora.

Atlantic

SCANDINAVIA

MUSCOVY RUSSIA

Baltic Sea

Gdansk

Vilnius

Minsk

POLAND

Warsaw POLISH-ASHKENAZI

Lublin

Lvov

Kiev

KHAZARS

Black Sea

Constantinople

Caspian Sea

PERSIA

Baghdad

JEWISH-ISLAMIC CULTURE

Jerusalem

ARABIA

ASHKENAZ

Cracow

Prague

Vienna

Frankfurt

Venice

FRENCH ASHKENAZI

Rome

Mediterranean Sea

EGYPT

SPANISH JEWISH CULTURE

Toledo

Cordoba

Kairouan

Fez

NORTH AFRICA

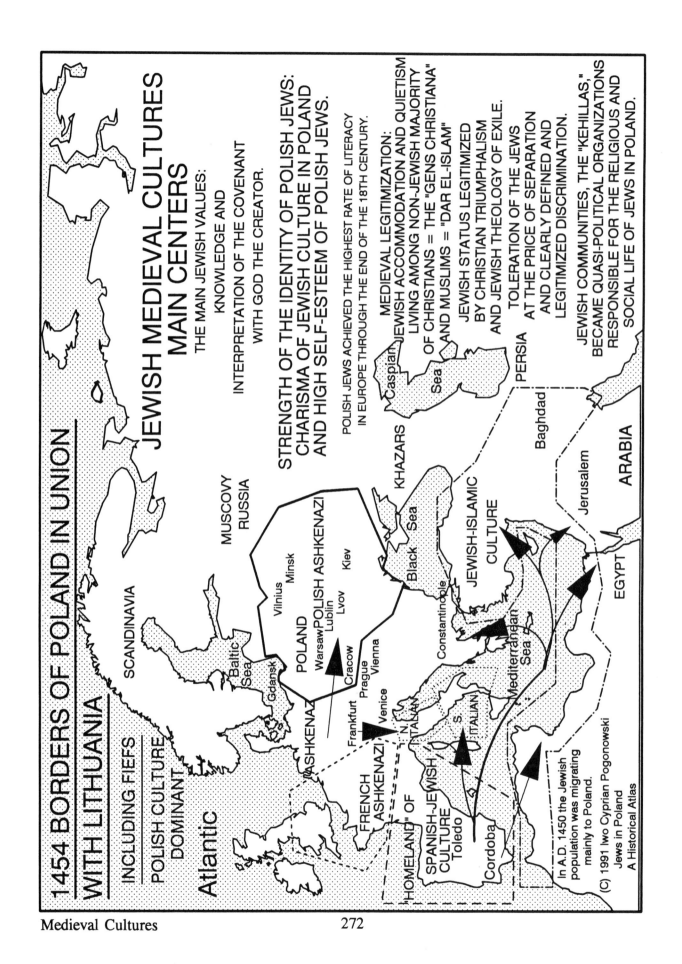

1454 BORDERS OF POLAND IN UNION
WITH LITHUANIA

INCLUDING FIEFS

POLISH CULTURE DOMINANT

JEWISH MEDIEVAL CULTURES
MAIN CENTERS

THE MAIN JEWISH VALUES:

KNOWLEDGE AND

INTERPRETATION OF THE COVENANT

WITH GOD THE CREATOR.

STRENGTH OF THE IDENTITY OF POLISH JEWS:
CHARISMA OF JEWISH CULTURE IN POLAND
AND HIGH SELF-ESTEEM OF POLISH JEWS.

POLISH JEWS ACHIEVED THE HIGHEST RATE OF LITERACY
IN EUROPE THROUGH THE END OF THE 18TH CENTURY.

MEDIEVAL LEGITIMIZATION:
JEWISH ACCOMMODATION AND QUIETISM
LIVING AMONG NON-JEWISH MAJORITY
OF CHRISTIANS = THE "GENS CHRISTIANA"
AND MUSLIMS = "DAR EL-ISLAM"

JEWISH STATUS LEGITIMIZED
BY CHRISTIAN TRIUMPHALISM
AND JEWISH THEOLOGY OF EXILE.

TOLERATION OF THE JEWS
AT THE PRICE OF SEPARATION
AND CLEARLY DEFINED AND
LEGITIMIZED DISCRIMINATION.

JEWISH COMMUNITIES, THE "KEHILLAS,"
BECAME QUASI-POLITICAL ORGANIZATIONS
RESPONSIBLE FOR THE RELIGIOUS AND
SOCIAL LIFE OF JEWS IN POLAND.

Atlantic

SCANDINAVIA

MUSCOVY
RUSSIA

Vilnius

Minsk

POLAND

Warsaw POLISH ASHKENAZI
Lublin Lvov Kiev

Baltic Sea

Gdansk

ASHKENAZI

Cracow

Prague Vienna

Frankfurt Venice

N.

FRENCH ASHKENAZI

"HOMELAND" OF

S.

ITALIAN

N. ITALIAN

SPANISH-JEWISH
CULTURE
Toledo

Cordoba

Mediterranean Sea

Black Sea

Constantinople

JEWISH-ISLAMIC
CULTURE

KHAZARS

Caspian Sea

PERSIA

Baghdad

Jerusalem

EGYPT

ARABIA

In A.D. 1450 the Jewish
population was migrating
mainly to Poland.

(C) 1991 Iwo Cyprian Pogonowski
Jews in Poland
A Historical Atlas

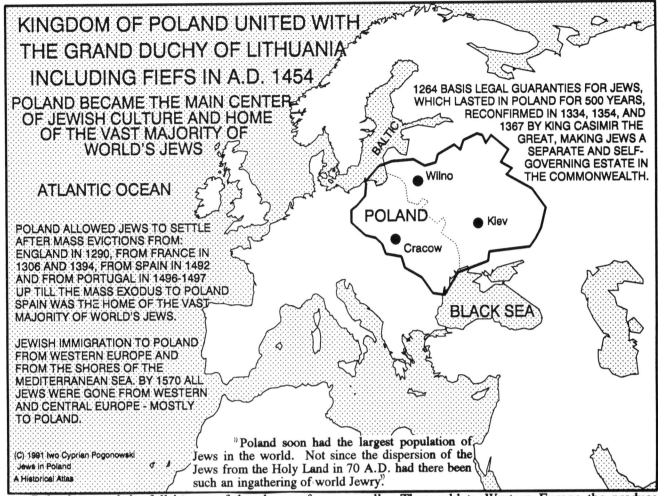

KINGDOM OF POLAND UNITED WITH THE GRAND DUCHY OF LITHUANIA INCLUDING FIEFS IN A.D. 1454

POLAND BECAME THE MAIN CENTER OF JEWISH CULTURE AND HOME OF THE VAST MAJORITY OF WORLD'S JEWS

ATLANTIC OCEAN

POLAND ALLOWED JEWS TO SETTLE AFTER MASS EVICTIONS FROM: ENGLAND IN 1290, FROM FRANCE IN 1306 AND 1394, FROM SPAIN IN 1492 AND FROM PORTUGAL IN 1496-1497 UP TILL THE MASS EXODUS TO POLAND SPAIN WAS THE HOME OF THE VAST MAJORITY OF WORLD'S JEWS.

JEWISH IMMIGRATION TO POLAND FROM WESTERN EUROPE AND FROM THE SHORES OF THE MEDITERRANEAN SEA. BY 1570 ALL JEWS WERE GONE FROM WESTERN AND CENTRAL EUROPE - MOSTLY TO POLAND.

(C) 1991 Iwo Cyprian Pogonowski
Jews in Poland
A Historical Atlas

1264 BASIS LEGAL GUARANTIES FOR JEWS, WHICH LASTED IN POLAND FOR 500 YEARS, RECONFIRMED IN 1334, 1354, AND 1367 BY KING CASIMIR THE GREAT, MAKING JEWS A SEPARATE AND SELF-GOVERNING ESTATE IN THE COMMONWEALTH.

BALTIC

Wilno

POLAND

Kiev

Cracow

BLACK SEA

"Poland soon had the largest population of Jews in the world. Not since the dispersion of the Jews from the Holy Land in 70 A.D. had there been such an ingathering of world Jewry".

Poland escaped the full impact of the plague of the Black Death which began in Western Europe in 1348 where it marked the end of an epoch and a turning point for the Jewish communities there. The plague followed fifty years of Jewish horror in Germany (1298-1348). The Talmud was denounced and various libels were spread. Massacres of Jews followed riots. Beginning in 1298 R. Asher ben Jehiel wrote that the pogroms would not leave a single Jew in Germany. Hatred of Jews reached unprecedented intensity exceeding even the period of crusades.

The Jews were seen as the originators of the Black Death. The opinion of 1348 of Pope Clement VI that "it is absolutely unthinkable that... the Jews have performed so terrible a deed" had no effect in Western Europe. Previous discrimination against Jews was implemented on a far more extensive scale. By the middle of the fifteenth century Poland was the safest place for Jews. There was political and economic foundation for the economic and social success of the Jews in the Kingdom of Poland which was united with the Grand Duchy of Lithuania and is shown on the map above including fiefs. The conquest of Constantinople by the Turks in 1453 made the overland trade route from Lvov to the new capital of Turkey very important. Jews served the economic interests of the noble citizens of Poland

well. They sold to Western Europe the produce from the Moslem East as well as Polish grain, lumber, and cattle. Jewish traders used overland, river and sea routes. Vistula grain trade records reflect these successful transactions. The Jews in Polish cities participated in all branches of commerce and competed successfully with Christian immigrants from Germany in local as well as the international transit trade. The Jews played an increasingly important role in the textile trade with Western Europe.

Jewish success led to tension with the Christian burghers and their trade guilds were often dominated by German immigrants. In 1485 a compromise contract was signed in Cracow. It did not prevent the riot of 1494 and resettlement of the Jews from the fortress of Cracow to the suburb of Kazimierz which became a very successful commercial and trade center. As Jews were turning to commerce in all major cities of Poland their competition against German immigrants became widespread.

By the end of the 15th century Polish parliament became bi-cameral and the supreme political power in Poland. These achievements were the first in Europe and proved to be very favorable for the Jews economically and socially as well as politically.

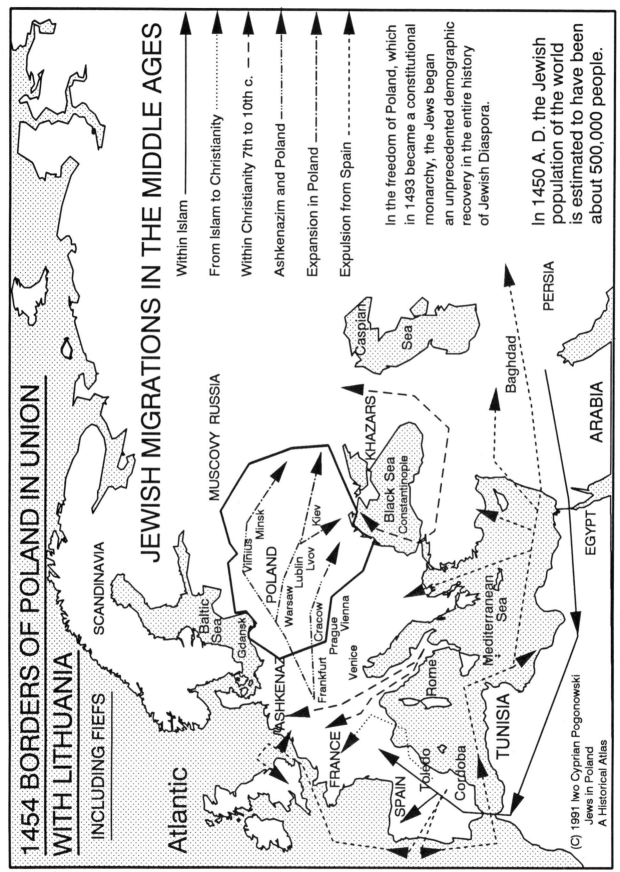

JEWISH MIGRATIONS IN THE MIDDLE AGES

1454 BORDERS OF POLAND IN UNION WITH LITHUANIA

INCLUDING FIEFS

Within Islam ⟶

From Islam to Christianity ········

Within Christianity 7th to 10th c. — —

Ashkenazim and Poland —·—·—

Expansion in Poland ⟶

Expulsion from Spain — — —

In the freedom of Poland, which in 1493 became a constitutional monarchy, the Jews began an unprecedented demographic recovery in the entire history of Jewish Diaspora.

In 1450 A. D. the Jewish population of the world is estimated to have been about 500,000 people.

Atlantic

SCANDINAVIA

MUSCOVY RUSSIA

Baltic Sea

Gdansk

POLAND

Vilnius

Minsk

Warsaw

Lublin

Lvov

Kiev

Cracow

Frankfurt

Prague

Vienna

Venice

ASHKENAZ

FRANCE

SPAIN

Toledo

Cordoba

Rome

TUNISIA

Mediterranean Sea

KHAZARS

Black Sea

Constantinople

Caspian Sea

Baghdad

PERSIA

ARABIA

EGYPT

(C) 1991 Iwo Cyprian Pogonowski
Jews in Poland
A Historical Atlas

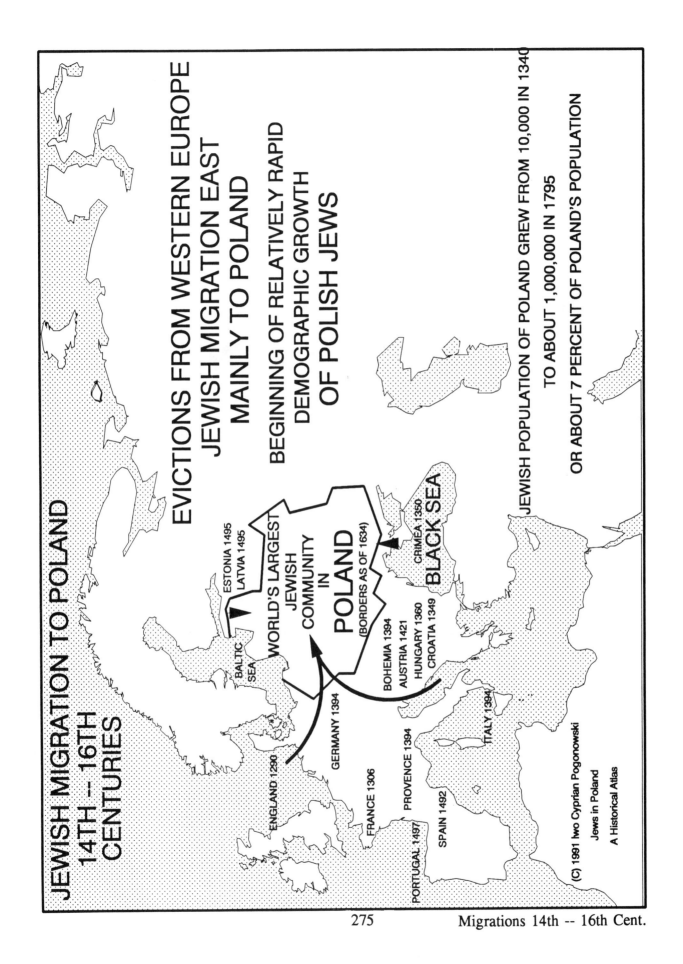

JEWISH MIGRATION TO POLAND
14TH -- 16TH
CENTURIES

EVICTIONS FROM WESTERN EUROPE
JEWISH MIGRATION EAST
MAINLY TO POLAND

BEGINNING OF RELATIVELY RAPID
DEMOGRAPHIC GROWTH
OF POLISH JEWS

JEWISH POPULATION OF POLAND GREW FROM 10,000 IN 1340

TO ABOUT 1,000,000 IN 1795

OR ABOUT 7 PERCENT OF POLAND'S POPULATION

BALTIC
SEA

ESTONIA 1495
LATVIA 1495

WORLD'S LARGEST
JEWISH
COMMUNITY
IN
POLAND
(BORDERS AS OF 1634)

BOHEMIA 1394
AUSTRIA 1421
HUNGARY 1360
CROATIA 1349

CRIMEA 1350
BLACK SEA

GERMANY 1394

ENGLAND 1290

FRANCE 1306

PROVENCE 1394

ITALY 1394

PORTUGAL 1497

SPAIN 1492

(C) 1991 Iwo Cyprian Pogonowski

Jews in Poland

A Historical Atlas

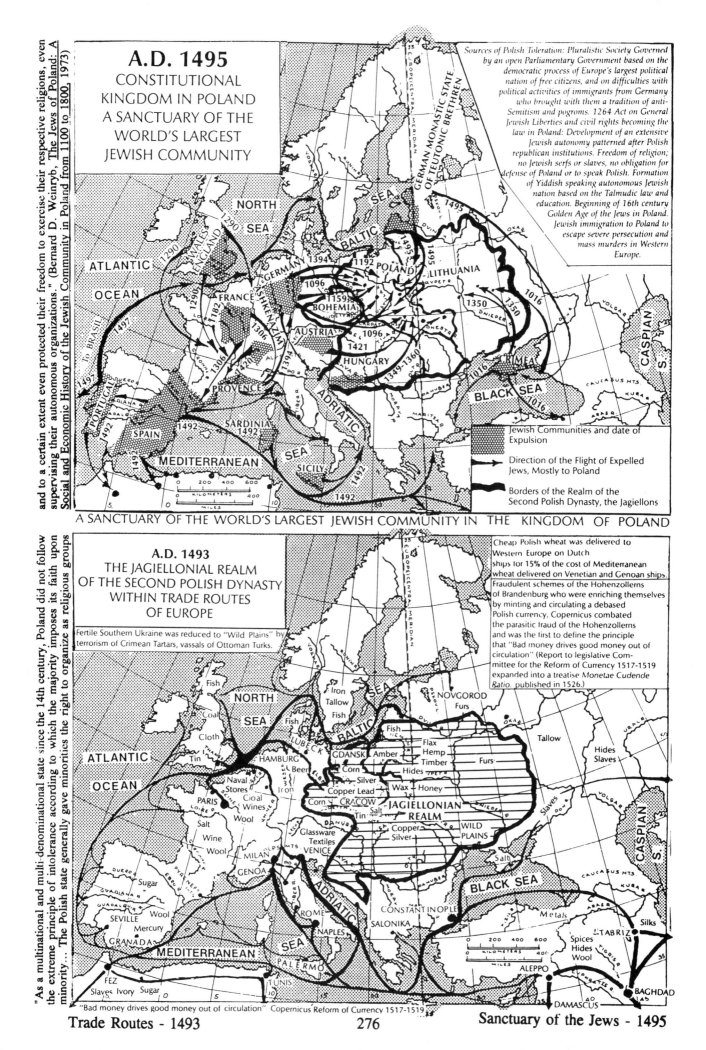

A.D. 1495
CONSTITUTIONAL KINGDOM IN POLAND A SANCTUARY OF THE WORLD'S LARGEST JEWISH COMMUNITY

Sources of Polish Toleration: Pluralistic Society Governed by an open Parliamentary Government based on the democratic process of Europe's largest political nation of free citizens, and on difficulties with political activities of immigrants from Germany who brought with them a tradition of anti-Semitism and pogroms. 1264 Act on General Jewish Liberties and civil rights becoming the law in Poland: Development of an extensive Jewish autonomy patterned after Polish republican institutions. Freedom of religion; no Jewish serfs or slaves, no obligation for defense of Poland or to speak Polish. Formation of Yiddish speaking autonomous Jewish nation based on the Talmudic law and education. Beginning of 16th century Golden Age of the Jews in Poland. Jewish immigration to Poland to escape severe persecution and mass murders in Western Europe.

and to a certain extent even protected their freedom to exercise their respective religions, even supervising their autonomous organizations." (Bernard D. Weinryb, The Jews of Poland: A Social and Economic History of the Jewish Community in Poland from 1100 to 1800, 1973)

Jewish Communities and date of Expulsion

Direction of the Flight of Expelled Jews, Mostly to Poland

Borders of the Realm of the Second Polish Dynasty, the Jagiellons

A SANCTUARY OF THE WORLD'S LARGEST JEWISH COMMUNITY IN THE KINGDOM OF POLAND

A.D. 1493
THE JAGIELLONIAL REALM OF THE SECOND POLISH DYNASTY WITHIN TRADE ROUTES OF EUROPE

Fertile Southern Ukraine was reduced to "Wild Plains" by terrorism of Crimean Tartars, vassals of Ottoman Turks.

Cheap Polish wheat was delivered to Western Europe on Dutch ships for 15% of the cost of Mediterranean wheat delivered on Venetian and Genoan ships. Fraudulent schemes of the Hohenzollerns of Brandenburg who were enriching themselves by minting and circulating a debased Polish currency. Copernicus combated the parasitic fraud of the Hohenzollerns and was the first to define the principle that "Bad money drives good money out of circulation" (Report to legislative Committee for the Reform of Currency 1517-1519 expanded into a treatise *Monetae Cudende Ratio*, published in 1526.)

"As a multinational and multi-denominational state since the 14th century, Poland did not follow the extreme principle of intolerance according to which the majority imposes its faith upon minority... The Polish state generally gave minorities the right to organize as religious groups

"Bad money drives good money out of circulation" Copernicus' Reform of Currency 1517-1519

Drowning of several hundred Polish Jews in Dvina R. near Polock by Ivan the Terrible.

A.D. 1576-1582

POLAND'S VICTORIOUS CAMPAIGN

IN WAR WITH

MUSCOVY RUSSIAN EMPIRE

OVER LIVONIA

Poland acts as a great power under leadership of Batory mobilizing adequate forces to defeat Russian invasion of Livonia by Ivan IV "The Terrible." **1**) Polish operations remove Muscovy's forces from Livonia. In **2**) 1577 reduce Dvinsk (Duneburg); 1578 Wenden decisive operations; **3**) 1579 reducing Polock 22,000 Knights in 100,000 force: raiding deep into Polesie **4**) Reducing Vyelkye Luki Stara Russa, building road to Polock.

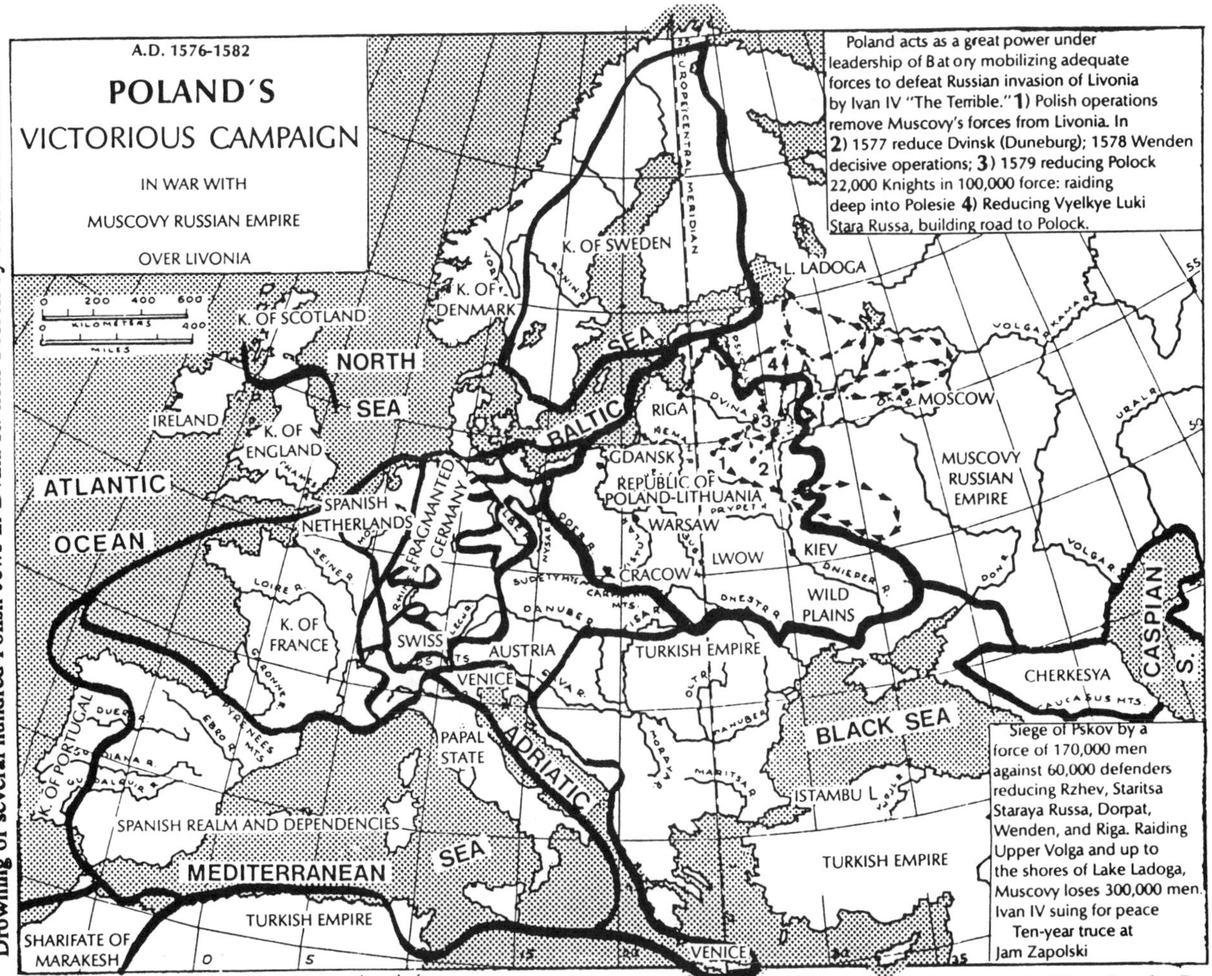

K. OF SCOTLAND
NORTH SEA
IRELAND
K. OF ENGLAND
ATLANTIC OCEAN
SPANISH NETHERLANDS
FRAGMANTED GERMANY
K. OF DENMARK
K. OF SWEDEN
BALTIC SEA
L. LADOGA
RIGA
DVINA R.
GDANSK
REPUBLIC OF POLAND-LITHUANIA
WARSAW
LWOW
CRACOW
KIEV
WILD PLAINS
MOSCOW
MUSCOVY RUSSIAN EMPIRE
VOLGA R.
CASPIAN S.
CHERKESYA
BLACK SEA
K. OF FRANCE
SWISS
AUSTRIA
VENICE
TURKISH EMPIRE
PAPAL STATE
ADRIATIC
K. OF PORTUGAL
SPANISH REALM AND DEPENDENCIES
MEDITERRANEAN SEA
TURKISH EMPIRE
SHARIFATE OF MARAKESH
ISTAMBUL
VENICE

Siege of Pskov by a force of 170,000 men against 60,000 defenders reducing Rzhev, Staritsa Staraya Russa, Dorpat, Wenden, and Riga. Raiding Upper Volga and up to the shores of Lake Ladoga, Muscovy loses 300,000 men. Ivan IV suing for peace

Ten-year truce at Jam Zapolski

Deep raids by Polish cavalry tying up Muscovy's main forces

Drowning of Several Hundreds Jews

1594-1596

NALEVAYKO'S UPRISING FOR CIVIL RIGHTS UKRAINIAN COSSACKS

The 1596 Union of Brest between Catholic and Orthodox Churches attempted to subordinate the Orthodoxy to Rome and to strengthen the ties of Byelorussians and Ukrainians with Poland. It was supported by the Orthodox Metropolites who hoped to obtain seats in the Senate of the Polish Republic. This was blocked by the Catholic clergy. The Union of Brest broke up the Ruthenian population into Uniates and Disuniates. It contributed to major Cossack uprisings against the Republic.

Nalevayko's uprising had religous and economical motives. Nalevayko was executed in Warsaw in 1597

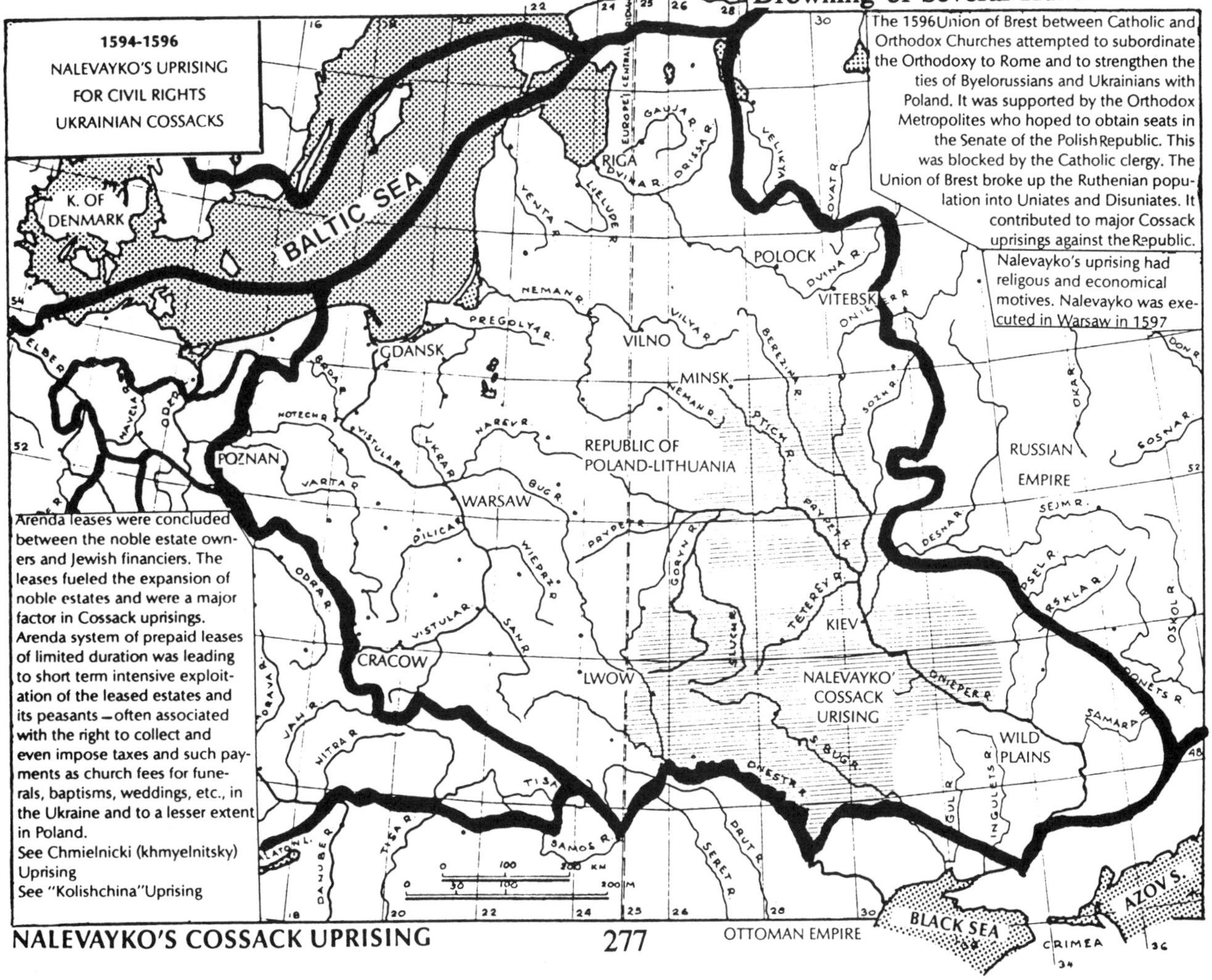

K. OF DENMARK
BALTIC SEA
RIGA
POLOCK
DVINA R.
VITEBSK
VILNO
MINSK
GDANSK
POZNAN
REPUBLIC OF POLAND-LITHUANIA
WARSAW
RUSSIAN EMPIRE
KIEV
CRACOW
LWOW
NALEVAYKO' COSSACK URISING
WILD PLAINS
OTTOMAN EMPIRE
BLACK SEA
CRIMEA
AZOV S.

Arenda leases were concluded between the noble estate owners and Jewish financiers. The leases fueled the expansion of noble estates and were a major factor in Cossack uprisings. Arenda system of prepaid leases of limited duration was leading to short term intensive exploitation of the leased estates and its peasants – often associated with the right to collect and even impose taxes and such payments as church fees for funerals, baptisms, weddings, etc., in the Ukraine and to a lesser extent in Poland.

See Chmielnicki (khmyelnitsky) Uprising

See "Kolishchina" Uprising

NALEVAYKO'S COSSACK UPRISING

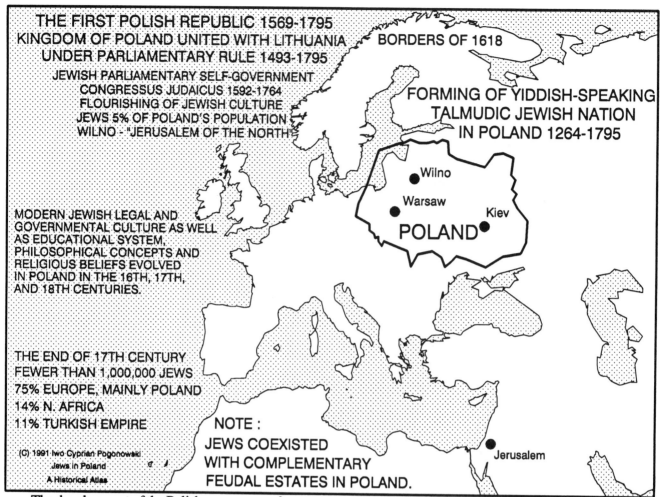

THE FIRST POLISH REPUBLIC 1569-1795
KINGDOM OF POLAND UNITED WITH LITHUANIA
UNDER PARLIAMENTARY RULE 1493-1795
JEWISH PARLIAMENTARY SELF-GOVERNMENT
CONGRESSUS JUDAICUS 1592-1764
FLOURISHING OF JEWISH CULTURE
JEWS 5% OF POLAND'S POPULATION
WILNO - "JERUSALEM OF THE NORTH"

BORDERS OF 1618

FORMING OF YIDDISH-SPEAKING
TALMUDIC JEWISH NATION
IN POLAND 1264-1795

Wilno
Warsaw
Kiev
POLAND

MODERN JEWISH LEGAL AND
GOVERNMENTAL CULTURE AS WELL
AS EDUCATIONAL SYSTEM,
PHILOSOPHICAL CONCEPTS AND
RELIGIOUS BELIEFS EVOLVED
IN POLAND IN THE 16TH, 17TH,
AND 18TH CENTURIES.

THE END OF 17TH CENTURY
FEWER THAN 1,000,000 JEWS
75% EUROPE, MAINLY POLAND
14% N. AFRICA
11% TURKISH EMPIRE

(C) 1991 Iwo Cyprian Pogonowski
Jews in Poland
A Historical Atlas

NOTE :
JEWS COEXISTED
WITH COMPLEMENTARY
FEUDAL ESTATES IN POLAND.

Jerusalem

The development of the Polish government-from-below in the form of an orderly national system of representation provided a model for Jewish self-government in Poland. The Act of Nieszawa of 1454 is viewed as the actual beginning of the Polish Nobles' Republic of the Kingdom of Poland united with the Grand Duchy of Lithuania and including Ukraine, Byelorussia, Prussia, and Latvia. The Polish parliament became bi-cameral in 1493, the first in Europe. The First Polish Republic was formally founded in Lublin in 1569. The number of noble citizens exceeded one million by 1618. Then the free Jewish population of Poland numbered 500,000 or 70 percent of all Jews and 5 percent of the population of the Polish state. Starting with the 16th century, Polish Jews became dominant among the Ashkenazim.

The 16th century is known as the Golden Age of Poland and of Polish Jewry. During the 16th century the Jews of Poland were given full autonomy and could issue their own laws. Thus, in the history of Diaspora the Jews had in Poland the only Jewish national parliament, the "Congressus Judaicus", (1592-1764) during the entire period between the Sanhedrin of antiquity and the Knesset of the modern State of Israel.

Poland remained for centuries the most important

country for the survival of the Jews. Modern Jewish legal and governmental culture as well as educational systems, philosophical concepts and religious beliefs evolved in Poland in the 16th, 17th, and 18th centuries. Jewish historians such as S. Dubnow (1860-1941) viewed the institutions of the autonomy of Polish Jews as the most important phenomenon in the history of the Diaspora. Fundamental Polish laws of 1422 and 1425 protected private property and due process. The last one named "Neminem Captivabimus" was equivalent to English Act of Habeas Corpus of 1685 and preceded it by 260 years.

Poland became the country of thr rebirth of the Jewish people. There they formed a Talmudic Jewish nation. The Talmud was used as the basic law of Jewish autonomy in Poland. A simple and universal handbook of the Jewish law, entitled Shulhan Aruch, was prepared by Joseph Caro, a Sephardic Jew, in 1565. Shuhan Aruch was completed, put in final form, and supplied with commentary by Moshe Isserles (Remu c.1510-1572), chief rabbi of Cracow and president of the Cracow yeshiva. Isserles' version of Shulhan Aruch was universally accepted by all Ashkenazi Jews in Europe. A synagogue named after Moshe Isserles and founded by his father was built in Cracow in 1553. It survived the Second World War.

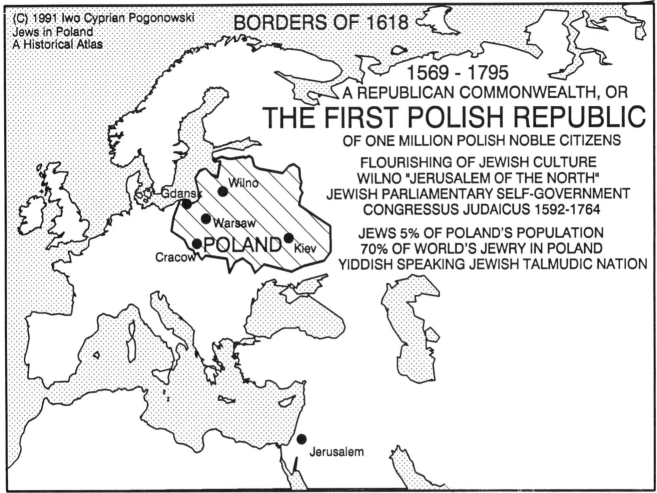

BORDERS OF 1618

1569 - 1795
A REPUBLICAN COMMONWEALTH, OR
THE FIRST POLISH REPUBLIC
OF ONE MILLION POLISH NOBLE CITIZENS

FLOURISHING OF JEWISH CULTURE
WILNO "JERUSALEM OF THE NORTH"
JEWISH PARLIAMENTARY SELF-GOVERNMENT
CONGRESSUS JUDAICUS 1592-1764

JEWS 5% OF POLAND'S POPULATION
70% OF WORLD'S JEWRY IN POLAND
YIDDISH SPEAKING JEWISH TALMUDIC NATION

Gdansk · Wilno · Warsaw · POLAND · Kiev · Cracow · Jerusalem

Starting in the 12th century anti-Jewish laws were enforced in western and southern Europe. These laws excluded Jews from land ownership, farming, and working in most crafts. Jews were taxed heavily and were not permitted to live in most towns. In those in which they could live they were restricted to designated streets or sections. Commerce, banking, and money lending were the main Jewish occupations. During the 12th to 15th centuries violent persecutions threatened Jews with extinction. Brutal persecutions of Jews occurred during the crusades, the plague of 1348-51, and during the intensification of Holy Inquisition (1215-1859). The Inquisition caused the death of millions in western Europe, including 40,000 Jews. It never was enforced throughout Poland as it was in Western Europe; the Polish parliament banned it in laws of 1552, 1562, and 1565.

The Statute of Jewish Liberties issued in 1264 in Kalisz, Poland, was reconfirmed by Casimir the Great in 1334, 1354, and 1367. The Polish Statute of Jewish Liberties lasted for 500 years and permitted Jews to become an autonomous feudal quasi-estate. The sociological study *The Jews in Polish Culture* by Aleksander Hertz (1961) described the Jews of Poland as a charismatic Jewish hereditary caste which encompassed 75 percent of world Jewry by 1790 and lasted until 1944.

Self-governing Jewish communities in Poland spoke the Yiddish language of the Ashkenasi Jews. They were free to speak their own language and did not experience any pressure to speak Polish. Poland was the freest country among the great powers of Europe in the Renaissance period. The Polish-Lithuanian state was the largest on the European continent. Poland was the pioneer of pluralism in Europe. Basic democratic ideals were crystallized in 15th- and 16th-century Poland, during the rise of east-central Europe under Polish leadership. These ideals included: the principle of government by consent, personal freedom, freedom of religion, and the value of self-reliance.

Jews in Poland had their own courts and were represented by a single lobbyist who negotiated with the Polish government on all matters, including the amount of taxes to be paid to the Polish Treasury. Jews were guaranteed personal freedom and the right to trade, equal with the burghers. Jews also worked in trades, banking, money lending, the leasing of inns, mills, and even collection of various state taxes. The national parliament of Polish Jews was the supreme authority over all European Jewry. It was known as the "Congressus Judaicus" (1592-1764).

279

GOVERNMENT STRUCTURE OF THE POLISH REPUBLIC

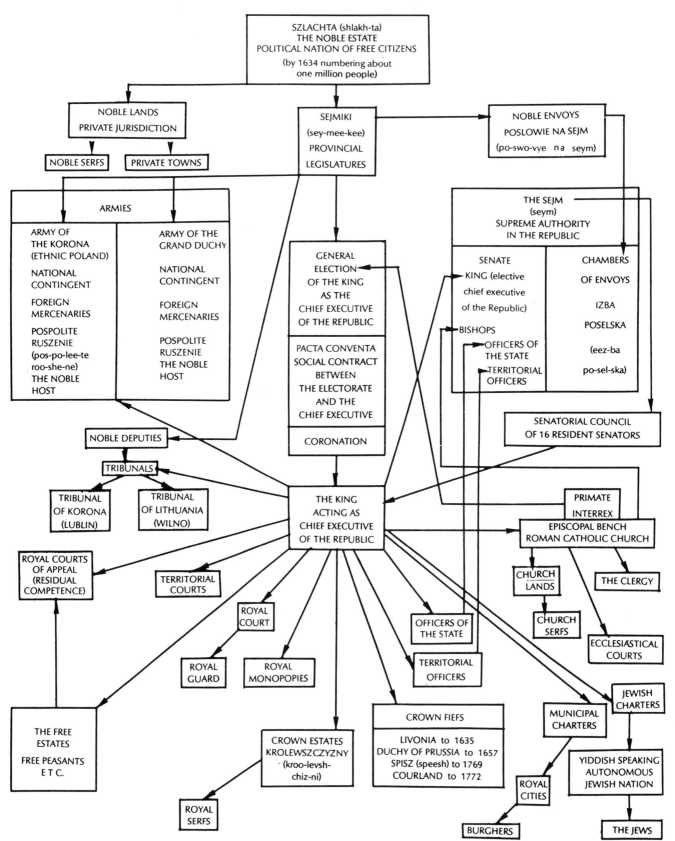

Jewish national parliament the "Congressus Judaicus" (1592-1764) was patterned after the Polish national parliament (1493-1795).

CENTRAL INSTITUTIONS OF THE FIRST POLISH REPUBLIC 1569-1795

Diag. of Government Structure of the Polish Republic.

AUTONOMOUS JEWISH GOVERNMENT

NOTE: JEWISH PARLIAMENTARY GOVERNMENT UNIQUE BETWEEN SANHEDRIN OF ANTIQUITY
AND KNESSET OF THE STATE OF ISRAEL
SELF GOVERNMENT OF YIDDISH SPEAKING JEWISH TALMUDIC NATION IN POLAND
WHICH NUMBERED 1,000,000 YIDDISH SPEAKERS BY 1795

GENERAL CHARTER OF RIGHTS AND PRIVILEGES GUARANTEEING FREEDOM AND SECURITY OF THE JEWS
BASED ON THE ACT OF KALISZ OF 1264

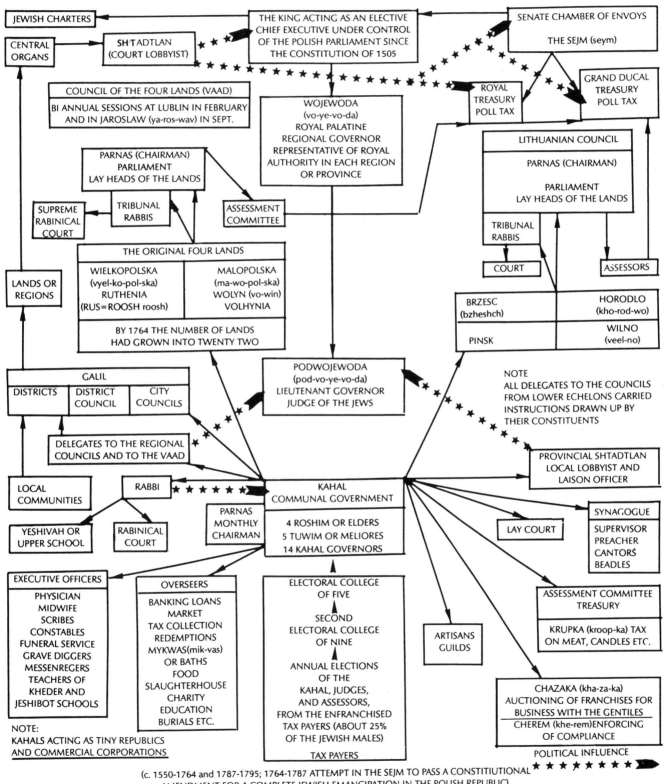

(c. 1550-1764 and 1787-1795; 1764-1787 ATTEMPT IN THE SEJM TO PASS A CONSTITIUTIONAL
AMENDMENT FOR A COMPLETE JEWISH EMANCIPATION IN THE POLISH REPUBLIC).

THE ORGANS OF JEWISH REPRESENTATIVE GOVERNMENT

Diag. of Autonomous Jewish Government in the Polish Republic.

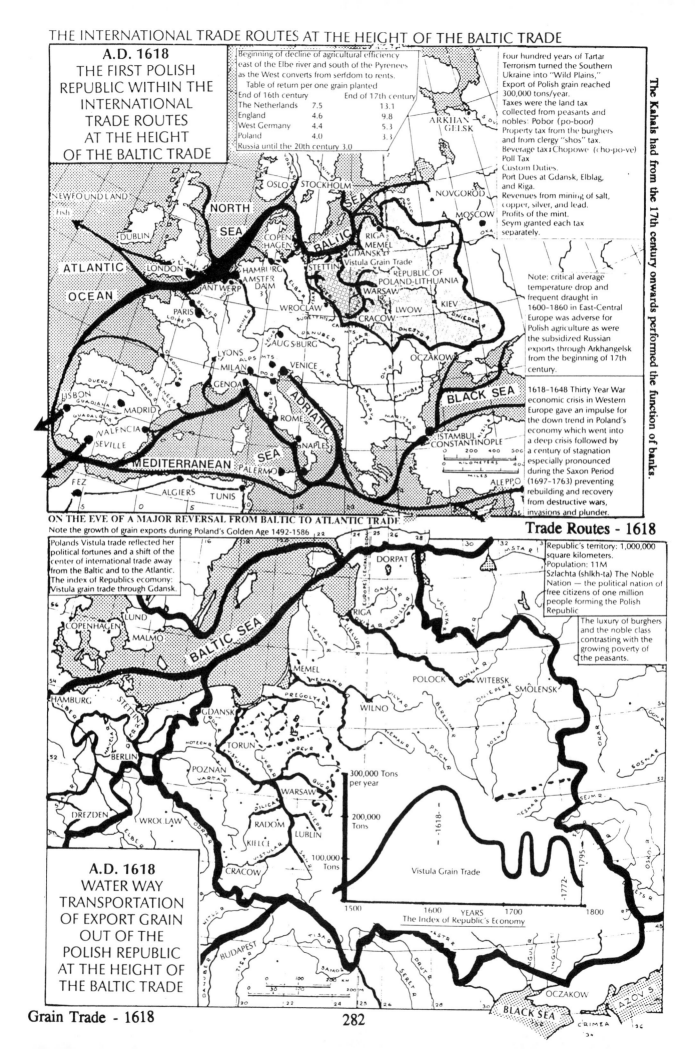

A.D. 1618
THE FIRST POLISH REPUBLIC WITHIN THE INTERNATIONAL TRADE ROUTES AT THE HEIGHT OF THE BALTIC TRADE

Beginning of decline of agricultural efficiency east of the Elbe river and south of the Pyrenees as the West converts from serfdom to rents.

Table of return per one grain planted

	End of 16th century	End of 17th century
The Netherlands	7.5	13.1
England	4.6	9.8
West Germany	4.4	5.3
Poland	4.0	3.3
Russia until the 20th century 3.0		

Four hundred years of Tartar Terrorism turned the Southern Ukraine into "Wild Plains." Export of Polish grain reached 300,000 tons/year.
Taxes were the land tax collected from peasants and nobles: Pobor (po-boor)
Property tax from the burghers and from clergy "shos" tax.
Beverage tax: Chopowe (cho-po-ve)
Poll Tax
Custom Duties.
Port Dues at Gdansk, Elblag, and Riga.
Revenues from mining of salt, copper, silver, and lead.
Profits of the mint.
Seym granted each tax separately.

The Kahals had from the 17th century onwards performed the function of banks.

Note: critical average temperature drop and frequent draught in 1600-1860 in East-Central Europe was adverse for Polish agriculture as were the subsidized Russian exports through Arkhangelsk from the beginning of 17th century.

1618-1648 Thirty Year War economic crisis in Western Europe gave an impulse for the down trend in Poland's economy which went into a deep crisis followed by a century of stagnation especially pronounced during the Saxon Period (1697-1763) preventing rebuilding and recovery from destructive wars, invasions and plunder.

ON THE EVE OF A MAJOR REVERSAL FROM BALTIC TO ATLANTIC TRADE

Trade Routes - 1618

Note the growth of grain exports during Poland's Golden Age 1492-1586

Polands Vistula trade reflected her political fortunes and a shift of the center of international trade away from the Baltic and to the Atlantic. The index of Republics ecomony: Vistula grain trade through Gdansk.

Republic's territory: 1,000,000 square kilometers.
Population: 11M
Szlachta (shlkh-ta) The Noble Nation — the political nation of free citizens of one million people forming the Polish Republic

The luxury of burghers and the noble class contrasting with the growing poverty of the peasants.

300,000 Tons per year
200,000 Tons
100,000 Tons
Vistula Grain Trade
1500   1600   YEARS   1700   1800
The Index of Republic's Economy

A.D. 1618
WATER WAY TRANSPORTATION OF EXPORT GRAIN OUT OF THE POLISH REPUBLIC AT THE HEIGHT OF THE BALTIC TRADE

WESTERN BORDER OF ARENDA ACTIVITY
▬ ▬ ▬ ▬ ▬ ▬ ▬ ▬

A.D. 1618
LANGUAGES
OF THE MULTINATIONAL
REPUBLIC OF POLISH NOBLES

Nobility of 10% and burghers of 15% spoke Polish throughout the multinational Republic; 450,000 Jews spoke Yiddish — a Germanic language (300,000 Jews lived in towns and 150,000 in the villages). For listing by size of the community of other language groups see the summary in the left bottom corner.

BALTIC SEA

ESTONIAN
ESTONIAN
RUSSIAN
LIVONIAN
RIGA
LATVIAN
LATVIAN
RUSSIAN
MOSCOW
LITHUANIAN
BYELORUSSIAN
WILNO
MINSK
HAMBURG
GERMAN
PRUSSIAN
POLISH
GERMAN
GERMAN
BERLIN
GERMAN
GERMAN
POZNAN
POLISH NOBLES' REPUBLIC
BYELORUSSIAN
BYELORUSSIAN
BYELORUSSIAN
SERBO-
LUSATIAN
WARSAW
GERMAN
CZECH
POLISH
POLISH
RUSSIAN
CRACOW
UKRAINIAN
LWOW
KIEV
UKRAINIAN
CZECH
SLOVAK
UKRAINIAN
BUDA
PEST
HUNGARIAN
VLACH
VLACH
TARTAR
TARTAR
BLACK SEA
CRIMEA
AZOV S.

Republic's Languages
Estimated total population of
11,000,000 on one million
square kilometers:

Polish   40%, 4.4M
Ukrainian   30%, 3.3M
Byelorussian   15%, 1.7M
Lithuanian   5%, .7M.
Others: Approx. 1.5M
Yiddish, German, Latvian,
Russian, Estonian, Armenian,
Prussian, Tartar, Livonian,
Slovak, Czech, and Gypsy
listed by group size.
M = millions

ARENDA TYPE OF PREPAID JEWISH LEASES OF GENTILE ESTATES

The western border of the area of Arenda activity is shown on the map above. About three quarters of the Jewish population of the Republic of Polish Nobles lived in the area of Arenda activity. The Arenda activity consisted of pre-paid and short duration Jewish leases of gentile estates complete with jurisdiction over the rural population which inhabited the leased property. Thus, the Christian peasants within Arenda activity were exploited and controlled by the Jewish Arendazh. He was in power "to punish by fines or by sentence of death" the peasants in the leased estates. Arendazh had the right to impose and collect taxes as well as church fees for baptisms, weddings, funerals, etc. and to control the very access to churches (these taxes and fees were resented by the local Christian peasants).

In 1581 in Lublin the "Congressus Judaicus" or the Jewish autonomous parliament in Poland forbade all Jews, under the penalty of anathema, to take Arenda leases in Polish ethnic areas, as shown on the above map. Polish ethnic areas were Catholic, so was the leadership community of the Republic of Polish Nobles. Thus it was in the area predominantly populated by Greek Orthodox Ukrainians and Byelorussians in which the Arenda activity functioned and eventually led to uprisings and massacres of Catholics and Jews especially in 1648 and in 1768.

When a Jewish entrepreneur called an "Arendazh" succeeded in securing an Arenda lease he then organized the exploitation of the leased estate in order to earn profit over and above the pre-paid amount of money. An Arendazh usually would bring with him his poorer relatives or acquaintances and settle them in the leased estate in order to run its various economic facilities such as inns, orchards, fish ponds, flour-mills etc. A Jewish entrepreneur or Arendazh would receive, for the duration of the Arenda lease, estates which often included a complex of small towns and a large number of villages. Small Jewish towns called "shtetls" were established in vicinity of Arenda activity. Jewish self-government assisted the lease holders in establishing procedures to renew their contracts with the estate owners and not to be subject to underbidding by other Jews. Within the area of Arenda activity Jewish population was increasing very rapidly.

283

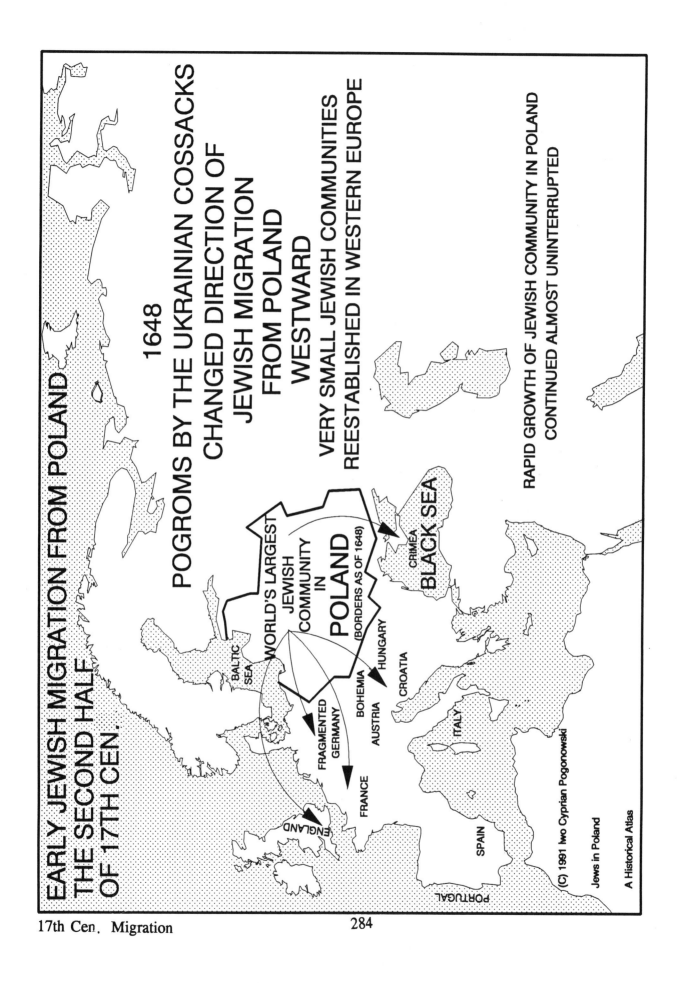

EARLY JEWISH MIGRATION FROM POLAND
THE SECOND HALF
OF 17TH CEN.

1648

POGROMS BY THE UKRAINIAN COSSACKS
CHANGED DIRECTION OF
JEWISH MIGRATION
FROM POLAND
WESTWARD
VERY SMALL JEWISH COMMUNITIES
REESTABLISHED IN WESTERN EUROPE

RAPID GROWTH OF JEWISH COMMUNITY IN POLAND
CONTINUED ALMOST UNINTERRUPTED

BALTIC
SEA

WORLD'S LARGEST
JEWISH
COMMUNITY
IN
POLAND
(BORDERS AS OF 1648)

FRAGMENTED
GERMANY

BOHEMIA

AUSTRIA

HUNGARY

CROATIA

ENGLAND

FRANCE

ITALY

SPAIN

PORTUGAL

CRIMEA
BLACK SEA

(C) 1991 Iwo Cyprian Pogonowski

Jews in Poland

A Historical Atlas

17th Cen. Migration

284

A.D. 1648-1651
COSSACK UPRISING
— THE END OF GREAT
POWER STATUS OF
POLISH NOBLES' REPUBLIC
UKRAINIAN COSSACK
UPRISING EXPLOITED BY
MUSCOVY RUSSIA, SWEDEN
BRANDENBURG AND TURKISH
MOSLEM OTTOMAN EMPIRE

Polish armies, were the sole defenders of the Jews, for the Jews and Polish nobility were allies against a rebellion which viewed them both as enemy.

Cossack Uprising

Cossack March

Ukrainian Cossacks rebelled against attempts to convert them into serfs and change their religion into Greek Catholic. Cossacks were ready to participate in an anti-Turkish crusade. When the Polish plans failed Cossack uprising broke out. Bohdan Chmielnicki (1595-1652) assumed the leadership; he was a former officer-scribe in the army of the Polish Republic (he failed to get satisfaction in court for his grievances against other Ukrainian nobles and himself committed an act of treason and desertion for which he faced a death sentence). 1648 march of the joint Cossack-Tartar forces started after concluding an alliance with the Khan of Crimea.
Muscovites supported Chmielnicki with men and money in order to weaken Poland and eventually annex Ukraine into the Muscovy-Russian Empire. Defeated by the army of the Republic, Chmielnicki accepted Muscovy protectorate which eventually led to abolition of Cossack self-Government.

0 200 400 600
KILOMETERS
MILES 400

SCOTLAND
NORTH SEA
IRELAND
ENGLAND
DUTCH REPUBLIC
ATLANTIC OCEAN
K. OF SWEDEN
K. OF DENMARK
BALTIC SEA
BRANDENBURG
SAXONY
300 GERMAN STATES
POLISH NOBLES' REPUBLIC
MUSCOVY RUSSIAN EMPIRE
CASPIAN S.
SWISS
HABSBURG EMPIRE
K. OF FRANCE
SAVOY
TRANSYLVANIA
MOLDAVIA
CRIMEA
CHERKESYA
1648 MARCH OF COSSACKS AND THEIR TARTAR ALLIES
WALLACHIA
BLACK SEA
ADRIATIC
PAPAL STATE
RAGUSA
K. OF PORTUGAL
CATALONIA
SPANISH REALM AND DEPENDENCIES
MEDITERRANEAN SEA
TURKISH MOSLEM OTTOMAN EMPIRE
SHARIFATE OF MARAKESH
MOSLEM OTTOMAN EMPIRE

Crimean Tartars — a Moslem vanguard of the Turkish Empire intended to weaken the Polish Republic but prevent rising of an independent Ukrainian Cossack state. Prolonging the war gave Tartars an additional opportunity to loot and take people for ransom. Tartars broke with the Cossacks at Zborow and Zwaniec while at Beresteczko they simply ran from the battlefield and left the Cossacks to suffer a crushing defeat.

The largest massacre of Jews since A.D. 117

1648-1651 COSSACK UPRISING — THE END OF GREAT
POWER STATUS OF POLISH NOBLES' REPUBLIC

A.D. 1648-1651
COSSACK UPRISING
LED BY
BOHDAN CHMIELNICKI
(KHMELNYTSKYY)
BATTLES AND PACTS
ENCOURAGING MUSCOVY ATTACK

Huge human losses including 120,000 Jews murdered and starved by the Cossacks, the **largest massacre of Jews since A.D. 117** Tartars murdering at Batoh of an entire captured Polish division after the Cossacks demanded the killings and refunded the ransom value of the Poles; huge losses of life and property throughout the area of Cossack uprising.

LIVONIA
K. OF SWEDEN
BALTIC SEA
RIGA
DENMARK
HAMBURG
WEST POMERANIA
BRANDENBURG
BERLIN
300 GERMAN STATES
SAXONY
KLAJPEDA
KROLEWIEC
PRUSSIA
GDANSK
POZNAN
WARSAW
K. OF POLAND
CRACOW
DVINSK
POLOCK
VITEBSK
SMOLENSK
MOSCOW
MUSCOVY RUSSIAN EMPIRE
WILNO
GRAND DUCHY OF LITHUANIA
MINSK
'POLISH NOBLES' REPUBLIC'
1648 MARCH OF COSSACKS AND THEIR TARTAR ALLIES
Cossack Uprising
Cossack March
BERESTECZKO
ZBARAZ
ZBOROW
ZWANIEC
PILAWCE
KIEV
BIALA CERKIEW
PEREJESLAW
KORSUN
YELLOW WATERS
UKRAINIAN COSSACKS
SICZ
BATOH
HABSBURG EMPIRE AUSTRIA
UKRAINIAN COSSACK UPRISING EXPLOITED BY MUSCOVY RUSSIA, SWEDEN BRANDENBURG AND TURKISH MOSLEM OTTOMAN EMPIRE
CRIMEA TARTARS THE "HORNETS NEST" OF TERRORISM
BLACK SEA
TURKISH MOSLEM OTTOMAN EMPIRE

BATTLES AND PACTS
1. May 1648 Yellow Waters
2. May 1648 Korsun
3. Sept. 1648 Pilawce
4. July-Aug. 1649 Zbaraz Siege
5. Aug. 1648 Zborow Pact
6. June 1651 Beresteczko
July 1651 Beresteczko
8. Sept. 1651 Biala Cerkiew Pact
9. June 1652 Batoh
10. Dec. 1653 Zwaniec pact
11. Oct. 1653 Moscow Sobor on annexation of Ukraine by Muscovy-Russian Empire
12. Jan. 1654 Perejeslaw pact between Cossacks and Muscovy on annexation by Russia of Ukraine east of the Dnieper River.

Bohdan Chmienlicki (1595-1652) assumed the leadership

Cossack Uprising - Details - 1648 -- 1651

285

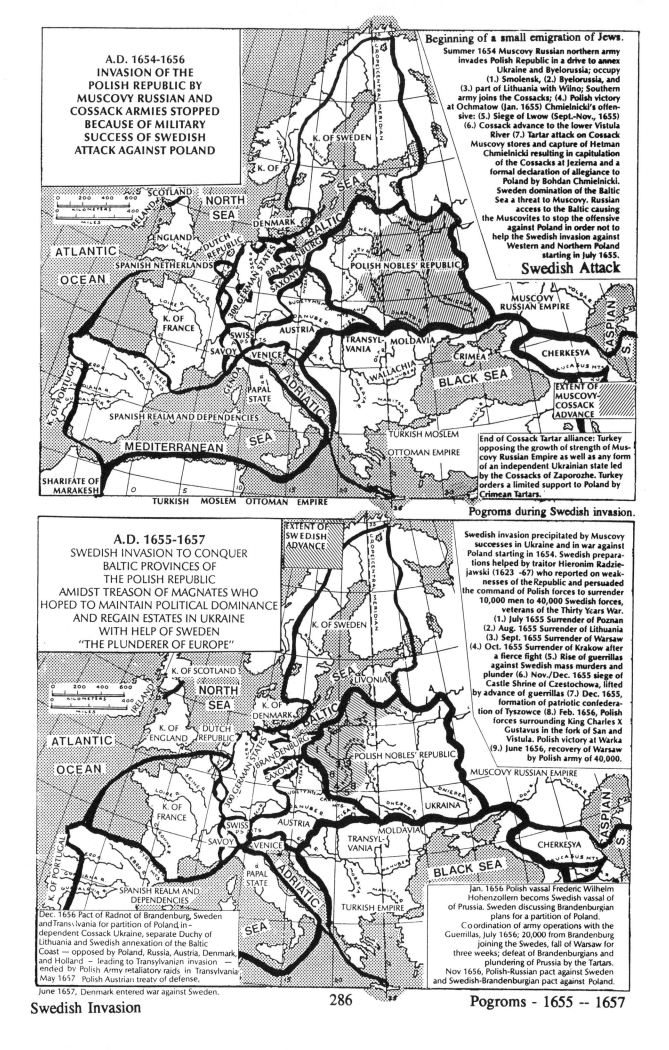

A.D. 1654-1656
INVASION OF THE
POLISH REPUBLIC BY
MUSCOVY RUSSIAN AND
COSSACK ARMIES STOPPED
BECAUSE OF MILITARY
SUCCESS OF SWEDISH
ATTACK AGAINST POLAND

Beginning of a small emigration of Jews.

Summer 1654 Muscovy Russian northern army invades Polish Republic in a drive to annex Ukraine and Byelorussia; occupy (1.) Smolensk, (2.) Byelorussia, and (3.) part of Lithuania with Wilno; Southern army joins the Cossacks; (4.) Polish victory at Ochmatow (Jan. 1655) Chmielnicki's offensive: (5.) Siege of Lwow (Sept.-Nov., 1655) (6.) Cossack advance to the lower Vistula River (7.) Tartar attack on Cossack Muscovy stores and capture of Hetman Chmielnicki resulting in capitulation of the Cossacks at Jezierna and a formal declaration of allegiance to Poland by Bohdan Chmielnicki. Sweden domination of the Baltic Sea a threat to Muscovy. Russian access to the Baltic causing the Muscovites to stop the offensive against Poland in order not to help the Swedish invasion against Western and Northern Poland starting in July 1655. **Swedish Attack**

End of Cossack Tartar alliance: Turkey opposing the growth of strength of Muscovy Russian Empire as well as any form of an independent Ukrainian state led by the Cossacks of Zaporozhe. Turkey orders a limited support to Poland by Crimean Tartars.

Pogroms during Swedish invasion.

A.D. 1655-1657
SWEDISH INVASION TO CONQUER
BALTIC PROVINCES OF
THE POLISH REPUBLIC
AMIDST TREASON OF MAGNATES WHO
HOPED TO MAINTAIN POLITICAL DOMINANCE
AND REGAIN ESTATES IN UKRAINE
WITH HELP OF SWEDEN
"THE PLUNDERER OF EUROPE"

Swedish invasion precipitated by Muscovy successes in Ukraine and in war against Poland starting in 1654. Swedish preparations helped by traitor Hieronim Radziejawski (1623 -67) who reported on weaknesses of the Republic and persuaded the command of Polish forces to surrender 10,000 men to 40,000 Swedish forces, veterans of the Thirty Years War. (1.) July 1655 Surrender of Poznan (2.) Aug. 1655 Surrender of Lithuania (3.) Sept. 1655 Surrender of Warsaw (4.) Oct. 1655 Surrender of Krakow after a fierce fight (5.) Rise of guerrillas against Swedish mass murders and plunder (6.) Nov./Dec. 1655 siege of Castle Shrine of Czestochowa, lifted by advance of guerrillas (7.) Dec. 1655, formation of patriotic confederation of Tyszowce (8.) Feb. 1656, Polish forces surrounding King Charles X Gustavus in the fork of San and Vistula. Polish victory at Warka (9.) June 1656, recovery of Warsaw by Polish army of 40,000.

Jan. 1656 Polish vassal Frederic Wilhelm Hohenzollern becomes Swedish vassal of of Prussia. Sweden discussing Brandenburgian plans for a partition of Poland. Coordination of army operations with the Guerrillas, July 1656; 20,000 from Brandenburg joining the Swedes, fall of Warsaw for three weeks; defeat of Brandenburgians and plundering of Prussia by the Tartars. Nov 1656, Polish-Russian pact against Sweden and Swedish-Brandenburgian pact against Poland.

Dec. 1656 Pact of Radnot of Brandenburg, Sweden and Transylvania for partition of Poland, in - dependent Cossack Ukraine, separate Duchy of Lithuania and Swedish annexation of the Baltic Coast — opposed by Poland, Russia, Austria, Denmark, and Holland — leading to Transylvanian invasion — ended by Polish Army retaliatory raids in Transylvania May 1657 Polish Austrian treaty of defense.

June 1657, Denmark entered war against Sweden.

Swedish Invasion

Pogroms - 1655 -- 1657

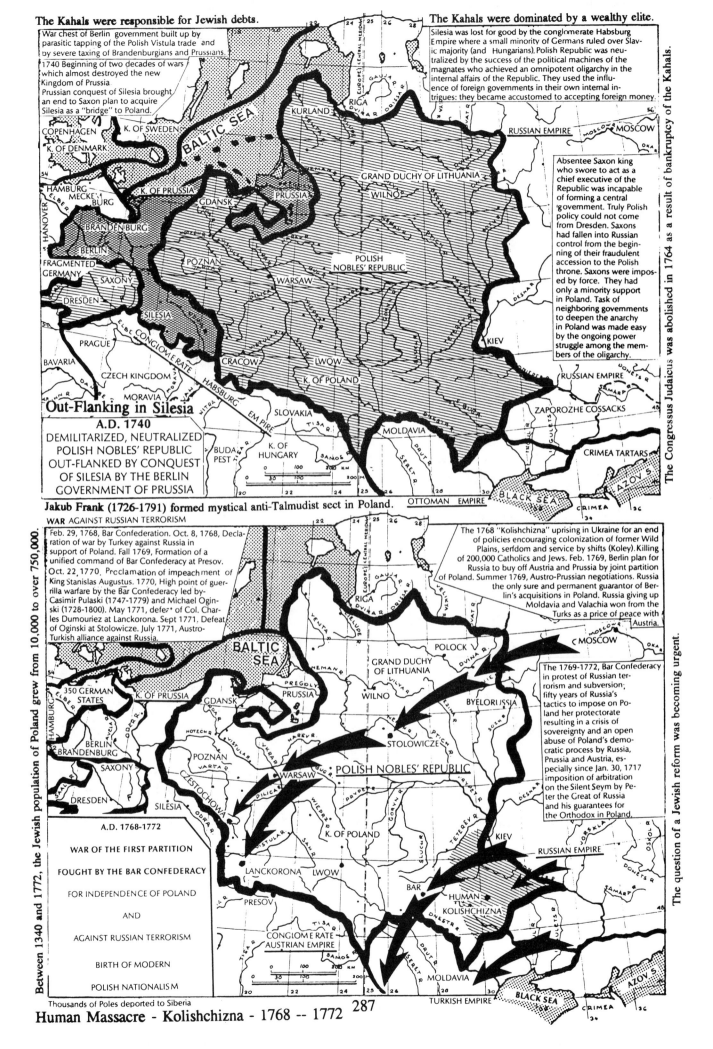

The Kahals were responsible for Jewish debts.

War chest of Berlin government built up by parasitic tapping of the Polish Vistula trade and by severe taxing of Brandenburgians and Prussians.

1740 Beginning of two decades of wars which almost destroyed the new Kingdom of Prussia.

Prussian conquest of Silesia brought an end to Saxon plan to acquire Silesia as a "bridge" to Poland.

The Kahals were dominated by a wealthy elite.

Silesia was lost for good by the conglomerate Habsburg Empire where a small minority of Germans ruled over Slavic majority (and Hungarians). Polish Republic was neutralized by the success of the political machines of the magnates who achieved an omnipotent oligarchy in the internal affairs of the Republic. They used the influence of foreign governments in their own internal intrigues: they became accustomed to accepting foreign money.

Absentee Saxon king who swore to act as a chief executive of the Republic was incapable of forming a central government. Truly Polish policy could not come from Dresden. Saxons had fallen into Russian control from the beginning of their fraudulent accession to the Polish throne. Saxons were imposed by force. They had only a minority support in Poland. Task of neighboring governments to deepen the anarchy in Poland was made easy by the ongoing power struggle among the members of the oligarchy.

The Congressus Judaicus was abolished in 1764 as a result of bankruptcy of the Kahals.

Out-Flanking in Silesia

A.D. 1740

DEMILITARIZED, NEUTRALIZED POLISH NOBLES' REPUBLIC OUT-FLANKED BY CONQUEST OF SILESIA BY THE BERLIN GOVERNMENT OF PRUSSIA

Jakub Frank (1726-1791) formed mystical anti-Talmudist sect in Poland.

WAR AGAINST RUSSIAN TERRORISM

Feb. 29, 1768, Bar Confederation. Oct. 8, 1768, Declaration of war by Turkey against Russia in support of Poland. Fall 1769, Formation of a unified command of Bar Confederacy at Presov. Oct. 22, 1770, Proclamation of impeachment of King Stanislas Augustus. 1770, High point of guerrilla warfare by the Bar Confederacy led by Casimir Pulaski (1747-1779) and Michael Oginski (1728-1800). May 1771, defeat of Col. Charles Dumouriez at Lanckorona. Sept 1771, Defeat of Oginski at Stolowicze. July 1771, Austro-Turkish alliance against Russia.

The 1768 "Kolishchizna" uprising in Ukraine for an end of policies encouraging colonization of former Wild Plains, serfdom and service by shifts (Koley). Killing of 200,000 Catholics and Jews. Feb. 1769, Berlin plan for Russia to buy off Austria and Prussia by joint partition of Poland. Summer 1769, Austro-Prussian negotiations. Russia the only sure and permanent guarantor of Berlin's acquisitions in Poland. Russia giving up Moldavia and Valachia won from the Turks as a price of peace with Austria.

The 1769-1772, Bar Confederacy in protest of Russian terrorism and subversion; fifty years of Russia's tactics to impose on Poland her protectorate resulting in a crisis of sovereignty and an open abuse of Poland's democratic process by Russia, Prussia and Austria, especially since Jan. 30, 1717 imposition of arbitration on the Silent Seym by Peter the Great of Russia and his guarantees for the Orthodox in Poland.

The question of a Jewish reform was becoming urgent.

Between 1340 and 1772, the Jewish population of Poland grew from 10,000 to over 750,000.

A.D. 1768-1772

WAR OF THE FIRST PARTITION

FOUGHT BY THE BAR CONFEDERACY

FOR INDEPENDENCE OF POLAND

AND

AGAINST RUSSIAN TERRORISM

BIRTH OF MODERN

POLISH NATIONALISM

Thousands of Poles deported to Siberia

Human Massacre - Kolishchizna - 1768 -- 1772

E. Zabłocki, *An Arendazh* (the leaseholder), *with a Tenant Farmer*
(see Arenda activity)

288

UNDER FOREIGN RULE

ECONOMIC AND POLITICAL

COMPETITION

1795 -- 1918

"Zionists were interested in having Jews settle in Palestine. They too were interested in building a nation. They played up news about anti-Semitism. Jews cannot feel secure living in Poland, they said. The love of the land of Israel has been central to Jewish thinking for millennia, but the Zionist movement was a consequence (not a cause) of the anti-Semitism."

"...The Jewish community did not support Polish nationalism. They sought a homeland in Palestine or autonomy in those areas of Eastern Europe where they were heavily concentrated. And a substantial number of Jews were revolutionary. As a handicapped people, they wanted a change."

Arthur Szyk, *The Statutes of Kalisz,*
Death of Berko Joselewicz at Kock, 1809

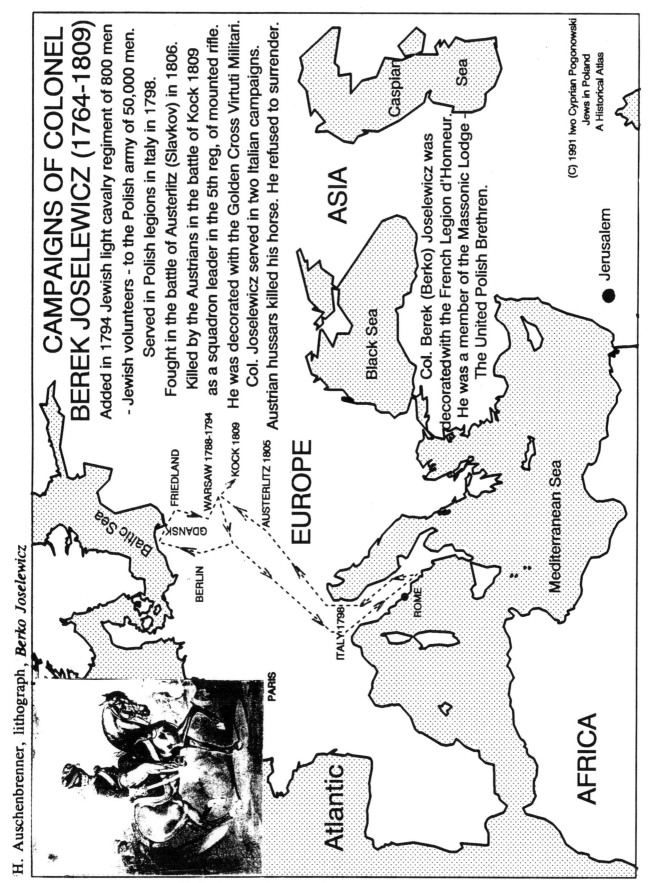

CAMPAIGNS OF COLONEL
BEREK JOSELEWICZ (1764-1809)

Added in 1794 Jewish light cavalry regiment of 800 men - Jewish volunteers - to the Polish army of 50,000 men.

Served in Polish legions in Italy in 1798.

Fought in the battle of Austerlitz (Slavkov) in 1806.

Killed by the Austrians in the battle of Kock 1809 as a squadron leader in the 5th reg, of mounted rifle.

He was decorated with the Golden Cross Virtuti Militari.

Col. Joselewicz served in two Italian campaigns.

Austrian hussars killed his horse. He refused to surrender.

H. Auschenbrenner, lithograph, *Berko Joselewicz*

Col. Berek (Berko) Joselewicz was decorated with the French Legion d'Honneur. He was a member of the Massonic Lodge - The United Polish Brethren.

ASIA

EUROPE

AFRICA

Atlantic

Baltic Sea

Black Sea

Caspian Sea

Mediterranean Sea

Jerusalem

FRIEDLAND

WARSAW 1788-1794

KOCK 1809

GDANSK

BERLIN

AUSTERLITZ 1805

ITALY 1798

ROME

PARIS

Col. Berek (Berko) Joselewicz - 1764 -- 1809

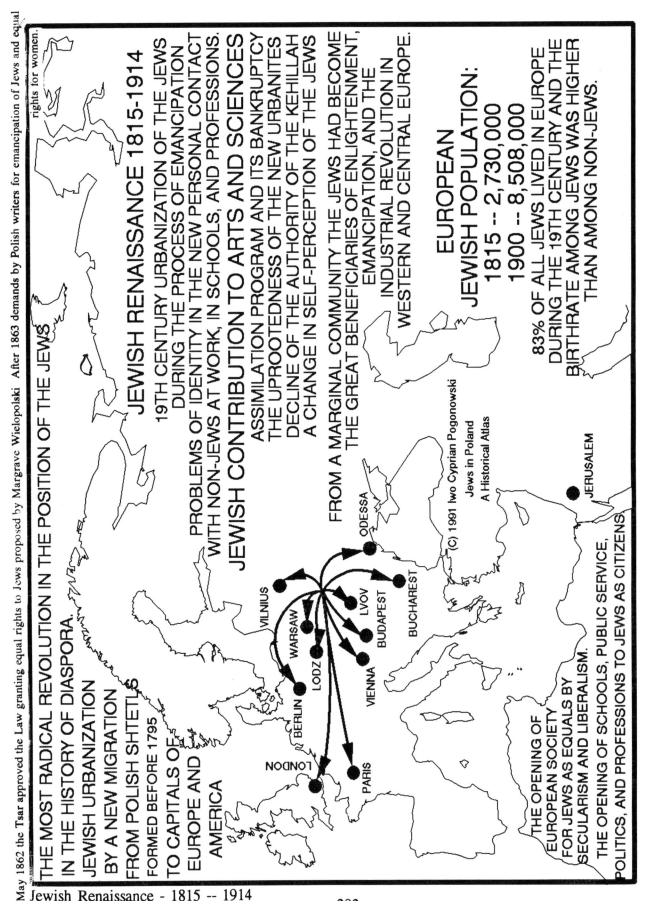

JEWISH RENAISSANCE 1815-1914

THE MOST RADICAL REVOLUTION IN THE POSITION OF THE JEWS IN THE HISTORY OF DIASPORA.

JEWISH URBANIZATION BY A NEW MIGRATION FROM POLISH SHTETLS FORMED BEFORE 1795 TO CAPITALS OF EUROPE AND AMERICA

19TH CENTURY URBANIZATION OF THE JEWS DURING THE PROCESS OF EMANCIPATION

PROBLEMS OF IDENTITY IN THE NEW PERSONAL CONTACT WITH NON-JEWS AT WORK, IN SCHOOLS, AND PROFESSIONS.

JEWISH CONTRIBUTION TO ARTS AND SCIENCES

ASSIMILATION PROGRAM AND ITS BANKRUPTCY
THE UPROOTEDNESS OF THE NEW URBANITES
DECLINE OF THE AUTHORITY OF THE KEHILLAH
A CHANGE IN SELF-PERCEPTION OF THE JEWS

FROM A MARGINAL COMMUNITY THE JEWS HAD BECOME THE GREAT BENEFICIARIES OF ENLIGHTENMENT, EMANCIPATION, AND THE INDUSTRIAL REVOLUTION IN WESTERN AND CENTRAL EUROPE.

EUROPEAN JEWISH POPULATION:
1815 -- 2,730,000
1900 -- 8,508,000

83% OF ALL JEWS LIVED IN EUROPE DURING THE 19TH CENTURY AND THE BIRTHRATE AMONG JEWS WAS HIGHER THAN AMONG NON-JEWS.

THE OPENING OF EUROPEAN SOCIETY FOR JEWS AS EQUALS BY SECULARISM AND LIBERALISM.

THE OPENING OF SCHOOLS, PUBLIC SERVICE, POLITICS, AND PROFESSIONS TO JEWS AS CITIZENS.

(C) 1991 Iwo Cyprian Pogonowski
Jews in Poland
A Historical Atlas

ODESSA
VILNIUS
WARSAW
LODZ
BERLIN
LONDON
PARIS
VIENNA
BUDAPEST
LVOV
BUCHAREST
JERUSALEM

May 1862 the Tsar approved the Law granting equal rights to Jews proposed by Margrave Wielopolski   After 1863 demands by Polish writers for emancipation of Jews and equal rights for women.

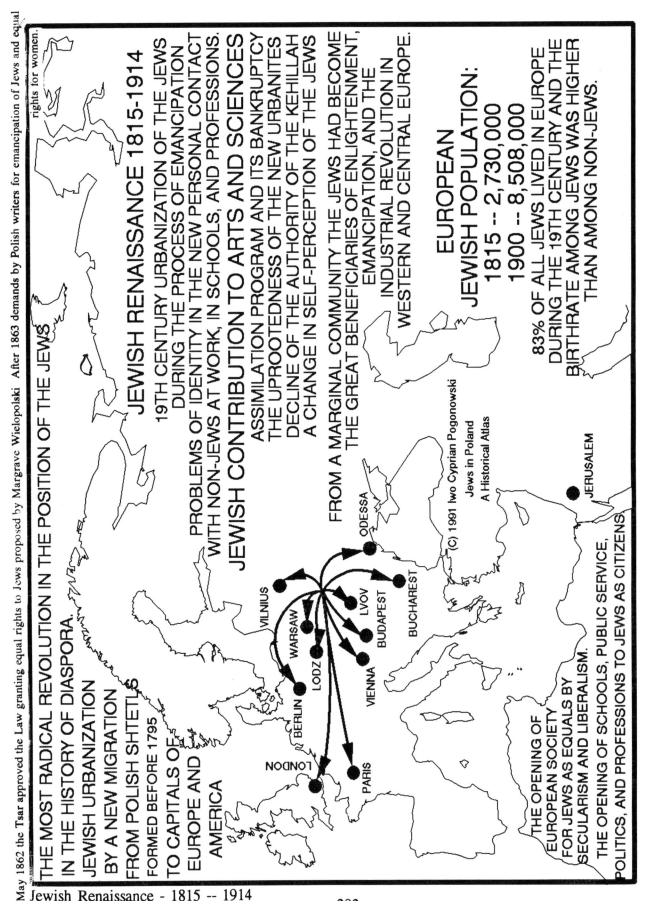

Jewish Renaissance - 1815 -- 1914

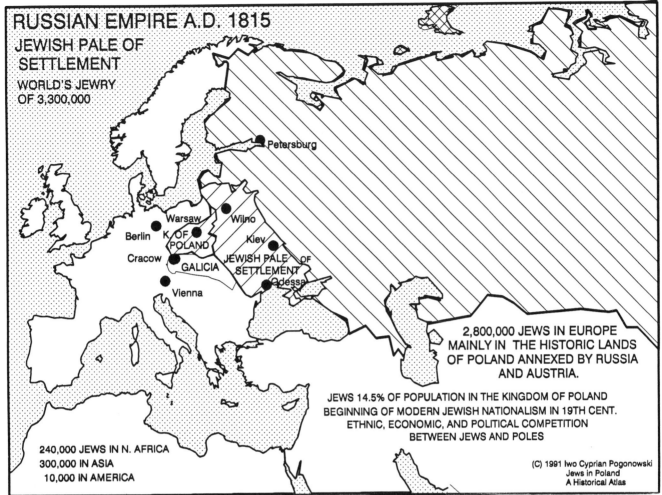

RUSSIAN EMPIRE A.D. 1815
JEWISH PALE OF SETTLEMENT
WORLD'S JEWRY OF 3,300,000

2,800,000 JEWS IN EUROPE MAINLY IN THE HISTORIC LANDS OF POLAND ANNEXED BY RUSSIA AND AUSTRIA.

JEWS 14.5% OF POPULATION IN THE KINGDOM OF POLAND
BEGINNING OF MODERN JEWISH NATIONALISM IN 19TH CENT.
ETHNIC, ECONOMIC, AND POLITICAL COMPETITION
BETWEEN JEWS AND POLES

240,000 JEWS IN N. AFRICA
300,000 IN ASIA
10,000 IN AMERICA

(C) 1991 Iwo Cyprian Pogonowski
Jews in Poland
A Historical Atlas

In 1795 the Russian Empire acquired one million or 80 percent of Polish Jews in its spoils from obliteration of Poland. The Russian myth that the small Jewish nation was dedicated to the destruction of the Great Russian nation might have had its roots in the memory of early slave trade and wars conducted against Kievian Rus by Turkic Khazars whose elite converted to Judaism (700-1016 A.D.). Russian policy was "to keep the Jews harmless" and to confine them in the Pale of Settlement in the provinces annexed from Poland.

The Polish Statute of Jewish Liberties and Jewish Autonomy were abrogated. The situation of the Jews seriously deteriorated. Similarly in the Polish provinces of Austria and Prussia (which acquired 15 percent and 5 percent of Polish Jews respectively) the governments in Vienna and Berlin discriminated against Jews and demanded that they accept German language and culture.

The Jewish school system in the shtetls of Poland produced the largest number of men of any group in Europe who could read, write, and count. Polish Jews were literate in Hebrew while Yiddish was the language spoken in Jewish communities in the former Polish provinces. In the 19th century many Polish Jews started to migrate to the cities of Austria and Germany where they made significant contributions to western culture and civilization. 1815-1914 was the century of the Great Jewish Renaissance, despite lack of pluralism in European societies and growing opposition to the emancipation of Jews. A history of Europe of this period cannot be written without mentioning the Jewish presence in literature, music, science, philosophy, psychology, painting, and journalism. Jews were prominent in the financial world as well as in the leadership of revolutionary movements.

During the 19th century Jews were emancipated in most of Europe. Russia was an exception. There the government was limiting the areas of Jewish settlement and enforced discriminatory policies. Jewish distinctiveness was still viewed in the Russian Empire in a religious context, based on the Jewish theology of exile and what is known as "Christian triumphalism."

By 1880 over 80 percent of all Jews lived in the territory of pre-partition Poland. By the end of the 19th century there were in the Russian Empire in the former Polish provinces about 6,000,000 Jews, including 1,300,000 in the Kingdom of Poland, 800,000 in neighboring Austria and 50,000 in the Prussian part of Germany.

293

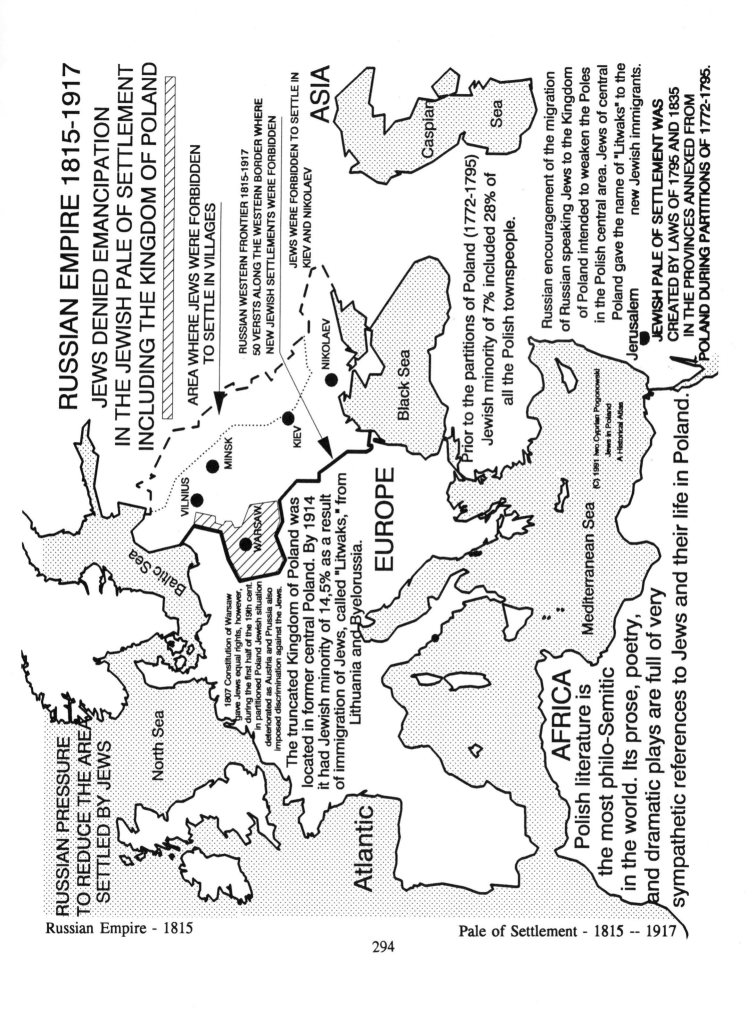

RUSSIAN EMPIRE 1815-1917

JEWS DENIED EMANCIPATION IN THE JEWISH PALE OF SETTLEMENT INCLUDING THE KINGDOM OF POLAND

AREA WHERE JEWS WERE FORBIDDEN TO SETTLE IN VILLAGES

RUSSIAN WESTERN FRONTIER 1815-1917 50 VERSTS ALONG THE WESTERN BORDER WHERE NEW JEWISH SETTLEMENTS WERE FORBIDDEN

JEWS WERE FORBIDDEN TO SETTLE IN KIEV AND NIKOLAEV

ASIA

Caspian Sea

Prior to the partitions of Poland (1772-1795) Jewish minority of 7% included 28% of all the Polish townspeople.

Russian encouragement of the migration of Russian speaking Jews to the Kingdom of Poland intended to weaken the Poles in the Polish central area. Jews of central Poland gave the name of "Litwaks" to the new Jewish immigrants.

Jerusalem

JEWISH PALE OF SETTLEMENT WAS CREATED BY LAWS OF 1795 AND 1835 IN THE PROVINCES ANNEXED FROM POLAND DURING PARTITIONS OF 1772-1795.

NIKOLAEV

KIEV

MINSK

VILNIUS

Black Sea

WARSAW

EUROPE

Baltic Sea

1807 Constitution of Warsaw gave Jews equal rights, however, during the first half of the 19th cent. in partitioned Poland Jewish situation deteriorated as Austria and Prussia also imposed discrimination against the Jews.

The truncated Kingdom of Poland was located in former central Poland. By 1914 it had Jewish minority of 14,5% as a result of immigration of Jews, called "Litwaks," from Lithuania and Byelorussia.

RUSSIAN PRESSURE TO REDUCE THE AREA SETTLED BY JEWS

North Sea

Mediterranean Sea

(C) 1991 Iwo Cyprian Pogonowski
Jews in Poland
A Historical Atlas

AFRICA

Polish literature is the most philo-Semitic in the world. Its prose, poetry, and dramatic plays are full of very sympathetic references to Jews and their life in Poland.

Atlantic

Russian Empire - 1815

Pale of Settlement - 1815 -- 1917

294

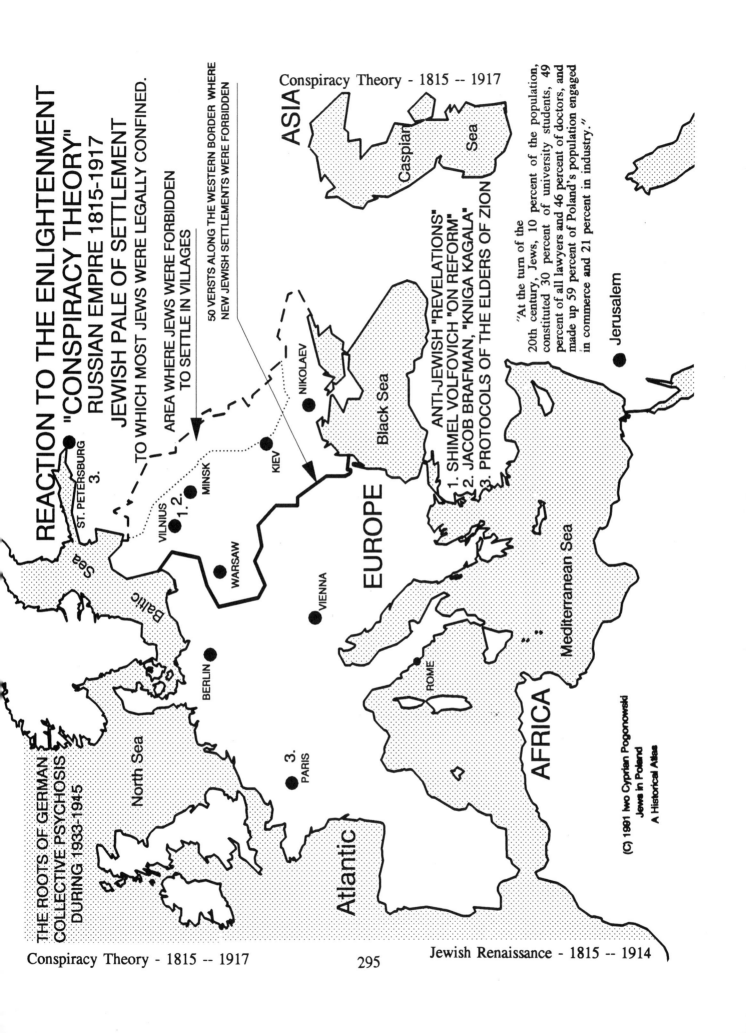

REACTION TO THE ENLIGHTENMENT
"CONSPIRACY THEORY"
RUSSIAN EMPIRE 1815-1917

JEWISH PALE OF SETTLEMENT
TO WHICH MOST JEWS WERE LEGALLY CONFINED.

AREA WHERE JEWS WERE FORBIDDEN
TO SETTLE IN VILLAGES

50 VERSTS ALONG THE WESTERN BORDER WHERE
NEW JEWISH SETTLEMENTS WERE FORBIDDEN

THE ROOTS OF GERMAN
COLLECTIVE PSYCHOSIS
DURING 1933-1945

Conspiracy Theory - 1815 -- 1917

ASIA

Caspian
Sea

ANTI-JEWISH "REVELATIONS"
"ON REFORM"
1. SHIMEL VOLFOVICH
2. JACOB BRAFMAN, "KNIGA KAGALA"
3. PROTOCOLS OF THE ELDERS OF ZION

"At the turn of the
20th century, Jews, 10 percent of the population,
constituted 30 percent of university students, 49
percent of all lawyers and 46 percent of doctors, and
made up 59 percent of Poland's population engaged
in commerce and 21 percent in industry."

ST. PETERSBURG
3.

VILNIUS
1. 2.
MINSK

KIEV

NIKOLAEV

WARSAW

Black Sea

EUROPE

VIENNA

Baltic Sea

BERLIN

North Sea

ROME

Mediterranean Sea

AFRICA

Jerusalem

3.
PARIS

Atlantic

(C) 1991 Iwo Cyprian Pogonowski
Jews in Poland
A Historical Atlas

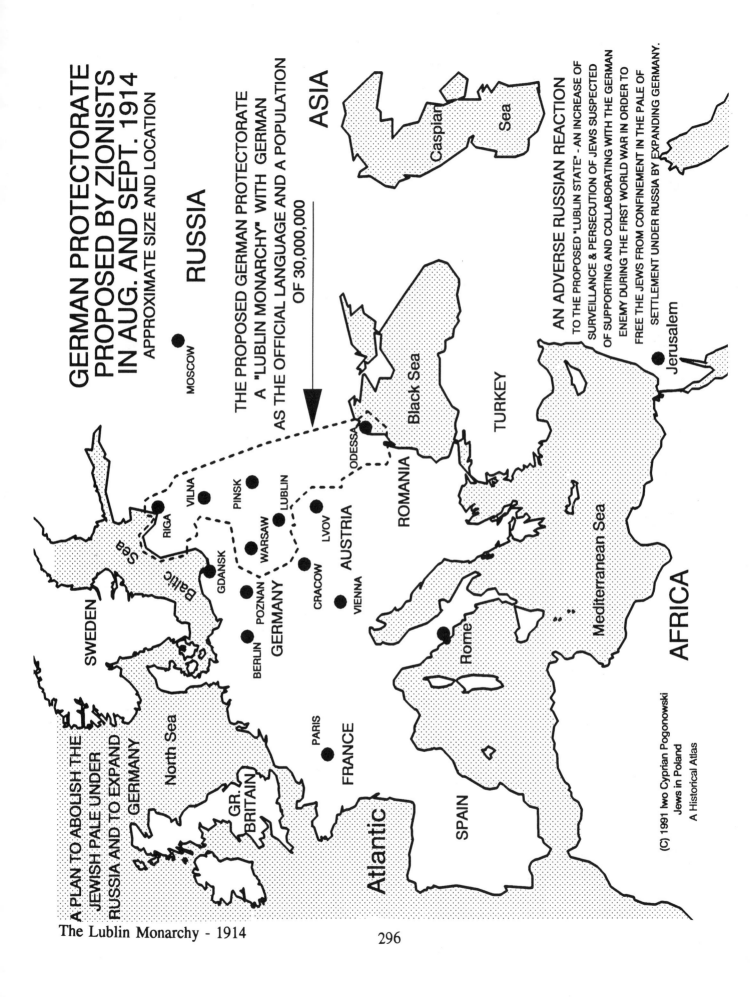

GERMAN PROTECTORATE
PROPOSED BY ZIONISTS
IN AUG. AND SEPT. 1914
APPROXIMATE SIZE AND LOCATION

THE PROPOSED GERMAN PROTECTORATE
A "LUBLIN MONARCHY" WITH GERMAN
AS THE OFFICIAL LANGUAGE AND A POPULATION
OF 30,000,000

A PLAN TO ABOLISH THE
JEWISH PALE UNDER
RUSSIA AND TO EXPAND
GERMANY.

AN ADVERSE RUSSIAN REACTION
TO THE PROPOSED "LUBLIN STATE" - AN INCREASE OF
SURVEILLANCE & PERSECUTION OF JEWS SUSPECTED
OF SUPPORTING AND COLLABORATING WITH THE GERMAN
ENEMY DURING THE FIRST WORLD WAR IN ORDER TO
FREE THE JEWS FROM CONFINEMENT IN THE PALE OF
SETTLEMENT UNDER RUSSIA BY EXPANDING GERMANY.

RUSSIA

ASIA

Caspian Sea

MOSCOW

Black Sea

TURKEY

Jerusalem

ODESSA

ROMANIA

VILNA

PINSK

RIGA

LUBLIN

LVOV

WARSAW

GDANSK

AUSTRIA

Baltic Sea

POZNAN

CRACOW

VIENNA

BERLIN

GERMANY

SWEDEN

North Sea

Rome

Mediterranean Sea

AFRICA

GR. BRITAIN

PARIS

FRANCE

Atlantic

SPAIN

(C) 1991 Iwo Cyprian Pogonowski
Jews in Poland
A Historical Atlas

The Lublin Monarchy - 1914

296

Pro-German Zionists formed the Zionist Association for Germany in 1897 and elected as its president Max I. Bodenheimer (1865-1940), who served until 1910. In 1902 Bodenheimer wrote a memorandum to the German Foreign Ministry in which he claimed that Yiddish, spoken by millions of East European Jews, who lived in the provinces annexed from Poland by Russia and Austria, was "a popular German dialect," and that these Jews were well disposed to Germany by linguistic affinity. Bodenheimer stated that Zionism was currently controlled by pro-German leaders, and that Germany's support for Zionist goals would be a boon to German ambitions in the Near East and would earn the gratitude of the entire Jewish people. "The influence of Jewry in foreign lands would accrue to the benefit of Germany..."

On Aug. 11, 1914, Bodenheimer submitted another memorandum to the German Foreign Ministry on the "concurrence of German and Jewish interests in the World War." On Aug. 17, 1914, the German Committee for Freeing of Russian Jews was founded by German Zionists including Max Bodenheimer, Franz Oppenheimer (1864-1943), Adolf Friedmann (1871-1933) and Russian Zionist Leo Motzkin (1867-1933). The German Foreign Ministry supported the founding of the new committee.

In Sept. 1914 the German Committee for Freeing of Russian Jews sent voluminous documentation about the Eastern Jews to the German Foreign Ministry and proposed establishment of a "buffer state" within the Jewish Pale of Settlement, composed of the former Polish provinces annexed by Russia. The new committee warned against the resurrection of a Polish national state and the danger of the Polish irredentist movement in the territories annexed from Poland by Germany and Austria. Thus, the Poles were the group to benefit the least from the establishment of the proposed new German protectorate.

The new buffer state was to have been dominated by some six million Jewish inhabitants, while other nationalities would counterbalance each other. The Jews would be most important because of their distribution, control of trade, and high literacy. Hatred of Russia and fear of other national groups in the buffer state would make them dependent on German protection and support. The new buffer state was to be a monarchy under a Hohenzollern prince from Berlin. Lublin was to be its capital because it was the seat of the autonomous Jewish national parliament, the Congressus Judaicus, before the partitions of Poland.

The population of some 30 million of the proposed buffer state or "Lublin Monarchy," was to be composed of autonomous groups of 6 million Jews, 8 million Poles, 11 million Ukrainians and Byelorussians, 3 1/2 million Lithuanians and Latvians, and under 1/2 million Baltic Germans. The official language, culture, and the officers' corps of the new monarchy was to be German.

Major Bogdan Hutten-Czapski, a "Polish-German" from Posen (Poznań) who was serving in the German General Staff, was assigned to evaluate the proposal for the new buffer state as a part of his task to encourage revolutionary and nationalist movements among the diverse ethnic groups which inhabited the former Polish provinces annexed by Russia in 1772-1795. On Hutten-Czpski's recommendation the proposal was rejected as utterly unrealistic. Eventually, the World Zionist Organization separated itself from the proposal.

Jewish philosopher and defender of the Eastern Jews, Martin Buber (1878-1965), at first supported the proposal for the Lublin state. Later he withdrew his support from the idea of a "Jewish state with cannons, flags, and military decorations." One of Buber's associates, Julius Berger, wrote that the whole proposal of the Jewish buffer state verged on criminal irresponsibility and that it was the product of an irresponsible political dilettantism, which resulted in an increase of negative attitudes of Poles towards the Jews. Berger felt that antagonizing the Poles was dangerous in view of the fact that nobody could predict who would control the politics of Poland after the war.

Bodenheimer and Oppenheimer were given a promise from Paul von Hindenburg (1847-1934) and E.F.W. Ludendorf (1865-1937) that German Jews would be used as trustees of the German military and civilian authorities in the occupied territories populated by Eastern Jews. The name of the Committee for Freeing of Russian Jews was changed to the Committee for Eastern Affairs. Even in this new form, the committee did not succeed in representing all German and Austrian Jews. However, after 1916, the committee acted as an anti-Polish pressure group in Berlin and kept on stressing the common interests of Jews and Germans in Poland. Oppenheimer, embittered by disagreements with other Zionists, told his audience, "We are Germans to the last drop of blood."

Martin Buber wrote in *Der Jude* (a monthly magazine) in the fall of 1917 that the Germans were losing importance for the Eastern Jews and that many Poles, who might be left in control, saw Jews as "parasites and uninvited guests, who sooner or later must leave Poland."

The idea of a Jewish Lublin state was used in German propaganda in the most sinister way during World War II. For example, of the 70,000 Jews delivered by the Vichy French to the Germans, many bought first class railroad tickets to travel from France to the "Jewish Lublin State" for re-settlement there. All of these people were murdered in Treblinka and in the vicinity of Lublin, where the Germans organized an extermination camp in Majdanek; there alone, in 1941-1944, some 200,000 Jews and 160,000 other Europeans, mainly Poles, were murdered. Max Bodenheimer died in 1940 in Palestine, a refugee from Germany.

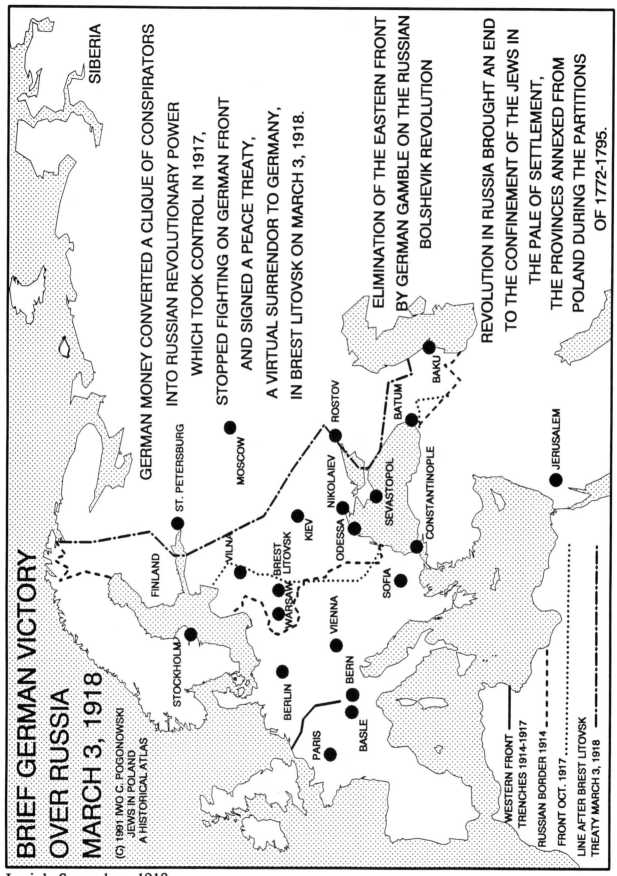

BRIEF GERMAN VICTORY
OVER RUSSIA
MARCH 3, 1918

(C) 1991 IWO C. POGONOWSKI
JEWS IN POLAND
A HISTORICAL ATLAS

SIBERIA

GERMAN MONEY CONVERTED A CLIQUE OF CONSPIRATORS
INTO RUSSIAN REVOLUTIONARY POWER
WHICH TOOK CONTROL IN 1917,
STOPPED FIGHTING ON GERMAN FRONT
AND SIGNED A PEACE TREATY,
A VIRTUAL SURRENDOR TO GERMANY,
IN BREST LITOVSK ON MARCH 3, 1918.

ELIMINATION OF THE EASTERN FRONT
BY GERMAN GAMBLE ON THE RUSSIAN
BOLSHEVIK REVOLUTION

REVOLUTION IN RUSSIA BROUGHT AN END
TO THE CONFINEMENT OF THE JEWS IN
THE PALE OF SETTLEMENT,
THE PROVINCES ANNEXED FROM
POLAND DURING THE PARTITIONS
OF 1772-1795.

ST. PETERSBURG
MOSCOW
ROSTOV
BAKU
BATUM
NIKOLAIEV
SEVASTOPOL
CONSTANTINOPLE
KIEV
VILNA
ODESSA
BREST LITOVSK
WARSAW
SOFIA
FINLAND
STOCKHOLM
VIENNA
BERN
BERLIN
BASLE
PARIS
JERUSALEM

WESTERN FRONT
TRENCHES 1914-1917 ————
RUSSIAN BORDER 1914 —— —— ——
FRONT OCT. 1917 ···········
LINE AFTER BREST LITOVSK
TREATY MARCH 3, 1918 —·—·—·—

Lenin's Surrender - 1918

298

German strategy to win the First World War was based on the elimination of the eastern front in order to concentrate on the victory in France. Dr. Helphand, born in the northern part of the Jewish Pale of Settlement in Berezino, between Vilnius and Minsk, a Social Democrat, played the most important part in Germany's eastern strategy. He provided the German government with the general plan of action in a memorandum of March 9, 1915 (please, see Part I, Appendix I, page 137). He established the German relations with the Russian revolutionary movement from the spring of 1915 to Nov. 1917.

German Foreign Ministry played the leading role in the policy of support of the left wing of Russian revolutionary movement by political and financial means throughout the war. The ministry felt that it could handle successfully the gamble of using revolutionary forces in Russia while opposing them at home. Russian revolutionaries main attraction was that they were enemies of the Tsarist regime and that they advocated the immediate cessation of hostilities and a separate peace with the Germans at any price.

A virtually unlimited German financial support to convert a clique of conspirators into Russian revolutionary power was handled mostly through an all-Polish Bolshevik team in Stockholm, Sweden. These contacts of Dr. Helphand, and trusted associates of Lenin (1870- 1924), were all born in the Jewish Pale of Settlement, which they resented with a vengeance. They included Jakub Fuerstenberg-Hanecki (1879-1937), Karol Sobelson-Radek (1885-1939), and Wacław Worowski-Szwarc (1871-1923). All of these men were dedicated to socialist revolution. They were prepared to use every means to achieve it.

The files of the German Foreign Ministry thoroughly document the four stages of the policy of the Imperial German Government towards the revolution in Russia. The first stage lasted from Jan. 1915, the time of the first records of German interest in the revolution, until its outbreak in March 1917. The second stage ran from March 1917 until the Bolshevik seizure of power. It includes the shipment by the Germans of Lenin and other Russian revolutionaries from Switzerland and Belgium through Germany and Scandinavia to Russia. The third stage covered the German reaction, in Nov. and Dec. 1917, to the Bolshevik seizure of power, and ended with the failure of Helphand's and Radek's plan for the peace conference on a neutral territory. The fourth stage consisted of the opening of the negotiations in Brest-Litovsk, a town under German occupation in Nov. 1917 and their conclusion on German terms on March 3, 1918. It was a humiliating capitula-tion, opposed by the great majority of Russians. It was forced upon Russia by Lenin and his associates in the Bolshevik leadership.

The peace treaty of Brest-Litovsk was concluded between Bolshevik government of Russia and Germany, Austria-Hungary, Bulgaria, and Turkey. The Bolsheviks surrendered to Germany and Austria 150,000 square kilometers of Poland, Lithuania, Latvia, and Estonia. The German states also occupied a major portion of the Ukraine and Byelorussia. Already, on Feb. 9, 1918, the Germans established a Ukrainian state, on territory overlapping Polish provinces, such as Chełm region, following earlier recommendations of Dr. Helphand. On Nov. 13, 1918, after the defeat of Germany on the western front, the Bolshevik government declared the treaty of Brest-Litovsk as null and void.

The pro-German activities of Dr. Helphand did not remain secret. Already on July 18, 1917, Russian Ministry of Justice under Prime Minister A. F. Kerensky (1881-1970) declared Lenin and the Bolshevik leadership guilty of high treason and produced evidence that the Bolsheviks received money from the German Government. Helphand was exposed as the German agent in the treasonable cooperation between Bolsheviks and the German Government. The Bolsheviks published their defense in the *Listok Prawda* (instead of *Prawda* paper) on July 19, 1917. They wrote that the documents used by the Ministry of Justice "were... the foul conspiracy by the pogromists and hired slanderers against the honor and life of the leaders of the working class." Lenin and Zinoviev were able to go into hiding in time. Leon Trotzky (1877-1940) and a number of other Bolsheviks were arrested. The whole Bolshevik party went underground.

Dr. Helphand made a fortune as an arms merchant and trader in strategic supplies, as well as a political consultant. In 1916 he was awarded the citizenship of Prussia as a "bearer of German civilization" and in recognition for his services to the Berlin Government. However, during the negotiations at Brest-Litovsk he offered in Stockholm his services to the Soviet Government and asked Lenin's permission to return to Russia. Lenin refused. By then the German Government ordered a close watch on Helphand's activities (this order was suspended on May 23, 1918). Helphand never returned to Russia. He died in Berlin in 1924 as the richest man in Germany. His associates of the all-Polish Bolshevik team of Stockholm all were eventually killed: Worowski in Switzerland in 1923; Hanecki, after a show trial, in Moscow in 1937: and Radek, in 1939, in a Soviet prison.

PRESSURES TO ESCAPE FROM EUROPE
SITUATION IN POLAND, BASIC FACTS BETWEEN WORLD WARS:
ECONOMIC CRISIS AND MASS UNEMPLOYMENT IN POLAND 1918-1939
GERMAN ECONOMIC BOYCOTT AND LOSS OF RUSSIAN MARKET
RESULTING IN ETHNIC STRIFE AND ANTI-SEMITIC RIOTS
DRAMATIC INCREASE OF THE NUMBER OF JEWS ON WELFARE FROM 20 TO 33 PERCENT (1921-1937)
ZIONIST STRUGGLE FOR HOMELAND IN PALESTINE
EXTENSIVE POLITICAL PLURALISM OF POLISH JEWS
A CHRONOLOGY

Aug. 27, 1897, Congress of Zionists was founded in Basel. World Zionist Organization was established and dues were set at one *shekl*, or one unit of each local currency, per year. (In 1935 Polish Jews contributed 405,000 *shekls*.)

In Sept. 1897, *Bund* was founded in Wilno as a national-separatist segment of Social-Democratic Party of Russia, in the provinces annexed from Poland. Their new slogan was: "Jews who are active in Polish society do not cease to be Jewish." In 1921 in Gdańsk, convention *Kombund* separated itself from social-democrats, and in 1924 refused to join the 2nd International as "too centralized and dominated by Moscow." *Bund* also opposed "Jewish clericalism." During the 1930s there were 50,000 *Bund* members in Poland. They received some financial help from the American Society of Friends of the *Bund*.

Between Aug. 1914 and Sept. 1916, Józef Piłsudski's legions of 12,000 men included 3.5% Jewish volunteers. However, international Jewish organizations opposed the independence of Poland.

Nov. 2, 1917, Balfour Declaration on Jewish right to a homeland in Palestine was issued. Organized Zionists numbered about one million.

In Oct. 1918, Zionist Proclamation of Copenhagen stated its demands: 1. Jewish Homeland in Palestine. 2. Full emancipation of the Jews in all countries. 3. Cultural, social, and political autonomy of the Jews in all countries of Jewish Diaspora.

Nov. 11, 1918, Independent Poland was re-established. Six concurrent wars on the borders of Poland were fought and won by the Poles between 1918 and 1922. Poland's borders were then defined.

Nov. 12, 1918, Zionists demanded a separate Jewish constitution, a Jewish national government including a secretary of state, and a formal Jewish state in Poland. Jewish Committee of Warsaw declared support for the government of Józef Piłsudski.

Feb. 18, 1919, Polish Prime Minister, Ignacy Paderewski, declared his government's support for "a complete emancipation of Jews in Poland, following the English and American example." Pressure was exerted on Poland to establish a Jewish state within the Polish state. Generally, however, the government of Poland was supportive of the Zionists and the conservative Aguda. The Poles appreciated the fact that Jews did not have territorial claims against Poland, like the Germans or Ukrainians, for example.

May 26, 1919, the U.S. press described current riots and general postwar public disorders in Poland as anti-Semitic pogroms. False evidence was used, such as the pictures taken in Kishiniov, in Moldavia, during a pogrom in 1905; also, false claims were made that the Russian pogrom of 2500 Jews in Homel was committed by the Poles.

June 28, 1919, Treaty on National Minorities was signed in Versailles. It required Polish government's protection and subsidies for Jewish education and religious activities. Full emancipation of the Jews was guaranteed by both Polish constitutions of 1921 and 1935.

Sept. 30, 1921, Jewish population in Poland was 2.8 million, in 1931 it was 3.1 million, and in 1937 about 3.5 million, including 330,000 legally repatriated (on the basis of Polish-Soviet pact of Riga, 1921) and about 450,000 illegal refugees from the Soviet Union -- all of whom were granted Polish citizenship. In 1921-1937 Jewish minority increased by 800,000, while 390,000 emigrated. In 1937 Jewish population in Poland exceeded 3.5 million people as a result of immigration and a high birthrate. Seventy five percent lived in towns - 1/3 in five cities: Warsaw, Łódź, Kraków, Lwów, and Wilno. Two-thirds of all Jews were store keepers, market stall keepers, peddlers, tradesmen, and the like.

Between 1918 and 1939, one-third of Jewish population worked mainly in commerce, crafts, and in light industry (garments, weaving, leather crafts, and food) -- only 0.7 % made a living in agriculture. Only 3.3% of Jewish population were in the entrepreneurial class; however, Jewish entrepreneurial class represented 46% of the entire entrepreneurial class (of about 85,000) in pre-war Poland. Jewish industrial proletariat represented only 8% of the total in Poland. The percentages of professionals in ethnic groups were: 6.6% of Jews, 6% of Germans, 5% of Poles, 2% of Ukrainians and Byelorussians.

In March 1922 a plebiscite was held in the Wilno area. Polish and Jewish votes for the incorporation of the area into Poland won the referendum.

In 1923, Jews in Poland controlled 80% of commerce and 50% of light industry and crafts. By 1935 these figures decreased to 52% and 40%, respectively.

Dec. 27, 1924, a decree on state monopoly of tobacco, alcoholic beverages, and matches was issued. On June 3, 1925, Jewish deputies staged a protest on behalf of Jewish merchants.

Between 1925, and 1926, about 26,000 graduates of pioneer trade schools, named *Hechaluc*, emigrated from Poland to Palestine. They were prepared to be farmers and soldiers ready to fight "for the defense and cultivation of land in Palestine."

July 4, 1925, the Ugoda, or a Polish-Jewish agreement, was concluded between the government and Jewish parliamentary representation, (the *Koło Żydowskie*), which affirmed its loyalty to the Polish government and its readiness to vote for the government's budget. The published twelve points of *Ugoda* spelled out the religious, cultural, and organizational privileges of Jewish communities in Poland.

In March 1926, Polish Prime Minister, Aleksander Skarżyński, stated the support of Poland for "Jewish independent state in Palestine, as large as possible, with an access to the Red Sea" (in an address to Nachum Sokołow, the president of World Zionist Organization). On May 27, 1926, Polish Ministry of Interior authorized Zionist activities, such as emigration and collection of money for colonization of Palestine.

Oct. 14, 1927, Polish government issued a decree on the responsibilities and prerogatives of the *kahals*: support of rabbis, maintenance of religious facilities such as buildings, synagogues, cemeteries, schools (*kheders* and *yeshibots*), ritual baths for women (*mikvas*), and supervision of the ritual slaughter (*shekhita*) as well as distribution of *kosher* meat. *Kahals'* responsibilities included the administration of the estate and various foundations of the community (*kehilla*), as well as charities for the poorest members. When Zionists, socialists, and conservatives competed for control of the *kahals*, Polish government sympathized with the conservative *Aguda Isroel* (which was considered an effective anti-communist guardian of the *kahal*.)

1929-1933, were the years of the most severe economic crisis in Poland. State railroads cashiered 3000 Jewish employees. Jewish share in wholesale of alcoholic beverages fell from 60% to 2%, of tobacco from 80% to 3%, and of salt from 50% to 4% -- all of which had been government monopolies since 1924. In 1929-1933 Jewish membership in the Communist Party of Poland dropped from 35% to 26%. The percentage of Jewish communists was the highest in small towns (70% and over).

In 1930 the aid totaling 150 million złotys sent by families residing abroad supported partly or fully every sixth Jew in Polish small towns the *shtetls*.

Between 1931 and 1934, Polish government provided the Zionists of "*Brith Trumpeldor*" and "*Bejtar*," with military training in Poland in camps at Rembertów, Andrychów, and Zielonka near Warsaw. In 1936 *Bejtar* had 52,000 members - 75% of them in Poland. British government pressed the Poles to stop this military training program of members of *Hagana* and *Bejtar*.

Feb. 4, 1932, Jewish representative demanded that the *Seym* writes off delinquent Jewish taxes of 1,200 million złoty and protested the reduction of nearly 1,300 state monopoly concessions on Jan. 1, 1932.

Oct. 14, 1932, the Zionist leader Włodzimierz Żabotyński, or Meir Jabotinsky, wrote on *Liberalism* in the Zionist newspaper the *Hajnt*, and discussed the origins of Polish anti-Semitism. He wrote that "-- speaking among ourselves -- we are flooding the universities, banks, as well as the medical and legal professions..."

Between 1933 and 1935, 8707 Jewish businessmen emigrated from Poland to Palestine, taking with them 226 million *zlotys*, more than the total Polish foreign currency reserve of 160 million. British authorities required the immigrants to Palestine to bring a minimum of 1000 British pounds.

Between 1933 and 1937, amidst the economic crisis anti-Jewish boycotts and riots, such as in Przytyk, Częstochowa, Brześć, and Mińsk Mazowiecki intensified. Between May 1933 and Aug. 1936 the *kahals* reported 1289 injuries resulting from these riots. [Note: two days of riots in Los Angeles ending May 1, 1992, involved 1370 injuries.]

THE LAST BLOSSOMING

OF JEWISH CULTURE

IN POLAND

1918 -- 1939

Between 1935 and 1937, British yearly quota for Jewish immigration to Palestine was gradually reduced from 24,000 to 1,600.

July 25, 1935, a non-Zionist International Territorial League "Freeland" was founded in London. In Jan. 1936 Lord Mellchet, the president of the federation of some 310 Jewish sport clubs "Makkabi," supported the "Freeland" program and proposed the emigration of one and half million Jews from Poland. "Freeland," or "Frajland," was bitterly opposed by the Zionists as an anti-Semitic diversion. Meanwhile, Polish diplomats tried to secure permission from colonial powers for yearly emigration of 30,000 Jews, which equaled the approximate natural yearly increase of Jewish population in Poland. The French were approached about opening Madagascar for immigration of Polish Jews.

Dec. 8, 1935, The Congress of the Small-holder (peasant) Party condemned all anti-Jewish disturbances and supported the formation of Jewish cooperatives and orderly Jewish colonization of Palestine, or any other acceptable land. A similar attitude was also expressed by the Polish Socialist Party.

March 27, 1936, the law on ritual slaughter, or *shekhita* (which at that time had virtual monopoly over meat market in Poland, while in other countries it represented no more than 3%) was passed. Beginning Jan. 1, 1937, meat products from ritual slaughter were to be sold exclusively in Jewish neighborhood stores. The Orthodox Jews protested that the new law limited their religious freedom, while the Zionists claimed that it was putting 100,000 Jews out of work. A complete ban on *shekhita* was never passed, and the law was never strictly enforced.

June 4, 1936, Prime Minister of Poland, General Felicjan Slawoj-Skladkowski, condemned anti-Jewish excesses, but said that economic struggle should go on (he used the word *owszem*, or "by all means," which offended Jews and many other people who were aware of the growth of anti-Semitism in Europe, and especially of the German atrocities towards the Jews, committed just west of Poland's border).

In Aug. 1936, Professor Stanisław Grabski stated that Poland was in dire need of industrialization and industrial employment for her excess agricultural population. He wrote that the pressure for the emigration of Jews was a mistake. Antoni Roman, Polish Minister of Commerce and Industry, noticed that merchants represented 5% of population of Poland, while in industrialized countries they represented 12 to 21%. Rabbi Tobiasz Horowitz, the leader of *Aguda,* was convinced that any significant improvement in the situation of the masses of poor Jews could be achieved only through strengthening of the entire Polish economy.

In Oct. 1936 Sir Herbert Samuels, an English-Jewish political leader, stated that in order to provide adequate living conditions for Polish Jews, a major improvement of Poland's economy was necessary; otherwise part of Polish Jewish population would have to emigrate.

Between Oct. 15 and Nov. 15, 1936, the *New York Wochenblat* was alarmed by the results of "charity gifts of millions of old clothes" to Polish Jews who immediately were selling 90% of used clothing and were flooding the flee markets in Poland. In this situation, unemployment increased in the garment industry, while money was made by New York businessmen who benefited from Polish transport subsidies.

In 1937 Jewish business real estate was worth ten billion złotys, or one-third of the total business real estate in Poland. Despite the flight of Jewish capital from Poland and general pauperization, the Jews paid 28% of income taxes, while they represented about 10% of the population.

In December 1937, fiftythree professors of the universities of Warsaw, Wilno, and Poznań signed a declaration "In Defense of Polish Culture." They protested against all forms of discrimination against Jewish students, such as separate sitting in classes and brawls in which many were wounded. The declaration condemned all excesses based on the extremists' belief in the messianic mission of the Jews as "a nation chosen to rule the world."

In 1938, Jews represented 33.5% of Poland's physicians, 53% of lawyers, and about 24% of university students, while constituting only 10% of the country's population.

May 4, 1938, a law was passed in Poland to regulate and limit the access of Jews to the legal profession.

July 5, 1938, in Evian an ineffective meeting of 30 countries was held. It was presided over by President F.D. Roosevelt and attempted to remove immigration restrictions existing in these countries, in order to help German Jews. The American plan required 16 years to be implemented and was called "Evian-Naive."

In 1938/39 Jewish press in Poland included 160 titles (11 scientific) - total daily circulation of 800,000, of which 180,000 were in Polish, the rest mainly in Yiddish. Among 103 professional theatres in Poland, 15 were Jewish. Earlier, the world-renowned institute of Yiddish philology (YIVO) functioned in Wilno. Other Jewish scientific institutions were located in Warsaw. Orthodox Jews believed that Yiddish should be used in daily life, while Hebrew should remain the holy language of liturgy. On the contrary, the Zionists felt that Hebrew should be the language of the future Jewish state.

In spring 1939 Włodzimierz Żabotyński (Meir Jabotinsky), the leader of Zionists Revisionists, and Abraham Stern, the leader of *Irgun Zwei Leumi,* came to the Polish Foreign Ministry with a request for a loan, weapons, and commando training. In May 1939 Żabotyński received financial aid in the amount of 212,000 *złotys* from Polish government. Military training of members of Irgun and Hagana resumed in Rembertów, Andrychów, and Warsaw. Żabotyński clearly stated that the aim of Zionists-revisionists was to create a Jewish state on both sides of the Jordan River.

In the 1930s, the British limited legal immigration to Palestine. The Zionists organized illegal immigration, *or Aliya-bet*, which was carried out by *Sherut-Israel* (the foundation of future Israeli intelligence, the *Mossad*). The name *Bricha* or escape, was used by clandestine groups which organized illegal departures of Jews from Europe, mainly from Poland, where this emigration was interrupted by the war.

At the beginning of 1939, Polish Ministry of Internal Affairs noted that because of British limitation of immigration to Palestine groups of Jews were leaving Poland as tourists, when in fact they were emigrants. An order was issued to the press censors to make sure that there would not be printed any reports or articles on departures of emigrants who pretended to be tourists.

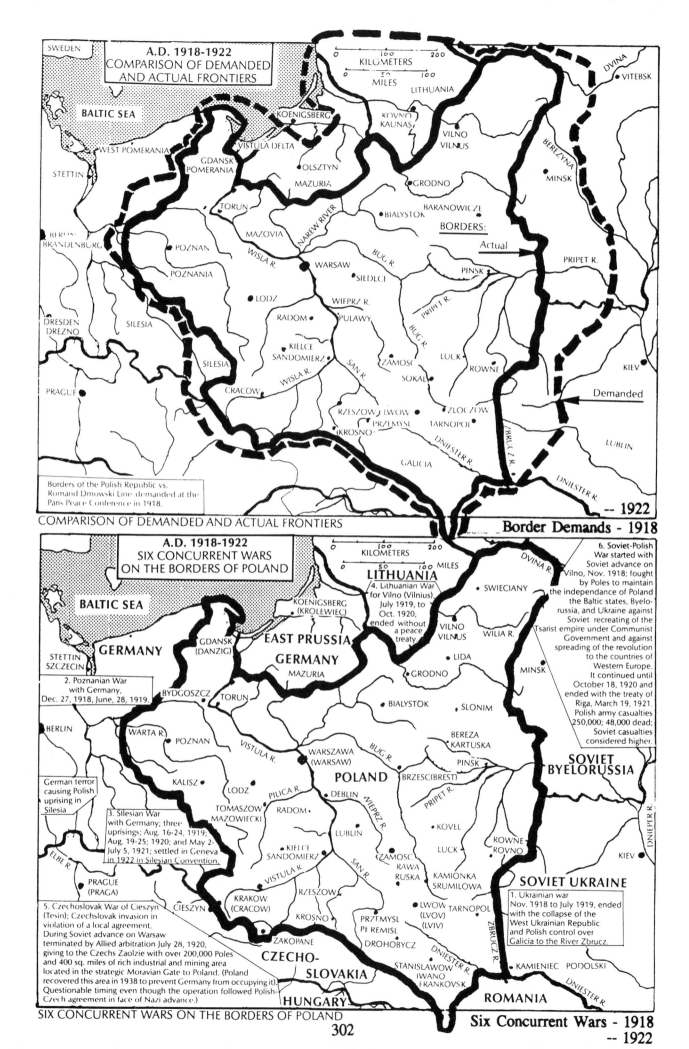

A.D. 1918-1922
COMPARISON OF DEMANDED AND ACTUAL FRONTIERS

KILOMETERS 0 50 100 200

MILES 0 50 100

SWEDEN

BALTIC SEA

WEST POMERANIA

STETTIN

KOENIGSBERG

VISTULA DELTA

GDANSK POMERANIA

OLSZTYN

MAZURIA

LITHUANIA

KOVNO KAUNAS

VILNO VILNUS

GRODNO

BEREZYNA

MINSK

VITEBSK

DVINA

BERLIN BRANDENBURG

TORUN

NAREW RIVER

BARANOWICZE

BIALYSTOK

BORDERS:

MAZOVIA

WISLA R.

POZNAN

POZNANIA

WARSAW

SIEDLCE

BUG R.

PINSK

PRIPET R.

Actual

DRESDEN DREZNO

SILESIA

LODZ

WIEPRZ R.

RADOM

PULAWY

PRIPET R.

PRIPET R.

SILESIA

KIELCE SANDOMIERZ

BUG R.

LUCK

ROWNE

KIEV

PRAGUE

WISLA R.

SAN R.

CRACOW

ZAMOSC

SOKAL

ZLOCZOW

Demanded

RZESZOW LWOW

PRZEMYSL

KROSNO

TARNOPOL

DNIESTER R.

ZBRUCZ R.

LUBLIN

GALICIA

DNIESTER R.

-- 1922

Borders of the Polish Republic vs.
Romand Dmowski Line demanded at the
Paris Peace Conference in 1918.

COMPARISON OF DEMANDED AND ACTUAL FRONTIERS

Border Demands - 1918

A.D. 1918-1922
SIX CONCURRENT WARS ON THE BORDERS OF POLAND

KILOMETERS 0 100 200

MILES 0 50 100

BALTIC SEA

STETTIN SZCZECIN

GERMANY

GDANSK (DANZIG)

KOENIGSBERG (KROLEWIEC)

EAST PRUSSIA GERMANY

MAZURIA

LITHUANIA

4. Lithuanian War
for Vilno (Vilnius),
July 1919, to
Oct. 1920,
ended without
a peace
treaty.

SWIECIANY

VILNO VILNUS

WILIA R.

DVINA R.

6. Soviet-Polish
War started with
Soviet advance on
Vilno, Nov. 1918; fought
by Poles to maintain
the independence of Poland
the Baltic states, Byelo-
russia, and Ukraine against
Soviet recreating of the
Tsarist empire under Communist
Government and against
spreading of the revolution
to the countries of
Western Europe.
It continued until
October 18, 1920 and
ended with the treaty of
Riga, March 19, 1921.
Polish army casualties
250,000; 48,000 dead;
Soviet casualties
considered higher.

2. Poznanian War
with Germany,
Dec. 27, 1918, June, 28, 1919.

BYDGOSZCZ

TORUN

LIDA

GRODNO

BIALYSTOK

SLONIM

MINSK

BERLIN

WARTA R.

POZNAN

VISTULA R.

WARSZAWA (WARSAW)

BUG R.

BEREZA KARTUSKA

PINSK

SOVIET BYELORUSSIA

German terror
causing Polish
uprising in
Silesia

KALISZ

LODZ

PILICA R.

POLAND

DEBLIN

BRZESC (BREST)

3. Silesian War
with Germany; three
uprisings; Aug. 16-24, 1919;
Aug. 19-25, 1920; and May 2-
July 5, 1921; settled in Geneva
in 1922 in Silesian Convention.

TOMASZOW MAZOWIECKI

RADOM

WIEPRZ R.

LUBLIN

KOVEL

ELBE R.

PRAGUE (PRAGA)

KIELCE SANDOMIERZ

VISTULA R.

SAN R.

ZAMOSC

RAWA RUSKA

LUCK

ROWNE ROVNO

KIEV

DNIEPER R.

KRAKOW (CRACOW)

RZESZOW

KAMIONKA SRUMILOWA

SOVIET UKRAINE

5. Czechoslovak War of Cieszyn
(Tesin); Czechoslovak invasion in
violation of a local agreement.
During Soviet advance on Warsaw
terminated by Allied arbitration July 28, 1920,
giving to the Czechs Zaolzie with over 200,000 Poles
and 400 sq. miles of rich industrial and mining area
located in the strategic Moravian Gate to Poland. (Poland
recovered this area in 1938 to prevent Germany from occupying it).
Questionable timing even though the operation followed Polish-
Czech agreement in face of Nazi advance.)

CIESZYN

KROSNO

ZAKOPANE

CZECHO-SLOVAKIA

HUNGARY

LWOW (LVOV) (LVIV)

TARNOPOL

PRZEMYSL PL REMISL

DROHOBYCZ

STANISLAWOW IWANO FRANKOVSK

1. Ukrainian war
Nov. 1918 to July 1919, ended
with the collapse of the
West Ukrainian Republic and
Polish control over
Galicia to the River Zbrucz.

ZBRUCZ R.

KAMIENEC PODOLSKI

DNIESTER R.

DNIESTER R.

ROMANIA

SIX CONCURRENT WARS ON THE BORDERS OF POLAND

Six Concurrent Wars - 1918
-- 1922

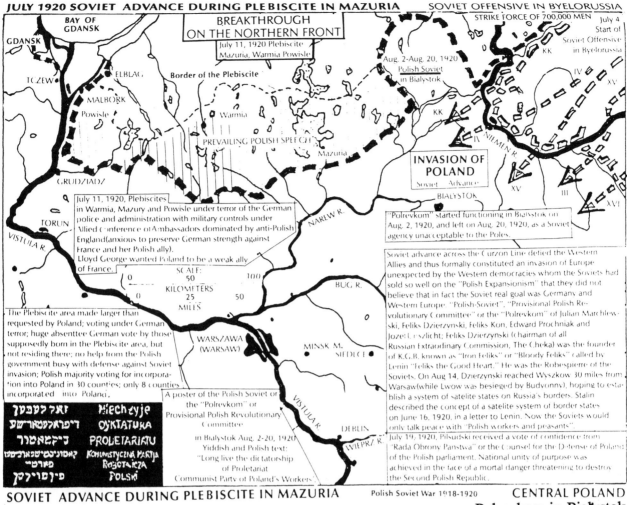

BREAKTHROUGH ON THE NORTHERN FRONT
July 11, 1920 Plebiscite Mazuria, Warmia Powisle

Border of the Plebiscite

BAY OF GDANSK

GDANSK
TCZEW
ELBLAG
MALBORK
Powisle
Warmia
PREVAILING POLISH SPEECH
Mazuria

GRUDZIADZ

July 11, 1920, Plebiscites in Warmia, Mazury and Powisle under terror of the German police and administration with military controls under Allied Conference of Ambassadors dominated by anti-Polish England(anxious to preserve German strength against France and her Polish ally). Lloyd George wanted Poland to be a weak ally of France.

TORUN
VISTULA R.
NAREW R.

SCALE:
0   50   100
KILOMETERS
0   25   50
MILES

The Plebiscite area made larger than requested by Poland; voting under German terror; huge absenttee German vote by those supposedly born in the Plebiscite area, but not residing there; no help from the Polish government busy with defense against Soviet invasion; Polish majority voting for incorporation into Poland in 30 counties; only 8 counties incorporated into Poland.

WARSZAWA (WARSAW)

BUG R.

MINSK M.
SIEDLCE

VISTULA R.
DEBLIN
WIEPRZ R.

STRIKE FORCE OF 700,000 MEN

Aug. 2-Aug. 20, 1920 Polish Soviet in Bialystok

KK
IV   XV

July 4
Start of Soviet Offensive in Byelorussia

NIEMEN R.

INVASION OF POLAND
Soviet Advance

BIALYSTOK

KK
IV
XV   III
XVI

"Polrevkom" started functioning in Bialystok on Aug. 2, 1920, and left on Aug. 20, 1920, as a Soviet agency unacceptable to the Poles.

Soviet advance across the Curzon Line defied the Western Allies and thus formally constituted an invasion of Europe unexpected by the Western democracies whom the Soviets had sold so well on the "Polish Expansionism" that they did not believe that in fact the Soviet real goal was Germany and Western Europe. "Polish-Soviet", "Provisional Polish Revolutionary Committee" or the "Polrevkom" of Julian Marchlewski, Feliks Dzierzynski, Feliks Kon, Edward Prochniak and Jozef Uns zlicht; Feliks Dzierzynski (chairman of all Russian Extraodinary Commission, The Cheka) was the founder of K.G.B. known as "Iron Feliks" or "Bloody Feliks" called by Lenin "Feliks the Good Heart." He was the Robespierre of the Soviets. On Aug 14, Dzierzynski reached Wyszkow 30 miles from Warsaw(while Lwow was besieged by Budyonny), hoping to establish a system of satelite states on Russia's borders. Stalin described the concept of a satelite system of border states on June 16, 1920, in a letter to Lenin. Now the Soviets would only talk peace with "Polish workers and peasants".

July 19, 1920, Pilsudski received a vote of confidence from "Rada Obrony Panstwa" or the Counsel for the Defense of Poland of the Polish parliament. National unity of purpose was achieved in the face of a mortal danger threatening to destroy the Second Polish Republic.

נאָר לעבּען דיקטאַטור פראָלעטאַריאַט קאָמוניסטישע פאַרטיי פון פויליקן

Niech żyje DYKTATURA PROLETARIATU Komunistyczna Partia Robotnicza Polski

A poster of the Polish Soviet or the "Polrevkom" or Provisional Polish Revolutionary Committee in Bialystok Aug. 2-20, 1920; Yiddish and Polish text: "Long live the dictatorship of Proletariat Communist Party of Poland's Workers"

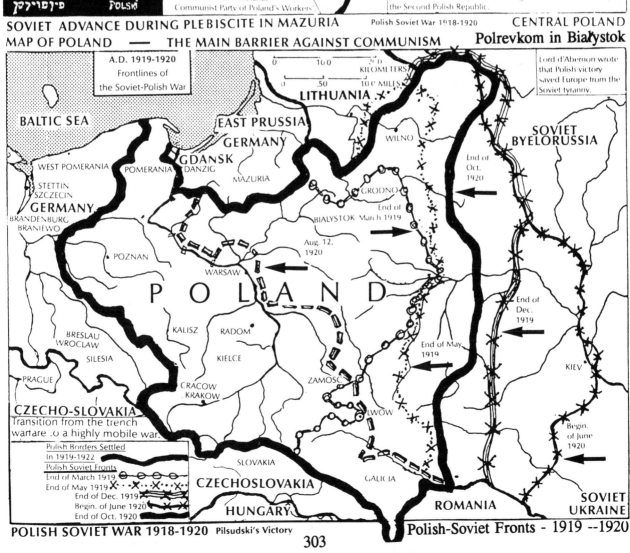

A.D. 1919-1920 Frontlines of the Soviet-Polish War

SCALE
0   100   200
KILOMETERS
0   50   100 MILES

Lord d'Abernon wrote that Polish victory saved Europe from the Soviet tyranny.

BALTIC SEA
LITHUANIA
EAST PRUSSIA
GERMANY
GDANSK
DANZIG
MAZURIA
WILNO

SOVIET BYELORUSSIA

WEST POMERANIA
POMERANIA
STETTIN
SZCZECIN
GERMANY
BRANDENBURG
BRANIEWO

GRODNO
End of Oct. 1920

End of BIALYSTOK March 1919

Aug. 12, 1920

POZNAN

WARSAW

P O L A N D

KALISZ   RADOM
KIELCE

BRESLAU
WROCLAW
SILESIA
PRAGUE

CRACOW
KRAKOW

ZAMOSC
LWOW

End of Dec. 1919

End of May 1919

KIEV

Begin. of June 1920

CZECHO-SLOVAKIA
Transition from the trench warfare to a highly mobile war.

Polish Borders Settled in 1919-1922
Polish Soviet Fronts
End of March 1919
End of May 1919
End of Dec. 1919
Begin. of June 1920
End of Oct. 1920

SLOVAKIA
GALICIA
CZECHOSLOVAKIA
HUNGARY
ROMANIA

SOVIET UKRAINE

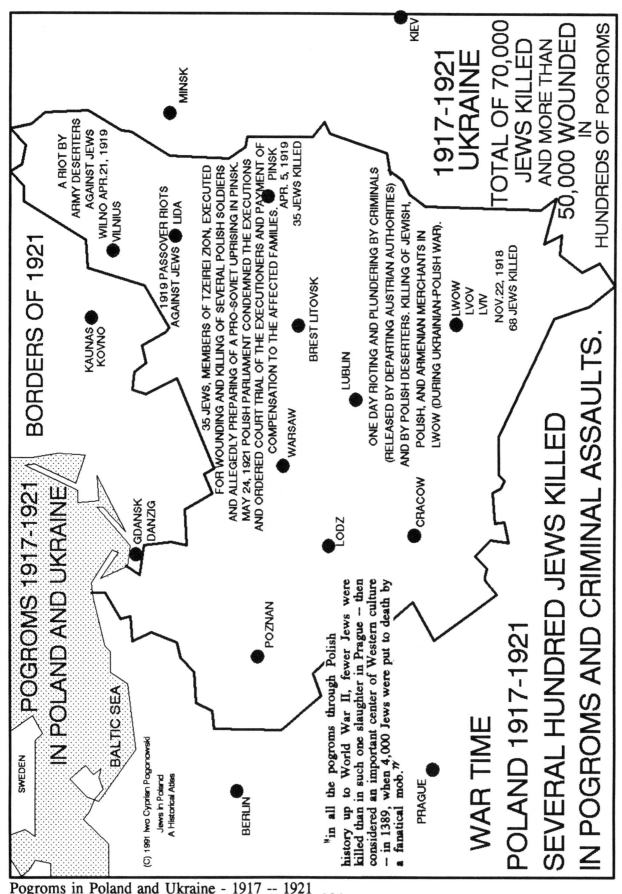

POGROMS 1917-1921
IN POLAND AND UKRAINE

BORDERS OF 1921

1917-1921
UKRAINE

TOTAL OF 70,000
JEWS KILLED
AND MORE THAN
50,000 WOUNDED
IN
HUNDREDS OF POGROMS

WAR TIME
POLAND 1917-1921
SEVERAL HUNDRED JEWS KILLED
IN POGROMS AND CRIMINAL ASSAULTS.

SWEDEN

BALTIC SEA

(C) 1991 Iwo Cyprian Pogonowski
Jews in Poland
A Historical Atlas

"in all the pogroms through Polish
history up to World War II, fewer Jews were
killed than in such one slaughter in Prague -- then
considered an important center of Western culture
-- in 1389, when 4,000 Jews were put to death by
a fanatical mob."

MINSK

KIEV

A RIOT BY
ARMY DESERTERS
AGAINST JEWS
WILNO APR.21, 1919

VILNIUS

1919 PASSOVER RIOTS
AGAINST JEWS LIDA

35 JEWS, MEMBERS OF TZEIREI ZION, EXECUTED
FOR WOUNDING AND KILLING OF SEVERAL POLISH SOLDIERS
AND ALLEGEDLY PREPARING OF A PRO-SOVIET UPRISING IN PINSK.
MAY 24, 1921 POLISH PARLIAMENT CONDEMNED THE EXECUTIONS
AND ORDERED COURT TRIAL OF THE EXECUTIONERS AND PAYMENT OF
COMPENSATION TO THE AFFECTED FAMILIES.   PINSK
APR. 5, 1919
35 JEWS KILLED

KAUNAS
KOVNO

GDANSK
DANZIG

WARSAW

BREST LITOVSK

LUBLIN

ONE DAY RIOTING AND PLUNDERING BY CRIMINALS
(RELEASED BY DEPARTING AUSTRIAN AUTHORITIES)
AND BY POLISH DESERTERS. KILLING OF JEWISH,
POLISH, AND ARMENIAN MERCHANTS IN
LWOW (DURING UKRAINIAN-POLISH WAR).

LWOW
LVOV
LVIV
NOV.22, 1918
68 JEWS KILLED

LODZ

CRACOW

POZNAN

BERLIN

PRAGUE

Pogroms in Poland and Ukraine - 1917 -- 1921

304

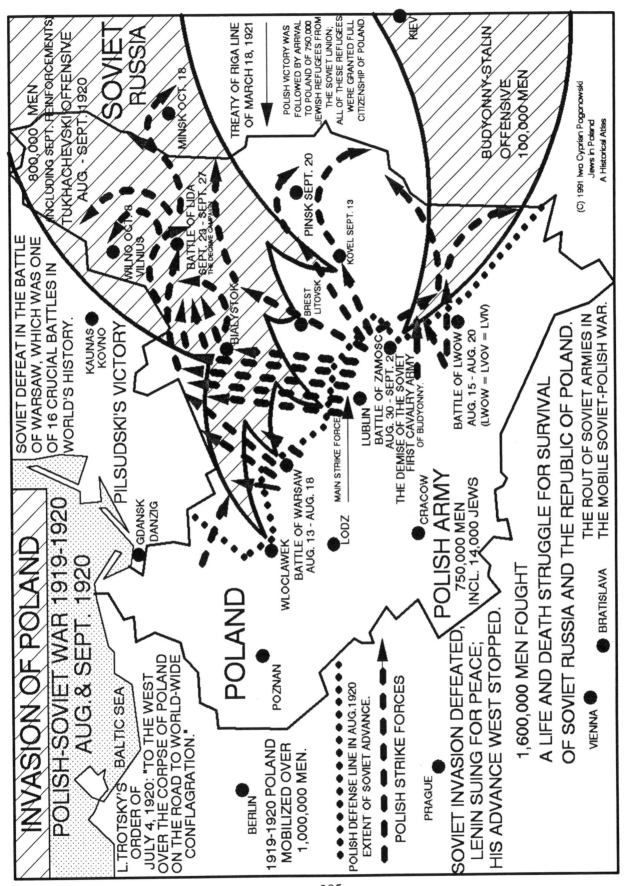

INVASION OF POLAND

POLISH-SOVIET WAR 1919-1920 AUG. 8 SEPT. 1920

PILSUDSKI'S VICTORY

L. TROTSKY'S ORDER OF JULY 4, 1920: "TO THE WEST OVER THE CORPSE OF POLAND ON THE ROAD TO WORLD-WIDE CONFLAGRATION."

SOVIET DEFEAT IN THE BATTLE OF WARSAW, WHICH WAS ONE OF 16 CRUCIAL BATTLES IN WORLD'S HISTORY.

800,000 MEN INCLUDING SEPT. REINFORCEMENTS

TUKHACHEVSKI OFFENSIVE AUG. - SEPT. 1920

SOVIET RUSSIA

TREATY OF RIGA LINE OF MARCH 18, 1921

POLISH VICTORY WAS FOLLOWED BY ARRIVAL TO POLAND OF 750,000 JEWISH REFUGEES FROM THE SOVIET UNION; ALL OF THESE REFUGEES WERE GRANTED FULL CITIZENSHIP OF POLAND.

BUDYONNY-STALIN OFFENSIVE 100,000 MEN

(C) 1991 Iwo Cyprian Pogonowski
Jews in Poland
A Historical Atlas

KIEV

MINSK OCT. 18

PINSK SEPT. 20

KOVEL SEPT. 13

WILNO OCT. 8 VILNIUS

BATTLE OF LIDA SEPT. 23 - SEPT. 27 THE DECISIVE CAMPAIGN

BREST LITOVSK

BIALYSTOK

KAUNAS KOVNO

MAIN STRIKE FORCE

LUBLIN

BATTLE OF ZAMOSC AUG. 30 - SEPT. 2 THE DEMISE OF THE SOVIET FIRST CAVALRY ARMY OF BUDYONNY.

BATTLE OF LWOW AUG. 15 - AUG. 20 (LWOW = LVOV = LVIV)

GDANSK DANZIG

BATTLE OF WARSAW AUG. 13 - AUG. 18

WLOCLAWEK

LODZ

CRACOW

POLISH ARMY 750,000 MEN INCL. 14,000 JEWS

POLAND

POZNAN

BALTIC SEA

1919-1920 POLAND MOBILIZED OVER 1,000,000 MEN.

POLISH DEFENSE LINE IN AUG. 1920 EXTENT OF SOVIET ADVANCE.

POLISH STRIKE FORCES

BERLIN

PRAGUE

BRATISLAVA

VIENNA

SOVIET INVASION DEFEATED, LENIN SUING FOR PEACE; HIS ADVANCE WEST STOPPED.

1,600,000 MEN FOUGHT

A LIFE AND DEATH STRUGGLE FOR SURVIVAL OF SOVIET RUSSIA AND THE REPUBLIC OF POLAND.

THE ROUT OF SOVIET ARMIES IN THE MOBILE SOVIET-POLISH WAR.

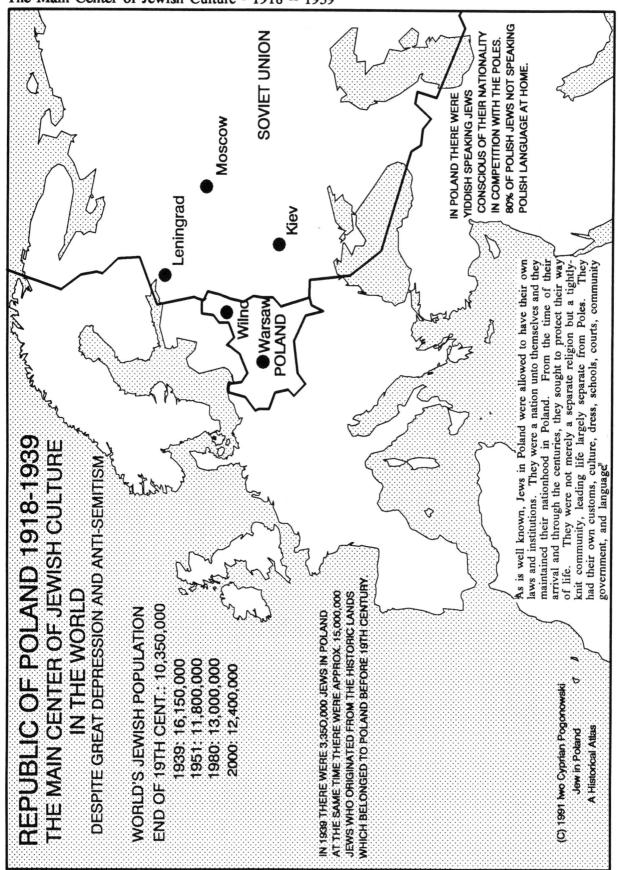

REPUBLIC OF POLAND 1918-1939
THE MAIN CENTER OF JEWISH CULTURE IN THE WORLD

DESPITE GREAT DEPRESSION AND ANTI-SEMITISM

WORLD'S JEWISH POPULATION
END OF 19TH CENT.: 10,350,000

1939: 16,150,000
1951: 11,800,000
1980: 13,000,000
2000: 12,400,000

IN 1939 THERE WERE 3,350,000 JEWS IN POLAND AT THE SAME TIME THERE WERE APPROX. 15,000,000 JEWS WHO ORIGINATED FROM THE HISTORIC LANDS WHICH BELONGED TO POLAND BEFORE 19TH CENTURY.

SOVIET UNION

Moscow
Leningrad
Kiev
Wilno
Warsaw
POLAND

IN POLAND THERE WERE YIDDISH SPEAKING JEWS CONSCIOUS OF THEIR NATIONALITY IN COMPETITION WITH THE POLES. 80% OF POLISH JEWS NOT SPEAKING POLISH LANGUAGE AT HOME.

"As is well known, Jews in Poland were allowed to have their own laws and institutions. They were a nation unto themselves and they maintained their nationhood in Poland. From the time of their arrival and through the centuries, they sought to protect their way of life. They were not merely a separate religion but a tightly-knit community, leading life largely separate from Poles. They had their own customs, culture, dress, schools, courts, community government, and language."

(C) 1991 Iwo Cyprian Pogonowski.
Jew in Poland
A Historical Atlas

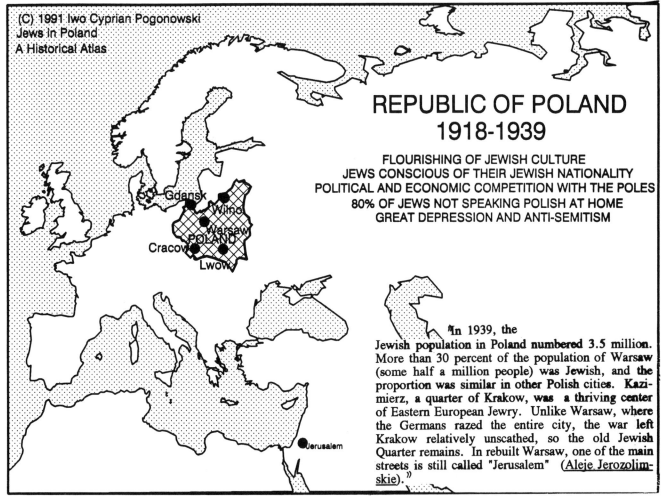

REPUBLIC OF POLAND
1918-1939

FLOURISHING OF JEWISH CULTURE
JEWS CONSCIOUS OF THEIR JEWISH NATIONALITY
POLITICAL AND ECONOMIC COMPETITION WITH THE POLES
80% OF JEWS NOT SPEAKING POLISH AT HOME
GREAT DEPRESSION AND ANTI-SEMITISM

"In 1939, the Jewish population in Poland numbered 3.5 million. More than 30 percent of the population of Warsaw (some half a million people) was Jewish, and the proportion was similar in other Polish cities. Kazimierz, a quarter of Krakow, was a thriving center of Eastern European Jewry. Unlike Warsaw, where the Germans razed the entire city, the war left Krakow relatively unscathed, so the old Jewish Quarter remains. In rebuilt Warsaw, one of the main streets is still called "Jerusalem" (Aleje Jerozolimskie)."

Competition between Jews and Poles was fostered and exploited by Austria, Germany, and Russia from the beginning of the 19th century. During World War I most international Jewish organizations opposed the independence of Poland. However, in the ethnic Polish areas many Jews supported the cause of Poland. After the Polish victory in 1920 in the war against the Bolsheviks, Jewish inhabitants of Vilno region voted with the Polish majority for union with Poland. Many educated Jews joined the ranks of Polish intelligentsia and took part in the cultural and intellectual life of Poland. There were 2,900,-000 Jews in Poland in 1930, including over 600,000 Jewish refugees from the Soviet Union. By 1939 there were 3,340,000 Jews in Poland and over 80 percent of them did not speak Polish at home. Masses of Jews in Poland considered themselves to be of Jewish nationality and most of them supported the idea of a Jewish national state. The number of Jews in Poland increased with influx of refugees from Germany.

In the Second Polish Republic (1918-1939) Jews had full civil rights, schools in Yiddish and Hebrew and their own press, theatres, libraries, clubs, etc. Again Jewish culture flourished in Poland as nowhere else. Jews represented 9 percent of the population of Poland and 30 percent of urban dwellers. During prewar persecution in Germany, Jews were sheltered in Poland and given help. Most outbreaks of Polish anti-Semitism resulted from political and economic competition between Jews and Poles and did not have racist character as was the case in Germany. The majority of Polish Jews supported the idea that as a separate nationality the Jews in Poland should enjoy complete autonomy in the tradition of the pre-partition Polish state.

The structural, economic, and cultural separation of Jewish Yiddish civilization constituted an issue which the Polish state could not solve on the basis of the concept of a nation-state which was supported by the majority of political parties in Poland. The Great Depression contributed to worsening of Christian-Jewish relations. An extremist press of limited circulation was spreading the conviction that the vast majority of Jews was irrevocably hostile to Polish independence. After 1935 it portrayed the Jews as an "alien element," the "Judeo-communist mafia," and as "rootless cosmopolitans spreading pornography."

Starting in 1939 the catastrophe of World War II brought the end of the Second Polish Republic and immense suffering to the Polish population. The Poles had only very limited possibility of saving the Jews. There was no Polish Quisling or Laval and no Polish complicity in the genocide of the Jews by the Germans. In occupied Poland individual Jews were saved while Jewish masses were exterminated.

307

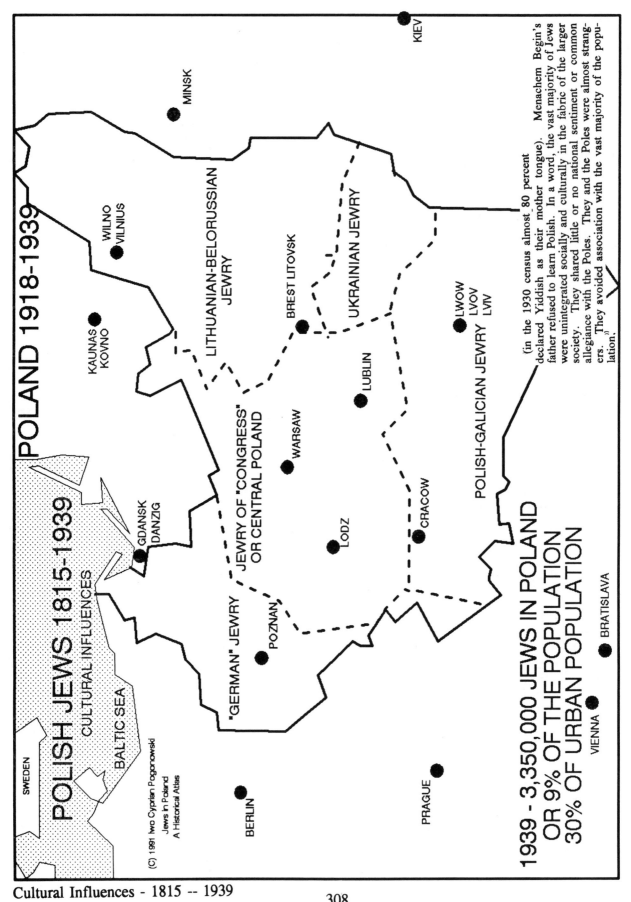

POLAND 1918-1939

POLISH JEWS 1815-1939
CULTURAL INFLUENCES

(C) 1991 Iwo Cyprian Pogonowski
Jews In Poland
A Historical Atlas

SWEDEN

BALTIC SEA

GDANSK
DANZIG

KAUNAS
KOVNO

WILNO
VILNIUS

MINSK

KIEV

LITHUANIAN-BELORUSSIAN
JEWRY

BREST LITOVSK

UKRAINIAN JEWRY

"GERMAN" JEWRY

JEWRY OF "CONGRESS"
OR CENTRAL POLAND

POZNAN

WARSAW

LODZ

LUBLIN

CRACOW

LWOW
LVOV
LVIV

POLISH-GALICIAN JEWRY

BERLIN

PRAGUE

VIENNA

BRATISLAVA

1939 - 3,350,000 JEWS IN POLAND
OR 9% OF THE POPULATION
30% OF URBAN POPULATION

(in the 1930 census almost 80 percent declared Yiddish as their mother tongue).   Menachem Begin's father refused to learn Polish. In a word, the vast majority of Jews were unintegrated socially and culturally in the fabric of the larger society.   They shared little or no national sentiment or common allegiance with the Poles.   They and the Poles were almost strangers.   They avoided association with the vast majority of the population."

Cultural Influences - 1815 -- 1939

308

Isaac Bashevis Singer (1904-1991), a winner of the Nobel Prize in literature, recognized a longstanding separation between Jews and Poles in Poland. He wrote an article titled "Jews and Poles Lived Together for 800 Years But Were Not Integrated." The article appeared in the New York-based Jewish newspaper *Forverts* on Sept. 17, 1944 under the pen-name Iccok Warszawski. He wrote: "Rarely did a Jew think it necessary to learn Polish; rarely was a Jew interested in Polish history or Polish politics." Refering to the Second Polish Republic (1918-1939) he continued "Even in the last few years it was still a rare occurrence that a Jew would speak Polish well. Out of three million Jews living in Poland, two-and-a-half million were not able to write a simple letter in Polish and they spoke [Polish] very poorly. There were hundreds of thousands of Jews in Poland to whom Polish was as unfamiliar as Turkish." He later wrote in Forverts, March 20, 1964 "My mouth could not get accustomed to the soft consonants of [Polish] language. My forefathers have lived for centuries in Poland but in reality I was a foreigner, with separate language, ideas and religion. I sensed the oddness of this situation and often considered moving to Palestine." (The above quotations are from Chone Shmeruk's *Isaac Bashevis Singer and Bruno Schultz* published in the Polish Review. Vol. XXXVI, No. 2, 1991: 161-167.)

Culturally and linguistically, Bashevis Singer was typical of Polish Jews in central Poland and eastern borderlands ruled by Russia during the partitions (1795-1918). Isaac Bashevis Singer is recognized by many as the Shakespeare of Yiddish literature. Born near Warsaw, he was steeped in Yiddish and did not know any Polish until the age of 15. Untill then, the Polish language was as unfamiliar to him as Chinese.

In Lesser Poland, or Galicia, annexed by Austria, Polish schools survived and the knowledge of Polish was much more common there, even among Orthodox Jews. Bruno Schultz (1892-1942) was among Jewish members of the Polish intelligentsia in Drohobycz, in eastern Galicia, as southeastern Poland was named by the Austrians. He wrote exclusively in Polish and was a prize-winning writer (Golden Laurel, Polish Acad-

emy of Literature, 1938) and graphic artist. The Yiddish press started publishing his prints in 1930. Bruno Schultz had more formal training than Bashevis Singer and was brought up in more cosmopolitan atmosphere. His language was Polish; he belonged to a generation of Polish Jews brought up in Polish. Bruno Schultz was a product of three interacting cultures, Polish, Jewish and German. Besides Polish, he knew German and no doubt understood the colloquial local Yiddish, which is a dialect of high German and was the "lingua franca" of Polish Jews.

Bruno Schultz was murdered by a German officer in a street in his native Drohobycz, where he taught high school (1924-1941). Had he accepted help from his Polish friends and left the Drohobycz ghetto, he could have survived. Generally, the Jews who spoke Polish well had by far a better chance to survive than the Orthodox Jews, who spoke only Yiddish well.

In the Jewish religious community some familiarity with Polish was necessary only for those Jews who had direct dealings with Poles in order to make a living. The fact that the vast majority of Polish Jews either did not speak Polish or spoke it very poorly contributed to the tragic situation of Jews in Poland under German occupation during World War II. A constant fear of being recognized by an inability to speak Polish like a native accompanied most Jews during the German genocide of Jewish people in Poland. Poor Polish language skills, next to "Semitic" appearance and circumcision, was among the characteristics by which Germans were able to recognize Jews.

Jews in northwestern and western Poland did not speak Yiddish. Their language was German. Before World War I most of them migrated west. The few who remained in western Polish provinces represented a very small percent of the Polish Jewry. These Jews used the German language as their own. However, their knowledge of German did not help them during the war. Most of them were murdered by the Germans, during the German genocide of the Jews in 1941-1944.

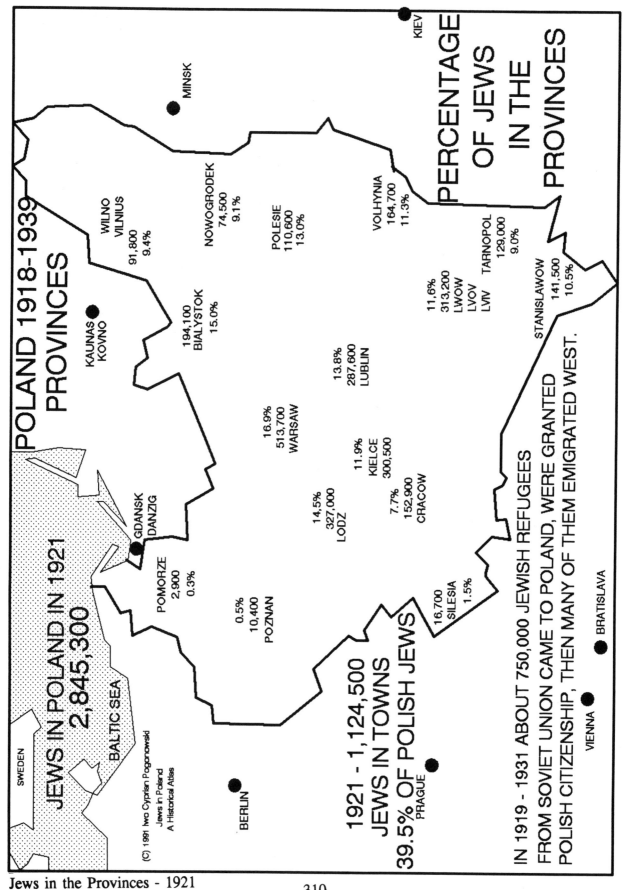

POLAND 1918-1939
PROVINCES

PERCENTAGE
OF JEWS
IN THE
PROVINCES

JEWS IN POLAND IN 1921
2,845,300

1921 - 1,124,500
JEWS IN TOWNS
39.5% OF POLISH JEWS

IN 1919 - 1931 ABOUT 750,000 JEWISH REFUGEES
FROM SOVIET UNION CAME TO POLAND, WERE GRANTED
POLISH CITIZENSHIP, THEN MANY OF THEM EMIGRATED WEST.

(C) 1991 Iwo Cyprian Pogonowski
Jews in Poland
A Historical Atlas

SWEDEN

BALTIC SEA

KIEV

MINSK

WILNO
VILNIUS
91,800
9.4%

NOWOGRODEK
74,500
9.1%

POLESIE
110,600
13.0%

VOLHYNIA
164,700
11.3%

KAUNAS
KOVNO

BIALYSTOK
194,100
15.0%

11.6%
313,200
LWOW
LVOV
LVIV

TARNOPOL
129,000
9.0%

STANISLAWOW
141,500
10.5%

LUBLIN
287,600
13.8%

WARSAW
513,700
16.9%

KIELCE
300,500
11.9%

GDANSK
DANZIG

LODZ
327,000
14.5%

CRACOW
152,900
7.7%

POMORZE
2,900
0.3%

POZNAN
10,400
0.5%

SILESIA
16,700
1.5%

BRATISLAVA

VIENNA

PRAGUE

BERLIN

Jews in the Provinces - 1921

310

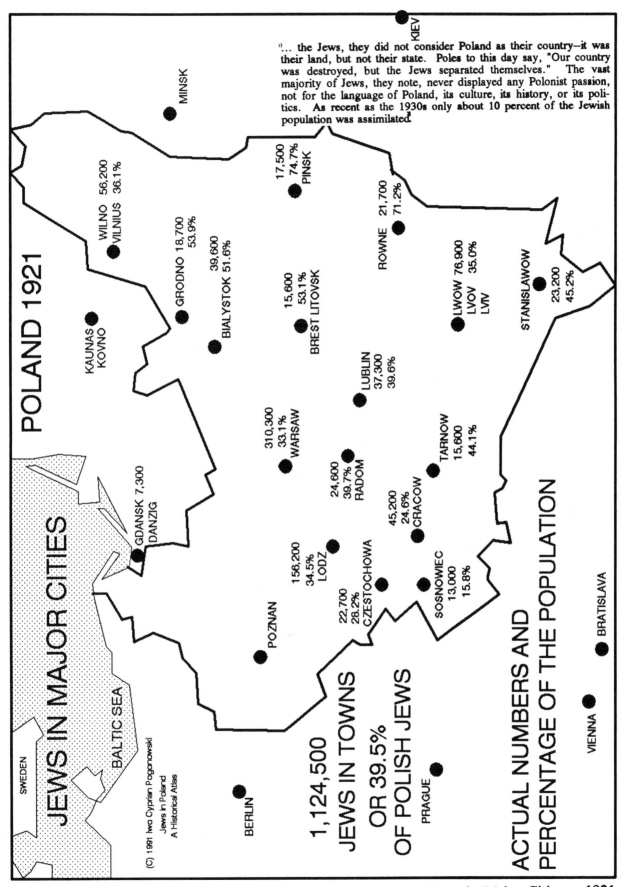

POLAND 1921

JEWS IN MAJOR CITIES

"... the Jews, they did not consider Poland as their country—it was their land, but not their state. Poles to this day say, "Our country was destroyed, but the Jews separated themselves." The vast majority of Jews, they note, never displayed any Polonist passion, not for the language of Poland, its culture, its history, or its politics. As recent as the 1930s only about 10 percent of the Jewish population was assimilated."

KIEV

MINSK

WILNO 56,200 36.1%
VILNIUS

17,500 74.7% PINSK

ROWNE 21,700 71.2%

GRODNO 18,700 53.9%

BIALYSTOK 39,600 51.6%

15,600 53.1% BREST LITOVSK

LWOW 76,900 LVOV 35.0% LVIV

STANISLAWOW 23,200 45.2%

KAUNAS KOVNO

LUBLIN 37,300 39.6%

310,300 33.1% WARSAW

TARNOW 15,600 44.1%

24,600 39.7% RADOM

45,200 24.6% CRACOW

GDANSK 7,300 DANZIG

156,200 34.5% LODZ

22,700 28.2% CZESTOCHOWA

SOSNOWIEC 13,000 15.8%

POZNAN

BALTIC SEA

SWEDEN

(C) 1991 Iwo Cyprian Pogonowski
Jews in Poland
A Historical Atlas

1,124,500 JEWS IN TOWNS OR 39.5% OF POLISH JEWS

ACTUAL NUMBERS AND PERCENTAGE OF THE POPULATION

BERLIN

PRAGUE

VIENNA

BRATISLAVA

Jews in Major Cities - 1921

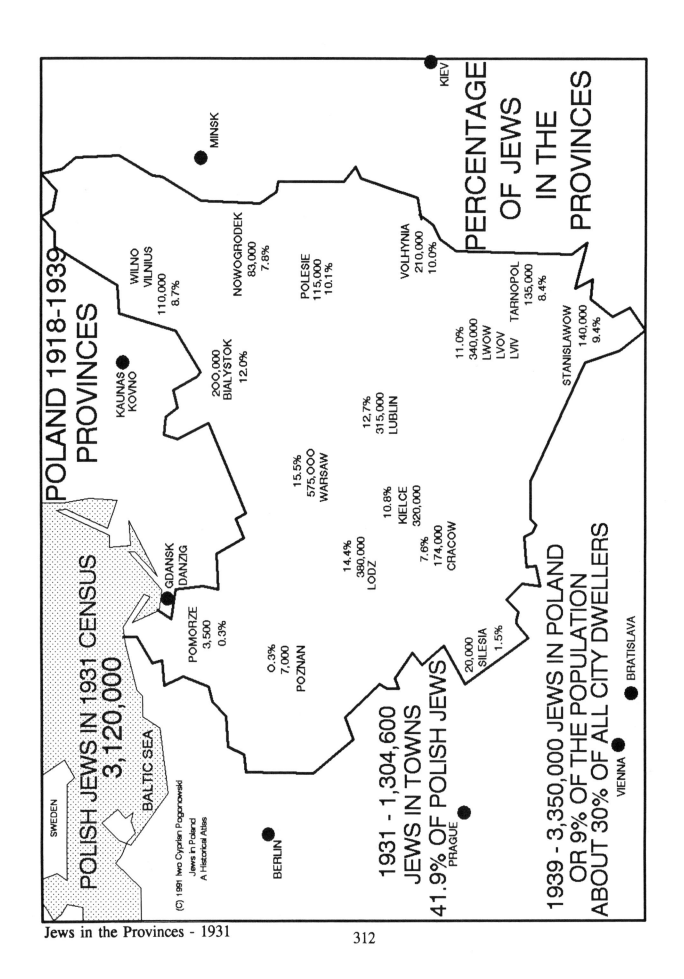

POLAND 1918-1939
PROVINCES

PERCENTAGE
OF JEWS
IN THE
PROVINCES

POLISH JEWS IN 1931 CENSUS
3,120,000

SWEDEN

BALTIC SEA

(C) 1991 Iwo Cyprian Pogonowski
Jews in Poland
A Historical Atlas

MINSK

KIEV

WILNO
VILNIUS
110,000
8.7%

NOWOGRODEK
83,000
7.8%

POLESIE
115,000
10.1%

VOLHYNIA
210,000
10.0%

TARNOPOL
135,000
8.4%

11.0%
340,000
LWOW
LVOV
LVIV

STANISLAWOW
140,000
9.4%

KAUNAS
KOVNO

200,000
BIALYSTOK
12.0%

12.7%
315,000
LUBLIN

15.5%
575,000
WARSAW

10.8%
KIELCE
320,000

14.4%
380,000
LODZ

7.6%
174,000
CRACOW

GDANSK
DANZIG

POMORZE
3,500
0.3%

0.3%
7,000
POZNAN

20,000
SILESIA
1.5%

BERLIN

PRAGUE

VIENNA

BRATISLAVA

1931 - 1,304,600
JEWS IN TOWNS
41.9% OF POLISH JEWS

1939 - 3,350,000 JEWS IN POLAND
OR 9% OF THE POPULATION
ABOUT 30% OF ALL CITY DWELLERS

Jews in the Provinces - 1931

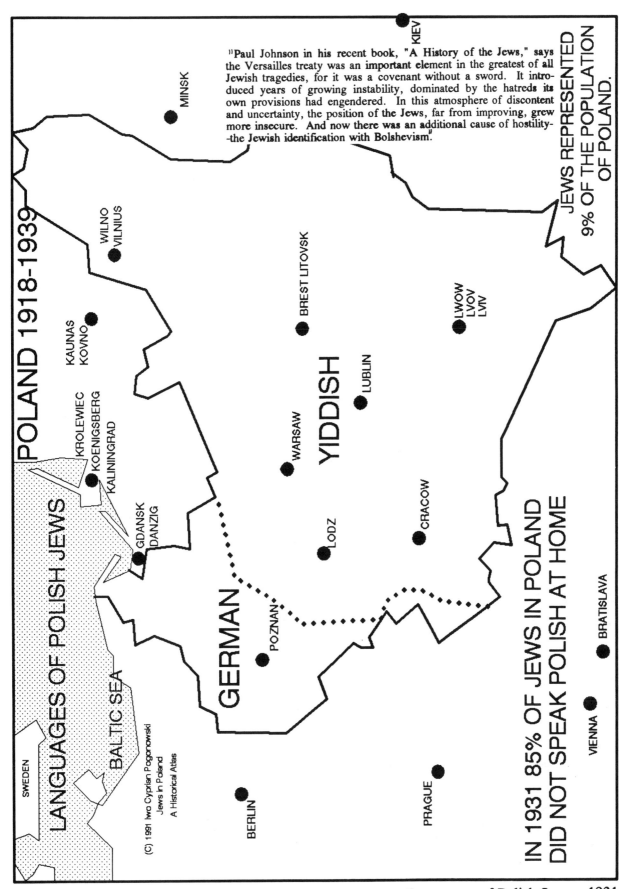

POLAND 1918-1939

LANGUAGES OF POLISH JEWS

"Paul Johnson in his recent book, "A History of the Jews," says the Versailles treaty was an important element in the greatest of all Jewish tragedies, for it was a covenant without a sword. It introduced years of growing instability, dominated by the hatreds its own provisions had engendered. In this atmosphere of discontent and uncertainty, the position of the Jews, far from improving, grew more insecure. And now there was an additional cause of hostility--the Jewish identification with Bolshevism."

JEWS REPRESENTED 9% OF THE POPULATION OF POLAND.

KIEV

MINSK

WILNO VILNIUS

BREST LITOVSK

KAUNAS KOVNO

LWOW LVOV LVIV

KROLEWIEC KOENIGSBERG KALININGRAD

LUBLIN

GDANSK DANZIG

WARSAW

YIDDISH

CRACOW

BALTIC SEA

LODZ

GERMAN

POZNAN

(C) 1991 Iwo Cyprian Pogonowski Jews in Poland A Historical Atlas

SWEDEN

BRATISLAVA

VIENNA

BERLIN

PRAGUE

IN 1931 85% OF JEWS IN POLAND DID NOT SPEAK POLISH AT HOME

Languages of Polish Jews - 1931

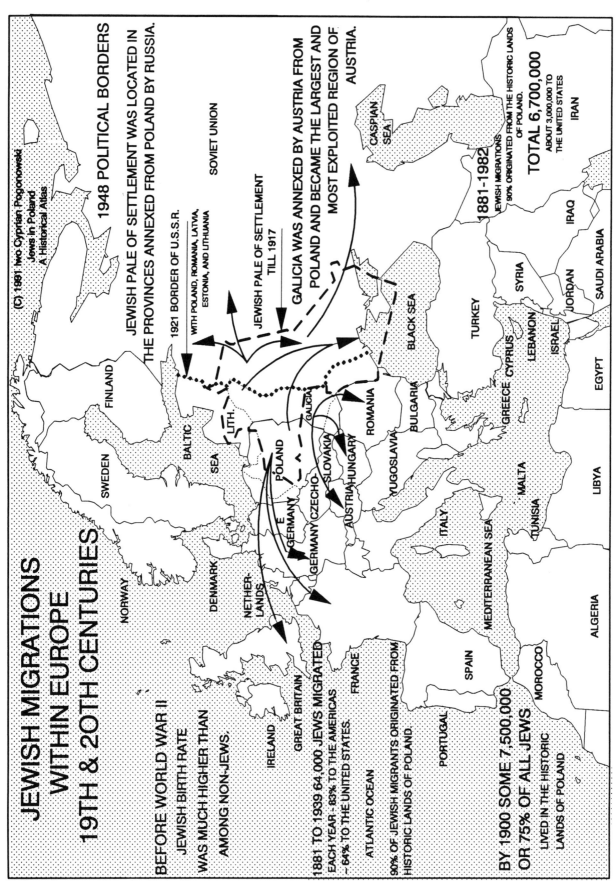

JEWISH MIGRATIONS WITHIN EUROPE 19TH & 20TH CENTURIES

(C) 1991 Iwo Cyprian Pogonowski
Jews in Poland
A Historical Atlas

1948 POLITICAL BORDERS

JEWISH PALE OF SETTLEMENT WAS LOCATED IN THE PROVINCES ANNEXED FROM POLAND BY RUSSIA.

1921 BORDER OF U.S.S.R.

WITH POLAND, ROMANIA, LATVIA, ESTONIA, AND LITHUANIA

JEWISH PALE OF SETTLEMENT TILL 1917

GALICIA WAS ANNEXED BY AUSTRIA FROM POLAND AND BECAME THE LARGEST AND MOST EXPLOITED REGION OF AUSTRIA.

1881-1982

JEWISH MIGRATIONS 90% ORIGINATED FROM THE HISTORIC LANDS OF POLAND.

TOTAL 6,700,000

ABOUT 3,000,000 TO THE UNITED STATES

BEFORE WORLD WAR II

JEWISH BIRTH RATE WAS MUCH HIGHER THAN AMONG NON-JEWS.

1881 TO 1939 64,000 JEWS MIGRATED EACH YEAR - 83% TO THE AMERICAS - 64% TO THE UNITED STATES.

90% OF JEWISH MIGRANTS ORIGINATED FROM HISTORIC LANDS OF POLAND.

BY 1900 SOME 7,500,000 OR 75% OF ALL JEWS LIVED IN THE HISTORIC LANDS OF POLAND.

SOVIET UNION

SWEDEN
NORWAY
FINLAND
BALTIC SEA
LITH.
DENMARK
NETHER-LANDS
GERMANY
E GERMANY
POLAND
CZECHO-
SLOVAKIA
GALICIA
AUSTRIA HUNGARY
ROMANIA
BULGARIA
BLACK SEA
YUGOSLAVIA
IRELAND
GREAT BRITAIN
FRANCE
ATLANTIC OCEAN
ITALY
MEDITERRANEAN SEA
PORTUGAL
SPAIN
MALTA
TUNISIA
MOROCCO
ALGERIA
LIBYA
EGYPT
GREECE
CYPRUS
TURKEY
LEBANON
ISRAEL
SYRIA
JORDAN
IRAQ
SAUDI ARABIA
IRAN
CASPIAN SEA

Migrations - 19th & 20th Cent.

SHOAH

THE GERMAN GENOCIDE

OF THE JEWS

1940 -- 1944

The Nazis believed in a life-and-death struggle of the German "master race" against the Jews, Slavs and Bolsheviks. The extermination of Polish, Soviet and other "eastern" Jews was a "practical step" in preparation of the eastern "living space" for colonization by the Germans. Eventually, the sick fantasies of the Nazi government in Berlin led it to its catastrophic mistake -- the invasion of the Soviet Union.

Ghetto Monument in Warsaw
Photograph

316

SOVIET FAILED STRATEGY FOR WORLD DOMINATION 1939-1945

BY UNLEASHING GERMANY AGAINST POLAND, FRANCE, AND GR. BRITAIN AND DEFLECTING JAPAN AGAINST AMERICA AND EUROPEAN COLONIES IN ASIA

SOVIET TRIGGERING OF WORLD WAR II WHICH RESULTED IN THE KILLING OF 50,000,000 INCLUDING GERMAN GENOCIDE OF 6,000,000 JEWS OR ONE-THIRD OF WORLD'S JEWRY.

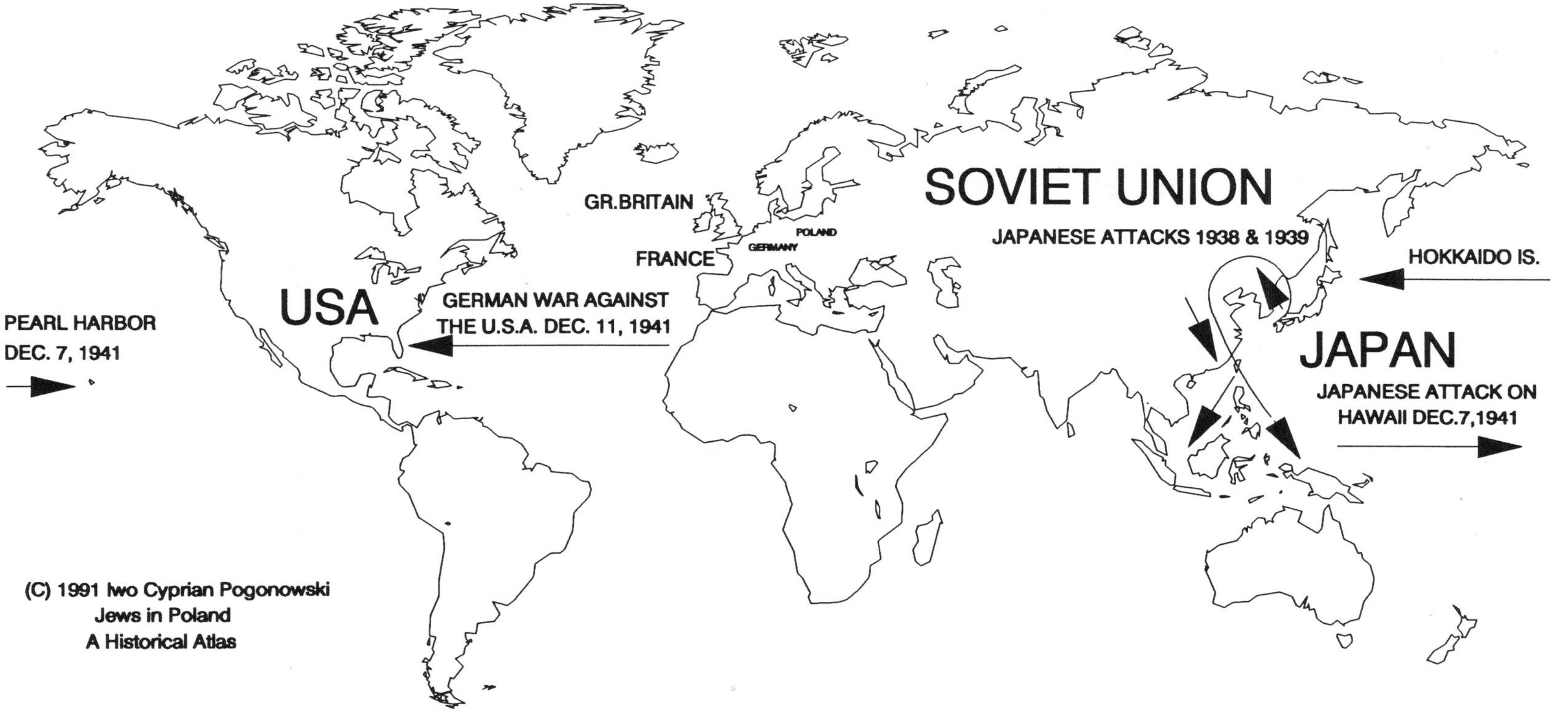

HOKKAIDO IS.

JAPAN

JAPANESE ATTACK ON HAWAII DEC.7,1941

SOVIET UNION

JAPANESE ATTACKS 1938 & 1939

POLAND

GERMANY

GR.BRITAIN

FRANCE

GERMAN WAR AGAINST THE U.S.A. DEC. 11, 1941

USA

PEARL HARBOR DEC. 7, 1941

(C) 1991 Iwo Cyprian Pogonowski
Jews in Poland
A Historical Atlas

IN 1939 THE SOVIETS HOPED FOR A PROTRACTED WAR OF ATTRITION BY GERMANY IN THE ATLANTIC BASIN AND BY JAPAN IN THE PACIFIC BASIN.

RESULTS OF FAILURE: COLLAPSE OF FRANCE IN 1940 & GERMAN ATTACK ON RUSSIA IN 1941 SOVIET FAILURE TO PARTITION JAPAN AND OCCUPY THE ISLAND OF HOKKAIDO IN 1945.

317

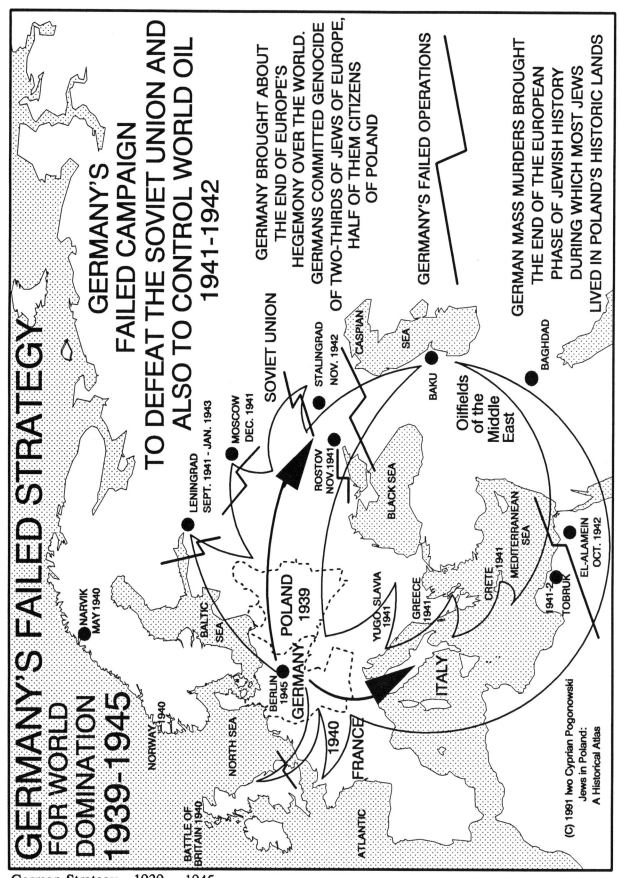

GERMANY'S FAILED STRATEGY FOR WORLD DOMINATION 1939-1945

GERMANY'S FAILED CAMPAIGN

TO DEFEAT THE SOVIET UNION AND ALSO TO CONTROL WORLD OIL 1941-1942

GERMANY BROUGHT ABOUT THE END OF EUROPE'S HEGEMONY OVER THE WORLD.

GERMANS COMMITTED GENOCIDE OF TWO-THIRDS OF JEWS OF EUROPE, HALF OF THEM CITIZENS OF POLAND

GERMANY'S FAILED OPERATIONS

GERMAN MASS MURDERS BROUGHT THE END OF THE EUROPEAN PHASE OF JEWISH HISTORY DURING WHICH MOST JEWS LIVED IN POLAND'S HISTORIC LANDS

SOVIET UNION

STALINGRAD NOV. 1942

CASPIAN SEA

BAGHDAD

BAKU

Oilfields of the Middle East

MOSCOW DEC. 1941

LENINGRAD SEPT. 1941 - JAN. 1943

ROSTOV NOV. 1941

BLACK SEA

NARVIK MAY 1940

BALTIC SEA

POLAND 1939

YUGO SLAVIA 1941

GREECE 1941

CRETE 1941

MEDITERRANEAN SEA

EL-ALAMEIN OCT. 1942

NORWAY 1940

BERLIN 1945 GERMANY

1940

FRANCE

1941-2 TOBRUK

BATTLE OF BRITAIN 1940

NORTH SEA

ITALY

ATLANTIC

(C) 1991 Iwo Cyprian Pogonowski: Jews in Poland: A Historical Atlas

German Strategy - 1939 -- 1945

318

Germany precipitated two world wars which destroyed European hegemony over the globe. Adolf Hitler (1889-1945), who played the crucial role in leading Germany during the second world war, was a personification of German racist megalomania. He set out to change the world balance of power dramatically in order to win a decisive victory of the "German race" over all other races, especially the "Jewish race" and the "Slavic race." The German government declared both of these "races" as "subhuman." Territorial expansion by conquest of Lebensraum, or "German living space," was the aim of German Nazi government at all times. Lands east of Germany were to be conquered and their Slavic and Jewish population was to be enslaved or exterminated and replaced by "racial Germans."

Adolf Hitler had mixed feelings about his own pedigree. He was born in Barnau, Austria, a son of second cousins. His father Alois was an illegitimate son of Anna Schicklgruber, who allegedly served as a maid in a Jewish household. She lost her job when she became pregnant. Eventually, Anna married Johann Georg Hiedler. Alois was adopted, but kept on misspelling the new family name as "Hitler." Alois, a custom official, was 52 when Adolf Hitler was born as a third child to his third wife, Klara Ploetzl, a farm girl. Adolf Hitler went to school near Linz. At first he made good grades but could not get along with his ill tempered father, whose illegitimate birth and possible Jewish ancestry annoyed the young Hitler. He cultivated a fierce pride in his German ancestry and race.

Hitler hated Jews and Slavs, the vast majority of the population of Austria and a threat to the small ruling German minority. In 1905, at 16 Hitler dropped out of high school and two years later went to Vienna where he failed the entrance examination of the Academy of Fine Arts twice. He blamed his failure on Jewish professors.

Hitler avoided steady work. Instead he often was homeless and lived on soup at charity kitchens. At first he shoveled snow, helped masons, and carried suitcases at the railroad station. Later he began to sell his advertising posters and for the rest of his life considered himself an artist. Hitler also developed a life-long interest in astrology and in the ancient Germanic pagan religion, which originated in Scandinavia. In 1913 Hitler failed the Austrian Army's physical examination as too weak, (apparently he was sexually impotent most of his life). In 1914 Hitler volunteered for service in the German Army, earned battle field decorations, was wounded in the leg, and temporarily blinded by poison gas.

After Germany's defeat, Hitler joined the National Socialist German Workers' Party in 1920, which was committed to "greatness of Germany." By 1923, he had an army of hoodlums, the "storm troopers," who wore brown uniforms and used swastika as their emblem. Hitler formed very clear and simple notions about life based on a crude interpretation of the theory of evolution and a belief that an alleged Jewish world-conspiracy was a deadly threat to a "natural" hierarchic order which should be dominated by the "German race." His near-lunatic beliefs helped him to become a skillful "Machiavellian" schemer, a calculating opportunist, and above all a power hungry politician, and organizer, who always thought that he knew what he wanted.

On Nov. 8, 1923, Hitler tried to seize the Bavarian government in Munich with a force of 2000 "storm troopers." He failed, was arrested, and sentenced to five years in prison for treason. In prison Hitler began writing his book *Mein Kampf* (My Struggle), in which he described the Germans as "the highest species of humanity on earth." Hitler believed that the wars for German

Lebensraum were an inevitable life-and-death struggle between races for the "survival of the fittest" from which Germany could not turn back without being "disgraced forever."

The *Protocols of the Elders of Zion* -- a fake and contrieved "plan" of the Jewish campaign for world domination -- became the essence of the Nazi regime. German racists scheming actually resembled the notions described in the *Protocols*. They also felt an utter contempt for humanity at large and conspired to achieve world domination by building a world-empire controlled by a small but highly organized and regimented people. German racists also glorified sinister means and destruction. Eventually, the German Ministry of Education prescribed the Protocols as one of the basic texts for schools.

By 1929, the Nazis had become an important political party in Germany and had a second private army, the battle ready "SS" or the "Schutzstaffel" (Elite Guard). In the July 1932 election, the Nazis received 40 per cent of the vote and became the strongest party in Germany. On Jan. 30, 1933 president Paul von Hindenburg appointed Hitler to be the Chancellor (prime minister) of Germany, which became the Third Reich. By then Hitler recognized himself in the prophesies published in France in 1550-1555 in an astrological calendar and in the Astrological Centuries by Nostradamus (1503-1566). He claimed that the word "Hister" or "Ister" (Latin for Danube River) really meant "Hitler." In 1935 Hitler appointed astrology as a "science of state" (Reischfachschaft) and in 1939 K.E. Kraft (1900-1944) as his astrology advisor to elaborate plans for military operations. When in 1941 Kraft began to predict failures, Hitler ordered him arrested. Kraft died in the Buchenwald concentration camp. Hitler turned to other astrologers for advice and in 1942 after getting unsatisfactory predictions he proclaimed astrology as a "useless science," but kept on worrying about the prediction "...from fields against Hister. In an iron cage the great one will be dragged..."

In 1942 Hitler told Himmler, "The discovery of the Jewish virus is one of the greatest revolutions that have taken place in the world. The battle in which we are engaged today is of the same sort as the battle waged, during the last century, by Pasteur and Koch... We shall regain health by eliminating the Jew." (*Hitler's Table Talk*, ed. H.R. Trevor-Roper, London, 1953, p. 332, as quoted by Norman Cohn, *Warrant for Genocide. The myth of the Jewish world-conspiracy and the Protocols of the Elders of Zion.*, Chico, CA: 1981.) Hitler compensated the looming prospect of military defeat by claiming that he was winning the greatest victory by exterminating the Jews of Europe whom he believed to be striving for world-domination everywhere and at all times. He saw Jews as bacilli and compared Christianity and Bolshevism with syphilis and plague. He loathed Christianity and Jews, "the evil anti-natural race" undermining the "original hierarchical order" dominated by the German "race." In 1945 Hitler kept on repeating the same nonsense in which he believed in 1920. He saw non-Germans as totally different, only "trying to be human beings, with a quasi-human face" -- in reality "sub-human, lower than any animal."

Before he shot himself on April 30, 1945, Hitler dictated his testament, which he ended with an appeal to the elite of the German nation "to merciless opposition to the world-poisoner of all peoples, international Jewry." The ardent support of Nazi government by the German people lasted until the bitter end. Hitler was worshipped as an incarnation of Germany and her most charismatic leader ever.

319

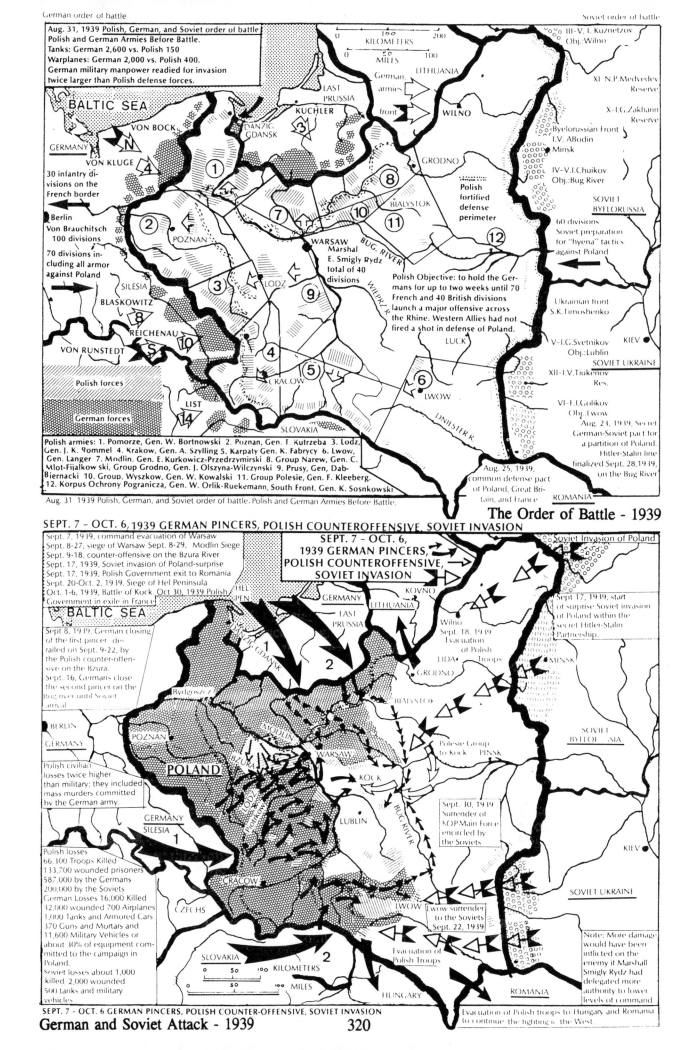

German order of battle — Soviet order of battle

Aug. 31, 1939 Polish, German, and Soviet order of battle
Polish and German Armies Before Battle.
Tanks: German 2,600 vs. Polish 150
Warplanes: German 2,000 vs. Polish 400.
German military manpower readied for invasion twice larger than Polish defense forces.

Polish Objective: to hold the Germans for up to two weeks until 70 French and 40 British divisions launch a major offensive across the Rhine. Western Allies had not fired a shot in defense of Poland.

Polish armies: 1. Pomorze, Gen. W. Bortnowski 2. Poznan, Gen. T. Kutrzeba 3. Lodz, Gen. J. K. Rommel 4. Krakow, Gen. A. Szylling 5. Karpaty Gen. K. Fabrycy 6. Lwow, Gen. Langer 7. Modlin. Gen. E. Kurkowicz-Przedrzymirski 8. Group Narew, Gen. C. Mlot-Fijalkowski, Group Grodno, Gen. J. Olszyna-Wilczynski 9. Prusy, Gen. Dab-Biernacki 10. Group, Wyszkow, Gen. W. Kowalski 11. Group Polesie, Gen. F. Kleeberg. 12. Korpus Ochrony Pogranicza, Gen. W. Orlik-Ruekemann, South Front, Gen. K. Sosnkowski.

Aug. 31 1939 Polish, German, and Soviet order of battle. Polish and German Armies Before Battle.

The Order of Battle - 1939

SEPT. 7 – OCT. 6, 1939 GERMAN PINCERS, POLISH COUNTEROFFENSIVE, SOVIET INVASION

Sept. 7, 1939, command evacuation of Warsaw
Sept. 8-27, siege of Warsaw Sept. 8-29, Modlin Siege
Sept. 9-18, counter-offensive on the Bzura River
Sept. 17, 1939, Soviet invasion of Poland-surprise
Sept. 17, 1939, Polish Government exit to Romania
Sept. 20-Oct. 2, 1939, Siege of Hel Peninsula
Oct. 1-6, 1939, Battle of Kock. Oct 30, 1939 Polish Government in exile in France.

Polish losses
66,300 Troops Killed
133,700 wounded prisoners
587,000 by the Germans
200,000 by the Soviets
German Losses 16,000 Killed
32,000 wounded 700 Airplanes
1,000 Tanks and Armored Cars
370 Guns and Mortars and
11,600 Military Vehicles or
about 30% of equipment committed to the campaign in Poland.
Soviet losses about 1,000 killed, 2,000 wounded
500 tanks and military vehicles

SEPT. 7 – OCT. 6 GERMAN PINCERS, POLISH COUNTER-OFFENSIVE, SOVIET INVASION

German and Soviet Attack - 1939

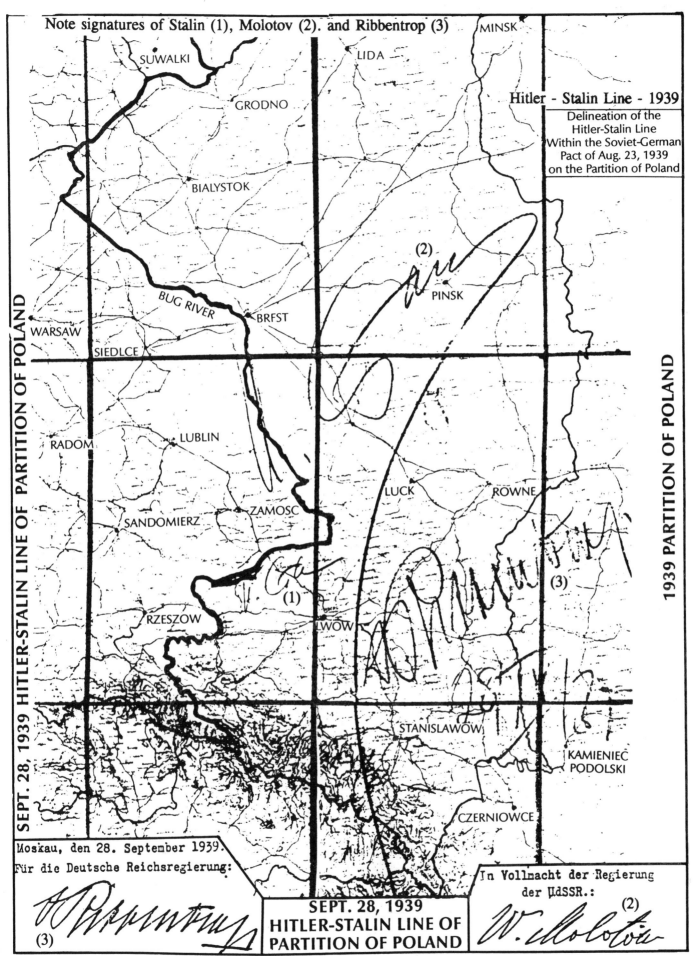

Map: Sept.28,1939 Hitler-Stalin Line of Partition of Poland.

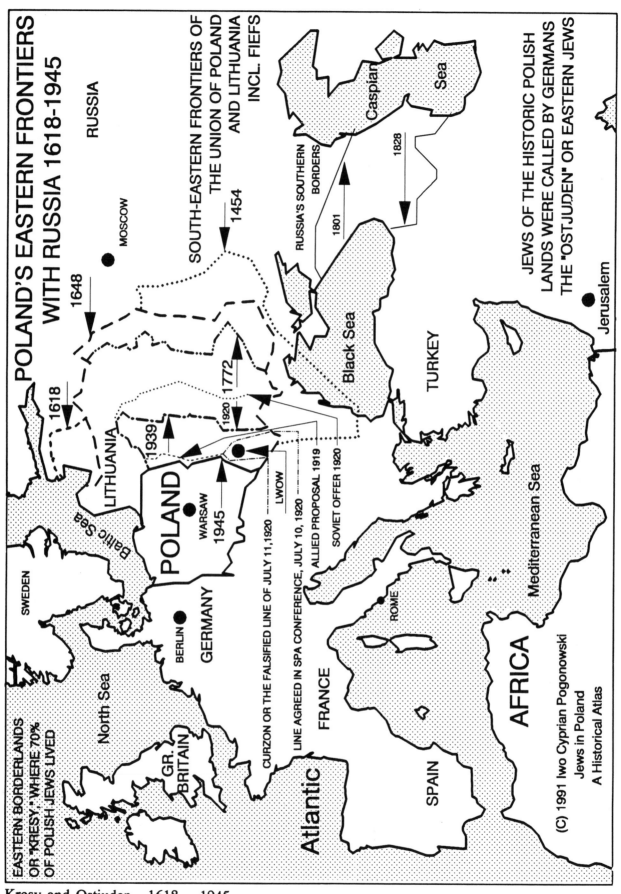

POLAND'S EASTERN FRONTIERS WITH RUSSIA 1618-1945

EASTERN BORDERLANDS OR "KRESY," WHERE 70% OF POLISH JEWS LIVED

SOUTH-EASTERN FRONTIERS OF THE UNION OF POLAND AND LITHUANIA INCL. FIEFS

JEWS OF THE HISTORIC POLISH LANDS WERE CALLED BY GERMANS THE "OSTJUDEN" OR EASTERN JEWS

RUSSIA

MOSCOW

1648

1618

LITHUANIA

1939

1920 1772

1454

RUSSIA'S SOUTHERN BORDERS

1801

1828

Caspian Sea

Black Sea

TURKEY

Jerusalem

POLAND

WARSAW

1945

Baltic Sea

SWEDEN

BERLIN

GERMANY

CURZON OR THE FALSIFIED LINE OF JULY 11,1920
LWOW
LINE AGREED IN SPA CONFERENCE, JULY 10, 1920
ALLIED PROPOSAL 1919
SOVIET OFFER 1920

North Sea

GR. BRITAIN

FRANCE

Atlantic

SPAIN

AFRICA

ROME

Mediterranean Sea

(C) 1991 Iwo Cyprian Pogonowski
Jews in Poland
A Historical Atlas

Kresy and Ostjuden - 1618 -- 1945

322

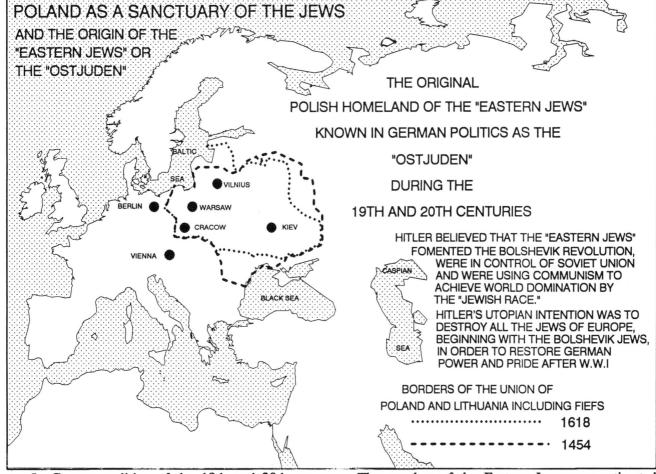

POLAND AS A SANCTUARY OF THE JEWS
AND THE ORIGIN OF THE "EASTERN JEWS" OR THE "OSTJUDEN"

THE ORIGINAL
POLISH HOMELAND OF THE "EASTERN JEWS"
KNOWN IN GERMAN POLITICS AS THE
"OSTJUDEN"
DURING THE
19TH AND 20TH CENTURIES

HITLER BELIEVED THAT THE "EASTERN JEWS" FOMENTED THE BOLSHEVIK REVOLUTION, WERE IN CONTROL OF SOVIET UNION AND WERE USING COMMUNISM TO ACHIEVE WORLD DOMINATION BY THE "JEWISH RACE."

HITLER'S UTOPIAN INTENTION WAS TO DESTROY ALL THE JEWS OF EUROPE, BEGINNING WITH THE BOLSHEVIK JEWS, IN ORDER TO RESTORE GERMAN POWER AND PRIDE AFTER W.W.I

BORDERS OF THE UNION OF
POLAND AND LITHUANIA INCLUDING FIEFS
················· 1618
- - - - - - - - - · 1454

In German politics of the 19th and 20th centuries the term "Ostjuden" or "Eastern Jews" referred to the mass of Jews who inha-bited Polish lands annexed by Russia and Austria during the partitions 1772-1795. In 1879 a professor at the university of Berlin warned that "a horde" of the Ostjuden will eventually become "controllers of Germany." Political importance of the German notion of the Ostjuden grew after assassination of Tsar Alexander II in March 1881, when pogroms in Russia drove waves of Jewish refugees to Vienna and Berlin, many of them en route to America. In pre-1914 Vienna Adolf Hitler developed a morbid fixation of the Ostjuden as a threat to the Germans.

The numerically small, German Jewish community saw the Ostjuden as many millions of "ghetto Jews: "physically filthy, medieval, une-mancipated, alien in appearance, manner, language, culture, and locked in their religious extremes such as Hasidism. Their side-locks and caftans made them look strange and very different from German society. After the Russian Revolution the defeated tsarist soldiers and politicians spread among the Germans the notion that Jews controlled the Bolshevik movement and the government of Communist Russia.

The number of the Eastern Jews was estimated at approximately 8 million before 1914. Thus, Germans feared that they will be overrun by "hordes" of the Ostjuden. After 1918 in the Weimar Republic the "Ostjudenfrage," or the question of the Eastern Jews, consisted of formulation of the policy on ways and means of eviction out of Germany of the unwanted Jewish immigrants. From 1933 on Hitler continued and radicalized the anti-Jewish policies of the Weimar Republic.

In Sept. 1938 at the Munich Conference Hitler said: "nine tenths of the Jews living in Germany had immigrated from the east during the last decades. Although they arrived with nothing, today they possessed 4.6 times as much as their hosts..." and he added that: "World Jewry...regarded the Jews in Europe as an outpost for the Bolshevising of the World. The Jews hated him because he had prevented further Bolshevising of Europe." On Jan. 21 1939 Hitler stated: "With us the Jews will be destroyed. Not for nothing had the Jews made Nov. 9, 1918 (communist revolution in Germany); this day would be avenged."

Killing by the Germans of 500,000 Eastern Jews in Soviet occupied territory of Poland between June and December 1941 started the German genocide of European Jewry on a massive scale.

323

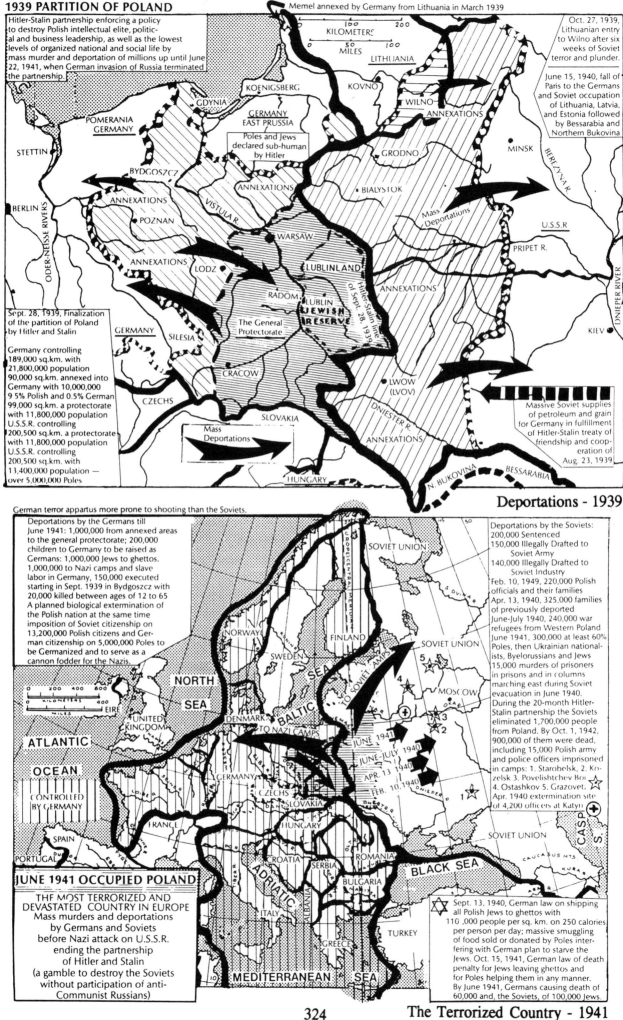

1939 PARTITION OF POLAND

Hitler-Stalin partnership enforcing a policy to destroy Polish intellectual elite, political and business leadership, as well as the lowest levels of organized national and social life by mass murder and deportation of millions up until June 22, 1941, when German invasion of Russia terminated the partnership.

Memel annexed by Germany from Lithuania in March 1939

Oct. 27, 1939, Lithuanian entry to Wilno after six weeks of Soviet terror and plunder.

June 15, 1940, fall of Paris to the Germans and Soviet occupation of Lithuania, Latvia, and Estonia followed by Bessarabia and Northern Bukovina

Poles and Jews declared sub-human by Hitler

Sept. 28, 1939, Finalization of the partition of Poland by Hitler and Stalin

Germany controlling 189,000 sq.km. with 21,800,000 population 90,000 sq.km. annexed into Germany with 10,000,000 9 5% Polish and 0.5% German 99,000 sq.km. a protectorate with 11,800,000 population U.S.S.R. controlling 200,500 sq.km. a protectorate with 11,800,000 population U.S.S.R. controlling 200,500 sq.km. with 13,400,000 population — over 5,000,000 Poles

Massive Soviet supplies of petroleum and grain for Germany in fulfillment of Hitler-Stalin treaty of friendship and cooperation of Aug. 23, 1939

Mass Deportations

The General Protectorate

LUBLINLAND

LUBLIN JEWISH RESERVE

Deportations - 1939

German terror appartus more prone to shooting than the Soviets.

Deportations by the Germans till June 1941: 1,000,000 from annexed areas to the general protectorate; 200,000 children to Germany to be raised as Germans: 1,000,000 Jews to ghettos. 1,000,000 to Nazi camps and slave labor in Germany, 150,000 executed starting in Sept. 1939 in Bydgoszcz with 20,000 killed between ages of 12 to 65 A planned biological extermination of the Polish nation at the same time imposition of Soviet citizenship on 13,200,000 Polish citizens and German citizenship on 5,000,000 Poles to be Germanized and to serve as a cannon fodder for the Nazis.

Deportations by the Soviets: 200,000 Sentenced 150,000 Illegally Drafted to Soviet Army 140,000 Illegally Drafted to Soviet Industry Feb. 10, 1949, 220,000 Polish officials and their families Apr. 13, 1940, 325,000 families of previously deported June-July 1940, 240,000 war refugees from Western Poland June 1941, 300,000 at least 60% Poles, then Ukrainian nationalists, Byelorussians and Jews 15,000 murders of prisoners in prisons and in columns marching east during Soviet evacuation in June 1940. During the 20-month Hitler-Stalin partnership the Soviets eliminated 1,700,000 people from Poland. By Oct. 1, 1942, 900,000 of them were dead, including 15,000 Polish army and police officers imprisoned in camps: 1. Starobelsk, 2. Kozelsk 3. Povelishtchev Bor 4. Ostashkov 5. Grazovet, Apr. 1940 extermination site of 4,200 officers at Katyn

JUNE 1941 OCCUPIED POLAND

THE MOST TERRORIZED AND DEVASTATED COUNTRY IN EUROPE Mass murders and deportations by Germans and Soviets before Nazi attack on U.S.S.R. ending the partnership of Hitler and Stalin (a gamble to destroy the Soviets without participation of anti-Communist Russians)

Sept. 13, 1940, German law on shipping all Polish Jews to ghettos with 110,000 people per sq.km. on 250 calories per person per day; massive smuggling of food sold or donated by Poles interfering with German plan to starve the Jews. Oct. 15, 1941, German law of death penalty for Jews leaving ghettos and for Poles helping them in any manner. By June 1941, Germans causing death of 60,000 and, the Soviets, of 100,000 Jews.

324

The Terrorized Country - 1941

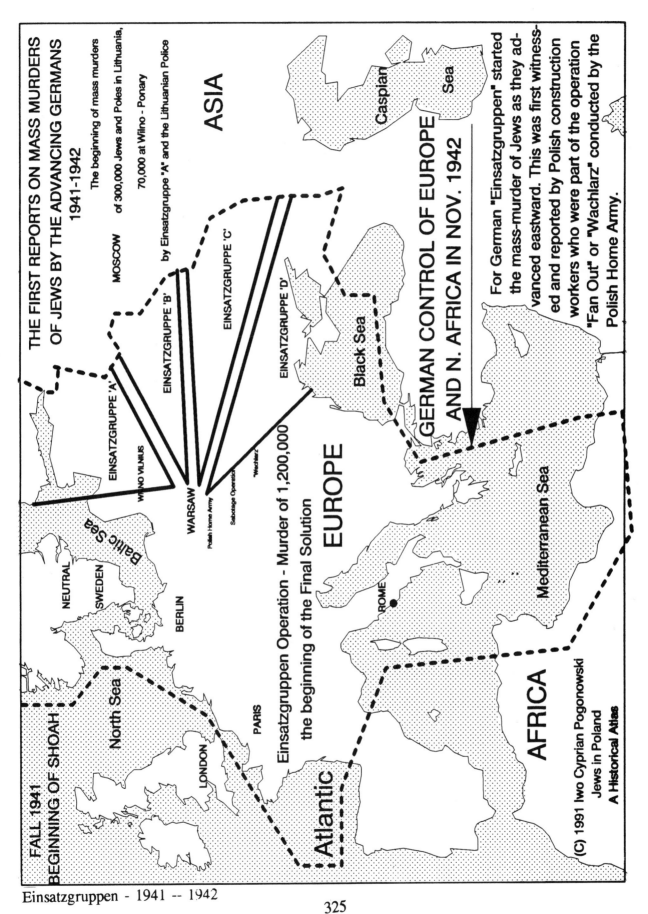

THE FIRST REPORTS ON MASS MURDERS OF JEWS BY THE ADVANCING GERMANS 1941-1942

The beginning of mass murders of 300,000 Jews and Poles in Lithuania, 70,000 at Wilno - Ponary by Einsatzgruppe "A" and the Lithuanian Police

ASIA

Caspian Sea

GERMAN CONTROL OF EUROPE AND N. AFRICA IN NOV. 1942

For German "Einsatzgruppen" started the mass-murder of Jews as they advanced eastward. This was first witnessed and reported by Polish construction workers who were part of the operation "Fan Out" or "Wachlarz" conducted by the Polish Home Army.

MOSCOW

EINSATZGRUPPE 'B'

EINSATZGRUPPE 'C'

EINSATZGRUPPE 'D'

EINSATZGRUPPE 'A'

WILNO VILNIUS

WARSAW

Polish Home Army

"Wachlarz"

Sabotage Operation

Black Sea

EUROPE

Baltic Sea

NEUTRAL

SWEDEN

BERLIN

ROME

Mediterranean Sea

Einsatzgruppen Operation - Murder of 1,200,000 the beginning of the Final Solution

North Sea

PARIS

LONDON

Atlantic

AFRICA

(C) 1991 Iwo Cyprian Pogonowski
Jews in Poland
A Historical Atlas

FALL 1941
BEGINNING OF SHOAH

Einsatzgruppen - 1941 -- 1942

325

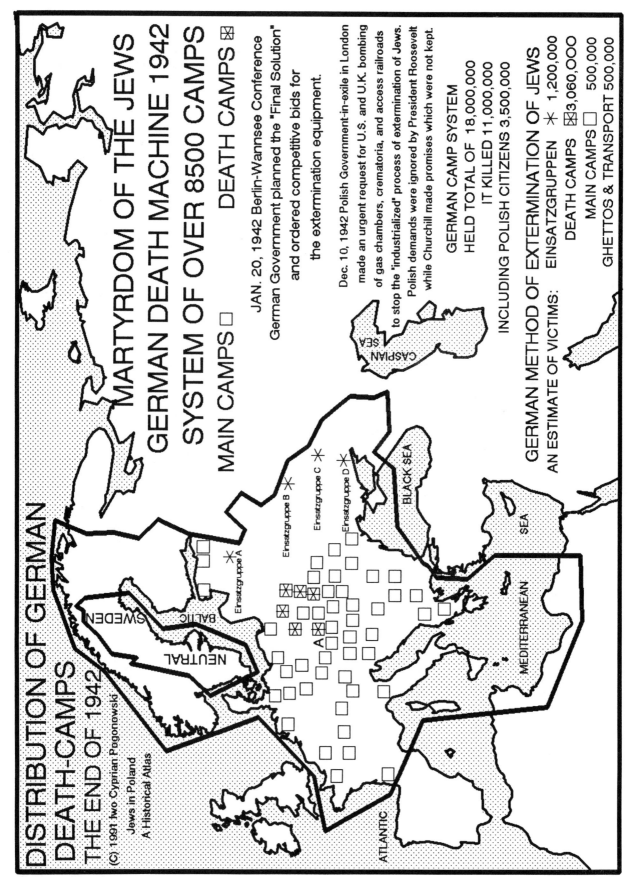

DISTRIBUTION OF GERMAN DEATH-CAMPS
THE END OF 1942

(C) 1991 Iwo Cyprian Pogonowski
Jews in Poland
A Historical Atlas

MARTYRDOM OF THE JEWS
GERMAN DEATH MACHINE 1942
SYSTEM OF OVER 8500 CAMPS

MAIN CAMPS ☐   DEATH CAMPS ⊠

JAN. 20, 1942 Berlin-Wannsee Conference
German Government planned the "Final Solution"
and ordered competitive bids for
the extermination equipment.

Dec. 10, 1942 Polish Government-in-exile in London
made an urgent request for U.S. and U.K. bombing
of gas chambers, crematoria, and access railroads
to stop the "industrialized" process of extermination of Jews.
Polish demands were ignored by President Roosevelt
while Churchill made promises which were not kept.

GERMAN CAMP SYSTEM
HELD TOTAL OF 18,000,000
IT KILLED 11,000,000
INCLUDING POLISH CITIZENS 3,500,000

GERMAN METHOD OF EXTERMINATION OF JEWS
AN ESTIMATE OF VICTIMS: EINSATZGRUPPEN ✳ 1,200,000
                           DEATH CAMPS ⊠ 3,060,000
                           MAIN CAMPS ☐ 500,000
                           GHETTOS & TRANSPORT 500,000

CASPIAN SEA

Einsatzgruppe A
Einsatzgruppe B
Einsatzgruppe C
Einsatzgruppe D

BLACK SEA

SEA

MEDITERRANEAN

ATLANTIC

SWEDEN
NEUTRAL
BALTIC

German Death Machine

326

An Anatomy of World's Sin of Omission Towards the Victims of the Holocaust.

A message from Jewish leaders in occupied Poland, it arrived in London in Nov. 1942.
Addressed to Ignacy Schwartzbart, a Zionist and Szmul Zygielbojm, a Bundist,
Jewish members of Polish National Council in London,
and to American Rabbis, Stephen Wise and Nachum Goldman

"We want you to tell the Polish government, the Allied governments, and Allied leaders that we are helpless against the German criminals. We cannot defend ourselves, and no one in Poland can possibly defend us. The Polish underground authorities can save some of us, but they can not save the masses. The Germans do not try to enslave us the way they do other peoples. We are being systematically murdered... All Jews in Poland will perish. It is possible that some few will be saved. However, three million of Polish Jews are doomed to extinction.

There is no power in Poland able to forestall this fact; neither the Polish nor the Jewish underground can do it. You have to place the responsibility squarely on the shoulders of the Allies. No leader of the United Nations should ever be able to say that he did not know that we are being murdered in Poland and that only outside assistance could help us."

This message was delivered to the Polish Government-in-Exile and to the following dignitaries in London: Anthony Eden, Foreign Secretary; Arthur Greenwood, leader of the Labor Party; Lord Selbourne; Lord Cranborne; Hugh Dalton, the Chairman of the Board of Trade; Ellen Wilkinson, member of the House of Commons; O'Malley, British Ambassador to the Polish Government-in-Exile; Richard Law, Foreign Affairs Under Secretary; Sir Cecil, the Chairman of the United Nations War Crimes Commission.

This message was brought to London by the Polish diplomat Jan Karski, eye witness to the German extermination of the Jews in the death camps and ghettos. Karski accomplished his mission and delivered the desperate message about the fate of Jews in occupied Poland to Allied leaders.

Dec. 4, 1942 The headquarters of the Council of Assistance for the Jews, code name *ZEGOTA*, was established in Warsaw under the auspices of the Polish Government-in Exile. Pre-war political leaders were in charge of the operation, which was unique in occupied Europe. Julian Grobelny was the chairman, Leon Feinr, vice chairman, and Adolf Berman, secretary.

Dec. 10, 1942 An urgent appeal to the Allies was made by the Polish Government-in-Exile, led by General Sikorski. It was primarily addressed to the governments of the United States and Great Britain. The appeal demanded a stop to the German genocidal operation by bombing the access railroads, gas chambers, and crematoria as well as to use of other measures of retaliation and punishment against Germany. The Poles cited the complete records of German crimes as reported on radio by Stefan Korbonski, the Head of the Directorate of Civil Defense in Warsaw, and by numerous emissaries from Poland. At the same time Polish reports were confirmed independently by the intelligence work of Allen Dulles in Geneva, Switzerland, where travelling German industrialists were cooperating with the U.S. Office of Strategic Studies (now the Central Intelligence Agency). Travelling German businessmen were insuring their personal security in the face of the dwindling prospects of German victory.

Polish government's requests for bombing access railroads leading to the extermination camps, as well as gas chambers, and crematoria were ignored by Washington and London.

May 13, 1943 Szmul Zygielbojm (1895-1943), a member of the Polish National Council, committed suicide in London in protest to the indifference of the Allies to the German genocide of the Jews in occupied Poland.

Aug. 1943 The Polish diplomat, Jan Karski, arrived in Washington and reported to President Roosevelt on the horrible situation in occupied Poland and on German genocide of the Jews.

Karski represented the Polish Government in speeches and conferences asking for immediate measures for stopping the German industrialized extermination process in order to save millions of Jewish and other victims. He contacted the Under Secretary of State, Adolf Berle, Attorney General Biddle, Supreme Court Justice Felix Frankfurter, Catholic Archbishops Mooneym and Strich, rabbis Stephen Wise, Nachum Goldman, and Waldman requesting their political support for the Allied bombing needed to disable the huge extermination plants in the German death camps in vain.

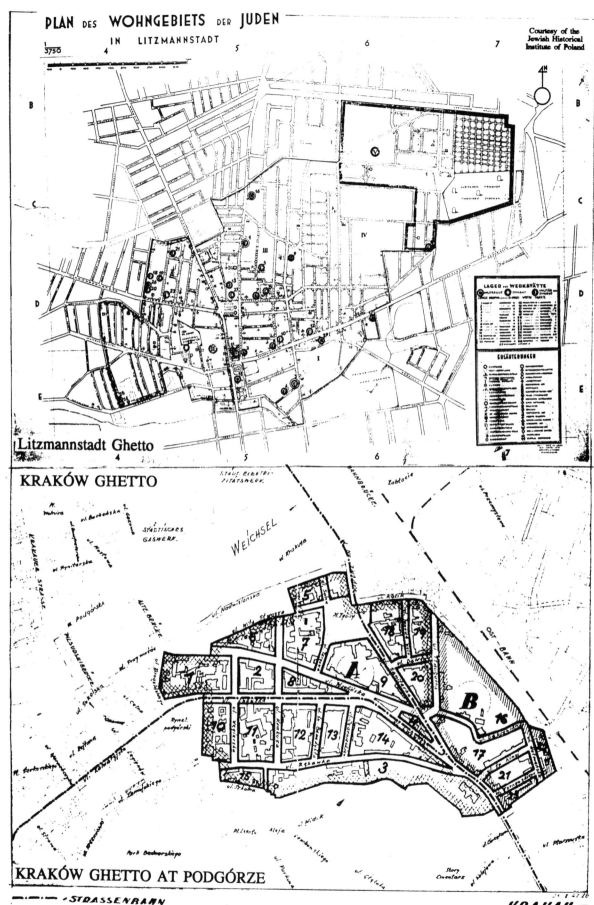

PLAN DES WOHNGEBIETS DER JUDEN
IN LITZMANNSTADT

Litzmannstadt Ghetto

KRAKÓW GHETTO

WEICHSEL

KRAKÓW GHETTO AT PODGÓRZE

STRASSENBAHN

GRENZE DES JUDENBEZIRKS 1. ABCHNITT **A**

2. ABSCHNITT **B**

Podgorze Judenbezirk

KRAKAU —
PODGÓRZE
MST: 7:5000

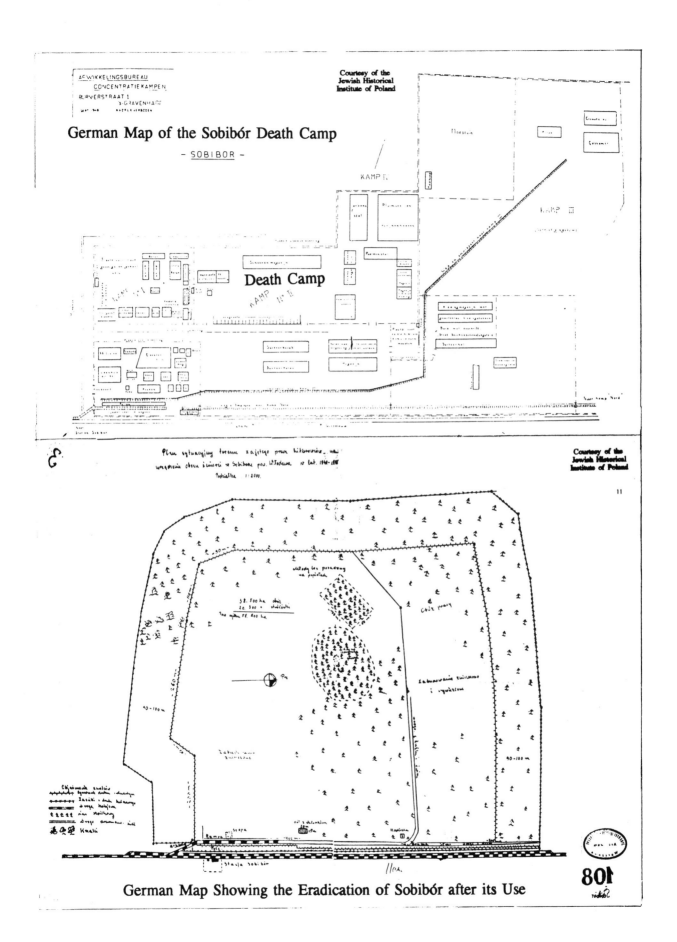

German Map of the Sobibór Death Camp

Death Camp

German Map Showing the Eradication of Sobibór after its Use

329

I.D. Card: *Kennkarte of Mrs. Cyla Bau*

(Józef Bau: "Czas Zbezczeszczenia," Ofset A.P., Tel-Aviv, 1990)

WARSAW GHETTO 1940-1943 A GENERAL MAP

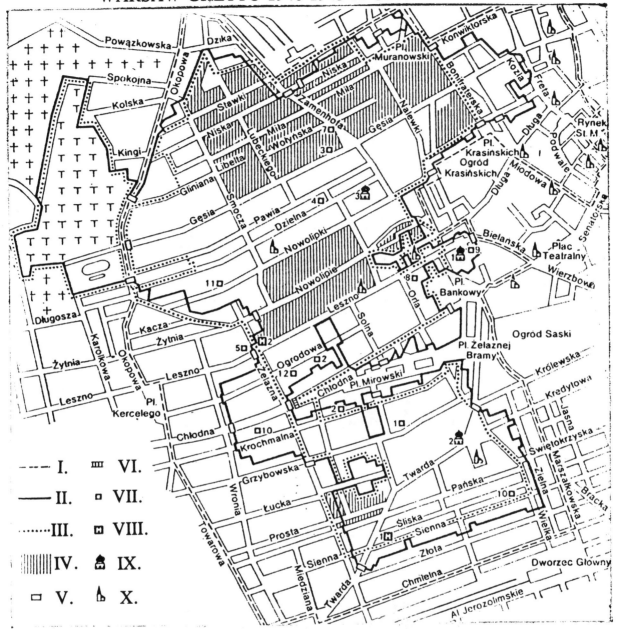

The German-Created Warsaw Ghetto 1940-1943 -- A General Map

Ghetto 1940-1942.
I. - extent in the middle of 1940
II. - ghetto borders Oct. 1940
III. - ghetto borders July 1942
IV. - ghetto at the beginning of
         the uprising on Apr. 19, 1943
V. - gates to the ghetto
VI. - bridges
VII. - institutions
VIII.- hospitals
IX. - synagogues
X. - churches

Synagogues:
1. The Great Synagogue on Tłomackie Street
2. Nożyk's Synagogue
3. Synagogue "Morija"

Institutions:
1. "Judenrat" Jewish Council
2. Jewish Ghetto Police
3. Jewish Jail (Gęsiówka)
4. Pawiak Prison
5. Courts on Leszno Street
6. Communal Labor Office
7. Post Office
8. Office for prosecution of usury and profiteering
9. Library, Jewish Studies Institute, and other offices
10. Dr. J. Korczak's Orphanage
11. Dr. E. Ringelblum's Secret Archives
12. Trade schools
Hospitals:
1. Berson's and Bauman's Hospital
2. Mosaic Faith Hospital in Czyste

WARSAW GHETTO

A Chronology of German Creation, Control, and Destruction of the Warsaw Ghetto

A report concerning the activity of a special German elimination troop:

Bogusław Jędruszczak

Mieczysław Jędruszczak

16 V 43

"Thus far 67 000 000 cu. metres have been demolished or blown up. 22,5 million bricks,5006 tons of scrap metal and 76 tons of copper were salvaged. part of debris will be left and,having been levelled, will be covered with ashe strewn with faeces and sown."

15 XI 40   Created November 15, 1940   Destroyed May 16, 1943

A report of May 24th 1943 by General J.Stroop"Out of 56 065 Jews seized,7000 were killed in the course of the campaign 6929 Jews were dispatched in Treblinka.—Except for 8 building the former ghetto has been entirely demolished.".

Warsaw Ghetto

First walls separating the Jewish population from the rest of the city's inhabitants started to be erected in May 1940.According to German communiqués the reason was a plague hazard.New rules and regulations issued daily introduced constant changes that contributed a great confusion among the frantic population moving to new locations. In 1940 displacement of people within the city has been estimated to reach over one million.

The Jewish district in Warsaw was officially proclaimed on November 15th 1940. The area of the ghetto was reduced from 5 to 4sq kilometres. Its borders ran along walls separating houses or courtyards, gates,doors and windows were blocked and walled up. 450 000 of Warsaw Jews,including thousands displaced from small towns of the Warsaw distrikt were crammed into the ghetto.

On November 20 th 1941 the area of the ghetto was reduced once again and subdivided into two parts-northern and southern.The two parts were linked by means of a wooden bridge over Chłodna Str.The wall was erected in the middle of the street,eliminating practically all contacts between the Jews and the Polish population.As of November 10th 1941 capital punishment has been introduced for Poles offering help to the Jews.

In the morning of August 12th 1942 a German communiqué announced the closing down of the so-called smaller,i.e. southern ghetto.Its entire population was ordered to move to the northern part before 6 p.m.of the same day. It represented another stage of the extermination of the Jews started with a deportation of 300 000 Jews from Umschlag platz of the Warsaw ghetto to the extermination camp in Treblinka.

In September 1942 new orders were given reducing the area of the ghetto to ca.18q.kilometre.The area was inhabited by 65 000 Jews.Outside the area delimited by Bonifraterska St, Gęsia St, Smocza St. and Stawki St.were located "shacks",i.e. blocks of houses reserved for work-shops exploiting labour of the ghetto Jews and carrying production in the interests of German enterprises.

What has remained from those years?

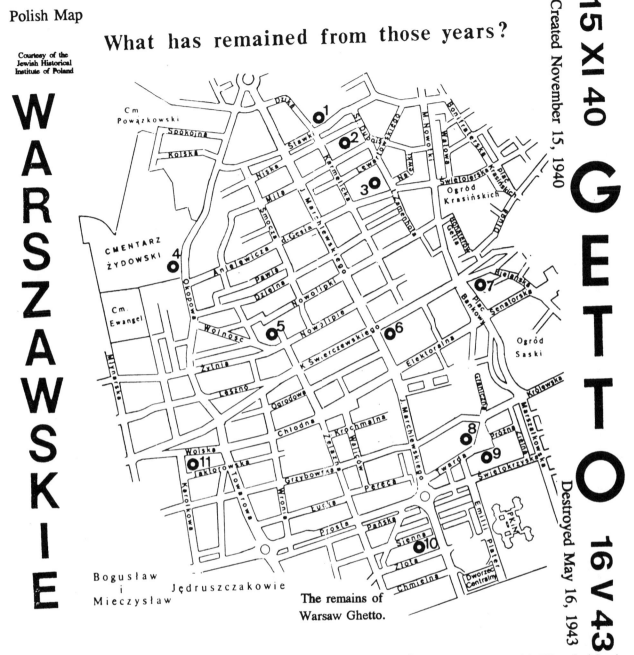

The remains of
Warsaw Ghetto.

WARSZAWSKIE

15 XI 40
Created November 15, 1940

GETTO

16 V 43
Destroyed May 16, 1943

Bogusław
i Jędruszczakowie
Mieczysław

1. 4. Stawki Street. - Umschlagplatz. Between July 22nd and September 21st 1942 the Germans deported from here 300,000 Jews to Treblinka.

2. 18 Miła Street. - The Monument of the Leaders of the Jewish Combat Organization of 1943.

3. Zamenhofa Street. - The Monument of the Heroes of Warsaw Ghetto.

4. 49 Okopowa Street. - The Jewish Cemetery.

5. 103 Żelazna Street. - Gestapo Bureau for Displacement in 1942 and 1943.

6. 115 Świerczewski Street, former 35 Leszno Street. The Jewish Theatre in 1941-1942 - now the cinema "Femina."

7. 3-5 Tłomackie Street. - The Jewish Historical Institute. In front of it there was the Great Synagogue of Warsaw.

8. 6 Twarda Street. - The Nożyk Synagogue - now the Jewish Theatre.

9. Grzybowski Square. - The All Saints Church - a plaque commemorating Rev. Fr. Marceli Godlewski who helped Jews in Warsaw Ghetto.

10. 55 Sienna Street to 60 Złota Street. - The remains of the ghetto walls.

11. 12 Jaktorowa Street, former 92 Krochmalna Street. - The building of the orphanage ran by Dr. Janusz Korczak in the years 1939-1940.

Warsaw Ghetto Remains - 1940 -- 1943

Belzec

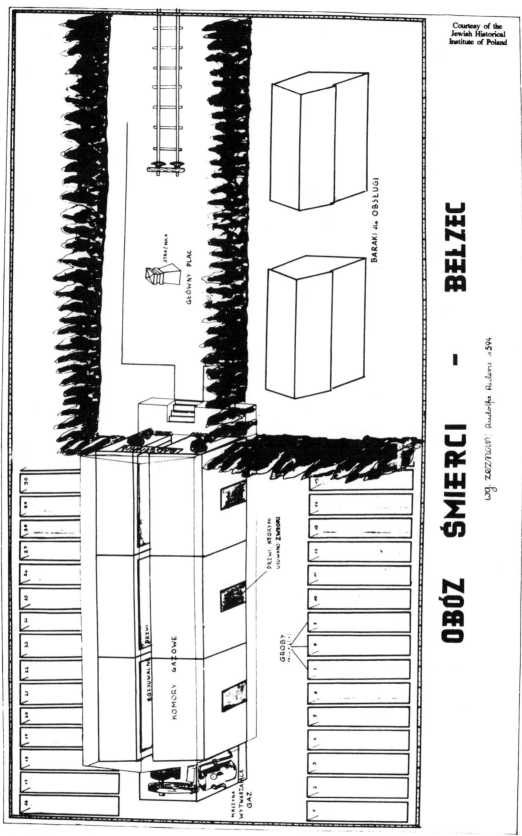

Belzec Death Camp (Reported)

334

OBÓZ ŚMIERCI TREBLINKA

LEGEND:

1. Administration
2. Guard house
3. Infirmary for guards
4. Parking lot
5. German quarters and weapons
6. Ukrainian guards
7. Zoo
8. Laundry
9. Well
10. Bakery & Storage
11. Storage of Jewish effects
12. Jewish barracks, kitchen, and work shops
13. Latrines
14. Stables
15. Chicken coops
16. Crematorium
17. Vegetable garden
18. Gas station
19. Masonry tower
20. Warehouse
21. Garage
22. Containers & bottles
23. Undressing area
24. Selection for gaseing
25. Sorting of victims' effects
26. Infirmary and crematorium
27. Main yard
28. Jewish court yard
29. Gas chamber
30. Main crematoria
31. Railroad terminal
32. Guard towers

German Map of Płaszów Concentration Camp

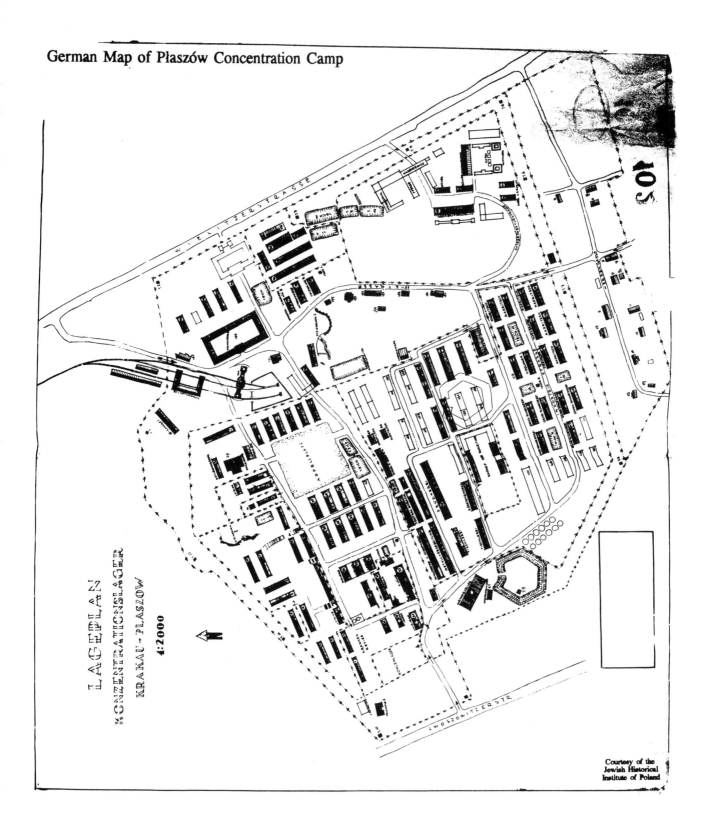

German Map of Płaszów

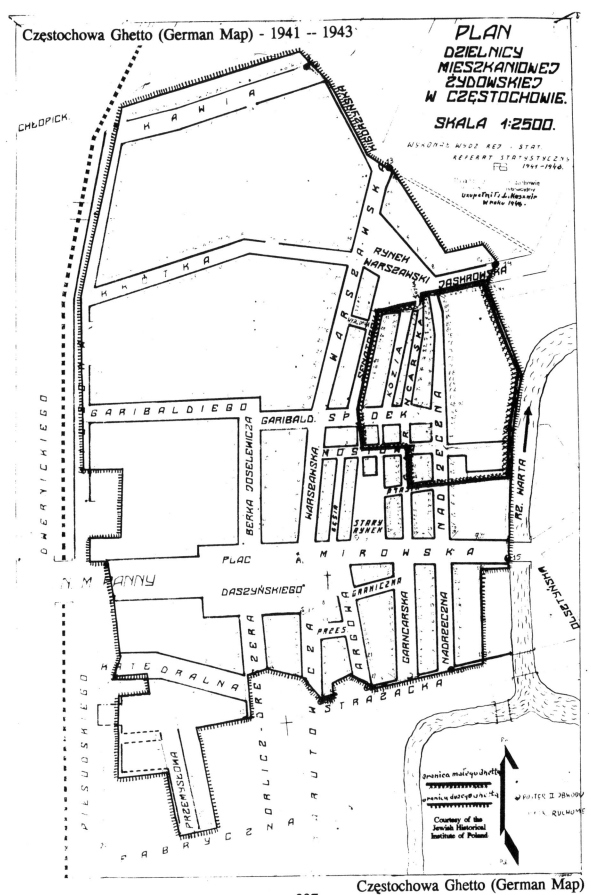

PLAN
DZIELNICY
MIESZKANIOWEJ
ŻYDOWSKIEJ
W CZĘSTOCHOWIE.
SKALA 1:2500.

Courtesy of the
Jewish Historical
Institute of Poland

Częstochowa Ghetto (German Map)

337

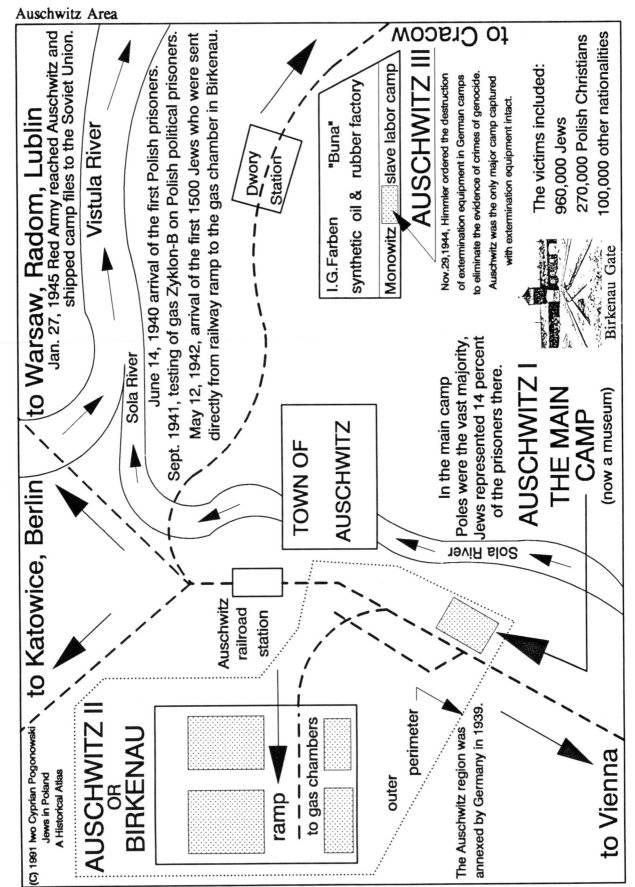

Auschwitz Area

to Warsaw, Radom, Lublin
Jan. 27, 1945 Red Army reached Auschwitz and shipped camp files to the Soviet Union.

Vistula River

June 14, 1940 arrival of the first Polish prisoners.

Sept. 1941, testing of gas Zyklon-B on Polish political prisoners.

May 12, 1942, arrival of the first 1500 Jews who were sent directly from railway ramp to the gas chamber in Birkenau.

Sola River

to Cracow

Dwory Station

I.G.Farben   "Buna"
synthetic oil & rubber factory

Monowitz   slave labor camp

AUSCHWITZ III

Nov.29,1944, Himmler ordered the destruction of extermination equipment in German camps to eliminate the evidence of crimes of genocide. Auschwitz was the only major camp captured with extermination equipment intact.

The victims included:
960,000 Jews
270,000 Polish Christians
100,000 other nationalities

Birkenau Gate

TOWN OF AUSCHWITZ

In the main camp
Poles were the vast majority,
Jews represented 14 percent
of the prisoners there.

AUSCHWITZ I
THE MAIN
CAMP
(now a museum)

Sola River

to Katowice, Berlin

Auschwitz railroad station

ramp

to gas chambers

outer

perimeter

The Auschwitz region was annexed by Germany in 1939.

AUSCHWITZ II
OR
BIRKENAU

(C) 1991 Iwo Cyprian Pogonowski
Jews in Poland
A Historical Atlas

to Vienna

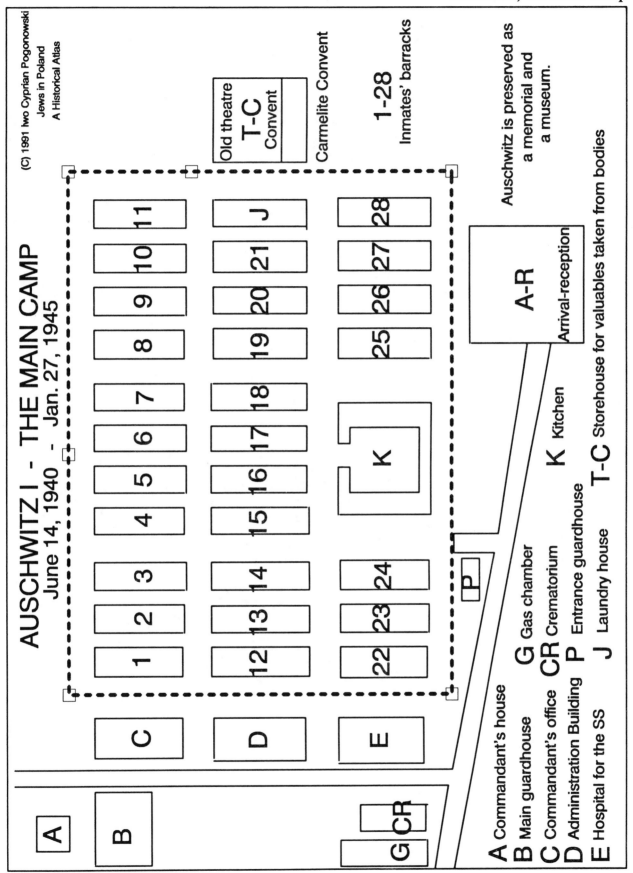

AUSCHWITZ I - THE MAIN CAMP
June 14, 1940 - Jan. 27, 1945

(C) 1991 Iwo Cyprian Pogonowski
Jews in Poland
A Historical Atlas

Old theatre
T-C
Convent
Carmelite Convent

1-28
Inmates' barracks

Auschwitz is preserved as
a memorial and
a museum.

A-R
Arrival-reception

A Commandant's house   G Gas chamber
B Main guardhouse   CR Crematorium   K Kitchen
C Commandant's office   P Entrance guardhouse T-C Storehouse for valuables taken from bodies
D Administration Building J Laundry house
E Hospital for the SS

German Map of the Sachsenhausen Concentration Camp

1. Concentration Camp 2. Brick Factory 3. DAW Factory
4. Camp Headquarters 5. SS Barracks
6. Headquarters for the Entire System of German Concentration Camps
7. Armory of the SS

1 Häftlingslager
2 Klinkerwerk
3 DAW – Deutsche Ausrüstungswerke
4 Kommandantur
5 SS-Kasernen
6 Inspektion aller KZ-Lager
7 Waffenlager der SS

Konzentrationslager Sachsenhausen – Übersichtsplan
In the concentration camps, Jews from Germany (who were highly assimilated) argued with the guards, "We're not Jews, we're Germans." And they said, "We want to fight for the Fatherland."

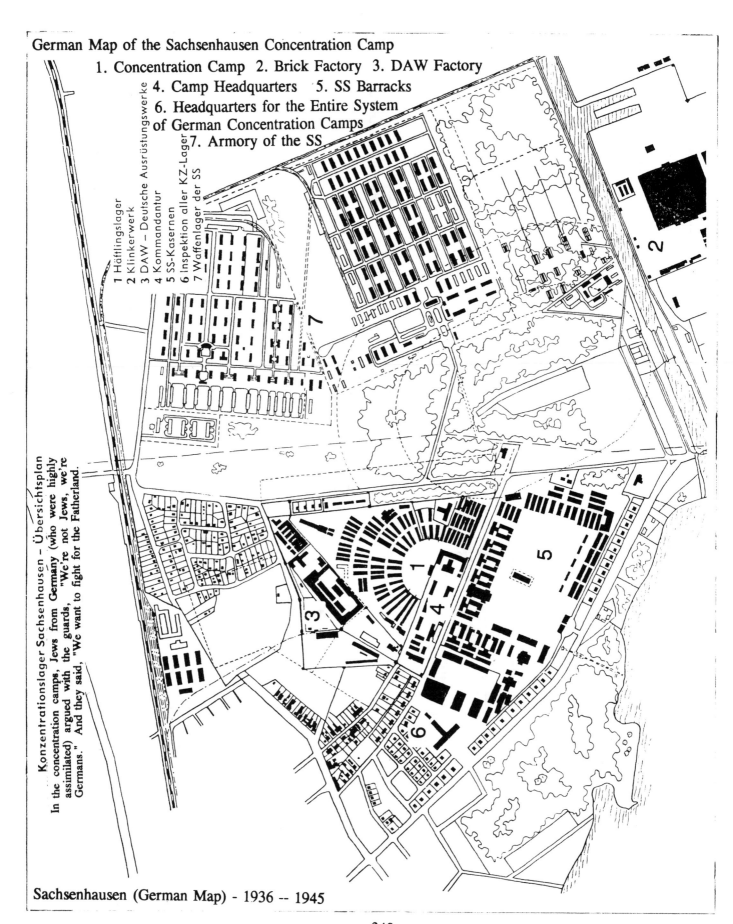

Sachsenhausen (German Map) - 1936 -- 1945

340

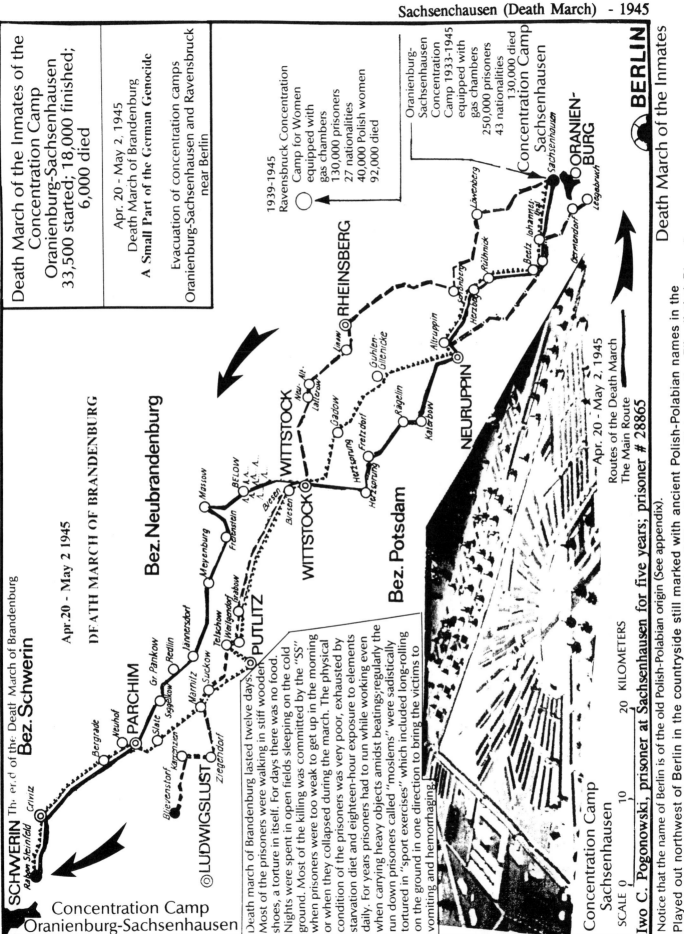

Death March of the Inmates of the Concentration Camp Oranienburg-Sachsenhausen
33,500 started; 18,000 finished; 6,000 died

Apr. 20 - May 2, 1945
Death March of Brandenburg
A Small Part of the German Genocide

Evacuation of concentration camps Oranienburg-Sachsenhausen and Ravensbruck near Berlin

1939-1945
Ravensbruck Concentration Camp for Women equipped with gas chambers
130,000 prisoners
27 nationalities
40,000 Polish women
92,000 died

Oranienburg-Sachsenhausen Concentration Camp 1933-1945 equipped with gas chambers
250,000 prisoners
43 nationalities
130,000 died
Concentration Camp Sachsenhausen

BERLIN

ORANIEN-BURG

Death March of the Inmates

Apr. 20 - May 2, 1945
Routes of the Death March
The Main Route

Iwo C. Pogonowski, prisoner at Sachsenhausen for five years; prisoner # 28865

RHEINSBERG

NEURUPPIN

WITTSTOCK

Bez. Potsdam

Bez. Neubrandenburg

DEATH MARCH OF BRANDENBURG

Apr. 20 - May 2 1945

Bez. Schwerin

SCHWERIN

PARCHIM

LUDWIGSLUST

PUTLITZ

Death march of Brandenburg lasted twelve days. Most of the prisoners were walking in stiff wooden shoes, a torture in itself. For days there was no food. Nights were spent in open fields sleeping on the cold ground. Most of the killing was committed by the "SS" when prisoners were too weak to get up in the morning or when they collapsed during the march. The physical condition of the prisoners was very poor, exhausted by the starvation diet and eighteen-hour exposure to elements daily. For years prisoners had to run while working even when carrying heavy objects amidst beatings; regularly the run down prisoners called "moslems" were sadistically tortured in "sport exercises" which included long-rolling on the ground in one direction to bring the victims to vomiting and hemorrhaging.

Concentration Camp Sachsenhausen
SCALE 0 10 20 KILOMETERS

Concentration Camp Oranienburg-Sachsenhausen

Notice that the name of Berlin is of the old Polish-Polabian origin (See appendix).
Played out northwest of Berlin in the countryside still marked with ancient Polish-Polabian names in the common language of Polish and Elbe River Slavs. "Polabian" literally means "living on the Elbe (Laba) River."

Notice Polish-Polabian names such as Pankow, Grabow, Gadow, and Below left by the original settlers of today's East Germany.

Map: 1945 Death March in Brandenburg; a Small Part of the German Genocide

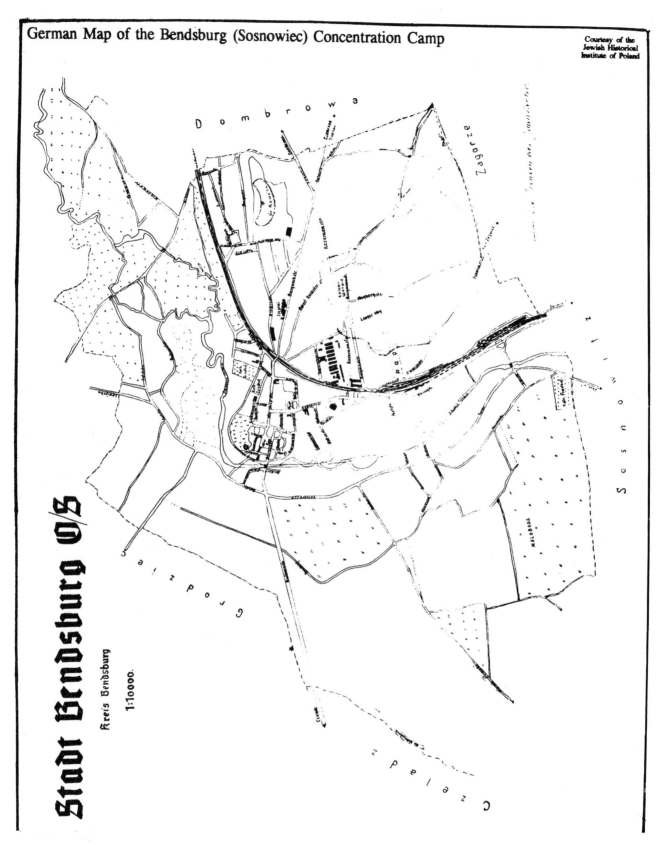

Bendsburg (German Map) - 1943

Bendsburg Ghetto - Sosnowitz (Germ.Map) - 1943

After capitulation a reprisal: Germans deported the entire population of Warsaw including thousands of Jews who were hiding on the "Aryan side" of the city.

Germans Mass Murdered the Population of Warsaw and the Soviets stood by Across the Vistula

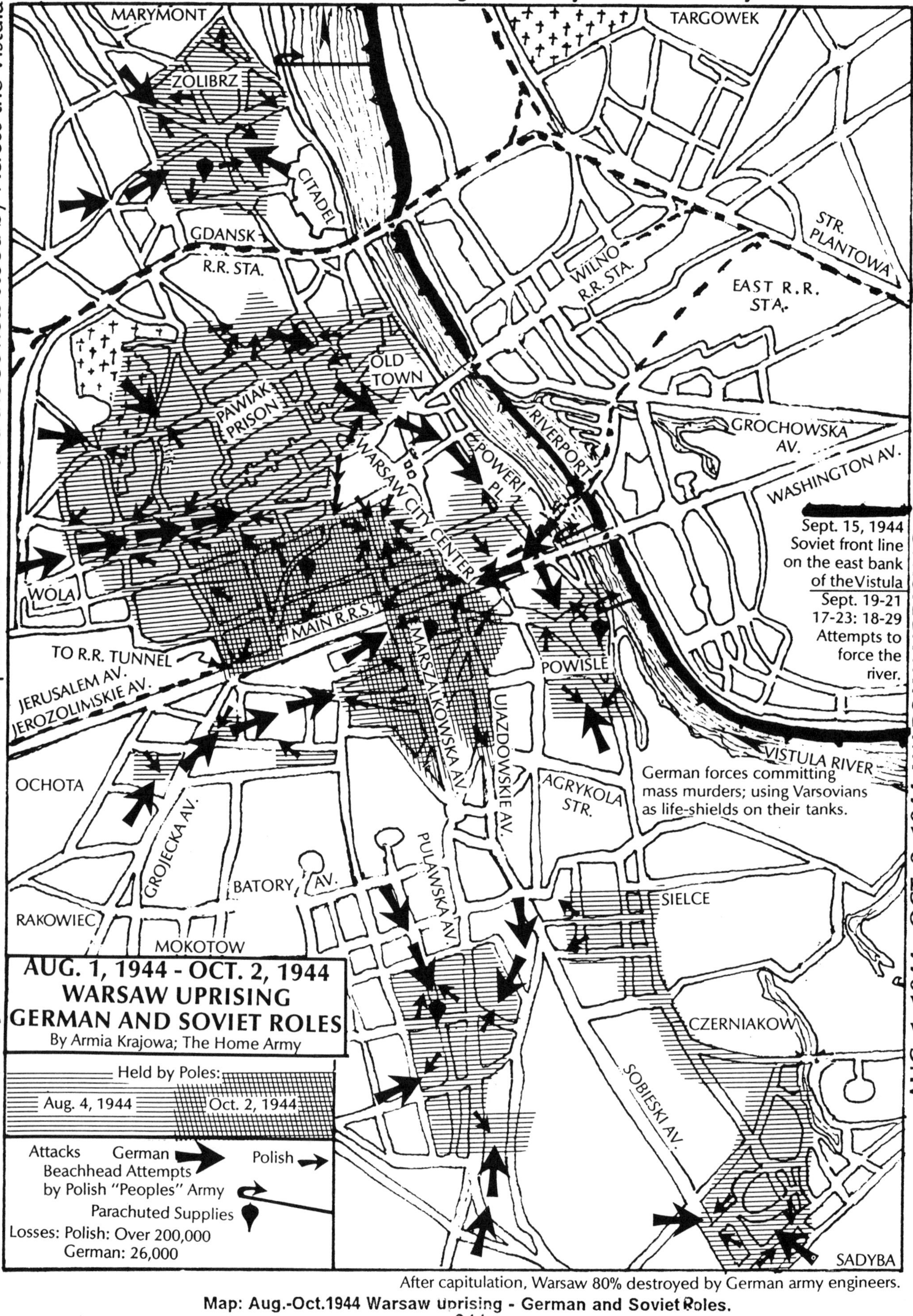

MARYMONT
TARGOWEK
ZOLIBRZ
CITADEL
GDANSK
R.R. STA.
WILNO R.R. STA.
STR. PLANTOWA
EAST R.R. STA.
OLD TOWN
PAWIAK PRISON
RIVERPORT
GROCHOWSKA AV.
WASHINGTON AV.
WARSAW CITY CENTER
POWERI PL.
Sept. 15, 1944 Soviet front line on the east bank of the Vistula
Sept. 19-21 17-23: 18-29 Attempts to force the river.
WOLA
MAIN R.R.S.
TO R.R. TUNNEL
JERUSALEM AV.
JEROZOLIMSKIE AV.
POWISLE
MARSZALKOWSKA AV.
UJAZDOWSKIE AV.
VISTULA RIVER
OCHOTA
AGRYKOLA STR.
German forces committing mass murders; using Varsovians as life-shields on their tanks.
GROJECKA AV.
PULAWSKA AV.
BATORY AV.
RAKOWIEC
SIELCE
MOKOTOW
AUG. 1, 1944 - OCT. 2, 1944
WARSAW UPRISING
GERMAN AND SOVIET ROLES
By Armia Krajowa; The Home Army
CZERNIAKOW
Held by Poles:
Aug. 4, 1944
Oct. 2, 1944
SOBIESKI AV.
Attacks German
Polish
Beachhead Attempts by Polish "Peoples" Army
Parachuted Supplies
Losses: Polish: Over 200,000
German: 26,000
SADYBA

AUG. 1, 1944 - OCT. 2, 1944 WARSAW UPRISING GERMAN AND SOVIET ROLES

After capitulation, Warsaw 80% destroyed by German army engineers.

Map: Aug.-Oct.1944 Warsaw uprising - German and Soviet Roles.

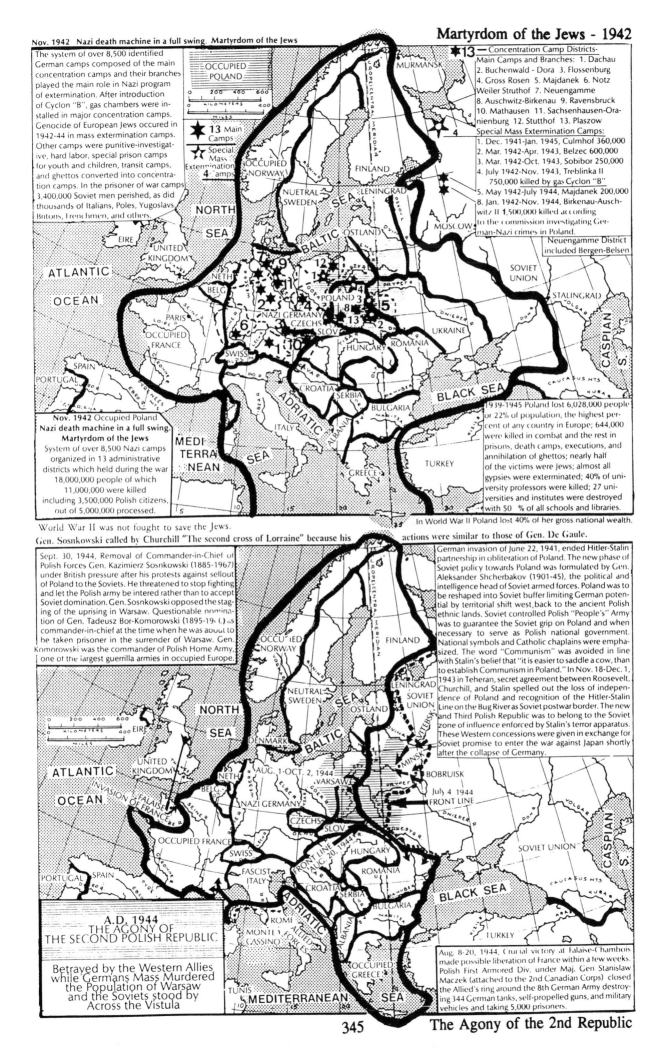

Nov. 1942 Nazi death machine in a full swing. Martyrdom of the Jews

The system of over 8,500 identified German camps composed of the main concentration camps and their branches played the main role in Nazi program of extermination. After introduction of Cyclon "B", gas chambers were installed in major concentration camps. Genocide of European Jews occured in 1942-44 in mass extermination camps. Other camps were punitive-investigative, hard labor, special prison camps for youth and children, transit camps, and ghettos converted into concentration camps. In the prisoner of war camps 3,400,000 Soviet men perished, as did thousands of Italians, Poles, Yugoslavs, Britons, Frenchmen, and others.

OCCUPIED POLAND
0 200 400 600
KILOMETERS 400

★ Main Camps
☆ Special Mass Extermination Camps

★13 —Concentration Camp Districts-
Main Camps and Branches: 1. Dachau
2. Buchenwald - Dora 3. Flossenburg
4. Gross Rosen 5. Majdanek 6. Notz Weiler Struthof 7. Neuengamme
8. Auschwitz-Birkenau 9. Ravensbruck
10. Mathausen 11. Sachsenhausen-Oranienburg 12. Stutthof 13. Plaszow
Special Mass Extermination Camps:
1. Dec. 1941-Jan. 1945, Culmhof 360,000
2. Mar. 1942-Apr. 1943, Belzec 600,000
3. Mar. 1942-Oct. 1943, Sobibor 250,000
4. July 1942-Nov. 1943, Treblinka II 750,000 killed by gas Cyclon "B"
5. May 1942-July 1944, Majdanek 200,000
8. Jan. 1942-Nov. 1944, Birkenau-Auschwitz II 1,500,000 killed according to the commission investigating German-Nazi crimes in Poland.

Neuengamme District included Bergen-Belsen

Nov. 1942 Occupied Poland
Nazi death machine in a full swing. Martyrdom of the Jews
System of over 8,500 Nazi camps organized in 13 administrative districts which held during the war 18,000,000 people of which 11,000,000 were killed including 3,500,000 Polish citizens, out of 5,000,000 processed.

1939-1945 Poland lost 6,028,000 people or 22% of population, the highest percent of any country in Europe; 644,000 were killed in combat and the rest in prisons, death camps, executions, and annihilation of ghettos; nearly half of the victims were Jews; almost all gypsies were exterminated; 40% of university professors were killed; 27 universities and institutes were destroyed with 50 % of all schools and libraries.

In World War II Poland lost 40% of her gross national wealth.

World War II was not fought to save the Jews.
Gen. Sosnkowski called by Churchill "The second cross of Lorraine" because his actions were similar to those of Gen. De Gaule.

Sept. 30, 1944, Removal of Commander-in-Chief of Polish Forces Gen. Kazimierz Sosnkowski (1885-1967) under British pressure after his protests against sellout of Poland to the Soviets. He threatened to stop fighting and let the Polish army be intered rather than to accept Soviet domination. Gen. Sosnkowski opposed the staging of the uprising in Warsaw. Questionable nomination of Gen. Tadeusz Bor-Komorowski (1895-19 C) as commander-in-chief at the time when he was about to be taken prisoner in the surrender of Warsaw. Gen. Komorowski was the commander of Polish Home Army, one of the largest guerrilla armies in occupied Europe.

German invasion of June 22, 1941, ended Hitler-Stalin partnership in obliteration of Poland. The new phase of Soviet policy towards Poland was formulated by Gen. Aleksander Shcherbakov (1901-45), the political and intelligence head of Soviet armed forces. Poland was to be reshaped into Soviet buffer limiting German potential by territorial shift west, back to the ancient Polish ethnic lands. Soviet controlled Polish "People's" Army was to guarantee the Soviet grip on Poland and when necessary to serve as Polish national government. National symbols and Catholic chaplains were emphasized. The word "Communism" was avoided in line with Stalin's belief that "it is easier to saddle a cow, than to establish Communism in Poland." In Nov. 18-Dec. 1, 1943 in Teheran, secret agreement between Roosevelt, Churchill, and Stalin spelled out the loss of independence of Poland and recognition of the Hitler-Stalin Line on the Bug River as Soviet postwar border. The new and Third Polish Republic was to belong to the Soviet zone of influence enforced by Stalin's terror apparatus. These Western concessions were given in exchange for Soviet promise to enter the war against Japan shortly after the collapse of Germany.

AUG. 1-OCT. 2, 1944
July 4 1944 FRONT LINE

A.D. 1944 THE AGONY OF THE SECOND POLISH REPUBLIC

Betrayed by the Western Allies while Germans Mass Murdered the Population of Warsaw and the Soviets stood by Across the Vistula

Aug. 8-20, 1944, Crucial victory at Falaise-Chambois made possible liberation of France within a few weeks. Polish First Armored Div. under Maj. Gen. Stanislaw Maczek (attached to the 2nd Canadian Corps) closed the Allied's ring around the 8th German Army destroying 344 German tanks, self-propelled guns, and military vehicles and taking 5,000 prisoners.

The Agony of the 2nd Republic

The Soviet offensive stopped for the purpose of allowing the routed German army to destroy Free Warsaw

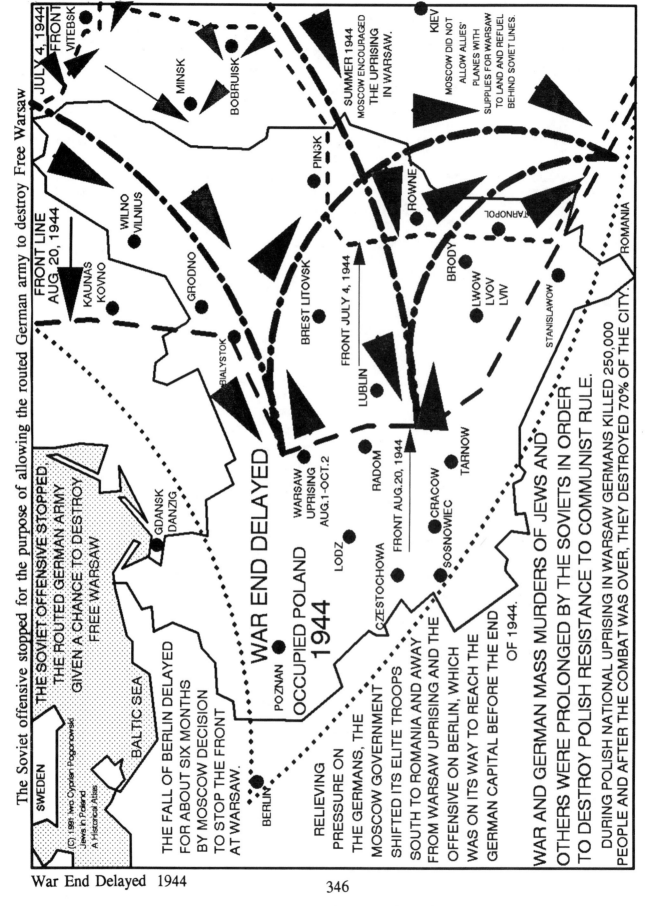

FRONT LINE JULY 4, 1944

FRONT

VITEBSK

MINSK

BOBRUISK

SUMMER 1944
MOSCOW ENCOURAGED THE UPRISING IN WARSAW.

KIEV

MOSCOW DID NOT ALLOW ALLIES' PLANES WITH SUPPLIES FOR WARSAW TO LAND AND REFUEL BEHIND SOVIET LINES.

PINSK

ROWNE

FRONT LINE AUG. 20, 1944

WILNO VILNIUS

GRODNO

TARNOPOL

KAUNAS KOVNO

BRODY

LWOW LVOV LVIV

BIALYSTOK

BREST LITOVSK

FRONT JULY 4, 1944

STANISLAWOW

LUBLIN

ROMANIA

TARNOW

FRONT AUG. 20, 1944

RADOM

WAR END DELAYED

WARSAW UPRISING AUG. 1 - OCT. 2

CRACOW

SOSNOWIEC

OCCUPIED POLAND 1944

LODZ

CZESTOCHOWA

GDANSK DANZIG

THE SOVIET OFFENSIVE STOPPED. THE ROUTED GERMAN ARMY GIVEN A CHANCE TO DESTROY FREE WARSAW.

SWEDEN

(C) 1991 Iwo Cyprian Pogonowski
Jews in Poland
A Historical Atlas

BALTIC SEA

POZNAN

BERLIN

THE FALL OF BERLIN DELAYED FOR ABOUT SIX MONTHS BY MOSCOW DECISION TO STOP THE FRONT AT WARSAW.

RELIEVING PRESSURE ON THE GERMANS, THE MOSCOW GOVERNMENT SHIFTED ITS ELITE TROOPS SOUTH TO ROMANIA AND AWAY FROM WARSAW UPRISING AND THE OFFENSIVE ON BERLIN, WHICH WAS ON ITS WAY TO REACH THE GERMAN CAPITAL BEFORE THE END OF 1944.

WAR AND GERMAN MASS MURDERS OF JEWS AND OTHERS WERE PROLONGED BY THE SOVIETS IN ORDER TO DESTROY POLISH RESISTANCE TO COMMUNIST RULE.

DURING POLISH NATIONAL UPRISING IN WARSAW GERMANS KILLED 250,000 PEOPLE AND AFTER THE COMBAT WAS OVER, THEY DESTROYED 70% OF THE CITY.

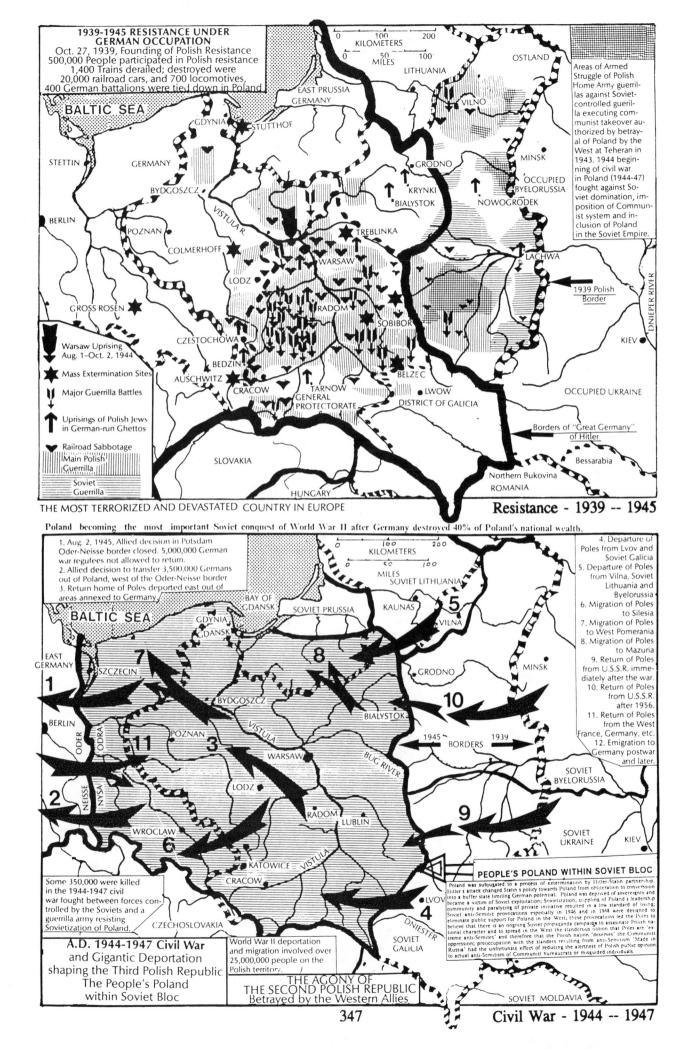

1939-1945 RESISTANCE UNDER GERMAN OCCUPATION
Oct. 27, 1939, Founding of Polish Resistance
500,000 People participated in Polish resistance
1,400 Trains derailed; destroyed were
20,000 railroad cars, and 700 locomotives,
400 German battalions were tied down in Poland

BALTIC SEA

Areas of Armed
Struggle of Polish
Home Army guerril-
las against Soviet-
controlled guerril-
la executing com-
munist takeover au-
thorized by betray-
al of Poland by the
West at Teheran in
1943. 1944 begin-
ning of civil war
in Poland (1944-47)
fought against So-
viet domination, im-
position of Commun-
ist system and in-
clusion of Poland
in the Soviet Empire.

OSTLAND
LITHUANIA
EAST PRUSSIA
GERMANY
VILNO
GDYNIA
STUTTHOF
MINSK
STETTIN
GERMANY
GRODNO
'OCCUPIED
BYELORUSSIA
BYDGOSZCZ
KRYNKI
BIALYSTOK
NOWOGRODEK
BERLIN
VISTULA R.
POZNAN
LACHWA
COLMERHOFF
TREBLINKA
DNIEPER RIVER
WARSAW
LODZ
1939 Polish
Border
GROSS ROSEN
RADOM
KIEV
SOBIBOR
CZESTOCHOWA
BELZEC
OCCUPIED UKRAINE
BEDZIN
LWOW
AUSCHWITZ
TARNOW
DISTRICT OF GALICIA
CRACOW
GENERAL PROTECTORATE
Borders of "Great Germany"
of Hitler
SLOVAKIA
Bessarabia
Northern Bukovina
HUNGARY
ROMANIA

Warsaw Uprising Aug. 1–Oct. 2, 1944
Mass Extermination Sites
Major Guerrilla Battles
Uprisings of Polish Jews in German-run Ghettos
Railroad Sabbotage
Main Polish Guerrilla
Soviet Guerrilla

THE MOST TERRORIZED AND DEVASTATED COUNTRY IN EUROPE   **Resistance - 1939 -- 1945**

Poland becoming the most important Soviet conquest of World War II after Germany destroyed 40% of Poland's national wealth.

1. Aug. 2, 1945, Allied decision in Potsdam
Oder-Neisse border closed. 5,000,000 German war refugees not allowed to return.
2. Allied decision to transfer 3,500,000 Germans out of Poland, west of the Oder-Neisse border
3. Return home of Poles deported east out of areas annexed to Germany.

4. Departure of Poles from Lvov and Soviet Galicia
5. Departure of Poles from Vilna, Soviet Lithuania and Byelorussia
6. Migration of Poles to Silesia
7. Migration of Poles to West Pomerania
8. Migration of Poles to Mazuria
9. Return of Poles from U.S.S.R. imme- diately after the war.
10. Return of Poles from U.S.S.R. after 1956.
11. Return of Poles from the West France, Germany, etc.
12. Emigration to Germany postwar and later.

BALTIC SEA
BAY OF GDANSK
SOVIET PRUSSIA
KAUNAS
SOVIET LITHUANIA
GDYNIA
GDANSK
VILNA
EAST GERMANY
SZCZECIN
GRODNO
MINSK
BERLIN
ODER
ODRA
BYDGOSZCZ
BIALYSTOK
POZNAN
VISTULA
1945   BORDERS   1939
WARSAW
BUG RIVER
NEISSE
NYSA
LODZ
SOVIET BYELORUSSIA
RADOM
LUBLIN
WROCLAW
SOVIET UKRAINE
KATOWICE
VISTULA
KIEV
CRACOW
LVOV
DNIESTER

PEOPLE'S POLAND WITHIN SOVIET BLOC
Poland was subjugated to a process of extermination by Hitler-Stalin partnership. Hitler's attack changed Stalin's policy towards Poland from obliteration to conversion into a buffer state limiting German potential. Poland was deprived of sovereignty and became a victim of Soviet exploitation; Sovietization, crippling of Poland's leadership community and paralyzing of private initiative resulted in a low standard of living. Soviet anti-Semitic provocations especially in 1946 and in 1968 were designed to eliminate public support for Poland in the West; these provocations led the Poles to believe that there is an ongoing Soviet propaganda campaign to assassinate Polish na- tional character and to spread in the West the slanderous notion that Poles are "ex- treme anti-Semites" and therefore that the Polish nation "deserves" the Communist oppression; preoccupation with the slanders resulting from anti-Semitism "Made in Russia" had the unfortunate effect of reducing the alertness of Polish public opinion to actual anti-Semitism of Communist bureaucrats or misguided individuals.

Some 350,000 were killed in the 1944-1947 civil war fought between forces con- trolled by the Soviets and a guerrilla army resisting Sovietization of Poland.

CZECHOSLOVAKIA
SOVIET GALICIA
SOVIET MOLDAVIA

A.D. 1944-1947 Civil War
and Gigantic Deportation
shaping the Third Polish Republic
The People's Poland
within Soviet Bloc

World War II deportation and migration involved over 25,000,000 people on the Polish territory.

THE AGONY OF
THE SECOND POLISH REPUBLIC
Betrayed by the Western Allies

347   **Civil War - 1944 -- 1947**

WOHNGEBIET DER
JUDEN
BETRETEN
VERBOTEN

Jewish Quarter:
Entry Forbidden

Poles were executed for entering the Ghetto, when they were bringing food for the starving Jews.

BRIHA

THE ESCAPE FROM EUROPE

1945 --

In 1944, the surviving organizers of *Briha* resumed the *Aliya-bet* (illegal immigration of Jews to Palestine) through the Romanian port of Constanca to Haifa in Palestine, as it was done before the war.

In 1945 some 40,000 *olim*, or immigrants to Palestine, used new western passages through Szczecin and Kudowa Zdrój. From there, they traveled west and south by trucks and buses. By the end of 1945, a Zionist Coordination Center was organized in Łódź; its central emigration department assumed the name of Bricha, which in turn established branches on border crossings. Thus, a code name *Khyzar*, or "bristle" in Hebrew, was used for Szczecin (Stettin) which in Polish means bristle market. The Polish branch of Bricha used the offices of "Polamt," or the Palestinian Office of the Jewish Agency in Warsaw. The central command of Bricha operated from Tel-Aviv and Paris.

In 1946 there were about a quarter of a million Jews in Poland, some 200,000 Polish Jews in Great Britain, and about 100,000 in Austria and West Germany. The daily rail transports of Germans leaving Poland, and travelling through Berlin to the British zone of occupation were augmented with up to 700 *olim*. The main reason for the Jewish exodus was the Soviet-staged pogrom of Kielce, which took place on the 4th of July 1946 (the American holiday was picked for a better propaganda effect). Polish public opinion condemned this hideous crime in which 42 people were killed. As an immediate consequence, 150,000 Jews left Poland, mainly through Szczecin and Kłodzko, (code-named *Dorom).*

In 1947 there were about 100,000 Jews left in Poland, and over 200,000 Polish Jews in West Germany and Austria. They waited for the admission of 100,000 to Palestine, as promised by the Anglo-American Commission. The rest hoped for visas to the United States, Canada, Australia and other countries. Life in the displaced persons' camps was often humiliating and conflicts arose between Bundists advocating return to Poland and Zionists insisting on immigration to Palestine.

In Nov. 1947 the United Nations authorized the partition of Palestine. The Zionists organized money collection for *giyus*, or Fund for Help to Fighting Palestine. All Jewish political parties supported the *giyus* drive. In Poland alone the drive brought 113 million *złotys*.

A military training camp for Hagana was established by Polish authorities in Bolków, near Wrocław. Soviet officers were among the instructors. Trainees were singing in Russian the *Fizkulturnyy Marsh* (Soviet Athletes' Marching Song). Between 130 and 150 trainees (generally 22 to 25 years old) were put through the ten-day course during which daily 10-hour activities were scheduled. Among the 2500 to 3000 people in the camp, there were also wives of the trainees, many of them Christian women, called in Yiddish *shiksas* (siksy in Polish).

On May 14, 1948, the state of Israel was founded, and its armed forces were established on May 28, 1948. They were based on the *Hagana* (the defense) and the Irgun Zwei Leumi (National Military Organization). The armed forces of the new state included 60,000 soldiers and officers.

Roman Kramsztyk, *Jewish Children in the Ghetto*

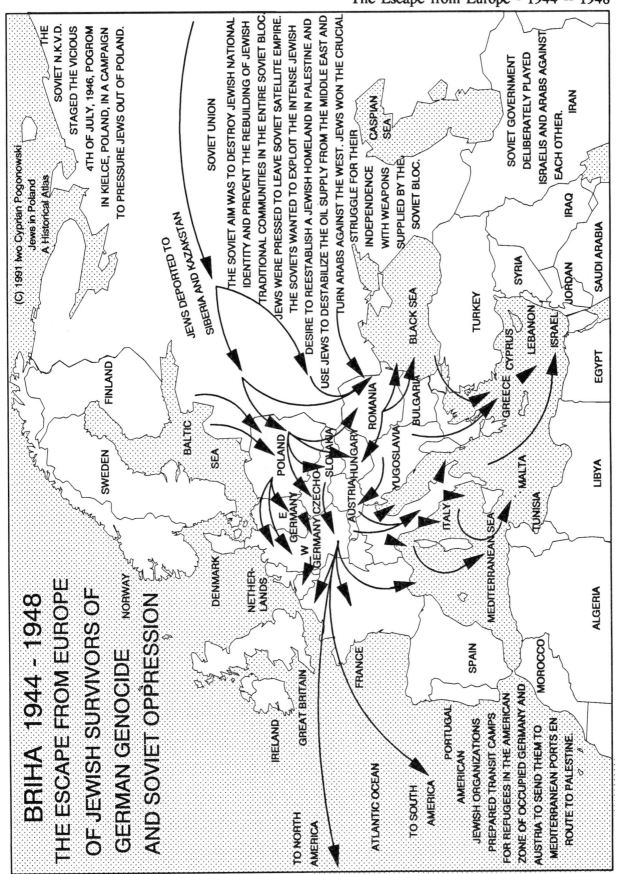

BRIHA 1944 - 1948
THE ESCAPE FROM EUROPE
OF JEWISH SURVIVORS OF
GERMAN GENOCIDE
AND SOVIET OPPRESSION

(C) 1991 Iwo Cyprian Pogonowski
Jews in Poland
A Historical Atlas

THE SOVIET N.K.V.D. STAGED THE VICIOUS 4TH OF JULY, 1946, POGROM IN KIELCE, POLAND, IN A CAMPAIGN TO PRESSURE JEWS OUT OF POLAND.

JEWS DEPORTED TO SIBERIA AND KAZAKSTAN

SOVIET UNION

THE SOVIET AIM WAS TO DESTROY JEWISH NATIONAL IDENTITY AND PREVENT THE REBUILDING OF JEWISH TRADITIONAL COMMUNITIES IN THE ENTIRE SOVIET BLOC. JEWS WERE PRESSED TO LEAVE SOVIET SATELLITE EMPIRE. THE SOVIETS WANTED TO EXPLOIT THE INTENSE JEWISH DESIRE TO REESTABLISH A JEWISH HOMELAND IN PALESTINE AND USE JEWS TO DESTABILIZE THE OIL SUPPLY FROM THE MIDDLE EAST AND TURN ARABS AGAINST THE WEST. JEWS WON THE CRUCIAL STRUGGLE FOR THEIR INDEPENDENCE WITH WEAPONS SUPPLIED BY THE SOVIET BLOC.

SOVIET GOVERNMENT DELIBERATELY PLAYED ISRAELIS AND ARABS AGAINST EACH OTHER.

CASPIAN SEA

IRAN

IRAQ

SAUDI ARABIA

JORDAN

SYRIA

LEBANON

ISRAEL

CYPRUS

GREECE

TURKEY

BLACK SEA

BULGARIA

ROMANIA

YUGOSLAVIA

AUSTRIA HUNGARY

SLOVAKIA

CZECHO

HUNGARY

EGYPT

LIBYA

MALTA

TUNISIA

ITALY

MEDITERRANEAN SEA

ALGERIA

MOROCCO

SPAIN

FRANCE

W GERMANY

E GERMANY

POLAND

BALTIC SEA

FINLAND

SWEDEN

NORWAY

DENMARK

NETHER-LANDS

IRELAND

GREAT BRITAIN

ATLANTIC OCEAN

TO NORTH AMERICA

TO SOUTH AMERICA

PORTUGAL

AMERICAN JEWISH ORGANIZATIONS PREPARED TRANSIT CAMPS FOR REFUGEES IN THE AMERICAN ZONE OF OCCUPIED GERMANY AND AUSTRIA TO SEND THEM TO MEDITERRANEAN PORTS EN ROUTE TO PALESTINE.

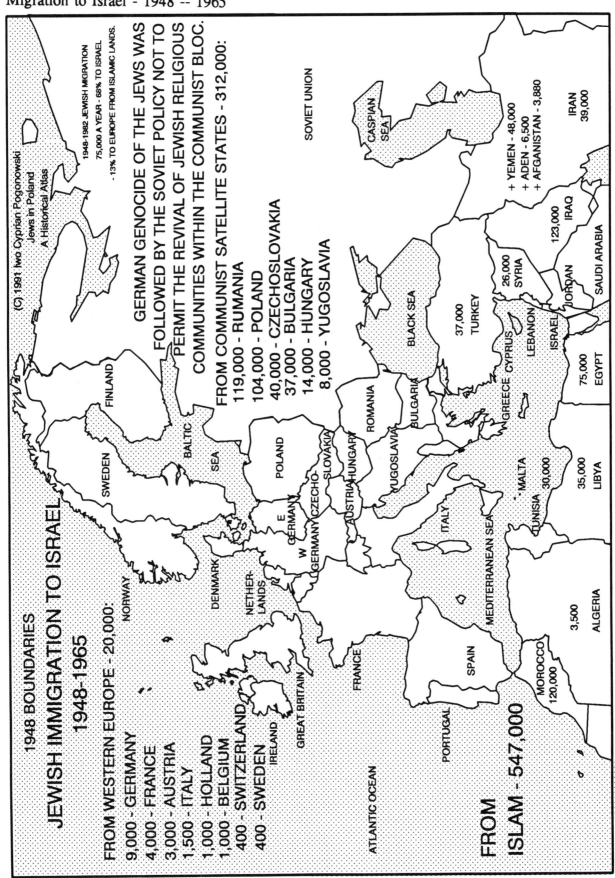

1948 BOUNDARIES
JEWISH IMMIGRATION TO ISRAEL
1948-1965

FROM WESTERN EUROPE - 20,000:

9,000 - GERMANY
4,000 - FRANCE
3,000 - AUSTRIA
1,500 - ITALY
1,000 - HOLLAND
1,000 - BELGIUM
400 - SWITZERLAND
400 - SWEDEN

(C) 1991 Iwo Cyprian Pogonowski
Jews in Poland
A Historical Atlas

1948-1982 JEWISH MIGRATION
75,000 A YEAR - 68% TO ISRAEL
- 13% TO EUROPE FROM ISLAMIC LANDS.

GERMAN GENOCIDE OF THE JEWS WAS
FOLLOWED BY THE SOVIET POLICY NOT TO
PERMIT THE REVIVAL OF JEWISH RELIGIOUS
COMMUNITIES WITHIN THE COMMUNIST BLOC.

FROM COMMUNIST SATELLITE STATES - 312,000:

119,000 - RUMANIA
104,000 - POLAND
40,000 - CZECHOSLOVAKIA
37,000 - BULGARIA
14,000 - HUNGARY
8,000 - YUGOSLAVIA

+ YEMEN - 48,000
+ ADEN - 6,500
+ AFGANISTAN - 3,880

IRAN
39,000

123,000
IRAQ

26,000
SYRIA

JORDAN

SAUDI ARABIA

75,000
EGYPT

35,000
LIBYA

30,000
TUNISIA

3,500
ALGERIA

120,000
MOROCCO

FROM ISLAM - 547,000

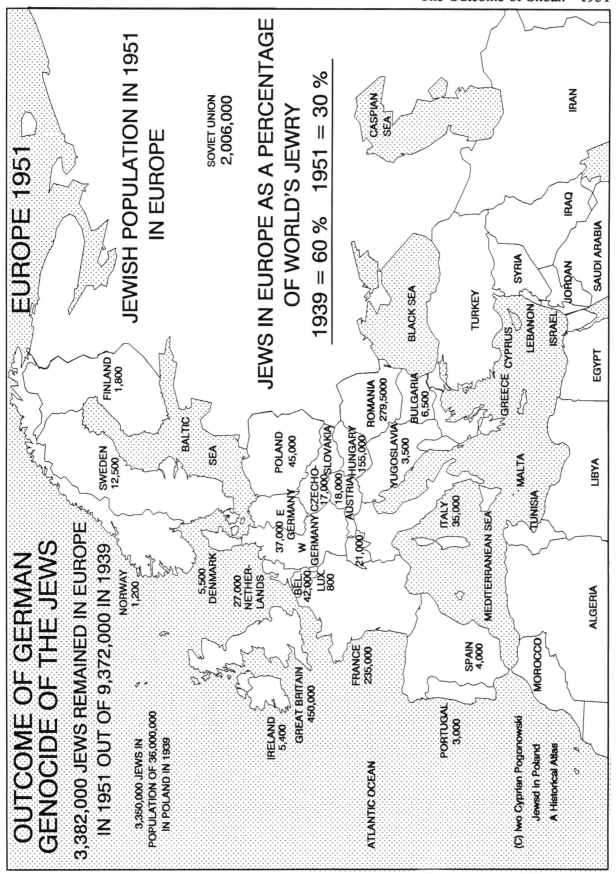

EUROPE 1951

OUTCOME OF GERMAN GENOCIDE OF THE JEWS

3,382,000 JEWS REMAINED IN EUROPE IN 1951 OUT OF 9,372,000 IN 1939

3,350,000 JEWS IN POPULATION OF 36,000,000 IN POLAND IN 1939

JEWISH POPULATION IN 1951 IN EUROPE

SOVIET UNION 2,006,000

JEWS IN EUROPE AS A PERCENTAGE OF WORLD'S JEWRY

1939 = 60 %   1951 = 30 %

FINLAND 1,800

SWEDEN 12,500

BALTIC SEA

POLAND 45,000

E GERMANY 37,000

W GERMANY

CZECHO-SLOVAKIA 17,000

AUSTRIA 18,000

HUNGARY 155,000

21,000

ROMANIA 279,5000

YUGOSLAVIA 3,500

BULGARIA 6,500

BLACK SEA

CASPIAN SEA

IRAN

IRAQ

SAUDI ARABIA

SYRIA

JORDAN

TURKEY

ISRAEL

LEBANON

CYPRUS

GREECE

EGYPT

LIBYA

ITALY 35,000

MALTA

TUNISIA

MEDITERRANEAN SEA

ALGERIA

SPAIN 4,000

MOROCCO

PORTUGAL 3,000

FRANCE 235,000

GREAT BRITAIN 450,000

IRELAND 5,400

ATLANTIC OCEAN

NORWAY 1,200

DENMARK 5,500

NETHER-LANDS 27,000

BEL. 42,000

LUX. 800

(C) Iwo Cyprian Pogonowski
Jewsid in Poland
A Historical Atlas

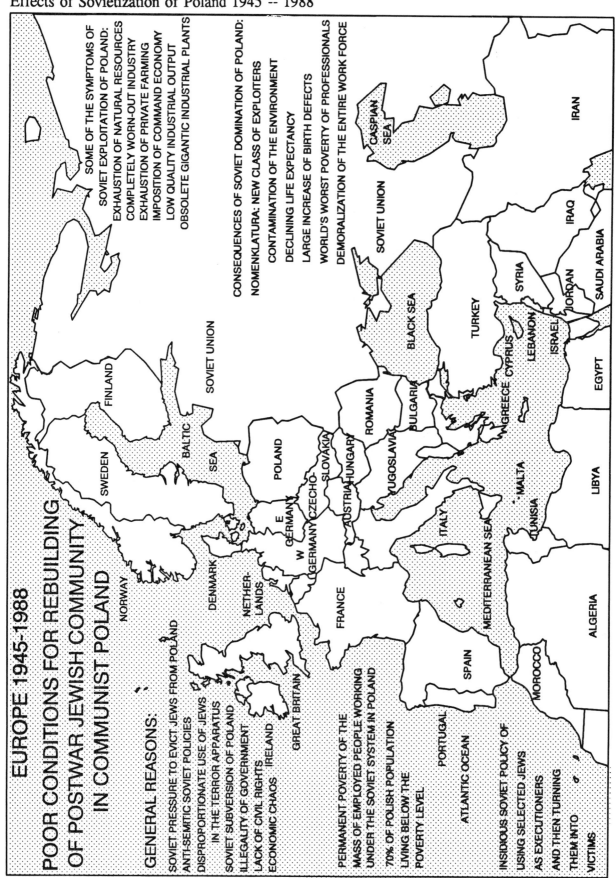

EUROPE 1945-1988

POOR CONDITIONS FOR REBUILDING OF POSTWAR JEWISH COMMUNITY IN COMMUNIST POLAND

GENERAL REASONS:

SOVIET PRESSURE TO EVICT JEWS FROM POLAND

ANTI-SEMITIC SOVIET POLICIES

DISPROPORTIONATE USE OF JEWS IN THE TERROR APPARATUS

SOVIET SUBVERSION OF POLAND

ILLEGALITY OF GOVERNMENT

LACK OF CIVIL RIGHTS

ECONOMIC CHAOS

PERMANENT POVERTY OF THE MASS OF EMPLOYED PEOPLE WORKING UNDER THE SOVIET SYSTEM IN POLAND

70% OF POLISH POPULATION LIVING BELOW THE POVERTY LEVEL

INSIDIOUS SOVIET POLICY OF USING SELECTED JEWS AS EXECUTIONERS AND THEN TURNING THEM INTO VICTIMS

SOME OF THE SYMPTOMS OF SOVIET EXPLOITATION OF POLAND:

EXHAUSTION OF NATURAL RESOURCES

COMPLETELY WORN-OUT INDUSTRY

EXHAUSTION OF PRIVATE FARMING

IMPOSITION OF COMMAND ECONOMY

LOW QUALITY INDUSTRIAL OUTPUT

OBSOLETE GIGANTIC INDUSTRIAL PLANTS

CONSEQUENCES OF SOVIET DOMINATION OF POLAND:

NOMENKLATURA: NEW CLASS OF EXPLOITERS

CONTAMINATION OF THE ENVIRONMENT

DECLINING LIFE EXPECTANCY

LARGE INCREASE OF BIRTH DEFECTS

WORLD'S WORST POVERTY OF PROFESSIONALS

DEMORALIZATION OF THE ENTIRE WORK FORCE

NORWAY

SWEDEN

FINLAND

BALTIC SEA

SOVIET UNION

DENMARK

NETHER LANDS

E GERMANY

W GERMANY

CZECHO-

SLOVAKIA

POLAND

AUSTRIA HUNGARY

ROMANIA

YUGOSLAVIA

BULGARIA

BLACK SEA

TURKEY

CASPIAN SEA

IRAN

IRAQ

SAUDI ARABIA

SYRIA

JORDAN

LEBANON

ISRAEL

CYPRUS

GREECE

EGYPT

LIBYA

MALTA

TUNISIA

MEDITERRANEAN SEA

ITALY

FRANCE

SPAIN

PORTUGAL

ATLANTIC OCEAN

MOROCCO

ALGERIA

IRELAND

GREAT BRITAIN

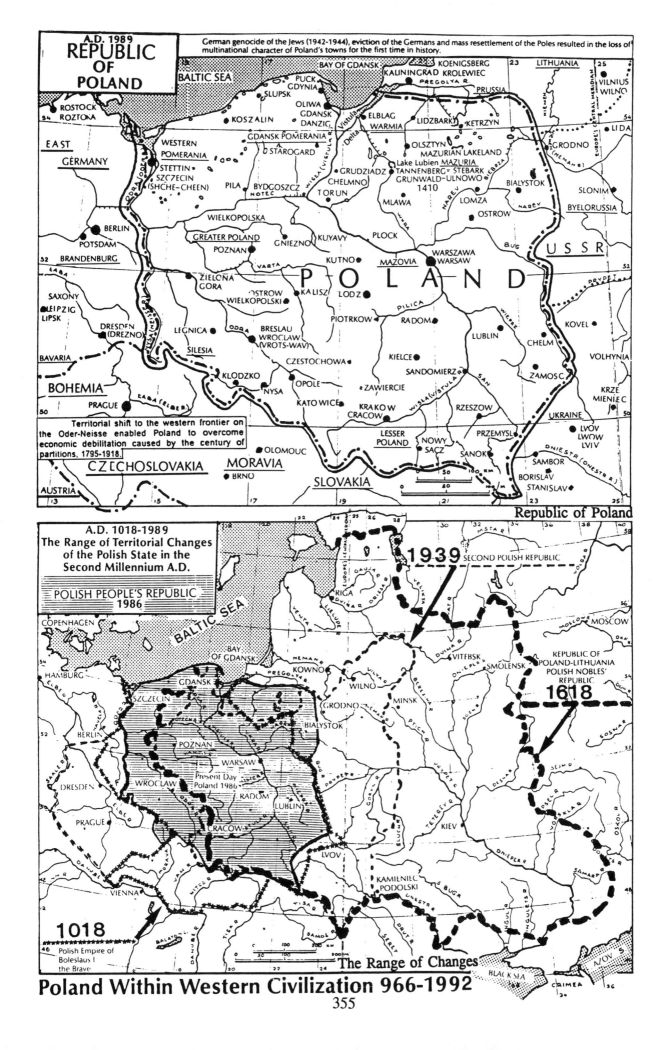

REPUBLIC OF POLAND

A.D. 1989
REPUBLIC
OF
POLAND

German genocide of the Jews (1942-1944), eviction of the Germans and mass resettlement of the Poles resulted in the loss of multinational character of Poland's towns for the first time in history.

Territorial shift to the western frontier on the Oder-Neisse enabled Poland to overcome economic debilitation caused by the century of partitions, 1795-1918.

Republic of Poland

A.D. 1018-1989
The Range of Territorial Changes of the Polish State in the Second Millennium A.D.

POLISH PEOPLE'S REPUBLIC 1986

1939 SECOND POLISH REPUBLIC

REPUBLIC OF POLAND-LITHUANIA POLISH NOBLES' REPUBLIC

1618

1018

Present Day Poland 1986

Polish Empire of Boleslaus I the Brave

The Range of Changes

Poland Within Western Civilization 966-1992

ITEMIZED TABLE OF CONTENTS

PART I - CHAPTER 1

PART I - CHAPTER 2

PART I - CHAPTER 3

PART I - CHAPTER 4

GERMAN ANNIHILATION OF THE JEWS

A CHRONOLOGY

BASIC FACTS AND TYPICAL EVENTS

Based on the Files of Nuremberg Trials of German War Crimes
the Commission Investigating German-Nazi Crimes in Poland,
and the Jewish Historical Institute in Poland

ILLUSTRATIONS, DOCUMENTS, AND ANNOTATIONS

358

PART III - ATLAS

JEWS IN POLAND

Poland in the Jewish History

A Historic Perspective

Maps and Graphs:

Early Settlements in Poland
966 -- 1264

The Crucial 500 Years
1264 -- 1795

Under the Foreign Rule
1795 -- 1918

The Last Blossoming in Poland
1918 -- 1939

Shoah - The German Genocide
1941 -- 1944

Briha The Escape from Europe
1945 -

Total: 287 items made up of 115 maps and graphs, plus 172 illustrations: paintings, drawings, documents (including official posters), photograpphs, newspaper titles and headlines (including cartoons).

Annotation Texts

Index 365-398

A Glossary:
Polish, Latin, and Hebrew*, and Yiddish** 399-402
(Terms used during centuries of contacts between Poles and Jews)

INDEX

366

369

377

378

380

- bills of exchange for cash 16, 79
- international letter of credit 80
- letter of credit 16
- originated in 15th c. Poland 80
- used by Jewish network of international credit 80
- used for safe transfer of money 79
- used in mobilization of large loans 79
- used throughout Europe 79
- travel check 16, 80

Manchester Guardian on German perverted ingenuity 129

Mannesman Industries exploitation of prisoners 133

manors in Polish agriculture 68

manpower shortage, German 95, 97, 105

manufacturing of weapons instructions 120

Margalit, Avishai, Professor of Philosophy, Hebrew University, Jerusalem 178
- *His Violent Career* The New York Review of Books, May 14, 1992, p. 18-24
- Yitzhak Shamir's career including his work with Abraham Stern

Mark, Ber, Jewish fighter 123
- author *Uprising in the Warsaw Ghetto* 123

marriages with Jews, forbidden in Germany 91

martyrdom of the Jews 326
- German death machine 1942 326
- system of 8500 camps 326

Martyrs of Charity 173-4

Marx, Karl (1818-1883) 18
- political economy 1859 18
- materialist history 1859 18

mass
- emigration as a solution to the Jewish problem 109
- media access, Poles and Jews 163, 171
- media, western shifting responsibility of genocide 136
- murders at Bydgoszcz 98
- murders committed by Germans 109, 174
- murders prolonged by the Soviets 346
- murders while Warsaw was destroyed 346

massacres
- of Jews 109, 273, 285
- of Polish officers 102-4
- the largest of Jews since A.D. 117 (in 1648) 285

Massada-like suicide 123
- at Jewish headquarters in the ghetto 123
- at Mila Street no. 18 in Warsaw May 8, 1943) 123
- moments before an escape passage was found 123

masses of Jews were only in historic Poland 135
- belonging to all levels of society

135
- poor and rich 135
- pious and secular 135
- rural and urban 135
- illiterate and highly educated 135

Mathausen concentration camp 94

Mazovia 75

Mazuria, Plebiscite of 303

McKinsey I.J. and Stanton B. 178
- *The Charisma of John Paul II* 178
- *To Poles, the Pope Is One of Their Own* 178

medical school, cadavers profaning 28

Medieval
- Jewish merchants, the Radanites 257
- period 11, 22
- slave trade 259-261

Mediterranean
- basin 13
- ports of embarkation for Palestine 351

Mein Kampf 97, 319
- on Germans as the highest species on earth 319

Mellon, John Seymour, wrote in 1919 168
- " It is all rot to say there are pogroms in Poland" 168
- " Jews are at the bottom of all Bolshevism in Russia" 168

melting pot 37
- in Israel 37

Meir, Golda 26

metropolitan of Moscow converted to Judaism 25

Mendala family murdered for boiling eggs for Jews 126

Mesopotamia 250, 256, 261

message from Jewish leaders in occupied Poland, fall 1942 327

Messiah 167

messianic
- longing of Jews and Poles 163
- mission of "Jews to rule the world" ridiculed 301

Michnów retaliation massacre of 250 Polish families 126

Mickiewicz, Adam 151, 165, 178
- Polish Romantic ideology 165
- *Of a Foreign Mother* by Jadwiga Maurer 178
- connection with the Jewish world 178
- *Encyclopedia Judaica* listed him as a Jew 178

Middle Ages 13, 14, 22

Middle East 13, 14, 133, 351
- destabilization of 133, 351
- oil-rich 133, 351

middlemen, Jewish 68

- between absolute rulers and their state administration 71
- between the nobility and the peasants 68
- flexible, with ability to mediate 71
- formed international credit network in early 17th c. 72
- not bound by ethics of the guilds 71
- paid with protection and privileges 72

Midstream, Monthly Jewish Review 23

midwife executed for delivering a Jewish baby 129

Miechów 120

Międzybóż 83

Mieses, Mateusz, *Of Jewish Descent* ("Z rodu Żydowskiego") 178
- *Patriotic Polish Families, Once of Jewish Blood*, WEMA, Warsaw 1991
- ("Zasłużone rodziny polskie krwi niegdyś żydowskiej")

migrations, Jewish
- after Ukrainian pogroms 284
- by the "Litwaks" encouraged by Russia 294
- helped spread north the cultures of antiquity 271
- mainly to Poland (dates) 272-6
- to capitals of Europe and America 292
- to Israel (1948-65), map of and numbers 352
- to Palestine 300
- to western Europe, a trickle 71
- within Europe, 19th and 20th centuries 314

mihya, or means of livelihood 69

Mikołajczyk, Stanislaw, *The Pattern of Soviet Domination* 170, 177
- on taxing British rule in Palestine by immigration of Jews 170
- *Rape of Poland* 170, 177

Mila Street no. 18, Massada-like suicide of Jews 123

militia, or Jewish police in the ghettos 88, 116

military-industrial complex, German 97, 98

military training camps for Zionists in Poland
- Andrchów 300-1
- Bolków near Wroclaw, 10-day course 349
- Rembertów 300-1
- Warsaw 301
- Zielonka 300

Miłosz, Czesław, writer, Nobel Laureate 28, 159, 169, 174, 176, 177
- *Anti-Semitism in Poland* 176
- German Nazism was not Christian at all 159
- on Holocaust as a qualitative jump, not a gradual increase 159
- on Holocaust created by German pagan movement 159

- on Holocaust millions of non-Jewish victims 177
- on Holocaust undergoing modifications 177
- on intellectuals of Jewish descent 176
- on Jewish Communists in top positions in Poland 176
- on Jewish roots of Adam Mickiewicz, (Kultura, Sept 1991, p. 19-33) 178
- on Jewish uniformed members of the apparatus and communist cadres 176
- on Jews as more reliable instruments of the Soviets 176
- on Jews blamed for Soviet terror and general poverty 176
- on Jews in the Polish Communist Party in 1945 176
- on Jews in the very cruel security police 176
- on Jews less inclined to Polish patriotism 176
- on obstacles to join Polish army by Jews in the USSR 176
- on recruitment of Jews to Polish Communist army in the USSR 176
- on socio-economic basis of anti-Semitism 159
- *Poland and the Jews* 169
- *W wielkim Księstwie Sillicianii* Kultura, Sept. 1991
- (In the Grand Duchy of Sillicania)

Ministry of Internal Affairs, Poland 1962 31
- card index of all hidden Jews 31
- defined hidden Jews 31
- evicted 30,000 people classified as Jews (1968-9) 31
- preparing for total elimination of Jews 31
- senior Jewish officials under sur-veillance 31
- under control of the Soviet KGB 31

minorities in Poland 25, 91
- Byelorussians 91
- German 91
- Jewish 25, 78, 91,
- Moslem 78
- rights 76
- Ukrainian 25, 91

Mińsk Mazowiecki 27, 125, 126, 300
- execution of 70 Jews by German police 126
- riots 300

Mińsk (Litewski) 102, 108, 129
- mass execution of Jews and Communists 108

Miro, M. "Remnants: The Last Jews of Poland 177
- Detroit Free Press, March 21, 1987 177

Mitoraj, Bronisław, betrayed and executed 128

mixed couples 22, 91
- *The intermarrying Kind* 22

"mixed" form of government 67
- developed in Poland 67
- open, free, decentralized 67

Mlawa execution of 51 people 111
- fifty Jews 111

- one Polish bystander who shouted: "They are spilling innocent blood." 112

mobilization in Poland
- March, 1939 95
- numbers in September 1939 96

Moczar, general Mieczysław (Mietek) 31
- born Nicolai Demko (ethnic Ukrainian)
- in 1939 recruited by NKVD
- led anti-cultural revolution 1967-9
- led anti-Jewish police faction 1962-9
- minister of internal affairs 1964-9
- potential successor to Gomulka, 1968 31
- secret police chief
- subservient to the KGB

modern
- early period 14

Modrzewski, Andrzej Frycz 63
- "De Republica Emendada" (1551) 63

Moffat, J. P. of the Dept. of State
- on buying off Germany in Eastern Europe 93

Mołczadź self sacrifice 114

Moldavia (Moldova) 300

Molotov, Vyacheslav M. (Skryabin, 1890-1982) 101
- Commissar of Foreign Affairs 101
- on joint German-Soviet attacks on Poland 101

Mongol
- Empire 85
- invasion of 1241 267
- people 85

monopoly
- decree on alcoholic beverages, matches, and tobacco 300
- rights, leases of, as a Jewish domain 69

Monte Cassino 33

Moravian Gate (to Poland) 94

"more Judaico," a degrading oath 73

Mościcki, Ignacy, President of Poland 165

Moscow 25, 26, 85, 100, 104, 123-4, 135, 277
- battle of 108, 135
- eviction of Jews in 1790 85
- front 108
- grand duke of 25
- had current information on Jews in Poland 124
- metropolitan of 25
- propaganda 123
- radio 95
- use of Polish as the language of civility and elegance (17th c.) 85

Moslem 78, 273
- as a derogatory term in German concentration camps 341

Mossad, Israeli Intelligence 301

- founded by *Sherut-Israel* 301
- operation of *Aliya-bet* 301

"most anti-Semitic country [Poland] 247
- in which anti-Semitism is transmitted with mother's milk"
- according to Itzhak Shamir 156, 178

Moszkowicz, Daniel led ghetto uprising, killed 126

Motzkin, Leo (1867-1933), Russian Zionist 297

Mrożek, S. Holocaust "a matter between Germans and Jews" only 173

multinational commonwealth, Poland (1386-1795) 13, 72, 86, 159
- where toleration was a part of the divine order 72

Mundelein, Cardinal 92

Munich 94-5

Muranowska Street tunnel 123

music used, for sadistic tortures 125

Muslim 13, 261, 272
- contempt of infidels 13
- "Dar El-Islam" 272
- emancipation 16
- population 13
- prisoners of war 16
- rule in Arab Spain 261
- Tartars 285
- territory 259

Mussolini, Benito 90

Muszyński, Bishop Henryk 34

Myednoye 104

Myślenice 27

mystical anti-Talmudist sect in Poland 287
- see Jakub Frank (1726-91) 287

myths in Germany 18, 255

mythological operas 18, 255

Naftul betrayed a Jewish hideout and caused executions 120

Nalewki Street Warsaw 101

name lists for death transports see lists

Narvik, Norway 33

Natan Hanover 84

nation, Jewish
- reestablished in Israel 37
- with extraordinary vigor and perseverance 37

national
- Committee, Jewish 22, 118, 120
- Council, Polish in exile 124
- Democrats 27, 28
- identity, Jewish 20, 307
- interest separation, of Poles and Jews 23

- mourning after WWII 30
- national values, Polish 115
- National Security Office of Germany 99
- Socialist Labor Party of Germany (1932 - 40% of vote) 134, 319
- Socialist Germany
- Socialist government
- Socialist Labor party, German
- Socialist regime
- -Socialistic party, German
- Socialists, Austrian
- socialists (Nazis) legally assumed power in Germany 135
- socialists popular in Germany till the end 135

nationalism
- Jewish, modern 20, 23
- Polish 21, 163

nationalist struggles 21

National Socialism 27
- at war with "Jewish-Bolshevism" 91
- claims of German superiority 27
- popular appeal of 27, 90
- very weak opposition to 90

nations, Polish and Jewish
- "the two saddest on earth" 157
- "their paths ... have parted forever" 157

nation-states 136, 168, 307
- concept of 307
- fall of the centralized 168
- fraudulent denationalization of minorities 136
- rejection of pluralism 136

natural selection 18

natural law 18

Naumann, Dr. German judge 128

Nazi Danes 111

Nazi German
- genocide 14
- government 14, 22, 27
- ideology of pan-Germanism 135
- murders 22, 27
- party 135
- plans to murder 11,000,000 Jews 89
- Sturm-Abteilungen (SA) 134

Nazi Germany 22

Nazi term 150,162
- not linked to Germany in America 162
- used to cover up German guilt in the genocide of the Jews 162

"Nazis are people from outer space" in America 162

"Nazis," as if Nazis were some sort of nationality 150

negotiations collective, Jewish 73-5, 78
- for political support 73
- for self-imposed restrictions 73
- for the sake of social peace 73
- with burghers 73
- with Polish treasury about taxes 74-5, 78

Neminem Captivabimus, Act of 62

New Canaan (New Kna'an) 257, 259
- name of Slavic lands given by Jewish slave traders 257

new German order 136
- any intelligent Pole a potential threat to 136

New York Wochenblat, (1936) 301
- alarmed by flooding Polish flee markets with used clothing 301
- on abuse of Polish transport subsidies 301
- on Jewish unemployment in Polish garment industry 301

Netherlands 66, 115

New Deal 92

New Orleans 161, 164

Newsweek
- on American Jews 22
- *The Intermarrying Kind* 22

Niepokalanów 107

Nieszawa, Act of 60, 278

Nietzsche, Friedrich 173, 217
- at war against mediocrity of men 217
- on execution of anti-Semites 217
- on his Polish ancestors 217
- on undergrowth of Germans, Slavs, and Jews 217
- on *liberum veto* 217
- on Martin Luther 217
- on misuse of his terminology 217
- on nature and civilization 217
- on supermen and subhumans 217
- on *uber-mensch* 173
- on Wagner's mythological operas 217
- unjustly accused of racism 217

Niezabitowska, Małgorzata 158, 163, 166, 177
- *Remnants, the Last Jews of Poland* 162, 166, 177

Nihil Novi Constitution of 1505 75

NKVD
- Jewish agents 122

"no salvation for Germans...Jews must be killed" 91
- Julius Streicher (in 1935) 91
- to "free mankind" 91

Nobel Prize 159, 309

nobility
- a political nation of one million of free citizens in the old Poland 15-66
- abolishing titles of 16
- citizen-soldiers 15
- commonwealth of 15
- dominant feudal estate 15
- formed government-from-below (democratic) 18, 82-3, 278
- Polish *szlachta* 16

noble citizens 66
- dominated Poland's economy 66
- main driving force of the old Poland 66

"no peace at any price" (1939) 96

Paulinów provocation and execution of 14 Poles 120

pawns to German princes, magnates, or towns 72
- Jews in late medieval Germany 72

"payers of royal tax" (Jews as) 72

peasants
- Austrian fled to Poland 86
- buying from and selling to Jews 167
- culture influenced Jews in villages 167
- exploited people in close contact with Jews 167
- relations with nobles and Jews 86
- Russian fled to Poland 86
- runaway foreign serfs obtained freedom 86
- serf escapes influenced partitions 86

Pecuła, Feliks executed for hiding Jews 125

Pecuła, Stanisław executed for hiding Jews 125

Peli, Rabbi Pinchas H. of Ben-Gurion University of the Negev 178
- "A time to speak out," *Jerusalem Post*, March 19, 1988 178
- on the new Jew no longer ready to be the eternal victim 178
- on the new Jew who rose from ashes of Auschwitz and Treblinka 178
- on satanically-contrived gas chambers 178

penal code
- on enemies of the Soviet state 100
- Soviet Russian 100

People's Poland within the Soviet Bloc 347
- effects of borders shift west 355

Persia 107
- Empire 256-7

Peter the Great 82
- brought a crisis of Polish sovereignty 82
- placed Saxon puppet on the Polish throne 82
- organized the modern form of Russian government based on the military-police rule

Philby, Kim British officer, Soviet spy 125
- NKVD-KGB general 125
- security chief in Gibraltar 125
- while Gen. Sikorski was killed 125

philo-Semitc weekly, "idolatrously" 177
- according to Jerzy Urban, gov. spokesman, himself Jewish 177
- Catholic weekly *Tygodnik Powszechny* of Kraków

philo-Semitic literature, Polish 294

Piast dynasty's original Polish lands 132

Pietraszewicz, Bronisław of the Home Army 128
- shot SS Gen. Fr. Kutchera 128

Pilecki, Witold (Tomasz Serafiński) 105
- organized resistance in Auschwitz (later tortued and murdered by the Soviets - he was known as one of the most courgeous men during the Second World War) 105

Pilica-Zamek reprisal execution 120

Pilichowski, "Czapa" killed in Warsaw Ghetto 123

Piłsudski 24, 28, 90, 158, 165-6, 173, 182, 303
- admitted and gave citizenship to 600,000 Soviet Jews 173
- a friend of Jews 165
- as a cult figure 158
- dedication to, by Arthur Szyk 182
- forced Bolsheviks back in 1920 166
- Marshal Józef 28
- offered free military transport to Jews 165
- opposed to quotas 28
- Polish Legions 24, 300
- support by "Rada Obrony Państwa" 303

Pińsk 116, 304
- execution of 35 Jews, allegedly Soviet agents (1919) 304
- Polish parliament condemned the execution (1921) 304

Piotrków 62, 100
- first ghetto in occupied Poland 100

Piotrków Trybunalski
a reprisal murder 117

Piper, Franciszek estimates of Auschwitz victims 132

Pipes, Richard 84-5, 40, 180
- *Catherine II and the Jews* 84-5
- *The Russian Revolution* 180

Pirow, Oswald 93-4

pisarz, or a clark 70

Pius XII, Pope 92

Planty Street no. 7, Jewish quarters in Kielce 134

plastic surgery 110
- to remove scars of circumcision 110

Płaszów concentration camp 134, 336
- commander sentenced to death by Polish court 134
- German map of, 336

pluralism 16, 19, 65, 82-3, 136
- as a historic mission 83
- based on multinational character 65
- idea of 82
- in Poland 279
- of Polish Jews 300
- rejection of 136

pluralistic

- civilization in Poland 83
- Polish state 78
- societies, self-destruction 37
- unity between absolutists neighbors 86
- values 82

Płudy 107

Podolia 14, 66-7, 83

Podolski, Michał executed for hiding Jews 125

pogroms
- accounts of 119, 147
- and criminal assaults against Jews (1917-1921) 304
- during Swedish invasion (1655-7) 286
- in Brzeziny, 1656 23
- in central Europe 20
- in Gabin, 1656 23
- in Kielce, 1946 134, 159, 349, 351
- in Kishiniov, 1905 300
- in Łęczyca, 1656 23
- in Lida, 1919 304
- in Lvov, assault on Jewish, Armenian, and Polish merchants in 1918 304
- in Odessa, 1905 had a record of extreme violence, 500 Jews perished
- in Pińsk, (35 Tzeirei Zionists executed in 1919) 305
- in Poland, 1917-1921, 104, 119, 304
- in Prague, Czechia, 1389 (4000 killed) 304
- in Russia 244, 300
- in Ukraine, more than 2,000 pogroms (70,000 killed) 1917-1921 168, 304
- Ukrainian (1648) 284-5
- in western Europe 20, 147
- resulting in 150,000 death in the Ukraine 168
- sporadic 73, 150

Polak, Dr. Fazimierz murdered 114
- while helping a Jewish patient 114

Poland 27
- abolishing titles of nobility in the 16th century 16
- adopted the first modern constitution in Europe 26
- as a federal republic 17
- as the European Middle-East 15
- autonomy in 15, 270
- basic ideas of democracy 15th and 16th c. 16
- bicameral parliament, 1493 15
- border country 13
- chief executive officer of 16
- Christian coexistence with Judaism and Islam 15
- civil and human rights 14
- Commonwealth of 15
- compact and powerful realm 17
- conflict of interest 23
- constitution of, Nihil Novi, or Nothin New About US Without Us" (1505) 22
- constitutional civic and intellectual liberty 17, 276
- Constitutional Monarchy (1493-1569) 276
- cosmopolitan character 15
- decline of 82
- decline and fall, end 18th c. 17
- deluge of invasions 22

- dismembering of 21
- distinctive civilization 14
- due process under law of 15
- economic decline 23
- emancipation offer to Jews and Muslims (1569) 16
- ethnic pluralism of 16
- exposed to Germanic threat 17
- fall of 21, 23
- favorable environment for Jews 14
- first partition 13
- first protestant vassal 16
- First Republic of 16
- first to stand up to German terrorism 162
- founding of the 1st Republic 1569 16
- four Christian confessions 15
- free of religious wars 16
- freedom of conscience 14
- freedom in 18
- freest state, 16th and 17th c. 17
- golden age 15
- greater freedom 14
- heaven for the Jews 158
- heaven for the poor and oppressed 17
- historic lands 13, 20, 21
- history of 18
- home of Jewish literature and philosophy 158
- in Jewish History, a Perspective 241
- indigenous democratic process 14
- intellectual fertilization 15
- intellectual leadership, pluralistic 31
- king as an elective chief executive 16
- King of 16
- Kingdom of 13, 27, 276
- lands of 19
- leader in protection of liberty 158
- legal system of 15
- -Lithuania, the state of 66
- lost in WWII half of her educated people 160
- massive influx of Jews 14
- more tolerable than elsewhere 13
- multi-denominational state 15
- no discriminatory taxes 14
- nobel citizens of 15
- obliteration of 18
- official documents in 6 languages 15
- the oldest republic 17
- of one million citizens (1569-1795) 15
- opposition to reforms 22
- "paradise of the Jews" 17
- parliamentary government 15
- partitions of, 1772-1795 14, 18, 84
- people of 18
- "pillar of justice" 84
- pluralism of 16, 19
- political autonomies 15
- political tradition 18
- power struggle 23
- powerful realm 17
- principle of a quality 16
- reach farmlands and forests 16
- rebellions 22
- reforms 22
- religious toleration of 16
- renaissance 15th and 16th c. 15
- republican government, 1454 15
- republican 19
- Russian neighbor of 16
- "sanctuary of the Jews" 17, 276
- safest country for the Jews 158, 273
- saved Jews from extinction 11,

387

388

394

Zyklon-B gas 108
- from hydrogen-cyanide crystals 108
- stock on 1945 for gassing 15,000,000 112

Żabotyński, Włodzimierz (Meir Jabotinsky), Zionist-revisionist leader 300
- on creating of a Jewish state on both sides of Jordan River 301

- on flooding of Polish universities by the Jews 300
- received financial aid from the Polish government (1939) 301

Żegota (see Żegota above), see Council of Assistance for the Jews

Żeromski, Stefan, writer (1864-1925) 294

Żmudziński, Capt. Tadeusz of the "blue" police 124
- served in Polish Home Army 124
- gave shelter and Aryan papers to Jews 124

Żyd (or zhid)
- as an opposite to "yevrey" 168
- origin of word from Venecian "giudeo" 266

Żółkiew ghetto 125

Żydokomuna (the Communist Jews) 158

Żydy do Palestyny 166

GLOSSARY OF
POLISH, LATIN, HEBREW*, AND YIDDISH** TERMS
USED IN CONTACTS BETWEEN POLES AND JEWS

aguna*	woman abandoned by her husband
aj-waj (ay-vay)	exclamation used mainly in the shtetls in Poland, see "Oy-Vey League"
aj waj mir!	emotional exclamation
akim	a pagan
akta grodzkie	official documents issued or filed with court in a town
apikores	heretic, renegade
areilim	non-Jew
arenda	a lease contract of monopoly rights
arendarz	arrendator, contractor
ashir*	a wealthy person
asygnacja	a payment order similar to a modern check
asygnacje	the system of payment orders similar to modern checking account, transfer of funds
asygnacyjny papier	paper (money)
asygnata	order of payment, cash order, voucher, bill of exchange
asygnować	to assign, to allot, to allocate, to bestow
asygnować fundusze	to appropriate, to budget, to allow, to transfer money, to issue an order of payment
asygnowanie	assignment, allotment, allocation, allocation, appropriation, allowance, budgeting, giving out an order of payment
aukcja	auction sale, competitive bidding, a price or rent increment
bachor**	Jewish child
bajgiele**	sweet pretzel
bal teszub*	renegade who returned to Judaism
bałabuste**	hostess, lady of the house
bałagan**	a mess, disorder, disorderly condition
bałaguła**	Jewish coachman
balchazaka*	holder of a hazaka
bankiele**	bankruptcy
bares gelt**	cash
belfer**	tutor

bet-ha-midrasz*	prayer house
bobe**	grand mother
bojne**	beans
bona moneta	coins with a high silver content
borg**	credit
borgować**	to give on credit
boruchy**	religious ritual
bosiny**	watch over a deceased
bronfen**	vodka
bube**	child
buntować się	to mutiny, to sabotage a monopoly, to refuse to render labor dues, to attack the arrendator, to produce own liquor
cc! (tz-tz!)	exclamation of admiration or irony
chajet**	tailor
chała**	ritual Jewish loaf
chałat**	coat worn by Orthodox Jews
chałupa	shack
chasyd*	Hassidim
chasydzka rodzina	Hassidic family
chasyne**	wedding
chazarnik**	pork eater
chazer**	pork
cheder (kheder)*	Jewish primary religious school
cherem*	anathema of the second degree
chewra, chewre*	a bunch of friends
chuchem*	sage
chypa**	wedding canopy
cipkie**	noodles
Congressus Judaicus	autonomous Jewish parliament in old Poland (before partitions); see Jewish Seym and Vaad Arba Arazot
currentis moneta	money with a high copper content introduced after 1663
cures**	trouble, unpleasantness
cyces**	fringes
cyganić	to cheat, to swindle, to sharp, to fool, to lie, to tell lies like a Gipsy
cygański	vagrant deceitful, fraudulent, thievish, tricky like a Gipsy

cygaństwo	deceit, fraud, confidence game, lie, vagrancy Gipsy style	gospodyni	landlady, hostess, housekeeper, woman in charge of dairy and poultry production on a manor
cymes**	delicacy	gosposia	servant, maid
czerwony złoty	golden ducat, worth up to 18 złotych	grojse**	big
czopowy	excise tax on liquor	gromada	rural community, village council
czynsz	real estate tax, rent, rental, rent-charge	grosz	1/100 złoty, hist. 1/30 złoty
dajon*	judge of religious cases	groszowy	cheap, inexpensive
detrachot*	commentary on cabalistic scriptures	grzywna	hist. 48 grosze, by the 18th cent. currency of account only, fine
dobra	landed property, a section of a latifundium, several klucze	gumienny	stockyard supervisor
dom	house	gumno	a barn, a threshing floor, a barn-yard
dozorca	caretaker, custodian, hist. supervisor	haman*	giant, feast of Purim
dozorca niewolnikow	slave-driver	hamanować**	to persecute
		handełe**	trade, commerce
dozorca więzienny	jailer	Hasid*	member of a religious movement, begun by Israel Ball Shem Tov, which emphasized piety and joyous communion with God
dozór	supervision, care, inspection, watch		
dwa	a couple		
dworek	small manor house		
dworka	servant maid	Haskalah*	Jewish enlightenment movement
dwornie	in a courtly fashion	hazaka (khazaka)*	license granted by a kahal entitling a person to hold monopoly on some economic enterprise
dwornik	assistant to podstarosta		
dwór	court-residence, mansion, manor, manor house		
		hazówkie**	prohibition to buy
dzierżawa	a leasehold, usually of real estate, rent, rental	hebrajski	Hebrew*
		hebrajszczyzna	Hebrew language, Hebrew culture*
dzierżawca	lessee of a dzierżawa	herb	coat of arms, crest
dzierżawić	to rent, to hold on lease	herbowy	heraldic, armorial
Edom*	Christianity	herst du!**	listen!
edomit**	a Christian	heter iska*	a legal circumvention of the biblical prohibition of loaning on interest
ekonom	steward of an estate, hist. general manager of a unit of a latifundium		
		hetman	a defense minister, a marshal, commander-in-chief
fajne berye**	to pretend to be an important person		
fanaberja	whim, vagary, fad	hetmanić	to command, to be at the head
faktor	factor	hetmaństwo	hetmanship, command
farfel**	noodles	hevra*	a mutual benefit society of people in the same occupation (incl. charity)
fein**	fine		
fejne bery**	a dignitary, an outstanding person	hrabstwo	county, a very large hereditary estate
ferfał**	lost	husyn**	fiance (male)
folga	a discount granted to a person owing some financial obligation, a relief	informacja	information, intelligence, an information bulletin
		instancja	a brief submitted on behalf of an accused person or a victim of some calamity, stage in a court system
folgowanie	leniency, indulgence		
folwark	a grange, hist. a feudal manor		
frokt	freight	instrukcja	order, instruction given to administrators
froktarz	freighter, owner of a frokt shipped by river boat		
		inwetarz	inventory, stock-list, hist. inventory of equipment, buildings, taxpayers, and income of a unit of a latifundium
furszpil**	a prelude to wedding music		
gabe, gabide**	man in charge of a philanthropy		
gałzen*	robber, cut-throat		
ganc git**	very well	Izrael	Isarel
ganew, ganef**	thief	jarmułka*	scull cap
gekeszenes ganef**	pickpocket	Jaśnie Pan	a title of an aristocrat used in the etiquette of Old Poland
		Jasne Panes**	plural of the above used by Jews
gedułt**	patience	Jehova*	the name of God
geld**	money, earnings, profit	jewrej (yevrey)*	Jew, Hebrew, correct in Russian, a pejorative and insulting term in Polish
geszeft**	business, earnings		
gewałt**	violence, rape		
git**	good	Jewish Seym	autonomous Jewish parliament in old Poland (before partitions); see Congressus Judaicus and Vaad Arba Arazot
git jur**	good year (greeting)		
gite nacht**	good night		
giten tag**	good day		
gitwoch**	good week (greeting)	jingieł**	boy
glik**	good luck	jupica**	Jewish male garment
glikste!**	just have a look!	kahał*	the governing council of a kehilla
goim*	non-Jews	kahalnik	a member of a kahal
goj (goy)*	a non-Jew	kałe*	fiance (female)
goja, gojka**	a non-Jewish woman	kapcan*	poor
gołd**	gold	kapconim*	poor people

400

kapure**	sacrifice, victim (of circumstance)	nucher*	foreigner
karczma	tavern, inn, (also once used as a general store, restaurant, and for social functions)	o wa! (o va!)	
		o we! (o ve!)	excl.: of irony or contempt
		o weh mir!	exclamation: it hurts me!
kasa centralna	master ledger	obywatel	citizen
kasa oszczędności	savings-bank	oh wej!	an impatient exclamation
kasztelan	senator, titular palatine	oj waj (oy vay)	exclamation with various connotations
katzin*	Jewish notable	oj wej mir! woe!	I am in trouble!
kehilla*	an organized Jewish community	ordynacja	a Polish estate that was not divided among heirs upon the death of the owner, but passed intact to one of them, not necessarily to the oldest son
kepełe**	head, brain, cleverness		
kidush*	prayer over vine		
kikać**	look, look in		
kirkut**	Jewish cemetery		
klucz	complex of manors and private towns		
klejne**	small	oszachrować**	to take in, to cheat
kługer**	smart, clever	oszczędność	economy, thrift, thriftiness, frugality
kofrim*	unbeliever	oszczędności	savings
komisariat	an administrative district	Oy Vey League	universities with large Jewish enrollment in the United States; see "Aj-waj"
komisarz	an official charged with a specific task		
konsens	a monopoly license granted by an owner of a town		
		Palestyna	Palestine
koszer*	cleanliness, according to Judaic rules	Pan	"Sir," title usually applied to a Polish nobleman, now applied to all grown men
koszerne*	tax for approval of kosher goods		
królewszczyzna	a royal land grant given for life	Pan dziedzic	country squire
kuczki**	feast of the tents	Pani	"Lady," title usually applied to a Polish noble woman, now applied to all grown women
kupno na raty	system of purchase by deferred payments		
		Pani dziedziczka	wife of a country squire
kwit kasowy	voucher	pejsy*	side curls
laszt	volume measure for grain, large, regional	pinkas*	communal minute book, congressional record of the *Congressus Judaicus*, the Jewish Seym, or the Vaad Arba Arazot
łapserdak**	Jewish male garment		
leśnik	forest warden		
liberum veto	unanimity rule in the Seym	pisarz	
litwak**	Jewish immigrant from Lithuania, Belorus, or Russia	prowentowy	clerk, bookkeeper, comptroller
		płacić na raty	to pay by installments
maca (matzo)*	flat, thin enliven bread	plajt**	bankruptcy
mahażyk*	a general arrendator	po żydowsku	in Yiddish, Jewish fashion
majdałe**	girl	pod chajrem**	on a word of honor
majne munes	my conscience	pod chejrymem**	on a word of honor
mame**	mother	podskarbi	state treasurer
mamełe**	dear mother	podstarosta	an administrator of the agricultural production of a manor
mamram* (memram, membron*)	bills of exchange for cash, an international letter of credit, used in Jewish international credit network, a travel check		
		podwojewoda	deputy provincial governor whose main function was to sponsor a "court of the Jews," which heard appeals from rabbinical courts and cases involving Jews and Christians
meches*	convert from Judaism		
mecyja*	very good, unusual thing		
mejlech*	king		
mełamed*	teacher in *kheder*		
mezuza, mezuze*	scripture in small container nailed to door or window frame	pogłówne Żydowskie	Jewish head tax in the old Poland
		ponieść satratę	to sustain a loss
mieszczanin	burgher, townsman	pręt	a measure of area equaling 7 1/2 ells
mihya*	means of livelihood	protekcja	protection, patronage, use of influence on behalf of a client or a business associate
minjen*	ten grown Jews as a minimum prayer group		
mishar*	commerce		
mishpoche*	family	purec*	noble man, rich man
mitzva*	a Jewish religious duty	rabin*	rabbi, Jewish clergyman
morejne*	an upper class Jew	rachunek	bill, count, calculation
myszygene**	crazy	rachunek bieżący	current account
naród szlachecki	the noble estate, the political nation of free citizens (numbering over one million people)	rachunki	financial accounts, book-keeping
		rachunki domowe	household accounts
		rata	an installment payment
		reb*	mister
naród starozakonny	Jews, the people of the Old Testament	rebe*	reverend (rabbi)
		rebbe*	a leader of a group of *Hassidim*, not necessarily a rabbi, whose authority was charismatic
naród wybrany	Jews, the chosen people		
nu (ny)	and, well, therefore	rejwach**	noisy commotion
		Sanhedryn*	Jewish tribunal

401

Sejm, or Seym	the Polish parliament, legislature, or diet
sejmik	regional legislative assembly, diet, the basic political power in the old Poland
shtadlan*	a Jewish lobbyist with the non-Jewish authorities (one represented all Jews in negotiations with the central government of the Polish Commonwealth)
siste!**	just look!
skapcanieć	to become poor
skarb	treasury
sługa	servant
służba	service, duty
służba folwarczna	the corps of manorial service employees
sohair*	merchant
spław	river trade
sprawiedliwość	justice, judicature, equity, fairness
starosta	foreman of a district, holder of a *starostwo*
starostwo	a royal land grant limited in time
staroszlachecki	of the ancient nobility
strata	loss
strawa	food, nourishment
suplika	a petition
sy git**	OK, it's a deal
syjonism	Zionism
syjonistyczny	Zionist
szabas (sabbath)*	weekly Jewish holiday, the sabbath, sabbath day
szbasówka**	1. tallow candle burnt ritually by Jews on sabbath 2. sabbath-day vodka 3. Jew's ritualistic cap
szacherki**	little swindles
szachermacher**	swindler, cheat, trickster, crook
szachraj**	swindler, cheat, trickster, crook
szachrajka**	female *szachraj*
szachrajstwo**	swindle, hanky-pinkie
szachrować**	to cheat, to swindle
szachrowanie**	swindle
szadchen**	marriage broker
szaddai*	strong, powerful
szafa pancerna	safe
szafarka	a woman steward
szafarz	a steward
szajgec* (shaygetz)	a Jewish boy
szajne**	beautiful, perfect
szamatha*	anathema of the third degree
szames*	janitor at a synagogue
szapszceświnik**	a renegade (an insult)
szejtewate**	silly, mixed up
szeląg	1/3 grosz
szikse*	non-Jewish woman
szlamazara**	sluggard
szlamazarnie**	sluggishly
szlamazarność**	sluggishness
szlamazarnik**	sluggish man
szmendryk**	stupid man
szmonces**	Jewish quip
sznaps**	vodka
szolem alejchem*	shalom, peace be with you
szóstak	1/5 złoty, 1/6 *tynf*
szra nyszt**	shut up! do not talk, be quiet
sztyl**	peace, quiet
szwarc jur**	a bad (black) year
szwindel**	swindle
szyliszes**	a legal confirmation of an engagement to marry
szytwa, szytwes**	partnership, *śitwa*
szynk	a bar
szynkarz	a bar-keeper, a barman
szyper	skipper, skipper of a river boat or flotilla of boats
talar bity	6 - 8 *złote*
tales*	ritual shawl
tanti	possessing much cash
targownik	market-tax lessee
tate**	dad
tatełe**	daddy
tojd**	death, the end
tref*	religiously impure object, food
trefnić*	to make impure
trefny	adj. from *tref*
tuchim*	an engagement to marry
tynf	18 silver *grosze* or 36 - 38 copper *grosze*
uj! (ooy)	exclamation
uniwesał	an edict
vaad*	council, legislature
Vaad Arba Aratzot*	Congressus Judaicus, *Jewish Seym*, originally The Council of Four Lands
Vaad Medinat Lita*	The Council of Lithuania
vaad galil*	a regional council, between the *kahal* and the Congressus Judaicus
waj giwalt!**	a fearful exclamation
waj mir!	an emotional exclamation
widdi*	prayer before death
włość	a large estate, a section of a latifundium including several *klucze*
wojewoda	governor of a province, also holding a seat in the Polish senate
wucher**	usury, usurer, money lender
wucherer**	usurer, money lender
wus is dues?**	what is it? what does it mean? what's going on?
yehidim*	non-arrendators, Jews without a contract with Polish noblemen
zamek	castle, *klucz* administrative headquarters
zaścianek	village of ennobled peasants
zejde (zeyde)*	grand father
złoty	basic Polish monetary unit
znak herbowy	nobelman's coat of arms
Żyd	Hebrew, Jew, grammatically correct in Polish, a pejorative and insulting term in Russian
Żydówka	Jewess
Żydówki	Jewesses
żydowski	Hebrew, Judaic, Jewish
żydowski język	Yiddish
żydowstwo	the Jewry, Jewish traits
Żydzi	Jews, Jewry

Note: the word "Żyd" in the Polish language gave origin to over one hundred nouns, adjectives, and verbs derived from it. Ample examples and analysis of the vocabulary created by contact of ethnic Poles and Jews are given in: Maria Brzezina, *Polszczyzna Żydów*, (Polish dialect of the Jews), Warsaw: Państwowe Wydawnictwo Naukowe, 1986

Henryk Pilatti, Death of Berko Joselewicz at Kock, 1809